MEN OF GOOD WILL

Volume I. MEN OF GOOD WILL
The Sixth of October
Quinette's Crime

Volume II. PASSION'S PILGRIMS
Childhood's Loves
Eros in Paris

Volume III. THE PROUD AND THE MEEK
The Proud
The Meek

Volume IV. THE WORLD FROM BELOW
The Lonely
Provincial Interlude

Volume V. THE EARTH TREMBLES
Flood Warning
The Powers That Be

Volume VI. THE DEPTHS AND THE HEIGHTS
To the Gutter
To the Stars

Volume VII. DEATH OF A WORLD
Mission to Rome
The Black Flag

DEATH OF A WOR

MEN OF GOOD WILL

Volume Seven

Book XIII. **MISSION TO ROME**

Book XIV. **THE BLACK FLAG**

Translated from the French for the first time, by GERARD HOPKINS

DEATH OF A WORLD

A WORLD

by **Jules Romains**

Alfred A. Knopf · New York · 1938

Originally published as

LES HOMMES DE BONNE VOLONTÉ

XIII. *Mission à Rome*

XIV. *Le Drapeau noir*

Copyright 1937 by Ernest Flammarion

FIRST AMERICAN EDITION

Copyright 1938 by Alfred A. Knopf, Inc.

Contents

13.
MISSION TO ROME

I.   Wanted—A *Rara Avis*. Who is Merry del Val?   3

II.   A Man of Resource   15

III.   The Comte de Mézan Advises   19

IV.   Will He Accept?   24

V.   Mionnet Comes in Contact with the Civil Power   35

VI.   Viaur and the Pundits   43

VII.   Eve of Departure. A Trip to M—. A Strange Visitor   58

VIII.   Wazemmes Gives His Allegiance to the Action Française   71

IX.   Louis Bastide in Despair. Françoise in Peril   81

X.   Mionnet Arrives in Rome   90

XI.   Jaurès is Discouraged   92

XII.   An Article from the *Temps*   105

XIII.   A Letter from Maykosen. The Situation in France   108

XIV.   Jerphanion Writes to Jallez about a So-called "Modern Youth Movement"   114

XV.   Extracts from Jallez's Answer   119

XVI.   First Contacts with Rome. The Baron de Fontmonge   120

XVII.	The Pleasures of Fear. Portrait of a Banker under a Shadow	130
XVIII.	A Day at the Vatican	140
XIX.	Dom Charles Magloire Makes a New Disciple	157
XX.	The Lighter Side of Religion	169
XXI.	Small-talk at the Lacchinis'	179
XXII.	Prelates Off Duty	185
XXIII.	The Questionnaire	188
XXIV.	Mionnet Writes His Report. Light on Merry del Val	193
XXV.	The Palatine, the Scagnozzo, and Paolina	206
XXVI.	Maykosen Writes from Rome. Further Lights on Merry del Val. The "Sect"	219
XXVII.	A Successful Demonstration	232
XXVIII.	Ortegal at Work: Genius Set Free	243
XXIX.	A Story without Proof	260
XXX.	A Highly Suspect Photograph	267
	Summary	280

Contents

14.
THE BLACK FLAG

I.	With Reference to a Particular Magnetic Field	285
II.	Jerphanion Becomes Confidential	292
III.	Why I'm Going to Get Married	295
IV.	Mionnet Feels Himself Abandoned	303
V.	A Surprising Summons	310
VI.	A Tiresome Letter	312
VII.	Merry del Val	316
VIII.	How a Man Refuses to Make Use of Certain Weapons	330
IX.	Pierre de Lherm on His Farm and, Later, with His Nephew	332
X.	Gurau; Current Affairs; Autumn in the rue de Chaillot	348
XI.	Gurau, Germaine, and the Future	354
XII.	Germaine and Mareil Face to Face with the Unseen. The Man Covered with Blood	359
XIII.	Germaine Baader and Marie de Champcenais Rub Shoulders in the Beyond	369
XIV.	Marie Finds New Happiness	372
XV.	"Four Days of Love at Bruges with an Egyptian Princess"	382
XVI.	One Hour of Love with a Woman Doctor of Rather Peculiar Tastes	398

XVII.	Quinette's Progress	417
XVIII.	Jallez Spends an Evening with Jerphanion and His Wife	427
XIX.	A Wanderer in London	452
XX.	The Black Flag	463
XXI.	The Little Professor with the Mongol Cheekbones	466
XXII.	A Swirl of Leaves before the Coming Storm	480
XXIII.	Murder, Far Off, of an Archduke	508
XXIV.	Extracts from a Confidential Report Addressed by Mionnet to President Poincaré, Dated July 4, 1914	517
XXV.	Maykosen Sees William II	521
XXVI.	The Gateway of History	529
XXVII.	Portrait of France in July '14	535
	Summary	550
	Index of Characters	*follows page* 551

DRAMATIS PERSONA

DRAMATIS PERSONAE

Since a number of the characters of *Death of a World* were introduced in the earlier volumes of *Men of Good Will,* the reader may find it convenient to refer to a list of Dramatis Personæ, with a short summary of the antecedent action in which each has participated. It is suggested that the best way to use the Dramatis Personæ is to refer to each character in turn when the reader reaches the point in the narrative where that character makes his first appearance (as indicated by page numbers following the names below). The characters who appear for the first time in *Death of a World* are not included in this list.

MANIFASSIER, LÉON (p. 3), is secretary to Gurau (see below), first associated with him in the affair of the oil-dealers.

GURAU, MAXIME (p. 3), is an honest politician with slightly tarnished ideals. A member of the Chamber of Deputies and an independent journalist, he has been politely blackmailed by a group of oil-monopolists headed by Champcenais and Sammécaud (see below) into dropping his opposition to their activities; in return, they have bought for him the control of a newspaper, the *Sanction.* Gurau's attempts to justify this to himself indirectly produce a strain on his relations with his mistress, Germaine Baader, who has been playing the market; Gurau declines to help her out of financial embarrassment, for fear that he might be accused of selling out to the oil-magnates to meet her debts. However, his importance grows in the political picture; he is in frequent contact with such men as Jaurès, Viviani, Briand, Clemenceau, Caillaux. His ambition is to become the leader of the Syndicalists in the workers' revolution which he anticipates—a bloodless revolution leading to a better order. His first step into national prominence is as Minister of Labour in Briand's Cabinet, from which he resigns early in 1910 over a matter of policy involving old-age pensions. The threatening international situation increases his interest in foreign affairs; he refuses Briand's offer of the Ministry of Labour in a new Cabinet, but later accepts the Ministry of Public Works under Monis. Meanwhile he has lost Germaine and become intimate with Mme Godorp, who maintains a fashionable salon. In 1911 he achieves his ambition of becoming Foreign Secretary (under Caillaux), and from here on he is in close touch with various international incidents. A man primarily of action, he is "practical" in the sense that he has learned the uses of hypocrisy; but fundamentally he is a man of good will. In or out of office, he works consistently for peace.

COURSON, FRANÇOIS (p. 3), Undersecretary in the Foreign Office, consults with Gurau at critical moments in foreign relations. A good Catholic, he is concerned about pro-German policy in Vatican circles, suggests to Manifassier that an unofficial representative be sent to Rome in the interests of France.

POINCARÉ, RAYMOND (p. 3), one of numerous historical figures introduced as characters in *Men of Good Will,* has succeeded Caillaux as Prime Minister. His ambitions and his relations with Gurau are discussed by Manifassier and Geoffroy (see below).

SAINT-PAPOUL, MARQUIS DE (p. 11), is a comfortable landed proprietor who has married money and has political ambitions. He has been elected to the Chamber of Deputies in 1910, from a provincial district where he has a country estate, as a Republican candidate of the Left.

MUN, COMTE ALBERT DE (p. 11), of the French Academy, has discussed labour problems with Gurau.

DRAMATIS PERSONAE

LAMBRON DE CRAUZE, MADAME (p. 16), confidante of Gisèle Godorp (see below).

GODORP, GISÈLE (p. 16), is a fashionable and ambitious woman of the Parisian world, who falls in love with Gurau and replaces Germaine Baader in his affections. She manipulates the influence of her salon for the advancement of his political career.

MIONNET, ABBÉ (p. 19), is a priest in his early thirties, a graduate of the Normal College, and a man who has given an impression of intelligence and reserve. Several of the other characters have interested themselves in his career, notably the Marquis de Saint-Papoul. Mionnet is the confessor of the Marquis's sister Bernardine; he has kept a written record of her confessions, which reveal a life of sexual frustration with pathological overtones. In connection with the financial difficulties of a tramway company in the town of M—, which involve the local Bishop, Mionnet is sent by his superior to investigate the trouble and avert a Church scandal. The outcome is successful; but he has a love-affair with his landlady's daughter; his reputation is endangered by rumours of this, which he effectively silences.

MÉZAN, COMTE DE (p. 19), prominent in Catholic and financial circles, has interested himself in Mionnet's career.

LEBAIGUE, MONSIGNOR (p. 37), is Mionnet's ecclesiastical superior who was instrumental in sending him to M—.

HACHENARD, DR. (p. 43), a radiologist who becomes interested in the experiments of Dr. Viaur (see below).

VIAUR, DR. ALBERT (p. 43), staff physician at Celle-les-Eaux, watering place near Paris (see Haverkamp, below), discovers that one of his patients can stop his heart temporarily. This leads to a series of interesting experiments which give promise of considerable importance in physiology, and reveal Viaur as a single-minded idealist with a first-rate scientific mind.

VAQUEZ, PROFESSOR (p. 44), heart-specialist invited to witness Viaur's experiments.

BABINSKY, PROFESSOR (p. 44), neurologist invited to witness Viaur's experiments.

PAILLETON, DR. (p. 45), neurologist with whom Viaur has discussed his cardiac experiments, and who is sceptical of Viaur's observations.

VIDALENQUE (p. 45), original subject of Viaur's experiments, is a waiter at Celle-les-Eaux; he has learned in the Foreign Legion that he can stop his heart-beat at will.

LAPIERRE, DENISE (p. 49), secretary at Celle-les-Eaux; a friendship arises between her and Viaur, and she volunteers as a subject for his experiments.

SÉRASQUIER, MONSIGNOR (p. 58), Bishop of M—, has been responsible for involving the Church in the tramway scandal. Mionnet finds him difficult to handle, but gains his confidence.

MANGUY (p. 66), Vicar-General at M—, who has been made the scapegoat in the tramway scandal.

WAZEMMES, FÉLIX (p. 71), is a naïve young man who has worked for several years in the employment of Haverkamp (see below). His previous activities include a mild career as a patron of the turf, and a pleasant love-affair with an older woman. A typical obscure son of the Parisian lower bourgeoisie, he has been useful to his employer in a minor capacity, and has no higher ambition than to be rich and have a famous actress for his mistress.

DRAMATIS PERSONAE

LAMBERT (p. 71), a friend of Wazemmes.

HAVERKAMP (p. 74), employer of Wazemmes, is the nearest French equivalent of the American Babbitt, but with important differences. As a real-estate promoter he has managed to build up Celle-les-Eaux, a highly profitable "health" spa near Paris, with a fashionable hotel and casino; his success arises from advertising the local waters, which are practically without distinguishing mineral properties, as being medicinally valuable. He has also participated in an under-cover deal in the disposition of disestablished religious properties. A man without a trace of Babbitt's sentimentality, he is hard-boiled but not ruthless; he conducts his love-affairs on an animal level, and with the same satisfaction that he gets from a good dinner; but he is genuinely in love with Paris. Recently he has bought an extensive property near Limoges which involves him in financial difficulties. At a consultation with Dr. Viaur he finds himself in reasonably good health.

BRIAND, ARISTIDE (p. 78), has been frequently introduced under his own name, in actual scenes reconstructed from history, and in imaginary episodes with Gurau. The attempted assassination of Briand has figured in a preceding volume.

MIRAUD, VICTOR (p. 78), uncle by marriage of Wazemmes, a philosophical craftsman who is a follower of Jaurès.

BASTIDE, LOUIS (p. 81), is a little boy who rolls his hoop through the streets of Paris in one of the most famous episodes in *Men of Good Will*. He is a pupil of Clanricard (see below), who tries to help his family when Louis's father is out of work. Louis takes the family situation to heart, goes to work as a delivery boy, meanwhile making a game of it in his vivid and introspective imagination. The richness of Louis Bastide's inner life is in absolute contrast to the poverty of his circumstances at home.

DRAMATIS PERSONAE

CLANRICARD, EDOUARD (p. 83), is an idealistic young Parisian school-teacher. Out of a genuine goodness of nature, which might be mistaken for naïveté, he has been a good Samaritan to Louis Bastide, his pupil. Through an article he writes on the loneliness of the young intellectual, he comes to know Jallez and Jerphanion (see below); to the latter he almost loses Mathilde Cazalis (see below), the girl he wishes to marry, but Jerphanion gives her up.

MAIEUL, FRANÇOISE (p. 86), has been introduced in a remarkable scene describing her birth.

JAURÈS, JEAN (p. 92), another character drawn from recent history, is the eminent Socialist leader. He too has been associated with Gurau, and many of the other characters are among his followers.

CHAMPCENAIS, HENRI, COMTE DE (p. 100), is the leader of the oil-magnates mentioned in connection with Gurau, and has also invested in Haverkamp's enterprises. Recently he has established connections with a ring of international munitions-makers headed by Zülpicher (see below). On a visit to Zülpicher's château he makes advances to Mme Zülpicher, which reveal him as a sentimentalist and perhaps a masochist.

ZÜLPICHER (p. 100) is an important munitions-dealer associated with Champcenais, discreetly prepared to take advantage of international crises.

MAURRAS, CHARLES (p. 103), the royalist and reactionary.

DUROURE, LIEUTENANT-COLONEL (p. 105), has appeared at a dinner-party given by Champcenais in honour of Zülpicher; he is an authority on artillery.

MAYKOSEN, ALFRED (p. 108), Russian by birth and American by naturalization, maintains a front as an international journalist; he

DRAMATIS PERSONAE

has supplied Gurau with inside information on probable diplomatic moves in Germany.

CAILLAUX, JOSEPH (p. 110), pre-war Minister of Finance, is another of the actual personages to appear in the narrative; he has advised Gurau to compromise with the oil-magnates. After becoming Prime Minister and making Gurau his Foreign Secretary, he negotiates with Berlin over Gurau's head. Subsequently Gurau is instrumental in bringing down his government; he is succeeded by Poincaré.

JERPHANION, JEAN (p. 114), the central character, not to say the hero, of *Men of Good Will,* has come to Paris in the fall of 1908 to study at the Normal College in preparation for a career as a teacher. He has brought from his home in the mountains of southern France, and from his peasant background, an honest ruggedness of character, an independent mind, a vigorous sense of humour. He is a tolerant sceptic who, like other young men of his time, sees all too clearly the shadows of coming events that are to immerse Europe in chaos. His long conversations with his friends Jallez (see below) and Clanricard are centred in the question that has occupied the minds of thoughtful young men throughout the civilized world in this century: What can we do about it? Jerphanion has seen some of his fellow-students throw themselves into causes and movements of various kinds, and he himself considers joining both the Freemasons and the Socialists. He gains considerable insight into the nature of parliamentary democracy as secretary to the Marquis de Saint-Papoul, a provincial member of the Chamber of Deputies; and in the course of a normal and healthy life he has a few love-affairs. He has accidentally learned of Jallez's love-affair with Juliette Vérand (see below) and is obliged to intervene tactfully on behalf of her husband, of whose existence Jallez had been unaware. Recently Jerphanion has become attracted to Mathilde Cazalis (see below), but offers to give her up because Clanricard has been deeply wounded by their relationship.

DRAMATIS PERSONAE

JALLEZ, PIERRE (p. 114), is Jerphanion's intimate friend and next to him in importance among the characters of *Men of Good Will*. Jallez and Jerphanion are good foils for each other: where the latter is objective, normal, sceptical, Jallez is introspective, poetic, subtle. Less successful than his friend in emotional relationships, because he demands more of them, Jallez has had a love-affair with Juliette Vérand that has brought unhappiness on both sides; and Jerphanion has tactfully intervened at one point to straighten out Jallez's affairs. But in their long conversations it is Jallez who reveals not only a deeper emotional nature, particularly in the memories of his adolescence, but also a greater originality in ideas. After taking his degree at the Normal College, Jallez becomes a free-lance journalist and makes a tour of Alsace and the Rhineland to write a series of articles on the frontier.

CLEMENCEAU, GEORGES (p. 174), another character from recent history, frequently introduced in accounts of international episodes.

PICHON (p. 206), Foreign Minister under Briand. Gurau refuses a post in the same Cabinet.

ORTEGAL (p. 243), a modernist painter who has appeared briefly at a literary gathering where Jallez and Jerphanion were present, and whom Jallez subsequently visits.

KATCHOWSKY (p. 248), described by Jallez, who meets him at Ortegal's, as resembling a "dubious, half-starved bohemian."

SAMMÉCAUD, ROGER (p. 349), one of the leaders of the oil-magnates, has been instrumental in sidetracking the opposition of Gurau. He conducts a long and elaborate liaison with Marie de Champcenais (see below), wife of his friend and partner, which ends in her having an abortion. Subsequently he spends a night with Germaine Baader (see below).

DRAMATIS PERSONAE

BAADER, GERMAINE (p. 354), is a successful actress past the first flush of youth, formerly Gurau's mistress, now—after a brief interlude with Roger Sammécaud—in the same relationship to the playwright Henry Mareil, who has been useful to the advancement of her career. They have recently spent a night at Celle-les-Eaux, Haverkamp's watering-place.

MARQUIS (p. 354), manager of the theatre where Germaine Baader is under contract.

MAREIL, HENRY (p. 355) (real name Lucien Wormser), is a fashionable playwright who succeeds Gurau as the lover of Germaine Baader. As a Jew, he had suffered at the time of the Dreyfus affair, and from the subsequent propaganda of the reactionary Action Française.

CHAMPCENAIS, MARIE DE (p. 369), wife of Comte de Champcenais, is a fashionable and fastidious, but rather light-minded woman who has let her sexual inexperience prey on her mind. Her husband's business associate, Roger Sammécaud, makes an intimate proposal which at first embarrasses her. The affair progresses, however, in Sammécaud's bachelor apartment in Paris, and on trips to the country and to England, until Marie becomes pregnant and has an abortion.

CERCOTTE, MADAME (p. 370), a fortune-teller whom Marie de Champcenais has consulted.

CHAMPCENAIS, MARC DE (p. 378), subnormal son of Marie and her husband, brought up in the French provinces and later sent to school in England.

LAFEUILLE, PIERRE (p. 390), a young law student introduced by Sammécaud to Gurau, later a member of the staff of Gurau's newspaper, where his articles proposing a state oil monopoly are cleverly disguised propaganda for the oil-dealers. Subsequently Gurau suppresses his alarmist article written at the behest of the munitions-dealers.

DESBOULMIERS (p. 394), one of the oil-magnates associated with Champcenais and Sammécaud.

QUINETTE (p. 417) is a humdrum bookbinder who becomes obsessed with the idea of committing a murder for its own sake. He selects as his first victim Augustin Leheudry, an obscure young man with no connections, proceeds step by step to gain his confidence, finally kills him in a quarry and makes identification impossible. In order to lay a red herring across his trail, he makes friends with an inspector of police, Marilhat (see below); in this connection he spies upon a radical society and reports to Marilhat. Quinette's other two victims, whose deaths the narrative has obliquely reported, were originally associated with Leheudry.

LEHEUDRY, AUGUSTIN (p. 417), a petty sneak-thief who sought refuge in Quinette's shop and became his first victim.

PARENT, SOPHIE (p. 417), Leheudry's mistress, whom Quinette has deceived after the murder of Leheudry.

JANITRESS AT 142 A FAUBOURG SAINT-DENIS (p. 417) originally rented an apartment to Quinette in the course of his first crime; her subsequent disappearance has been noted in the press.

ALBERTE, MADEMOISELLE (p. 417), has appeared as hostess at a dinner-party where a guest mentions, in another connection, the quarry where Leheudry was murdered.

MARILHAT (p. 421), inspector of police with whom Quinette has established contact; he has made Quinette the recipient of several confidences, and has never suspected him.

DRAMATIS PERSONAE

VÉRAND, JULIETTE (formerly Juliette Ezzelin) (p. 454), is first introduced as a casual customer of the bookbinder-murderer Quinette. The young wife of a humdrum office clerk, she is passionately in love with Jallez, who breaks off their affair and fails to re-establish it, leaving her desperately unhappy. Her husband shows her an anonymous letter, in which he learns of her love-affair, as she returns from a meeting with Jallez, clinging to her fragment of happiness; a scene follows in which she makes her husband promise not to follow up the information. At a subsequent meeting with Jallez he upbraids her for not having told him of her marriage, but continues to make love to her. She has recently divorced her husband and resumed her maiden name.

CAULET (p. 435), comrade of Jallez and Jerphanion at the Normal College, fond of practical joking.

CAZALIS, MATHILDE (p. 435), a young school-teacher who frequents the Wednesday evening discussion group led by Sampeyre (see below), where several young men have been attracted to her. Almost engaged to Clanricard, she jilts him for Jerphanion, who later gives her up; then she has a brief affair with Laulerque (see below). Sampeyre advises her to come to an understanding with Clanricard, and she has now married him.

MACAIRE (p. 480), the Saint-Papouls' dog, an animal of charming and original personality.

SAINT-PAPOUL, BERNARDINE DE (p. 480), eccentric old-maid sister of the Marquis, who studies the lives of the saints with a mixture of piety and secular curiosity. She somewhat maliciously misleads Jeanne, the nervous eighteen-year-old daughter of the Marquis, as to the nature of the sexual act. Her confessions, of which Mionnet keeps a record, contain frequent references to Jerphanion.

DRAMATIS PERSONAE

SAINT-PAPOUL, CLÉMENCE (p. 480), wife of the Marquis de Saint-Papoul.

PAULETTE (p. 487), mistress of the Marquis de Saint-Papoul.

LOMMÉRIE, MONSIEUR DE (p. 487), is a Catholic financier who has engaged Haverkamp to negotiate the secret purchase of a disestablished religious property.

LOMMÉRIE, ROLAND DE (p. 487), son of the above, is an army officer on duty in Africa.

ALLORY, GEORGE (p. 489) (real name Abraham David), is a snobbish and empty novelist who has failed in his ambition to be elected to the French Academy; in his disappointment he has explored the ramifications of vice, and attempted suicide.

MASCOT (p. 490), member of a secret society to which Laulerque (see below) belongs.

LAULERQUE, ARMAND (p. 490), a young radical, has joined a secret society organized for violence in political action, for which he has gone on several missions. The society's part in the attempted assassination of Briand, together with various suspicious matters which he learns, undermines his confidence in its revolutionary effectiveness. Laulerque has been in love with a Croatian girl who is a fellow-member of the secret organization; also he has had a brief love-affair with Mathilde Cazalis.

KARL, MONSIEUR (p. 490), another member of the secret society with whom Laulerque has worked, in connection with the purchase of real estate in the south of France.

SAMPEYRE (p. 493) is an intellectual liberal in middle age, a follower of Jaurès, and mentor of a group of young idealists who meet at his house on Wednesday evenings to discuss peace, politics, and labour. He has patched up the romance of Mathilde Cazalis and Clanricard.

BENOÎT-COTRU (p. 500), the family from whom Haverkamp bought the Limoges property.

NANTHIAT (p. 500), manager of the factory at Limoges which Haverkamp has acquired.

GEOFFROY (p. 513) is in the civil service, an important man on Caillaux's staff; he is instrumental in persuading Gurau not to resign from Caillaux's Cabinet at a critical moment, has arranged for a significant mission to the Vatican, and has otherwise been on the inside during the progress of pre-war diplomacy.

The foregoing paragraphs have been prepared by George Stevens.

BOOK THIRTEEN:
MISSION TO ROM

Chapter

1

WANTED—A "RARA AVIS." WHO IS MERRY DEL VAL?

Manifassier had reported to Gurau, the very day after its occurrence, the conversation he had had with Courson.

Gurau was inclined to lend a favourable ear to anything that came from Courson, but on this occasion, though admitting that what had been said was "extremely interesting," he pointed out that it scarcely justified a direct approach to Poincaré.

"He would think from my asking such a thing that I had something definite to report, some serious communication to make. One can't just go to a man with a neat mind like his and say: 'Look here, a rumour has reached me—' If I did that, he'd never treat me seriously again."

Not that he would have minded, in itself, taking the initiative. He was only too glad of any pretext for continuing the political flirtation which for some months now he had been carrying on with Poincaré. Besides, anything connected with the Church excited him. The idea that he might find himself, however indirectly, however casually, mixed up with ecclesiastical affairs, inevitably appealed to him, quite apart from any personal interest he might take in the matters at issue; and he would have welcomed an opportunity, other things being equal, of letting the Prime Minister see that though, for the time being, he was out of office, he had lost none of his vigilance and was as closely in touch as ever with his private sources of information. But he was anxious not to give the impression of being an officious busybody, ready to make a great to-do about nothing.

". . . I must wait for the right moment."

The right moment happened to turn up a day or two later. One morning Poincaré, whose natural affability was becoming more marked as the presidential election approached, accosted him in one of the corridors of the Chamber with a kindly smile and an air of being less preoccupied than usual. Their talk turned almost at once to foreign affairs.

Poincaré was uneasy about the Balkan war which had just broken out. It was not the actual progress of hostilities that troubled him, for he was of the opinion that, despite inevitable changes of fortune, the Balkan states would ultimately emerge victorious. True, they were not allies of France, but they were the friends of Russia and, in a general sense, inspired by Russian diplomacy. In many ways too—for example, in the matter of military tactics—they might be considered as the pupils of France. Their victory would mean a weakening of the power and the prestige of the Central Empires, thereby strengthening the hands of French politicians. But he could not help wondering whether the present conflict might not have a far more serious sequel directly involving French interests:

"Look at what's happened already. First you get the Italo-Turkish outbreak, and then, with only a year between, this. The one follows logically from the other, and behind it all is the general state of simmering that's been going on in that part of Europe ever since October 1908, and even earlier. . . . What's it all going to lead to? I'm always haunted by the fear that Austria may decide to take a hand."

"And Russia?"

Poincaré's immediate reaction to the question was a slight shrug. The next moment, however, he tried to offset the significance of this gesture by saying, in a tone which was eloquent more of non-committal politeness than deep feeling and seemed to express not so much a personal conviction as the current official attitude:

"Russia's always prepared to listen to reason."

Gurau, encouraged by the cordial atmosphere of their interchange, tried hard to find out whether, during his visit to Russia in the preceding August, the Prime Minister had not, in fact, gathered any hints of the impending Balkan trouble. Wasn't it true that Sazonov had already had wind of something? The general view was that he was a man with a bold realism of outlook and a restless intelligence. There were many, indeed, who saw no little danger in a mind so ceaselessly active.

Poincaré side-tracked the question with a few amiable generalities. Hurriedly he set himself to develop his theme, and his voice took on again its earlier note of precision. "The important thing for us," he said, "is to be ready for anything. No matter what happens, nor where, we must not let ourselves be taken by surprise."

"Your saying that reminds me," interjected the former Minister, "that I want to ask your advice about something rather disturbing, something rather odd, that has come to my ears."

Without mentioning Courson by name, he recounted the various warnings he had received about the situation in Rome.

"The source of my information is thoroughly reliable."

The precise form of the communication Gurau deliberately left vague. From the way he spoke, it might equally well have been something picked up in conversation, something imparted to him by letter, or contained in a document of undoubted authenticity. If it were the last, he made it quite clear that he had no intention of letting it out of his hands. He indicated, in the friendliest way possible, that anyone less kindly disposed towards the Prime Minister than himself might have used what he knew to ask some very embarrassing questions in the Chamber and so stage a dramatic come-back on the political scene.

Poincaré listened with deep attention. When next he spoke, it was, first of all, to thank Gurau for the attitude of friendliness and loyalty which he had adopted in the matter, an attitude which was exactly what he would have expected from their former relationship (though, in fact, he had nothing to fear from a public debate on the subject). Next, he admitted that unfortunately he had only too good reason to believe that what the other had been told was true. He, too, had been in receipt of certain reports, some emanating direct from French agents on the spot, unofficial persons living in Rome, others reaching him in a more roundabout fashion, but of no less trustworthy a nature. For example, there were persistent rumours current both in Vienna and in Belgrade of a number of activities on the part of the Roman Curia which were quite clearly inspired by hostility to France, to the Triple Entente, and to the smaller powers who were their friends. Sazonov had expressed similar uneasiness when they had met last August in St. Petersburg. The trouble was that all these rumours were so vague, so inconsistent, so obviously stamped with the hall-mark of gossip. If Gurau could really fill the gap by supplying detailed and definite information, he would certainly be rendering his country a great service. Another and more serious weakness in the French position resulted from the absence of any machinery which would enable the government to discuss matters frankly with the Holy See or, in case of necessity, make representations in the proper quarters.

"I don't for a moment imagine that it's practical politics to think of having an accredited ambassador at the Vatican. Our breach with Rome may or may not have been a wise step, but it's too late to think of that now. At some future date we may be able to take a different line without incurring the hostility of anti-clerical opinion, but the time's not yet."

Gurau could not help noting with a little private thrill of admiration the way in which Poincaré had framed his words so that, while remaining true to his personal convictions, he could have repeated them quite safely in the hearing of his Versailles constituents of all parties.

"Have you anything to suggest?" continued the Prime Minister.

Gurau replied, with well-simulated spontaneity, that when he had been at the Foreign Office he had once played with the notion (in fact, he had done nothing of the sort) of entrusting somebody with a special and confidential mission to Rome.

"I don't know . . . but I used to wonder whether it might not be possible to find someone in the ranks of the French clergy—I'm quite sure a layman would be no good—someone of intelligence and initiative, not yet too well known, and of undoubted patriotism. . . ."

"Yes," interrupted Poincaré, "yes. . . ."

". . . And capable of understanding that the interests of the faith have nothing in common with the intrigues of the Austrian and German parties at the Vatican. . . ."

"Yes, yes. . . ."

". . . Someone who would think it just as natural to help us by combating such intrigues as others find it natural to further them."

"Good. And what precise instructions, may I ask, would you have given to your envoy?" Poincaré smiled.

"I've never worked out the details . . . the idea's still quite vague in my mind . . . but the kind of thing I had in view, once we'd found the right person, was to get him settled on the spot in such a way that, without involving himself in any kind of conspiratorial secrets, he could be sure of not attracting undue attention. His position as unofficial agent would, of course, be known to nobody, except, perhaps, to our Ambassador at the Quirinal."

"Go on. . . ."

"My idea would be that by virtue of his cloth he could mix freely in ecclesiastical circles, hear what was being said, get into touch with influential persons. . . ."

"Yes. . . ."

"The whole scheme may, of course, be moonshine. . . . For all I know, Vatican circles may be even more impenetrable than we think . . . but we do know that leakages occur, if only because a certain amount of talk reaches our ears. I find it difficult to believe that a man of ability and tact, whose whole time would be given to the business, couldn't give us more and better information than just Tom, Dick, or Harry. Perhaps his chief value would be in assembling the various odds and ends of news that reach us at present without order or discrimination, and so providing us with sufficient material on which to base an attitude."

At this point Poincaré remarked that perhaps one of the results of having more detailed information available might be to diminish the fears of the government in this matter of Rome. He wondered sometimes whether it was really worth while attaching so much importance to Vatican activity in the international field, except where purely Church affairs were concerned—whether, indeed, any such activity existed at all.

". . . In all my dealings with ecclesiastics, I have always been struck by the narrowness of their outlook. Where international politics are concerned, I'm inclined to believe that their reactions don't go much beyond arguing something as follows: 'This or that government has just played us a nasty trick, or looks like being a nuisance. This or that government, for the moment at least, is well disposed. . . . How can we defend ourselves against such and such a threat or get such and such a concession? . . .' Usually the whole thing boils down to ensuring the appointment of some particular man as archbishop or bishop, where they are dealing with a country in official relations with Rome, or, where they aren't, of guaranteeing a degree of freedom for religious instruction, or working for the repeal of some measure that bears hard on Catholic propaganda. . . . It may, perhaps, go as far occasionally as saying: 'How can we pay so and so out? . . .' Generally speaking, I should say that their interests are extremely limited, very prosaic, and definitely egocentric. I've got an impression, too, that even the governments which one would regard as most naturally inclined to work hand in glove with their clergy treat them in fact as very junior partners. They may be willing to protect them, to make use of them—for the very good reason that no possible weapon should ever, in theory at least, be ignored—but they don't really trust them, and certainly don't treat with them on a basis of equality. . . . I'm still more certain that the Papacy as it is today is very unlikely to initiate a policy on the grand scale, a great Continental movement à la Richelieu, Metternich, or Bismarck . . . or bring to fruition the seeds of a great European plot against the French nation."

"But, my dear Prime Minister, didn't you yourself just now produce the phrase: 'pay so and so out'? And is it so wholly unreasonable to attribute to the Vatican a desire to 'pay out' the France of today for the wrongs it believes itself to have suffered at her hands in the past —especially if it can persuade itself that in so doing it will be acting for our final good and may succeed in bringing the French people back to a chastened mood of Christian repentance after having served as an object lesson to the rest of the world? . . . Is it unreasonable to picture the Vatican as moved by such intentions and bringing to their execution the patience which has always characterized the policy of the Church? . . ."

"It might be so . . . though, as a matter of fact, the France of today is less likely to inspire such thoughts of vengeance than the France of yesterday. . . ."

He was, however, fully in agreement with his visitor that it would be the height of folly to assume *a priori* that any facts which might emerge on inquiry must be unimportant. Even if the Vatican were not playing, on the contemporary scene, that role of mysterious plotter and worker of mischief which was the favourite figment of so many heated imaginations, even if it were not the centre of intrigue which it was popularly supposed to be, it might, all the same, yield information which would put us on the track, indirectly, of other movements. At any rate, as had so often been pleaded by those who argued for a re-establishment of diplomatic relations, it formed an admirable observation post.

After a moment's silence he continued, with an air of deep thought:

"The whole thing really turns on the question of personalities . . . and the sooner we face that, the better. The Vatican may not have the means it once had of making a policy effective . . . but it certainly has some, and assuming that there happened to be on the spot a man of ideas, a man of *one* idea, a man of iron will, suffering from a sense of grievance, however little justified—it wouldn't be lack of means that would stand in the way of his influencing events. With far weaker weapons at his disposition, such a man could do much—a Richelieu, a Ximenes, even a Mazarin, who for ten years had lived with an oath of vengeance to inspire him, a man who had said: 'I will work for the punishment of France because France deserves punishment, and because by so doing I shall be working too for the glory of the Church and the edification of Christendom. I will take every opportunity of helping her enemies, of injuring her and her friends, especially since, as it so happens, this renegade land has only heretics whom she can call her friends. . . .' The real point is, does such a man exist? I am prepared to admit that Pius X is not a 'political' Pope, that his grievance against us and against others is not likely, where he alone is concerned, to express itself in long-distance plotting. But don't let us forget Merry del Val. Who, precisely, is he? What goes on in his head? Is it he, perhaps, who plays the part of Richelieu or Mazarin in this affair? . . . If he were to do so, then the political nullity of his Pope, the note of pure and simple piety which, as all are agreed, marks the character of the sovereign pontiff, would be far from disadvantageous to his Minister. He would have complete freedom of movement and a convenient screen as well. Yes, the more I think of it, the more certain I am that the whole problem centres on this one point. . . . If we come down to brass tacks, the whole job of your emissary would be to clarify our knowledge of Merry del Val. That would be quite enough for us. Who is this Merry del Val? Is he the kind of man who might evolve a policy and follow it out? If he is, then it is essential for us to know what that policy is, though I have very little doubt, alas, of its nature. . . . I agree with you that for such a mission a cleric is indispensable, but he must be a man capable of taking the widest possible views, and he must be able to give us absolute guarantees of loyalty. Have you anyone in mind?"

Gurau admitted that he had not.

The Prime Minister sat deep in thought, gazing before him at a point slightly above the level of his head. His eyes were shining, and he was manifestly excited by the turn the conversation had taken. He seemed quite oblivious of the time.

"Look here," he said suddenly, with one of his frankest smiles, "I'd like to go more thoroughly into all this, but I can't; I'm too busy. I wonder if you'd do me a favour and take over the job yourself. . . .

I'm not saying that as an excuse for shelving it; on the contrary, my asking you to do such a thing is proof of the importance I attach to it. . . . I want you to go ahead exactly as though you were a member of the Cabinet. Choose your man, make your plans, and you can rely on me to back you up."

Gurau thanked him for this evidence of his trust and declared that he was in thorough agreement about the necessity of narrowing down the point at issue as far as possible. Unfortunately, the more delicate and important the task, the harder would it be to find the right man.

". . . The mere fact that we've got to sound opinion without giving away what we're after makes it all very much more complicated."

"Of course we mustn't give away anything!" exclaimed Poincaré.

He added that he would consult a connexion of his who was a Bishop—without, naturally, going into details—a man of assured integrity and, if he might use the phrase without appearing to be pretentious, a thoroughly "loyal Republican."

He thought too that he might put out a feeler in certain directions among Catholic, though liberal-minded, members of Parliament.

". . . I'm thinking, for instance, of men like Denys Cochin, the Comte de Mun, or, if the worst comes to the worst, the Marquis de Saint-Papoul. He hasn't the influence they have, I know, but he's by no means a fool, and he's in touch with a great many people. . . . On the whole, de Mun would be best . . . I'd rather do nothing without his approval."

Gurau replied that he was on very good terms with the Comte de Mun, and thought highly of him. (He had been deeply impressed by the talk they had had in 1910 about women home-workers. It occurred to him, moreover, that M. de Mun's influence in the forthcoming presidential elections would be considerable. It was not, therefore, difficult to understand why Poincaré felt so tenderly towards him. . . .) His relations with M. Denys Cochin were friendly, though far from intimate. M. de Saint-Papoul he scarcely knew.

Two days later Gurau was able to buttonhole M. de Mun as the latter was coming out of a committee. Looking at the honest, sensitive face before him, he felt there should be no difficulty in seeing eye to eye with his Catholic colleague so far, at least, as general principles were concerned.

In a friendly, almost deferential tone he asked him what he thought about the anti-French schemes which, according to reliable observers, were being hatched in the shadow of the Vatican.

M. de Mun replied that he thought the rumours in question were exaggerated. The Pope harboured no views antagonistic to France; quite the contrary, in fact. Those who thought him capable of supporting any intrigue could know very little about him.

"The Pope is a saint! Liturgical problems, music, pure theology, are what interest him. Politics and political machinations bore him and make him nervous."

Gurau pointed out very quietly that the Pope's saintly qualities were not in question. The virtues of Pius X, as well as his detachment from worldly affairs, were personal to himself. The real danger lay in his leaving too free a field to the politicians of his entourage, and there was only too good reason for suspecting some of *them*.

M. de Mun, his voice taking on a faintly ironical inflexion, replied that it was to deal with precisely such dangers that diplomacy had been invented. If France was in a worse position to deal with them than other countries, France had only herself to blame.

Gurau admitted that the rupture of relations with the Vatican might, quite possibly, have been a mistake, adding, however, that it was not a mistake that could be repaired at a moment's notice, and that the fact that France had no minister accredited to the Holy See was no reason for standing aside and doing nothing about any plotting that might be going on. M. de Mun spread his arms and gave a slight shrug, indicating by the gesture that though he might deplore the situation in which France found herself, he could see no way out of the difficulty.

But Gurau pressed his point:

"Is there nothing you think we could do?"

M. de Mun pursed his lips.

"I'm afraid not. Some of my co-religionists, of course, who have occasion to go to Rome, regularly use their influence to make things easier. But they can do very little."

Gurau slightly altered his line of approach:

"Don't you think that, short of bringing pressure to bear, we might at least have better sources of information, might at least try to get a clearer view of what is going on?"

Once again M. de Mun made an evasive grimace.

"From information that has reached me," continued Gurau, "I gather that many bishops and monks of Teutonic origin, resident at Rome, make no bones about serving the interests of their country. . . . Their chief activity in this line, I suppose, lies in keeping their government informed, should necessity arise."

"Is there any reason to suppose that the French bishops and monks don't do the same?"

"Are you sure they send us all the information we need?"

"That I can't say. . . . Perhaps it's not their job to do so."

"Or perhaps they don't think it is. . . . That's precisely what I'm afraid of."

Gurau thought a moment; then:

"There is, in Rome, occupying a post of the highest importance, one man in particular about whom I am—shall we say—extremely curious and not a little nervous . . . and I'm not the only one. . . ."

"Meaning—?"

"The Cardinal Merry del Val. . . . Rightly or wrongly, I believe it to be very important indeed for us to know what he's up to."

"Possibly; and that is where a good ambassador would be of the greatest value."

"I can only repeat what I said before—that we have no ambassador and are not likely to have one in the immediate future. . . . But if I understand you correctly, you yourself are not altogether easy in your mind about the feelings and intentions of Merry del Val."

"His feelings towards us are not likely to be very warm. As to his intentions—I have no authority for thinking that they are particularly villainous. . . ."

"You admit, though, that it might not be without some value for us to know just what they are?"

"Possibly."

"Suppose I asked you straight out something like this: What steps ought we to take to find out what they are . . . now, at once . . . without waiting for him to disclose them to some future and hypothetical ambassador? . . . In other words, how are we to set about instituting an inquiry on the spot, a deliberate and discreet inquiry? How would you answer?"

"You have taken me by surprise."

"You can suggest nothing?"

"Are you thinking of something on strictly non-official lines?"

"Maybe."

"Non-official or not, success would depend upon the Cardinal's willingness to receive an emissary and confide in him."

"Can you think of no other way of carrying out an unofficial inquiry?"

"You mean by getting other people to talk? . . . That would lead to all sorts of complications."

Neither M. de Mun's tone nor the little smile which accompanied it was very encouraging. Gurau felt that he would gain nothing, for the present at least, by pressing his point.

"Will you so far oblige me, my dear sir, as to think the matter over? . . . I need hardly point out that what we have been discussing must be regarded as strictly confidential."

Chapter

A MAN OF RESOURCE

"Nothing doing with him," thought Gurau. "I'm pretty sure he wouldn't categorically deny that there is a danger, and he certainly wouldn't go so far as to approve a plot, hatched and blessed by the Holy See, to crush a France once ruled by Combes and now ruled by Poincaré. But he's against our doing anything to try to unmask an enemy who may be lurking in the respectable surroundings of Rome. He belongs to that over-courteous section of the community which has brought to a fine art the employment of exquisite manners as a way of escape from any difficult situation. There are moments when I'd gladly punch their gentlemanly heads for them."

He returned to the Chamber and sat down at his desk without, at first, looking about him. After a few minutes, however, his eyes began to wander. M. de Mun had also returned. Gurau could see him out of the corner of his eye, seated between two fattish members with pendulous cheeks, pink, bald heads, and rolls of fat above their collars. He noted again the enigmatic façade presented by the man's moustache, eyes, and general appearance of well-born military retirement; by the honest glance of that level gaze which, in its obvious aptitude for the thorough understanding of certain sides of life, reminded him of the expression to be seen at times on the faces of young girls brought up in a good family.

"There's a core of hardness in the fellow," he reflected, and felt suddenly critical of all those men and women who are usually described, a little too unthinkingly, as "decent." "Even he isn't altogether displeased at the thought that our anti-clerical Republic is in trouble, that circumstances have combined to show it the *reductio ad absurdum* of its errors. Oh, I'm sure he wouldn't like to think that the proof might land us in disaster. No doubt he hopes that Providence will step in to save us at the last moment, or a miraculous and national repentance—perhaps both. . . ."

Seated there with his arms crossed, he watched the light of the Chamber falling like a sad and not unpleasing drift of rain upon a speaker to whom no one was listening.

The names mentioned by Poincaré flitted through his mind: Denys Cochin . . . Saint-Papoul.

He turned his head. He had caught sight of another man, very different from M. de Mun, occupying a desk several rows away, towards the back of the room and in the left-hand segment of the horseshoe: a thin, tallish man, dressed in funereal black, unneighboured, and with several dispatch-boxes in front of him. From his down-drawn brows it was clear that he, unlike his colleagues, was actually listening to the speaker, despite the noise of private conversations all around him and the feeble quality of the voice that was trying to dominate the babble.

Gurau was on the barest nodding terms with the Marquis de Saint-Papoul. He thought he looked a bit of an old fool, but was secretly inclined to agree with Poincaré that he had close ties binding him to many different worlds—feudal aristocracy, Church, and moneyed middle class. Neither his activity at question time nor his reputation as a committee-man had been of a sort to compromise M. de Saint-Papoul. There was no reason not to believe that he wielded a good deal of backstair influence. Colleagues quite frequently asked him to act as their substitute, and on more than one occasion Poincaré had been seen chatting to him in a corner.

Gurau noticed that the Marquis was in mourning. "Of course. He lost his father-in-law early in the autumn, or so I seem to remember. I forgot to send him a line of condolence. . . . Too late now." If what Mme de Crauze and Gisèle had told him of the father-in-law were true, the Marquis must now be in control of an enormous fortune, a fact which certainly was not calculated to diminish any influence he might already have. To do him justice, there was nothing in his appearance—mourning excepted—to lead one to suppose that he was any different from what he had been last summer. That certainly was a point in his favour, and fitted in well with the general impression he gave of being abler than he looked.

Acting on a sudden impulse, Gurau decided to go and sit next to M. de Saint-Papoul. The Marquis gave signs of evident surprise and showed that he was profoundly conscious of the honour that was being done him. He half got up and bowed from the waist.

"My dear sir . . ."

Gurau, with a gesture of friendly intimacy, signed to him to be seated.

Although there was no one near them, he began to talk in a low voice:

"I want to ask your advice—your very confidential advice. . . ."

The other nodded with a conspiratorial air.

Gurau made a movement of the chin towards the ministerial benches.

"It's about something Poincaré's got deeply at heart. . . . You can take anything I say as coming from him. . . . Both he and I know that, for all your republican sympathies, you've got a good many connexions among the clergy."

The Marquis nodded in modest agreement.

"That being so, you're in a better position than most to do us a great service. Can you think of anyone among your clerical friends to whom the French government—I'm not mincing matters, but please keep what I say to yourself—could entrust a delicate mission abroad? The kind of man we're looking for must be absolutely reliable, very intelligent, used to dealing with people, and a true Frenchman at heart—by which I mean that he must be able to see that there are circumstances in which a man can, and should, serve his country in spite of her mistakes, must be capable, too, of realizing that the interests of true religion are not identical with the interests of those people who, at home or elsewhere, use religion as a mask or a shield. He needn't occupy a high place in the hierarchy; in fact, we'd prefer someone who was not in the public eye—a young man for choice. If you can think of anyone," he added, "who roughly fills the bill, I'd be grateful if you would put him in touch with me. If he impresses me favourably, if I think he can give us the necessary guarantees, I'll tell him what it is we have in mind. Do you think you can help?"

M. de Saint-Papoul, after much frowning consideration, assured Gurau that he would give the whole matter immediate consideration and would be the soul of discretion. If he could have forty-eight hours, he would be able to give some sort of general answer.

"Three days, if you like; five, even!" exclaimed Gurau. "What we're asking of you is something of extreme delicacy. Take all the time you need, my dear sir."

The Marquis in reply made a gesture which at once expressed his gratitude and indicated that he was fully aware of the seriousness of what had been proposed.

"In forty-eight hours," he repeated, "I shall be in a position to tell you what I think."

"It's almost too good to be true," thought Gurau as he went back to his own seat; "provided he really has a wide circle of acquaintances and knows which note on the keyboard to strike."

Chapter 3

THE COMTE DE MÉZAN ADVISES

M. de Saint-Papoul had, in fact, almost at once decided which was the right note to strike. His decision was due, however, less to natural astuteness than to the limited nature of the keyboard at his disposition.

The truth was that he knew comparatively few people—few, that is, who could be held to rank above a fairly low standard of usefulness. Among the clergy, in particular—leaving out of account the provincial canons and country priests of his acquaintance—his intimates were far from numerous.

Listening to Gurau, the idea had immediately come to him: "Just the thing for the Abbé Mionnet!" and "This is a matter about which Mézan, if only he would, if only I dared ask him, could give excellent advice."

It was between these two poles—Mionnet and Mézan—that, as soon as Gurau left him, his thoughts began to oscillate.

About Mionnet his conscience was not quite easy. "Considering the way he helped my election, I've not been very polite to him, not acted really even with common decency. . . . It must be more than a year since I had him to dinner. I'm not actually certain whether or no he's back for good from that job he was doing in the country. Bernardine may have mentioned seeing him at Saint Thomas's, but if so, I can't have been paying attention."

From another point of view it seemed to him that a little preliminary talk with Mézan—quite apart from putting him *au fait* with the Abbé's present situation—would give him the ammunition he needed before making a frontal attack upon Mionnet.

"However little I may be inclined to confide in him, I shall be able to tell from his reactions what sort of a chance I should have with Mionnet—or with anybody else. He's so well in with all that world!"

The trouble was that he couldn't be really frank with Mézan. M. de Saint-Papoul was not the man to take lightly the promise of discretion which he had made to Gurau. It must never be said that a leader of the extreme Left had reason to regret taking a Gascon gentleman into his confidence.

Of course, if it came to that, Mézan was a gentleman, too, and, what was more, a friend. He could safely be put upon his honour. But the very reasons which lent weight to his advice made any promise he might give suspect. Were his wife and Bernardine right in believing the story that Mézan was bound by close ties to the Society of Jesus, that he had actually at one time been a "secret member," with the prerogatives, but also with the obligations, that such a relationship entailed? If they were, then his word of honour to a friend would certainly not stand in the way of his putting his fellow-members on their guard.

One day, under the genial influence of a cigar and a glass of armagnac, Saint-Papoul had taken his courage in both hands and frankly attacked Mézan on the subject. The latter had replied with a laugh. "Oh, I know that's what people say," he had answered, "and from certain things I have seen, I gather that a lot of your friends believe it. But surely you don't?—that, I confess, would surprise me. . . . Really, I can't help smiling. Not that I mind; just the contrary, in fact. I'm regarded as a bit of a mystery . . . people are a little frightened of me. A vague sense of power that never quite comes into focus has a way of reacting upon the popular imagination. You see it in the fact that certain business men put it about that they are Jews, or that, in other walks of life, there's advantage in having the reputation of holding high office with the Masons. . . . The truth is—yes, the real truth—that persons such as I am supposed to be exist only in the novels of Eugène Sue. . . . If you started that line of talk with people who know about these things, they would merely shrug their shoulders. It's not worth serious consideration for a moment . . .

though that doesn't mean," he added with a slight change of tone, and as though in parenthesis, "that you won't meet plenty of secular clergy, decent priests not too highly gifted with intelligence, who, for some unknown reason, have a perfect obsession about the Jesuits and will assure you with a knowing wink that the Society has its agents everywhere, that you will find them disguised as bearded officers of the Grand Orient itself. . . . Well, that's the first point. The second is this—for there's never, as they say, smoke without fire—that I did, as a young man, play with the idea of becoming a Jesuit, that I actually spent eighteen months in the noviciate. As things turned out, I found I couldn't stand it—not so much the actual discipline as the moral atmosphere, which is very intense and puts a terrible strain on the nerves. . . . Perhaps, too, my superiors considered that I was lacking in flexibility or resistance. I was going through one of those periods, not uncommon in youth, when the health, especially as it affects the nerves, is not yet stabilized. The real reason, of course, was much simpler: I had no vocation. Nevertheless, I have always had a weakness for my friends of the Society and have always felt strongly attached to them. As someone once said to me, with perfect truth: 'They've got everything in their favour: intellectual subtlety and military courage; freedom of movement combined with a rigid discipline. They may be said to be an amalgam of all that is best in the Benedictines and the Foreign Legion. . . .' I've sometimes made a retreat with them, and I do what little I can to further their interests. If the occasion arises and I ask them a service, they treat me as a privileged person, and I say that knowing full well that it is one of their rules to be all things to all men."

Was that the whole truth? M. de Saint-Papoul would not have liked to take an oath that it was. In any case, he still felt that he must go carefully. The Count was certainly a good Frenchman, of that there could be no doubt. Should necessity arise, he might even give considerable rein to his patriotic sentiments. There had been an occasion when, in the Marquis's hearing, he had commented severely on the number of Germans who were invading the Society. But how far could this independence of judgment be relied upon? Mézan might be willing to deplore certain errors to be found within the Society, or, more generally, within the body of the Church, and yet refuse to countenance any intrusion of the civil power into the administrative field of religion.

M. de Saint-Papoul came, ultimately, to the conclusion that he would not be taking too great a risk in seeing Mézan and, in the course of conversation, asking him about Mionnet. Circumstances would show whether he could allow himself to go a little further without incurring a charge of foolhardiness.

It was not difficult to find an excuse for paying Mézan a visit. For some time past the Count had been trying, without much success, to get some directorships for the Deputy from Périgord. As soon as he had come into the Montech money, the difficulties had grown less and he had actually got him appointed to two boards, though by that time Saint-Papoul was no longer in need of the financial aid represented by directors' fees and percentages. Life is like that. Of one of these boards M. de Mézan was not himself a member. It was quite natural, therefore, that M. de Saint-Papoul should take his advice about some little awkwardness connected with his new duties.

He went to see Mézan the next morning in the latter's office at the Banque du Nord. After disposing of the point which he had used as a pretext for his visit, he led the conversation to the subject of Mionnet. He learned that the Abbé had completed his mission to M— some months previously; that he had so far succeeded in his task as to cause serious offence to a certain number of people and make a good many enemies. Attempts had even been made to "entangle" him with a woman—much to the amusement of M. de Mézan. But taken all round, the affair had ended as a great personal triumph for the Abbé. He had shown that he possessed many various qualities, not least a gift of initiative and a power of interpreting instructions which, had things turned out badly, might have done him considerable harm, but which, in fact, had had the effect of giving him an assured position.

"It is entirely owing to him that the Bishop is still there, though he had been more or less instructed to get rid of him. Still, he made up for that by laying about him, in other directions, with a pretty strong hand."

The Abbé had not returned to Saint Thomas's. A special Department of Social Studies had been created for him under the Archbishop's immediate patronage. He had also resumed his lectures at the Institute. But there was something rather unreal now about his academic activities.

"You mark my words," said M. de Mézan with a knowing look, "he won't grow old in the service of education. That young fellow's made for a more active life."

M. de Saint-Papoul was delighted with what he heard. The news seemed to him to be highly encouraging.

He ventured a comment:

"You think he's the kind of man to whom one could entrust a delicate mission—something a little bit out of the ordinary?"

The Count glanced at him inquisitively.

"Have you got something of the sort in mind?"

"Oh dear me, no!"

It occurred to him, however, that a flat denial was not perhaps, in the circumstances, a very astute move.

"I mean, one never knows. In view of the increasing improvement in the relations between the State and the Church, an occasion might arise for the government to seek the co-operation of the clergy . . . and in such a case we politicians might find it useful to have someone up our sleeves. It's always as well to know on whom one can rely."

Chapter

4

WILL HE ACCEPT?

On his way to the Palais Bourbon after luncheon, M. de Saint-Papoul passed the Archbishop's palace and left there a message for the Abbé Mionnet. In it he asked him to come and see him next morning about ten o'clock, at the rue Vaneau, if that wouldn't be too inconvenient, "in order to discuss a matter of considerable urgency."

Mionnet was punctual to the second. The Marquis found him looking rather fatter, but what chiefly struck him was the maturity and increased authority of his manner. His hair, he thought, had slightly receded from his forehead.

He apologized profusely for his recent neglect.

"My parliamentary work takes up a great deal of my time, and then I have had a certain amount of domestic trouble . . . a sad loss. . . . We have been seeing nobody. . . . I hoped you would have proposed yourself, quite informally. . . . But I've been following your career, even though from a distance. I know all about your success."

Having thus re-established contact, he thought it best to go straight to the point.

"I have a certain proposal to make to you. Whether or no it comes to anything, I must ask you to treat everything I say as being in the strictest confidence."

The tone of his voice was rather gloomy, but quite calm, and he stroked his moustache with his hand while he spoke, as though he were savouring the pleasure that his words gave him.

"What I am about to tell you is known only to the Prime Minister, one other eminent man of affairs, and your humble servant. . . ."

Fearing that the last words might seem slightly vainglorious, he corrected himself with a faint air of hesitation:

"And even I don't know the whole of the affair . . . no . . . there are details of which I have not yet been informed . . . so you see. . . . To cut a long story short, the French government has under consideration a mission abroad, for which it needs the services of an ecclesiastic of assured intelligence, character, and, of course, ability. . . . You at once occurred to me."

Mionnet thanked him, but added that no doubt the government would want somebody more important than himself, somebody who carried more weight.

"Far from it. . . . What you call 'weight' is not at all what they are looking for. It's—"

M. de Saint-Papoul, narrowing his eyes, seemed to be seeking the precise word needed to mark the antithesis. But it escaped him.

"Can you tell me what the object of this mission would be?"

"For the moment, no."

"Then I don't see—"

"It is quite impossible, I fear . . . but I can at least assure you that it would be in the highest degree honourable . . . that it would very much redound to the credit of anyone who could carry it through successfully. You don't really think, do you, that a man like the Prime Minister, like Monsieur Poincaré, would suggest to a priest something of which he need be ashamed?"

Mionnet assured him that the thought had never crossed his mind, but pointed out that he could hardly be expected to give an answer if he didn't know more about the matter in question.

"Naturally you will know, in good time. But, for the moment, it is your general attitude about which we want some indication. . . ." He narrowed his eyes again, but this time with the suggestion of a wink. "You have already shown, in connexion with this business at M—, that you can take risks and assume responsibility. You can hardly be surprised, after what happened there, that your name came up for discussion."

As a matter of fact, surprise was the last emotion that showed in

Mionnet's manner. But he seemed in no mood to buy a pig in a poke.

"Can't you at least tell me whether the matter concerns the Church directly or indirectly?"

"We should hardly approach a man like you if it didn't."

"Do you know whether the ecclesiastical authorities have been informed and, if so, whether they are agreeable?"

The Marquis raised his hand in a slow and solemn gesture. It was difficult to guess whether he meant it to imply that he was really ignorant or was merely pretending to be so.

"I don't know. . . . They certainly will be informed if the necessity arises. That point the Prime Minister must be allowed, in his wisdom, to decide."

The Marquis could not help noticing with surprise how the mere fact of being in the dark about a subject helps one to frame answers of prudent astuteness. What a great resource, he decided, that must be in diplomacy!

"The point is for me of fundamental importance," Mionnet insisted. "I am perfectly ready to run risks, but not the risk of finding myself one fine day at variance with my superiors. . . . Besides, if I am to accept a mission, I must be free to do so, and that means that I must get the necessary authorization and give my reasons for asking it. For the moment I say nothing about the regret I should feel at having to give up my work at the Department of Social Studies just as it is getting under way . . . and my lectures at the Institute."

The Marquis seemed to be sunk deep in thought. For two whole minutes he said nothing, but several unfinished gestures which he allowed himself showed how profoundly his mind was working.

"I have the impression," he said at length, "that you entertain no deep-seated repugnance to the matter in question." Ever since he had become a Deputy, M. de Saint-Papoul had enriched his normal vocabulary with certain "weighty" turns of phrase, such as he heard every day in the Chamber. "You wish to be made acquainted with the nature of the contingencies that may arise, as is perfectly natural. . . . I shall mention your name *in certain quarters*"—the phrase "in certain quarters" gave him a little thrill of pleasure—"I may even put you in touch with an individual occupying a position of the highest possible importance. He will decide how much he wishes to tell you. You will be able to talk to him with absolute frankness. Are you prepared for me to do this?"

Mionnet replied that he was.

There was a session of the Chamber that very afternoon. M. de Saint-Papoul went over to where Gurau was sitting, thus repaying the very flattering visit which he himself had received.

It was not without a feeling of pride that, bending towards his ear —for he noticed near by the fat face of the Deputy Courtalon—he murmured:

"I told you that I hoped to be in a position to give you my views within forty-eight hours. I am ready to give them now."

"Splendid!"

Gurau turned towards the Marquis and gazed at him in admiration.

"If I'm not mistaken, I think I've got the very man for you."

"Well done!" For a moment Gurau surrendered to the pleasure we all feel when circumstances enable us to do justice to someone we have previously underrated. When that happens, we are apt deliberately to go too far in the opposite direction. "What a man of resource he is!" he thought. "Who would think it from looking at him?"

The Marquis explained that though the man in question—who was far from being a nobody—had been sounded and had not replied with a flat refusal, a good deal still remained to be done before he could be brought to give any definite undertaking.

"Let's go somewhere quiet and talk," said Gurau.

They left the Chamber. The former Minister had taken the Marquis by the arm. M. de Saint-Papoul, walking out under the eyes of his colleagues, was conscious of a pleasant sense of importance.

He began by giving a description of his *rara avis:* a man of considerable culture . . . college-trained, with a degree . . . still in the hey-day of youth . . . a Professor at the Catholic Institute . . . in charge of an important department which had been specially created for him, and as such directly responsible to the Archbishop. He had already carried through with conspicuous success a difficult mission entrusted to him by his religious superiors . . . a man who, so everybody said, would certainly be one of our next bishops.

"Superb!" exclaimed Gurau. "But aren't you afraid that a man of such distinction may refuse to entertain our proposals? He'll think them unworthy of his consideration."

"That," retorted M. de Saint-Papoul shrewdly, "depends upon the precise nature of what you have to offer. You forget, my dear sir, that I myself am in ignorance of its details and so am hardly in a position to undertake to persuade him. It depends too, I imagine, on the kind of reward, immediate or future, with which you can dazzle him."

Gurau suggested that, as the session did not look like being very interesting, they should adjourn to his apartment, where they would find his secretary and former assistant, Manifassier, whose advice might be useful.

His apartment was small, situated on a first floor of the rue de Galilée and not ten minutes' walk from where Gisèle was living.

M. de Saint-Papoul was aware of a slight feeling of disappointment at hearing that the "secret" was to have yet another initiate, and one of no very high social distinction.

Gurau, for his part, was surprised to find himself showing such zeal for a matter of trivial importance which promised little in the way of personal benefit to himself. The fact remained that he was both excited and interested. Oh well, even if it were nothing but a relaxation, that was no reason for not going on with it.

The first result of the three-cornered conference which took place in Gurau's apartment—the study of which, furnished by Mme

Godorp on the lines of something she had seen at the Autumn Salon, gave on to a quiet, largish courtyard adorned with several grass plots —was to advance M. de Saint-Papoul's knowledge of the project.

He discovered that the mission entailed residence in Rome, and that its object was to unmask the activities of an anti-French cabal working there. He approved the plan without reserve. He was already too deeply committed to be able to question the main lines of the enterprise.

He suggested that he should bring these gentlemen and the Abbé in question—whose name was Mionnet—together at his own house in the rue Vaneau.

". . . Why not tomorrow evening? It would give me great pleasure if you would dine with me, quite quietly. Naturally, not a word must be breathed before the ladies, or before my son. After dinner we can adjourn to my study."

The invitation was accepted. But Gurau, whose tendency to do better than best sometimes led into unnecessary subtleties, proposed that the general meeting should be preceded by an interview between this Abbé Mionnet and Manifassier.

"You're about the same age. You will be able to talk to each other with perfect frankness. You will see at once where we shall be most likely to meet resistance. It'll mean that we shall have much less preliminary work to put in tomorrow night."

The idea did not particularly appeal to M. de Saint-Papoul, since it would deprive him of the pleasure of presiding over the first meeting between these gentlemen and his protégé. He offered, however, to give Mionnet the message at the same time as he invited him to dine.

Alone with Manifassier, Gurau pointed out that it would be lacking in cleverness—meaning by cleverness the *gradual* approach—if they told this Abbé Mionnet straight away that the mission on which he was to be engaged would be "directly aimed at Merry del Val."

"For them he is the Pope's *alter ego*. After Pius X, he is the most important figure in the Church. They would be terrified at the idea of attacking him. They must get used to the idea slowly. The best thing would probably be to let them discover for themselves that he is the centre of the plot. In your place, I should describe the mission in the most general terms, as a reconnaissance. Let him think that he is going to Rome to find out what he can, to keep his ears open, to discover where the danger lies, but don't let him suspect that his conclusions are being dictated to him in advance."

After saying that, Gurau bade his collaborator a friendly farewell. He had only just time to dress. Mme Godorp was giving a dinner to certain artists and men of letters.

The two young men were soon on the friendliest terms. Gurau's anticipations were proved so far right that the trip to Rome, mentioned by Manifassier in a most casual tone as something which he would gladly have undertaken himself had it come his way, soon lost much of its mysterious character. Furthermore, Mionnet felt it incumbent on him to impress this acquaintance of his own generation with a sense of his own adventurousness. If he foresaw any personal risks in the affair, he must be frank about them.

After first saying that, if he were a free agent, he would accept, without further discussion, a job which in itself would be amusing enough, he begged Manifassier to consider his actual situation, the obligations which beset him on all sides, the people he would have to humour.

Together they set themselves to solve his difficulties. Mionnet showed himself perfectly willing to accept those proposed by Manifassier, merely pointing out the particular obstacles they would have to surmount.

After half an hour of desultory talk (the interview, begun in the office next to the "boss's" in the rue de Galilée, was continued in the course of a stroll in the direction of the Trocadéro gardens), Mionnet confirmed the conclusion to which he had come after weighing the whole problem carefully—and which bore out what he had already said to M. de Saint-Papoul—that he could not possibly go without, in some way or other, first obtaining the permission of his superiors.

". . . Not of them all, naturally, but of some. . . . Put yourself in my place. I don't want the thing to become a matter of public discussion, but it is essential that when, as sooner or later it must be, my business in Rome is discovered and the inevitable awkwardnesses arise, there should be persons in Paris in a position to say: 'We knew all about it. You can take it from us that the young man accepted this task from the highest possible motives. We shouldn't like him to suffer because of it.' "

They concentrated on this part of the problem. As is usual in such cases, they wasted a good deal of time in elaborating ingenious plans which were momentarily amusing but of little real value. They even found it fun to cap each other's subtleties.

Little by little, first one, then the other, narrowed the search to the dimensions of a single idea which seemed remarkably astute and which, maybe, chiefly attracted them because it lent itself to continual embellishment—the sort of idea which is a fine excuse for endless conversation.

Instead of letting Mionnet go off quite unprotected, like a poor devil without shelter, without lightning-rod, at the mercy of any sudden revelation which would leave him naked, would it not be better to swathe him to the neck in some kind of defensive system?

Mionnet had mentioned in passing, and without the slightest trace of irony, the work he was doing for the Archbishop at the Department of Social Studies. What was to stop them from founding in Rome some little Department of Studies or Research? It might, for instance, be called "Department of Franco-Roman Studies." There would be a fine Honorary Committee or list of Patrons, crammed with high-sounding names of the sort to lull all suspicions—a handful of eminent gentlemen drawn from the Catholic world, from the ranks of Academicians and Members of Parliament, renowned equally for their patriotism and for their loyalty to the Church; a few great ladies; possibly one or two bishops. The enterprise would be put forward as a modest attempt to fill by private initiative the gap caused by the absence of official representatives and to smooth the way towards a better future. What more natural for its director than to clear up misunderstandings, to break down obstacles that might stand in the way of happier relations? And if experience showed that there were people actually engaged in fomenting trouble and making difficulties, no one would blame him for doing what he could to put a spoke in their wheel. What shadow of a pretext would the Curia have for taking offence?—unless it was prepared to admit that its conscience was not altogether clear.

How get such a Department started? It oughtn't to need a magician's wand. Why shouldn't the ball be started rolling by a handful of respectable if not very distinguished people drawn, if the worst came to the worst, from among M. de Saint-Papoul's connexions? For such a purpose, they could play the Marquis himself as a trump card. Such a nucleus once got together, they could look about for a few striking figure-heads. The money side of the business would present no difficulties. If the Quai d'Orsay were willing to foot the bill for a mission, it could hardly object to putting up the little extra needed to float the Department of Studies. And then, of course, one ought to be able to touch the decorative ladies and gentlemen of the committee for something.

The actual organization of the Department would be a rather more difficult problem. To give it genuine value would need subtlety. The general lines to be followed were clear enough: a single star performer and a company of "walking gentlemen," the star performer to be kept well out of the limelight while attention was concentrated on the walking gentlemen. "We've got the star all right," said Manifassier. As to the supers, no doubt the gentlemen of the committee would be delighted to find jobs for a few of their hangers-on. Nothing to worry about there. They would be completely insignificant. The supers—a superannuated canon, perhaps, and a provincial registrar—would be employed to collect a certain amount of harmless information and to distribute some tracts of a definitely Catholic complexion in preparation for M. Camille Bellaigue's [1] next visit. Under

---

[1] A critic and author noted for his bourgeois blamelessness.—TRANSLATOR'S NOTE.

cover of such trivialities, the man who mattered would carry on his work. The camouflage of the Department would furnish him with opportunities for getting into touch with people, for making useful contacts, and with an adequate excuse for embarking on indiscreet inquiries—"It's all to help the work of the Department, Monsignor" —while the existence of such an organization would make it possible to receive the apparently casual visits of shady characters with stories to sell, with whom, otherwise, it might be unwise to get into touch.

There should be no fear of detection provided the business were carried on with reasonable care. Detection is usually the result of persons beginning to wonder: "What the devil's this French Abbé doing here?" Once his presence could be logically accounted for, it was extremely improbable that his various movements would severally arouse suspicion. And if, by ill luck, the truth should leak out—such a leakage could only be partial—the consequences would be less grave than they otherwise might be. His actions could always be put down to an excess of zeal.

In fact, the idea of starting such an organization thrilled them. Neither of them had ever been to Rome, but they had read books about it, and they found no difficulty in envisaging the kind of small street in which the Department of Studies might open its modest doors. It would be, obviously, on the slopes of one of the hills; but of which? It must be neither too close to, nor too far from, St. Peter's, so as to profit by proximity and, at the same time, avoid the embarrassments consequent upon being caught up in the Vatican machine.

The plan was their joint child, but it was Manifassier who supplied the boldest strokes and the happiest embellishments. Mionnet took a hand in the game, but without making it clear just how far, actually, he was prepared to go. He was careful, more than once, while not in any way departing from the amicable tone of their conversation, to underline the fact that he had no intention of letting the Department of Franco-Roman Studies bring ridicule on the Department of Social Studies, which probably had given Manifassier his initial idea, but which Mionnet was very proud to have started and which he treated with a high seriousness.

Manifassier was careful to set his fears on this score at rest.

Mionnet declared that after much thought he didn't see how it would be possible either to set the Department of Studies going or to arrange for his own departure for Rome, unless they first took into their confidence, at least partially, somebody like Monsignor Lebaigue, under whose instructions he was at present working. There were too many risks involved, risks both of fact and of conscience, for him to dispense with such a minimum of caution. Besides, if it came to that, Monsignor Lebaigue was a man of great breadth of mind and undoubted patriotism. They could be sure that if he opposed the project, it would be for reasons which they could not justifiably ignore.

Finally they agreed to submit the idea of the Department to the full session to be held that evening at the Marquis's house. It would be up to Manifassier to describe the scheme in detail and reply to objections. Mionnet's part would be confined to declaring that, should such a Department be founded, he would be willing to go to Rome, subject, of course, to the tacit approval of Monsignor Lebaigue, to whom the whole plan would be submitted confidentially as coming direct from the Prime Minister.

Chapter

5

MIONNET COMES IN CONTACT
WITH THE CIVIL POWER

The dinner took its course without any notable incident. Mlle Bernardine made her presence felt both by Manifassier, who sat on her right, and by Gurau. She couldn't quite make out why they were there. She suspected that her brother was aiming at some political post more important than a seat in Parliament, and that he was trying to enlist the support of these two gentlemen. She thoroughly disapproved of any such ambition, mainly because she regarded her brother as quite unsuited to hold office. She therefore looked with no particular favour on the newcomers and addressed several questions to them which concealed an acrid malice beneath an appearance of childish irrelevance. One thing worried her a good deal—the constant use of the word "Minister" in addressing M. Gurau, who, as appeared from his own words and from the general trend of the conversation, was, in fact, not a minister at all. Not but what she knew that a great many people passed as titled whose claims to the distinction were completely bogus. Anyhow, he had nice manners and a pleasing appearance. Mlle Bernardine decided, in a fine flight of fancy, that he must undoubtedly be the bastard of some great family.

After dinner the four men withdrew into the Marquis's study. M. de Saint-Papoul was careful to see that the door was properly closed, and then handed round cigars and brandy. (Mionnet took a cigar, but refused the drink.) They sat in four armchairs drawn close together, leaning forward, elbows on knees, hands held before them.

When a gratifying atmosphere of conspiracy had been thus established, Gurau, who had already, during dinner, had several promising preliminary exchanges with Mionnet, opened the proceedings by saying: "It is a great pleasure for me, sir, to make your acquaintance. . . ." Then:

"You and Monsieur Manifassier have already met, and examined the question. No doubt you wish to communicate to us the results of your discussion."

Manifassier introduced their great invention—the *Department of Studies*. M. de Saint-Papoul appeared to be greatly impressed and declared that they could rely on his good offices. Gurau seemed at first a little uncertain. He suggested that the ornamental gentlemen whom they intended to appoint to their committee might be a bit slow in getting off the mark as well as embarrassing later, if, indeed, they didn't form an insuperable obstacle to any useful activity being undertaken. The fact, however, that the two young men were in complete agreement on the point impressed him, and he withdrew his opposition.

Being anxious to contribute something of his own to the scheme, he proceeded to dwell on the importance of developing an efficient system of communications.

There could be no question of transmitting reports through the normal channels of the Department of Studies. Not that the Abbé Mionnet would be forbidden to justify his presence in Rome by adding an occasional harmless memorandum to those of the "superannuated canon" and the "provincial registrar." But his serious reports must be forwarded by some other route which would have to be carefully arranged in advance to avoid all danger of miscarriage. (Gurau had not forgotten the diverted dispatches which had enabled Courson to discover so much secret history.) He thought it best that they should not go direct to the Ministry, where, no matter what precautions might be taken, there was always a chance of their falling into the hands of some subordinate. Mionnet had better address them personally to him, Gurau, and he would see that they got to the Prime Minister. ("By that time," thought Gurau, "I may have replaced Poincaré at the Foreign Office.")

"Or better still," he added, "let him send them under double cover to Manifassier, and then my name on the envelope won't attract attention."

At this point Mionnet put an objection which, he said, had suddenly occurred to him. They had agreed that it would be safer to keep him in a junior position so far as the Department of Studies was concerned. But in itself the Department wouldn't cut much ice, and the nominal directors would figure as comparatively obscure officials. Wouldn't his actual superiors, and, indeed, all those who were taking an interest in his career, find it rather odd that he should accept so unimportant an appointment? Wouldn't that fact alone tend to arouse suspicion?

The ex-Minister replied that he didn't think the risk was a very grave one. Anyhow, if he understood the proposal aright, Mionnet would be installed only with the tacit permission of Monsignor Lebaigue; in which case, at least the prelate under whose orders Mionnet directly came would realize the true position.

But Mionnet appeared unconvinced. He pointed out that he received his instructions from others as well as from Monsignor Lebaigue; from the Rector of the Catholic Institute, to name only one; and that there could be no question of taking everybody into their confidence.

For his own satisfaction, Gurau translated this argument of the Abbé's as follows: "Officially, in the eyes of my superiors and my colleagues, I shall find myself in the position of having accepted a very mediocre job after having held others which entitled me to hope for great things. My whole future, therefore, which does not depend solely on Monsignor Lebaigue, may be jeopardized. What compensation have you to offer me?"

When, therefore, a little later, M. de Saint-Papoul left the room— to look for a diary in which he had jotted down some addresses and names of people in Rome—he took the opportunity to whisper to Mionnet that when, a few hours previously, he had told Poincaré that he thought they had found the right man, he had been careful to raise the question of an "ultimate reward." The Prime Minister had replied—and he had told Gurau nothing that he did not know already—that since the breach of the Concordat, the State was clearly not in a position to further a churchman's official career, but that all the same there were ways, and, in view of the fact that he had increasingly to wink at infractions of the law, more and more ways; that it was always possible to strike a bargain, and that, paradoxical as it might seem to promise favourable consideration at Rome for a man who had been working against the intrigues of the Roman wire-pullers, he could almost certainly promise that something would be done in the present case, especially if, at the outset, the approval of someone high up in the hierarchy—of Monsignor Lebaigue, for instance—should have been obtained.

"I don't think I am going too far," added Gurau in a low voice, "when I say that, at the very first opportunity, the question of bestowing a cardinal's hat on you will be raised and very urgently pressed. The chances of success, let me point out, will be all the greater if, as a result of your activities, the attitude of the Vatican to France, and the relations between ourselves and the Holy See, shall meanwhile have taken a turn for the better."

Mionnet, without the slightest trace of affronted virtue, answered, also in a low voice, that he must be given a little more time to think things over, but that, whatever his answer, it should be given with a minimum of delay.

At this point, M. de Saint-Papoul came back.

As soon as Gurau was in possession of Mionnet's decision—which reached him the next day and was in the affirmative, though only provisionally, since it must, in the last analysis, depend upon the attitude of Monsignor Lebaigue when the position had been explained to him—he rang up the Prime Minister.

"I've managed to get our Roman scheme moving. I'll come along and talk it over at any time you like to name. If you don't mind, I'd like to bring Manifassier along too, since, by this time, he knows more about it all than I do. The details are complicated, and he has discussed them all with the man in question."

"Right; send Manifassier along first. I won't bother you if it's not necessary."

Poincaré saw Manifassier the same day (which was a praiseworthy act on his part, for the presidential campaign was in full swing, and the business of manœuvring for position had reached its critical stage).

He listened, interrupting only to put a few short questions on points of fact.

When the other had finished, he said politely, but without any great warmth:

"I congratulate you. You have put a lot of ingenuity into this scheme of yours. But I think it fairer to tell you quite frankly that you won't get away with it. If you had got the support of Monsieur de Mun it would be different. But I doubt whether you'll get it now. Without the help of somebody like him, it'll take you weeks and weeks to get a committee together, and then weeks and weeks more before you can establish your Department of Studies. Meanwhile there'll have been more than enough time for the alarm to be sounded and for the enemy to take his defensive steps. The scheme's no good unless it produces results quickly. There's a phrase, you know, for describing this sort of thing, and that's 'being too clever by half.' There's another objection. A scheme like yours will end by damping down any keenness that your envoy—whether it's this fellow or somebody else—may have. You thought it better, you say, not to mention Merry del Val, or the Merry del Val problem, to him directly. In arguing thus, I think you showed an error in psychology. You were afraid of frightening him off? Well, but if he's the man to be frightened so easily, he's no good to us. . . . It seems obvious to me that the business will cease to have any dramatic interest for him. It'll no longer be an adventure, an exciting puzzle to solve, and become merely a matter of dull routine reporting, without any kick in it. . . ."

He paused; then, with a sudden change of tone:

"Let me have a look at this young Abbé of yours."

"Here, sir?"

"Yes—or at my private address if he'd rather, and if you think it would be less compromising for him."

"All right, sir. What day, and at what time?"

Poincaré glanced at his appointment-book; then, with a faint smile:

"Tomorrow, eight o'clock," he said.

"I haven't got you up too early?"

"Oh no, sir; six o'clock's my usual time, unless I've been very late the night before."

"Good. Sit down."

The Prime Minister himself sank into a chair. In a series of rapid glances he took the Abbé's measure.

"You know roughly what we expect you to do, but I'm not sure that you've had it all very clearly explained. Actually, the job's a good deal less vague, and a good deal more interesting, than you possibly know. Quite simply, it's a question of finding out what Cardinal Merry del Val—the most influential man in the Church, that is, from a purely temporal point of view—is up to. Let me make one point clear at the outset. To a man as intelligent and as well educated as you, I needn't stress the fact that we are not for a moment concerned with religion as such. France today is by no means hostile to the Catholic faith. . . . We are interested in 'Monsieur' Merry del Val simply and solely as a politician, and in so far only as he is busy acting, unknown to us, in a sense hostile to our interests. For us, for France, the solution of the problem is of capital importance. You were, I understand, at college, and studied history. I needn't, therefore, point out to you that, as Europe is today, a man like Merry del Val, deliberately pursuing an anti-French policy, would be in a position to do us very considerable damage. Anything is possible. He may be full of the most Christian feelings towards us; on the other hand, he may dislike us, but without any great violence of feeling; he may, temperamentally, be incapable of sustained hate or long views . . . that is precisely what we want to know. You may say that it seems odd our turning to you for this information. I don't mind admitting that a good deal has already reached us. But we have no one as yet who has specialized in the question. One may have a hundred reports, but so long as they lack synthesis and verification, any conclusions drawn from them must remain conjectural. A historian like yourself must know that the diplomatic service of today —or, for that matter, of any day—is not exclusively manned by men of profound intelligence, by men intent on analysing any fact that comes their way with a sort of scientific intensity. Our embassies contain more keen dancers than keen investigators. That's the position. If you don't think the problem among the most intriguing that it is possible, at this moment of the world's history, to imagine; if the job doesn't excite you, there's no reason at all for you to take it on. We must try to find someone else. All we ask is that you should respect the secret of a project which you can communicate to other persons only at the risk, to however small a degree, of betraying your country. . . . If, on the other hand, you feel that you have here a magnificent opportunity of exercising your intelligence, and at the same time of doing your country a service which we shall not forget, go ahead. . . . But, for heaven's sake, drop this Department of Studies business. It's really too childish. And it's a bit cowardly. This is the kind of job one either takes or leaves alone. It's no good taking shelter behind illusory defences which won't, in fact, lessen the risk, and will diminish any credit that may accrue to you from the work."

Mionnet replied that the Department of Studies had not been his idea, and that he had agreed to it without enthusiasm. He added that, now he had a clearer idea of what was expected of him, the mission seemed extremely exciting. He was not afraid of the risk. For the moment he did not see how a simple French abbé could become sufficiently intimate with the second most important person in the Church to read his secret thoughts. But if the Prime Minister saw no essential absurdity in the idea, presumably the thing could be done.

No doubt, when the time came, he, Mionnet, would receive detailed instructions, advice, and the necessary assistance. There could be no question of his own keenness, nor of the spirit of curiosity which he would bring to the task.

He ventured to make an allusion to the necessity of confiding in Monsignor Lebaigue, but he mentioned it less as something necessary for his own peace of mind than as an additional guarantee of the success of the scheme.

The Prime Minister replied that he would think that aspect of the matter over, and would see Monsignor Lebaigue if he thought it wise to do so.

Chapter

VIAUR AND THE PUNDITS

Hachenard observed to his friend Viaur that he seemed very nervous.

"And I always thought you were such a cold-blooded devil! What are you frightened of? You're bound to get *some* results. After all, none of the experiments I've been at have ever failed. Let us assume for the sake of argument that you bring off only half what you did that first time I came to Celle. Half—a quarter . . . even so the effect would be enormous, quite enough to knock them sideways. They expect a great deal less than that. After all, you've not announced with a great flourish of trumpets that you're going to revolutionize the world, or even that you're staging a staggering display. It's merely a question of a couple of neighbours, as it were, dropping in to take note of 'one or two rather curious little facts.' "

The very light of the laboratory, entirely artificial, taken up and absorbed on all sides by flat dull surfaces and dingy, dirty colours—except for occasional metallic reflections almost equally gloomy—this light, alternating with sudden masses of deep shadow, and so different from the atmosphere in which he was accustomed to work, gave Viaur a sick feeling in the pit of the stomach. "What an ass I am!" he thought; "I ought to have got used to it by now, considering the number of times I've been here. But I can't help it. If I had to work every day in a place like this, I should feel as though I were in a photographer's dark room, or a submarine, or an astrologer's sanctum. . . . An odd sort of state of mind for a man of science. . . ."

Out loud he said:

"What gets my goat is going to all this trouble, and putting you to it as well, for a couple of second-raters."

"Don't exaggerate. I admit that Robertet isn't a Vaquez. But he's got a sort of reputation for laboratory work. The general opinion is that he'll be elected to the Academy of Sciences." He laughed. "I say advisedly: 'of Sciences'—next year. He's produced, at the lowest estimate, two or three quite nice little gadgets—not enough to get himself into the text-books, but you'd hardly expect a Professor of Medicine to be as ingenious as the inventor of the latest toy or mayonnaise whisk, would you? Janteaume isn't a great genius either, and he doesn't use his hands much; but, what with his paper, his review, his collection, to say nothing of the fact that he's an Academician, he's extraordinarily influential. Better men than he listen when he talks. I agree that, in terms of absolute value, it would be a greater thing to convert Babinsky. But Babinsky would be quite useless so far as getting your stuff known is concerned. . . . Janteaume's a talker, and that's all to the good; he's always meeting people, and if you're lucky enough to tickle his fancy with your experiments, he'll ride them like a hobby-horse and make it a matter of personal vanity to get them talked about . . . old Babinsky and his Olympian self-sufficiency! . . . You know perfectly well you wouldn't like Janteaume to get his knife into you. Well, it works both ways, don't you see?"

While Hachenard wandered about, testing each detail of his machines, in a sudden access of meticulous solicitude, they discussed the degree of importance that ought to be attached to what Viaur bitterly described as the "defection" of Babinsky and Vaquez, regarded as an omen or a symptom.

Hachenard maintained that the "defection" had been reasonable. Babinsky, who was just going off on a journey, had asked them to wait for his return. That was perfectly natural. A busy man, with a lot of packing to do and papers to put in order, isn't in the right mood for a test demonstration. "That's all you think about, but they've got other irons in the fire." Vaquez had said that he was perfectly willing to accept the invitation provisionally, "for some date after Babinsky's return," but that it was difficult, so far ahead, to fix definitely a convenient day.

"Put yourself in his place. He may suddenly find himself with an important piece of work to do. Would you rather have him fix a day and then call it off at the last moment?"

Viaur wondered whether, when they learned that Janteaume and Robertet had been in first on the experiments, Babinsky and Vaquez might not, perhaps, be offended.

"I don't think so. Whatever you do, there's a risk. You didn't want to wait any longer, and I must say I sympathize with you there. The great thing is to let the news of the experiments get around. If all goes well and you begin to be talked about, it's they who'll be sorry they were so lukewarm, and nervous lest you hold it against them. For the Lord's sake, don't start worrying about inessentials!"

But there was something else worrying Viaur. Might not Pailleton have done him a bad turn with his chief, under pretext of taking a hand in the affair?

"Why should he? That's a perfectly gratuitous assumption. If you aren't careful, old man, you'll be getting persecution mania. You'll be saying next that Pailleton crept in here by night and loosened this nut so as to get us a bad contact. . . . But look here, you won't do yourself any good if you let our two bright boys know that you got 'em here as second-best. If they find it out for themselves it won't matter. By that time they'll have done their stuff. . . . And here's another piece of advice: don't on any account be carried away to show them your other results. I know you. . . . If things go well, you'll get carried away, you'll think you've got the world at your feet. . . . If things go only half well, you'll want to make up for 'em by showing something else. . . . No, no, and again no. At the very most you can make some vague allusion to 'work in progress.' . . . Where are you off to now?"

"There's something I wanted to say to Vidalencque and the girl."

"Stay here. There's nothing you need say to them. You'll only get on their nerves. You're getting on your own."

"I'm afraid they may get worked up hanging about in that waiting-room. Don't you think it would calm them down if I went and had a word or two with them? I'm not going to bother them—only chat a bit."

"A nice cheerful companion you'd make! Sit down. And don't look at the clock as though you'd got a train to catch. They're ten minutes late—I know it. Well, that's better than if they were ahead of time."

"How do you make that out?"

"Because if they were early, it might be to say: 'We didn't want to let you down, so we just came along. Frightfully sorry . . . unforeseen engagement . . . only got five minutes. . . . Just run through the business as quickly as you can.'"

The two pundits did not at once take the chairs that had been pushed forward for them. They wasted a considerable time in removing their overcoats. Janteaume apologized politely for their late arrival. They had arranged to come together in Janteaume's car, but Professor Robertet had been delayed by "a very important piece of work."

Janteaume was no substitute for Babinsky so far as size went, though there was a certain dignity about him. He had a prominent stomach, a Bourbon profile, a fat face, the smooth surface of which was broken by a trace of whiskers, no moustache, and a pair of well-shaped ears which he was for ever fingering. The tone of his voice and the expression of his eyes exuded a benevolence which had all the appearance of having been put on that morning with his collar. Obviously, he trotted it out for everybody.

Robertet, with his eyeglasses, his little chin-tuft, his high collar, his small black tie, his mincing voice, and his angular features, was more like a head clerk than any head clerk had a right to be—like, in fact, a character actor playing the part. His chief anxiety on entering a room was, clearly, to avoid being ignored. It betrayed itself by the way he had of stepping back to let others go first, by his manner of attracting attention with a little flutter of the hand, by the sort of undulating movement with which he insinuated himself into the front row of a crowd, by a slightly exaggerated way of speaking.

They did not remain seated. They kept on asking what it was they were to be shown, as though they had come without the least idea of what they were to see. Viaur and Hachenard seemed to be inextricably confused in their minds. Just as one of their hosts made an effort to answer their questions, Robertet would suddenly evince an enormous interest in one of the radiological instruments before him and want to have it explained. Or Janteaume would express sudden curiosity about the career of a radiologist and would start questioning Hachenard on what he made, on what his expenses were, on the dangers of his profession.

By dint of patient tact, the two men brought their guests' attention back to the matter in hand. But the questions showed no sign of diminishing in number. So Viaur was going to show them some of his experiments, introduce them to some of the people on whom he had been trying out his theories? How many? Two? That wasn't many. Had he been experimenting in a wider field? Yes? Good. Where were the two persons in question? Waiting in a near-by room (what else should they be doing?). Who were they? Did Viaur know them? Both of them employees at Celle-les-Eaux? An odd coincidence, that. So Viaur knew them well, did he? His relations with them were not solely those of a hospital doctor with his patients.

They said nothing to show that they held this fact against him, but it was clear that it worried them a bit. They would have preferred a couple of subjects recruited in a—what was the word?—in a more "regular" manner.

Hachenard, who was more self-controlled than Viaur, and whose training as a physicist gave him greater presence of mind, explained the nature of the experiments which he and his friend were about to present, the main point of which would be to concentrate within the minimum time the greatest possible weight of demonstrative evidence. X-ray records would be taken of each of the subjects in quick succession, and Hachenard had so arranged things that the results could be observed with the least possible difficulty. Without moving from their chairs the two learned gentlemen would be able to *see* the slowing-down process of the heart.

He went on to explain the system of double and simultaneous recording which he and Viaur had elaborated. (Viaur interrupted to say that the merit of this contraption was almost entirely Hachenard's.) In the absence of a cardiograph, which would have hampered the X-ray exposure, a sphygmograph, attached to the subject's wrist, would trace on squared paper the frequency of the heart-beats. Further, thanks to a double-keyed instrument which he had invented, one of the demonstrators, without taking his eyes from the screen, would be able to ensure that each systole and each diastole was duly shown upon the registering drum. This second record, in so far as it presupposed the intervention of the operator, would not offer the same guarantees as the former, though that, in its turn, would show only indirectly the beat of the heart. Genuine proof would be got from a comparison of the two records. The variations in pulse-rate to be observed would be so considerable that even an approximate agreement of the two graphs should suffice to make the point good.

What more brilliant method could they desire than this triple verification of the same phenomenon—direct observation, key-board recording, and automatic trace? (There was no reason why they shouldn't start the whole test over again, at a later stage, with an ordinary cardiograph substituted for the X-ray.)

Hachenard was anxious that the first experiment should be confined to the X-ray method alone, which would make for simplification and would have the advantage of not dissipating the attention of the observers. "It would be much better," he said to himself, "to begin with something on broad lines. If our two friends actually see on the screen the representation of Vidalencque's arrested heart-beats, they'll be properly bowled over. The rest of the business'll be as easy as pie." Viaur's mind was working along similar channels. He spoke less than his friend, but he was far more nervous. With his eyes fixed on the faces of their two visitors, he tried to forecast what their reactions would be.

Janteaume glanced at the instruments, made a dissatisfied grimace, and looked at Robertet. Robertet returned his look, examined the instruments in his turn, and echoed the grimace, though with an added expression of scornful competence.

It was he who spoke first, his rather shrill little voice taking on a false note of friendliness:

"Is it really worth while, my dear colleague, putting so much machinery in motion? We've hardly reached such an advanced stage yet. Surely the thing can be done much more easily. We've come here to establish a perfectly simple fact. Bring in your subjects. We both of us know how to listen to a heart. I can assure you that if the phenomenon is as clearly marked as you say it is, we shall very soon detect it."

Janteaume, much relieved, expressed a similar view, though with greater heartiness. Hachenard only with difficulty kept himself from exclaiming that if his instruments were not to be used, there was no point in setting the scene of their experiments in his laboratory. He refrained, however, from a fear of dragging in his own professional pride as a radiologist. He contented himself with pointing out that to see a case of muscle contraction on a screen was just as simple as to note it through the medium of the ear, and more immediate. He realized, however, that the two pundits had no confidence in his mechanical ingenuity. "If I insist, they're quite capable of believing that I've fixed things in such a way that they won't be able to detect the trick."

He motioned to Viaur that they had better agree.

"Which shall we begin with?" asked Viaur.

Hachenard, who was immediately conscious of a great many mutually contradictory reasons for choosing one or the other of their subjects, felt that they might as well trust to luck.

"With—oh, I don't know—with the girl."

Viaur brought in Denise Lapierre. She seemed excessively nervous. She gazed at him with appealing eyes.

The two important-looking gentlemen bowed slightly. She scarcely dared to glance at them.

"I have a feeling that nothing'll happen," she said.

Viaur bit his lip. Her words, he thought, were unfortunate.

The two gentlemen reassured her in a few carefully chosen words, as though she were about to undergo an operation.

"What have I got to do?" she asked Viaur nervously.

"Why, take off your blouse, of course. . . . Here, wait a moment." She pouted, seemingly on the verge of tears.

"I don't feel like it today, honestly I don't. Besides, what's the use, since I've told you that nothing'll happen?"

He did not wish to be sharp with her. On the other hand he felt shy about using the friendly, intimate tone which was usual between them. "They already look as though her appealing ways had made them suspicious. They'll end by getting the idea that we're nothing but a troupe of country-fair jugglers." He was careful, therefore, to remain distant with her. But the only effect of this was still further to unnerve the girl.

Finally she agreed to take off her blouse. Robertet asked for a stethoscope. There wasn't one. Neither Viaur nor Hachenard had thought of providing so elementary an implement for use in a demonstration which was to be conducted by means of the subtlest mechanical contrivances. The two pundits exchanged one of those hateful smiles which, on the faces of examiners, succeed in freezing a candidate's blood in his veins.

"It doesn't matter," said Robertet, with the suspicion of a sigh. "I suppose you've got a towel?"

But this, too, they had failed to provide. Hachenard, however, discovered one in the cupboard of a neighbouring consulting-room. The incident increased the general sense of uneasiness.

Robertet took the towel and spread it on his knees in readiness. Then he turned to Denise Lapierre:

"Come here, please."

Then, addressing Viaur:

"What is it you want us to notice?" he asked.

Viaur forced his voice to remain calm. "The normal frequency of this girl's heart-beat," he said, "is somewhere between seventy-five and eighty—rather less, as a matter of fact; seventy-five and seventy-eight would be more accurate." He managed to maintain the objective attitude of the demonstrator, but his voice trembled. ". . . She is not subject to much spontaneous or reflex variation of rate. Before I began experimenting I never found it to be below seventy-three. Now, the effect of voluntary checking, to show the possibility of which is my sole object, has been to reduce the pulse to something under fifty—and that after a course of gradual training extending over about three months, neither very violent nor very continuous. She can produce this slowed heart-beat when told to, after an initial pause of about two minutes. Progress has been by fits and starts. Up to the end of last month fifty-eight was the best she could manage; then at the beginning of this month there was a sudden deceleration to forty-eight or forty-nine."

Neither of the two examiners made a sign. It was almost as though they had heard nothing at all. Robertet had taken hold of the left hand of Denise Lapierre, who stood before him, with an air of great distress, occasionally pulling up the shoulder-strap of her chemise with her right hand, which had remained free. He seemed not even to be taking her pulse.

He got up, pulled down the top of her chemise, after first modestly spreading the towel upon her chest, and then, thrusting beneath her nose a half-bald head that gave off a smell of rancid brilliantine, went through the process of listening to her heart.

"Very rapid action," he said. "A good deal nearer a hundred than eighty, I should say."

"Really!" exclaimed Viaur. "I must say you surprise me. . . . Would you like my watch?"

"Thank you, I have my own."

But he made no use of it. Instead, removing his head from its pleasantly feminine resting-place, he made way for Janteaume.

While his colleague was listening, he put several questions to the girl:

"Did you run at all on your way here? . . . No? . . . Have you been here long? . . . Ah! . . . You haven't by any chance been taking coffee—strong coffee? . . . Or anything else—anything special?"

Janteaume, too, scorned to have recourse to his watch.

"Yes," he said, raising his head, "the heart action is very disturbed." He glanced paternally at the young woman and patted her cheek. "Perhaps we're a little upset. . . ."

"Do you mind if I try?" asked Viaur, who for the last few minutes had been struggling with his impatience.

He listened to the girl's heart, ostentatiously making use of his watch.

"Rather less than twenty in fifteen seconds . . ." he announced with affected nonchalance; "nineteen and a half, to be precise . . . that's to say, seventy-eight to the minute."

"Yes," remarked Robertet, as though Viaur's statement had confirmed his own observations; "she's calming down now. . . ."

"Would you like to see whether we can get a voluntary deceleration?" asked Viaur.

"Certainly."

"Come, my dear," went on Viaur in a lower tone, "there's nothing to be afraid of, just concentrate, and try to slow down your heart as much as you can."

"Now? At once?"

There was a trace of anxiety in his tone as he answered:

"Yes . . . make it beat as slowly as you know how."

"But—oh, I'm still so nervous!"

"Try just the same."

The four men remained silent. Hachenard, who was standing a little behind Denise, kept his eyes fixed on their visitors. "When we've become pundits," he wondered, in a sudden access of rage, "shall we be just such another couple of nasty old buffoons?"

Denise, her face tense and remote, her eyes half-closed, was trying to abstract her attention from the scene and to concentrate on the task before her, which consisted in no less than attempting to do something which once, perhaps, had been natural, but which mankind, after a thousand years of progress, had forgotten. She would have given anything to succeed, to avoid causing her good, dear friend a disappointment which, she felt, would be a serious matter for him. Now and then, after a more than usually spiritless effort, her features would show a faint quiver, and when this happened, she would shake her head as though to say: "I know I shan't bring it off."

"Now come along," said Viaur again, close at her ear. "Do just what you always do. . . . It'll be all right, you'll see. . . . Are you ready? . . ."

He leaned forward, applied his ear to her chest, and said to Robertet:

"Just come here a moment. . . ."

Robertet took his place and listened.

"It's not quite so good as usual," Viaur explained with feverish excitement. "I don't think it's much below fifty-five. . . . But this time you really must time it. . . ."

He held out his watch to the professor, or, rather, pushed it into his hand; then, as the latter took no notice, held it up at some distance from his eyes. Robertet, with a rather vague look, raised his head and beckoned Janteaume to take a turn.

"Obviously she's a good deal quieter now," he said, trying to keep his naturally acid voice from assuming an aggressive inflexion. To hear him, one would assume that Viaur's whole object was to establish the fact that here was a heart which could become "a good deal quieter" after a period of excitement.

Janteaume made a sign with his hand to show that he wanted the watch. He made as though to proceed to a meticulous test.

"I've just counted precisely fifteen beats in a quarter of a minute, which gives a complete rate of sixty."

"It's actually increasing again," Viaur explained. "As yet I've trained her to slow the action only for very short periods. . . . The curve has very sharp variations. You ought to have done your counting a moment or two ago."

"These gentlemen," said Hachenard in a cold, bitter voice, "could have followed what's happening quite comfortably on the screen and then verified the results at their leisure on the cardiographic chart."

The two gentlemen did not even take the trouble to contradict. They seemed so far in complete agreement that the same indulgent smile showed at the same moment on both their faces. It said as clearly as any words would have done: "Dear young people, we're not in the least annoyed. At your age it's natural enough to get worked up. Our job is to apply the cold douche of common sense."

"Any use trying her again?" asked Viaur of his friend, between clenched teeth.

"I don't think so . . . what's the good?"

"Shall I fetch in Vidalencque?"

"Yes."

Before repeating the experiment on the waiter, Viaur plucked up what courage he could still muster and said:

"I really must insist, gentlemen, that this time one of you listens the whole time."

Janteaume indicated that he was ready to yield pride of place to his colleague, but the latter waved aside the proffered honour. It fell, therefore, to Janteaume to officiate.

"Buck up, Vidalencque . . ." Viaur began, but Robertet interrupted him in his most acid tones:

"Excuse me, but is it absolutely essential that you issue instructions to your subject?"

"Of course not . . . that's to say . . ." Viaur was clearly disconcerted.

"Don't you think," went on Robertet, this time addressing Janteaume, "that it is important to guard against the hypothesis of personal influence, of the kind of direct suggestion practised by the Nancy school?"

Janteaume solemnly nodded agreement. Viaur tried to argue:

"Just as you wish, sir, of course. But if the phenomenon occurs it doesn't seem to me any less remarkable just because you like to explain it by the theory of suggestion."

Robertet shook his head with the air of a man who knows his own mind.

Viaur stepped back. "All right, I won't interfere. Please conduct the test yourselves."

Janteaume applied his finely modelled ear to Vidalencque's chest. He seemed to be waiting for some sort of an order from Robertet. But his friend said nothing.

A minute passed. At the end of it Janteaume remarked rather hesitatingly:

"It's certainly odd."

"What's odd?"

"There's a kind of muted quality about the sounds. It's just as though there had been a deceleration, a very marked deceleration. . . . Listen for yourself."

Robertet took his place. He tapped the man's chest and moved his ear from point to point. He seemed annoyed. He said:

"Leave off breathing!"

The order was unnecessary. For the last ten seconds Vidalencque had not been breathing at all. He reached the maximum point of strain. His face showed a complete change of expression.

Robertet, now that he was listening no longer, looked at him. So did Janteaume. The two pundits were clearly perplexed. Viaur and Hachenard had the impression that fortune stood poised upon a knife-edge, and that very little would send it tumbling down on the right side.

Vidalencque, with a sudden sharp movement began to breathe again. Beads of sweat stood on his forehead. He glanced at Dr. Viaur as much as to say: "I've done my best."

"Listen again, gentlemen," said Viaur, "and you will note the return to a normal rate."

They listened—first the fat Academician, then the bearded professor. The professor tugged at his beard and looked at the ground.

He asked Vidalencque one or two questions about his antecedents. The waiter, who wasn't sure what Viaur wanted, replied with a certain show of embarrassment. Robertet did not push the cross-examination very far.

Finally the visitors remarked that they would not detain the two subjects longer and dismissed them with thanks.

They wandered up and down the laboratory, as though they wanted to make a pronouncement or start a discussion, but didn't know quite how to begin. Once or twice, as they approached each other, they exchanged a half-finished sentence, muttered rather than spoken. Viaur and Hachenard stood apart saying nothing. They ventured an occasional quick glance, Viaur nervously, the radiologist with an expression of mockery.

The two distinguished strangers seemed suddenly to take note of the time and to remember an urgent appointment elsewhere. They asked for their coats and in the bustle of putting them on dropped a few rather disjointed remarks. Most of them came from Robertet:

"It's all very interesting of course . . . worth investigation. Everything's worth investigation. . . . Too soon to draw conclusions. . . . Your second subject's a bit abnormal. I've come across cases no less odd than his in my own experience . . . but there's seldom much of scientific value to be learned from freaks like that. It's a field particularly open to trickery. One can't be too careful."

"Well, that's that!" exclaimed Viaur in a little burst of anger when the two experts had taken their departure. "We've certainly wasted our time, if we haven't done worse. Robertet hadn't even the grace to admit that he was impressed. Come across similar cases, has he! . . . I nearly said: 'If you have, then why on earth haven't you mentioned them, why haven't you done something about them, instead of filling hundreds of pages with a lot of nonsense wrapped up in pseudo-scientific language? . . .' Have you ever read his work on the variations of temperature noted in the farmyard hen during twenty-four hours? . . . It's enough to make you split with laughter! . . . It says

precisely what everybody's always known: it embodies no discovery
and gets nowhere; it could all be said in ten lines of straightforward
French . . . instead of which he fusses about with a hundred pages
of calculations and graphs and perfectly infantile prosings. . . . Why
wouldn't he have anything to do with your instruments and those
diagrams we'd prepared? I suppose he's jealous."

Hachenard did his best to cheer him up.

"After all, the great thing is that the experiment wasn't a failure.
At least they can't say that. . . . They were more deeply impressed
than you think. . . . They didn't want to say anything before they'd
had time to think over what they'd seen. . . . They had to be solemn
about it. . . . But a train's started in their minds all right . . . particularly in Janteaume's . . . I could tell that because he didn't say
much."

Chapter

7

EVE OF DEPARTURE.
A TRIP TO M—.
A STRANGE VISITOR

The tray of a trunk was balanced precariously across the arms of a chair; two piles, one of linen, the other of papers, stood side by side on a table. On the floor were several pairs of shoes and two heaps of books. A handsome new soutane on a hanger hung from the top of a bookcase. Collars and other details of attire were scattered here and there awaiting disposal. In the middle of the room was an open trunk, brand-new, smelling of glue, and as yet almost empty. A second, smaller trunk, or rather valise, had already been closed.

"I've still more than twenty-four hours before me—twenty-six, to be precise. The main part of my packing will be finished by this evening. Tomorrow morning I shall devote to minor matters and to getting my ticket from the travel agency. After lunch I shall do some errands and pay a few farewell calls. Everything's panning out very satisfactorily."

He pottered about, his mind agreeably occupied the while with thoughts of many things—practical details, anticipations of his Roman adventure, memories of northern Italy (the only part of the country of which he had some experience), and the recent impressions which he had gathered at M—.

It was but two hours since he had stepped off the train. The idea of the trip had suddenly occurred to him the previous Monday as he was coming away from Poincaré, who had spared him ten minutes for a second interview. "Monsignor Sérasquier always said that if I ever went to Rome he would give me some addresses. . . . Well, why not? . . . His introductions might come in very useful, especially in the circles with which I shall have most to do. . . . Besides, it would be nice to see him again, to say nothing of M—. I could spend a couple of nights there . . ." (he smiled to himself) "but not at the Pension Roubier."

It was mid-winter, but pleasant, open weather, misty and not too wet. Everything at M— was as he remembered it. The Saint-Charles quarter was musical with the rhythmic sounds of harness-makers and smithies. Coming thus from Paris, he realized that this little eddy of liveliness, stressing, as it did, the underlying sleepiness of the place without breaking it, making for charm but never for excess, was an effect not easy of attainment and therefore to be enjoyed as a casual recreation.

The upper town, though the trees had lost their greenery, was charming as ever and, doubtless, as secret. Close to the station a new shop, a sort of modern department store, had been opened. Seven or eight persons whom he met in the street raised their hats. With several others he took the initiative.

Monsignor Sérasquier seemed rather older and rather thinner. The unyielding pride with which he had resisted his illness and the disagreeable onsets of the world had lost something of its rigidity. He was at once less restless and less magnificent. The marks of weakness in voice and face had become established in a final permanence, had made contact with physical characteristics of profounder origin, with those unaccented traces which are the normal accompaniment of old age. At sight of Mionnet he had expressed the greatest pleasure.

"We'll have dinner here this evening together, just the two of us, and a good gossip. Tomorrow as well, luncheon and dinner. You must spare me tomorrow, I insist. There's a good early train the next morning which you can take. Better still, you must stay here; that's much the simplest plan. I've got a spare room that's not being used. You've taken a room at the hotel? Don't bother about that; I'll send my man for your bag, and he can explain that I'm keeping you here."

Their several talks had been long and various. The Bishop, less preoccupied with his personal dignity than when Mionnet had known him first, delighted, in fact, to surrender to a few hours of affectionate intimacy—a pleasure of which, for the moment, he appeared to be almost entirely deprived—had lost nothing of his great gift of pleasing. He told a great many stories, most of them old, about people whom he had known in his youth or knew of by hearsay. A few, rather newer, showed that he had retained his power of acute observation. Most of them concerned churchmen, but the laity played its part in his anecdotes, and even, occasionally, women. He never cheapened himself by having recourse to ambiguity or dirt, the mainstay of country curés in such matters, and particularly popular at public dinners. (On these occasions there is always some old fat-faced priest who guffaws his way through the meal as he strives to cap his neighbours in the matter of smut, and cocks his eye knowingly at the maid to see whether as she took away his plate she heard his latest and duly enjoyed it.) He made reference to certain characteristics of feminine psychology which he had the good taste not to attach, overtly, to any experiences of his own. The subject led him on to venture a few remarks on the confessional. He gave it as his opinion that the sophisticated were apt to exaggerate the importance, psychologically speaking, of the information obtainable by priests in confession.

" 'What profundities of the human spirit, especially of the female spirit, don't they have the chance of sounding! . . .' That's the line usually taken, but, to my mind, it's only true given certain conditions. The first is that the priest in question must have a natural flair for such things, a curiosity which no mere training will ever give him; the second, that he must be in a position to verify, to check, his observations by other less direct means. Do you really think that anyone can get a reliable idea of women from simply hearing them in the confessional? They're too good actresses for that, and the circumstances offer too good an opportunity for the display of their gifts. For a man, I admit, who has watched them when they're not, as it were, on show and then hears their carefully arranged admissions, it may be in the last degree instructive. Given that prerequisite, the priest can read them as no one else can. He's got, you see, a double approach. The layman's nowhere by comparison."

He regretted that the dignity of the sacred office made it impossible for a priest of talent to write a book of maxims and characters dealing with women, "in the manner of La Bruyère or La Rochefoucauld. . . . Anyone with a bit of feeling for style could make something of a theme like that." He examined Mionnet out of the corner of his eye, as though wondering whether, as a college graduate, he might feel tempted by such a suggestion.

All around them, as they sat each on one side of a table which, without extra leaves, could easily seat twelve guests, lay the vast spaces of the dining-room. The occasional entrances and exits of the butler alone disturbed their almost royal solitude.

The Bishop caught Mionnet eyeing the walls and the high ceiling. "Yes," he said, "it is pretty big. . . . I don't often dine alone. . . . I usually have my secretary, or the secretary-general . . . or somebody . . . visitors. . . . What I really like is tête-à-tête like this . . . although in some ways I feel that I'm the sort of man who ought to live surrounded by a court. . . ."

In the course of their next meal the conversation turned to a discussion of the qualities which make a man contemptible or fine. The morals of this descendant of the counts of Sérasquier were, in general, based less on the teachings of the Church than on the traditions of chivalry. In his eyes the human ideal was the "man of honour," the man who could be blindly trusted, who would never betray a friend or a leader, or even a subordinate. His hatred was reserved for the disloyal, for men incapable of constancy, false friends, false servants, treacherous leaders. It was easy to guess that he found it easy to forgive the weaknesses, even the vices, of those who satisfied his rather elementary standards of conduct. His clerical training, however, showed in the way, which sat rather uneasily upon him, of admitting that a certain diplomatic astuteness, a possibly wide distinction between what a man thought and what he said, between what he felt and what he allowed himself to show, played a necessary part in the art of living. Boasting of his honesty, insolent perhaps in his attitude to others, the rather crude squire that he once had been had had superimposed upon him this later training, and it had been so successful that, quite probably, he no longer perceived the resultant incongruity. (He thought of himself, indeed, as erring on the side of frankness.) Mionnet, who was young enough to note such encroachments of the acquired training upon the raw material of character, found himself wondering with amusement how far the superimposition had proceeded in his own case.

Another trait in him which Mionnet noted, attributable to the same influence, was the assumption on his part (it had by this time become a sort of childlike belief) that a man of the Church had not the same obligations of behaviour to the rest of the world as to his fellow-clerics. Not that he found himself bound to his colleagues by anything like a system of reciprocal duties, but that they, and they only, appeared to him in the guise of genuine equals, as men worthy of respect. Duty towards members of the laity he recognized as something that might be serious, even exigent, but it remained essentially an act of grace, a gesture as of the master to the pupil. It was the duty that bound a man to his inferior, almost the duty of a senior to a junior; it resembled the attitude of a father to his child, though the layman in question might be twice his age, might, conceivably, be his father or his mother. Only to the wearers of his own cloth was the priest bound, within limits, to speak the truth—and even then only with due respect to the promptings of tact and prudence, considerations which could never be ignored—the truth, that is, in the sense that it implied complete frankness, the giving to another of a certain hold over one's mind. The truth, in his view, was never obligatory towards members of the laity except in so far as it might serve to correct their errors, or when, as dogma, it was spelt with a capital T. In such cases the layman could claim it as his right as a child might claim food; but he must accept it with due respect and without displaying either preference or repugnance. All he could regard as his right was truth in the mass. The consideration of delicate or doubtful points involved in its statement, the possibility of modification in its details, were not his business. This attitude might be described, in other words, by saying that he recognized many duties towards laymen, but *never the duty of giving an account of his actions* (and this held true even in such matters as taxes or tramway administration, lay and temporal though these things might appear to be). Any account that he did give would be as an act of grace only, or such as might be forced from him by the detestable machinations of the times.

But, strongly though he held these views, they did not prevent Monsignor Sérasquier from inveighing against the Orders; from styling himself a Gallican (in the grand manner of the seventeenth century); from hinting that the Republic in its recent squabbles with the Church was far from having been the only offender; from maintaining that the Freemasons in office had shown greater patience than the kings had ever done; from declaring, when he knew that Mionnet was about to leave for Rome, that he "would learn a thing or two there about the bad turns that the Vatican was preparing against France." When he spoke like this, the patriotic Frenchman, easily suspicious, and ill at ease at the thought of Italian popes and their train of dignitaries, almost, one might say, the anti-clerical, showed through the Bishop's mask with an effect that was strangely inconsistent. But Monsignor Sérasquier was no more proof than other men against harbouring contradictory thoughts, though he carried off the difficulties of the situation better than most, for he liked to let his mind work as the mood took him, in movements of wide generalization, and was comfortably immune from awkward pricks of conscience such as might have made another man ask himself: "Is that consistent with what I said yesterday?" or "Am I not, perhaps, forgetting the other side of the question?"

Listening to him, watching him against the intimate background of his house—which he liked to belittle as a poor, middle-class place —noticing the way in which his mind reacted (a mind that had lost its first vigour, to be sure, but that still gave glimpses of the magnificent natural endowment which underlay it), Mionnet was led to ask himself more than one question, but in particular this: "Has he faith? And if so, what form does it take with him?"

It was impossible to imagine him standing at night in his library, tormented by abstract questionings, weighing difficulties, seeking aid from the works of the Fathers and the philosophers; or shivering at dawn in his oratory, beseeching God to help him in his struggle against doubt. But impossible though it might be to visualize such moments, they might exist. It is so dangerous to say with certainty what a man will or will not do when there is no one there to see. But it did seem improbable.

"I can imagine him praying, but as a man conscious of his own grandeur, a little distrait, official even in his solitude, speaking to God with a purely formal assumption of humility, as to someone on whom he has a right to rely, someone who only through sheer perversity could fail to regard him as a person of outstanding importance— rather like Louis XIV at his devotions. There is probably something about Monsignor Sérasquier which makes its easier to understand a man like Louis XIV. . . . Besides, I am sure that he deliberately refuses to admit to his mind any thought that might embarrass him, as a good woman, concerned for her reputation, refuses to let her mind dwell even on the possibility of infidelity. . . . He can always, too, fall back on the comforting thought that, in all ages, there are specialists whose duty it is to argue victoriously against all attacks made against faith. The mere fact that there are still so many eminent persons both within the Church and outside it who continue to believe proves that a man can believe without running the risk of being considered a half-wit. . . . And having gone so far, he no doubt dismisses the matter from his mind."

Mionnet's forthcoming departure for Rome seemed to interest the Bishop deeply. But he was polite enough to accept the account of his mission which had officially been given him (this being the one that Mionnet and his "protectors" had finally agreed upon). Its main lines were as follows.

The Abbé had decided to apply himself seriously to a doctoral thesis which he had been planning for several years on "The Foreign

Policy of the Papacy in the Nineteenth Century." In order to consult the relevant documents he must spend some time in Rome. His object was to work in the great libraries, to get access, if possible, to the papal archives, to have interviews with those actors in the events with which he was to deal who were still living, or with persons who had known them. The French Foreign Office, in view of the fact that the subject of the thesis might have an interest for it, had kindly provided him with certain letters of introduction and would, in various ways, make things easy for him.

Monsignor Sérasquier had listened to his guest's account of the matter with an air of unquestioning benevolence, though not without letting it be seen that he had his own views about it all. He thought for a moment or two in silence, a faint smile upon his lips.

"I will give you one or two addresses," he said at last, "which you can use or not as you like."

One of these was that of a certain Baron de Fontmonge, Councillor of the Belgian Embassy, in the Piazza della Trinità dei Monti. (Mionnet did not like to ask whether it was the actual Embassy which was situated on the Piazza della Trinità dei Monti nor whether it was the one accredited to the Quirinal or to the Holy See.)

The other address was that of a Monsignor Dougérin, at the Canonica.

"There are a lot of other people I could introduce you to, but these seem to me the most suitable for your purpose. I will write to them tomorrow."

He added, without seeming to lay much stress on his words (though a brief onset of twitching in the muscles of his face and a dragging down of the right-hand corner of his mouth gave the lie to his assumed detachment of tone):

"You are going to Rome to pursue your studies. But naturally you will take the opportunity of informing yourself about a number of things. . . . Many of them will have a certain bearing on the matter of your researches. You will find the people whose names I have given you well informed. . . . They will receive you well, as coming from me. . . . The only piece of advice I have to give you is this: don't make yourself too conspicuous. . . . In Rome they are quick to notice strangers."

Mionnet learned a little later that since the departure of Manguy opinion in Catholic circles at M— had quieted down considerably, although there were still a good many people who upheld the late Canon. The scandal of the tramways had subsided. There had been a certain amount of consolation for those who had not got away unscathed ("and I suffered more than most," said the Bishop) in the knowledge that M. de Quingey and others who had expected to profit from the discomfiture of their predecessors had, in their turn, begun to lose money.

Before going out to dine in a small hotel in the rue du Vieux-Colombier, much patronized by the clergy, where he had for some time been in the habit of taking his meals, Mionnet decided to tidy up his room a bit. Not that he expected a visitor, but the idea of coming back and finding the place looking like a battlefield was repugnant to him. He replaced the tray in the large trunk and closed the lid. The objects which still remained to be disposed of he pushed out of sight in a corner behind a chair.

There was a knock at the door. He imagined that the porter had brought up a letter. Laying down a shoe which he was holding in his hand, on top of the trunk, next to a hammer with which he had been mending one of the locks, he went to the door and opened it.

He saw before him a young-looking priest, not very tall, with a bright, intelligent face lit by a pair of keen and restless eyes. He did not know him. The visitor bowed.

"Monsieur?"

"The Abbé Mionnet, if I am not mistaken?"

"Yes."

"I'm afraid I'm disturbing you. . . ."

"Well, I was just going out. . . . Whom have I the honour of addressing?"

The stranger, who was holding his hat in one hand, made with the other a sweeping, evasive gesture as though to minimize the importance of what he was about to say.

"My name is Robert—the Abbé Robert . . . but it will convey nothing to you. . . ."

Though he accompanied the words with a smile, there was a determined look in his eyes. He made a movement towards the interior of the room.

"I should very much like five minutes' talk with you, but I fear my visit is not very timely."

"The fact is I'm starting on a journey almost at once. . . ."

"I know," said the other, with a conspiratorial air.

". . . And unless it is a very urgent matter . . ."

"It happens that it is . . . a matter of considerable importance. . . . I said five minutes; three will be enough. . . . What I have to say concerns this journey of yours."

Mionnet looked the stranger up and down, then signed to him to enter. He removed the shoe and the hammer from the lid of the trunk, cleared a chair, and pushed it forward. Backing towards the table, he stood there, leaning against it, his arms folded.

His visitor refused the offer of the chair. His glance took in the trunk and the other evidences of impending departure. He sighed faintly and then, without any attempt to instil mystery into his voice:

"Please take what I am about to say," he remarked, "in the nature of an anonymous warning."

He smiled.

"It is very unlikely that we shall ever meet again. But if we should do so, I should be glad if you would not go out of your way to recognize me."

He made a quick little movement with his right hand as though to dismiss the matter once and for all.

". . . Treat me as an unknown friend. . . . Give up this journey. . . ."

Mionnet did not reply at once. A number of different ideas formed with lightning rapidity in his mind.

At last, "Why should I?" he asked.

With an air of great politeness the other spread his arms, bowed slightly, and smiled.

"Unfortunately," he replied, "I must ask you to take what I am saying on trust."

"No doubt, sir, I should be pleased to do so if I had the honour of knowing you better. . . ."

The young man repeated the gesture, but said nothing.

With a careful assumption of innocent wonder, Mionnet continued:

"I confess I am puzzled to make out the exact significance of this warning. Is it that you think the actual journey may be dangerous? Is it my plan of staying in Italy that you wish me to abandon? Have you heard of any inconveniences that may await me there? Or do you merely mean that I oughtn't to be leaving Paris, that I have work here to do? That last consideration might, I admit, carry a certain weight with me. . . ."

At each question the self-styled Abbé Robert made the same evasive gesture, which took the form of the movement of the arms which he had already twice repeated, though this time it was never completed. Then he said:

"All I can tell you, sir, is that my determination to approach you has been dictated simply and solely by a desire to serve your interests."

Mionnet moved away from the edge of the table, straightened himself, inclined his head slightly, and, in the tone of a man putting an end to an interview, remarked:

"Very good. I am grateful to you for coming. . . . I will think over what you have said."

Mionnet was more preoccupied with this visit than he liked to admit, and when, next morning, he went to see Monsignor Lebaigue, he told him about it.

"It certainly is tiresome," said the prelate.

He got him to describe the Abbé "Robert's" appearance. But Mionnet's account was lacking in detail.

"Such a visit," he said, "might be accounted for in many different ways, as, no doubt, you are aware, all of which are worth serious consideration. If we had time we ought probably to try to find out something more about it, but you're off this evening."

"You still think I should go just the same, Monsignor?"

The prelate considered the question.

"Yes. . . . If you put off your journey it will look too much as though you were yielding to intimidation. Any suspicions there may be in certain quarters would merely be confirmed. . . . It may have been only an attempt to sound you, to make you speak. . . . You didn't give anything away?"

"Nothing, Monsignor."

"Listen to me," went on Monsignor Lebaigue, biting his thumbnail twice as he spoke. "This business has a queer look to me. I should be surprised if there were anything much behind it. . . . It may have been just some crazy free lance acting without authority. . . . I will make a few inquiries through official channels. It may not be the first time that fellow's tried it. When you get to Rome you'll be in a better position to see. Be careful. You'll soon feel whether or not instructions have been given to put a spoke in your wheel."

Monsignor Lebaigue remained silent for a few moments, a frown on his forehead; then he began to laugh. He took out his pencil and hunted about for a scrap of paper.

"I'm going to give you an address."

In the middle of a piece of paper he wrote, in his firm, elongated, rather decorative script:

Dom Charles Magloire,
Sant' Anselmo.

"I can't remember the exact name of the street. . . . San Saba— San Sabina—something like that, I think. But you won't have any difficulty in finding it. It's somewhere on the slopes of the Aventine. You'll like the walk, it's magnificent. . . . Let yourself be seen with this Dom Charles Magloire . . . work up an intimacy with him if you can. He's not difficult to handle, provided you're willing to listen to him without arguing. Get him to introduce you here and there. Make it clear that you've chosen him as your guide, philosopher, and friend."

Mionnet permitted himself an understanding smile.

"May I ask you, Monsignor, the precise object of these precautions?"

The prelate burst into a guffaw of laughter.

"I guarantee that if there's any organized espionage on your movements, your watchers will have something to puzzle their brains over. . . ."

"Ought I to ask his advice about my thesis?"

"That's immaterial. He won't be interested in it except in so far as it fits in with his own particular mania. . . . Generally speaking, go out, at least at first, as little as possible. Confine yourself to the most innocent occupations. . . . And don't throw your memoranda into the waste-paper-basket."

Chapter 8

WAZEMMES GIVES HIS ALLEGIANCE TO THE ACTION FRANÇAISE

The 16th of January was an important date in the life of Raymond Poincaré, for on that day the plenary session of the Left groups, meeting at the Senate, turned him down in favour of Pams as official Republican candidate, by 323 votes to 309 at the third count. He was forced, therefore, to choose between two alternatives: either to withdraw from the contest, or to allow himself to be put forward by the Right parties, a decision which would inevitably have a very great effect upon the general policy of the country in external as well as internal affairs.

But the date was, relatively, of no less significance in the political life of Wazemmes, since at nine o'clock that evening he joined the Action Française.

The step had been in preparation for some considerable time. It was over a year ago that Lambert, of the rue des Gardes, had undertaken to convert Wazemmes to what he, Lambert, with a fine air of nonchalance, was pleased to call the "party of truth."

Lambert, of the rue des Gardes, served in the men's outfitting department of the Maison Dorée. He was also one of the Camelots du Roi. His membership of the organization dated from the Conservative schism in the Sorbonne. He had more than once painted in glowing colours to Wazemmes the delight of being an active Camelot. There was the fun of having mysterious orders passed on to one by a pal, or of finding laconic instructions in sealed envelopes left in the porter's lodge: "Meeting at such and such a place at such and such an hour. Destroy this paper"; the pleasure of feeling oneself one of a secret society, of being involved in street brawls—with the added thrill of having a serious, a dignified, purpose. When a fellow's a

Camelot, he doesn't play the games he used to, English and Boers, or Japanese and Russians, behind the piles of road-mending material in the rue Stephenson. He's in a real plot, he's fighting for the truth. Heads get broken in good earnest. One's up against the cops—with drawn clubs, too—or the hooligans employed by the Reds and the Freemasons against patriotic Frenchmen. There's pretty serious damage done; chaps go home with black eyes, or with "a crack on the skull, take my word," or with an arm that may be useless for the rest of the week. Some don't go home at all, because they spend the night in a cell. Lambert, of the rue des Gardes, had already done six nights in the lock-up, but he'd never had a real sentence, a fact which had helped him to keep his job, but, on the other hand, prevented him from really shining in the organization. For the delights of glory were not the least of those prized by these gallant youths, nor was fortune niggardly in rationing them. The papers were full of their exploits, the least of which was enshrined in the official gazette of the movement and described in terms usually reserved for the great deeds of history. No act was too trivial, no witticism too weak, to escape admiring reference. Many were invented that had never occurred or been spoken. On gala days great ladies mixed freely with them, "duchesses and princesses, honour bright, real slap-up skirts, dolled up to kill, with royal blood in their veins, women, if you understand what I mean, 'of the house of France,' and don't you forget it, me lad! And they behave as though you were one of themselves, too. Even in the eighth-arrondissement section, which isn't my own, there are two sons of a count who call me by my Christian name just because we were in a scrap together. It's 'Lambert here, I say, Lambert . . . let me introduce my friend Lambert. . . .' In my own section, of which I'm one of the oldest members, my word's law. Pity I can't do a couple of weeks in the jug, but my old folks'd have a fit if I did. I shouldn't bother about losing my job, the committee would find me another and help me out, too, meanwhile. The men who run the show are hand in glove with a whole lot of high-ups, employers, bankers, and chaps like that, who just do anything they want. They've only got to give the word and the money comes tumbling out—as is only right and proper."

Lambert's information was weakest on the purely theoretical side. He knew it was important, but had not given it much thought. He could repeat, of course, the chief article of faith, which was that the present régime was rotten; that the Republic, better known as "the old Sow," had for God knew how long been leading France to destruction; that the ministers and, without a single exception, the deputies were nothing but a lot of common crooks who were being paid good money by foreigners to betray their country; but that all would be well the moment the King returned, escorted by his loyal and patriotic supporters. Such an event, it was implied, might happen any day now, but nobody seemed to mind waiting a bit, since the period, with its intolerable humiliations, presented an unrivalled opportunity for the exercise of wit and the enjoyment of fun such as might never occur again.

Generally speaking, the "program" found in Wazemmes a willing participant. Not that he had any particular love of street brawls or went out of his way to get a crack on the head, but he was given to understand that the existence of a Camelot was not exclusively made up of pitched battles, but largely consisted in noisy demonstrations, and even in quite peaceful meetings between four walls, at which heroism could be manifested by a chap's shouting seditious songs until he was hoarse. He flattered himself that he hadn't got a bad voice and could remember the tunes fairly easily. What chiefly attracted him, however, was the atmosphere of "class," the flavour of aristocratic worldliness, that hung about the whole thing. For some time now, it is true, he had ceased to think of himself as made of the same stuff as the "people," but the "people" weren't always so ready to note the difference and had an uncomfortable way of treating him as one of themselves. He didn't, to be sure, want to appear "stuck-up," he was perfectly willing to show sympathy with the aspirations of the lower orders, but on condition that the proper distance was observed. Anything that would help to prevent undesirable confusion, that would mark, in a visible and permanent fashion, the difference between himself and his neighbours, at once recommended itself to his consideration. A fellow might be taking a cup of coffee or a glass of white wine at the bar of a corner café in a crowd of young workmen, errand-boys, and newspaper-venders, with a loutish sort of a proprietor behind the bar, who was not very good at noting social distinctions. But only let him say casually: "I'm a monarchist," or "We Camelots," or "As my friend Count So-and-So was saying to me the other day at our section meeting," and the odds were that the necessary difference would at once be established. There might be a few ugly looks, but looks of some sort there were bound to be. One or two of the bystanders might guffaw or shrug their shoulders, but there would be an immediate sense in the company that he belonged to a different class—a superior class, needless to say. It would be up to him, of course, to choose his moment—not, for instance, to assert himself in too rowdy a place where the surprise produced by his words might take the form of a smack on the jaw, but that wasn't the kind of company, anyhow, in which he would be likely to find himself.

There were advantages, too, where nice little bits of skirt were concerned. If a fellow said: "I'm one of the Camelots du Roi," the little chicken would at once think that he was a viscount at the very least, or anyhow a "real gentleman" who was well in with the "swells," and if it so happened that he was passably good-looking, with nice manners, well . . . even if the skirt in question turned out to be the daughter of a militant Socialist, it was more than likely that she'd lose her head.

Of course, there was one's boss to be considered. What would he say when he found out that one was a member of the Action Française? If only he belonged himself, all would be well. Whenever Wazemmes found himself echoing Haverkamp, he felt extraordinarily easy in his mind, and he never embarked on an enterprise about which Haverkamp had not given him instructions, or in the conduct of which he could not take Haverkamp as a model, without an uncomfortable twinge of conscience. Haverkamp, to be sure, betrayed no sympathy for the hooligans of the extreme Left, and had no tolerance for the indiscipline of the workers. He, too, was one of "nature's aristocrats." . . . It would be a red-letter day indeed if, once he had won his spurs in the Action Française, he could bring along his boss as a prospective member!

Something, however, had kept him hesitating a long time. One Sunday when he happened to be sauntering in front of the Church of Notre-Dame-de-Clignancourt, he had heard a lot of young people offering the party paper for sale. The next day he had asked Lambert who they were. "Some of the Camelots," came the answer, and Wazemmes made a face. Everyone has his peculiar susceptibilities, however absurd they may be. To sell papers in the street, to take pennies from the hands of casual passers-by, had always stood to Wazemmes as the lowest of low occupations, fit only for social outcasts and on a level with collecting cigarette stubs, clipping dogs, and nosing about in dust-bins. . . . How was it possible to scavenge about among dust-bins, even in the name of the house of France, without losing all sense of superiority? It was no good for Lambert to say that he had often hawked the *Action Française* in the streets, that the sons of a count could be found selling it in front of Saint-Pierre-de-Chaillot and Saint-Philippe-du-Roule, Wazemmes couldn't get over his repugnance. The knowledge that the Duc d'Orléans himself was in the habit of eating salted spiders wouldn't make the thought any the less revolting.

"It's all settled. I've spoken about it to the section officers. You'll be let off selling papers," Lambert had told him quite recently. "I couldn't give the true reason—it wouldn't have done you any good right at the beginning so I said you'd promised your uncle never to sell papers in the street. They said your uncle was an old tike, but they realized that you couldn't just give him a kick in the pants. You see, our people have a great respect for the family."

The meeting in the course of which Wazemmes's membership was to become an accepted fact was held in Dr. Albérand's drawing-room on the boulevard Barbès. On that particular evening the doctor was to be out on a round, the details of which his family could discover by reference to his engagement-book. It would keep him away from home until after eleven. But if the room itself was free of waiting patients, the traces of their recent presence was still in evidence. Between the chairs, the carpet, and the pictures on the walls floated a faint exhalation made up of body odours, the smell of disinfectants, and a less definite exhalation which brought a dim reminder of dust, old clothes, and the dark recesses of cupboards.

On such occasions Dr. Albérand's son, Gaston, a law student, was in the habit of using the big drawing-room to entertain his political friends with the connivance of his mother and his sisters. His father had a shrewd inkling of what was going on, but preferred to remain, officially, in ignorance. He himself had Right sympathies. He was not ignorant of the fact that his son was a Camelot, and though he didn't much like the idea, he felt qualms about exerting his authority, especially as, so far, he had not suffered professionally from Gaston's antics.

Those present were: Lambert, of the rue des Gardes; a law student called Duc, or Ducle, a friend of the son of the house; a young gentleman with a hyphenated name, impressive-sounding but difficult to remember—Wazemmes had no chance to find out what profession he followed, but noted with intense care his every word and gesture, so anxious was he to learn the manners of the great world (gradually he became aware that he was called Hervé de la Bresche des Broons); and a man of the name of Octave Poisson, who was presented to the company three separate times as an "ex-revolutionary" who had become disgusted by the demagogues of the Left and who had now returned to political sanity and the touching allegiance of the French people to their kings. Octave Poisson's means of support were no more visible than those of Hervé de la Bresche des Broons, but they could hardly be the same. (Interrogated on the subject by Wazemmes after the meeting, Lambert said shortly: "Don't you worry about him.")

The evening began with a long discussion—the details of which escaped Wazemmes—on the responsibility incurred by two hypothetical young men in the matter of organizing some recently initiated service. This was followed by the admission of the new member, which was effected without formalities or speeches. He learned that he would be regarded as "permanently enrolled" in the last week of the month. He would be told later what obligations membership entailed.

Next he had to listen to some of the ritual songs of the Camelots and was even permitted to take part, which he found the best way of learning them. Though he was not normally shy and had a good opinion of his powers as a singer, he felt a good deal of awkwardness. These young gentlemen, especially Hervé de la Bresche des Broons, impressed him. But he soon noticed that Hervé de la Bresche's voice, strong and manly though it was in ordinary speech, took on the shrill quaver of extreme old age as soon as he began to sing, no matter how hard he might try to keep it steady. This fact put Wazemmes in countenance again.

They began—on the principle of giving honour where honour is due—with what might be called the Hymn of the Camelots du Roi.

> Long life to the Camelots, mother of mine,
> Long life, and more strength to their hands!
> Than flouting the law there is nothing so fine.
> Long life, and more strength to their hands!

with its refrain:

> Long live the King, to Hell with things Republican!
> Long live the King, the dirty Sow shall swing!

Mention of the Sow led, by natural association of ideas, to a song in her honour, the words of which ran as follows:

> When the Sow shall swing from the nearest lamp,
> All Paris will dance
> As much as she wants
> And the world will laugh.

And then the second verse:

> Briand will float, as he always does,
>   And Jaurès will swill
>   Till he's managed to fill
>   That belly of his,

the words of which Octave Poisson bawled with proletarian gusto.
But Hervé de la Bresche des Broons, perhaps because he had the soul
of a poet, or because he came from Brittany, shouted out that they
mustn't forget Botrel's "Up, Lads!"

> We come from Brittany's fair land,
>   Loyal to our King,
>   Our King!
> Our fathers fought with sword in hand
>   To serve their King,
>   Their King!
> Armorica, where shore and sea
>   Run still with the blood of chivalry,
>   Sing! Sing! Sing!
> Up, Breton lads! Long live the King!

At the last line all rose with a single motion and stood, arms outstretched, as though waving hats.

Up to this point Wazemmes had been conscious of a certain fur-
tive pleasure, not untouched by shame, as he yelled sentiments which
he could not but regard as almost obscene. (The vision of Uncle
Miraud, seen vaguely and afar—sad, disappointed, outraged—was
heavy on his conscience. He tried to blot the face from his memory,
as a schoolboy, on his first visit to a brothel, tries to blot his mother's.
Haverkamp's, too, was there, less remote, but more enigmatic. The
smile upon its lips was ambiguous; did it betoken admiration or
pitying contempt? "Go to it, my boy," or "Will you never grow up?")
But the song of the Breton lads made him feel grand again, filling
him with a sort of lyric frenzy. A surge of emotion for "France of
the olden time" swept into his little gutter-snipe soul. He felt him-

self the fellow and companion of the Musketeers, of La Tour-d'Auvergne,[1] of all the ancient chivalry of France fighting and marching its way across Europe. His heart thrilled to the vision of plumes and the sound of trumpets. Not that those odd, respectable words "King," "throne," stood to him for anything actual at all. They were more incomprehensible, if that were possible, than the Immaculate Conception or the Sacred Heart of Jesus. They lodged in his brain with all the incongruity of a piece of old furniture on a subway platform. Not to mince matters, though he found the word "throne" exciting, there was something a little frightening about it too. The short, sharp vocable made him think of other, not very agreeable words to which it had a phonetic resemblance: bone, stone, moan, groan. . . . A frightened memory flashed into his mind of cruel, forgotten things, the kind of things he had read about in history books, of torture chambers and gibbets and men dying in remote dungeons. Fortunately, a lyric fervour swept him free of all such morbid obsessions.

This emotion reached its crisis with the arrival on the scene of the three ladies. Albérand's mother and two sisters came into the room. Mme Albérand was smiling, but she held a finger to her lips. The two young girls, each with a tray in her hands, started to carry around glasses of orangeade. To Wazemmes they seemed ravishingly beautiful.

"You've sung enough now," said their host's mother with an air of charming severity. "We shall be turned out of the house by our landlord, who's a furniture-dealer, a Jew, and a Freemason."

The young people, who were already on their feet, fell silent, and bowed with an assumption of Old World courtesy, which seemed to come as natural to Octave Poisson as to Hervé de la Bresche des Broons, though perhaps he put into it a trifle more of conscious nonchalance. They helped themselves to the proffered drinks.

---

[1] La Tour-d'Auvergne distinguished himself in the Revolutionary wars and was named by Bonaparte in 1800 *"le Premier Grenadier de France."*—TRANSLATOR'S NOTE.

Lambert introduced Wazemmes. Young Albérand announced to the company that his sisters belonged to a society of young royalist women.

Wazemmes held out a moist and trembling hand. It came to him that the life of a Camelot was a tangled skein woven of fights with cops and meetings with glorious young girls of the highest possible social standing. The intoxication which came with the thought was as violent as that which he had known, in earlier days, as he came from Rita's door in the October twilight—and a good deal nobler.

Chapter

9

LOUIS BASTIDE IN DESPAIR.
FRANÇOISE IN PERIL

Louis Bastide, in his little room, was going through a period of despair. He knew that it would be long-drawn-out. There was no reason to suppose that the prospect would look more cheerful when he went to bed at eleven or when he awoke next morning.

He was seated before a table not more than two feet square, covered with a dark green cloth, and pushed anyhow against the wall facing his bed. Luckily, since the bed was short, there was room for the table between its foot and the window. Naturally, whenever he stretched his arm or raised his elbow, he came into sharp contact with the metal rails.

It was his work-table. He loved it, and the thought of it filled him with pride. He had been profoundly troubled by a stain on the cloth made by an overturned ink-well. He had failed to remove it entirely from the material, and it had soaked into the wood beneath. But today this disaster seemed comparatively trivial. That very afternoon his schoolmaster had announced the mathematical order of the class. An official announcement of results is always an impressive affair, and during the moments that preceded it, Louis had been conscious of nothing but a fever of anticipation. Presentiment had made his knees feel like water. But the shock of the fact had been worse even than the agony of waiting, or, rather, the fact had been so cruelly catastrophic that it had presented itself to his consciousness in the form of one anticipation the more, inexorable, terrifying. First, so-and-so; second, so-and-so . . . one after another the places were called, but the name Bastide remained absent. Each place thus announced increased the depth of his dizzy plunge without arresting it.

. . . Seventeenth! Louis had been seventeenth! The master had betrayed surprise, but only for the briefest of brief moments. Apparently he had overcome his disappointment very quickly. Later, going over the paper, he had said: "The problem you failed entirely to solve. As to the theorem, your figure was extremely badly drawn. You showed your bisector BC as a dotted line; but you argued as though it were the line BC, which is one of the lines containing the angle. . . ."

It was bad enough to have made a mistake which, with a little more attention, a little more careful thought, might have been avoided. But it was far worse to have to admit that he did not understand mathematics. It couldn't have been worse if he had been compelled to realize that he had an incurable disease, like cancer, of which the papers were so often full; incurable and at the same time shameful, like this syphilis that people were always talking about.

Of course, he did understand the stuff a little, about as much as the backward pupils, as much as those at the bottom of the class to which he was sinking so headlong. But he did not understand it thoroughly, and not to understand it thoroughly was as bad as not understanding it at all. Louis Bastide knew quite well that there was a passage of four and a half lines at the bottom of page 59 of the geometry book which last December, just before Christmas, he had failed to grasp. In order to go on, in order to give himself the chance, or rather the illusion, of understanding what followed, he had behaved as though he really did grasp those four and a half lines (after bravely trying them first this way and then that; after going back to them several days running; after grinding away at them with endless, agonizing concentration, all the way from the rue Damrémont to Chaptal). But to "go on" like that, as though he had grasped something that he had not grasped at all, was merely to play a trick on himself. Now that he was at page 72, Louis was suddenly thwarted, suddenly thrown out of step, by a sense of remorse at the way he had scamped the difficulty of page 59. His feelings were rather like those of a man who realizes that he has paid for a purchase with counterfeit money.

If he had been rich, he would have taken private lessons, would have got somebody to explain the difficulty. But would even that have been a sure way out of the tangle? It often happens that a schoolmaster explains one obscurity only to erect another in its place: and one just hasn't the courage to say that one doesn't understand a second time.

"Do you mean to say you don't see it yet?" his master had exclaimed irritably last Wednesday, when he was going over on the blackboard the previous day's lesson. Louis knew perfectly well that he hadn't really "seen," but what could he do? When, in the privacy of his own room, his head between his hands, and the bitter taste of his penholder in his mouth, he had gone over and over again the phrase which he could not understand, what was there left for him to do? He was alone. He could not turn for help to his father, who had never learned mathematics and who, anyhow, was dozing preparatory to going to bed because he was tired out by his day's work—poor Papa, who, old as he was, spent the whole day tying up parcels of books none of which he would ever read.

The awful thing was not being able to understand when he had embarked on a career in which, if he didn't understand, he would sooner or later have to face disaster. He could go on pretending for a time, could try to go on passing the counterfeit money, but eventually the fraud would be discovered. Already it had been discovered, for what else but discovery was this shameful, depressing "seventeenth" about which he hadn't yet dared to tell his mother? When would he be brave enough to mention it? Tomorrow morning, perhaps, when he got up—for at least he would have had a night's sleep, haunted though it would have been by a sense of impending terror, like that of a criminal.

What ought he to have done, a year ago, when M. Clanricard had pleaded so hard with his parents: "You can't stop his schooling when

he's so intelligent and such a hard worker. Let him try for a scholarship at the College of Chaptal. If he fails, we can talk the matter over
again"—what ought he to have done then? His father had found a
job as a packer in the publishing house of Guérin and Son. The family had felt a return of confidence. The future had looked less threatening. There was nothing very foolhardy about letting the boy stay
at school awhile longer. "You can see for yourselves," said M. Clanricard, "how increasingly difficult it becomes to make a living in the
manual trades, and then, all the time he's serving his apprenticeship,
he'll be making nothing. I wouldn't give you this advice if I wasn't
sure that he had gifts." Dear Monsieur Clanricard, how he had deceived himself! How blind affection had made him! And it was he
who had chosen the College of Chaptal as goal, although he knew
how great a part mathematics played in the curriculum.

Louis felt that by dint of hard work he could have succeeded in
almost any other branch of scholarship. He was good at French,
though he found the more advanced syntax and the longer phrases
rather frightening. He could learn history without difficulty. He was
one of the top boys in German and English despite his faults of accent
and pronunciation. Up to the present even the various branches of
science had not really stumped him, because they had not as yet involved him in complicated formulæ. But what good could all this do
him now that he had been placed seventeenth in mathematics?

Wasn't it almost dishonest to let his parents go on feeding and
keeping him in the belief that he was destined for a brilliant future?
If he said to them now: "I don't understand mathematics; I can't go
on . . ." they would just think that he was going through one of
those periods of idleness common to boys of his age, that he was fed
up with books, and wanted to play in the streets like an errand-boy
or enjoy himself with a lot of other young people in a factory.

Louis Bastide let his mind dwell seriously on the thought of death.
Not that he even remotely contemplated either killing himself or
going out of his way to get killed. But he couldn't help reflecting
that if death came his way he would welcome it as a relief. It wasn't

on the means of death, which might be intolerably painful, that he brooded, but on the idea of death itself as a way of escape from life, as a quick solution of all difficulties.

What he complained of about life was not that it exacted too heavy a price for the pleasures it afforded. He was not by nature exigent, and his Christian upbringing had convinced him that human beings have few rights in this world.

What he complained of—and never had the fact seemed so obvious to him as this evening—was the difficulty of ever being satisfied with one's own efforts, of avoiding remorse, of being able to live without a continual sense of self-criticism, no matter how hard one might try. How was it that so many people seemed to be perfectly satisfied? Was it that they knew better how to act? Was it that circumstances were kinder to them? For instance, if they were incapable of understanding mathematics, circumstances might not force them into becoming members of a college in which a knowledge of mathematics was indispensable. Or if they were badly educated—and there were a lot of badly educated people, people worse educated than Louis, even in mathematics; at this very moment there were fifteen boys who had taken places lower than seventeenth—their circumstances might be such that the fact would not distress their parents.

Was it possible, perhaps, not to worry, just to take life as it came? He had heard people say so and boast of it. But he didn't see how such an end could be compassed. He might refuse to play, might allow himself no relaxation, might punish himself, deprive himself of all pleasure, but that wouldn't alter the fact that he was responsible, that the load on his shoulders must remain heavy. Who could understand mathematics for him, or pass examinations in his place? Who could guarantee him against having some day to face the sad and disappointed eyes of his father and his mother, against being compelled to realize that he and he alone had been the cause of their long years of fruitless sacrifice?

That was why death seemed such a boon. It does seem probable that when a boy is dead he can cease from worrying about his responsibilities, cease troubling his head about finding ways out of inextricable tangles, be free of all difficulties for ever and ever . . . unless, of course . . . unless . . .

Mme Maieul looked at the sleeping Françoise. Was she asleep? Her cheeks were very red, her breathing short and quick. The little face twitched now and then as though the child were still half awake, as though she were forcing herself to sleep. Perhaps even so young a child as she is already capable of willing itself to sleep, no matter what the obstacle. Maybe already one of those divisions of nature is operative that at a later stage become so terribly marked, between what the body wants and what, in fact, it gets.

Was she still in pain? Probably. In her stomach and her head almost certainly. Her forehead was so hot and so red! Tiny beads of perspiration seemed trying to form, but as yet they were scarcely perceptible. Had she dared, Mme Maieul would have taken Françoise's temperature again in the hope of finding that it had dropped a further one or two points. But to do so would have been sheer selfish cruelty. Two hours ago the thermometer had marked 40° C., and only half an hour since, when the doctor came back, 39.8°. He had not seemed as anxious as he had on his previous visit. "It looks as though there's a little intestinal poisoning; she's probably eaten something that disagreed with her. . . . Don't let her temperature frighten you. At her age it has a way of shooting up for nothing at all. There doesn't seem to me to be any reason to fear that she's in for a serious illness. . . ." But he had spoken in an almost conventional tone, as though repeating a well-worn formula. A little later there had been a noticeable change in his voice—a trace of irritability, of annoyance: "It's very odd. I've been having a number of cases like this recently among my patients. . . ." (His patients were mostly children about Françoise's age.) "So far, very few have turned out serious. . . . It's almost as though there were a mild epidemic about."

"But what sort of epidemic? . . ."

"Hanged if I know . . . a kind of intestinal flu to which children seem particularly susceptible this year. . . . But that's only guess-work on my part. . . ."

"But, doctor, she's hardly been out the last few days. She's not been playing with other children, and she's certainly been near nobody who's sick. . . ."

"Ah."

He didn't say that none had turned out to be serious, but only that very few had. Perhaps some of his patients had died. "Some children, of course, are very delicate. He didn't seem at all frightened about Françoise when he came that second time; but this morning he certainly frightened me."

Two years and two and a half months. Poor little masterpiece! So lovely a face, already eloquent of gentleness and pride; such beautiful eyes behind their lowered lids; lips slightly parted, the upper ever so little projecting above the lower, and forming themselves into one of those pouts one calls adorable because it marvellously contains the hinted signs of so much—of so much, particularly, that is still to come—of young girlhood treasuring the possession of just such a grimace with which, as with a weapon of tried proof, to express disdain of some unworthy suitor.

It occurred to Mme Maieul with a sudden stab of pain, that earlier in that very day—perhaps two hours ago, perhaps four—Françoise had found herself at a parting of the ways, a point of divergence marked by a terrible simplicity (in later life, the cross-roads of existence have a way of being more complicated, more subtly difficult); two ways, and no more than two, had lain before her—to the left, death; to the right, life. How many times had she already passed by such crises of direction in the course of her short life? How soon would the next one be upon her? How brightly watchful childhood must ever be! Never for a moment must the choice be mistaken. When the slope of the road led the wrong way it must be resisted, and sometimes the descending hill was precipitously steep, while the right way, for the moment, seemed like a wall unscalable. And older folk, those who were there already, could see it all before their eyes and yet do little more than see. At most they might help to prevent the sleeping, feverish scrap of humanity from falling down the steep place. Each time it would be harder to let her go because of the crises already met and passed with honour. Good luck, blessedly efficacious in the past, must arm the doubting spirit for the future. The longer its record grew, the more precious seemed its promise. Mme Maieul let her imagination dwell on a Françoise fallen ill at ten or at fifteen, on a Françoise in danger of her life at eighteen. . . . What courage it needed to see so far ahead those partings of the way and to march towards them with a gay step! Happy those mothers who paid to Providence more than lip service. "I will do all that it is my duty to do," think such favoured women, "all that I can. But the final decision, each time, must be in the hands of God"—which meant: "On Him I shift the ultimate responsibility"—that is to say, the only responsibility that really counted. What a relief that must be for the anguished heart!

"I too know how to pray," she told herself; "at a pinch, with the help of a little auto-suggestion, I can make myself believe that my prayer will take effect. But what I can't do is to shuffle off on God the responsibility that I know to be my own."

Dr. Périer was walking the hundred yards that separated two houses in the rue de Berlin whither he had received an urgent summons.

His mind was full of little Françoise Maieul, whom he found enchanting, was extremely fond of, and would hate to see die. He did not think that she was in any great danger. But he was always nervous where children were concerned. He spent his whole day tending their ailments; he had, as the saying goes, "saved" hundreds. But he had trained himself never to look too far ahead, never to assume that they would be saved, even when their symptoms and his experience augured the best. "I have specialized in a terrifying field," he used often to reflect; "I am like a man working with the most delicate materials, the finest silk, muslin, or gauze. . . . One never knows when it is going to tear."

He let his mind dwell on this world, or rather this species, made up of children, with its own natural laws, its peculiar dangers, in which he, Périer, important, familiar, yet always a stranger, spent his life. It was so easy to think of children as ends in themselves, without regard to the grown-ups they would one day become. The end of childhood had a way of seeming like the end of an existence sufficient to itself. What happened to them afterwards was in the nature of a metamorphosis which, almost in spite of oneself, one knew would occur, though when it did, one's interest in the business would be at an end. These epidemics were constantly falling out of a clear sky, to rage like a mild gale through the world of children. There is something fundamentally reassuring about the idea of an epidemic. Without the background of an epidemic to which it could be referred—its death-rate was remarkably low, and, as it were, an indirect consequence—the case of Françoise Maieul would have been very much more disquieting. Périer thought of Hippocrates, of the monumental hypotheses in which that great man's common sense had been crystallized, of the way in which, in age after age, their truth had again and again been proved. But at this point in his reflections the train of his thought was broken by the opening of a door in response to his pressure on the bell-push, and by the warm gust, as it were, of confused anxiety that came to meet him from the suddenly revealed interior.

MIONNET ARRIVES IN ROME

When he got out of the train at the Termini station, Mionnet decided to leave his luggage in the cloak-room, and set off in search of a hotel. He had in his pocket two short lists of addresses, one given him by Monsignor Lebaigue, the other by one of his colleagues at the Catholic Institute. But he had made up his mind not to use either of them. The houses recommended to him were obviously such as catered specially for the needs of the clergy and other devout-minded persons, and where, into the bargain, the majority of the visitors would be French. He had no wish to spoil the effect of his arrival in Rome by immersing himself in an atmosphere which he knew only too well. His position as a foreigner and the objects of his journey entitled him to a freedom of action which he intended to enjoy to the full. To reinforce these arguments was the fact that Monsignor Lebaigue had put him on his guard against the "special" surveillance of which he might quite possibly become the object from the moment of his appearance in the city. To establish himself at once in one of the five or six houses to which a French abbé might be expected to find his way would be to make the task of those who might be eventually saddled with the duty of watching his movements rather too easy.

He had taken with him nothing but a small hand-bag which would attract no attention. At the entrance to the station he had some difficulty in escaping the clutches of the hotel porters, cab-drivers, and other importunate strangers.

He identified the Piazza di Termini on his map and smiled to find how like it was to the station square of any big nineteenth-century provincial town. In spite of the cold there were a good many people walking about. Boys were crying the latest editions. He reached the Via Nazionale. He had noted in his guide-book the address of a good second-class Swiss hotel, situated at No. 104 of that street. He knew from experience that Swiss hotels in Italy are, as a rule, both clean and cheap.

At the Hôtel de la Paix et Helvétia he was offered, for four francs, a room facing on the street which seemed sufficiently Swiss to be encouraging, sufficiently Italian to be charming. He took it at once and went back to the station for his bags.

As he crossed the Piazza di Termini his attention was caught by the cries of the news-venders, and he glanced at the headlines. One of the papers announced as the great event of the day a "Heroic Enterprise by Six Bersaglieri in Lybia," but another reported the election of "Raimondo Poincaré" as President of the French Republic.

"My protector," thought Mionnet, and allowed himself a little thrill of personal pleasure.

Chapter

11

JAURÈS IS DISCOURAGED

"Dine with you? I should be delighted. But this evening's impossible. I don't mean I'm going somewhere else; far from it. I'm just snowed under with work on the paper. You've got something you want to talk to me about, something important? . . . I rather suspected as much. . . . Well, look here, come and pick me up at the offices of *L'Humanité* about eleven o'clock. We'll go somewhere near for a drink and a chat. Then, if I'm wanted, they'll know where to find me. But don't bother, they won't disturb me without very good reason."

At that late hour the Café du Croissant was deserted, except for two scrubby little men at the bar who were more concerned with their own affairs than with the appearance of strangers. The newcomers sat down on the bench which stood with its back to the entry. A blast of cold air came in through the window. It took some minutes for Gurau, who was sensitive to minor discomforts, to forget it.

Jaurès seemed rather out of breath. His puffy, puckered eyes gave evidence of fatigue.

"So Poincaré's offered you the Foreign Office?" He corrected himself with a guffaw of laughter: "Or, I should say, he's made Briand offer it? . . . And you want to ask my advice, eh, before giving an answer one way or the other? That's very nice of you. I am deeply touched. You know that according to the *Echo de Paris* I'm a very ill counsellor, and that I'm almost automatically wrong in everything I say. . . . In your own interests, then, it might be better for you to do the exact opposite of anything I suggest."

On the same note of friendly chaff Gurau replied that he reserved to himself the right to disobey Jaurès, but that, whatever the upshot, he attached great value to this conversation and expected to get from it a good deal of light on his own immediate problems.

"If I listened merely to the promptings of my own judgment"—and Jaurès leaned his head forward a little—"I should say, without going any further into the business, what are you doing up that street?"

"Of which are you most distrustful, the owner or the captain?"

Jaurès started to laugh. "Of both."

"But there are a lot of people who think you have a weakness for Poincaré."

Jaurès raised his arms slightly and seemed to be carefully considering his reply.

"I can't help admitting that in intelligence he's superior to a great many others, and in character too. What I deplore is that he should put these qualities, should put his personality, which is strong and, in its own way, attractive, at the service of an ideal the nature of which, I fear, is only too obvious."

He paused a moment, then, again raising his arms in a gesture:

"And to think that they could find no one but Pams to put up against him! Pams, a man with everything against him, yes, everything—natural inferiority, a lack of culture and intelligence as far beyond competition, it seems to me, as his material wealth, that very wealth itself and the rather comic way he got it—far more comic than Félix Faure's pelt and leather business—even his name, which is like nothing so much as the noise made by a child's pistol. Nothing absent, in fact, that the heart of a music-hall song-writer could desire. You must admit that the Radicals are a perfectly fantastic lot of idiots. Here they are, in charge of the Republic, which owed its foundation to them, doing their level best to turn it into ridicule. It's almost as though they were trying to furnish their worst enemies with weapons to turn against them. What better could Maurras have invented than the candidature of Pams? . . . And that was the only alternative offered! I must say there was a good deal of excuse for those of us who preferred to vote for Poincaré."

Gurau, who had been one of those referred to, felt grateful to Jaurès for this absolution. Lowering his voice and leaning sideways towards his neighbour, Jaurès continued:

"Many Radicals, it's no good blinking the fact, are a good deal lacking in morality. . . . The party has permitted an infiltration by very doubtful elements, and the highest posts are by no means the least affected. Our idealistic fight at the time of the Dreyfus Affair, and our consequent victory, opened our ranks to a mob of scamps and profiteers. The professional politicians, who lay low when things were difficult, have got back into the saddle. . . . About that, Péguy is perfectly right. . . ."

Gurau remarked that that, perhaps, was not so much a vice peculiar to the Radical Party as the working of a law of history. It is natural that debased characters should rally to a successful group and exploit it. The party in power has always, in every period, attracted to it people who see in politics nothing but a way of getting places and profits, and the result makes itself felt from the highest to the lowest, from minister to road-mender.

Jaurès replied that the duty of leaders ought to be to control a stampede perhaps inevitable in itself and keep it within reasonable bounds.

They spoke of Léon Bourgeois. Gurau pointed out, not without irony, that Bourgeois, who might easily have rallied round himself the majority of the Republican votes, had not only, as often before, shirked the duty laid upon him, but had actually taken an active part in favour of Poincaré's campaign.

"Yes," said Jaurès, "Bourgeois's is an odd case. He's the kind of man whose public career is always at the beck and call of his private life. . . . There's the question of his health, for instance, which is genuinely bad, though not so bad as he conveniently makes out. He's certainly not one of those heroes who's likely to have himself carried into the front line on a stretcher. . . . There are his sentimental complications. . . . Incidentally, I was told something which I find it

very difficult to believe, about his refusal to be a candidate. Haven't
you heard?"

Jaurès put the question with a sidelong glance. And his eye seemed
to permit itself the luxury of a little ironic and malevolent twinkle—
much as a man might permit himself an occasional night out. Perhaps at that moment he was priding himself on knowing how to be
as spiteful as the next man, on being able to show that if he was bitter
it was because he saw things so clearly, on being in a position to prove
that he had not been taken in by the course of events. But try though
he might, he remained the "decent fellow" he always was, without a
trace of venom.

Gurau protested that he had not the slightest idea to what his
friend was alluding.

"Oh, well, then, it seems—not that I really know anything about
it—but I had it from someone who's pretty close to him, who's really
on very confidential terms with him—it seems that he told this friend
of his when he was being urgently pressed to stand, that he wasn't the
least bit interested in the prospect of becoming President of the Republic—that what really appealed to him was something quite different—you'll never guess what. . . ."

"No; tell me."

"Why, being elected to the Academy! . . . You see he felt that if
he accepted the Presidency it would mean having to give up the
Academy . . . and—well, he preferred giving up the Presidency!
. . . What have you got to say to that? Pretty shocking, eh?"

"Yes, if it's true, and, by God, I wouldn't like to swear it wasn't!"

"That's just about how I feel. It's the kind of thing one would say
was impossible . . . and yet the probability is that it's true."

They remained silent, deep in thought, both of them, but with
smiles on their lips, Jaurès with his eyes fixed on the corner of the
ceiling opposite, Gurau looking at the table.

"It's only a trivial matter," went on Jaurès, "and, like most historical sayings, it was probably invented. But, like them, it has a
symbolic value. What hope is there for a régime, for a country, where

at such a time of peril, when the future of all of us is in the melting-pot, the biggest figure in the biggest party can be represented, without too great a show of improbability, as formulating his duty in terms like that? Corneille, thou shouldst be living at this hour!"

This decline of the Radicals, this disappearance of all heroic idealism from their policy, seemed to him to be connected in some way with a change of heart among the bourgeoisie.

"While the Affair was on, the behaviour of a part of the bourgeoisie was magnificent and really encouraging. Today, almost without exception, they have entirely changed round. Fear has killed in them every generous impulse. Their heart is no longer in Democracy. Deep down they regret having established the Republic. They've even abandoned their one-time liberalism. They have adopted many of Maurras's ideas as their own . . . with the flag left out. They support the régime because there's no alternative, and probably because it's convenient. But under cover of the Republic they fully intend to fight as hard as they know how against the logical development of its principles. And to do so they wouldn't mind going, if need be, as far as a war. Look at the terrifying uproar there's been all this last year about military pensions; remember the wave of flag-wagging that's sweeping the country, all the hectoring talk that's come from the lips of those one would have least expected to behave like that. . . . And don't forget that disgraceful reinstatement of Paty du Clam carried through under the pretext of healing old wounds. It's nothing but a rehearsal of mobilization. And they'll vote the three-years law. They don't want an army of reservists, a national army. What they want is a regular army, trained to take the offensive. Obviously an army of reservists is no good for an offensive. All it's good for is to fight foot by foot in defence of an invaded country. . . . To cut a long story short, they're undoing everything we've spent our lives in doing. In the words of the old saying, 'Reaction is flowing at flood stage.'"

Gurau remarked that Jaurès seemed in a gloomy mood.

"Well, I am. . . . I feel thoroughly discouraged . . ." confessed Jaurès, squaring his shoulders and then letting them droop once more.

"I try not to show it, and I'm fighting on as best I may. But to a friend like you I don't mind confessing the truth. . . . I often feel as though I were living in a nightmare, swimming with the last ounce of my strength against a current that is too strong for me, that is carrying me away, carrying all of us away."

Truth to tell, he sometimes questioned whether in fact France were still a democracy.

"The other day one of my 'young men' on the *Humanité* brought me the first draft of a piece of work he's been engaged on for some months. In its present state it's too technical and too heavy for publication in the paper—to say nothing of the trouble it would get us into with some of our friends. I don't quite see yet how I can make use of it. Put shortly, the object of this piece of work is to demonstrate, with all the relevant facts quoted and everything scientifically presented, that since the beginning of the century, and in particular during the last five or six years, most of the powers of the State have, in this country, passed quietly and without any fuss into the hands of a small group of financiers and heads of industrial trusts. I say advisedly powers of the State and not merely economic control, because the barrier that once separated economics from politics has broken down. It is a view, I admit, that confirms the Marxian theory, but it goes further than Marx. Marx saw capitalism as a gradually developing system. . . . What actually seems to have happened, without any of us noticing it, is something in the nature of a complete revolution. The royalists make a great song and dance about wanting to strangle the 'old Sow,' but there's really no need for so much shouting, for all this while the old Sow has been, in fact, bound and gagged very efficiently by a lot of silent gentlemen in morning coats. You can take my word for it that it's a pretty startling document. I can't give you the details offhand . . . but the fellow's made some very extraordinary discoveries. Do you know Guillain?"

"What Guillain's that? Do you mean the one who preceded me as Minister of Public Works some time ago under—who was it now?—Méline?"

"That's the man. . . . He was Vice-President of the Chamber, too, in Combes's time. Well, you probably won't believe me when I say that for some days now—ever since reading this document, indeed—I've been asking myself whether Guillain isn't the most powerful man in France at the present time."

Gurau confined his reply to a smile. Jaurès continued:

"I'm perfectly serious. . . . It's not my way, as you know, to joke about things like that."

"I know that Guillain is a big gun in the financial world. Still . . ."

"When, some while back, you were at the Office of Public Works, didn't you have a chance of seeing just how powerful he is?"

Gurau hardly liked to confess that he had considered his tenure of that minor office as merely a temporary halt in the antechamber of political success, and that he had left most of the work to his staff. He only said, therefore:

"I was there such a short time . . . and then, you see, the money magnates were so suspicious of me that they probably lay low until I cleared out." (As he spoke he was conscious of a vague memory of some rather gross scandal to do with accounting that Manifassier had nosed out. Gurau recollected having given a free hand in the matter to his collaborator, who had probably not made things any too easy for the individuals in question. Doubtless they had managed to drag the business out until the arrival of his successor.)

"Well, then," Jaurès went on, "let me remind you, if you've forgotten, that Guillain was, at one and the same time, president of the Steel Cartel and of a new body called the Federation of Metallurgic and Mining Industries; that's to say, of the two most powerful combines in the whole economic system. He had under his hand all the steel magnates, all the metallurgical federations, all the mines, all the manufacturers of war material—you get that point?—and in addition he had a more or less direct say in a large number of affiliated industries—electrical and chemical concerns, and organizations connected with transport and navigation. Not only that; his word was law in a great many banks, the funds of which are so deeply sunk in these industries that they are faced with the choice of controlling them or being controlled by them. . . . This vast network of business disposes annually of sums far in excess of the total budget of the country, and the directors need account neither to Parliament nor to public opinion. Their general meetings, as you must realize, are a joke, and the boards of directors consist entirely of the directors' creatures, or of decorative nobodies who form a screen for the real masters, and whose names occur regularly, with minor variations, in connection with a large number of businesses. I've mentioned only Guillain; but the work on which my young collaborator has been concentrating—a work, let me repeat, of the highest objectivity, the purpose of which is to gut and collate a large number of official documents emanating directly from the people concerned: regulations, annual reports, bulletins, prospectuses, etc.—this work of his cites dozens of names which —and this is the remarkable fact—mean absolutely nothing to the man in the street, arouse no suspicions, and incur no public hatred whatever, though the bearers of these names actually concentrate in their persons all the power and all the wealth and, more important still, all the liberty of action in the country. Just suppose for a moment that you or I tried to rouse a public meeting to indignation by mentioning names like Darcy or Pinot, Peyrimhoff or Mallet . . . wouldn't our efforts fall flat? No one would have the slightest idea whom we were talking about. Why, you must admit that even to you they signify next to nothing."

"I certainly admit that I should have to think a good deal, marshal odds and ends of impressions and suggestive details."

"Precisely. Stendhal would have phrased it by saying that they produce no crystallization. And how could they? The newspapers never mention them—and why? Because they control the newspapers, either as owners or as men in a position to withhold advertising expenditure. They're just clever enough to prefer real but hidden power to a compromising publicity. All they demand of the press is that it should keep its mouth shut, or detract attention by making a great how-de-do about nothing in particular, like Fualdès's organ."

Listening to this tirade against the press, Gurau was conscious of a slight feeling of embarrassment, though he comforted himself with the reflection that any reproaches he could make against his own action in this matter would be mild and, in any case, would refer to a period now long since past. But at this very moment Jaurès continued, without, apparently, any mischievous intention (though the very fact that the allusion was involuntary made it harder to hear unmoved):

"Among all these names kept so deliberately in the background, one can't help noticing one or two that, little by little, and from one year to another, come to the surface—like magic imps in a bottle. Take one, for example, which, I confess, I'd never so much as heard mentioned—de Champcenais—does it convey anything to you?"

"It's vaguely familiar . . ." said Gurau, feeling rather nervous about what was to follow.

"A year or two ago he was a mere nonentity, a man with no discoverable connections in the business world, an oil magnate, one among many. One finds his name cropping up here and there in various documents. . . . Then his activities seem to increase . . . he burrows about underground. . . . He appears suddenly as interested in some big armament deal, is mentioned in connection with one of the big banks, and in other affairs of the like nature. This fellow de Champcenais, it seems, drags about with him—unless it's the other who does the dragging—a big foreign industrialist, a man interested in the arms traffic—I can't remember his name, it's something rather German-sounding—I've got the word Zürich in my head and it's made me forget it—but, anyhow, these hints of international deals leave a nasty taste. . . . You see, what it all comes to is this. If things are as I paint them, what becomes of Democracy, Parliament, Universal Suffrage? . . . Bah! . . . They've got their men in Parliament, and elsewhere, in more important positions still. It's merely a matter of choosing—they can always pay, and in subtler ways than by cheque, ways that don't need to be hushed up either, administrative appointments carrying a good salary, positions as legal adviser to some big company or other. They have their representatives everywhere, and everywhere they can pass on their instructions and dictate their vetoes, in committees, at Cabinet meetings. . . . It's pretty depressing and humiliating to see names cropping up in the lists prepared by my young friend, names the owners of which, if we didn't exactly respect, we didn't, at least, see any good reason to look at askance: Etienne . . ." (Gurau was conscious of a sharp twinge; he knew that Etienne was to be included in the new Ministry, probably at the War Office) ". . . Millerand . . ." (Thank Heaven! So far at least, Millerand hadn't been mentioned) ". . . the sinister Doumer, who very nearly defeated Fallières seven years ago and all but brought us to the brink of a war with Germany; and ten others. Don't forget, either, that Guillain is a personal friend of Poincaré's. Why, Poincaré himself, whom, in general, I regard as a man of honour, was once" (he stressed the words "was once" in a tone of sceptical irony), "was once municipal lawyer at Saint-Gobain—which is one of the appointments in the gift of those gentlemen!"

He made a sweeping gesture indicative of disillusion and weariness. Gurau, who had once more begun to breathe freely, was pondering how best to make a significant rejoinder when Jaurès continued:

"How can universal suffrage meddle with this sort of thing and correct abuses of such magnitude? It knows nothing of them, because it's to somebody's interest that nothing should be known. If anyone started out on his own to denounce the system, he'd be looked at as an irresponsible journalist or a political blackmailer. . . . In face of such an enormous combination of powerful influences there's nothing we can do . . . that's what gets me down. One realizes suddenly how helpless one is. . . . For instance, I shall go on fighting the Three-Years Act: I shall make speeches, write articles—with what result? It will get onto the statute book. And why? Because the gentlemen we've been discussing have decided in the secrecy of their deliberations that it shall. . . . I shall go on fighting the threat of war—"

He left the sentence unfinished, shrugged, and sighed.

Gurau set himself to chide him gently, arguing that under the influence of his recent reading of the article they had been discussing he tended probably to paint the picture in unnecessarily sombre colours. Had not he, Jaurès, more than once maintained, notably in the course of a conversation they had had one day—surely he couldn't have forgotten the occasion?—when Gurau had been to ask his advice—had he not maintained that the power of money was fortunately a complex and contradictory phenomenon, that to a very considerable degree it neutralized its own efforts, so that in the maelstrom of its activities reason had still a chance of making itself felt, of choosing the better way, and determining the ground on which it would offer battle?

"I'm not questioning the clear-sightedness of your young collaborator, nor the reliability of his information. But it may be that he is rather too much under the influence of a system. From what you tell me, he is a full-fledged Marxist."

"Certainly he's a Marxist," Jaurès agreed, "and you know what my personal feelings are about any too rigid attempt to apply the ideas of Marx. But though Marxism may have led my young friend to discover and integrate his facts, the facts themselves are not the product of Marxism. No, my friend, they exist only too truly. . . . And if we try to persuade ourselves that they are not of capital importance, then it is we who are guilty of bad faith. We shall be deliberately shutting our eyes. Our belief in the rational ought not to prevent us from calculating the chances of the irrational."

It surprised Gurau that Jaurès, reviewing the forces in the field and drawing from his survey the conclusion that there was well-nigh nothing to oppose to the ranged might of finance, should have forgotten the element provided by organized labour.

"Far from it—certainly I have not forgotten it. My argument was based upon the traditional weapons of Democracy. Organized labour is an entirely new item in the account."

"So much the better. It may be able to make up for the deficiencies of the rest."

"I should like to believe it. But I'm afraid this is one of my black days. Many of your trade-unionists—and I say 'your,' not, God knows, because I want to dissociate myself from them, but merely because I wish to stress the peculiar rights you have acquired in the labour world—seem to me to have evolved a rather disquieting view of the role to be played by the workers; very disquieting, I should say, given the circumstances of our immediate future. I seem to hear them crying: 'Down with Democracy,' just as loudly as Maurras, for different reasons, admittedly, but no less bitterly, and declaring that, when it comes down to brass tacks, it matters very little whether the system of the country is a monarchy or a republic. More than one of them, if pressed, would admit that they prefer the idea of a monarchy based on trade-unionism and the corporative state to that of a parliamentary republic. Without realizing it, they are bringing grist to the mill of extreme reaction, and, as I see it, the royalists are just laughing up their sleeve. It is at the very moment when the cause of Democracy and Peace, abandoned by a bourgeoisie that has denied its Revolutionary past, ought to be closing its ranks against the converging attacks of its enemies, that the most active elements of the labour movement are putting up a pretence of taking no interest in the struggle. That, it seems to me, is the most sinister of all the aspects of the situation. . . ."

"Well, after all that," said Gurau a little later, "I don't think I need repeat my question."

"What question?"

"Whether or not I am to participate in the new Ministry. . . . Everything you've just said shows me that I ought to keep out of it."

Jaurès seemed to rouse himself from a deep reverie. "Really? . . . Then I was wrong."

"What do you mean—you were wrong?"

"Since they've offered you the post—go ahead and take it."

"Do you mean that seriously? Why should I?"

"To stop somebody else getting it."

"You honestly think, then, mockery apart, that I could make a good job of it?"

Jaurès, his head once more cocked towards his left shoulder, appeared to be weighing the argument with scrupulous exactitude.

"You won't, unfortunately, be able to put much of a spoke in their wheel . . . but if you can influence events even a little, that'll be better than nothing. . . . The Three-Years Act, of course, will get through. Any attempt to oppose it would be merely beating the air . . . and it won't directly concern you. But, at least, where foreign policy is concerned, you won't add fuel to the fire. And you'll be in the best possible position to tread out the sparks. . . . I believe in you, Gurau."

Jaurès's face brightened. It was as though that word "believe" had released the current of his normal thinking, dammed for the moment by the working of some evil charm. With a rapidity which Gurau found surprising he reverted to a point of view which, though it did not deny the dangers ahead, refused to sit down under the threat and expressed renewed confidence in the power of effort. His optimism was like some great bird smoothing down its feathers and trying its wings after a storm of rain. With fearless eyes he seemed to take in the prospect of the times, to weigh and evaluate the mass and surge of history.

"Does he, I wonder, notice the illogicality of his self-contradictions?" wondered Gurau. But he himself was not immune to the belief in humanity which burst now, like music, from the man opposite. "Perhaps in this, more than in anything else, he deceives himself. If so, it's a deception I would willingly share. By dint of such magnificent lies mankind has scaled the heights!"

Chapter

12

AN ARTICLE FROM THE "TEMPS"

(From a military correspondent)

I have been reading recently an admirable and substantial pamphlet of 64 pages from the pen of Lieutenant-Colonel Duroure, entitled "The Army and the Next War." It is an off-print from a series of articles which has been appearing in the *Revue Militaire Générale,* and it comes at an opportune moment. Colonel Duroure, whose lectures at the Staff College will long be remembered for the deep impression that they made, is at pains to remind us of a number of truths on which military men will be agreed, but about which public opinion is insufficiently instructed and which still meet with a great deal of stubborn resistance in Parliament. But more than this, he denounces certain fallacies which, if they found ready acceptance among those responsible for our destinies, might rapidly lead to a catastrophic situation.

The most dangerous of these fallacies concerns *quantity*—or rather, for there can be no question of our resigning ourselves light-heartedly to a position of numerical inferiority—to the habit of estimating the number of troops available on mobilization without reference to their *quality.* Those who pretend to calm our fears and seek to dissuade us from the necessity of making renewed efforts merely by computing the total roll of our active and reserve forces, as though these two categories were comparable in terms of quality, are preparing for us a terrible day of disillusionment.

Lieutenant-Colonel Duroure, with a power of reasoning which is remarkable for its vigorous phrasing and rises at times to almost poetic heights, points out that the next war will be determined by its *initial drive.* The swiftness and strength of this drive will dominate every consequent operation and may be decisive for the whole campaign. I should like to draw attention in particular to the magnificent passages on pages 37-9, in which, with a clarity of analysis worthy of a great doctor combined with the prophetic fervour of a visionary, the author brings before our eyes the advance of the opposing armies to the first—and perhaps the last—great battle of such a war.

In the light of these pages and of the evidence—painful at times to read—which he adduces, it is clear that if we are prepared, as we have been ever since the initial error was made in 1905, to rely on a regular army of mere skeleton proportions, imperfectly trained and instructed, owing to shortness of the time at their disposal—especially where arms of precision are concerned—we shall merely be condemning ourselves in advance to defeat. What use can our reserves hope to be, slowly collected and badly equipped, despite the excellence of our machinery of mobilization, needing, as they would do, several weeks to assemble and re-entrain, if in the meantime a decision should already have been obtained, to say nothing of the only too probable hypothesis that the actual mobilization of reserves would be upset and dislocated before completion by the advance of an enemy who had emerged victoriously from the *initial drive*?

I am not altogether prepared to accept the Colonel's pet theory of a fusion of all arms in a kind of *homogeneous group* organized with a view to maximum offensive mobility. I am inclined to think, as I always have done, that our 75's, in spite of their relative cumbrousness, may still give an excellent account of themselves, both when acting independently and in support of infantry. That certainly is the lesson which would seem to emerge from the present hostilities in the Balkans, though it is open to Colonel Duroure to retort that his method has not been put to the test in that campaign, and that, had it been, the results would have been staggering.

At any rate, this pamphlet, full as it is of enthusiasm and good sense, is a timely publication. Not only does it prove that our higher command is intellectually alive to the needs of the moment, but it provides a fine crop of decisive arguments for those of our more enlightened statesmen who have undertaken to pass through Parliament, the members of which are too often ill informed and influenced unduly by electoral policy, the Three-Years Act, which is the essential preliminary to any scheme which can hope to guarantee the national safety.

A LETTER FROM MAYKOSEN.
THE SITUATION IN FRANCE

(Translated from the German)

The event which I felt able to predict to Your Majesty has, in fact, occurred. M. Raymond Poincaré has been elected President of the Republic. It is not my intention to rehearse the circumstances which the newspapers have already made familiar, nor do I think that overmuch importance should be attached to the intrigues which preceded the election. All that part of the business was, as they say here, *de la frime*.[1] What is, however, remarkable is that almost all the conservatives and nationalists voted solid for Poincaré, opposition to whom finally centred in the irreconcilable elements of the Left, and the Freemasons.

Your Majesty knows already what I think of the man. He is gifted with a fine practical intelligence and an extraordinary power of working. His memory is prodigious. It is said that before going on an election tour he learns twenty speeches by heart and can deliver them faultlessly as the proper occasion arises. He is shrewd and patient. He is capable of pursuing a favourite scheme over a long period of years without betraying any part of it that is not essential to the success of the undertaking. He has one passion only—ambition. But where that is concerned he is insatiable. It would be wrong to assume that even now he has got everything he wants. He is undoubtedly anxious to play a great role in the history of his time; and from what I know of the man there can, unfortunately, be little doubt of the way in which he conceives that role. In fact, he hardly troubles to hide the nature of his intention.

It does not seem likely that his policy will find much opposition at home. The last few years have seen a great many changes in France,

[1] These words appear in French in the text.

which are not always understood abroad because of the erroneous views held there about the internal disagreements which are rife in this country. Such disagreements, though much diminished in intensity, are still matters to be reckoned with, but it would not be difficult to divert opinion from them by appealing to the sentiment of national prestige and greatness; and it seems not unlikely that a government determined to exploit this aspect of the French character might find fewer obstacles in its way than another. Each time I travel through the country I find an increase of jingoism. I'm not thinking now chiefly of the parties which have always held that any efforts to maintain peace are merely a shameful symptom of weakness. What strikes me chiefly is that the people one meets casually are less and less averse to admitting that the present situation seems soluble only in terms of a war, which, naturally, will give France an opportunity of revenging herself for the disasters of the last. Everywhere one goes one comes on reviews of troops and public ceremonies, each one of of which serves as an excuse for popular manifestations and inflammatory speeches. The army is greeted on all sides with acclamation. Gone are the days of anti-militarism. The recent fighting in the Balkans has been interpreted in a sense highly flattering to French hopes and French pride. There is a general feeling that in matters of diplomacy Germany is becoming more and more isolated, and that, militarily speaking, French strategy and French equipment have given proof of their superiority. The newspapers, too, are busy persuading the public that great strides have been made in aviation.

The Ministry which Poincaré has just summoned is very unlikely to put much of a brake on his activities. Everyone is convinced that the new Presidency will inaugurate a period in which relations between the Executive and the responsible ministers will be very different from what they have been hitherto. Without doing violence to the Constitution, the President can make full use of his official powers, which are much like those of a constitutional monarch. But in addition he will exercise every scrap of personal influence that he possesses, and personal influence can have great weight, especially in foreign politics, as we have reason to know from the example of the late King of England. The Prime Minister, Briand, seems to have one object and one only: to be returned to office as often as possible, and to keep himself there no matter what the majority in Parliament may say, what the current view of politics may be, or with how many powerful influences he may have to compound. He is not unlike B.[1] His ambition differs from Poincaré's in that it seems to find complete satisfaction in the success of these manœuvres. It is obvious that he ridicules the idea of playing a historic role. If anyone pushes this country into war, it will not be he, but it would be dangerous to assume that he would do much to prevent others doing the pushing if Poincaré and public opinion were against him. He is regarded here as a *jouisseur*.[2]

He has appointed as Foreign Minister Maxime Gurau, a man I know well and about whom I wrote a great deal to Your Majesty during the critical weeks of '11. He has genuine distinction of character and a mind capable of taking wide views. In private life he is an individual of undoubted honesty. Unfortunately, he has an almost feminine sensitiveness which puts him at the mercy of his impressions and makes him extremely vulnerable where his self-respect is concerned. The humiliations to which he thinks he was subjected in '11, as a result of which he resigned in the following year, have made him an almost declared enemy of Germany, though before those events occurred I know that he was animated by a sincere desire to avoid a conflict between the two countries. It was in 1912 that he came under the influence of Poincaré, who, by means of flattery and promises, enlisted him as an ardent supporter. From what I heard at the time, and from what has happened since, it seems pretty certain that his dramatic resignation in January of that year was deliberately engineered by Poincaré in order to bring about the fall of Caillaux, who stood for a policy of agreement, and to set his own feet on the first rung of the ladder which was to lead him to the highest office in the State.

[1] There is no means of identifying the individual meant.
[2] In French in the text.

Since that time Gurau has been completely caught up in the political machine. But, for all that, he remains one of the very few people sufficiently intelligent to see what a disaster for the whole world a war would be. Of that I fully convinced him in the old days, as too that the idea of any war being short and conducted on the principle of the offensive (a fallacy which is still to be met with very widely here) was wholly absurd. I feel pretty sure that he would be willing to lend an ear to any reasonable argument, especially if it were accompanied by a certain amount of personal flattery which would enable him to forget the affronts which he received in '11. Unfortunately, he has more intelligence than character, and, in view of the fact that he is dominated by Poincaré's terribly strong will, it seems more than likely that he must ultimately give way. If he does so his reasons will be wholly different from Briand's. (The pleasures of power are not sufficient to satisfy him, and he might be as keen as Poincaré to play a historic role, though in a very different sense.) But the weakness of his character is seen clearly in this, that he has allowed himself to be seduced by a character stronger than his own, and one that he knows will, in all probability, be hostile to his own cherished convictions, instead of taking a stand against it.

It would be unwise, therefore, to rely too much on him as a means of preventing Poincaré from pursuing his tortuous course across the length and breadth of Europe. The really important things will be kept from him even more completely than they were in Caillaux's government. But since the new President of the Republic will be careful not to rub him the wrong way, there is no reason to suppose that the two men will fall out.

The other ministers are of no importance, with the single exception of Etienne, the Minister for War, who has given his word to get the Three-Years Act through Parliament. He is a dangerous man, and the big industrialists and arms-manufacturers are entirely in his hands. (Think of him as resembling S.) He is not, however, sufficiently corrupt to make it possible to act upon him from outside by means of money. In any case, it is extremely difficult in France for a man, however venal he may be, to accept money from Germany if he occupies a position of any prominence. I am for ever coming on evidence that this side of the business is being badly mishandled. I had an opportunity the other day of seeing a list of subsidies actually paid. In almost every case they were to complete nonentities who can exercise scarcely any influence on events. That sort of thing is described here by the phrase *jeter son argent par les fenêtres*.[1] The only persons who might safely be approached in this way with advantage are certain extreme revolutionists. But it would be a mistake to exaggerate their hold on the public. Apart from them, the few politicians and journalists capable of being bought would prefer to sell themselves to Russia, which pays well and is less bound by red tape in these matters, or to the Balkan States. They know that if the worst comes to the worst and they are found out, no one will hold them guilty of treasonable practices. Indirect bribery is a different question altogether. But it is slower in producing results, and there, too, Russia has many advantages.

And now that I have touched on Russia, let me say that almost unimpeachable evidence has fallen into my hands to the effect that, during his trip last August, Poincaré, as I suspected, both received and gave a number of perfectly formal undertakings. But Your Majesty is doubtless in full possession of authoritative information about that. In the event of what has come to Your Majesty's ears not tallying with my version of the circumstances, I beg respectfully that Your Majesty will have me told so, in order that I may institute further inquiry. From what I can discover it appears that Poincaré extracted a promise to the effect that the troops on the frontier should be reinforced, and the construction of strategic railways pushed forward.[2] In return for this he promised money, of course, but more than this, the passing into law of the Three-Years Act, and the unconditional support of France should Russia become seriously involved in the Balkans. It

[1] In French in the text.
[2] The reference is to the Russo-German frontier, the garrisons of which had been partially withdrawn in 1910. Strategic railways behind the frontier had long been contemplated, but never completed.

was probably this latter point that induced Sazonov to engineer the new Balkan war.

A few days ago I managed to get a glimpse of a dispatch sent to the Quai d'Orsay last November by the French Minister in Belgrade. It contained the following significant passage which I quote from memory, not having had an opportunity of making a copy: "In the opinion of the King of Servia a Balkan war will inevitably bring about an Austrian cataclysm. The only question, therefore, to be decided is whether such an outbreak should be provoked now or whether it had better be delayed for a few more years." And, a little further on: "It goes without saying that but for Russian encouragement, Austro-Servian relations would never have reached their present grave state of tension. . . . The Servians are persuaded—and nothing will shake their belief—that Russia is prepared to stand solidly behind them in defence of their country against Austria, since Servia is the pivotal point of the struggle between the Slav and the Germanic ideals." All of which fully confirms my views of the part played by Sazonov.

To return to the Three-Years Act. Its passage through Parliament is assured. It would, I am sure, be a mere waste of money to attempt to subsidize any opposition to it. On the other hand, may I respectfully suggest that though Your Majesty should take all necessary steps for the increase of the fighting forces by 120,000 additional men, it would be well not to lay this proposal before the Reichstag before the French measure has reached the statute book—a matter, at most, of two or three weeks.

As I have already had the honour of informing Your Majesty, my plans are to take a short trip in Italy, where I think it not unlikely that I may pick up some interesting scraps of information. Should Your Majesty feel curiosity about any particular points on which I might be able to throw light, I should esteem it a favour to receive Your Majesty's instructions at the earliest possible moment. (I prefer that N. should be kept out of this little affair.)

Meanwhile, with all due respect, I subscribe myself

Your Majesty's most humble, obedient servant.

Chapter

14

JERPHANION WRITES TO JALLEZ ABOUT A SO-CALLED "MODERN YOUTH MOVEMENT"

. . . .

I am becoming terribly bored at La Rochelle. I realize that, without my knowing it, my unconscious had been reckoning on a year as the maximum period of my stay in this rather dreary exile, not counting holidays. If it finds out in the next few months that somebody has been having a game with it, and that the same depressing round is about to begin again, there'll be the devil to pay.

In general I hold that, life being short, and wasted opportunities beyond recall, uninteresting episodes should never be permitted to exceed one year. The returning seasons have a distressing way of underlining the fact that everything to be seen here has been seen already and that the people I meet have a melancholy sameness about them.

. . . .

This colleague of mine passed on to me the articles in question. You must, given the advantages of your situation, have seen them when they first appeared. I am amazed that you have said nothing about them. Can it be that you find them unimportant? I am perfectly willing to agree that the inquiry has been conducted in a highly tendentious manner, but even so, even admitting the absurdity of suggesting that this rather too carefully drilled and rehearsed bit of choral singing really represents the views of modern youth, the fact remains that the thing is symptomatic. After all allowances have been made for the part played in it all by deliberate manipulation, it is a sign of something; and it does make one think.

I confess that reading the stuff plunged me in gloom, I'd almost said an agony of gloom, and I longed to know what you thought about it all. There's nothing I wouldn't give for one of our old saunters through Paris so that we could thoroughly hammer out the question between us.

You see, when all's said and done, there's a good many of these chaps, and though it's pretty obvious that they've been selected with some care, they do come from a pretty wide variety of social strata. However carefully they may have been brought together, the fact that such a bringing-together was possible implies certain similarities and points of contact already in existence. I should like to think that the principle of cohesion had been operated by two or three influences, always the same, making themselves felt over a wide field; but what I find disquieting is that these influences crop up in such widely divergent directions, and that they can apparently rely on such unquestioning obedience. It's almost as though one were hearing the same lesson twenty times repeated.

If I were to express what I feel in words of one syllable, I should say: "How can a man of our age, of our time, think like that?" (How can a Frenchman suddenly become a Persian?) When the ways of thought of an older generation disgust me, I am ready to make allowances. But this is a case of my own contemporaries, who think of themselves as being just as modern as I think of myself, with just as much claim on the future.

Everything that I love and revere they hate and despise. Everything I hate and despise or think of as out of date they value above rubies. The future that they seem to desire, that they are doing their level best to prepare—to prepare, incidentally, for us—freezes my blood with horror and sets me bristling with fury. It is not so much the actual things they propose, stripped of all circumlocution, that I find hateful and antipathetic, as their way of thinking of these things, their arguments, admitted or implied, their assumptions, the mental atmosphere in which they live and which colours all their theories.

They proclaim their admiration for "action." I, too, admire action, and hope that one of these days I shall be in a position to act. But their passion for action is the result, merely, of their hatred of thought. They refuse to admit that action should be dictated by thought. If I said to them: "You're on fire to do something; splendid! There's no lack of work to our hands. We've got to reorganize society from top to bottom, but, of course, in accordance with our thinking, since so long as there are men capable of using their brains, it is only by such use that they can rise superior to the animals," they wouldn't budge. That's not what they mean by action. Action, for them, is at the very opposite pole to thinking. In their view it is what prevents a man, saves a man, from thinking, what forcibly corrects the results of thinking. Put bluntly—more bluntly than they usually like to put it, because they are devotees of verbal mystification and a "noble pathos" —what they mean by action is, in private life, playing games, running a business, spending as little time as possible over books, especially "serious" books; in public, getting ready for war, sooner or later waging it, and in the meantime re-establishing social order, for which purpose they seek to obtain control of the police and the civil service, as well as of the army, which they never cease acclaiming. It is cracking the workers' skulls if they strike and disposing as quickly as possible of the leaders who persuade those workers to think honestly about the conditions of their lives (conditions that don't seem too bad so long as they don't think); it is bringing into line the school-teachers with their comic ideas of instructing the "people" in ideas, the ideas of the great thinkers of the past, instead of confining themselves to what is asked of them—namely, teaching a lot of little brats arithmetic, spelling, and respectful obedience. And if this re-establishment of order takes too long, they are ready to plump for war, for essential "action," the specifically heroic remedy which will make short work of the mob and sweep away every vestige of "ideas."

They make a great parade of admiring Bergson, because to them Bergson and his disciples represent the claims of action and instinct over thought, the denunciation of the "errors of intelligence," the argument that intelligence is incapable of understanding life or of legislating for those who are anxious to live.

They are anti-intellectualists, not so much from an excess of intel-lectuality as because they see in the intelligence the spear-head of thought, and because they realize that thought deprived of such a weapon would no longer be very dangerous, might indeed be fooled by any kind of lie, every kind of mythology. They have a particular horror of irony—for they remember that it was irony that once upon a time led the attack against all those abuses and injustices in which, safely encircled, the old society held sway. Voltaire, Renan, France? —for them these are no less than Satan and his children. They profess a respect for Catholicism, but certainly not because of any Christian or universal ideal that it embodies. They see in it, or think they do, a means of protection for the mind against the products of the mind, for social order against subversive criticism. They love their country, though not for the reasons we do; just the reverse, in fact, for they value those very ingredients of patriotism which make it suspect to us: hate and distrust of foreigners; the setting of the claims of the nation above those of humanity; of tradition against progress; the glorification of the virtues of obedience, and, above all—this, indeed, is the head and front of their whole movement—the keeping of the people in a state of hysterical tension and so making war possible the moment those who control the people think it desirable.

You may call me every kind of a simpleton for admitting it, but such a possibility never entered my head. When we used to take our philosophical saunters, you and I, from the College to the Sorbonne, when we gazed into the future from the house-tops or from the plat-form of the Sacré-Cœur, it never occurred to me as conceivable that so many young fellows of our age had thus sold their souls to the past, had bargained away their blood for that of their elders.

Figure me, therefore, in far-away La Rochelle standing aghast. I don't say to myself: "It's you who are deceived"—oh no; what I say is: "Can it be that you are out of touch with the majority of your generation, with the spirit of the age? Is it possible that while you, and a few others like you, whom you took for a mighty army, were marching bravely towards the future, the main body of your contemporaries, like Panurge's sheep, were all the time rushing down a steep place, without a word to us of what they intended to do, to the abyss of ancient errors and ancestral absurdities?"

Made restless by this anxious questioning, I took a walk down by the harbour. I wanted to stop all the "common" people that I met, young workmen, young sailors, and say to them: "The bourgeois of this generation have gone off the rails, have lost their senses. Fear of losing their paternal heritage has stolen their wits. Tell me that with you it is not so—comfort me!" But I did not dare. I am not sure that they would have grasped the urgency of my question, that they would have understood how important it was for them to make an answer. Anyhow, they don't know. That's what makes the situation so tragic: those who could answer think it to their interest to answer wrong, while those who might answer right have not learned how to do so.

Do, please, send me just a line of encouragement.

. . . .

. . . .

I have read, or rather glanced at, a few of the replies to the questionnaire you refer to, but I made the mistake of not taking the business seriously enough. I don't mean this ironically. I know too well how these tricks are worked. If you wanted me to (and if my work on *Paris-Journal* left me the time) I could easily organize, here and now, a nation-wide inquiry from which it would emerge that, for instance, most young Frenchmen are Buddhists, or that French-women are noisily demanding a return to polygamy. Thinking the matter over, however, I am inclined to believe that your anxiety is justified.

. . . .

The truth probably is that at any period an inquiry conducted in similar quarters and with a similar intention would have produced results just as depressing and just as discouraging for the future; would have made you exclaim, in just the same way: "What a generation! What a future to look forward to!" And yet the future has a way of proving that the "young" who really influenced it were, all the time, quite a different young from what we had supposed.

. . . .

16

FIRST CONTACTS WITH ROME.
THE BARON DE FONTMONGE

Mionnet felt justified in allowing himself two or three days of idleness before setting seriously to work. His mission had been organized on the most generous lines. He was in no way bound. Certain results were expected of him, a certain length of time had been placed at his disposition. A first period of three months had been vaguely mentioned, but this, if necessary, would be prolonged. During this time Mionnet would receive a modest subsidy (five hundred francs a month), which would be sent through the post. While in Rome he would have to take orders from nobody, report to nobody, give an account to nobody. It was for him to make all necessary arrangements, when and how he would. He had in his pocket (in addition to a permission to celebrate Mass, which, sooner or later, he would have to get countersigned—Monsignor Lebaigue had warned him of this Roman custom—by the Vicar-General, though he needn't bother about that yet, since there was no reason for him to say Mass for some considerable time) several short lists of addresses: one forwarded by Manifassier and drawn up by Courson and the staff of the Ministry; the second given him by Monsignor Sérasquier; the third emanating from Monsignor Lebaigue. A final list consisted of various names collected from a number of sources. His letters of introduction came to no more than two: a few lines scribbled and enclosed in an envelope, and a visiting-card, addressed to a couple of unimportant persons. Word of his arrival would have been sent directly to a few other individuals. If he didn't put in an appearance, they would, naturally, be surprised; but no day had been fixed for his visits.

His desire to become acquainted with Rome in the irresponsible mood of a common tourist had a good deal to be said for it. It was no bad thing that he should get a first and independent idea of this city into the secrets of which he would have, later, to insinuate himself with skill and cunning. The sooner he could begin to feel at home, the less likely would he be to make mistakes. Besides, it would give him a footing as a serious student.

He was careful always to carry his guide-book, but intended to use it as little as possible—only, in fact, to identify on the map the places he visited and the principal monuments. He would postpone until later all thought of serious sightseeing, the often onerous duties of the conscientious globe-trotter.

His first two days were spent, therefore, in wandering widely. He, as it were, "sniffed" at the city, welcoming the unexpected and storing up the impressions thus gained in his memory. Needless to add, no information that he had gained in the course of his previous reading altered the fact that he found many things very different from what he had anticipated.

One particular characteristic of Rome he found "amusing" and definitely conducive to thought. It was this: that the city seemed to consist of a vast "containing circumference" proper, of great age, and partly in ruins, which was very imperfectly filled by scraps and groups of urban material, dating from various periods, and in very various states of freshness or decay. They seemed to him, these agglomerations, to have been popped down haphazard, to have no particular connection one with another, to give an impression of having been abandoned, even those that appeared to be of quite recent construction, sometimes jostling one another as though by accident or inadvertence, sometimes nestling in cosy proximity or turning backs on one another; a clutter of buildings besieged and half submerged by solitude.

He was delighted, too, by the arrangement of the hills; in the first place because he was constantly having to fit them with their appropriate names (and such names, redolent of history!); secondly because several of them were difficult to identify, to distinguish one from another. Now he would find himself on some sweet and gentle slope, now in some dip of the ground between adjacent summits, the whole variation of contour so slight that his memory of the map alone persuaded him of its existence. There were heights, too, so important-seeming, so individual, that he was amazed to find that they belonged to the same general system as their neighbours, and "supplementary" hills admitted to the freedom of the city only after the original Seven, and yet so perfectly suited to their environment, so obviously worthy to be included in the majestic company, that he could not but feel a sort of retrospective resentment at the thought of their belated admission.

About the modern town he could not make up his mind. For the present he withheld judgment. It was not unpleasing, but it was a little like some provincial lady visitor finding herself there by accident, ill at ease, sitting on the edge of her chair, and ready to depart with as little protest as she had come. It was not that there were no points of contact, no passages of transition, between it and the Rome of an older day. There were places at which modernity seemed to have emerged naturally from age, but others where it thrust itself into prominence with a mixture of shamefacedness and uncomfortable bravado, so that there seemed no good reason why it should have chosen one spot rather than another, why it had stretched so far or stopped so short. The general result was to make the wanderer wonder at his very first saunter, here at a group of new houses lost in a wilderness of weeds and white dust, there at a spick and span suburb cheek by jowl with mouldering ruins.

What struck him about the Papal City was the odd way in which it was placed; or, rather, he could not help realizing that the lack of all logical necessity in its topographical situation must recently have become more and more obvious, in proportion as the changes in Rome had caused certain quarters to dwindle while others grew, had cut across, diverted, or lessened the importance of certain arteries of the city's life. In the immediate neighbourhood of the Vatican, as in many other places, he felt that the initiative of the original designers had rather too easily come to terms with circumstances, more than one of which must always have been accidental, while others had latterly disappeared altogether.

The Tiber itself, in its passage through this heart of civilization, had lost much of its historic majesty, to assume the appearance of a stream dividing rather unevenly a decent Southern town, old, dusty, sleepy, and but half alive. It seemed strange that the Trastevere should have accumulated so vivid a tradition about itself. Everywhere he had to get himself accustomed to finding that names were more magnificent than the things they stood for.

In the course of these, his first, wide-flung saunters, Mionnet found himself wondering—he knew it was too soon to ask such questions, but he could not resist their onset—what chances this Rome that he had before his eyes might hold, at first view, for a stranger arriving there saddled with a task such as his. Nothing there, he decided, that still had claims on life was of more than natural size; nothing, except a few ruins rendered harmless by age, made a man feel small. The Vatican, of course, flanked by the dramatic vastness of its great Basilica, might subdue the spirits of a simple soul by its mere appearance, more particularly of a simple clerical soul, conscious of its own unimportance in the hierarchy and overcome at the thought of finding itself here at the very centre of the world. But Mionnet was less overwhelmed by the material fact than delighted at the hint it gave of internal complications. Seen from outside, this solid mass had the absorbent, tortuous, confused look of a coral reef.

Curious though he was about the place (it was one of the quantities to which he had not as yet affixed any number in the equation of his life), he curbed his impatience and refrained as yet from visiting it in detail. "That must be for later. . . . At the moment I must be content with a general view of things. There must be no exceptions to that rule. It would never do to get my proportions wrong."

He did no more, therefore, than take a hurried walk round the interior of the Basilica, idle away a few moments in St. Peter's Square, watch the guards on duty, and scrutinize the people who were going into the building or waiting at the Bronze Door.

Gazing at the heaped accumulation of the fabric, at the Oriental splendour of this Palace round the foot of which the Colonnade of St. Peter seemed flung like Scheherazade's necklace, he found it amusing to let his thoughts take a personal turn. "Inside there," he reflected, "is the man I'm after, and here am I, commissioned to probe his secret. It's all rather fun."

(He had just read in the papers of Gurau's appointment to the Foreign Office. To know that behind him stood both Poincaré and Gurau, not only the Élysée but the Quai d'Orsay as well, well, that was rather fun too.)

The thought of all this complicated world of Rome, and of the long-drawn test of patience that lay before him, conjured up in his mind a vision of difficulties in the grand manner—difficulties that would be the product of deliberate inertia, of silence and subtle courtesy, that would be put in his way by past masters in the art of delay and avoidance, all those many varieties of dissimulation that are possible only for people with unlimited time at their disposal.

Mionnet watched the folk he met in his daily walks, in the business thoroughfares and on the Corso, in the Via Nazionale, in the poorer quarters, and in the streets that lay about the Vatican. The practical man with a plan of campaign in his pocket, making direct assault on certain chosen points, would be condemned to inevitable failure. He who would succeed must learn to waste time, to be patient, to idle, to rejoice in apparently useless conversations, to take in good part the side-tracking of his intentions, and clues that led nowhere, to enjoy subtlety for subtlety's sake, to pick up dropped hints rather than put pointed questions. He must learn to regard nothing as *a priori* useless, no chance meeting as sterile. He must be ever on the watch for chances, like one of those sportsmen in the south of France who would rather wait endlessly for their prey, knowing the likely spots and keeping their eyes skinned, than run themselves out of breath in useless pursuit. In short, he mustn't for a moment make the mistake of thinking himself back at M—.

One chance isn't much, perhaps; but chances have a way of accumulating, and one sometimes leads to another. This warped and capricious crop must be harvested in its own way.

He congratulated himself on not having at once made his presence known. The delay of a few days was neither here nor there. Anything that might give him a general impression, however vague and sketchy, that might, however inconclusively, determine his attitude, was better than premature action.

On the morning of the third day, as he was returning from a hurried visit to the Trinità dei Monti, it flashed into his mind that he must be quite close to one of the addresses that had been given him. He rummaged in his pockets. M. de Fontmonge, whose name figured on the Sérasquier list as Counsellor of the Belgian Embassy, lived just opposite. It must be his private residence. The house was small, narrow-fronted, built in an agreeably old-fashioned style, and standing near the corner of the square.

"Monsignor Sérasquier has warned him of my impending arrival. . . . It would do no harm to leave a card as a first step. It will give me a little breathing-space; and I don't suppose that the mere sight of my card will set him talking. . . . Now, where is it?"

He rang the bell, gave his card to the maid who opened the door, and made as though to turn away. But the servant, after glancing at his name, insisted on his entering the house. Had she been forewarned by her master? Was she suspicious of the visitor's intentions? Or was she afraid that he might think he had been turned from the door? He allowed himself to be persuaded.

He was received at the end of a few moments by M. de Fontmonge.

"I was just off to the Embassy. I'm extremely glad not to have missed you. Our cousin Sérasquier has written such a lot about you. Do sit down, there's time for a few moments' conversation."

M. de Fontmonge was a man of about fifty, with large, dark-brown eyes, set deep in his head beneath bushy pepper and salt eyebrows. He had a huge moustache of the same colour, a large nose, and the general appearance of a country squire. He wore a well-cut suit of some heavy English material. The rustic burr in his voice was faintly noticeable. He sounded the final *r's* of his words rather like the German *ch:* the word "presque" became in his mouth "sièche"; and each of his phrases was, as it were, strung out on a melodic line, the structure of which was unvarying—a series of rather heavy, equally marked vocables, a sort of rhythmic, measured progress leading up to a single syllable that was much lighter and broader than the rest, sometimes to more than one, marking a pause before a fresh sequence of quick, descending notes, so that the whole phrase sounded like one single word carrying, usually about its middle, a strong tonic accent.

The room in which he received the Abbé was largish, irregular in shape, and with a rather low ceiling. One end of it abutted on the master's study, the other on the drawing-room. The house stood high, and the windows of the room gave onto a magnificent city landscape with the Piazza di Spagna in the immediate foreground, a panorama in which the dominating tone was composed of ochre, the tints of roof tiles, and of silver. There were almost as many towers and domes visible as people huddled in the houses at their feet. The whole compact mass of buildings showed no gap, nor was there a corner of the general sweep but had an air of familiar intimacy and legendary splendour. And yet against the unbroken uniformity each several monument stood out detached and beautiful, and the light seen and depicted by so many master painters shed a peculiar glory on buildings, distant hills, and sky.

The two men chatted for about ten minutes. M. de Fontmonge, whose eloquence marked him as a great talker, expressed his mind soberly and without superfluous ornament. His phrases were simple, clear-cut, and logically organized. He did not repeat himself. Transcribed exactly as spoken, his words would have provided a lucid, if not particularly elegant, text. They reminded the listener, from time to time, of one of those exercises to be found in "French Conversation in Twenty Lessons." But the speaker's accent, an occasional Belgian turn of phrase, and now and then a guffaw of laughter gave to the whole a strongly individual character.

"Have you been here long? . . . Where are you staying? . . . At a hotel? . . . Who told you about it? . . . Have you been warned that gentlemen of your cloth ought to be especially careful? . . . Ever since the present Pope took office, a remarkably efficient police system has been instituted. . . . No sooner is the presence of a strange priest reported than he is shadowed. I'm not joking. It's the Vatican, not the Italian government, that looks after these things. Most of the landlords and landladies and keepers of family pensions patronized by the clergy are now affiliated to the 'black' police. They make regular reports, and pay particular attention to all newcomers. There are also a number of inspectors who move freely about the city. The reason given is the advisability of keeping a watch on public morals. I am, myself, by way of being an old inhabitant of this city. I knew it during the last years of the late Pope. Morals at that time were, I admit, pretty loose. There were a lot of stories going round about the cardinals. One used to see in the streets—and elsewhere—a pretty odd-looking lot of priests. They hailed from all over the place, and there was no city in the world where a man in clerical dress had less to fear in the matter of interference. But things have been made so difficult for them now that a great many have left. The rest are careful to lie low. The present régime demands an almost apostolic level of virtue. The princes of the Church are expected to set an example. . . . Of course, there are other reasons, too, for all this watchfulness. Relentless war is being waged against modernism . . ." (M. de Fontmonge pronounced the word "modernism" with a peculiarly harsh sibilance) "and against all liberal tendencies, especially such as come from France. . . . You, as a Frenchman, will have to take extraordinary precautions if you want to escape attention. Not that I suspect you of any moral looseness, but we foreigners like to feel that we are free, don't we? . . . Tell me again the name of your hotel."

"The Hôtel de la Paix et Helvétia."

"Where is it?"

"Via Nazionale, close to the station."

M. de Fontmonge seemed to be ransacking his memory. He looked very serious. Then he rose, went across to his desk, opened a drawer, and consulted something, a directory, perhaps, or a note-book, turning its leaves without taking it from its place. When he came back again, he was deep in thought.

"Mm—I've no information about that hotel. Only, be careful. Are you going to stay there the whole time?"

"Oh no, certainly not."

"Where are you thinking of going?"

"I really don't know."

"One other thing. Where have you arranged to say Mass?"

"I haven't thought about it yet. I probably shan't say it as often as I do in Paris."

"When you want to, and in case you don't know where to go, I can show you a little Belgian chapel where you will be undisturbed."

"But first I shall have to get my permit countersigned by the Vicar-General. I'm told that is customary here. . . ."

"It may be customary . . . but there is no reason why you should observe the custom, because my compatriot will not dream of asking to see your permit. I can assure you of that. . . ."

They went out together, parting on the doorstep, after Mionnet had given his word to come to dinner one day soon. M. de Fontmonge would drop him a line.

". . . Not to your hotel, but to the post-office in the Hotel Continental building opposite the station. . . . I will try to get one or two interesting people for you to meet."

M. de Fontmonge went down the Trinità dei Monti steps towards the Piazza di Spagna. (Mionnet realized suddenly that it was to the Papal court that his host was accredited, that the Embassy was on the Corso, and could be reached from here in five minutes by way of the famous Via dei Condotti.) He himself went back by the Via Sistina.

As he walked, his thoughts were active:

"Why does he seem to attach so much importance to this particular aspect of the question? Why is he so nervous about me? He can know nothing about my reasons for being in Rome except what he has learned from Monsignor Sérasquier. . . . Did I, perhaps, say more than was wise to Monsignor Sérasquier? Or . . ."

To this question he had two answers. One version ran: "Haven't all these people, perhaps, got a slight touch of persecution mania?" the other: "It's perfectly obvious now that the fellow who came to see me in Paris was an agent of this secret police. Naturally they have 'contacts' abroad. It was an attempt to intimidate me. If that's so, my presence in Rome must be widely known. No matter what precautions I'd taken, they'd have very soon been on my tracks."

It was at such moments that he got a sense of reassurance from the thought that he had both Poincaré and Gurau behind him.

Chapter

17

THE PLEASURES OF FEAR.
PORTRAIT OF A BANKER
UNDER A SHADOW

During the days that followed he knew the peculiar thrill of a man who realizes that he is the object of watchful attention, is for ever on his guard, but can never get direct proof of what he suspects.

He would turn his head sharply when walking. Sometimes he would stop abruptly at a corner or before a shop-window, so as to let some questionable individual he had noticed get in front of him. When he went to the post-office in the Continental Hotel building (he had at once written to Manifassier giving this as his address), he took a roundabout route, and only asked for his letters when he saw that nobody was within listening-distance of the window.

The impression that he had of being followed remained vague, and he met it by reverting to his old habit of seeking solitude. He had to admit that in many ways he felt freer here than he had ever done in Paris. In this city a priest was the most ordinary and uninteresting of objects. He might have idled away his time, his hat pushed back, his hands behind him, his soutane half unbuttoned, yawning and eyeing the women, and nobody would have paid him any particular attention.

There were, however, certain decisions that he needs must take. Where, for instance, should he settle? Fear of finding himself in some trap for priests led him to bide his time. He suggested a weekly arrangement to the landlord, which, it being out of season, was accepted. He decided, also, to buy an Italian abbé's hat at the first possible moment. He would use it only in certain circumstances. It wouldn't, of course, be sufficient disguise to protect him from the glances of the informed, but simple precautions, like small strokes of luck, are sometimes extremely helpful.

Still, all this was by way of being preliminary and accessory to his main object, which was to get on with his job. It was essential that he make a beginning soon. The goal seemed a great distance off, the ways of approach as yet indiscernible.

In order to give a sign of life to his Paris chiefs and temper their impatience, he sent to Manifassier a short personal letter, couched in general terms.

When they had parted, it had been agreed between them that they should communicate in this way (the recipient to destroy the letter after reading, if he thought it advisable to do so) whenever it was necessary to discuss some private scheme or for either of them to ask a favour of the other.

Mionnet made it clear in a few lines that he thought it better to go slowly at first, so as to avoid foolish mistakes. He asked also to be informed whether the substitution of G. for P. at the Ministry in any way modified the original plan of campaign.

That done, he set himself once more to study his lists. Dom Charles Magloire. . . . Wouldn't he be the best person to start with, in order, at the outset, to throw his invisible watchers off the scent? At the top of Courson's list appeared the name of a Mme Lacchini, Via Liguria, doubly underlined, and followed by a note, in brackets: "(absolutely reliable)."

Mionnet felt too lazy to tackle this Dom Charles Magloire so soon. He therefore chose Mme Lacchini for the first round.

He found the Via Liguria in one of the new quarters that had been built on the site of the Villa Ludovisi, a high-pitched district approached by the handsome Via Veneto.

The Lacchinis' house, with its small garden, was rather like one of those Riviera villas that stand on the slopes above Cimiez. The neighbourhood gave the impression of being a smart suburb, a sort of sum-

mer resort. It was a part of Rome to which Mionnet had not yet penetrated. Its air of sleepiness and moderate comfort was not without a
charm of its own.

It was eleven o'clock in the morning. (Mionnet could not have
said exactly why he had chosen this time, which was the same as that
at which he had called on M. de Fontmonge.) After a short wait he
saw coming towards him a lady of middle age, still handsome, full-
figured, brown-haired, who might, for anything to the contrary, have
been an Italian. But her gestures and the first words that she uttered
made it perfectly clear that she was French. She greeted Mionnet as
though the whole household had been impatiently awaiting him for
the last few days and had begun to get nervous at his non-appearance.

She spoke quickly, flitting rapidly from idea to idea. She seemed
nervous. She asked a question, but did not wait for the reply. All of
which gave an impression, not of idle prattle, but of a woman labouring under some strong emotion. For the second time since their meeting she said:

"We've so much to talk to you about."

She changed her seat, then got up suddenly. "I only hope my husband hasn't gone out!"

She rang the bell and sat down again. But when, at the end of three
seconds, no servant appeared, she jumped up again and went off to
look for her husband.

Mionnet found himself in a drawing-room which, by two case-
ments and a French window, gave onto the garden. It was square in
shape and fairly large. The furniture varied considerably in quality.
A few pieces were obviously old and valuable; others, of no particular age, were mean and florid in style. Odds and ends of things in the
worst possible taste were dotted here and there, giving to the whole
interior an effect in which relics of a rather debased elegance and
signs of crudeness more properly the appanage of recent wealth
played an equal part. The ceiling, framed in a cornice of flabby
rococo design, was covered with a sort of mythological sea-scape,
centring on a half-nude goddess, very fair as to the hair and rather

short as to the body. "The lady of the house," reflected Mionnet, "is dark."

Mme Lacchini reappeared, a look of despair on her face. Her husband had just gone out. She expressed surprise, since he had not taken leave of her. Perhaps he had had an urgent summons to his office.

Noticing, as she entered, the Abbé's look of curiosity at his surroundings, she said hurriedly:

"We live in quite the pleasantest part of Rome. . . . The whole quarter is new. Our house was built only a few years ago. . . . We used to be right down in the city, near the Corso. You'd never believe how much fresher it is here. In summer there's no comparison. It takes my husband very little longer to get to his work, and he sleeps infinitely better. Of course it's only in summer that we're here—during the hottest months."

Mionnet learned, little by little, that the husband owned a bank (doubtless one of those discreet-looking banks with an extremely solid clientele); that he belonged to an old Roman family noted for its Catholicism, but also for its liberal ideas; that he had inherited from his father a deep love of France; that the father had been one of the bankers to the Vatican under Pope Leo XIII, with whose ideas he was in close sympathy; that the son had inherited from his father the responsibilities of the family business and had kept up the old connection even under the present régime, though falling more and more into disfavour because of his French views, his French wife, and the growing power at the Papal court of the enemies of France.

"They can't now endure anybody who does not share their hatred of France. Certain Frenchmen have been left undisturbed in their positions, but only because, whether prelates or others, they are bad Frenchmen who are willing to deny their country and overwhelm it with curses. . . . My husband, who is not a Frenchman at all, would never consent to do that even at the time of the Combes affair. 'There have always been people like that,' he said; 'the same sort of thing happened with the royal house of Savoy and with Bismarck. . . .'

Well, you know what these princes of the Church are like, always smooth and subtle in their methods. They have left in my husband's hands a few petty odds and ends of business, but, generally speaking, they have dismissed him. . . ."

At this point in their conversation the front door was heard to open and close, and M. Lacchini came into the room. He had not gone to the bank at all, but had merely been quite near by, to the post office in the Via Ludovisi.

He was a small man, tending to fat, with a very short neck, a pear-shaped head, and black hair that was getting thin. His face was of a dirty sallow complexion and covered with a network of fine wrinkles; his eyes, dark and dull, but sufficiently sharp, beneath creased and heavy lids. He spoke French very fluently, but with a strongly marked accent which one felt to be an inseparable part of the man. Normally it took the form of a slight lisp, a trill of syllables from the end of his tongue, though any sudden emotion had a way of sending his voice down into his throat.

He repeated what his wife had already said, speaking of the Papacy much as Corsicans speak of Bonaparte, with a sort of possessive familiarity. Pius X still remained for him a type of those church-men who are to be met with in every corner of Christendom, men whose origins are public knowledge, the stages of whose careers have been publicly discussed, whose weaknesses are the common property of all. On the whole M. Lacchini appeared to look on him as a decent enough man, rather provincial, even countrified, in outlook, extremely pious, obstinate to a fault in matters which interested him, but apart from them easily taken in, and this not so much because his mind lacked subtlety as because he was entirely ignorant of the modern world. He was just a good parish priest with a great love of plain-chant and liturgy. The banker bore him no personal grudge in the matter of his disgrace.

Mionnet had a feeling that the view of Pius X commonly accepted in Rome was not very different from that current in Paris. The probability was, therefore, that it more or less represented the fact. Was there similar agreement about Merry del Val? How did people account for the fact that a lasting and apparently confidential relationship was possible between men about whom the least that could be said was that they were utterly unlike? Mionnet felt that it was too early to put such a question directly. He waited until the name of the Secretary of State should crop up naturally in the conversation.

But for the moment M. Lacchini seemed concerned with certain private grievances and confined himself to making charges only of an impersonal nature. What he said amounted, in fact, to this: that it was "pretty cheeky" of the Vatican to behave worse towards France than towards any other country, seeing that most of its money came from France, and that without the contributions made, in various forms, by French Catholics, the finances of the Papacy would long ago have been in a bad way. But M. Lacchini's lisping phrases were constantly cut short by his wife's petulant interruptions, which he as constantly corrected, with the result that their joint explanations had the effect of leaving their visitor more bewildered than before.

So far as he could make out, M. Lacchini, at the time when he had stood high in Papal favour, was particularly concerned with the material interests of the Vatican in France (collecting funds and seeing that they were transferred to Rome, or arranging to have them deposited or invested on the spot—it was not very clear which). This work necessitated constant visits to Paris, and it was on the occasion of one of these that he had made the acquaintance of Courson. They had discussed many things together, but now they were reduced to an exchange of letters. To judge from the face he made as he said this, the banker was not over-fond of committing confidential matters to writing.

"I'll tell you something about all that later," he said.

Neither he nor his wife appeared to have the slightest uncertainty about the reason for Mionnet's presence in Rome. They were urgent in their insistence that he be ceaselessly on his guard. But their warnings did not take exactly the same form as M. de Fontmonge's. "Don't believe anything unless you know precisely who your informant is.

Don't listen to strangers. You'll find yourself besieged by people with their pockets crammed with the most extraordinary stories; you'll be bothered out of your wits by them. Put yourself in our hands. . . . We'll set you on the right track. . . . We'll see that you meet the right people."

Mionnet observed quietly that he hoped to avoid the good offices of busybodies, since no one had any right to assume that he wanted to hear anything about anyone. He hinted that he relied completely on the discretion of the Lacchinis. But he noticed that they seemed to attach little importance to his protestations. Did they think that he would find it impossible to keep his secret, or was it, perhaps, their opinion that it might do less harm than he thought if the enemy got wind of his mission?

"When all's said," he reflected, "I'm nothing but a Northern barbarian. It may be that in this land of subtlety the greatest wisdom consists in not holding one's cards too carefully hidden, but in letting one's opponents get a glimpse of one's hand—especially of such a hand as mine . . ." and he smiled to himself at the idea of P. figuring as a bearded king, and G. with the insolent eye of the knave.

He asked whether the Lacchinis knew a certain Dom Charles Magloire, a Benedictine, who lived at Sant' Anselmo.

Husband and wife seemed surprised, exchanged several words in Italian, and repeated more than once: "Dom Charles Magloire . . . why of course, of course!" until, finally, encouraged by M. Lacchini's approving nod and sallow grin, his wife hastily continued:

"Oh yes, we know him . . . but why do you ask? He is very well known in Rome. That's to say, he's hardly ever to be seen in society, but people talk of him a lot—especially now, because he's not quite right in the head."

She explained that he was an inoffensive individual, very learned, but very fanatical. He was the last person in the world to complain of the encroachments and excessive powers of the Papacy or the intrigues of the Vatican! The truth was, of course, that he lived with his head in the clouds, or, rather, in the Middle Ages. He dreamed of a day when the Pope should become once again, not only monarch of the Papal States—that was a mere nothing—but the supreme suzerain of Christendom, of a Christendom, moreover, reunited and greater than it had ever been. He was always getting mixed up with incredible plots to bring about the fusion of the Churches. He had approached the Orthodox Greeks, the Anglican bishops, the Swedish communions, and even the Zionist Jews. It was impossible to say how seriously he ought to be taken. A lot of people believed that it was nothing but a private fantasy of his own, that most of the negotiations existed only in his imagination or, at best, that he was in touch with only two or three poor devils without any authority at all to treat of such matters, while the really important folk whose names were for ever on his lips regarded him as a joke or fobbed him off with a few meaningless phrases. The fact remained, however, that he had organized several mysterious conferences in Rome which had been attended by some of the cardinals. More than this, he had presented to the Pope, shortly after the latter's election, one of the leaders of the Zionist movement, and no one could deny that the Holy Father had later made certain public pronouncements favourable to the Palestinian Jews. There was more reason than one why the Pope should feel drawn to this visionary. They were both men who belonged by temperament to an earlier age, and the same simplicity of heart marked their attitude to life. They knew nothing of the modern world and took refuge in dreams. Without exactly sharing those of the Benedictine, or even believing them to be practicable, Pius X had undoubtedly a kindly feeling towards the man who entertained them. They flattered, not so much himself personally, for he was entirely without ambition, as his sense of the greatness of the see of Saint Peter, his rather simple desire for absolute domination, his profound conviction that the representative of God on earth, if he is the Father of all men taken as individuals, is still more naturally the Father of all men taken together, of all nations and all peoples, and that this paternal function must be held to extend to every aspect of life. Temperaments such as his pay but lip service to the famous distinction between temporal and spiritual.

Nor had the entourage of the Pope any reason to look askance at the good Dom Charles Magloire. Quite the contrary. The Benedictine's goings-on were too well known to worry anybody. And besides, the more the Holy Father's eyes could be blinded by sweet-smelling smoke, the more dreamers there were to hold the front of the stage with their discussions about Gregorian chant and the pronunciation of Latin, about infant Communion and the union of the Churches, the more free would the politicians be to *"sviluppare le proprie combinazioni."*

Listening while the banker droned on, obviously delighted by this opportunity of giving rein to his own subtlety (he wagged an impatient finger at his wife's attempted interruptions), Mionnet mentally gave full credit to the man who had made him the recipient of such reliable information, and acknowledged the cleverness of Monsignor Lebaigue.

He next tried to get a similar "sidelight" on Monsignor Dougérin, the "Canon of St. Peter's."

"What's the name?—Doudgérin? . . . Monsignor Doudgérin? . . ."

Husband and wife again began questioning each other in Italian, but the exchange between them this time was more hesitating, more laborious, and interrupted by little irritable exclamations such as: "Of course not! . . . What on earth are you thinking of!"

Finally they so far agreed as to declare that they had heard tell of "Monsignor Doudgérin," Canon of St. Peter's, had even perhaps met him on some occasion, but that beyond that they knew nothing of him. They seemed, they said, to remember that he had been a friend of Father Tyrrell's, the famous Jesuit who had died a few years ago in a state of excommunication.

The tone in which they gave this information had taken on a suddenly casual note, which seemed to indicate that a person so different from their other acquaintances was little likely to interest Mionnet.

In view of this change in their attitude, he forbore to mention any of the other names which figured on his lists. He did not even mention the Baron de Fontmonge.

"We'll arrange some meetings for you, a few quiet little dinner-parties . . ." said Mme Lacchini. "You can rely on us."

On his way home from their house, under a driving rain which blew in his face all along the Via Veneto, he decided to buy a thick note-book with large pages (he was a man who loved note-books). In this he would jot down each day whom he met and where. It looked as though so many people were going to volunteer information that he would have difficulty in keeping them all apart in his memory.

The contents of this new book would in no way encroach upon that of a certain dark red book, nor on that of a certain green book, both of which still accompanied him in his trunks. From them too, had their size permitted, he would never willingly have separated himself, although one at least was secured with more than usual care. Every evening on returning to his hotel he was at pains to assure himself that the japanned steel box was where he had left it at the bottom of his trunk. The advantage of a pocket note-book was that he could keep it by him no matter how carefully he might be watched. But in any case he must be more than ever careful to keep his eyes open.

Chapter

18

A DAY AT THE VATICAN

By the same post he received an answer from Manifassier and an invitation to dinner from the Baron
de Fontmonge.

The substance of Manifassier's letter was as follows: "Keep on as
before. When you have enough material for a report, send it me in
the form of an official letter. Double envelopes are now useless."

M. de Fontmonge's note indicated that there would be other guests,
asked particularly to meet Mionnet.

"What with all these contacts that are being arranged for me, I
shall very soon become compromised. It is time to cover my tracks
a bit. I must really throw myself into the arms of Dom Charles
Magloire."

He wrote him a polite letter and said that he should do himself the
honour to call in two days' time. One of the paragraphs contained the
following phrase: ". . . I am one of those who have felt the charm
of your enthusiasm . . ." and in signing himself he was careful to
use the word "admiration."

After he had posted the letter, an idea came to him. "Why shouldn't
I spend tomorrow having a good look at the Vatican? Better employ
the blameless curiosity of the simple tourist while I have a chance.
Once I've got to know too many people and have heard too many
stories about Tom, Dick, and Harry, once our good friend Dom
Charles Magloire has made me free, as he very well may do, of the
secrets of the seraglio, I shall no longer be able to go there, guide-
book in hand, without being assailed at every turn by too many re-
minders of reality, too many thoughts of petty intrigue. Certain

states of grace have a way of not being repeated, and it would be a pity to miss an opportunity. . . ."

He took no more than a cup of black coffee when he got up, and by a quarter past nine was installed in a small café on the Piazza Rusticucci, facing the colonnade of St. Peter's. He ordered a cold meal to be served to him in the open air (for the interior of the restaurant was dark and damp), and washed it down with a white Castelli Romani. The weather was deliciously bracing. The colonnade was bright with sunlight, and the gestures of the Bernini statues seemed amply justified, if insufficiently serious.

Several saunterers showed in the immensity of the two squares, local residents and early visitors. The restaurant-keepers and hawkers of souvenirs kept their eyes open for possible customers and embarked upon so patient a series of manœuvres, so subtle a campaign of approach, that the prospect of eventual profit was clearly made doubly delightful for them by the added sport of a difficult capture adroitly organized.

Just before ten o'clock Mionnet, meekly following the information contained in his guide-book, crossed the Piazza di San Pietro obliquely and had no difficulty in finding, to the left of the Basilica, the arcade immediately opposite the Bronze Doors, which gave access to the museums.

He had taken a good deal more wine than food and felt cheerful, brisk, slightly drunk, and free of all heaviness.

The way seemed to him particularly easy to find since he had only to follow the other visitors. It led him through tiny squares, narrow alleys still enveloped in icy shadow, and a number of cloisters. The buildings about him, clean, solid, and austere, reminded him more of a castle than a church. He saw groups of ushers and guards so extravagantly dressed that they seemed to be there for no other purpose than to astonish the tourists.

It was only when he began to think about the matter and had looked up once or twice at the towering Basilica that he realized that in fact he was making the circuit of the apse, in order to reach a long interior walk lying between the Palace and the Gardens. At last he reached the entrance to the Museums, took his ticket, and mounted the staircase in the direction of the Sala a Croce Greca.

He had five hours before him, since he meant to stay in the Museums until they closed. (He had already promised himself a meal of some sort between three and four, either in the same restaurant or another on the same square, to be accompanied by a white wine of some different brand, in which the fatigues of the intervening hours would be deliciously dissolved. Nothing like being thoroughly tired when one wants to sort one's impressions.)

He made use of his guide-book only occasionally, and then very sparingly. What he aimed at doing on the occasion of his present visit was to get a general idea of the lay-out of the place and identify the main objects of interest. For this purpose he relied upon chance combined with a minimum of method. He glanced at his book whenever he had to choose between two possible directions, when he wanted to be sure where precisely he was or to verify the authorship of some work of art which had caught his attention.

He stopped before the most famous monuments with a little flutter of mental recognition, as who should say: "So there you are!" But he avoided, without much difficulty, indulging in long æsthetic meditations or critical appraisements. He refused to be an awe-struck student, rehearsed no well-conned lesson. These works had been created, had they not, in their time, to give pleasure? Later they had been collected also to give pleasure—the sort of pleasure a man may take in sauntering and chatting with his friends, or in feasting at a table in the company of prosperous men and handsome women.

He let his eyes dwell on the charming intricacies of the shell-like Belvedere. He took his stand at the entrance to one of the great rooms and allowed himself to be dazzled by the dwindling vista of galleries.

A ceiling here delighted him; a Venus there, deep in her niche, was pleasantly exciting.

In places a vast window gave onto a courtyard or a garden. Sometimes, close at hand, precipitous spaces opened at his feet, leading the eye through secret glories of dazzling light to catch, far down, a wilderness of lovely shapes. At times he saw before him great dwindling tiers of windows, joining, far off, yet other tiers; a series of horizontal lines, gently drawn to a perspective point; corners that closed the view; roofs spread out beneath a brilliant sky; a vast complexity of buildings, overlapping, interpenetrating, hinting at endless possibilities of movement for favoured initiates (bare-headed, their feet in sandals or heelless shoes).

Mionnet's thoughts turned to Tibet, to Lhassa. He dreamed that here, through a window, he had been permitted to view the greatest lamasery of the world; a well-kept lamasery in which was no smell of rancid butter or human sweat. And what a sky!

From another window—where the outside vista was reflected in a long gallery of gilt-framed mirrors—he got a passing impression of Versailles. But it was a Versailles more secret than its prototype, longer inhabited, impregnated with a deeper refinement of living, and much less theatrical, since here the Basilica and its colonnade alone were theatrical, and, caught up in the intimacies of the Palace, he could forget them, could abandon them without a qualm, to the gaping crowds. Ah well, let them "do" their sights and goggle their eyes. The stage was set, and someone had got to pay for it all. But for the poor actor life was not always beer and skittles! . . . Just as well that the wretched human ocean should break in foam about the gorgeous promontory and think to go no farther. . . . Each day the tide would ebb with the brainless regularity of nature, leaving each day a line of spume upon the sand—spume that was made of minted gold and silver. And from those shallows of scattered coin someone, perhaps, would make new Venuses to rise for the joy of one or two. If the wretched human ocean could ensure that, what more need one ask of it? Now and again, perhaps, there might emerge a great man or a fair woman meet to be shown the splendours that are hidden from the common gaze. But, on the whole, what further claim could the stupid herd make, in justice, upon its masters? Was it not given already more than its deserts, didn't it get twice its money's worth, in those superb displays, over-strong wine for weak heads, the beauty of which was justification enough if justification were needed?

Turning from one of these windows, Mionnet found himself suddenly in a gay riot of naked men and women. Nowhere in the world was there gathered so fair a show of lovely nudities; nowhere had the glories of pagan nature suffered so little from the thwarting hand of modesty. No breasts of goddesses here chipped into shapelessness, no men insultingly castrated. Not here were the gifts of God pilloried for laughter or marked for punishment. The vigour of the flesh and its desire, all the sweet armament of love, had been respected, not torn like malignant growths from the living body. Fig-leaves, indeed, there were, but serving to cover rather than to hide. And what so tenderly they draped showed as some precious fruit, some fresh and fragile harvest of the flesh. At sight of them the heart grew gay with laughter. About the great noble chords of marble they ran like a wanton tune endlessly repeated. Not without cause had they been made so huge and so agreeably moulded. The very whiteness of their untinted plaster, as of something that gloried shamelessly in its very artificiality, setting itself of deliberate intent to catch the wandering eye, seemed evidence that bashfulness itself was caught here in self-mockery. Whoever it was who had made these late additions had done so surely in a spirit of malicious glee, thinking no doubt of the women's eyes, wanton as well as innocent, that would range these pleasant fields. For them no doubt it was that such care had been taken, in concealing detail, to leave unmodified the form! Whoever had thought of all this had been at pains to show while seeming to conceal, laughing the while—as only those unwedded still can laugh—in anticipation of all the fancies, gaily indulged or solemnly rebuked, that would throng the charming heads of endless women down the ages.

Mionnet whispered to himself, casually and as they came to him, the names of the popes of the great age: Julius II, Leo X, Clement VII, and Alexander Borgia, he who least of all should be denied . . . of others, too, less easy to remember (what was their order?): Sixtus IV, Nicholas V, Paul III. (Only with the Council of Trent had the bad times come.) Not from those times, indeed, dated the fig-leaves, so new, so rich in subtle provocation. The great men of the past had given asylum with a clear conscience, had offered opportunities for praise and appraisement by connoisseurs of brilliance, to all these bosomed Aphrodites and Dianas, these magnificently equipped presentments of Apollo, of Antinoüs, of Heracles, rescued by miracle from the fanaticism of the earliest Christians. "Leo X, Cardinal at fourteen, Pope at forty. . . ." How charming it was to evoke the images of those young cardinals, chatting at their ease before such statues! . . . ("Come and see my latest acquisitions," the Pope might have said, or: "How much better the courtyard of my Belvedere looks now. . . .") Here would be one, a scholar, quoting Greek, identifying a goddess from some mirror in her hand or jewel in her hair, there an exquisite polishing an epigram in honour of Praxiteles; and others, too, whose mistresses from Borgo Nuovo, Trastevere, or Tivoli glowed with but twenty summers. And since they too, the young cardinals, were themselves but thirty or eight-and-twenty, it would be but natural, and from no desire to play perversely on the strings of scandal, that they would see in the sculptured figures and in the painted ornaments of life a commentary on living and a call to live; that they would look upon the forms of ancient goddesses with eyes that remembered and compared, congratulating themselves on the sureness of their taste, regretting that they had been too easily pleased, or wondering anxiously whether the Roman girls had not shown a sad falling off since the days of the emperors . . . and such thoughts they would not have kept silent for themselves, but would have spoken as occasion suited, as the familiarity of their friendships or the mood dictated.

What a number of statues here of Antinoüs and Apollo, of the young Hermes and the youthful Bacchus! Greece in those days had been once more in fashion, and men had deeply pondered Plato. That world of prelates had been a world of males, full of youths in their first bloom, born of a race where beauty is the rule, with, for their choosing, a host of boys, the youngest of the young, and a world to live in where curious manners were accepted as the norm. Might one not suppose that now and again these figures of Hermes and Antinoüs, not yet festooned with fig-leaves, had inspired witticisms of a certain kind; nay, more, had urged to passionate vows, serving as themes for madrigals sung to the glory of Alcibiades?

For such things Michelangelo and Raphael had shown a sympathy, tracing curious subtleties, ambiguous truths, hinting at strange resemblances. They had made clear the likeness between some Cardinal's mistress and a goddess of the ancient world, between that same mistress and a saint in paradise, between a youth of the Greek age and some young noble of the Papal Guard, between a maiden and a boy. It was they who had built bridges of strange reference to link past with present, who had hammered curious intricacies of beauties and of loves.

"Cardinal at fourteen; Pope at forty. . . ." At a turn of a corridor, in the embrasure of a window from which he could see a dwindling vista of façades, Mionnet repeated the phrase.

Aristocracy! That had been the age of aristocracy; the only one. None but the "best" are safe from exploitation by their fellows. There are dreary periods in which the "best," threatened on all sides by the stupidity of the world, must shut their secrets firmly in their breasts (as it might be in a japanned steel box). Others there have been, still far removed from the great epochs of the past, in which, though concessions to stupidity had still to be made, a man might still talk allusively to friends, might taste the rare pleasure of subtle insinuations, read meaning in a smile or in a whispered word (exchanged before a Hercules with his club or the soft curve of Aphrodite's knee).

"Cardinal at fourteen . . . Pope at forty. . . ." Beyond the windows stretched the Roman sky-line. Above the Sabine Hills the heavens hung bright. About power sought for its own sake there is something plebeian. It is a thing of tedious duties. It satisfies a vulgar thirst in nature. In the drunkenness it gives there is a sense of weariness and sweat. For all his greatness Napoleon had been caught in a round of servile tasks. Power for him had brought no freedom. He had differed from the office clerk or the day-labourer only in being bigger.

Power is a good only if it serves to build a secret dwelling-place for pleasure; if it makes possible the accumulation of spoils for the life within. The true solution was there, framed in the opening of that window. Power successfully achieved had there its image: a system of palatial detachment; a network of "princely" dwelling-places and secret corridors, flanked by something strong and sturdy, beyond the might of the outside world to penetrate; defences of stone, and, better still, defences of beliefs.

To revel in magnificence apart. To relish on the palate the sense of living in a citadel set deep in luxury; to share such sense with a chosen few. The point of power is not to get drunk on solitude. Life in "society," when society consists only of the best and excludes severely all who are unworthy, is the pleasantest of all lives. Versailles failed because at Versailles society was too much mixed: a superfluity of fools. The weakness of all aristocracies of birth lies in the crude, the childish, mechanism by which they are recruited. The risk is too high of their producing swarms of fools. A true aristocracy arranges matters in subtler and more mysterious ways. It works by no fixed rules and by many different reasons. I make this man a Cardinal because he is talented; that man because he is the son of a Prince, and himself marked by distinction. . . . You because you are no less distinguished, though the son of a shepherd. . . . You because you are rich, because possessions have brought to you an easy manner and a quick intelligence. . . . You because you are handsome. . . . You because you are learned in classical inscriptions and together we shall have some charming talks on that most important of subjects. . . . You because you are a friend of the King of Poland and can help my political schemes. . . . You . . . for no particular reason, but just because it is good sometimes to indulge a whim.

Nor should women play too great a part in any aristocracy. Beautiful women in marble or in paint of course there must be to make pleasant our sauntering steps. Women, too, as many as you like, of flesh and blood for the delights of love, or to grace a feast and lend pleasure to our talks. But they must not control life, not be its reigning queens, filling galleries and rooms with their gossip and jealousies and intrigues! There will be quite enough female intrigue without encouraging it! . . . So long as they are confined to the secrecy of the bed they don't so much matter. The Cardinal returning from his mistress forgets before he reaches home half of what she whispered to him, and when he enters the council chamber he is back in a world of men where the ideas of men are all that matter. "Incidentally," reflected Mionnet, "that's one of the reasons—though I never thought of it before—for the superiority, so often admitted, of the policies of the popes over those of kings. The policy of the Louvre, of Versailles, of the Tuileries, was too often dictated by women. . . . The policy of the Vatican, even in the period of most extreme indulgence, never."

His visit to the Rooms of Raphael, to the Loggie, coincided for Mionnet with the point of highest intensity attained by this cerebral intoxication, which, though it may have been helped in its earlier stages by the wine of Castelli Romani, no longer owed anything to such adventitious causes.

Thoughts followed daring thoughts in rapid succession, disdaining proof, finding sufficient justification in their mere existence, in the radiance in which they moved, the vibration that they imparted to the mind.

"How right I was to choose the Church as my career! My instinct was a true one. It provides just the asylum I need against the prejudices of the modern world. No wonder that I find Monsignor Sérasquier so sympathetic. What nonsense all this undergraduate talk is:

truth; duties towards society; solidarity of man! Truth means thinking straight; not allowing oneself to be exploited by others. . . . The
general ruck of mankind has no rights at all. So far as I am concerned,
it is part of the natural environment of my life, like the soil or the vege-
tation of the earth. But the possibility of such an attitude was lost
when the best among men allowed themselves to be influenced by
the fear of being unjust. What is justice? A cancer. In accepting my
condition as a clean, well-clothed, well-nourished, educated member
of society, I am unjust in my relation to the Negro in the deep heart
of Africa, since he remains naked, filthy, unenlightened, and half
starved. Similarly I am unjust in my relation to the sheep whose flesh
I eat, to the bean-stalk that is stripped for my pleasure. We are unjust,
all of us, in our relation to the monkeys, who, maybe, had just as much
right as man to the empire of the world; to ants, to microbes whose
natural aspirations we frustrate; to the very air, since we steal its oxy-
gen. The argument based upon equality of rights, upon 'reciprocity,'
is a slippery slope down which the mind of man rushes to inevitable
absurdity.

" 'All very well,' it will be objected, 'but how dare *you* make such an
admission, you, a minister of a religion which preaches charity and
justice?' There are those who enjoy the irony of such a situation. But
when all's said, no force of nature can be used unless it has first been
harnessed, first been trapped, and every trap needs its bait. If the
Socialists got power tomorrow, they would dictate to the masses in
the name of freedom. . . . When a trap begins to fail, one changes
the bait. . . . To realize that men must be deceived in order to be
led is but to admit the working of a natural law. The master of a
sailing vessel cheats the wind every time he tacks in its teeth. I cheat
my organism by getting myself vaccinated. . . . No one today will
really face the implications of these elementary concepts. There was
a time when the 'best' were at one in their attitude towards them,
when they wouldn't even waste time discussing them, but now who
is there will venture to question them if only in the privacy of his
secret thoughts? The moderns are nothing but a lot of fools in their

desire for 'sincerity.' Everyone wants to make everyone else believe in his sincerity, and what does that signify if not that the good life has been once again invaded by the standards of the gutter? In the old days it was generally understood that the 'best' were concerned only with what they themselves wished. To conform was the mark of inferiority, and conformity in the general run of mankind there needs must be, since men can be influenced only through their beliefs. . . . If they can't be influenced, can't be used, better destroy them out of hand. The Red Indian has been destroyed and a whole host of animal species. . . . Not that their masters need be other than kindly and well-intentioned. . . . The Church! the gentlest of all the dominations, and the least costly. In a sense it is madmen like Dom Magloire who are right. Think of the Church compared with the great military dictatorships! . . . One of these days the world will find itself with a collectivist State on its shoulders. . . . Then we shall see!"

As he was walking down the little staircase leading to the Sistine Chapel, he became suddenly conscious, not only of a weakness in the knees sufficiently accounted for by long hours of toiling round the galleries, though normally he would not have expected to feel it quite so soon, but, more especially, of a little secret stab of interrogation, or rather of the onset of a small host of questions. He knew some of the little pests of old. Many a time he had had to drive them back into their lairs.

"In choosing the Church as a career, didn't you perhaps forget that you were living in the twentieth century? Weren't you fooled by a dream touched with the iridescent hues of history? The Church you entered was, in fact, a phantasm. It ceased to exist in any real sense ages ago. . . . How much of the great traditional Church remains in the Church today? Has not the façade of charity and justice encroached upon the essence of the organization until nothing of the latter remains? Aren't you too, just a little, the victim of your own idealism?"

As a rule he left the question unanswered. But today he felt in a mood to look such gloomy problems in the face and chose to take advantage of the place and hour.

"That there is a suspicion of anachronism I am prepared to admit. But who is there who does not like sometimes to dress up the world in which he lives from the wardrobe of history? . . . But there is more in the business than mere suggestion. . . . The glory of the Church is still a reality. Difficulties beset it, but it revels in difficulties. It knows full well that fools will never understand. . . . It wages constant war against the dullness that assails it from within. The thrill that comes from maintaining a position endlessly false is as the breath of life to it. . . . Need to resolve the discords keeps it ever on the watch. After all, what better careers are there? Business? . . . Bah! Politics? . . . Nothing but labour and a sweating of blood, even when one's got to the top, dirt and the livery of the gutter. The politician lives continuously beneath a sword of Damocles, is for ever exposed to all the blasts of heaven; no existence within the 'secret palace' there; no hierarchy in which to lie entrenched. . . . The army? A bad joke if ever there was one, as things are today. Lieutenant in a line regiment until one is thirty-eight, and ultimately retirement on a colonel's pay in some tiny country town. . . . What else, then? Vice-chancellor of a university? . . . To be an archbishop is better fun, to be a cardinal more splendid still. I can think of no better way of facing the creeping horrors of old age. . . . Besides, I'm not equally qualified for all employments. Gifts I have, but they are strictly limited. . . ."

But the peace of mind thus won was of short duration. Another new-born snake of doubt raised its venomous head:

"The fact that you were willing to come here on such a mission as in fact is yours proves beyond question that you don't believe, that you never have believed, in the survival, in however modified a form, of this glorious Church. Had you done so, would you have been willing to serve the temporal power against this world of Rome? And what a temporal power!—a government at the beck and call of the masses!"

For a while he stood nonplussed. He was on the point of admitting that much he could not explain had determined his choice of a profession. A man with a certain background of culture, a man trained to use his brain, is apt to treat himself as a problem. He likes to see clearly into his motives, to construct an intellectual image of himself that shall at least be plausible. But in doing so he is, perhaps, as far from the truth as the author of a thesis on, say, "The Politics of Richelieu."

"What is there to prove that I did not make that momentous decision as most men make the most important decisions of their lives, from confused and various motives, some puerile, some profound, but none that really square with the reasons publicly given?"

It was a sobering thought. His mind turned to his "Green Book" which had a certain evidential value. If the Green Book proved nothing, could it be because he, Mionnet, had already started inventing reasons, putting forward plausible excuses, even before he had allowed himself to act? Had he lied to himself as a precautionary measure? Poor Green Book!

Suddenly an idea of which till that moment he had had no inkling set his spirits once more soaring:

"What if, in the weeks to come, I become convinced—it's quite possible I might—that this Merry del Val, whom I am here to unmask in the interests of a temporal power, is working, not for another temporal power, but for the Church, for the restoration and glorification of the Church, the Church that is the centre of my world, the true Church, my Church?"

What a dramatic turn-about of roles that would be for the spirit working in solitude! What a test for the sincerity of his convictions!

"And it's just as possible as anything else. There's no particular reason why this Spaniard of a great house should desire the triumph of the Central Empires for their own sake. . . . It may be, of course, that he's nothing but a mercenary hireling working for pay, or a fool, a coxcomb, set on assuaging a petty spite against France, or flattered by the attentions of the national enemy. . . . But then, on the other hand, it may be that his is a fine and daring spirit wholly wedded to the Church's cause, that to serve the Church he may be willing to sacrifice all else, himself included. What then?"

Yes, what then? . . . If Mionnet found out that Merry del Val was indeed such a hero, what would he do?

It was a thrilling problem, apt to make a man feel his full stature, to savour the freedom of his choice, to realize the part his will could play in the mechanisms of the world.

"When I've assembled my information, when I feel in a position to draw my conclusions, and if my conclusions square with this new assumption, what shall I do? What decision shall I make?"

The man pondering this question was the man who remembered full well that once he had "saved" Monsignor Sérasquier.

"To save Merry del Val" was a phrase that he could shape only half jokingly even in the secrecy of his heart. He didn't, of course, really believe in it. Not for a moment could the fate of Merry del Val really depend upon anything that he might do. But . . . well, the Government of the French Republic was not to be sneezed at . . . it had very real means at its disposition. It was strong enough, surely, to be able to suppress an enemy denounced by one of its agents, or at least to make life very difficult for him, to render nugatory most of his scheming. . . . The attitude of that government in the business in hand, its indifference or, on the other hand, its keenness, the violence of its reaction, would largely depend upon what he saw fit to report. . . .

"In other words, where shall I let the ultimate decision be made? In Paris? Or in my head? In Paris, where the facts which I transmit will speak for themselves without my playing any part more personal than that of a faithful recording instrument? Or here, in my head, where the same facts will be weighed in the balance of my judgment, retained or rejected, interpreted by myself in the office of sovereign judge, so that the reports I send will be no more than the tactful record of my own conclusions?" He put the question, but as yet he could find no answer.

But uncertainty on such a scale has in it something of magnificence. Not everyone can face decisions of such weight. To put so high a question here beneath the roof of the Sistine Chapel, gazing at the image of a great muscular God separating light from darkness, had about it something of the pleasure fitting to an aristocrat. Such a situation was not altogether unworthy of those princes clothed in purple who, from the depths of hidden palaces, had led the peoples of the world.

"Oh, it isn't in tune with the modern world! Faced with such thoughts, the poor manikin of the modern world would tremble like a leaf, would fear he might go mad. The poor modern manikin thinks of himself naturally as a servant—no need to hammer the fact into him with a stick—as a slave for ever charged with duties, for ever set on guard, responsible to others for everything he does or even thinks. The poor modern manikin feels guilty of treachery if he so much as dreams of making a decision for himself—of treachery to his country, his Church, his party, or his class. . . . When he chooses, it is always at second hand, and always between two duties, the duties of a slave who is bound by obedience to this or that. Which had I better obey, he thinks, the law voted by the Freemasons or the imperative mandate of the bishops? Under no circumstances can he be conceived of as a power treating on a level with his equals, no matter how high his place in society may be. For his place is always within a system. In no smallest feature does it resemble that of a 'sovereign and independent monarch.' Where are you, Prince de Condé, Mazarin, Wallenstein, men who could say: 'There is the King of France, there is the King of Spain, there is the Emperor, there is the Church, and there am I. What is my point of view in all this? What will redound most to my interest, my glory, what will satisfy my heart and head, what will further my choice and my policy? . . . The things, the forces, involved, that is another question. It is for me to decide how to play my game, how to manœuvre between powers greater than my own, relying on one more than on another, allying myself here or here, setting others to court me, according to the play of circumstance. . . . My honour as a gentleman compels me not to break, without sufficient reason, my given word, to prove false to my oath or my *allegiance;* that I know full well, and I expect the same consideration from others. But that, just because I happen to be a 'Frenchman,' I have no right to associate myself with the King of Spain against the King of France when I, Condé, think it good, reasonable, and honourable so to do, that I am to be held guilty of treachery because my view of things and my line of conduct differ from those of the King of France, *that* I do not understand; that I hold to be a dream of fools.' "

The tormented figures of Michelangelo, half-arrested in a sort of tranquillity, spread across walls and ceiling, filling the place with something of the grandeur of a tomb. But in the spaces between floated, half-glimpsed, a bevy of embryonic forms. A light mist of allegory. When Mionnet's eyes ceased to wander and became focused in sudden attention upon the painted figures of the chapel, these ghostly forms which he had allowed of their own accord to take shape seemed to superimpose themselves on the frescoed figures. From this junction of two imaginations emerged something vague and symbolic, as a dream will linger still, for the waking sleeper, in the borderland of consciousness. The kings, the prophets, and the sibyls seemed charged with a new and allusive significance. Those who decided, those who announced, those in whose hands it lay to deal out life or death. The ladder of principalities and powers rising to its goal in Him who was All-Powerful . . . and beneath them the multitude of the lost, chastised and rejected by Him who reigns on high.

Miserable multitude! Much to be pitied—and yet how much? Have they not themselves produced the furies whose victims they are? They cry aloud for comfort and relief, and care not how it comes. The whole responsibility of the "princes" consists in so directing the furies that they shall at least serve some purpose.

For, as with so many Sibylline Oracles, the phrase "to save Merry del Val" could be read in several different ways. And one of them, it didn't take much to imagine, meant the vast movement of peoples creeping to grips and death. . . . Those clusters of cascading bodies symmetrically projected to the gulf, there on the end wall, beneath the eyes of an angry God, mightn't they figure as tormented hosts set asunder by the Judgment of War, clinging to the down-tipped scale, and rolling helter-skelter to the pit?

While he sat at his second meal in the restaurant on the Piazza Rusticucci, Mionnet's thoughts came down once more to earth.

"All very fine to wonder what one will do in a situation which hasn't as yet materialized. . . . It's certainly one way to avoid being taken by surprise. . . . But I can't help thinking that I am, perhaps, a shade too previous."

Save Merry del Val? Rather like counting one's chickens before they're hatched. Get him first, and then talk of saving.

"Get him . . . I?"

He let his eyes travel once or twice between the table at which he sat and the vast mass of the Palace opposite. His conclusion this time differed from that he had drawn when he had paid his first visit to this scene. Then it had been: "Not bad"; now it was: "What fun!"

Chapter

19

DOM CHARLES MAGLOIRE
MAKES A NEW DISCIPLE

His first contact with Dom Charles Magloire left on him an impression of fantastic and almost burlesque adventure.

Everything about it seemed the prelude to odd episodes and strange incidents. He made his way to the monastery in which the Father lived through the old quarters of the city lying along the Tiber. He came to a halt in the Piazza Bocca della Verità, which at that time had not yet been tricked out with the present rather melancholy little garden, but, with its three monuments looking as though they had been left casually lying about on the ancient, dusty earth, seemed a perfect expression of that rather grand and historic melancholy—made familiar, however, as though the centuries were but one's dead relatives—which in those days was the marked characteristic of Rome.

Just inside the monastery wall he fell in with a very old, very small monk, deaf, with a pink and white complexion, who insisted on acting as his guide and who, as a result of changing his mind every other moment, and perhaps because his memory was feeble, seemed to forget that Mionnet's object was to find Dom Charles Magloire, and continually pointed out to him, with a great deal of conversation, here a new wing, there a chapel, opening odd doors, doing the honours of the refectory, breaking their progress to elaborate some detail he had forgotten, intent on finding Father This, the Bursar, Father That, the cook. All of which did not prevent Mionnet from getting glimpses, often surprising and at times almost heart-breaking in their exquisite beauty, of odd corners of Rome which he found it not always easy to identify. Those roofs down there belonged surely to the Trastevere? And wasn't that the campanile of Santa Cecilia? But what, then, were those ruins? What that little hill seen so strangely against the sky?

"Monte Testaccio!" asserted the old monk; but was he reliable? He must go out but rarely, and in the many years of his life there had been plenty of time in which to confuse the details of his daily view.

At every few steps Mionnet found himself thinking: "What exquisite peace! How the effect of it is to make everything look different, to make a revolution in all normal values! Surely this is how the great things of the world ought to be seen, far off and in ruins, by a man who possesses nothing but a heart at peace and dreams of paradise!"

On their way back he stopped for a moment or two at San Saba. From there his gaze could take in a wider sweep of ruins than ever before. They stood there, a confusion of stone at various levels, here rising high, there plunging to deep foundations, so long an integral part of the site, so overgrown with grasses and garden shrubs that the emotion they stirred in him—poignant in its intensity—was less one of sorrow at dilapidation than of wonder at such long survival.

After a while he took his way down into the hollow where lay the Circus Maximus. The sight of the gas-works filled him with a sudden sense of wonder, so that it came to him how even the gasometers, set high against the slopes of the Palatine, had all the appearance of things left over from a past age, fallen to ruin, majestic in decay, as though they, too, had once been called into being by the will of emperors. As he followed a deserted path that skirted the wall of the Jewish cemetery, a wretched yellow cur dashed past him with a jam-tin tied to its tail. The noise of the tin bumping along the ground was quite different from that which would have been made by a saucepan. The dog seemed less like the frightened victim of a practical joke than some fantastic messenger galloping along with news and making use, in some odd way, for greater speed, of an auxiliary engine.

Gazing thus at the deep depression of the Circus Maximus and at the complex contours that joined it not only to the Palatine and Aventine hills but to the parts about the Cælian Mount and the ruined

levels towards the south-east, Mionnet became aware how many
sweet surprises of pure topography Rome still held in store for him,
since the sheer quantity of details with which the ground was covered
not only made a general impression of shape and plan, but drew the
eye with sudden passages of eloquence, which, limited though they
might be in extent, somehow gave the tone to all the rest, so intimate
were the relations subsisting between the masonry and the natural
accidents of the ground on which it stood.

For several days Mionnet and Dom Charles Magloire were constantly in each other's company. Or so it seemed, for they were seen
together in all sorts of places, and a hundred witnesses could have
been called on to attest that the Benedictine had no companion more
apparently deferential, no protégé so fondly cherished, as a certain
young French Abbé, very tall and very dark of skin.

Mionnet looked far taller than when he was alone, for Dom
Charles Magloire was short and stocky, not so much square-built as
cylindrical. And his tubular body was surmounted by a bearded face
perched on an almost invisible neck, so that his general appearance
was that of an old Marseilles sea-captain. But though his accent had
retained something of its native fullness and heaviness, it had acquired as well a certain Italian quality. Whenever, for instance, he
became excited—which was not seldom—he would suddenly place
a strong tonic accent on one of the interior syllables of a word (where
it would fall naturally in the Italian equivalent); and his final *r's*
took on a prolonged, almost threatening roll which was quite foreign
to his native tongue. Italy, too, was certainly responsible for the sudden introduction of a markedly gentle phrase, with which, after a
particularly emphatic, not to say violently domineering passage, he
would, as it were, caress his interlocutor, so that he seemed to be
waiting upon his good humour, or the accident of his mood, for a
reply.

Dom Charles Magloire's first concern was to make Mionnet visit
every nook and cranny of the Sant' Anselmo Library, where he in-

troduced him to the librarian in charge. He took great pains himself
to point out to his companion the shelves which contained the books
which treated of the politics of the more recent popes—for the subject
of Mionnet's thesis had roused him to a great show of enthusiasm;
he had at once equated it with his personal preoccupations, and
Mionnet's intelligence had at once become for him a plot of precious
ground on which only the most carefully chosen seed must be allowed to fall.

A little later they spent a long day together in the Vatican. They
met early one morning by the Saint Angelo Bridge (Mionnet had
suggested fetching his companion from Sant' Anselmo, but this
would have involved a long detour, and Dom Charles, refusing this
excessive show of politeness, had himself proposed the alternative
meeting-place). They entered the Palace by the Bronze Doors and
hurried through the corridors and across the courtyards.

In the course of their walk Dom Charles Magloire had had a few
words with a strangely garbed individual, ending the brief conversation by a slight inclination of the head, or rather with an exchange
of salutes, a smile, a barely noticeable narrowing of the eyes. Mionnet
got a certain thrill out of the windings of their route, which seemed
to bear out his theory of "interior complications," and from a feeling
that he had been suddenly promoted to enjoy the privileges of an
initiate.

They reached the Vatican Library by a private door. Dom Magloire
introduced him successively, and in the warmest terms, to three
scrittori whom he knew personally. Each of these scrittori showed
them the department over which he himself presided, though he was
careful, *en route,* to point out the beauties and treasures which were
the common pride of all the officials of the place. So thoroughly was
this done that the visitors found themselves being shown the same
object more than once, and courtesy demanded that Mionnet should
express on each occasion the same delighted surprise. Thus it was that
he had to go into ecstasies before a number of horrors presented to
Popes Pius IX and Leo XIII by the then "head of the French nation."

He admired the tact with which the scrittori set themselves to please him by a reminder of the past generosity of his countrymen, while, by using the convenient phrase "head of the nation," carefully refraining from stressing the fact that in less than a century France had declined from a Kingdom into an Empire set up by plebiscite, and from an Empire set up by plebiscite into a middle-class Republic, to say nothing of its situation at the moment, which had no name in any language fit to describe it.

Not only was he shown for his admiration the manuscripts displayed here and there in glass cases, but especially precious examples, such as the Vatican Virgil, were produced from locked cupboards. His guides went so far in their expression of confidence that they allowed him to handle a papyrus of the sixth century. By their aid, too, he was enabled to decipher a signature of Saint Thomas Aquinas.

It appeared, however, that the library was poor in modern works treating of the question that he was ostensibly there to study. He commented on this fact to Dom Charles Magloire, but the Benedictine reassured him with a smile.

"Just wait!"

He took him into the Archivio Segreto and introduced him to the custodian, who appeared to be a personage of considerable importance. This gentleman, after politely asking what Mionnet was working at, summoned a subordinate to whose care he committed his two visitors with many expressions of courtesy. Meanwhile Dom Charles Magloire explained that the "Secret Archives" were secret only in name, since the last Pope had, in fact, thrown them open to the public.

"But," he remarked, lowering his voice and winking, "certain documents have, of course, been removed."

He added, however, that he could arrange for an exception to be made in Mionnet's favour, so that he should see all he needed for his work:

". . . on condition, naturally, that you are discreet in your use of the material. Not that with a man of your calibre the question really arises. . . . The more one learns about certain things, the less one wants to publish them unnecessarily. . . ." (He spread his arms.) "Here you will find everything you want—everything!"

Mionnet affected to be delighted, as though, by introducing him to the Secret Archives, his companion had set flowing the sealed fountain, the abundant source of all the truths of which he longed to be made free. Very quickly he set himself to consider the assistance he might expect to obtain from this collection in the task upon which he was really engaged. "Shall I be allowed to see contemporary or even very recent documents? Certainly not, Dom Magloire or no Dom Magloire. . . . Would it be possible to strike up a friendship with one or other of the archivists and chance his showing me something of importance? . . . Hm! Not very likely that Merry del Val leaves his correspondence to be collected in a place like this. The only papers here are out of date. . . . I might, of course, pick up a certain amount of interesting information from talk, but not directly. As well expect a man to get on the tracks of Poincaré's secret intentions by chatting to the Keeper of State Documents."

The chief benefit of all these visits lay in the fact that he would manage to get the entrée into a number of places; would grow to be regarded as a man whose comings and goings, whose thirst for curious information, had a perfectly honourable explanation; would get to know people who could introduce him into ever more intimate circles. Best of all, by frequenting the company of Dom Charles Magloire he would win a sort of comic notoriety which would serve him better than any disguise.

On their way back from the Archivio Segreto they met, at a corner of one of the corridors, a prelate whom Dom Magloire addressed as Monsignor Valensine or Valensini, and to whom he presented Mionnet in the warmest possible terms.

"He is His Holiness's Auditor," Dom Magloire explained as they continued their walk, ". . . one of the Palace officials. As such he has access to the Pope's secret antechamber. He is a very important personage. The particulars of all candidates for bishoprics pass through his hands. He will get his hat very soon now."

One evening Dom Charles seemed to have been seized by a sudden scruple:

"Look here, I don't want what I am doing to hinder you from sounding other possible sources of information. . . . I'll take you tomorrow to the Victor Emmanuel Library, which is in the old Jesuit College, near the Corso. . . . It is the national library of Italy. We don't, as a rule, very much like going there. Still, I happen to know one of the librarians, and I will introduce you."

Perhaps he wanted to show Mionnet what a wide circle of acquaintances he had. It was, indeed, remarkable that this monk from the Aventine, whom one would have been inclined to believe sunk in a dream-world of his own, knew so many different people (he referred to a great many more in conversation) and seemed proud of the fact.

Mionnet consented to go to the Victor Emmanuel Library. He noted the cordiality with which the Benedictine and his friend the librarian greeted each other. In general, however, he expected little from the visit.

"He's a Freemason," said Dom Charles as they came out.

"Really!"

"Yes, there's a great number of them here in official positions."

While they moved about together on these various visits, Dom Charles Magloire never left off talking. He was a man who asked few questions. Rather, he seemed one of those who immediately make up their minds about any stranger they are thrown with, adding detail to their first impression, if need be, in the course of their acquaintanceship, but always in accord with their original assumption, never modifying conclusions by observation, but following, throughout, the dictates of their imagination. The most he ever did was, now and then, to fall silent, or occasionally give a nod to express interest.

His passion, clearly, was the making of proselytes. Not that he ever troubled to elaborate his theories. Quite possibly he was incapable of doing so. They were his life, the breath of his nostrils. They fell from him piecemeal. So natural were they to him that he never dreamed that to others his allusions and sallies might be lacking in lucidity or coherence. He was quite unable to understand that others might find any difficulty in grasping what he meant or might wish to question his statements. He seemed convinced that every sane man must think as he did. Nothing he said was apparently designed to persuade. He spoke always as though to the obviously converted. (Just as, when Catholics talk together, they never argue about fundamental dogmas, referring to them as to things beyond dispute.) At most, his words were allowed occasionally to act as flicks of the whip, designed to awaken a slumbering belief.

If Mionnet had not already been put on the scent by the Lacchinis, he would have found considerable difficulty in reconstructing the views of his protector. Even knowing what he did, he found it difficult, at times, to recognize them in conversation.

Dom Magloire seemed entirely ignorant of the realities of modern politics, or rather they did not interest him. He was also as far removed as possible from being what is known in the Church and generally in the world today as a "politically-minded man." He was guilty of the crudest mistakes. He would have been amazed to learn that the King of England and the Emperor of Russia had not, as monarchs, precisely the same powers or the same position. He saw no difference between Socialists and Anarchists.

At the same time he dreamed of investing the Pope with authority greater than had ever been enjoyed by any of his predecessors. This was to begin by a union of the Churches. The Pope was to become once more the head of a united Christendom. To hear Dom Magloire, one would gather that this ideal was on the point of being realized. All that stood in the way was a certain amount of pride and self-interest. But his schemes did not end there. There was, according to him, a strong movement among the Jews aiming at the reconciliation of the Old and the New Testaments. The Pope would begin by declaring himself protector of Zionism and of the persecuted Jews throughout the world. This suzerainty would, little by little, extend into the realm of matters spiritual. For the extreme separatists there could, of course, be little hope. It must never be forgotten, however, that the burlesque ceremonies dear to the Masons and the ridiculous titles to which they were addicted, as well as the legends current among them, such as that of Hiram, formed a link with mediæval Christendom and Jewish antiquity.

There remained the Moslems and a few others. Dom Charles Magloire had very little to say about the Moslems. He really seemed to consider them in the light of "natives" who would have to be converted *en masse* when the problems of the "civilized" world had been settled.

Mionnet listened obediently, in the hope that later he would be able to question his talkative friend about, or rather to divert the flow of his conversation towards, the subjects he had at heart. More than once he tried to set him talking about Merry del Val.

It appeared that Dom Charles was not fond of him, regarding him as an opportunist politician, without heart, incapable of generosity, and a prey to megalomania. Perhaps it was that he found him rather too "aristocratic" for his taste. But a further ground of hostility was soon apparent. Dom Charles insisted in a highly significant way on the fact that Merry del Val was in the hands of the Jesuits, that he never so much as lifted a finger without first taking counsel with them, and that since his appointment the "White" Pope had had far less say in the concerns of the Church than the "Black."

"Here's a nice state of affairs," thought Mionnet. "By taking Dom Charles as human stalking-horse and lightning-conductor, I immediately proclaim myself to all and sundry as an enemy of the Jesuits. One can, it appears, be an ultra-papist and an anti-Jesuit at one and the same time. Really, life looks like becoming a little too complicated."

It was clear to him, as time went on, that there was no method in Dom Charles's prejudice against the Jesuits. (There was precious little method, if it came to that, in anything about him.) Many of the Company were his friends, some almost partisans and disciples.

Merry del Val stood for him as an expression of all that was bad in the Jesuit attitude (from which fact it appeared that there was something good in it as well). He was not, however, openly at variance with the Cardinal Secretary of State.

"I see him from time to time. We occasionally have a rare set-to. He doesn't want to figure as my declared enemy, so he pretends to treat me as a joke. I repay him in kind, and sometimes, I don't mind telling you, my fine gentleman laughs on the wrong side of his mouth."

Mionnet understood that Dom Charles accused Merry del Val of having, more than once, "put a spoke in his wheel," and held him responsible for certain set-backs which his great plan for the fusion of the Churches had received.

"Just because he had an English mother, he claims to know more than anyone else about the Anglo-Saxons. He wants to go carefully in the matter of England and says that I shall only make an enemy of her if I try approaching the Anglican Church direct. He is quite incapable of feeling enthusiasm for any cause. He probably thinks that enthusiasm is crude. He looks at everything with the eyes of a diplomat. You've only got to look at him to see that—as you'll agree when you meet him . . . with his well-cut soutane, his silk stockings, and the expensive shoes that he gets sent him from London. . . . I honestly believe his greatest ambition is to look as much like an English ambassador as possible."

"You would say, then, that he is more friendly to England than he is usually given credit for being?" asked Mionnet, trying hard to turn the conversation onto the Cardinal's political likes and dislikes. But the attempt was not very fruitful. It was a subject in which Dom Charles Magloire was very soon out of his depth. He appeared barely to suspect the existence in Europe of two great political groups in a state of ever increasing antagonism, or to realize that the Vatican could play an important part in the struggle. His interest in England was confined to the Anglican Church and to the hope that the Archbishop of Canterbury might be induced to make his submission to Rome. Similarly, Russia meant only the Orthodox Church, the local parish priests, the Holy Synod, and the difficulty of getting round such subtle Oriental barbarians.

More than once he spoke of Pius X himself. His attitude towards the pontiff was one of affectionate admiration:

"Mark my words, you're young, and you'll live to see his beatification."

But his respect did not exclude a certain amount of free criticism. He regretted, for instance, that Pius X was so obstinate, and it wouldn't have taken much to make him admit that this obstinacy was to a large extent due to stupidity:

"He attaches enormous importance to such questions as infant Communion. . . . It's absurd. . . . I wish you could have seen him last year—how time does fly! it's almost exactly twelve months ago— receiving the children who had come from France to bring him thanks for the Eucharistic Decrees! . . . There were tears in his voice when he made them his little address. . . . I don't deny it was all very touching; but at that time of all times! . . ."

For at "that time" Pius X had not been doing all he should to support the efforts of Charles Magloire. He didn't seem to realize that the day when he would be in a position to receive in St. Peter's representatives of all the congregations of Christendom assembled to confide to the hands of the Supreme Pontiff the reunion of all the Churches and the restoration of Christ's kingdom on earth, something would have happened that was more important than the mild march past of a lot of little urchins, two by two, in the Sistine Chapel.

At that point in the conversation Dom Charles shrugged his shoulders indulgently. The impression he gave was of a practical man, a realist who looked for results, complaining affectionately of a dear good Pope brim-full of sanctity, but a little too much obsessed by innocent dreams.

From these days of close companionship Dom Charles Magloire drew the conviction that he had found a new disciple, the most serious, perhaps, of all his disciples. What he particularly liked about

Mionnet was that he was such a good listener, a quality exemplified by the fact that his comments were marked by a high intelligence and that his objections, never foolish in themselves, always yielded to appropriate argument.

Mionnet spared no pains to strengthen this conviction. He expressed the desire to say his Mass occasionally in the little new chapel at Sant' Anselmo where Dom Charles usually said his own. He also asked his friend to recommend him a confessor.

"I'll be your confessor myself—if you would like me to be," replied the Benedictine.

Chapter

20

THE LIGHTER SIDE OF RELIGION

His assiduous attendance on Dom Charles Magloire did not prevent Mionnet from cultivating the various other contacts he had set himself to make.

A very few days after he had been asked to dine by the Baron de Fontmonge, he received a similar invitation from the Lacchinis. This was followed, the next week, by an evening party, given also by the Lacchinis, attended by a numerous and brilliant gathering, and offered as a mark of courtesy to a travelling American financier called Goldberg whose family had been converted to Catholicism and who was passing through Rome on his way to Pozzuoli and Sicily to visit certain of his industrial enterprises.

He also called on Monsignor Dougérin, Canon of St. Peter's, to whom he had been given an introduction by Monsignor Sérasquier.

He found it a busy and a fruitful time, distinguished too by several picturesque incidents, such, for instance, as his discovery of the scagnozzo.

He continued to live at the Hôtel de la Paix et Helvétia. When he was not dining out he took his meals in one or another of the little restaurants that he had marked down in the course of his walks. He realized that the arrangement was not the best possible, but its drawbacks were not serious. He was pretty sure that no one at the hotel was bothering about him. The owners were openly contemptuous of the Papal police, and took far more interest in the occasional arrival of a German tourist. Eating at small restaurants was cheap, and, provided one liked pasta, soup, and fried dishes, did not mind the taste of oil, and had no very high standard so far as the quality of the meat went or the cooking of the vegetables, one could fairly soon get used to the diet, which, almost everywhere, had an honest rustic savour about it.

At the Fontmonge table he made the acquaintance of the Baroness —a large, good-natured lady; of the son, a silent and difficult young man, very much a fish out of water; and of a daughter, who was a real beauty. (There were two other daughters, both married, one of whom lived in Brussels, the other in Vienna.) As to the beauty, she exhaled a pleasing aura of laziness which communicated itself to the admiration with which others regarded her. She goaded the intelligence to no activity. "If I were in love with her, and a poet into the bargain," thought Mionnet, "I should have to drive away all the most hackneyed epithets and terms of praise as one drives away a cloud of flies from a fruiterer's stall in the summer." Not that there was anything banal about her good looks. What was rare about her came from her perfection, the perfection of a type which seems to have no place in it for psychological complexity or romantic questioning. "I've never seen such dazzling fairness. Her complexion is all lilies and roses. She's as full-figured as a Flemish Madonna. . . ." The remoteness, the ambiguity, of her glance and of her smile, however, seemed out of tone with the rest of her characteristics, though not to the extent of making her seem mysterious.

More than half of the dozen guests were Belgians domiciled in Rome. Two others were of the same nation, temporarily in Italy, where they had business interests. The last couple, who were accompanied by their wives, belonged to the world of diplomacy. Mionnet learned from one of them that he was a Portuguese and that he knew the Fontmonges through friends of both, Belgians living at Lisbon, where they ran some large industrial concern (connected with transport). In the course of the same conversation he discovered, what he had not formerly known, that a large part of the industry of Portugal was in the hands of Belgians. The other, a Rumanian called Cotinescu, had lived a long while in Paris and had a great repertoire of pungent stories, which he told in a very beautiful golden voice and with a careful assumption of unconcern, while the Belgians greeted the points with a chorus of devastating laughter.

Most of these stories had to do with the world of the Vatican and its various ramifications in the capitals of Europe, and, generally speaking, with the affairs of the Church. Indeed, the whole conversation of the table seemed to turn on such matters. If it showed signs of becoming diverted, the host took great pains to bring it back again, probably for the benefit of the Abbé. A few of the stories, without being exactly indecent, had implications which the laughter of the Belgians drove home, though at the same time it gave to them an air of innocence. The "beauty" seemed in no way disconcerted, nor did anyone else appear to feel the slightest embarrassment on her behalf. She smiled at the right places, though it was impossible to say whether she was really amused or whether she was merely following suit, as we do when a joke made in a foreign language escapes us, though we see our neighbours doubled up with mirth. Mionnet found himself thinking of Alexander VI, though why of him rather than of some other pope of the great age he could not have said. There was no historical reason why he should do so. But he could so clearly see her seated opposite Alexander VI at some intimate supper attended by the princes of the Church, in a room adorned with classical statues of Venus temporarily undraped for the occasion.

The evocation of this scene gave a style to the anecdotes, most of which, otherwise, would have been sufficiently wretched. M. Cotinescu told several which he had picked up during his stay in Paris. He claimed to have had an intimate friendship with the last Papal Nuncio, Lorenzelli, and to have known the notorious Montagnini, the Nuncio's former secretary, who had remained in Paris after the departure of his chief. If the Rumanian diplomat could be believed, Lorenzelli, at the height of his reputation, when he moved freely in the Parisian society which he loved so well, had been a man of great charm, though rather over-fond of money and in constant need of it. He had taken bribes—quite naturally, perhaps, seeing what his position was; but his demands in this line had been exorbitant and had led to his making many enemies. He had, for example, demanded from one lady a sum of three hundred thousand francs in consideration of a bishopric being conferred on a certain Vicar-General in whom she took a friendly interest. As a result of her shrill outcries, he had compromised for one hundred and fifty thousand.

This story, told with much wit by Cotinescu, provoked delighted response on the part of the Belgian guests and led to a light-hearted discussion of the question of which cost more, an Opéra dancer or a bishop. The "beauty" listened to it all quite unmoved. The youth was busy emptying his plate and devouring great hunks of bread. Mionnet was asked for his opinion without the question being made to seem in any way impertinent or pointed. The assumption seemed to be that they were all good Catholics together, who could enjoy a joke among themselves. It would only have needed the sudden appearance of anyone suspected, however little, of Freemasonry to produce an atmosphere of extreme respectability and of the utmost deference towards Mionnet.

Montagnini, according to the Rumanian, had been a queer fish who had profited by the confidential mission entrusted to him by Rome after the departure of the Nuncio to start a regular campaign of defamation. Not only politicians, whether republicans or not, not only the French prelates, including those most loyal to Rome, but even the families of the aristocracy whose devotion to the cause of the Church could be least impugned had figured in his confidential reports, not seldom in an extremely scandalous light.

". . . Not that they weren't witty. Here's one instance which I happen to remember—I suppress the proper names of the individuals concerned, because," added the Rumanian as though excusing himself, "that sort of thing's not quite in my line. Here it is" (and he continued, speaking slowly and stressing each separate word):

" 'The gentleman known here as Count X is well known as a member of several clubs—the Île de Puteaux, the Bois de Boulogne, the Société Hippique, the Union Artistique, and the Yacht Club, but he does not belong to the Jockey Club, the Royal, the Agricole, and still less to the Union—a fact which speaks volumes as to the woman he has married.' Don't you find that last phrase quite delicious, coming after an enumeration which, as it were, sums up all that is smartest and most typically Parisian in French society? . . ."

He was clearly expecting applause. But the Belgians, who had looked for something more toothsome, seemed unable to get the full flavour of the words to which he had drawn their attention. If they were to have a sample, they would, frankly, have preferred something really scandalous.

". . . But wait," continued the Rumanian, "that's not all. 'His baptismal name,' adds a note, 'is, quite simply, X. His wife, a certain Princess Z, a German, and a member of the reigning family, had urgent need of a presentable husband. To fit him for the post, they made him a Count.' Urgent need of a presentable husband! . . . What an exquisite touch! . . . And, to fit him for the post, they made him a Count! . . . Really, it's as good as anything in Voltaire!"

The Belgians were only too glad to show their appreciation of the words "presentable husband." They repeated "presentable" with a kind of burlesque exaggeration, and one of them remarked that it was the politest synonym for "cuckold" that he had ever heard.

Cotinescu expressed it as his opinion that Montagnini's anxiety to smirch the reputations of well-known people with scandalous gossip, most of which can have had next to no interest for the Roman authorities, had been a blind to cover his own blackmailing activities.

". . . I have it for certain that he was one of Merry del Val's creatures . . ." (Mionnet became more than ever attentive) "and that Merry del Val is enough of a cynic to have recourse to any kind of weapon. . . . But I am pretty sure that the Monsignor did a good deal of work in his own private interest. . . . I'm told that several people were called upon by someone with no official position who showed them the report affecting themselves. It was for them to decide whether they would like it quietly got rid of . . . and at what price."

He further suggested that it was from pure spite and to revenge himself on certain people (particularly on those who had been unwilling to accept his figure), as well as to leave behind him after his departure an inextricable web of scandal, that the Monsignor had allowed the French police to lay hands on the famous cigar-boxes containing 3,032 separate reports. He may even have arranged the details of the search. One could believe anything of such a man.

"It would have been so easy for him to have hidden the boxes somewhere where they would never have been found. The whole thing was perfectly childish. One thing is beyond all doubt—that he was expecting his house to be searched. He might just as well have had a lot of dynamite cartridges on the premises. He knew that what he had got would provoke no less of an explosion and would involve a host of victims. There was sufficient material in what they found there to set the whole country by the ears, spatter everybody with filth, and produce a state of modified civil war. There was one report, for instance, which informed 'Monsieur Piou,' that Clemenceau was for sale, but that his price would be high . . . and another, dated a few days before the Presidential elections of 1906—gracious! that's already seven years ago; how time does fly!—which stated in the most unambiguous fashion that Monsieur Doumer, one of the candidates, and quite possibly the next President of the Republic, was saddled with debts and wanted the highest position in the State simply and solely in order to balance his private budget. . . . You see the devilish cleverness of the whole thing? . . . The dynamite had been timed to explode after Doumer's election. . . . And what do you say to his leaving about a very confidential letter from an eminent Roman prelate whom we all know . . ."

(In a very low voice, and turning towards M. de Fontmonge and one of the Belgians who lived in Rome, he mentioned a name which Mionnet could not catch.)

". . . which contained references to the acknowledged mistress of this prelate as well as to two young girls and to two Roman ladies in all of whom this large-hearted gentleman appeared to take a special interest, while hoping that their existence would not come to his mistress's ears? . . . What do you say to that for a way of helping the police of a 'Freemason' government to discover the secrets of his most intimate friend?" (The Rumanian never for a moment raised his voice, but put the question with his normal air of unconcern and in his most honeyed accents.) "My own private opinion is that he wasn't any too fond of his most intimate friend, and that he counted on the Sovereign Pontiff, who is not accustomed to treat matters of morals lightly and would have been horrified to see all this dirty linen washed in public under the very eyes of the enemies of the Church, cooking his intimate friend's goose for him. . . . And that's precisely what would have happened but for Merry del Val."

The Baron de Fontmonge interrupted at this point to observe that, making full allowance for Montagnini's love of scandal, he couldn't have invented all he put into his reports.

"I never said he could," retorted Cotinescu. "The intimate friend's letter was undoubtedly genuine. . . ."

"I was thinking about the report on Doumer. I know for a fact that before the elections Doumer, who was known to hold high office in the Masonic movement, had been negotiating with Merry del Val with the object of getting the support of the Right parties against Fallières, thereby being guilty of black treason against the Republicans."

One of the Belgians asked whether the same sort of thing hadn't just been happening in connection with Poincaré's election. The Baron de Fontmonge, with a glance at Mionnet, replied very briefly that he knew nothing whatever about that.

Mionnet collected all sorts of details about the way in which, according to these gentlemen, the Papal police in Paris were organized. Their chief, it appeared, was an officer with the title of *promoteur,* who kept in close touch with the Archbishop and his staff. Cotinescu had been on terms of friendship with the *promoteur* at the time of his residence in Paris—a certain fellow called Adam ". . . who might, I assure you, have walked straight out of Balzac."

There was no reason to suppose that this intricate organization had been discontinued. At the time to which Cotinescu referred, the *promoteur* had had his spies everywhere, and counted a number of police officers on his pay-roll, as well as certain female agents drawn from the ranks of women who kept hotels patronized by the clergy. He had had the bishops watched. "And to think all this was going on at home, too!" thought Mionnet. "I never dreamed of such a thing. Oh well, where ignorance is bliss—" His mind turned to the hotel in the Saint-Sulpice quarter where he had been in the habit of taking his meals all last winter. Was there any man or woman there whom he might consider, now, to have been suspect? The landlady herself, perhaps? . . . As to the "Abbé Robert," it was pretty obvious who his employer had been.

There followed a discussion, conducted with much apparent knowledge, on the difference between the ecclesiastical police of Paris and of Rome. Not all the guests were in complete agreement on each of the facts adduced. One of them maintained that the Watch Committee, instituted by Pius X immediately after his election, and composed of three Seminary directors, was still functioning; and that the "terrible triumvirate" (all triumvirates, thought Mionnet, are terrible) continued to play an important part in the life of the city. Cotinescu, on the other hand, held that the Watch Committee was a thing of the past, and that a system of *promoteurs,* subtler and more discreet, had been adopted in Rome as in Paris.

It was at this point in the evening's talk that the word *"scagnozzo"* had come up. At first Mionnet could not make out what curious animal was meant by the term. His neighbours employed it half jokingly, half nostalgically, in a tone of melancholy regret. Ah, the scagnozzo! How much less picturesque existence in Rome would be without that familiar figure! Not to have known a scagnozzo was to have missed that odd, dreamlike quality which once had marked the Eternal City. Each of the guests contributed some salient characteristic of the genus scagnozzo and trotted out some story to illustrate it. He seemed to have been the equivalent—with certain added refinements and subtleties of his own—of the Neapolitan cab-driver, the Venetian gondolier, and the Parisian street urchin. . . .

". . . and the Montmartre art student," added Cotinescu.

Was he still to be met with? Opinions differed on that point. The Watch Committee had done its best to do away with him, but the type died hard.

"You won't find one anywhere; he's completely vanished!" said some.

"Nonsense!" retorted others. "As soon get the bedbugs out of a Calabrian inn as destroy the Roman scagnozzo."

"But," Mionnet plucked up courage to ask of the mistress of the house, who sat next him, "what exactly is a scagnozzo?"

She laughed indulgently, but with a suspicion of embarrassment:

"Don't you really know? It's not easy to describe. You've got to know the type to understand. Perhaps the best way of explaining would be to say that the scagnozzo was a kind of bohemian priest, drawn from many places, but mostly from abroad, and living no one knew how. It's true that they've almost entirely disappeared. They'd say a Mass for anyone for a lira."

"For fifty centesimi!" put in the oldest of the resident Belgians.

"For fifty centesimi, perhaps."

"And they'd do other things as well. . . ."

"Possibly."

The good offices of the scagnozzo formed the subject of another batch of anecdotes. Many of them, dealing with persons whose identity remained anonymous, were probably traditional. Others, centring on some dignitary of the Church who was still living and well known, were, perhaps, no less so. The narrator never failed to declare that it was "absolutely true," but a hoary air of antiquity hung about most of these stories. Even those least likely to be false had become, as it were, stylized.

Mionnet was thoroughly enjoying himself. Now and then he let his mind wander to some of his more high-souled and enthusiastic colleagues in Paris. "If only they could be here, listening to all these tales of cardinals, recounted without any show of indignation, just as though they were the most natural things in the world! Poor dears, what a shock they'd get! But of course they never would be here."

He imagined, too, the state of mind of certain anti-clerical journalists dropping in on such a conversation, like a dog with its nose in a bowl of soup, knocked over by the Heaven-sent gift, gobbling up the delicious morsels till they were sick. "That's what the Church is like!" they'd prattle. "Didn't we always say so? Now we've got 'em! . . ." As though this sort of talk proved anything against the Church! As though trivialities of this kind could affect the Church's long views and wide understanding, could keep it from adding stone by stone to its centuries-old fabric, or patching it where patching was necessary. . . . Heaven save us from fools!

Such scandal might be no more than a sort of Roman folk-lore, a variant of the street-wit of Brussels, but, for all that, it delighted him to think that the Rome of the Renaissance popes was not altogether dead.

He had enough of the critical spirit, however, to realize that all this talk of Roman ways came from highly suspect quarters. "It's as though I were to derive my ideas of the leaders of the Third Republic from the conversation of a lot of French conservatives. . . ." With the single exception of good old Dom Charles Magloire, the people with whom he had come in contact, profess themselves good Catholics though they might, were all, more or less, anti-papists, enemies of the Vatican, and, to a certain extent, anti-clericals too, though they didn't know it.

He determined, therefore, to listen to every kind of gossip that came his way, boring though much of it might be. But he was not the man to let others dictate what he should think about it all or what he should report to whomever it might concern.

Chapter 21

SMALL-TALK AT THE LACCHINIS'

At the Lacchinis' quite a different tone obtained.

Those present were almost entirely Italian. Conversation was kept at a serious level. A certain superficial familiarity of manners—rather as though the company consisted of people who had known one another since childhood—was combined with an extreme reserve wherever real views were concerned. Here, too, a number of stories went round, but what they betokened was not so much high spirits as a rather fine-drawn bitterness. Mme Lacchini alone showed any sign of exuberance.

As at the Fontmonges', and especially on the evening when Mionnet was asked to dinner, his hosts had obviously arranged things, in the matter both of guests and of the subjects chosen for discussion, so that he might get as much information as possible. He felt that an effort was being made to convince him that the activities of the present régime had been directed, from the very first, against France. It had been born of an Austrian intrigue. It had been greeted by a cry of joy long famous in Rome: "The reign of Pius X will be the reign of Austria," which had escaped the Ambassador of the Dual Monarchy on a certain winter's day of 1904.

A Monsieur Berletti, one of the deputies of the Italian Parliament, told how, during the Tangier crisis, an important Pole, one of his intimate friends, had been received in audience by Cardinal Gotti, Prefect of the Propaganda and consequently one of the most powerful men in the Vatican. Gotti, taking the Pole for a loyal subject of Austria, had said to him in a tone of confidential jubilation: "We're perfectly happy now. The fate of the Church in France no longer worries us. The Republic is doomed. In less than three months Germany will declare war, or manage to have it declared against her. France, of course, will be beaten. One of the conditions of peace will be the re-establishment of the Concordat. On that point we have His Majesty the Emperor William's formal promise."

M. Berletti, M. Lacchini, and some of the others present amused themselves by giving a list of members of what they called the *"partito tedesco"* at the Vatican and in the quarters most nearly in touch with it. One by one the names of various cardinals were mentioned. "But you've forgotten so-and-so . . . and how about the former Nuncio at Vienna?—I can't just recall his name." The persons cited were, one and all, the most celebrated members of the Sacred College and the Papal court—holders of influential posts, heads of congregations, directors of secretariats. Some, such as Gotti, Angelo di Pietro, or Steinhuber, had been German in sympathy from the first (Steinhuber was actually German by birth). Others, like Vanutelli (Serafino) or Vives y Tuto, the Spanish Capuchin, had needed a little persuasion. But they had finally been won over. Nor did the occupation of Rome by the *"tedeschi"* stop there. The Palace officials, the various prelates, and the holders of humbler posts, all were their creatures. They controlled about sixty religious houses in Rome. Many heads of orders took instructions from them. Furthermore, hatred of the anti-clerical régime in France, and a desire to revenge themselves for the expulsions, had led several heads of orders whom nothing less would have attracted to Germany—many of them were Frenchmen by birth—to join forces with the *"partito tedesco."* So whole-hearted had this movement been that all, whether they were Assumptionists, Dominicans, Franciscans, Spiritains, or Capuchins, had forgotten their disagreements and joined the conspiracy. In former days there had been a house—not far from the Lacchinis'—a little lower down the hill, in the Via Quattro Fontane ("quite close to me," thought Mionnet), where the conspirators had met (they still did, asserted Bonfigli, the journalist), and where some of the most violent of the many campaigns against France had been hatched. As for the Jesuits, it would be perhaps a slight exaggeration, despite the rather sinister figure of Wernz, their General, and a few others, to say that they were in the hands of Germany, since the Jesuits are never in anybody's hands. But though they might hesitate to surrender their liberty of action, they worked more often than not in complete agreement with the *"partito tedesco."*

Mionnet was asked whether he had had a chance of seeing a copy of the *Correspondance de Rome,* founded by Monsignore Benigni, who had been rewarded for his pains by several high offices.

He replied that he knew it only by repute. That was a pity, he was told. Bonfigli offered to let him look through a file of the paper.

"You read Italian?"

"A little."

"It would be necessary only for the first issues. Since then the paper has been printed in French, doubtless in order to get subscribers all over Europe. It's rather like the sort of bulletin circulated by certain business houses. Its appearance isn't up to much, but the contents are exceedingly clever."

Mionnet was assured that he would find there an incomparable collection of calumnies, false news, attempts at blackmail, imaginary interviews, abuse of all sorts, marked by extreme coarseness of expression and dictated by hatred of France and of everything to do with France. He would learn, for instance, that France had subsidized the anti-clerical and anti-monarchical agitation in Italy (a curious combination; no one would have thought that there was so strong a bond between the house of Savoy and the Church); that it was France that had engineered the assassination of the King of Portugal and fomented the plots against the King of Spain. Her finances, however, he would gather, were in a hopeless state, her army disorganized, and her people ripe for revolution. The much advertised cessation of religious persecution?—a bad joke. Churches were being closed every day. A condition of rot was spreading through the whole country. Eyewitnesses were quoted to prove all this. The expression "Paris, the Turk of the West," occurred frequently in the columns of the *Correspondance.* As to the Entente Cordiale, it was nothing but an invention of the Freemasons, a concern run by the Jews of England and France. The only prospect open to sincere Christians was the ultimate reconversion of France, like any other barbarous people, by missions . . . but that would come later! (after her defeat, it was implied, in the next war).

Someone else asked Mionnet whether any attention had been paid in France to the Eucharistic Congress held in Vienna in 1912. The cynicism of the "German party" had reached heights where the comic had gone hand in hand with the sublime. What had been the theme chosen by the Jesuit Father entrusted with preaching the official sermon? "The Relations of the Holy Eucharist with the House of Habsburg." Many eminent voices had been raised to declare that the hopes of the Holy See were set on Germany. Was it surprising, after that, to hear Pius X popularly referred to as the "Pope of the Triple Alliance"?—of a Triple Alliance of which Italy was ashamed to remain a member.

In the course of an evening party given during the following week, Mionnet managed to have one or two more intimate conversations. He met again a few of the dinner guests and made a number of fresh acquaintances. He tried to get some information about Merry del Val, whose name had not been much mentioned on the former occasion. Was he the head and front of the conspiracy? Those he asked seemed, after a little reflection, to admit that he was. Did not Merry del Val's official functions and the control which he exercised in all matters of Papal policy point to him as the responsible agent? They all, oddly enough, agreed that the influence of Pius X in these matters, for all that he was known as the "Pope of the Triple Alliance," could be discounted. But thinking over the various answers he had got to his question, Mionnet was of the opinion that the views expressed had been based on prejudice rather than on evidence. Merry del Val still remained for him a mysterious figure.

A Senator of the Kingdom of Italy, named Rivalta, to whom Mionnet had just been introduced, told him that the Secretary of State, speaking one day in French to an international group, had boasted that he had organized the Congress of German Catholics at Strasbourg for the sole purpose of getting a dig at "those French swine." (Senator Rivalta was careful to stress the word "swine" so as to make it clear that it was a quotation.) Nor was the Cardinal, it seemed, particularly fond of the movement towards democracy in Italy. In 1909, at the time of the Catalonian insurrections and the execution of Ferrer, he had announced his intention of approving publicly of the sentence of death. When he was told that if he carried out his plan, it might mean riots in Rome, he had cried: "I shall do it all the same. Italy can go hang!"

But, to be just, it must be admitted that he had been in bad odour for two years with Austria, because of the way he had bearded Aerenthal over the appointment of Granito di Belmonte as Nuncio in the teeth of Austrian opposition. He had never had an interview with William II, nor tried to have one. He had given audience once to von Bülow and once to Bethmann-Hollweg, but there was reason to suppose that these meetings had been little more than formal expressions of courtesy.

In Italy itself he was in favour of the struggle against the anticlerical and revolutionary elements; but there was no sign that he was trying to get either the internal or the external policy of the Kingdom into his hands. He had been against the formation of a Catholic party: *"Cattolici deputati, si; deputati cattolici, no,"* he had said, offering the phrase as a slogan to the various members of Parliament who came to ask his advice. Even now, when, despite this, the Catholic Party seemed bent on getting itself organized, the Cardinal had not weakened in his hostility to the movement.

"But," insisted Mionnet, "wouldn't it be nearer the truth to say that he belongs to no party? Wouldn't you say that his only passion is how best to further the interests of the Church?"

"Perhaps."

Elsewhere, in the alcoves of the drawing-room, as soon as it was known that he was curious about everything to do with Merry del Val, he was treated quite gratuitously to indiscretions of another kind.

One such conversation, in particular, took place between three or four gentlemen who were standing in front of one of the windows at some distance from the main groups of guests and well out of hearing of the ladies. Their remarks, exchanged in low voices, were couched in a tone of restrained mockery.

"Did you never hear the MacWrench story? . . . In France, naturally, not much is known about it. . . . You must get someone to tell you. . . . Who was MacWrench? . . . Quite a somebody, eh, Astolfo? A presentable sort of chap, actually one of the court chamberlains—a *cameriere di numero*—with, unfortunately, a weakness for '*fiammiferi*,' as a result of which he got into trouble with the police. The Secretary of State, who had been at school with him in Birmingham and felt, no doubt, under certain obligations in the matter, did a good deal to help him."

Somebody else added:

"I'd be careful, though, if I were you, about mentioning it too freely. It wouldn't make you too popular with some people."

A moment later Mionnet was made the recipient of another observation. At the time he did not trouble his head much about its implications; indeed, he was disinclined to take it too seriously, since the speaker from whom it came seemed rather too intent on making a witticism of the kind that is meant "for gentlemen only":

"The higher ranks of the hierarchy fall into two main groups. I don't refer to the 'pro-Germans' and the 'pro-French,' but to the 'pro-men' and the 'pro-women.' Until you get that clear, you won't understand anything."

Chapter

22

PRELATES OFF DUTY

The first time that Mionnet went to see Monsignor
Dougérin, Canon of St. Peter's, he was received in
that dignitary's small flat in the Canonica—spotlessly clean, reasonably comfortable, and decently furnished; the sort of place that might
have belonged to a middle-class bachelor in a small business, or to a
chaplain in one of the large Paris schools. But a few days later his
latest acquaintance asked him to dine at Fagiano's, in the Piazza
Colonna, to meet a certain prelate, Monsignor Z—, requesting him,
at the same time, to "forget the gentleman's name."

This Monsignor Z—, a Frenchman by origin, but for many years
domiciled in Rome, seemed to be living more or less in disgrace, a
state of affairs which appeared to have had its origin when the present
Pope was first raised to the Chair of Saint Peter. ("Another man with
a grudge," thought Mionnet. "I'm seeing rather too much of people
with grudges.")

Monsignor Dougérin himself had already been eloquent about his
grievances in the safe privacy of his private rooms. At Fagiano's he
developed and elaborated what he had already said. Mionnet soon
realized that the conversation would add little to what he wanted to
hear. Still, though the subjects of discussion might be a little disappointing, there was something subtly amusing about the scene in
which they were set. It had never, in the wildest stretches of his
imagination, occurred to him that he would find himself one evening
in Rome seated opposite two prelates in an alcove of a restaurant,
surrounded by gilt mirrors and faded plush, and within reach of be-
jewelled women and gentlemen in evening dress, who, like themselves, were accommodated with discreet tables in obscure corners

and seemed to find nothing odd in seeing three respectable-looking clerics enjoying an intimate little dinner in which liqueurs and cigars played a by no means unimportant part.

The grievances of Monsignor Dougérin and his friend were connected with the "internal" affairs of the Church. They reproached Pius X with having continued and intensified a movement started during the previous century by Pius IX, which, though not shelved, had at least been modified by Leo XIII; a movement marked by autocracy and fanaticism, tending, on the one hand, to destroy the liberties of the national Churches, which they had enjoyed as semi-independent organizations, in the interests of the Pope, whom a new doctrine, quite at odds with the age-old tradition of Catholicism, was bent on turning into an absolute sovereign; and, on the other, to set the Church in opposition to the modern world and the modern outlook, to make it face backwards, to turn it into a rigid anachronism instead of giving it sufficient suppleness to permit of its further evolution. Such a movement, they maintained, no matter from which of these two angles it was regarded, must end in death—death from suffocation or death from petrifaction.

It was not difficult for Mionnet to guess that both his companions had been involved more or less seriously in the modernist adventure and could not forgive Pius X for the harsh way in which he had broken it up. Neither of them seemed personally to have suffered severely, but many of the principal victims had been their intimate friends. On two separate occasions Monsignor Z— made significant reference to Tyrrell.

Mionnet felt secretly surprised that it should have been Monsignor Sérasquier, himself of such unblemished orthodoxy, who had given him an introduction to Monsignor Dougérin. But as the discussion proceeded, it became clear to him that the grievances of the two men, though superficially alike, proceeded from very different attitudes of mind. It was Monsignor Z—, the friend of Tyrrell, who seemed tarred with the modernist brush. Monsignor Dougérin's dissatisfaction came from a feeling of Gallicanism outraged by an unprecedented triumph of ultramontane policy. The difference between the two being thus accounted for, Monsignor Sérasquier's recommendation no longer seemed strange.

"I'm probably compromising myself again," thought Mionnet, "though I don't see quite how. . . . Perhaps things aren't turning out so badly after all. I'm still covering my tracks, though possibly without meaning to."

The old subject of the Jesuits was again brought up, and of Merry del Val as the creature and instrument of the Jesuits. Monsignor Z— stated definitely that the Cardinal had a Jesuit confessor whom he saw daily. The two prelates, however, were responsible for no other revelation of importance. The tone of the conversation remained more or less austere, and Mionnet dared not side-track it into more personal channels.

Chapter

23

THE QUESTIONNAIRE

During this time Mionnet wrote twice to Manifassier and received two answers.

In his own letters he asked to be excused for having sent so little information. He explained that it seemed best to him to go slowly, carefully categorizing his sources of information and striking, as far as might be possible, a balance between them all. If the authorities at home wanted quicker results, he begged his correspondent to let him know. He alluded to the steps he was taking and the contacts he was establishing, without, however, going into details or mentioning names. He said that there was considerable danger of drawing conclusions too soon, and a great temptation to do so, since people in Rome seemed more than willing to serve him up ready-made generalizations. He confined himself to a bare reference to the "German party."

Manifassier's replies, which doubtless reflected the views of Gurau, and quite possibly those of Poincaré as well, were to the effect that Mionnet's scruples were thoroughly approved, and that his wish to go no faster than he thought wise was understood.

A few days after the arrival of Manifassier's second letter, and before he had had time to answer it, Mionnet learned from the Italian papers of the fall of the Briand Ministry. The news came to him as a shock. "How will it affect me?" he wondered. "Will Gurau remain at the Quai d'Orsay?".

It was at this moment that Manifassier's third letter reached him.

Dear Sir:

I have been instructed to enclose the accompanying short question-naire. You will, of course, use your own judgment in filling it in. No one here wishes to stampede you. I should, however, be grateful if you would let me have your replies, whether complete or not, within ten days at the latest. Please make them as definite as possible. You can postpone until later dispatches, composed more at leisure, any doubtful points, and any arguments or proofs which you may think necessary to amplify or explain your immediate statements.

No doubt you have read in the papers of the fall of the government. M. Gurau will not be included in the new list of ministers. He is, I may tell you, far from being sympathetic towards what seems to be the now prevalent attitude in government circles. But since he is still on excellent terms, personally, with the President, it would be simpler, perhaps, if your reply, this once at least, were sent through the usual channels.

The questionnaire, in longhand on a single sheet of paper, was written in a neat, clear script which Mionnet, though at first he at-tributed it to Gurau, decided a moment later to be that of President Poincaré himself.

It comprised five questions, separated by wide blanks:

1. What is the personal background of Cardinal Merry del Val?

2. When did he first come into favour with Pius X?

3. Why and how has he retained this favour? How complete is it? On what terms is he supposed to be at present with the Holy Father?

4. What is the present position of Cardinal Rampolla? Is he a pos-sible competitor of, and successor to, Merry del Val?

5. What does the "German party" consist of? Is it organized?

The questionnaire and its covering letter had on Mionnet the effect of a thunder-clap.

He wasn't, then, to be allowed to pursue, at his own sweet will, the pleasant, the charmingly diversified, amble proper to the historian in pursuit of research, the compiler in search of material. He had got to produce, and that with the least possible delay, results; results, too, by which he would be willing to stand. He remembered vividly how he had felt years ago when facing a written examination—just so long, just an hour or two, to get down on paper "all he knew."

He felt the action upon himself of a will the keen edge of which made it imperious. For more than an hour he remained closeted with the questionnaire, doing nothing but contemplate each question separately, first one, then another, and conscious all the while of the fact that they teased his mind.

He realized that, for the moment at least, he could answer no one of them. An hour before he had flattered himself that he knew "a lot." This "lot," put to the test, revealed itself as exactly nothing.

He saw, too, that the glorious freedom of appreciation on the possession of which he had plumed himself, the margin of discretion which he promised himself, had now been narrowed, had now been confined, to a point at which it could be said scarcely to exist any longer. No more convenient vagueness. He had got to put down in black and white what he believed to be the truth of a series of facts, or to lie, knowing that each lie could be pinned definitely down. No room any longer for elasticity of interpretation, for vague approximation. His reply must be close-packed, with no interstices through which might slip a "perhaps" or a "possibly."

"Why should he have written it all out in his own hand—if indeed the hand is his? Isn't he afraid I might make illegitimate use of such a holograph? He trusts me, it seems. . . . Perhaps it is that men of great force of character disdain the use of petty precautions. Perhaps they bank on the loyalty inspired by such a display of confidence. . . . He has only seen me twice, once for twenty minutes, once for ten. No doubt he thinks that was sufficient to sum me up. . . . Maybe he's right. Possibly he knows better than I do myself that there are certain abuses of confidence of which I could never be guilty. . . . Of course, too, if he hadn't written it all out himself, he'd have had to dictate it to someone. But to whom? To some underling whose indiscretions would be more to be feared, because they'd be made more irresponsibly."

He set about clearing his mind for action. Quickly, but with as little confusion as possible, he passed in review the resources at his disposition.

There was his pocket diary in which he had carefully noted down every piece of information of any importance which had come his way. But scarcely any of its contents could be used without further inquiry and verification.

Then there were the people he had met, and might, at need, try to meet again; the localities to which he had access, and the things he had chanced to find there.

He tried to survey with calm efficiency every thing and every person: the Vatican; the Archivio Segreto; the Freemason keeper of the Victor Emmanuel Library; the journalist Bonfigli; the Rumanian diplomat; Berletti, the deputy; Rivalta, the Senator; Monsignor Z—; the Belgians, etc. . . . For fear of omitting anything, and in spite of his dislike of excessively methodical habits, he began to jot down on paper various ideas as they occurred to him. He marked with a cross all those names which seemed to him to represent sources of information so far but partially tapped, or points of departure for further journeys of exploration. The journalist Bonfigli, for example, and Senator Rivalta must have numerous contacts. Faced by certain definite inquiries, even though they couldn't themselves supply the answers, they would at least be able to tell him which were the right doors to knock at.

The same would be true, within limits, of Dom Charles Magloire, while a prelate like Monsignor Z—, who had been so long settled in Rome, must have seen, with his own eyes, many strange happenings in Church circles.

The trouble wasn't going to be the lack of information but its

richness. So much of what had come his way was mutually contradictory, and there was no time to sift out the true from the false. Ah,
it was to be no longer a question of learning how to idle, to weave
subtleties, to imitate the Provençal sportsman waiting patiently and
unmoved for the game to come his way. He'd got to work at full
speed, as though the house were burning over his head . . . botch up
a job in a week which he would have liked three months to finish off
properly.

But it wasn't a bad thing, sometimes, to work as though the house
were burning. It gave one a sense of drive, a feeling that one was
cutting one's way through stubborn obstacles.

The following thought also came to him:

"Running about as I shall be doing these next few days, I shall be
the cynosure of all eyes in Rome. If the 'black' police don't get wise
to me this time, they must be a pretty futile lot."

Chapter

24

MIONNET WRITES HIS REPORT.
LIGHT ON MERRY DEL VAL

Eight days later, in the evening, with the assistance of a scrap of paper on which he had noted the results of his various activities, jotting down, as they occurred to him, the names of places and people additional to his original list, he recapitulated the labour of a week. He was not displeased with the success he had attained. He had managed to have interviews, some of more than an hour's duration, with thirty-four persons, twenty of whom had been previously unknown to him. In the search for documentary evidence he had paid thirteen visits to libraries, archives, and files of newspapers. The work had been done in a mood of pleasurable excitement which he had found delightful, though this had not prevented him from exercising all necessary care, a consideration he felt he owed it to his reputation to observe.

He decided to spend the night going through his notes and preparing his answers. His Italian-Swiss room being cold, he wrapped his legs in the coverlet of his bed.

Towards dawn he read through the following text, putting to it the last finishing touches:

1. Question: What is the personal background of Cardinal Merry del Val?

Merry del Val (Rafael), Cardinal with the title of Santa Praxedes, was born on October 10, 1865, in London. He was the youngest son of Rafael Merry del Val, a Spanish diplomat of aristocratic antecedents.

Educated first at Baylis House (Slough, England); later in Belgium at the Jesuit colleges of Notre-Dame de Namur and Saint-Michel de Bruxelles; later still, in England again, also under Jesuit influences, at St. Cuthbert's College, County Durham. He completed his studies at the Gregorian University in Rome. All this moving about was due to the necessities of his father's diplomatic career. Merry del Val holds doctorates in philosophy, theology, canon and civil law. He was ordained priest on December 30, 1888. It is said that he intended to be a Jesuit, but his family, and the Jesuits themselves, with whom he has never ceased to be extremely intimate, had other ideas for him. He confessed one day, to an old companion who had remained on friendly terms with him, that his ambition was to die Archbishop of Toledo, primate of Spain.

2. *Question: When did he first come into favour with Pius X?*

The rise of Merry del Val had already been rapid under the previous pontiff. It seems to have been due to three causes: the fact that the first years of his ecclesiastical career happened to coincide with the presence of his father in Rome as Spanish Ambassador to the Vatican, where he was looked upon with particular favour; the esteem felt for him by his former masters, the Jesuits; the fact that his aristocratic manners were peculiarly sympathetic to Leo XIII, who was himself of aristocratic descent. It was by that Pope that he was appointed, while still a young man, as President of the Academy of Noble Ecclesiastics, the school of diplomats where future nuncios are trained.

At the moment (July 3, 1903) when Leo XIII was struck down by the illness which was later to prove fatal, Merry del Val was deputy to Cardinal Volpini, Secretary of the Consistory, the second of the Congregations of Roman Cardinals (after the Holy Office). By right of office, Cardinal Volpini was Secretary of the Conclave which would be summoned on the death of the Pope. He himself, however, died suddenly on July 17, 1903. Since it was impossible to announce this news to the dying Pope, the candidates for the tiara, of whom there were a great number, asked the Cardinal Camerlingo, Oreglia di San Stefano, on whom devolved by right the duty of acting as interim pontiff, to appoint a successor to Volpini. But Oreglia, who was himself a candidate, fearing to favour a rival or to make enemies by giving to one of his colleagues a post which would be of such importance at the forthcoming elections, or for other reasons still, having to do with the "German party," which we shall be studying later, preferred to keep matters in suspense, that is to say, to allow the young deputy Merry del Val—who, being neither a Cardinal nor Italian nor old enough, could not offer himself as a candidate, and who, for all these reasons, might be expected to be sufficiently docile—to become *ipso facto* secretary of the Conclave. This state of affairs materialized three days later on the death of Leo XIII.

During the extremely agitated Conclave which saw the election of Cardinal Sarto, after the Austrian veto had been declared against Rampolla, Merry del Val, who had been placed by fate in a position of importance, found it possible to render certain services to the victorious party and to establish claims over those now in power. Despite this, however, his final elevation would not have taken place—not so soon, at least—but for one last piece of luck.

Pius X, once enthroned, had the greatest difficulty in finding anyone suitable to hold the office of Secretary of State. Rampolla, who had held it under Leo XIII, clearly could not retain it, after a rebuff made more serious by the circumstances in which it had been administered. He remained, however, sufficiently powerful to prevent any of his friends from accepting it, and to make his enemies fear his vengeance should they do so. One after another, eleven cardinals refused the post, though for many of them, like Agliardi, for instance, whose gifts were, at most, mediocre, the offer must have far transcended anything of which they had ever dreamed. For two months Pius X laboured in vain to fill the office, and his failure to do so undoubtedly intensified his sense of an isolation made all the more hard to bear by the fact that the terrible burden of the Pontificate had been laid on him unsought. During all this time the Secretary of the Conclave, true to tradition, had remained the new Pope's right-hand man, dealing with all the routine matters of the department pending the

appointment of a Secretary of State. He was very young. He was not
an Italian. But the duties which he had performed in connection with
the Conclave carried with them the right to a red hat. The Pope was
perfectly free to choose whom he would as Secretary of State, the sole
necessary condition being that the man selected should be a Cardinal.
Pius X, therefore, fell back on Merry del Val. At the Consistory of
October he was made, at one stroke, Cardinal and Secretary of State.

While, therefore, one cannot altogether dismiss the theory that the
individual in question plotted, or got others to plot, this turn of
affairs, such a conclusion is not the only one possible.

3. *Question: Why and how has he retained this favour? How complete is it? On what terms is he supposed to be at present with the
Holy Father?*

Once raised so unexpectedly to the position of chief collaborator of
the Pope, Merry del Val was clever enough to make himself necessary
but not troublesome. He was careful to keep his activities strictly
confined within the limits of his office. Until then the Secretary of
State had usually regarded himself as a Prime Minister with a finger
in every pie (Rampolla is a good example). Merry, on the other hand,
held the view that his field was simply and solely foreign affairs. This
self-denying ordinance on his part was the more welcome since Pius
X, primarily a "religious" and not at all a "political" Pope, wanted
to have his hands left entirely free in matters of religion and to be
spared the tedium of politics. Of course, in the very nature of things it
has been impossible to keep the two fields of activity entirely separate.
It has happened that in dealing with certain states (France, for instance) the Vatican has found it necessary to subordinate matters of
policy to considerations of faith. On the other hand, situations have
arisen in which political prejudices have dictated its religious attitude.
But there has never been the slightest friction between the Pope and
his minister, since the personal views of the Secretary in matters of
politics have, seemingly, led him to court those governments with
which, for the moment, the Holy See has had no quarrel either in

religious matters or in matters touching the temporal interests of the Church; while, at the same time, those states against which the pontiff appeared to have a grievance, either purely religious or in connection with the temporal interests of the Church, have been just those which normally roused the antagonism or mistrust of the Secretary of State.

I think I ought to point out that it is not at all necessary to attribute to Cardinal Merry del Val personal prejudices in political affairs deriving from his own background as a Spanish aristocrat or from his Jesuit upbringing. Everything he has done is explicable on the basis of his concern for the well-being of the Church; nor is it safe to assume that his private preferences or dislikes have dictated his policy in tightening the bonds between the Church and certain governments rather than others. Similarly, as no one doubts that the present pontiff is passionately concerned for the destiny of the Church, it is but natural that the two men, each working whole-heartedly in his own way for the same cause, should find each other highly sympathetic. At the same time it is equally clear that under another pope, as deeply devoted as Pius X to his Church, but with definite views of his own on politics, the Cardinal might have found things more difficult and have felt his liberty of action considerably curtailed, or that, with a different Secretary of State, Pius X might have found his political sympathies differently aligned. Still more certain is it that a different kind of pope and a different kind of secretary of state, given the same historical circumstances, might have reacted quite otherwise, and thereby imparted to events a complexion of quite another shade.

Setting aside certain rather inconsistent rumours, there is no reason to suppose that, up to the present, there has been any serious difference of opinion between Pius X and Merry del Val on essentials, nor does it seem likely that, in the normal course of events, there ever will be.

The many strongly marked contrasts between the characters of the two men do not in any way weaken their mutual understanding; indeed, the fact that there are so many tends to bring them together as complementary personalities. For instance, it is not impossible that a pope coming, like Pius X, from humble parents and generally admitted to be extremely simple in his own outlook and to have no claims to worldly wisdom may, at times, have felt a certain timidity in dealing with a man of such aristocratic origins, such fine distinction, and such diplomatic astuteness; may even have led him to follow his minister's advice without question in matters of high importance. But whereas between two men of the same generation such timidity might, sooner or later, have turned to bitterness or antipathy, the difference of age has resulted in the Pope's adopting towards his minister an attitude of fatherly pride and benevolence.

The best chance for the Cardinal's enemies would have been to attack him on matters of faith or of private conduct, for there the Pope is neither timid nor a time-server. But the minister sets up to be neither a theologian nor a dogmatist, and he has always been careful to follow his master's lead in both fields, to the point of accepting its possible international repercussions, without permitting himself to question their least detail. In fact, he has always behaved here as a man knowing himself to be without the competence necessary to draw his own conclusions. Not only is this attitude of his highly satisfactory to the Pope, but it could hardly fail to discourage the Cardinal's enemies, no matter what their own reactions may have been to the pontifical position.

In matters of private conduct it does seem, if one can believe current stories, that Merry del Val's opponents could justifiably hope to find him vulnerable. But, so far as I can make out, nothing has happened. It may be that proof has been lacking, that others besides the Cardinal have felt themselves on dangerous ground or have believed that he possessed against them weapons as effective as those they could employ against him, with the result that there has been a general conspiracy of silence bred of the fear that certain matters might come to the Pope's knowledge, the possible charges being of so delicate a nature that even the most spiteful have hesitated to speak directly of them to the Sovereign Pontiff and have remained content to let him get wind of them by the roundabout way of general gossip.

5. Question: What does the "German party" consist of? Is it organized?

The "German party," as it exists today, seems to have had its origins in the intrigues which preceded, accompanied, and followed the Conclave of 1903. Ever since that time it has presented two main features: its centre of action is Rome, and it has connections and ramifications all over Central Europe.

Before the Conclave an agreement was come to between the Cardinal Camerlingo Oreglia and Puzyna, Prince Bishop of Cracow, which had as its object the defeat of Rampolla in his character as the favoured candidate of France and Russia, and the election of a pope who would be sympathetically inclined to the Central Powers. This was to be either Oreglia himself, should circumstances prove favourable, or somebody else, such as Sarto, the Patriarch of Venice, who, it was thought, would become an easy tool. This arrangement no doubt accounted for Oreglia's refusal to nominate a successor to Volpini, since it must have been thought that young Merry del Val, as secretary of the Conclave, would prove malleable and might, at a pinch, even consent to form one in the plot.

During the Conclave the intrigue underwent a double development. After the first ballot Oreglia, by refusing, on his own authority and without consulting the Conclave, the employment by those cardinals who favoured it of the *accesso* (a special form of the ballot), probably prevented Rampolla, who then headed the list, from securing a clear majority.

After the second count, when it seemed almost certain that Rampolla would win on the next ballot, in spite of Russian blundering, Puzyna brought into play the famous Austrian veto. As is well known, the Conclave made a show of not at once submitting, and a number of votes in the third count went to Rampolla. But that was only a face-saving manœuvre, and, in fact, Rampolla's bolt was shot.

During the autumn following, Taliani, former Nuncio at Vienna, a friend of Puzyna's, and personally very hostile to France, undertook the formation of a secret society of cardinals which had as its object to continue the work of the Conclave and maintain the political orientation of the new régime unchanged. It is said that, in addition to Oreglia, the following clerics were members of this group: Aiuti, de Pietro, Agliardi, Trieppi, Pierotti, and a number of others, most of them, be it noted, men who had served as nuncios in one or other of the German-speaking countries. Oreglia, it seems, acted as a connecting link between this group and the Pope on the one hand, and, on the other, the affiliated members outside Rome, of whom the most prominent were Puzyna, Prince Bishop of Cracow, whom I have already mentioned, Gruscha, Archbishop of Vienna, Kopp, Cardinal Bishop of Breslau, Katschthaler, Archbishop of Salzburg, and Skrbenski, Archbishop of Prague.

Generally speaking, this organization is still in being, though the personnel has to some extent changed. The German party has made several new recruits, among others the Cardinals Serafino Vanutelli and Vives y Tuto. In Rome itself it can rely upon an impressive array of sympathizers and agents. It has its creatures in the various departments of the Palace and in all the more important offices. Of the religious houses, sixty are German, as are the heads of several of the orders. A number of others, who are not, entertain bitter feelings towards France on account of the severe measures taken by the French government against the religious congregations and feel sympathetic towards those I have mentioned. Nor should we forget the many unattached priests, several of whom may well be engaged on confidential missions in the city. I will send you later more detailed information on these different points.

It is not easy to determine how Merry del Val stands in regard to the German party. Has he been, from the very first and of his own free will, one of their creatures? Has he only gradually drawn closer to them? Or, on the other hand, has he become increasingly independent of the party while maintaining an appearance of sympathizing with a certain number of its objects?

The whole question is complicated by a further point—the assumed existence of the "Triumvirate."

This Triumvirate (which must be distinguished from a far less important one which controls the city's ecclesiastical police) remains wrapped in mystery. Its composition is said to be Merry del Val himself, Vives y Tuto, and Gaetano de Lai, the eminent theologian (two Spaniards and an Italian).

The theory is that since the very first days of the present Pontificate these three men have secretly shared between them the whole government of the Church, Merry del Val taking foreign affairs as his department, the other two making themselves responsible for all matters of faith and internal discipline.

The alleged existence of this Triumvirate at once raises a difficulty. In handing over to Merry del Val the field of politics proper under a Pope who takes no interest in such things, the other two partners of the concern are giving him complete control of one entire department. He, on the other hand, has left them with a property already heavily mortgaged, since there can be no doubt whatever of the lively interest shown by the Pope in everything that concerns faith and morals. The most they can hope for is to fill the roles of privileged counsellors.

The connection between the Triumvirate and the German party raises a second difficulty. Vives y Tuto is popularly supposed to belong to it. Are we, then, to conclude that he represents its interests within the Triumvirate? Is it his duty to keep a watch on Merry del Val, whom the others suspect of pursuing rather too independent a policy, and to make him toe the line?

Remember, too, that it is quite possible that all this talk of a "German party" and of a "triumvirate" may be nothing but the dramatization natural to a people avid of conspiracies. It is more than likely that the whole thing really boils down to nothing more than sympathizers loosely grouped, and influences vaguely interconnected, without there being any genuine organization at all.

Since I am anxious to keep you informed of everything, I ought, perhaps, to mention two bits of gossip which may be entirely without foundation, and which you may well be inclined to suspect, living as you do in a world where personalities occupy a less important position in politics than they do here.

The first has reference to the part played in the past, and perhaps to be played still more in the future, by the subsidies given to various persons by certain governments. It is a current reproach among well-informed persons that France has too much neglected this particular means of influencing opinion.

The second piece of gossip takes the form of hinting that the grouping of persons based upon a similarity of ideas, on national, political, and dogmatic likes and dislikes, is crossed and superseded by sympathies of a very different kind taking their origin in a certain community of habits and tastes of a peculiarly intimate nature. I should have ignored all such suggestions were it not for the fact that they are continually stressed and repeated by men who have the reputation of being sober critics and experienced observers of the Roman scene. Once they feel that they can talk freely, they all tell the same story. I think it must be at least allowed that this odd factor may be of weight in a small number of cases, and that it serves to explain certain events which otherwise would be incomprehensible.

If the first of these two pieces of information is found to be reasonably accurate, some use might, I think, be made of it. Nothing, however, can be done about the second. Still, a knowledge that both exist ought to serve as a warning not to attach too great or too unqualified a value to the official attitude of the persons concerned.

Mionnet had hesitated some time before writing these last two paragraphs. He conjured up a vivid picture of the probable expression on the President's face produced by this conclusion of a report drawn up by an ecclesiastical correspondent, and he could not resist the temptation to include it, although he would not be there to see its effect.

He read through his dispatch once more from beginning to end to judge of it as a whole.

"I haven't really done what I meant to do. . . . So much for all my good resolutions! . . . So much for the man who had reserved to himself the right of 'saving Merry del Val'! . . . I haven't kept a firm hold on my material. Something seems to have driven me on, to have taken charge of my pen. Not, I think, any concern for the wording and phrasing of what I have written, not even a conscious desire to produce an effect, except, possibly, in the last few sentences. What, then, can it be? . . . Something very odd, very incongruous, which I can't help recognizing as a feeling for the truth. The fact is I've not been able to resist the necessity, once I'd got down to it, of bringing to bear on all this agglomeration of evidence the keenest possible intellectual application, the most objective and honest sifting of which I was capable. And since thinking of it in that way meant finding words for it, here am I, after all, setting down the truth without meaning to! . . . And now that it's there in black and white, the Devil himself couldn't make me alter a line of it. . . . It certainly is very curious that lying, in a case like this, should present such extraordinary difficulties to a man of my temperament . . . and that I should find it so hard to give up the peculiar pleasure I feel at this moment in reading what I have written and finding it accurate. What margin of free manœuvre have I left myself now, should I decide later that I genuinely want to 'save Merry del Val'? . . . Of course I haven't definitely accused him of anything . . . I've left myself, left him, one or two small, very small, loopholes of escape, but only so far as 'truth' permits. I'm afraid I've got a long way to go yet before I realize my ideal of a really determined character!"

Chapter

25

THE PALATINE, THE SCAGNOZZO, AND PAOLINA

The letter from Manifassier which Mionnet had just found waiting for him at the post-office contained the following paragraph, which, indeed, formed the gist of the message:

"M. P. has asked me to tell you that he has been enormously impressed by your report (so have I, for that matter, not that I expect my humble opinion can be of any value to you). He said several other very flattering things about you—one in particular, that if ever the Embassy were re-established, it would be a real tragedy to think that your appointment would be against all precedent, since obviously you are the very man for it. So now you know! I rather think he's waiting until he's got a free moment in order to go over your dispatch more in detail with a view to asking you several further questions. In short, you are in the highest favour. No need for you to worry about whether you're to be kept at your post, nor whether you'll get the help necessary for the proper running of your show. My boss's successor has even gone so far as to say that he'll open a credit account for you if you think it might help you to force certain doors or get additional information. You would, of course, have absolute freedom to use such funds as you should think fit. So you see that the change of Ministry hasn't affected you. If, too, as you seem to suggest in one of your paragraphs, you find it possible, sooner or later, to win over to our side some of the more influential folk in Rome, the people here are only too anxious for you to go into the whole matter in detail and let them know the kind of sums you think would be necessary. I needn't warn you to tread very carefully. Go on using me as your letter-box until further notice. Employ double envelopes if you'd rather; but it's not absolutely essential."

Mionnet re-read this passage several times, rolling it round his tongue. He was a bit surprised that Gurau's successor—it was Pichon —should not have transferred the office of "letter-box" to one of his own staff. He reflected, however, that the arrangements at the Paris end were none of his business. Then, feeling that he deserved a little recreation, he decided to banish all thought of politics from his mind and to take a stroll on the Palatine, which, so far, he had been able to examine only hastily in passing.

On his way thither, and even after he had reached the summit of the hill, he amused himself by occasionally recapitulating certain portions of his report. "I wonder," he thought, "whether it was this the President liked so much," and, a moment later, "Or that? . . ." His phrases took on for him now a new air of authority, spoke to him in the confident tones of partners in an acknowledged masterpiece. "To see history being made, to be in the thick of things, to be an actor in the great pageant—ah, that's life!" He thought with pitying disdain of the mere student of the past he might have been—a scholar disputing with some fellow-specialist in Jena about the name of one of the negotiators of the Treaty of Westphalia.

He realized at once that his first impressions of the place had been fully justified. Certainly the Palatine was the most thrilling of all the sights of Rome, the place above all others capable of rousing a temperament like his to enthusiasm, of fascinating him with its associations.

According as one looked at it, it could figure as a garden run to waste about a kernel of old ruins, or as an agglomeration of ruins set in gardens. There was just the right amount of fallen glory—sufficient to calm the spirit without depressing it. The casual wanderer could take his pleasure here without feeling oppressed by the relics of the past, without feeling like an insect caught in some monstrous monument to a dead world. In the Forum one was obsessed by a sense of destruction, but not here. The ruins on the Palatine did not, as elsewhere, produce the effect of being lost in the surrounding scene, did not depress the visitor with a sense of all-enveloping melancholy, but seemed set about the place like picturesque objects in a park. Somehow the whole setting appeared to have come once more into its own, to be fulfilling a definite function, so that it impressed itself upon the mind of a visitor as a type of ideal town-planning. Why, the stranger might ask himself, did not every great city have some such large open space, easily accessible, charged with historical associations, raised above the surrounding streets, closed to wheeled traffic, kept only for pedestrians who were willing to waste occasional hours, leading nowhere, but ideal for leisurely sauntering, for reading, for idle dreaming; a place for lonely contemplation at the heart of packed and busy thoroughfares?

Solitude and height. The Palatine was a lofty hill, well shaped, sweeping upwards to a spacious summit, and surrounded on all sides by steep escarpments falling sheer to the plain beneath, with precipitous paths and high-perched belvederes, and balconies opening onto space. It was like a tower, like the lofty platform of some monument dominating the huddled town.

There was something about this curious wilderness that partook at once of open country, of suburban quiet, of a museum set under the sky's wide sweep, of an abandoned cemetery, of a market-garden, of an open-air restaurant. There was about it the air of one of those patches of grass and flowers framed in grey walls and lovingly tended by the caretaker of some historic castle. Mionnet could not help thinking of the sheltered walk at M— whither he had loved to climb at the day's end from the "lowest part" of the town.

Now and then a countryman would stop for a moment, outlined against spaced old trees; the cumbered masonry at his feet, and all around him the luminous air. He would fall quite naturally into the attitude of people seen so often in pictures and engravings of Italian landscapes popular between 1750 and 1850. In such compositions there is always a solitary form motionless against the view. If it is a woman, she carries a basket on her head; if a man, he leans against a fountain or the shaft of a broken pillar, gazing about him with an air of familiarity and detachment. "It is here that everything one reads of in books has happened. We are shepherds, peasants, wandering musicians; but, first and foremost, we are the guardians of these ruins, placed here to bear witness to the past."

Smothered in a dark luxuriance of leaves, a few trees had still retained their buds, and the grass between the half-buried masonry was starred with tiny flowers. The northern belvederes looked onto deep gulfs of shadow still damp with winter moisture. From the Forum rose a faint subterranean smell, as though the stuff of history lay rotting underground. But the southern belvederes lay already in full sunlight. Between the two the springtime of the Palatine ran riot, dark cold and limpid warmth commingled; flowering grass and ancient stones covered with inscriptions: AVIT. IDEMQUE. PROBAVIT. . . . In such a scene love must automatically find a place. It remained but to determine in what form it should appear, what garments it should wear, what pose adopt. It would have been pleasant, Mionnet thought, among these hillside paths, to be a layman and in love.

For some minutes he had noticed, not far from him, another ecclesiatic of shabby appearance, who seemed to be taking the same walk as himself. Each time that Mionnet stopped, he stopped too. His air was aimless. He looked now at some tombstone, now at a flowering shrub, without seeming to attach much importance to what he saw. After a while, and still keeping his distance, he began to smile and nod his head.

He was thin and quite young. He was dressed like an Italian. His shabby soutane hung lower behind than in front. His face looked yellow, but it was partly hidden beneath several days' growth of beard. The bristles, however, did not conceal the hollowness of his cheeks. His eyes were dark and shining.

Mionnet felt irritated by this constant proximity and tried to shake the stranger off. For a moment he thought he had succeeded. He had turned sharply to his left, taking a path at random through the trees. Very soon he came to a clearing where several ways met. The sun struck pleasantly through the young leaves on a little group of what looked like flagstones or tombstones half buried in the ground and leaning crazily together. Patches of old moss and a few weathered capitals completed a scene at which it was impossible not to look.

Mionnet gave a start. The grubby priest was close behind him and was saying in the most friendly manner possible, and in correct but sibilant French, that he must have missed his way, since there was nothing to be seen there and the path did not lead back to the city.

Mionnet was not surprised at being addressed in French. He was wearing his Paris hat, having long ago given up using the one he had bought. He might have snubbed the intruder, but it suddenly occurred to him that here before him was a scagnozzo in the flesh. Wasn't this a Heaven-sent opportunity for making the acquaintance of the type? What risk did he run more severe than having possibly to part with a lira? There was nothing to compromise him in such a meeting.

It came to him—after all he'd heard at the Lacchinis' and the Fontmonges'—as just conceivable that the fellow might be a tool of the "black" police, set to shadow him and bait a likely trap. But even if that were true, it was no reason for keeping him at a distance. It merely meant that he would have to watch his step pretty carefully.

In reply to this opening, therefore, Mionnet declared that he had no intention of going back to the city, and that, in fact, he was but taking a casual saunter.

"Would you like me to show you the Palace of Caligula? I can describe it all splendidly. It's very interesting."

Mionnet replied that he knew the Palace of Caligula. He resumed his walk, choosing his own direction. The only notice he took of the scagnozzo, who meekly followed, was to ask him:

"Where does this path go? . . . Do you know what this ruin's called? . . . Which church is that down there?"

He very soon felt certain that the scagnozzo was quite ignorant of his identity—unless he was acting a carefully studied part, an assumption that his whole appearance made extremely improbable. The man exhaled an air of degradation too complete to have been assumed. It was obvious that he looked on the French Abbé as a Heaven-sent opportunity, but only for trivial personal gains. His cunning was as crude as his indiscretion. He seemed extraordinarily anxious to get Mionnet to admit that he had arrived the day before with a band of pilgrims from the neighbourhood of Lyons, and that he was to be four days in Rome. He offered himself as a guide for Mionnet's leisure hours during that time. He would show him everything in much pleasanter conditions than he would find if he had to trail around with a crowd of tourists behind a professional cicerone dripping platitudes. He would do it all for a reasonable sum down— say fifty lire for the four days. Too much? Well then, how about forty? The French always had money to burn; he had lived in France himself and he knew. Forty lire was nothing for a Frenchman, though of course since the Separation the clergy weren't as well off as they used to be. Thirty, then. No doubt the French gentleman was curé of a big parish, where the least important service must bring him in more than that.

Mionnet was careful to give only evasive answers, couched in a tone of pleasantry. He encouraged his companion to prattle about himself. He learned in this way that the scagnozzo had been born at Salerno of a noble and "very rich" family which had come originally from Naples, and that one of his sisters was married to a Neapolitan count. He had lived for several years in France—he was reticent about the circumstances—in the Alpes-Maritimes. According to his story, he had been assistant priest at the Cathedral of Nice (where his special duty had been the confessing of Italians from the Old Town), and later locum at Lucéram during the curé's absence on sick-leave. He had got into trouble there as a result of "local spite," and from that time had dated the beginning of his misfortunes.

At a further stage in their conversation Mionnet, who had carefully led the talk back to Lucéram and its affairs, managed to get from him a few more details. "Local spite" had taken the form of a rumour that he had been the "fancy boy" of a very rich lady from abroad; that the lady in question had settled down in Nice simply to be near him; that that wasn't by any means all, since, the lady being thoroughly depraved, unspeakable orgies had been staged, sometimes in her villa, sometimes in the priests' house—orgies to which had been lured young girls from the neighbourhood, and, in particular, the Children of Mary. These charges—wholly unfounded, he need hardly say— had been merely a pretext. What the people had really objected to had been the Abbé's Italian origin.

"You see, they simply loathe Italians!"

On their way down the eastern slope of the hill, Mionnet tried to rid himself of his companion by offering him two lire; but the latter, with a sudden mysterious drop of his voice, asked whether "it would interest him to pay a visit to an old and extremely pleasant house situated near the San Sebastiano Gate."

Mionnet, a little uncertain what the object of this particular opening might be, let it be seen that he was waiting for further details. But the scagnozzo confined himself to veiled references. The people of the house, he said, were quite charming. If the gentleman would allow him to make the introduction, he would be sure of an enthusiastic welcome. If he didn't like it, he needn't stay. But the odds were he would like it enormously.

The nature of the proposal became clearer when the stranger added:

"No one need see us going there. I will wait for you this evening by the entrance to the Colosseum, close to where we are now. It'll be quite dark except for a moon. The family's highly respectable. The father's head gardener to a marquis attached to the court."

Then, as though reading the other's thoughts and fears:

"It'll be a nice little memento of your visit," he said. "I know the way perfectly. . . . If you are nervous, leave your money behind. But you'll need about thirty lire."

His last words were prompted by something he detected in the expression of his companion's face:

"It's not at all what you think. Don't go by your experiences in France. You'll find yourself welcomed by a real nice family. If I didn't think them nice people, I wouldn't take friends there."

Mionnet realized with considerable pleasure that the scagnozzo was leading him towards what was, after the Palatine, one of the most individual, the most secret, of all the quarters of Rome. It comprised an extensive region lying between the Colosseum, the San Sebastiano Gate, the Baths of Caracalla, and the gate leading to Saint Paul Without the Walls, a sort of waste land that looked surprised at finding itself within the circuit of the city limits. Mionnet had been through it by day. Lanes, thick with dust a few hours after rain, led between long old walls, themselves little more than dust solidified, which might have been the boundary marks of country estates. Above them, here and there, a house roof could be vaguely glimpsed. Southern trees were set about in scattered groups, and an occasional cypress, a solitary yew, seemed islanded in wastes of sky. Cross-roads were few and far between. Now and then a country cart, drawn by a mule, passed slowly, starting little swirls of dust that settled into a thin mist upon the air. Or it might be a hired cab taking tourists to the Via Appia, the skinny horse, with hanging head, ambling at something between a walk and a trot which was just sufficient to shake its hind quarters into spasmodic movement and set the bells upon its collar jingling. One could imagine behind the long walls market gardeners living their quiet lives protected by the walls of Aurelian from their melancholy neighbours of the Campagna, but separated from the city of today by a wilderness of ruins; or impoverished families of the old noblesse, many of them little better than peasants, lying there hidden away from the cares and duties of society, coming back into the world only on great occasions, hugging themselves in the pride of their vast old houses and wide lands kept still intact at the very heart of Rome.

More than most places in the city it set the mind dreaming of that Rome to which older travellers had come seeking the sentimental thrill of decaying grandeur, prepared to gape in wonder at so many things once great, now humbly dreaming, at famous sites resigned and ruined, reduced to a nameless dust hedged in by fields and shadowed by tall trees, symbols of what all around must come to in the end, rich with a promise of final peace, of something transcending mere collapse, to which the monuments still standing must ultimately attain. The whole scene was a precious gift from Heaven for those who sought to find less the deep heart of melancholy than the pleasing contrast which it made to present happiness, who could feel grateful to life for holding tenaciously and without fuss to the background of its former triumphs, springing like flowering grasses from the fissures of a dead world. What better fate for the ghosts of ancient loves and pleasures and fair vices than to find a last home behind the vista of old walls, tracing on memory's page a fading souvenir of youth and vigour, as though intent on proving that man is something more than a plaything of time's passage, more than the scattered dust of his own activities? There is peculiar pleasure in feeling thus man's mastery over time where all around the earth is buried in the rubbish of dead glories, set for the human eye to scan at leisure in the bright glow of morning hours.

Mionnet felt beneath his feet the dusty surface of the lane that lay, almost like a pointer, straight in the pathway of the moon, which, true to the other's promise, had risen, punctual to the tryst. Shadows lay beside them as they walked, here of a wall, there of a clump of trees, a sharp-edged patch of blackness, more welcome here than in the northern lands, trailing long arabesques of shade, or feathery tufts like thickset ostrich plumes. Elsewhere, glimpsed above the top of a wall, hidden deep in a garden, the window on the first floor of some house shone with a single light behind its panes. Alone there, perhaps, a single watcher, gazing towards the west, could see afar the Colosseum, dimly shining, a pattern of light and shadow beneath the moon.

They came to a courtyard leading off to their right into dim mysteries of a garden, and then suddenly close on their left, two blocks of building. The one farthest to the side had two storeys. It was hard to make out its details, for it faced away from the moon, and none of the windows were lighted; but it was just possible to note a certain beauty of line that graced it. The block straight ahead consisted of but a single floor, and the moonbeams struck at an angle across the fronting wall. It was a building of a very simple type. Lights burned behind two of the windows.

They were introduced into a large room, one end of which served its rustic owners for the purposes of eating, while the other was furnished as a drawing-room. A man was seated there with two very young children. The woman who had admitted them, and whom now they could see better, was dressed very neatly in working-class clothes, a black bodice adorned with a chain and pendant of gold, a black skirt hanging in many folds above several thicknesses of petticoat. She was bare-headed. Her smiling face was smooth and brown-complexioned, thin too, and wrinkled. In age she might have been about forty. The husband, scarcely older, was a man tending to fat. Clearly he had changed his working-clothes for a black suit, grown too small, which made him look as though he were dressed for Sunday. He wore a golden chain across his waistcoat, and a thick wedding-ring on his finger. In the drawing-room end of the apartment one whole space of wall was occupied by a large, low divan, above which presided one of those strips of cheap tapestry on which are represented well-known monuments or views of famous cities, picked out in crude colours. This particular example had as subject the Tiber above and below the Castle of St. Angelo.

The two children were seated on the matting which formed the covering of the earth floor. They were playing, or rather, it would be truer to say, were occupying themselves with as little noise and movement as possible. They were arranging dominoes so as to form lines of ramparts, the shape of which they changed from time to time.

On the walls of the room hung several sacred images and two or three pictures apparently representing scenes from the Risorgimento.

The whole atmosphere of the house was one of respectable domesticity, eloquent of the fact that its owners were happy and contented in their social status—an old-fashioned virtue which flourishes in periods of stability and security of tenure, when, in however small a way, there is some prosperity to be enjoyed, though here it was of such modest proportions that in more northern climes it would have taken on the appearance of poverty. But at the time with which we are dealing such virtue was commonly to be found among the people of Italy.

Introductions were reduced to the bare minimum, merely, as it were, glanced at in passing. The scagnozzo and the couple of the house had immediately embarked on a voluble conversation conducted in low tones and in what was probably the Roman dialect, so that Mionnet could understand very little of what was said. It was punctuated with smiles, friendly nods of the head, and an occasional understanding glance at Mionnet. It seemed to be composed of platitudes about the weather, trivial small-talk, and remarks of which he appeared to be the object, each of the several themes alternating with the others at the will of the speakers.

Finally the woman disappeared and returned in a moment or two, pushing before her a young girl who would have been taken for about twenty in Paris, though here, in Rome, she was probably not more than fifteen or sixteen. She had dark brown hair, a pale skin, and good features, though the oval of her face was a shade too strongly marked. The general effect was of considerable beauty, in spite of a precocious tendency to softness and plump lines. She smiled rather shyly, gazing at the visitors with frank but far from impertinent curiosity. There was nothing equivocal about the pride with which her mother displayed her charms. As to the father, he kept his eyes half-lowered as though he had had but a small and unimportant share in the work which the newcomer was good enough to view with approval.

"You like her?" asked the scagnozzo in his ordinary tone of voice.

"She is charming!"

The reply was marked by a note of sincerity as well as of politeness.

The young girl sat down rather timidly on the extreme edge of the divan. There was an attempt at general conversation. Mionnet tried his Italian. Every now and then the scagnozzo put in a word to make his meaning clear and to explain to him what was said in return. Each of the persons present managed to talk with animation, though nothing definite was said by anyone. The young girl, who was called Paolina, spoke little but regarded the company with a sort of secret smile.

Taking advantage of a moment's silence, the scagnozzo leaned towards Mionnet and, without taking the trouble to lower his voice, said in French:

"You like to sleep with her tonight?"

Mionnet, a little nonplussed, fumbled for an answer. At last, his eyes on the young girl, he said:

"Well, I don't know. . . . I think I'd rather come back tomorrow in daylight. . . . Wouldn't that be better?"

The scagnozzo seemed worried.

"Perhaps it would . . ." he said. "But you'll give me a little something now?"

"Yes, yes, of course."

"How much?"

"We'll settle that later. You can be easy on that score."

The scagnozzo gave a sigh and appeared to resign himself with the air of a man who has perhaps expected rather too much. He stroked his cheek with his hand, and the grating sound of the stubbly beard could be distinctly heard. Then, turning to the mother, he explained something very rapidly. It was the woman's turn to look worried. The girl left off smiling; then, as though changing her mind, smiled again, but with a rather constrained expression, while she glanced from one to the other of the two men.

Mionnet plucked the scagnozzo by the sleeve. "Tell them I want to be sure, before I arrange to come back tomorrow, that the girl won't mind."

No sooner had the scagnozzo translated the words than an expression of happy relief appeared on the faces of the two women. Encouraged by her mother, the girl smiled at Mionnet as though she had been his affianced bride.

They went home by another road. The moon threw their shadows before them. So deep was the silence that it was difficult to believe that they were within the boundaries of a great city. The only sound was the song of birds, among which Mionnet thought he could recognize the nightingale. The air was filled with the smell of dust, crushed leaves, and burning wood. Mionnet, who knew nothing either of Africa or of the East, decided that the night had "something Arabian" about it. He felt full of kindliness for every form of life that was not boring. He thought of the coming afternoon. It might, with luck, be perfect. Many different arrangements of circumstance, he told himself, might equally deserve the qualification of excellent, provided one was not fool enough to generalize.

Chapter

26

MAYKOSEN WRITES FROM ROME. FURTHER LIGHTS ON MERRY DEL VAL. THE "SECT"

(Translated from the German)

I must beg Your Majesty's indulgence for not having sooner sent Your Majesty what news I had. But since arriving here, I have had a great deal to do in order to probe more deeply into certain questions which it is my ambition to master fully. I have found Rome more confusing than ever. The place is like a basket of slippery eels. Each time I have felt on the point of drawing some definite conclusion, some conversation I have had or some fact that has come to my notice has made it necessary for me to start my investigations all over again.

I will jot down my results in order.

1. *Intrigues with France.*—Despite the interested denials which have been given on more than one occasion to Your Majesty's government, and despite the lying statements quite recently made by San Giuliano, first to the Chamber and then to the Senate, where he had the effrontery to assert that the Triple Alliance stood four-square to all attacks, the secret treaty with France is more than a mere legend. It dates as far back as 1902! This particular piece of treachery, therefore, is more than ten years old! Your Majesty will no doubt remember the many protestations of love and loyalty which he has received from Italy during that time. To be precise, it was signed in July 1902 by Prinetti, who has behaved throughout like the lowest kind of scoundrel. I cannot too strongly stress the importance of Your Majesty's bearing all this in mind and treating with extreme caution everything that comes from Italy. As people I adore the Italians, but as politicians they are the most slippery creatures in the world. It amazes me that anyone can be found still willing to sign agreements

with them. The treaty has never been denounced. It provides for the neutrality of Italy in the event of war breaking out between France and Germany. Many people here believe that since Giolitti's departure it has been elaborated by the addition of new articles and by arrangements of a military nature. However that may be, it is quite certain that Poincaré hopes to get more. Should war come, he would make the most strenuous efforts to loose Italy against Austria—which wouldn't, unfortunately, be very difficult. Hatred of Austria has remained a very vivid reality in this country, and it must be admitted that the policy of the Dual Monarchy has not always been of a kind calculated to lessen it. The main charge against it is that it has been supercilious. Italian policy is the product of a curious mixture, not easy to capture in words, of calculation and nervous self-love.

A view very generally held here, and very dangerous, is that the victory of the Central Empires in a European war would result in an intolerable extension of Austrian influence towards the south, which would make life impossible for Italy; and that, on the contrary, the defeat of those Empires, however slight, would inevitably lead to the break-up of Austria-Hungary. Apart from the fact that Italy would thus be rid of an oppressive neighbour, there is a lively hope here that she would get a slice of the corpse. At the moment the tendency here is to think that the slice would be all the bigger if Italy had had a hand in the killing. Germany can hope to keep her as an ally—and to prevent her from passing completely into the enemy camp—only if she can give a secret undertaking that the Empire of Francis Joseph will be dismembered as the result of a friendly agreement, and that a fair share of the victim will go to Italy. There is, of course, always the risk that she might sell such an agreement to Austria, but it is difficult to see what she would get in return.

French intrigues have a strong backing in Freemasonry, which is very strong here (it is said that the King himself is a Mason), and in the support of the parties which are heirs of the makers of the Risorgimento. The influence of these is considerable, even since the elections which have increased the power of the Right. The anti-clerical movement in France has certainly not prejudiced her in the eyes of a country that has had as many difficulties as Italy with the Papacy and is still officially at odds with it. The people, more superstitious than religious, are not very respectful towards the higher ranks of the hierarchy, which it has known too long and has seen at too close quarters. They certainly are not going to lose much sleep over the grievances of the Vatican against the French government. The fact, too, that the present Pope is thought to be very friendly towards, as well as indebted to, Austria makes it easier for Italian patriots to understand the attitude of France. Given a quarrel between the Pope and Austria on one side and France, anti-clerical and anti-Austrian, on the other, their sympathies would naturally be with the latter.

2. *The Catholic Party.*—The only thing that might profoundly, and at once, modify this attitude of mind, would be the organization of a strong Catholic party. Ever since the clever manœuvrings of Count Gentiloni, the elements of such a party have been to hand. The best observers think that this is the line that ought to be worked, and that the only way of ensuring that Italian politics will be inspired by feelings at least approximating to those felt by the Vatican for the Central Empires—in other words, the only way of making capital for international politics out of the fact that the population of Italy is Catholic—is to support the creation of a powerful Catholic party, which would take its orders from the Vatican and could easily keep in touch with the similar parties in the German-speaking countries. With such a party in existence, it would be much easier to persuade the majority of Italians that their place is naturally beside the Catholic inhabitants of Austria and South Germany and not beside those of France, riddled as they are with atheism and Freemasonry. France could, in that case, count only on the anti-clericals, who are already beginning to go out of fashion, and the revolutionaries and Socialists, who form but a small minority, and certain of whose leaders might be bought.

I have examined this argument pretty closely, and on the whole I think it is sound. If I may refer for a moment to a suggestion which has been transmitted to me as coming from Your Majesty, I should like respectfully to say that in principle the idea of distributing fresh subsidies as suggested seems to me a good one. But I take leave to point out that great care must be taken to avoid certain blunders. K.'s touch has been rather too heavy. May I say, in the strictest confidence, that he seems to me the wrong man for the job. He outrages the feelings of some by treating them crudely as though they were just so many individuals up for sale, or else he lets himself be cheated by others who take his money and then follow their own line. It is important to realize that this movement for a Catholic party contains many strictly honest persons who will only be antagonized by ill-advised suggestions of bribery.

3. *Merry del Val, the Vatican, etc.*—The whole situation is complicated by the position of Merry del Val. Many people here maintain that it is impossible to understand what he is after. The only thing certain is that he has never modified his opposition to the formation of an official Catholic party. Nevertheless, since his appointment as Secretary of State he has undoubtedly encouraged Catholics to take part in Parliamentary elections and in Italian political life generally. He has often, and quite openly, received in audience deputies who have come to ask his advice. K. goes so far as to suspect him of playing a double game. For two pins he'd suggest that he had sold himself to France—which is only another example of his over-subtlety.

Personally I can see only one explanation: the Cardinal is afraid lest, once definitely formed into a party, the Catholics may choose their own leaders and embark upon a policy which may not necessarily be the one that he himself thinks best. He believes he can keep a closer hold on them under the existing system. In particular he is nervous lest, in order to steal the Socialists' thunder, they might be tempted to play the demagogue—a prospect which, above all others, fills him with horror.

The possibility of a close alliance, however, between a Catholic party in Italy and its opposite number in the German states is not sufficiently attractive to outweigh with him the objections to which I have referred. And while I am on this subject, I should like to take the opportunity of commenting on a peculiarly crude error of judgment which has been expressed by several persons—not excluding a number in the immediate entourage of Your Majesty—and which might have very serious results. Those to whom I allude always talk as though Merry del Val had been got hold of once and for all; as though the Central Empires had but to raise a finger to set him working for the triumph of their policy. To think in this way is a grave mistake. I have good reason to know that he has already been seriously annoyed—and I am not now referring to the affair of Granito di Belmonte—because certain decisions were taken without his advice having first been asked on the principles involved, for he is not such a fool as to let himself be deceived by a mere show of consultation. If he thinks that certain people are playing with the idea of establishing between the Catholics of the Germanic lands and those of Italy a system of direct contacts which will have the effect of keeping him out in the cold so far as any action of importance may be concerned, he will undoubtedly be hostile to any orientation of policy in that sense.

Generally speaking, it would be the height of folly to throw away a trump card such as he represents. Cardinal Merry del Val has in the past rendered very great services—sometimes without meaning to, I admit—to the cause of the Central Empires. Many of Your Majesty's grandest projects for the salvation of Europe—now, alas, growing every day less likely to be realized—would undoubtedly have found in him an able and intelligent supporter. Given favourable circumstances, he may still, and even more than ever, be of the greatest assistance. But it is essential to treat him, and through him the Papacy, as a completely independent power, inspired by its own ideals and ready to co-operate with those whose views and whose interests are identical with its own, though never with an ally who regards it as a subordinate partner.

What I have just said of Merry del Val—and it is truer still of the Pope, in so far as he can be said to take any interest at all in politics—does not apply to persons of lesser eminence. I am all in favour of continuing the subsidies, but the list must be revised and proof of effective loyalty provided in the case of each recipient. Direct and even blunt interrogation might not be entirely out of place now and then. For this is one of the rare instances in which the method which I criticized so harshly just now could be usefully employed.

4. *The "Sect."*—Your Majesty cannot but know that for some time now I have been doing my best to get to the bottom of this problem, knowing, as I do, the importance which Your Majesty and certain august persons dear to Your Majesty attach to it. I am convinced that the difficulties most in the way of my getting a clear view of the position are due to the successive changes which have taken place within the organization itself; changes of the nature of which most of the members are themselves ignorant and which are of such a sort that no sooner has an inquirer got definite information on one particular point than the point in question is found no longer to correspond in any valuable sense to the reality.

One of the objects of my coming to Rome has been to meet somebody who may, I think, be able to throw light on this particular business. My expectation has proved itself to be well founded. Your Majesty will, I feel sure, forgive me if I mention no names. The individual in question made me certain confidences only on the explicit assurance that I would breathe no word of his identity to any living soul. Rightly or wrongly he believes that his personal safety depends upon the strict observance of this condition. Besides, Your Majesty will fully understand that the trust shown in me on this occasion is due entirely to the reputation I enjoy of never betraying my sources of information when asked not to do so.

One point seems to me to have been established beyond all doubt, and that is that the Archduke H. has been the fountain-head of the whole fantastic enterprise. The well-known mystic fanaticism of his character makes this at least probable. It is not, however, at all certain that he has not recently come under the influence of somebody else. Whether that is so or not, his own romantic tendencies and the kind of reading to which he is addicted would alone have sufficed to set him on a course so far removed from common sense.

It seems that at first there was nothing in the whole business but the noble illusion of an idealist. There is no need for me to remind Your Majesty that at the dawn of the present century there were, among those called by fortune to great responsibilities, many who were bound by a common feeling that civilization could be saved from disaster only if an effort were made to stop the armaments race and to lay the foundations of a durable peace. That, for instance, was certainly the ambition of Nicholas II, who, for all his weakness and mercurial disposition, may well have been sincere, even if his ministers were not. I have a lively recollection of the noble ambition which on a certain memorable occasion Your Majesty was good enough to mention to me, the object of which was, though by other means, more solidly based and marked by greater political genius, to guarantee no less the common future of Europe. It is not, therefore, surprising that the Archduke should also have listened to the dictates of conscience in the belief that they represented the will of God.

So far as I can understand it, his original intention, naïve perhaps, but innocent of all evil design, was to recruit in secret a sort of Order of Chivalry, consisting as far as possible of highly placed persons in various countries who would undertake, each in his own sphere, to rally all available forces against any danger that threatened, or looked like threatening, the cause of Peace. This fact has led certain people to declare that the "Sect" was an offshoot of Freemasonry. This I believe to be untrue. It may be that in its early days the movement took advantage of the accident that some of its members were Masons. But the method of enrolment was quite different, as was the way in which its resolutions were made known to the individuals composing it. It has nothing in any way resembling the meetings or ceremonies of the lodges. If an analogy is to be sought, it is much more with the

Italian Carbonari. The theory is that each member knows only the member who introduced him, from whom alone he receives his instructions. This holds true right through the organization. Another rule is that of implicit obedience *"perinde ac cadaver."* Was it the Archduke who drew up these rules? I have no means of knowing. If they have been rigorously applied, it is not difficult to see what immense power they must have put into the hands of the man or men at the head of the chain, or, rather, at the invisible centre of the network. Which makes it all the more necessary to find out the identity of the leader or leaders.

The first change occurred shortly after the movement was initiated. It seems to have had the effect of introducing terrorist methods instead of, or in addition to, the purely moral action at first envisaged. But nobody knows who was responsible for this highly important innovation. It was probably some individual or individuals—I lean to the belief that it was a single man, and I am trying to get on his tracks—who succeeded in dominating the Archduke's mind. Another possibility is that the new tendency first manifested itself among those who occupied a position as distant links in the chain, in which case there was no necessity to convert the Archduke to their views, since his orders—if it is indeed he who gives them—could have been profoundly modified without his knowing anything of what had happened. My own opinion is that, in fact, the Archduke has ceased for some time to be the effective head of the movement, and that the real leader is to be sought elsewhere. Who, then, is it? And what object is he pursuing? It may well be that the object has changed no less than the methods. Many of the acts attributed to the "Sect" bear a striking resemblance to the kind of thing that revolutionaries, concerned less to safeguard the peace of Europe than to provoke a general breakdown of Society, might have inspired their followers to bring about.

It has, of course, in popular opinion, been made responsible for a great deal more than it has performed. The only actual achievements which I have been able more or less to verify (I mean achievements on a grand scale, since quite possibly the "Sect" may have had a hand in a great many more or less trivial incidents) are, first, the kidnapping about which you already know, which so profoundly disturbed the court of Vienna, although at the time it was found possible to keep the facts from the public and to put about a more or less harmless interpretation to satisfy those whom it was impossible altogether to keep in the dark; and, secondly, the last attempt against the King of Italy. About the incident in which Your Majesty takes a more personal interest, I have not yet been able to discover anything definite. Some of the members are convinced that the attempt was timed for the Singer funeral, and that treachery alone was responsible for the breakdown of the arrangements. There is a story going about that the traitor has since been executed by some of his assistants. But this may be nothing but bravado on the part of the leaders. It should be noted that the organization of the "Sect" and the inability of the members to control the action of their chiefs make it easy to give currency to such forms of bravado, the object of which is to maintain the prestige of the invisible leaders and the morale of their scattered troops.

I have thought a great deal about the question put by Your Majesty: if the role of the Archduke can be ascertained beyond all shadow of doubt, would it not be possible to bring direct or indirect influence to bear on him, first by letting him know that his participation is common knowledge, and then by prevailing upon the Emperor and his entourage to take energetic action for the suppression of this intolerable state of affairs? But the situation is a good deal less simple than it appears. The Archduke may flatly deny the charge and show himself to be seriously offended by the suspicion. It is unlikely that he has allowed any material evidence to be accumulated against him, and it is certain that he has many accomplices in court circles by whose help he could easily be whitewashed. At the same time, I have an impression that as a result of this atmosphere of terror which has been carefully fostered and given a foundation of fact as well as of fancy, the Emperor, and a good many others as well, are thoroughly frightened, if not actually of the Archduke, at least of his associates, and would prefer to leave the situation in its present ill-defined state, provided they could get a *quid pro quo* in the form of an assurance of their personal safety. One mustn't, either, dismiss entirely the possibility that the Archduke is a prisoner in the hands of his followers and quite incapable of opposing their schemes except at the risk of his own life.

I have spoken so far only of the first change which has taken place in the policy of the group. But it seems that quite recently this change has been followed and complicated by another, even more disquieting, since it appears to have brought into play a whole new group of forces and to be fraught with political consequences that may be of the utmost seriousness. I have no formal proof of what I am about to tell you, and I am not prepared to swear that those from whom I have derived my information are not confusing several organizations which, in fact, have nothing to do with one another. In this world of secret agitators, so rich in madmen and visionaries, nothing is harder than to disentangle the real lines of connection. Even those most nearly concerned frequently have the wildest ideas about what is happening.

What is certain is that in the various geographical divisions of the Dual Monarchy, but especially in the more southerly districts, secret societies, numerically very powerful, have come into existence with the object of destroying the Empire and liberating the so-called "oppressed" nationalities. The most dangerous of these societies are situated in Croatia and the Dalmatian provinces. They are in constant touch with their agents in Servia, many of whom are in official positions and can help with money and influence. It is inconceivable that the Imperial police are ignorant of the existence of these societies, but so far they have been extraordinarily slack in dealing with them. The man here in Rome from whom I have got all this information maintains that these organizations form part of the general network centring in the "Sect"; or, to be more accurate, that they consist of members of the "Sect" who, though at first taking their orders from the central office, have tended more and more to adopt a purely selfish attitude and to further the attainment of the ends which most nearly concern themselves—namely, the emancipation of the various southern nationalities; a development which has come about quite naturally as a result of the many new recruits who have been made to the movement and who have brought with them their own peculiar political preoccupations. There is reason to believe that the original leaders, who never contemplated either this nationalist agitation or the dismemberment of the Empire, are fully alive to the danger. But these southern groups have acquired considerable power, not only as a result of their numerical strength, but because the lines of communication upon which the central authority has to rely to make its orders known are so long and so complicated that it has been found impossible to keep the outlying members in proper subordination. There has even been talk of a schism. Quite possibly there has been one, but if so, it has probably been less effective than was hoped, by reason of the extremely complex interconnection of all these many different intrigues. What seems most likely is that at the present moment not only the Archduke H., but other members, too, of the Imperial house, as well as a number of high functionaries both in Vienna and in the provinces, are more or less *emberlificotés* [1] and find themselves thoroughly compromised with a lot of scoundrelly agitators who are concerned only with the destruction of the Empire. Things seem to have come to such a pitch that nobody knows with whom or against whom he is conspiring, nor of whom he should be suspicious. As a result, the intrigues between Vienna and the south have reached a stage of unbelievable confusion. At various times various people are suspected of being involved, and it is pretty certain that a good many bargains have been struck and a good many people fooled. The only elements who stand to gain in the long run are those composed of the internal and external enemies of the Empire, who have nothing to lose by an accentuation of the present state of chaos. (Among the external enemies, Italy must now, I fear, be included.)

[1] In French in the original text.

I am convinced that if there were a strong man in Vienna, he could throw light on the whole business and quite possibly destroy the evil, but only on condition that he had his hands completely free. He would find himself, at a very early stage, up against highly placed individuals who, though they may never have sworn allegiance to the "Sect" or to any subversive organization connected with it, have all the same allowed themselves to be drawn into taking part in intrigues, into countenancing secret interviews, and into negotiating with the conspirators. Such is presumably the case of the heir to the throne, the Archduke Francis Ferdinand. Who has been responsible for getting him into such a position, frankly I do not know. Your Majesty has probably more information than I have on this particular point. I have heard it said that he has been deeply interested in the Slav agitation within the Empire; that he means, immediately after his accession, to rally the Slav elements to the monarchy by making them big concessions (possibly at the expense of Hungary, which is antipathetic to him); that in order to prepare such a policy he is anxious, as soon as possible, to win the goodwill of the leaders and agitators of the south; and that, as a result of all this, he has been forced to compromise himself in a number of necessarily secret negotiations and, unfortunately, has delivered himself into the hands of individuals who are a good deal clearer-sighted than himself. It is possible, too, that, believing himself to be threatened by the activities of the Archduke H., whom he doubtless holds responsible for fomenting the nationalist movement in the south, he has wished to be first in the field.

To sum up, I don't think I exaggerate when I say that the situation is extremely serious. It would be foolish to treat the business as no more than a fairy-tale. Should Your Majesty see any way to direct the attention of the persons most nearly concerned to this highly important problem, I respectfully urge Your Majesty to do so, in the interest not only of the Dual Monarchy, Your Majesty's ally, but in that of the Central Empires and of European Peace, which is gravely jeopardized by the present state of affairs.

I will not hesitate to keep Your Majesty informed should I learn anything further during the remainder of my stay here. But I think it unlikely that I shall be able to make many new discoveries unaided, though I may be able to learn the identity of the unknown leader. I have already a clue, though not a very reliable one. I suspect that he is of Asiatic origin.

So far as concerns the special subject of the nationalist Slav movement in the southern provinces of the Empire, I think I may be able to get a certain amount of information from Cardinal F. I am ready to see him myself if such a course seems likely to be fruitful. But he would have to be warned of the nature of my inquiries and show himself well disposed towards me.

Meanwhile I await Your Majesty's orders and take leave to subscribe myself

Your Majesty's must humble and most obedient servant,

MAYKOSEN.

Chapter

A SUCCESSFUL DEMONSTRATION

Viaur saw Hachenard waiting for him at the platform exit, holding in his hand a largish roll of printed matter. Contrary to his usual habit, he seemed nervous.

"Your train is late."

"It often is. But it doesn't matter. Have you got everything ready?"

"Yes."

"You've had the photographs enlarged?"

"Yes. One of the series, the one showing the carpenter's scar, hasn't come out any too well, though."

"Still, I hope it shows something?"

"Oh yes; and the others are excellent."

"No last-minute snags?"

"No. Pujac wants us to start at three instead of two forty-five."

"They're all going to be present?"

"I think so. Three or four extra ones are turning up unexpectedly, drawn by curiosity. Not a bad sign, that. Young fellows, contemporaries of our own. They asked me whether you'd mind. I took it upon myself to say you wouldn't. How about your subjects?"

"They'll all be there, I think. I noticed five of them on my train. The other two swore by all the Gods that they'd be on the next one."

"Do they all know where the hospital is?"

"I gave them each a paper with directions."

They walked down the boulevard Saint-Michel, gay with young leaves and brightened by crude sunlight shining from a blue sky dotted with white clouds.

"So everything's all right?" said Viaur.

"Yes. . . ."

"I shouldn't have thought so, to look at you."

"Oh, that's only because I've got all the details to see to. I want to be certain we've forgotten nothing."

"What's that in your hand?"

"I was just coming to that. It's a copy of *Science in the Modern World*. I bought it this morning. Your article's in it; the article, I mean, that that fellow Henry Champeaux wrote after he'd seen you."

Viaur felt suddenly very nervous. "How's it come out? . . . All right?"

"Oh yes. . . . You must read it for yourself . . . while we're having lunch, if you like."

Viaur wished to be reassured at once. "Not too idiotic, I hope?"

"No. It's obvious that he's a chap with a scientific training who knows his stuff. All the part where he describes how you came to undertake your experiments, and the reasons that led you to attach importance to your first observations, is very well done, very lucid, though it's a bit spoiled by one or two grandiosities."

"Grandiosities?"

"Yes—I mean, as though he'd been writing an obituary notice of Pasteur. He speaks of you as though you were a man of genius. I don't say you're not, but it makes everything rather awkward, don't you see?—mortgages the future, as it were. . . . What he says, too, about your actual experiments is quite good. It's the end I like least."

Viaur was conscious of a little stab of anxiety. "Oh! Why?"

"Well, he's rather gone off the deep end about it all. Those in the know, of course, will realize that it's nothing to do with you, but all the same there's an uncomfortable stunt feeling about the business. It would be a pity if those who are still unconvinced but not actually hostile were unnecessarily antagonized, and it's also rather foolish to put an extra weapon in the hands of our declared enemies."

"You're putting me in a blue funk! What is it he's been saying?"

"Oh, I don't suppose it seems anything very out of the ordinary to him—just in the day's work. All these journalists are the same. They assume that the public's become so indifferent to newspaper stories that nothing short of some tale of a miracle will get its attention at all. . . . He says that you've shattered the whole existing fabric of physiology and medicine . . . that this discovery of yours is the most revolutionary thing since—oh, I don't know when—Pasteur or Claude Bernard. . . . For two pins he'd undertake that you could cure any illness under the sun in next to no time. He certainly says things that, taken at their face value, make pretty stiff going. He mentions cancer. According to him, you're the kind of chap who'll be coming along in a week or two with a cure for that. It's a pity you didn't get him to show you his stuff before it was printed."

"But this is awful!"

Viaur looked utterly miserable.

"Nonsense! You exaggerate things so. I'm merely warning you of a possible danger. I've no doubt you'll get a chance of putting things right later."

By this time they had crossed the boulevard Saint-Germain. To Viaur's jaundiced eye the sun, the white clouds, the fresh green of the trees, had a look of insolent cruelty.

"Where are you taking us?" he asked. Their walk suddenly seemed to him useless and full of weariness.

"To a little eating-place I've found near the Halles. We'll feel better after a bite. There's heaps of time. The photographs and the rest of the stuff are waiting for us at the hospital."

Very quietly, but relentlessly, like a man who can't keep off his favourite idea, he went on:

"Why on earth did you let this article appear?—so soon I mean. A little later it wouldn't have mattered so much. You see, it looks as though you're trying to force the scientists' hands . . . making a turning movement so as to catch public opinion in the rear. It's almost as though you were saying: 'I've made a tremendous discovery, but all the jealous fools who work in the same field don't want to give me the credit for it.' . . . In two or three years' time, if the opposition hadn't been silenced, there might be some point in taking that line, but not now, not when things are just beginning, not when you're on the eve of getting a hearing from the Academy of Medicine and the Academy of Science . . . before your results have even been published. . . ."

Viaur had an uncomfortable feeling of guilt. When he spoke, it was in the tone of a man trying to make the best of a bad job:

"It was all Marquenat's fault, really."

"What do you mean? He didn't make you get the thing published, did he?"

"Of course not. . . . But he's been getting on my nerves, blundering round like a bull in a china-shop."

"You were pretty pleased about him at first."

"Naturally! He was charming when I went to see him at the hospital, and later, in the rue de Courcelles, where he lives. He came to see me. He saw exactly what I was after. He asked me to give him a few hints. He wanted to try some of my experiments himself. He said: 'You're opening up tremendous possibilities. You're a pioneer. . . .' He got me to go along to his place twice to help him with quite an interesting though not particularly important test which he'd worked out. . . . And then a few days ago it suddenly occurred to me what he was up to."

"What he was up to?"

"He wanted me to go shares. Put bluntly, the proposal was this: 'Don't be in too much of a hurry to publish your results. Slow everything up. Work over some of your experiments again. Then we'll add a few little things of mine and make a joint announcement. In that way it'll be a huge success. I'm only about ten years older than you, but I'm already regarded as more or less of a bigwig. My name will carry a good deal of weight. Anything with which I'm associated will have to be taken seriously. I can pull strings and save you years of struggle. . . .'"

"I knew nothing of all that," said Hachenard thoughtfully.

Viaur got more and more excited. "Of course you didn't! If I were going to go shares with anyone, it would be with you. . . ."

Hachenard made a gesture of protest.

". . . I offered to, and it was only right I should, but you refused
to hear of it. But you can't stop me from mentioning you when I give
an account of what I've been doing. Still, if I didn't share the glory
with you, who have been helping me for months, constructing apparatus and making all sorts of suggestions, I certainly wasn't going
to share it with this rotter, this fat quack, who knows perfectly well
that he's contributed nothing to my discoveries, but who prides himself on 'being in with people,' on having influence and position and
reputation . . . who's willing to make a deal . . . exchanging his
credit for my discovery, cooking up a sort of joint product . . . with
himself, needless to say, well to the front, and me bringing up the
rear in tow, hardly noticeable. . . . At first it would be 'Marquenat
and Viaur,' but in a few months I should conveniently drop out. The
world would hear of nothing but Marquenat's ideas, Marquenat's
discoveries, Marquenat's results. . . . Viaur? Oh yes, a fellow who
helped him in a small way, who prepared the ground. . . . 'Just look
at his background,' people would say; 'resident doctor at Celle-les-
Eaux . . . a medical attendant at a watering-place. . . . Medical attendants at watering-places don't revolutionize the science of physiology. . . . Pretty decent of the other fellow to let his name even
be mentioned. . . .' Protest? Fight? What good would that do?
'Another of these failures with a grievance,' it would be said, 'always
going round grousing about how they've been robbed and misrepre-
sented . . . and now, to make matters worse, he's ungrateful. . . .'
Nobody bothers about the facts in such cases. . . . Very soon I should
be no more thought of than the man whose name appeared with
Dumas's on the title-page of *The Three Musketeers*. Nobody now
even remembers who he was. . . . No, thank you! Any kind of
blunder'd be better than that, any kind of difficulty. I don't mind being smothered under organized opposition, under the whole damned
profession, if it comes to that . . . but I won't be made to look like a
fool, and a cuckold into the bargain."

"I quite see that," said Hachenard, tapping the magazine with his
finger; "but why the article?"

"Because once it has appeared, however badly written, in a magazine like this with a circulation of anything up to three or four hundred thousand, Marquenat's welcome to offer me his collaboration. I shall no longer be odd man out."

Hachenard made a grimace indicative of doubt.

". . . Marquenat'll be furious. No good counting on him after this. I've no doubt he thought his offer perfectly reasonable and even generous. You can't blame him; it's the way of the world. Still, no good crying over spilt milk. You'll have to get along without him. The real trouble is the effect it's going to have on the others. I can't help thinking you might have gone to work rather more cleverly. This stuff'll get written up in all the papers, and you know what they'll make of it! Oh well, the essential thing is to see that this afternoon's demonstration comes off. If the audience can be got to go home this evening reasonably convinced, the battle will be more than half won."

A house physician led them through the corridors with a great show of politeness:

"You'll be in the lecture-hall on the second floor. We thought it would be more comfortable, especially as there won't be many people there."

Two orderlies had been requisitioned to carry the apparatus and the documents.

Upstairs they found about fifteen people awaiting them, and three or four more turned up after they had arrived. Hachenard, who knew almost everybody there, introduced his friend. The audience was composed of two professors, four doctors belonging to the hospital, several students, two of whom were women, and several former house physicians who had been invited by their young friends. There were no old men present. Even the professors looked anything but pontifical.

Viaur found the atmosphere sympathetic. All these people, keen as mustard, would probably make things pretty difficult. He would be under fire from all sides at once, would have to face objections shot at him by quick-witted questioners, each one of whom would have had time to couch his question in the most damaging terms, would be free to choose the moment and the place of his attack. He would have no more than a moment or two in which to think of a reply as competent and as well informed as the question prompting it, and capable of satisfying and, if possible, of discomfiting the adversary without too seriously alienating his sympathy, while at the same time winning the approval of the rest of the company. In short, it would be a battle of one against fifteen. The one, to be sure, would not be entirely alone, since he would have at his side a faithful and vigilant friend; but even if that friend could give him, apart from technical assistance in the experimental part of the business, the moral support of his presence, could possibly help him in the actual answering of questions, he certainly couldn't take his place when it came to an exchange of intellectual blows, couldn't build up for him that sense of personality, that atmosphere of mental dominance, which, even though it be false—for there are quacks who can give the impression of genius voicing the bright spirit of truth, just as there are geniuses who have all the appearance of being quacks—brings to the support of every argument and every truth a something which has nothing to do with the purely rational quality of what is said.

But if Viaur was supremely aware of all the dangers awaiting him, he found them, on this occasion at least, profoundly stimulating. The battle was going to be worth fighting. If he won it, he would be spared many more in the future. There were enough people involved to make it certain that the business wouldn't be scamped. They weren't going to be content with just sneering it out of court. The bigger an audience, of course, the more liable it was to evince the foolish insensibility that is one of the products of crowd psychology; but to set against that, it shared those other characteristics of crowds —spontaneous generosity, sincerity, and a large sense of justice. Between the extremes of the too few and the too many, who could say whether there mightn't be a numerical mean, the precisely right number of informed auditors, varying according to the particular occasion? Taking everything into consideration, Viaur was inclined to think that the fifteen or so persons gathered to hear him gave exactly the best combination of intimacy and impersonality, of publicity and concentration. It was the ideal numerical mean, surely, equally far removed from the little huddle of friends and the crowd incapable of assimilating any subtlety of presentation because its touch was too coarse, or of following a reasoned line of argument because at any moment a wave of emotion might cloud its collective mentality.

We all know what it is to be seized by a sort of superstitious anticipation at the outset of some enterprise. We feel suddenly that everything's going to be all right or all wrong. And no matter how sophisticated we be, however well armed by scientific knowledge against the false significance of mere succession, it is difficult for us not to find in past experience some support for such a superstition. Haven't we all of us known what it is to feel a tonic note, as it were, dominating a series of events lying immediately before us, so that the whole succession is set in the same key, no matter how independent, how accidental, each single term may appear to be? We are convinced that the general tone is to be so-and-so, and in fact, as things turn out, it is.

Nor can such a feeling be entirely explained by our own mood of the moment. For a man may well embark upon a train of actions or events full of light-hearted confidence, only to feel almost immediately that things are going to turn out wrong. And the opposite is no less true.

Viaur had not started the day with any very definite sense of optimism. That morning, thinking of what lay before him, he had seen no reason for cheerfulness, and later Hachenard's words and the whole business of the article had worried him into a fever of apprehension. On the other hand, it is only fair to point out that not for a single moment had he felt as fearful for the outcome of the afternoon's demonstration as, given his temperament, he well might have done. Once inside the lecture-hall, seeing the expectant faces and shaking proffered hands, giving a last look at the "human material" of his experiments, waiting humbly, as he had been already told, in a neighbouring room, he felt a growing confidence in the outcome, a confidence with which his reasoning faculties had nothing to do beyond registering the fact of its existence. "It'll be all right"—the words formed themselves almost audibly—"there's absolutely no reason why it shouldn't be. These people have come here to take note of an event of the highest importance. My 'subjects' are here to make possible the manifestation of that event. Obviously they're in excellent form. My photographs are first-rate, my explanations well formulated. There's nothing particularly wonderful in a physiologist occasionally making a discovery and demonstrating it to the satisfaction of his hearers. Mankind is not entirely made up of blundering fools. I have had my share of difficulties; it's only natural that success should come my way at last."

And in fact the meeting went off very well indeed, not to say excellently. The little secretary, Vidalencque, the other waiter from the Palace Hotel, and a fourth subject as well decelerated and accelerated the action of their hearts—Vidalencque, still the star performer, even achieving a complete stoppage—sufficiently to satisfy those among the audience who already knew something, at least by hearsay, of the experiments and to stagger the few to whom this particular series of demonstrations had come as something quite new. All four, and a fifth, a Mme Empuis, produced admirable examples of vaso-dilation and constriction, as well as of diminished blood-flow, each phenomenon being accompanied by a rise in the subject's temperature and produced in direct response to the word of command of one or other of the doctors in the body of the hall. Finally, and particularly in the case of the fifth subject, there had been a remarkable display of arterial control, completed in less than two minutes and duly tested by the Pachon method.

Two of the sets of photographs had been especially admired, and their evidence had been borne out by the actual presence in the flesh of the individuals whose reactions they purported to record. The first had been the one that showed the day-to-day progress of a scar, from its earliest stage to complete formation; the second giving a similar "life-history" of a wart from the moment of its first appearance. It had been possible in both instances for the audience to observe on the bodies of the individuals concerned, brought there by Viaur for this very purpose—a carpenter from Celle and a young dressmaker—the precise condition of both the scar and the wart. The two cases showed with equal precision a daring extension of the experimenter's method. When Viaur had first happened on the carpenter, the man had been suffering from an accidental wound in the calf of the left leg caused by the fall of a plane. The injury was already a fortnight old, had a nasty look, and was showing considerable reluctance to heal. There seemed little likelihood that the infection would spread, but the wound's slowness in closing was somewhat abnormal. The doctor had at once realized that he had there to his hand an admirable opportunity of trying an experiment which he had long been planning. He had therefore contented himself with merely neutralizing the effect of the poison by the simplest possible method of local disinfection (he had done nothing beyond bathing the wound with warm water), while at the same time proceeding to an intensive stimulation of what he called the "voluntary centres of nervous energy." The scar-formation which had followed hardly merited the adjective "miraculous," but it had been sufficiently rapid (the enlarged photograph showed the whole process in all its stages) to provoke the admiration of his listeners.

In the case of the wart, the blemish had been produced on a patch of perfectly clear flesh (proved to be such by a dated enlargement) as the result of a process of "voluntary imitation" (the wart "imitated" had also been photographed), a process having much in common, allowing for the additional fact of voluntary or at least of "deliberately" voluntary provocation, with certain instances, already well known, of the transmission of small tumours by a sort of mental contagion. Viaur was now undertaking to make the wart dwindle and finally disappear altogether, by a similar method.

Short of accusing Viaur of being a cynical impostor surrounded by accomplices—an idea that apparently occurred to no one—it was difficult not to view his results with a certain degree of amazement. No less difficult was it not to realize the various long-distance possibilities opened up by such a series of tests. The members of the audience, particularly the younger ones, seemed well aware of the implications. Muttered comments could be heard coming from all corners of the room: "It's nothing short of revolutionary. . . ." "The whole question will have to be gone into afresh. . . ." "It looks as though there's not a single pathological symptom that wouldn't, in some degree, be amenable to the method. . . ." "It's a real challenge to the whole theory of passivity on which nineteenth-century medicine has been built! . . ." etc.

More than one drew attention to facts already well known which suddenly seemed to fall into place round this new discovery, like the orderly hierarchy of the old feudal service. The Nancy school was mentioned. It was admitted that insufficient attention had been paid to it. Charcot came in for a degree of belated approval. Even the old theory of mesmerism was seen now from a new angle.

Not a few turned out to have long ago suspected some possibility of the sort. "I always said . . ." "I never used to believe the stories one heard . . ." "Long ago, in 1904, in an article I contributed to the *Semaine médicale* on the cures at Lourdes, which I had been studying, I said . . ." "Last year, at the beginning of my course, I pointed out . . ."

"You just wait," whispered Hachenard to Viaur in the pause that preceded the drawing up of a report on the demonstrations, which those present agreed in thinking necessary and were one and all anxious to sign, "they'll all turn out to have anticipated you. But that's a very good sign. Whatever you do, don't damp their ardour!"

Chapter

28

ORTEGAL AT WORK:
GENIUS SET FREE

The naked woman with the pendulous breasts was seated obliquely in the Empire chair of unvarnished wood. The striped silk with which it was covered showed an indentation just where it was subjected to the pressure of her shoulder. To the right stood a deal table on which were grouped a guitar, a pair of curling-tongs, a folded newspaper set on end, a cheap thermometer, and one of those cards of buttons sold by haberdashers on which are fixed twenty or so buttons of identical design but varying sizes. This card was resting against a large box of matches so placed as to show the whole extent of its top surface.

Ortegal stood to the left of his easel. His stocky body was encased in a brown sailor's jersey, and a stumpy pipe of large dimensions was stuck in his mouth. Now and then he traced a very faint line, extending over almost the whole stretch of his canvas, with the long stick of charcoal which he held in his hand. Sometimes it was as near as possible straight and continuous, or broken here and there; sometimes it took the form of a very simple curve. At the moment his canvas—white, smooth, and of considerable size—contained nothing but five or six marks of this kind. So far they seemed to bear no obvious relation either to one another or to the general group composed of the naked woman and the table with its contents. Each one of them, however, was remarkable—so far, that is, as such an elementary form could be remarkable—from the sureness and subtlety with which it was put in. At no point had the charcoal been too heavily applied, at no point had it left the surface or faltered in its progress. If the guiding hand had paused, the effects of hesitation were not visible. It had continued on its way without perceptible uncertainty, finishing its task with perfect evenness of touch. The lines obviously, to anyone taking the trouble to look closely, were very beautiful lines, in the way that the crosses of *t's,* the curves of capitals, or the square flourish beneath the signature of a fine writer may be beautiful, or that a triangle drawn by a skilled student on a blank page may be good to look at, while his neighbour's remains ugly by reason of a heavy touch, a smudged appearance, lack of vigour, mistakes of direction, or general incompetence.

Ortegal, notwithstanding, was going through a bad time. The particular stage which his work had reached was one that he always found hateful. It might continue for a long time, it might pass almost at once, according to circumstances. A "long time" in such a connection would be an hour or an hour and a half. (In that case, he usually gave up working and went for a stroll in the Luxembourg Gardens, unless, providentially, a friend dropped in to distract his mind.) "Almost at once" meant a few minutes. For Ortegal this stage in the progress of a piece of work had little to do with what his hand was engaged on at the moment (that was of no importance; the odds were that there would be nothing to show); little to do even with the ideas that flitted in and out of his head (his mind was always active, and his ideas were much of a muchness at any given moment). No, its distinguishing mark was a feeling, disagreeable and only too easily recognizable, a feeling that *this time* he didn't know what he wanted to do. The feeling was so strong that Ortegal always had the impression that never before had he felt quite like that. As a matter of fact, each occasion was the exact counterpart of its predecessors. It was only the duration that differed.

This state of mind had absolutely nothing to do with the sense of impotence of which so many, writers especially, complained. Ortegal was always quite sure that he could do anything he chose. But what was it he wanted to do?—that was the question. He might have a vague idea, might see various ways in which his picture could develop. He might do this, then that, then something else . . . after which further progress would become purely mechanical. He had long ago given up bothering about the details of execution. It was one of the triumphs of modern painting that, once a composition was started, nothing stood in the way of its completion, since nothing outside the picture itself could create difficulties, neither rules nor model. The only danger, once the thing was under way, was a loss of verve, a hesitation in the hand similar to the sudden hesitation of a walker brought up sharp by a hole in the road. But the fear of that didn't worry Ortegal. His hand was always capable of drawing something, had always some impish impertinence in reserve, some memory from far-off days when he used to do copying in the galleries; days so far distant, inspiration so unexpected, that no one ever dreamed of tracing the influence to its source (sometimes not even Ortegal himself, for his hand had often a keener gift of remembrance than his brain); a quotation which was all the harder to identify since it was brief and inopportune. Who would have the astuteness to realize that, having half completed the curve of a guitar and being suddenly overcome by the fear of flatness, he had broken off and introduced quite literally the upper lip seen in some woman's head by Correggio? Or that, faced by the arid desert represented by the left-hand corner of his canvas, and recoiling from the too easy resource of filling it with a smear of grey paint, he had suddenly made it come alive by introducing what was no less than a bit from some skirt by Titian which he had copied in the old days, the "memory" of which was a living part of his fingers, just as three notes of a song sung in childhood are a living part of a man's unconscious mind? Most of the time he never bothered to trace the idea to its root, never even showed any curiosity about this manual recollection. He just didn't care.

No, the difficulty was to rouse in advance any interest whatever in the picture that he might or might not embark upon. "This? That?" Ortegal put the question to himself while his charcoal idly traced a faint, fair line which committed him to nothing. . . . The problem of "This? That?" bored him; and the alternative "This? That?" bored him no less. Odd how the same difficulty kept on cropping up. And yet Heaven knew he had not become a painter by accident. Ever since his childhood he had done nothing but scratch and scribble and daub. To have at his disposal some bare surface like a sheet of paper, and in his right hand something that could make marks—a pencil, a pen, a stick dipped in ink, a scrap of chalk; to cover the sheet with any sort of figures, with arrangements of light and shadow, had always been for him an instinctive occupation that had never lost its power to interest, a satisfaction such as others find in picking their noses. And if today he didn't spoil thirty sheets of paper a day with aimless scribbling, it was only because his agent had solemnly warned him against being too prolific in his output (however fugitive and formless). A charwoman might always rescue them from the waste-paper-basket and sell them, with the result that his "market" would eventually suffer. Occasionally he would forget this good advice, and then his mistress would call him to order, collecting for destruction the pieces of paper which he had so inadvertently made valuable.

But what always, in anticipation, filled him with a sense of disgust was not the itching of his hand to be at work, but the thought of all the stuff he'd got, willy-nilly, to get onto the canvas (that wretched piece of canvas leaning a little backwards on his easel, for all the world as though it were some blank face in a pillory). Each time, he was overcome by the appalling sensation of boredom which he used to endure at the École des Beaux Arts in Barcelona when, to satisfy his professor or to enter for a compulsory end-of-term competition, he had had to work up some wretched "Battle of the Horatii and the Curiatii." More than once he had tried to get out of the difficulty by setting himself rather more fantastic compositions, but he knew now that bits of a naked woman, thrown together with half a guitar and a thermometer, the whole done in the flat, could be just as tedious in the execution as any Horatii and Curiatii of the strict academic tradition.

What a pity it was that the moment just before he had to begin work couldn't last for ever; the moment in which he first "set" his subject! He would say to the naked model: "That's how I want you —no, more this way—now cross your legs, and let's see a bit of your body-hair. Throw those shoulders of yours back." And then he would walk up and down, his pipe stuck in his mouth. The guitar would be lying quite alone on the table like a household cat. His public would enjoy seeing it again. "It's a genuine Ortegal, all right," they'd say. But somehow the cat-guitar had got to be made to come alive. He must put some odd, some unexpected object between its paws. Suddenly he would bethink himself of the button-card which he had seen the other day swimming about among the spools of thread in the work-basket. . . . He loved playing with objects, presenting them in curious ways, making comic juxtapositions, relishing the mysterious satisfaction he got from the contemplation of curious shapes. . . . But, after all, such satisfaction was no more than the rather patronizing amusement of a great lord watching a lot of dancing peasants. The Spanish hidalgo throws a coin or two to the gypsies, and then tells them to clear off.

But the real underlying cause of his irritation was Jan Levisson's visit. The man had gone, leaving the studio icy cold and filled with draughts.

In two months the contract would expire. If, meanwhile, Ortegal caught a bad cold it would be to the old devil's interest. He'd be easier to deal with that way, wouldn't try to get the two thousand a month raised to three; wouldn't fight against having to produce thirty canvases instead of twenty-five; wouldn't feel up to contesting that infuriating, that obviously tricky clause about giving the man an option on everything, whether he chose to take it for exhibition or not. "I've still got twenty-two things of yours put away in the back shop. I've hawked them round London and Berlin and Stockholm—it's no good; they always come back. Naturally, I prefer to hang onto them rather than bring your prices down. Lucky for you my business is as firm as a rock. What would happen to you if you were being handled by some miserable little fellow who lives from hand to mouth? . . ." etc., etc.

What was this Jan Levisson up to? Not an easy question, that, to answer. Trying to get better terms out of him? Probably not; there were limits to the dirt that even he would dabble in. Putting him on his guard against Katchowsky, who had been smelling round this last week or two with vague talk of a commission? ("Pity you're tied up with Levisson! What terms you could get from someone else—from me, for instance! Levisson's a back number; when he's got to choose between something of Bonnard's and something of yours, it isn't you who get the extra shove! What you need is someone who'd carry your stuff and no one else's.")

But there was something else at the back of Levisson's head. What was it he'd said?—"It's your most recent things I find it hardest to get rid of. You're not like other painters. The more they repeat themselves, the more solidly do they dig themselves in. . . . No one could accuse you of repeating yourself . . . that's the last thing they'd think of saying. But they do say that So-and-so and So-and-so have recently been doing pretty well in your style, that they've even carried it further than you. You've not got your public properly in hand. It's not enough for them that others don't outdistance you; you've got to be always outdistancing them."

Ortegal was not given to what he privately called "reflection." He had a mistrust of reason, never having felt the need of it even in practical affairs. He thought in inspired flashes. Some incident from his past would suddenly come into his mind, or he would be struck by some private whimsy, by something overheard. He would sniff round it cautiously, carefully feeling his way. He was as mistrustful as an old peasant at a fair. He let others do the talking. At heart he trusted nobody absolutely. He always thought of the things that happened to him as out of the common run; or maybe he had grown to regard life as like that—a sequence of more or less arbitrarily connected incidents. No good trying to understand. If the cards fall right, so much the better. The great thing is to go while the going's good. Never risk losing luck by asking why; never try to get the better of it. The golden rule is not to get on the wrong side of people who might do one a good turn, not to inquire into their reasons. Why had the village priest got the idea of making him into an artist? Simply because he had been a pretty little boy and the old man had been keen on him—anyhow, that's what it had looked like. . . . An artist! What did the poor fellow think he meant by "artist"?

Not that he'd got to go out of his way to find how best to please people, or think too far ahead. Leave that to the Academicians; let them deceive themselves with the belief that they're giving the public what it wants. Ask the public what it wants and it'll say just those damn fool daubs that the Academicians can produce; but produce them, and they leave it cold. No good asking why. The public doesn't know.

How do acrobats manage to please their public? Not one spectator in a thousand is capable of saying in advance what trick will give him the greatest pleasure, the greatest thrill. If he could, he wouldn't be thrilled. The applause comes only when the thing's done. Once the applause is an accomplished fact, of course, the acrobat can try to argue things out. This "goes," he can say to himself; that doesn't. One turn, perhaps, may have gone well all winter and then may suddenly cease to draw. The applause grows less; the thing's been seen too often. It's up to the performer to find something else, but he'll be a fool if he relies on the public to show him what.

How do the women manage who are most successful in love, who can get men just where they want them, for whom men will do all sorts of idiotic things? Do they spend months and years working out a technique of pleasing? Do they consciously try to realize in their own persons the type most attractive to men? No, or, rather, only second-rate women do that, women who aren't really alluring, the sort of women who prompt men to say: "She'll do as well as another." But that's not the way things work with the women men go mad about. It just happens that some little haphazard gesture of theirs, some trick of the body, some expression of the lips, glance of the eyes, tone of the voice, have an extraordinarily exciting effect on the men they meet, drive them crazy, make them groan with delight. Theirs not to reason why, not even to criticize the result. A woman would be quite wrong if she considered a man, even in the privacy of her thoughts, as a fool just because, for instance, what excited him most was the tip of her ears, or a beauty-spot she might happen to have on her breast, or the way she put her foot on the edge of the bath. "He's an ass. A naked woman with the figure of a statue leaves him absolutely cold: but that ridiculous beauty-spot of mine will set him rolling on the floor with ecstasy! . . ." Doubtless there are reasons for such things, but it's no good trying to understand them. One's just got to face the fact, and if the fact is profitable, so much the better.

One day, not so very long ago, Ortegal had been feeling particularly low-spirited. He had been going through a bad time financially—not catastrophic—he had never known what it was to be down to bed-rock—but bad enough. He had taken a walk through the flea-market of Saint-Ouen. At that time he didn't know Paris very well; he was discovering it by fits and starts, getting odd little stabs of pleasure in the course of his wanderings. He hunted out corners which no one had ever told him about or of which he'd heard only by accident from his concierge or at the dairy. In this way he came occasionally on bits of the city which reminded him of Madrid or Barcelona, but chiefly of Madrid. He would look round, half hoping to see donkeys and crowds of barefooted children.

On this particular day, sauntering through the flea-market, which reminded him of the *sastro,* he noticed in the window of a junk-shop —it wasn't one of the open booths under the trees, but a sort of permanent erection on the opposite side of the path—he noticed one of those distorting mirrors which form part of the stock-in-trade of amusement parks or which one sees in the foyers of music-halls or in the passages leading to the bar. It was not the first time that he had seen such a mirror or that he had taken count of the odd things it did to the human face. But he had never before felt, as he did now, that it meant anything to him personally. It may have been that this speci-men was curved in an especially subtle way. Ortegal, who knew nothing whatever about physics, would have been hard put to it to say whether the curve in question was convex, concave, or anything else with a learned name. But the effect on the human face set him suddenly thinking. Reflected from that curious surface, it became oddly lengthened, though neither unduly thin nor yet with an appearance of painful compression. It became, not ridiculous, but mysteriously elegant, strangely sad. The upper part of the body was whittled away to a dwindling thinness till it looked like the body of a saint in the porch of a mediæval cathedral. Features tapered away into nothingness beneath foreheads magnificently monstrous, swelling between narrowed temples, foreheads of melancholy visionaries. Lips looked thin and scornful, as though formed to speak meticulously words of utter disenchantment. Cheeks and jaws lost all hint of the animal; chins became delicate, necks thin and fragile; hands took on an exquisite thinness, looked for all the world like the front paws of sleeping greyhounds.

An air of charm hovered over the reflected images. Three slum children, a biggish girl and two boys, not actually in rags but nearly so, had stopped behind Ortegal and were looking too. They saw themselves reflected in the mirror, and the strange gentleman. Instead of short and stocky, with a round, sly face, he appeared long and thin, with an expression of aristocratic kindliness touched with melancholy. They themselves looked taller than usual, but thinner too, and though their poverty remained, it had taken on a mysterious, suggestive quality. They might have been three starving princes who had been kidnapped by travelling mountebanks. Standing there together, they set the mind curiously wondering.

The afternoon had at first been sunny, but now thin clouds had drawn across the sky. A soft light, grey-blue and diffused, had settled on the day and, seen in the mirror, took on a quality of refined and strange nobility in tune with the human figures, bathing the distance in a luminous glow that made unrecognizable the details of the scene.

Ortegal moved on, but the thought of the mirror obsessed him. He could think of nothing but what it had shown him. He felt compelled to re-create not only the fact of what he had seen, but the mysterious world into which it had led his imagination, the poem that had never been read, the song that had never been heard.

He had sought to fix his vision, first in pencil on a sheet of paper, then in paint on a canvas so that he might catch the precise tone of grey-blue light; then, once more on paper, on sheets of increasing size and with coloured chalks; finally, once again on canvas. He composed vague scenes; or rather, for in themselves they had no importance, scenes seemed to emerge from the figures of his picture. It was the figures, the inhabitants of this noble, this curiously sterile and melancholy world, that he knew at all costs he must find and capture. They changed as he worked, and as the scene itself altered, it gave to them a growing definition. But it was as though they were all seen through a transfiguring medium. Looked at with attention, they appeared as the creatures seen in the mirror, the man dressed like some strange person of adventure, and the three young kidnapped princes.

Just when he had satisfied the need that had driven him to work, and was beginning to get bored, a friend had come in, and later still, another friend who had some mild pretensions to being a critic. They had been voluble; they had been curious.

The whole business had ended in his holding an exhibition. There had been exclamations of delight from the lovers of art; there had been critical articles—the first really good and important ones ever devoted to him (the word "genius" was freely used); there had been his first contract with a dealer; he had struck up friendships with men of letters who set themselves to explain his achievement with references to Greco, to Byzantine art, to Amenhotep IV, and who referred to him as a "really remarkable metaphysical poet."

There had been two or three other similar occasions in Ortegal's career when he had, as it were, been "offered the goods on a plate." One day, for instance, not knowing what to do while waiting for a model, he had amused himself by drawing on his canvas a number of straight lines which met at a point chosen for no particular reason fairly near the centre. They were as straight as he could make them and regularly spaced—rather like lines on a compass card. In this way he found himself left with about eighteen acute angles, the sides subtending which opened out towards the edges of his canvas. Next he shaded each alternate angle and ended by producing just such a design as he had been accustomed to scribble when he was a small boy. The effect of the whole was that of a circular fan. He had got thus far when the model arrived. He told her to take off her clothes and sit down. There before him was a naked woman and the rough sketch of a fan. He set himself deliberately to superimpose upon the design a drawing of the model, adapting the latter to the "accidents" of the compass card, breaking it up and reassembling it according to the edges and angles, the geometrical symmetry, the alternate darks and lights of his fan. Once more friends had turned up, literary friends, including one with mild pretensions to art criticism. A new school, a new epoch in the history of painting, had been born.

Again and again the same thing happened: a momentary whim to start with, followed by the excitement of giving it its head, combined with the knowledge that he would go on until he got bored (which would be soon enough) and then stop. And somehow people had always turned up at the right moment, had got very much more excited than he had ever done over the results of his mood, and had started talking. His instinct had warned him never to contradict them and never to let himself be carried away without first being sure of them. What he felt didn't matter.

To be sure, he had been careful to spread the idea that his moods were of supreme importance, that they led the way in matters of contemporary taste, at least in advanced circles, circles that were haunted by buyers and collectors and speculators in artistic "futures." A man has only got to start backing the market value of pictures, no matter what the pictures may be, to become at once both credulous and apprehensive. He lets himself be guided by the most unreliable of signs, is constantly on the look-out for portents, and fully believes in omens. A painter has only to bring him luck once or twice to assume in his eyes an almost godlike stature. And from then on, it is fairly easy for the painter to forecast the trend of the market, since, to a large extent, he can control it.

That, of course, is all as it should be. Only the fools complain. Painting can be precisely what its practitioners want it to be. It is the painters who matter, not painting in general. Some will never be anything but bores, no matter what they do. They may work for ten years on the same picture, putting into it a life-time of knowledge and skill. The result will be politely acclaimed as "very fine," but no one really cares two damns about it. Such men's "handling" is completely without interest, has nothing at all to say to anybody. And it'll say no more in ten years than it would in ten minutes. No one's going to fall in love with a woman by spending ten years looking at her eyes and her nose if his first impression is that her eyes and her nose are those of an English governess.

Contrariwise, there are painters whose lightest touch is capable of fascinating. No need for such men to work. In fact, if they work too hard they are apt to give themselves away, or if they let their natural appeal be overlaid by the paraphernalia of academic composi- tions. Ingres, for instance, had a delicious touch which is apparent in the most casual of his sketches. It is only in his *Apotheosis of Homer* that he becomes a bore. And that picture cost him months of work.

In spite of his native shrewdness, Ortegal could not help having in- creasing confidence in, if not his star, at least his powers. He was not far from believing himself possessed of an irresistible charm. He was like a woman who knows that she is indescribably attractive whether she be smiling, crying, yawning, or spitting out a cherry-stone. But he wanted to adventure further even than he had done so far. He knew that at bottom he was still timid. Each time he put across some new fantasy he was nervous of the result. He watched for the first reactions of the public with a sinking feeling in his stomach. He was ready at any moment to throw up the sponge. Worse than that, deep down he knew that he didn't dare to give full rein to his fantasies. The ones he chose to risk were already "in the air." It needed more cheek than he possessed to go further than that.

The best fantasy of all, the highest proof of his belief in himself, would be to give his hand perfect liberty of action, to let it do exactly as it wanted, as it did when he sat idly scribbling while he chatted with a friend or discussed some piece of business or found himself at some tedious party. "Let's have done once for all with Horatii and Curiatii. The beauty of my work has nothing to do with its subject. To believe otherwise is to be on a level with Caro-Delvaille and Dagnan-Bouveret and Reichshoffen with his endless studies of cuirassiers. Beauty in matters of art comes from the way the hand moves across a surface, no matter what it's doing, whether it's tracing half a profile or the volute of a column or an arithmetical figure, or determining the placing of a white space between two lines or two blocks of shadow. Why not face the fact squarely, since everything else bores me? Everything else is merely duty, merely a set task. If it's really me that people like in my work, and not the pretexts which make that work possible, oughtn't they to like best what comes most naturally to me, what I haven't got to force myself to produce? As one likes the smell of a woman's body, her armpit or the cleft of her thighs; as one squirms with pleasure at the way certain women from Rumania or the Argentine pronounce their *r's* when they talk French?

"The danger is that one will give offence—that's the trouble—one can't risk doing that, can't risk giving the lie to the literary gents and the highfalutin critics who are so busy explaining the great mysteries —talking about one's 'implacable logic,' saying that one's the 'most intellectual painter since Leonardo'—making it as clear as day that one's following in the footsteps (or almost, not entirely, because of course there's one's individuality to be considered) of Riemann and Bergson and the fellow whose name ends in -ski. One must never start making fun of the fourth dimension or absolute space. Safer to sit puffing at one's pipe. Or, if one does, it must be in such a way that they'll say they haven't really gone deep enough into what one's doing, haven't achieved the last analysis; that there's more in one than even they had thought. . . . And so it goes on."

Ortegal indulged in these sage reflections without any real feeling of contempt for his disciples. After all, there is something in the theory of unconscious genius. Bees, it seems, build combs of a mathematical complexity beyond the power of geometricians to calculate. A woman who smiles in a certain way resolves many complicated problems of modelling and perspective and light, quite apart from what her smile means. There's no reason why a painter, without any deliberate intention, shouldn't discover the same truths as Riemann or Bergson or the fellow whose name ends in -ski. If competent critics say he does, it's none of his business to deny it. He must just believe them as he'd believe a doctor who told him that his heart was "a magnificent organ."

While all this had been going on in his mind, Ortegal had laid aside his stick of charcoal and had been mixing on his palette a particular shade of grey faintly touched with plum-colour and a curiously tawny quality (he was proud of his "inimitable greys"). With a hand which even boredom could not rob of its sureness of touch, he described on his canvas a more or less straight and almost horizontal brush-mark, about two or three millimetres thick and some thirty centimetres long, roughly corresponding with his sense of the model's forearm, though he made no effort at all to evoke its actual form. This brush-mark held no interest for him. It was merely a temporary expedient, a trumpet note to summon fantasy, a point of departure.

There was something far from disagreeable in feeling the spontaneous uprush of deep mysteries and hidden truths. The prophets of the Old Testament must have felt rather as he was feeling now. God, to go further still, if He existed, must feel like that. If, meanwhile, one starved to death it wouldn't, of course, be quite so amusing, although one can usually get round even hunger. A glass of white wine taken on an empty stomach is almost as stimulating as a beefsteak. No, what wouldn't be amusing would be to remain obscure. It's not easy to find a substitute for fame, for the admiration of one's fellows, for the way they look on one as a source of ultimate truths and deep mysteries, almost as a god. Not easy, short of doing something violent, like taking opium or hashish or ether, as some of one's pals do; and even then it doesn't last!

Not that it looked as though he were particularly threatened at the moment with obscurity, judging by the last notice in the *Argus,* nor with starvation either, if it came to that, for all Levisson's warnings. Only yesterday he had given his broker instructions to buy five more Rio Tintos, which would make twenty in all. "What would poor old Van Gogh say . . . or poor Gauguin? . . . A bit comic when one comes to think of it. I'm taking their revenge. And the old Academicians of the Institute would gape if they knew about my Rio Tintos."

Ortegal, his brush in his hand—a fine brush which he held with the tips of his fingers—looked at the smear of "inimitable grey" which he had just set on the canvas, and touched it lightly. He was conscious of a sudden feeling deep down in himself, as though something had broken, the last ligament that held his audacity in check. The little sack containing that audacity, though punctured more or less severely in the past, had always been prevented from ever completely emptying itself. Now at last it was going to be allowed full liberty to spend the last drop of its secretions. . . . What a delicious feeling!

The brush moved towards the right and a little upwards. It described a letter, then another: $a, x;$ next, the sign $+$, followed by other letters and algebraic signs such as Ortegal had vaguely noticed at odd times and found amusing and exciting. He more or less knew the sense of some of them, such as "plus," "multiplied by," "equal to." Of others he happened to know the name—as, for instance, "to infinity," though the significance he attached to them was little more than vaguely astronomical. Of others, such as "larger than," "less than," "function of," he knew neither the names nor the meanings, though his eye had retained a pretty exact idea of their shapes and of their relative position among the horde of other signs.

The whole made a firework display of signs, an algebraic posy, bursting into florescence towards the upper right-hand corner of the canvas, the highest point in a jet of water, but a jet that struck obliquely upwards and not perpendicular, and the drops from which, *a's* and *b's, c's* and *x's,* plusses, minuses, zeros, and infinitudes, scattered and fell in glorious freedom from such degrading things as the law of gravity. At a little distance from this, so that it looked like an egg balanced on a jet of water, Ortegal put in an object which began by being a circle, to become later a circle penetrated by a cone, or, rather, entwined with a cone, since, the better to consummate their union, the figures abandoned any attempt to be three-dimensional. That done, the brush jumped suddenly to the point symmetrically opposite—namely, the left-hand corner of the canvas—where, in three bold strokes, it outlined an eye which might equally well have been a navel, though, on the whole, an eye was what it most resembled.

"Yes, a charming fancy—but then again, no, it's not a question of saying whether it is charming or not. The point is, it's me, or rather it's mine, a product of me. Take a sweet-smelling shrub, any part of a sweet-smelling shrub; crush one of its leaves, cut the stem, press out a single drop of sap. . . . The smell is always there, and if it so happens that you like the smell, that of all the smells in the world it is the one you most delight in, any scrap of the shrub will give it to you. Let it do what it will, it can't help oozing its essence, can't help yielding what most in all the world you love.

"What a sense of pride it gives you to feel yourself just like such a shrub! Of all sources of pride it is the most intimate, the one most nearly identical with your self, most closely bound to the very substance of your being. The pride of other men is something relatively external to themselves, pride in their work or in the power that enables them to produce that work. But with them the work is of prime importance. With each new work their whole fortune is at stake. But that means that they are never free from the obsessing terror of doing less well than their best! A champion may achieve some great feat, say an eighteen-foot jump, but ever after he dare not fall below that, has no right to fall below that. Each successive jump has got to be eighteen feet, or more. For the rest of his life he is condemned to strain himself, to kill himself, in an effort to beat his own record. . . .

If he drops ever so little beneath the standard he has set himself, not only does his reputation suffer, but his pride begins to slink off. A frightful fate if one really thinks of it!

"Whereas I, from now on, am absolutely safe, with no mark fixed by something external to myself which I have got to reach or pass. I can just let myself go. At this very moment I am doing exactly what I want to do, doing it as naturally as my skin sweats on a hot day. If you really have genius, you have it always and everywhere. Even your excreta are precious. . . . What people say may not be so wrong after all."

Chapter

29

A STORY WITHOUT PROOF

After acknowledging the receipt of Manifassier's letter by a short note in which he expressed himself as much gratified by the compliments which the other had passed on to him, Mionnet began to look each morning for the arrival of a new questionnaire. Nothing, however, came. He began to wonder whether it was not, perhaps, his place to write first, if only to offer a few suggestions about the amount of the proposed bank deposit and the ways in which it could best be used. He was still wondering when he heard again from Manifassier.

This new letter was more ambiguously worded than any of its predecessors had been. Obviously the writer had been at great pains to ensure that, if it went astray, no one not in the secret would be able to guess precisely to whom or to what it referred or whence it came. Mionnet could not help smiling, so unlike Manifassier was this procedure. There could be no doubt that the writing was his, though the signature had been replaced by a flourish.

He re-read the text several times with careful attention, until he felt satisfied that he had plumbed the mystery.

The writer, after excusing himself for a long silence, which had been due to many preoccupations, asked him to take up again and push as far as possible the inquiry into "those events of the past to which reference had been made in the last fifteen lines of the third section" of his report, and at the same time to take the opportunity of finding out whether it might not be possible to "discover and exploit evidence of similar weaknesses on the part of the same person, but more recent." A definite connection had at once been noted between the fifteen lines of the third section just mentioned, and the closing paragraphs of the fifth, which, in any case, seemed to promise "possible developments." He was asked to pursue "diligently" both lines of inquiry and to "leave no stone unturned in an effort to get definite information, something more reliable than impressions or mere rumours."

He was urged particularly to collect all available information about the individual who had been the subject of the second paragraph of the fourth section—about his character, about his intimates, and about the best means of getting into personal touch with him. One phrase, even more carefully disguised than the others, seemed to indicate that it might be decided to approach the gentleman in question independently of Mionnet. It was important, however, that the latter should know this, since it might happen that in his own attempts to achieve an interview he would stumble on evidence of this parallel manœuvre and be tricked into an unfortunate expression of surprise.

Finally, he was again invited to ask for a subsidy if he thought such a step necessary.

"Well, well," so the President hadn't just been content to "take the famous clauses as read." He had, apparently, gone into them with the greatest care and considered meticulously the use that might be made of the information they conveyed. "Well, well"; it was all very odd. Unfortunately the President did not quite realize the nature of the difficulties involved.

As a matter of fact, before this last letter had reached him, Mionnet had been trying to clear up certain obscurities, those in particular which shrouded the so-called MacWrench affair, about which he had heard for the first time at the Lacchinis'. He had not lost sight of it during the feverish week he had spent assembling material for his report. Indeed, it was owing to information which had come his way at that time that he had been enabled to formulate the famous paragraphs with a reasonable degree of confidence. But so many other urgent questions had pressed upon his attention that he had not as yet adventured far in this special direction. There was the added difficulty that though the persons of his acquaintance seemed ready enough to fire off witticisms at the expense of the MacWrench business, they were less so to offer proof or to elaborate their rather vague innuendoes.

During the days immediately following his walk on the Palatine, and before he knew that he was going to be asked to make the inquiry his prime preoccupation, he had, for reasons of personal satisfaction, gone pretty carefully into the question, working along fairly obvious lines. "So far as I understand it, whatever it was that happened happened at some time relatively recent and was for a while the talk of Rome. If things went as far as gossip indicates they did, there must have been some reference to them in the press, particularly in the anti-clerical papers and the comic magazines."

Where better than in the Victor Emmanuel Library could he find the files of these newspapers and consult them at his leisure? Thither, therefore, he bent his steps.

He had ready to hand certain definite starting-points for his inquiry, unless, of course, his informers had been on a hopelessly wrong track. The scandal had taken place under the present Pope and in the early years of his pontificate. There was no doubt about the identity of the principal actor, except that by some the name was spelt MacWrench, by others MacWrenth. Legal action of some sort had, it appeared, been taken. There were those who maintained that the proceedings had been cut short as a result of Merry del Val's personal intervention, though according to another version, sentence had actually been pronounced. However that might be, a close bond had been proved to exist between this MacWrench and the Secretary of State, and there was reason to believe in the existence, in the background, of a whole secret group united by tastes of a very special kind.

To begin with, Mionnet went carefully, page by page, through the files of two Roman daily papers and of those of the comic sheets which he could get hold of (others, the names of which had been given him, were not available in the library) covering a period beginning with the second half of 1903 and ending with the last three months of 1905.

He devoted special attention to the gossip columns, the general news items, and the law reports. Not a trace of MacWrench could he find, nor of any name resembling his. In this way he wasted two entire afternoons. The "Freemason" librarian, to whom Mionnet had been introduced by Dom Charles Magloire, noticed the concentrated way in which the French Abbé was working and came over to him more than once with offers of help. Mionnet, however, did not dare to explain frankly what he was after and confined himself to putting a number of general questions: "Is there a daily of more extreme Left sympathies than this one?" or "Which is the best-informed of the Roman papers, especially in matters of trivial daily and local occurrence?"

Acting on the advice of the librarian (who was obviously eaten up with curiosity to know more: "If only you'd tell me precisely what it is you want to find out, I should be in a better position to help . . ."), he spent the third day consulting two other sets of back numbers. But he had no more success than before. He had started work quite early in the morning, for his self-imposed task had taken on the characteristics of a sporting event. A little before noon he succumbed to a sense of hopelessness. "It's all been just talk. . . . There may have been a hint of scandal, but it never became public. Neither the law nor even public opinion was ever directly involved."

Suddenly, however, he found himself noting a very odd fact. From the collection which he was at the moment examining—a file of the *Popolo Romano*—occasional pages were missing. The issues concerned all belonged to the third quarter of 1905. He went over the whole collection again from the beginning of the year, making a note of the missing pages. Quite possibly the mutilations had occurred as a result of bad binding. (There were other indications that this might be the case; for instance, two whole issues were wrongly placed.) But examining the sheets more closely, he found evidence going to prove that the missing portions had been deliberately torn out. In two or three cases this was perfectly obvious.

Mionnet turned once again to the files he had been examining during the preceding days. For all the dates corresponding to those of the suspect numbers of the *Popolo Romano* some of the other dailies were intact, others a page short. Those that were intact he took the trouble to read from end to end, and in no case did he find the faintest reference to a MacWrench scandal. Where mutilation had occurred he noticed that it had been most thorough in the issues belonging to August 20.

The deletions in the comic papers showed, on close scrutiny, far more numerous still. But the parallelism of dates was here more difficult to establish, and in any case meant less.

This process of collation, though it was more hasty than he would have liked it to be, filled a good three hours. He had taken no intermission for luncheon.

The excitement of his discovery was somewhat modified by a sharp sense of humiliation. "How came it that I went through all these files yesterday and the day before without noticing the fact that several pages were missing? It doesn't say much for me as an investigator."

Just before closing-time he succumbed to the temptation of submitting his difficulties to the librarian:

"Look what I've found—quite by accident. Odd, isn't it?"

The librarian showed no very great excitement. He couldn't help admitting that certain pages were missing, and that here and there undeniable traces of removal could be found. But obviously he was not anxious to push the investigation further.

"Oh, you know how it is—probably some item of news somebody wanted—the text of a recently promulgated law, or a railway timetable. . . ."

"What about the comic papers, though?"

"A dirty picture, perhaps. . . ."

"Or an attack on somebody?"

"Possibly."

Mionnet pressed his point:

"Have you ever known cases where pages have been removed because they contained things that certain persons might find disagreeable?"

"Plenty! For instance, where a question of nobility was involved."

"What exactly do you mean by that?"

"Some story about a family using a bogus title, or gossip about honours recently purchased from the Pope."

"But how could anybody using the library tear out a whole big page like this one, for instance, without being seen by the official on duty?"

The librarian smiled and lowered his voice: "There are people who specialize in that kind of work—are employed to do it. They become very clever at it. If they're noticed they just slip the attendant something. We can't always be keeping an eye on the staff."

Mionnet was on the point of asking whether there was such a thing as an official law gazette, and where he might see it. (He had found no mention of any such publication in the catalogue of the Victor Emmanuel Library.) But he didn't want the librarian to think that he was merely nosing out scandals, and feared lest he might awaken his suspicions. It occurred to him also that even if such a gazette did exist, it would probably contain nothing but a bare mention of the case, assuming that the matter had ever got into court at all. If the proceedings had been stopped—as seemed most probable—there would be no reference to them at all. August 20—or, rather, the 19th —to which the mutilated sheets had drawn his attention, must have fallen during the recess in the law-courts. Any notice in the public press could have been little more than a statement that a grand jury had failed to find a true bill, with possibly some editorial comment on the circumstance. It was almost certain that there would have been no publication of a verdict.

After these long days spent in the library, his hunger for documentation was considerably assuaged. Outside, the spring weather was at its best; already it was almost uncomfortably hot. Mionnet knew from experience how pleasantly the afternoons could be spent in the house of the gardener and was loath to let such opportunities slip by. There he would find cool rooms and youthful passion, leafy peace and the song of birds. Paolina was always more pleased to see him in the day-time than at night, when an insidious sleepiness was apt to make her sulky.

It didn't need much, therefore, to make him postpone for the present his inquiries into the matter of MacWrench. Besides, after all, he was still constantly meeting people and keeping his eyes open for the chance of picking up odds and ends of information. He went to parties given by the Lacchinis and the Fontmonges, lunched and sometimes dined in their houses, was invited right and left.

Things had reached this stage when the fresh letter from Paris came to spur him to renewed energy.

Chapter

30

A HIGHLY SUSPECT PHOTOGRAPH

That afternoon, as he sat in the tramway on his way to Paolina, his mind was full of it. He had promised, the previous evening, to pay her a visit, and he was anxious to be as good as his word, even though this recall to duty had just arrived.

Some weeks ago he had come to a highly respectable and by no means exacting arrangement with the gardener's family, to the details of which the young girl had not been made privy. The scagnozzo had expressed himself satisfied with a further commission of fifty lire and now considered the account between them as closed. Mionnet had told him that his pilgrims had returned to France, but that he himself had been left behind to make arrangements for the arrival of a second batch. The story did not serve its purpose very well, since Mionnet found himself faced with the necessity of once more getting rid of the scagnozzo, whose pockets were bulging with the addresses of hotels, family pensions, and small restaurants, to say nothing of other places of interest, and who was anxious to involve his colleague in immediate negotiations with the proprietors of these various institutions in readiness for the promised influx of new visitors. Mionnet had to warn Paolina's mother that he would be downright angry should he find the man in her house when he came to visit Paolina. For the scagnozzo had taken to hunting him out there and would wait, making polite conversation with the mother, in the living-room, with its vast divan and its tapestry view of the Castle of St. Angelo, until the Frenchman should have finished making love to the daughter in the neighbouring bedroom.

While he waited for a No. 16 tram at the corner of the Via dei Serpenti, Mionnet saw coming towards him a big strapping priest, by no means old, dark-complexioned, with an insolent air, a pair of black eyes, and a well-modelled, fattish face. He was neither very well shaved nor very well dressed, but his general appearance approximated more to a state of careless elegance than of shabbiness. A collar of doubtful whiteness showed above the neck of his soutane, and as he approached, he inserted between the collar and his rather fleshy neck two plump fingers, with the air of a man who is rather out of condition and feels the heat.

Very courteously he raised his hat. " 'Ow do you do? . . . You are, I 'ope, well?"

He started to laugh at his efforts to express himself in a foreign language. Then he continued, this time in well-pronounced Italian, which Mionnet, to whom that tongue had now become familiar, found no difficulty in understanding.

"If I were not afraid of being a nuisance, I would ask permission to walk a little way with you."

Mionnet looked the newcomer over. The man's face and figure were vaguely familiar. Where had he seen them?

"To whom have I the honour of speaking?" he asked in French.

"To a student like yourself," the other replied in Italian. "I have seen you, the last few days, working at the library." A mischievous smile showed on his lips. "I met you once before. . . . I was in two minds about coming to see you at your hotel. . . ." After a slight pause he added, as though he were repeating a password: "the Paix et Helvétia. . . ."

Mionnet, faintly bored by the incident, inclined his head. "Is there something you wish to say to me, sir?"

". . . There is something I wish—to sell you."

"To sell? To me? I must ask to be excused. I can think of nothing at the moment that I wish to buy."

A No. 16 tram was approaching. Mionnet stepped into the roadway. The ecclesiastic followed him and very rapidly hissed in his ear:

"It is something I think you might find very interesting. I know that you are very curious about the Cardinal Secretary. You will never find anything half so useful for your purpose. It is a unique document."

Mionnet jumped onto the tram.

A few days later he was dining at the Lacchinis'. The guests were not numerous, but they were all intimate friends of the host and hostess. The most important person present was an Archbishop from Tuscany who was on a visit to Rome, a very close friend of Giacomo della Chiesa. The meeting had been arranged by Mme Lacchini as the result of a wish expressed by Mionnet, consequent upon his receipt of Manifassier's letter, to find some means of approaching the Archbishop of Bologna. Throughout the evening, however, the prelate showed the greatest reserve. No one made any attempt to draw him out. The real object of the introduction was to bring Mionnet to his notice and so facilitate an interview at some later date.

Just as Mionnet was leaving, Mme Lacchini made an opportunity to exchange a whispered word with him in the entrance hall.

"You were approached in the street the other day by an Abbé, weren't you? . . . He mentioned a document? . . . It's a matter of the utmost delicacy. . . . I hardly know what to advise. You must be very careful how you deal with the man in question. He's out for what he can get."

"A scagnozzo?"

"Ah, so you've found out the meaning of that word? . . . No, he's not exactly a scagnozzo. . . . But several of his friends are. He was formerly employed by the 'black' police. He was dismissed for some reason I don't know. He's got a great deal of information, and is much feared."

"In other words, a blackmailer?"

"If you like to call him so . . . but such things are not regarded in quite the same light here as elsewhere. . . . On the whole, I think you ought to hear what he has to say . . . but be careful. . . ."

The next morning about ten o'clock, as Mionnet was working in his room, word was brought that an ecclesiastic was asking for him at the street door. He went down.

It was the large, dark-complexioned priest. He carried a brief-case under his arm.

"I wonder whether you could spare me a few moments, Monsieur Mionnet?"

They went into a small sitting-room, furnished in pitch-pine, which was completely empty.

The visitor opened his case, which appeared to contain in its two compartments a very considerable number of miscellaneous papers, some printed, others in manuscript.

While his plump fingers were engaged in delicately searching a bundle of documents, he said:

"You are familiar with the appearance of the Cardinal Secretary of State? You would have no hesitation in recognizing him?"

Mionnet, who had never met Merry del Val, knew pretty well from portraits what he looked like. For some time he had been so deeply preoccupied with the thought of him that his features were clearly imprinted on his mind.

"Of course," he said.

"Then look at this."

The visitor had extracted from the bundle a largish photograph, about five by seven inches in size, pasted on a piece of thick grey cardboard and wrapped in a double covering of tissue paper. This he undid, displaying a dull-finished bromide proof which, despite its clearness of detail, was an enlargement of a smaller original.

He pushed it under Mionnet's eyes, keeping a tight hold of it with his right hand, the thumb and three last fingers of which gripped it like the hooks of a metal frame. His nails were black.

The scene represented was a very strange one, comprising two figures set against what appeared to be the terrace of an Italian summer villa. There was a balustrade. There were a number of shrubs. There was an expanse of sky. The two figures were bare-headed and dressed in what appeared to be soutanes, though cut on lines of extreme elegance and made, apparently, of fine black silk—a cross between a soutane and a dandy's dressing-gown. Each wore round his waist a loosely knotted girdle of some extremely rich material. There was no sign of dignity about either of them. One of the two, slightly taller than the other, showed a bald crown between two patches of hair brushed flat, though in spite of this he appeared to be a remarkably handsome man of mature years. His right arm lay along, or, rather, supported in a kind of embrace, the shoulders of his companion, a slim youth of quite extraordinary and quite unusual beauty. At the same time he held between his teeth a morsel of the flesh of some fruit—a peach, perhaps, or an apricot—which, leaning towards the upturned face of his young friend, he appeared to be offering to the parted lips, the expression of which might equally well have accompanied a smile, a kiss, or a swooning sigh.

"You recognize him?" asked the visitor.

Mionnet was forced to acknowledge that the features of the taller and elder of the two figures were remarkably like those of Merry del Val. But what struck him most of all was the unlikelihood of such a document being genuine, and the cynical insolence which alone could put it forward as such. With a slightly ironic intonation (all the conversation had so far been conducted in Italian, which Mionnet now spoke fluently if not very correctly) he said:

"And what precisely is the history of this photograph? Where, may I ask, was it taken?"

"At Castel Gandolfo, last summer. In the villa where the Cardinal lives during the hot weather."

"And who or what is the young man?"

"An Abbé from the Academy of Noble Ecclesiastics. If you buy the photograph, I will tell you his name."

"How came the picture to be taken? And by whom?"

"By another young priest from the Acadamy who was staying at the villa and sharing in the—diversions."

"How did it come into your hands?"

The visitor's smile was a delight to see. He accompanied it with a slight shrug.

"I'd rather you didn't ask me that. I have my secrets."

"And you actually expect me to believe that it's genuine?"

The other's face became at once very serious. His expression of surprise was almost painful in its intensity.

"But it is! There can be no possible doubt of it. There's not a trace of retouching. All that's been done is to enlarge the original to five by seven. The negative is two and a half by three and a half. It is extremely clear, having been taken by an admirable miniature camera of German make."

"You own the negative?"

The other hesitated; then:

"Yes," he said. "If we come to terms about the price, I will show you the negative before the money is handed over. You know that a print can be faked easily enough, but that the slightest attempt to fake a negative shows up at the very first glance?"

"I know nothing whatever about it. I've never dabbled in photography. But I do know that nowadays there are ways of faking everything."

Mionnet thought for a moment or two.

"You would part with the negative?" he asked at length.

"Possibly. It would depend upon the price."

Silence fell between them.

"Even though the negative may not have been faked," said Mionnet, breaking it, "it would have been perfectly easy to get two men to pose for such a scene. There are plenty of people sufficiently like the Cardinal. . . ."

The visitor, who was still holding the photograph, now gave it a long look as though he were calling it to witness his indignation.

"As like as all that? Feature for feature? Quite impossible! You can't seriously suggest such a thing! Bare-headed like that, and in broad daylight! It's a good enough likeness to serve as a passport photograph! Besides, they'd have had to find someone to take the part of the young man, whose name I've promised to give you."

There was once more an interval of silence.

"Does the Cardinal know of the existence of this picture?" asked Mionnet.

The other stood for a moment deep in thought. When, at last, he replied, it was in a tone of complete frankness:

"Yes."

"Has he made no effort to get hold of it?"

"There have been negotiations. We have not, however, been able to come to an understanding."

"The devil you haven't! That means, I suppose, that you were asking an enormous price?"

"Nothing exorbitant, I can assure you."

"But he has preferred to let the photograph circulate freely?"

"I'll be honest with you. It has occurred to him that he might gain nothing by buying it. What's to stop me from having other prints made and keeping some of them after selling this one?"

"He wouldn't run that danger if he could get hold of the negative."

"Don't be too sure—it's perfectly possible to take a copy of a negative which will be just as good evidence as the original."

"In that case, there's nothing to prevent your playing exactly the same trick on me?"

"What would it matter to you if I did keep an extra print or even a copy of the negative? I shouldn't, as a matter of fact, because I'm honest, but if I did, it wouldn't hurt you. You'd have your document just the same, and you would be free to use it as you liked. The two situations are entirely different."

Mionnet had to admit to himself that the argument was irrefutable.

"There's another thing," went on the big, dark-skinned man, replacing the photograph in its tissue-paper wrappings; "between you and me, I don't want to come to terms with him." His face took on a sudden expression of brooding violence and hard relentlessness. "I hate him. He did me about the worst injury one man could do another. I want revenge. I'm a man of my word, and if I'd sold him the picture, I should have kept nothing back. I should have bartered my revenge for gold."

"But, all the same, you would have sold it if he'd been willing to pay your price?"

The visitor raised his arms and shoulders in a gesture that seemed to say that there are limits even to heroic sentiments.

"I've something else to ask you. What reason had you to suppose that I was sufficiently interested in the Cardinal to be willing to buy a document of this description—setting aside, for the moment, all question of its genuineness?"

The other, who all this time had been carefully putting the photograph back in its place and now closed the brief-case, faced the question with one of his ambiguous smiles.

"It wasn't difficult to guess. You have made no attempt to conceal your activities. From the first moment of your arrival in Rome you started asking all and sundry about the Cardinal. For the last few days you have been making great efforts to get at the truth of the MacWrench affair."

"You know about that business?"

"I most certainly do."

Mionnet spent a moment or two in thought; then he, in his turn, smiled. "Are you in a position to tell me why it is that the files of the Roman daily papers all have certain pages missing?"

"I may be."

"Do you think it might be possible to find a perfect set of these papers anywhere?"

"I think it highly improbable."

"Who, do you think, was responsible for having these pages removed?"

"The black police, obviously."

"Will they have destroyed them?"

"Not all, perhaps."

"By which you mean—?"

The visitor smiled. "There may be people who belonged to the black police once but do so no longer, and they may have set aside some of these pages—who knows?"

"To save them from oblivion?"

The other burst out laughing. "Precisely!"

"And their work was so well done that it might still be possible to find some of the missing pages?"

"Not altogether impossible . . . but the ones I have are not very good."

He seemed to think a moment, for after a second or so he added:

"If you buy the photograph, I will do my best to get you one or two really good examples of these pages. I can promise nothing; but if they're to be had, you shall have them—as a little something extra thrown in."

Mionnet had done some thinking too.

"Might it not be possible," he suggested, "to get hold of them separately, without the photograph, to begin with?"

"I should have to think about that. . . ."

"Would the price be high?"

"No."

"About how much?"

"A thousand lire, I should say . . . for the two most important pages."

Mionnet gave a start. "But that's an enormous figure! How much are you asking for the photograph and its negative?"

"Fifty thousand lire."

"You must be mad!"

"Not at all. Fifty thousand lire is nothing for a document of such unique value. Governments spend fifty thousand lire for much less than that."

Mionnet's attitude had suddenly become cold and distant. He said nothing, but showed by his expression that he wished to put an end to the interview.

The other made no attempt to insist. He got up and held out his hand. His parting words were:

"Think it over; it's really an extraordinary chance."

The next day, at the same hour, Mionnet was again told that "the Abbé who was here yesterday" was downstairs asking for him.

"Have him shown up."

Late on the previous afternoon he had been to see Mme Lacchini and, without describing the nature of the document, had told her of the unknown priest's offer.

"He's a man called Ginorini," she had said. "I spoke to my husband about him this morning. It is generally believed that he has some incriminating evidence against the Cardinal . . . but since it was the Cardinal who had him dismissed from his post, it may be that he is merely trying to get revenge. My husband takes the very natural view that he is not a man to be trusted. Nevertheless, it is quite possible that the documents in question are genuine. One can never tell with people like that. He has several times tried to market them. If you really want them badly, you wouldn't, of course, dream of giving him the price he asks. . . . You'd have to go into it much more thoroughly and beat him down a lot. . . ."

The big, dark-skinned fellow came into Mionnet's room, his brief-case under his arm.

"Have you thought over what I said?" he asked jovially, taking off his hat.

"Yes . . . and I've come to the conclusion that at the price you name, even assuming that you can give me full guarantee of authenticity, the offer doesn't interest me. . . . In the first place, it's quite incredible that, even if the person concerned should have been guilty of the unbelievable foolishness of letting such a photograph be taken, you should have got hold of it, negative and all!"

Ginorini shook his head.

"Do you think I got it for nothing? . . . Besides, as no doubt Mme Lacchini informed you, I was at one time in an official position. . . . It hasn't occurred to you, perhaps, that in those circumstances a man may get chances of picking up things of considerable importance?"

He glanced round the room.

"At the time I am speaking of, there would not have been an object in this room that I couldn't have got hold of if I'd wanted to. If you do decide to buy the picture, take my advice and catch a train home that same evening. (I shan't give you away, but it would be better to be on the safe side.) . . . Get it into safe keeping somewhere . . . in the strong-room of some bank . . . preferably in another city"—he winked—"Bologna, for instance."

Two important considerations flashed into Mionnet's mind. He gave expression to them one after the other:

"How is it that no one's managed to get it from you before this, and without bothering to pay for it? . . . It wouldn't, surely, be difficult . . . you go about everywhere with it on you. . . ."

"Perhaps attempts have been made. But that's all over. Why? Because it's known that I am armed and that I shouldn't have the slightest hesitation about defending myself. The police force in question doesn't like having to do with armed men. If you're thinking of taking the photograph to another city, go armed. And don't forget to mention quite casually to the people in your compartment that you are armed. Then you won't have any trouble."

"There's another question I was about to put to you. . . . You referred—and I think I know why—to Bologna. . . . Why haven't you already found someone likely to be interested in this photograph in, let us say for the sake of argument, Bologna?"

"I can't answer that just now. Later, perhaps, I may be able to explain."

Neither spoke for a while. Then Ginorini, in a quite different and much sharper tone of voice than any he had hitherto used said suddenly:

"I can see you don't trust me. . . . I am going to give you proof of my bona fides. . . . I am in a mood to make you, here and now, a little present—the truth about the MacWrench affair—and it won't cost you a centime. Take a pencil, if you please, and make a note of what I'm going to tell you. Edgar Henry MacWrench, employed as one of the Palace Chamberlains from the 1st of July 1904—get that down, it's important—was caught *flagrante delicto* with a boy, a young match-seller, at midnight on the 16th of May 1905. . . ."

"*Fiammiferi!*" exclaimed Mionnet to himself. "Now I understand!"

". . . and condemned on the 19th of August (make a note of it) to a sentence of three months' imprisonment. . . . The match-seller got two and a half months in a reformatory."

"The 19th of August," thought Mionnet; "and it would have been reported in the newspapers of the 20th. . . . Excellent. . . . Still, strictly speaking, it proves nothing. . . . A blackmailer who had invented the whole thing would surely have taken the precaution himself to tear out the pages to prevent anyone trying to verify his facts."

"That same day," went on the other, "Merry del Val telephoned to a Monsieur Eddings, American chargé d'affaires—you can spell Eddings?—asking him to keep all reference to the affair out of the English and American papers. MacWrench was an old and very intimate friend of his. They had been inseparable ever since they were students together at Birmingham. He was not his only friend. MacWrench was on the most affectionate terms with the Cardinal Vincente Vanutelli, the younger of the two brothers of that name, and well known for his anti-French feelings—and had accompanied him on his mission to Ireland. The whole group, you see, was involved. The Pope, in spite of his blind belief in Merry del Val, would have broken every one of them. . . . The miracle they achieved was keeping the Pope from ever getting wind of the affair. . . . Oh, they had to be pretty slick. . . . They actually succeeded in getting MacWrench acquitted on appeal . . . so that even if some mention of the business had got to the Pope's ears at last, they could always say: 'It was a devilish plot organized by the enemies of the Church. . . . You can see for yourself. . . . The Court of Appeal has declared his innocence."

He struck the cover of his brief-case with his fingers. "There's no

Court of Appeal where my photograph is concerned."

He made a wide gesture with his arm and went on:

"I'm in no hurry. Take your time. . . . I don't imagine that you go about with fifty thousand lire in your pocket. No doubt you'll have to talk the whole thing over with others. But do what you can to verify my account of the MacWrench affair. If you can prove that I've lied in the slightest particular, you shall have the photograph for nothing."

SUMMARY

Gurau interests Poincaré in the Roman danger, and the President entrusts him with the handling of the business. Gurau gets no help from the Comte de Mun, but manages to enlist the services of the Marquis de Saint-Papoul. The latter, after consulting the Comte de Mézan, offers to the Abbé Mionnet a mission the nature of which is entirely unknown to him. After a conversation with Manifassier, a dinner at the Saint-Papouls' to meet Gurau, and a short interview with Poincaré, Mionnet accepts the mission.

Viaur, with the help of his friend Hachenard, submits the results of his experiments to two pundits of the medical world.—Mionnet takes a short trip to M——, where he has several intimate talks with Monsignor Sérasquier. He receives a strange warning.—Wazemmes is enrolled in the Action Française.—Louis Bastide broods miserably over his failure to shine in mathematics.—Françoise Maieul turns a dangerous corner.—Mionnet arrives in Rome.

Gurau consults Jaurès; Jaurès's discouragement; the decline of the Radicals; the new power of the capitalists.—Lieutenant-Colonel Duroure champions the Three-Years law.—Maykosen describes for William II the political situation in France; Poincaré, Briand, Gurau.—Jerphanion is seriously anxious about the mental attitude of a French youth movement.

Mionnet discovers Rome—its hills, the Tiber, the Vatican.—He is received by M. de Fontmonge, who strongly urges him to be careful. He calls on the Lacchinis, who also warn him, but against dangers of a different kind.—Mionnet makes a prolonged tour of the Vatican Museums. He meditates upon the greatness and the continuity of the Church. The Popes of the Renaissance. "Save Merry del Val."—

He becomes one of the faithful adherents of Dom Charles Magloire. Librarians and archivists. The reunion of the Churches.—Mionnet dines at the Fontmonges' and listens to several anecdotes bearing on the Church. At the Lacchinis' the conversation turns on the German party and the MacWrench affair. At Fagiano's restaurant he listens to the grievances of a Gallican and a modernist.—He is suddenly spurred to renewed activity by the receipt of a questionnaire from Poincaré. He sends a long report in reply: Merry del Val, Giacomo della Chiesa, the German party.—On the Palatine he meets the scagnozzo who introduces him to Paolina.

Maykosen sends to William II a long report on the Italian situation: the secret treaty with France; Merry del Val; fresh light on the Organization.—Viaur, still with the assistance of Hachenard, carries through a brilliant demonstration of his theories.—Ortegal goes through a bad time. Charm. His contract with Jan Levisson. The distorting mirror. The compass card. The Rio Tintos. Genius set free. —Mionnet undertakes, without success, an inquiry into the Mac-Wrench affair. Ginorini offers to sell him a very curious photograph, and makes him a present of the facts about MacWrench.

BOOK FOURTEEN:

THE BLACK FLAG

Chapter

1

WITH REFERENCE TO A
PARTICULAR MAGNETIC FIELD

"Well, it was time."

"Time for what?"

"Time we did something drastic about getting together again like this. You've promised me two whole days; we must spend them entirely together."

"Except tomorrow evening; remember, I told you . . ."

"I make no exceptions; you must get out of that."

"I can't, honestly."

"Oh yes, you can. You've often said that when it was a matter of real moment between friends, nothing ought to be allowed to stand in the way, no excuse should be regarded as valid. Please! You just must put off that engagement. I'm terribly serious about it."

"What a child you are!"

"Perhaps. It takes such a long time for two people to get back to where they were before. Don't you realize that? It's a whole hour since we met, but we're only just beginning to get on the old terms. It's rather awful when one thinks of it. I honestly believe we should have had a more interesting conversation if we'd been complete strangers. How do you explain such an odd state of affairs?"

"It's probably that where we're concerned you demand more. You take our old relations as the standard and compare the present with the past."

"All the more reason for not cutting short a meeting to which I've looked forward for so long. We shall get back to the old intimacy just about when we've got to part again, tomorrow evening, you see if we don't. We shall suddenly discover all sorts of things that we want to say to each other."

They had passed the Arc de Triomphe at the Carrousel and were now walking along the centre path of the Tuileries Gardens.

Jallez stopped, pulling Jerphanion gently by the sleeve.

"Let's have a good look. There's something different about you."

"I'm older."

"No, it's not that."

"Perhaps I'm fatter?"

"Don't be a fool . . . it's some tiny detail. . . . Ah, I've got it! It's your beard; don't you wear it differently?"

"Yes."

"It's shorter, surely, and not so thick?"

"Yes, quite accidentally, I assure you."

"Accidentally?"

"I took too much off when I was trimming it some time ago, and then I got fiddling about with it until the only thing left to do was to alter its whole shape. There was a period when it had almost completely vanished, but it's grown since then."

A few paces farther on he reverted to a thought which he had already put into words:

"I may not look older, but time's passing and we're all of us getting on. Another year gone. It's awful! Do you remember that visit you paid me in my native mountains? The wonderful days we had? Can you still see in imagination the inn where they made us an omelet on the great stove? Say you can."

"I can, extraordinarily clearly—just as though I were there now. The two tables where the peasants sat with their whips and their sticks . . . and their hats. One down the middle of the room, the other against the wall. I can still taste the wine. . . ."

"Good! I like to hear you say that. . . ."

". . . and still recapture our mood, the way we felt as though we were masters of time, riding the years like a horse. And I can see again the country we walked through, and feel my blister, and remember how I actually enjoyed its hurting me, and revelled in the exhaustion of my limbs. And after our meal, when you got us both going again, there was a sort of lightness in my head, a devil-may-care spirit of laughter, a blister on my foot, and, between the two, my legs, which felt like a couple of bits of string. Never fear, I shall remember it as long as I live. . . . You tried to teach me a mountain song, which I found amazingly beautiful, an expression of patience and strength and mastery passed on from father to son down the ages. . . ."

"Well, old man, we've never really met since then, not what I call meeting, with time to talk at length and at leisure. If that's to be the rhythm of our lives, it's all too horrible to contemplate. We shall reach sixty without ever having had more than a week together."

"Circumstances may change."

"I hope to God they do. . . ."

"We must wait and watch."

"And think of the hardening of the arteries."

"Which is already well on its way, eh?"

"That kind of thought makes one want to let everything go hang, all the so-called serious things of life, the duties and the tasks which eat up one's life without leaving anything to show for the effort, to abandon everything for the chance of *doing* something, something that shall resist the action of time, some piece of knowledge mastered, perhaps, some line of study established. The great thing is to be able to recognize at first sight just those actions which will count most in the years to come, which will give one a feeling later on that one has made the best of one's time, has filled it full to bursting. And they're far from being the kind that the immediate circumstances of one's life, the discipline of one's days, indicate as being the most significant. When I'm fifty, when I'm sixty, what shall I most regret not having done now, this very year, this very summer? What shall I reproach myself with not even having had the idea of doing? That's the tragic problem; nothing else matters two hoots. When we look back on it all, the things that now seem so important, the preoccupations and plans and calculations of today will have shrunk to the dimensions of the merest trivialities and cheats of time. . . . In such matters you've always been more reliable than I. It's you to whom I must look for advice and inspiration."

While the words poured from him, they were both of them looking, or seeming to look, at the children playing ball between the trees. But Jerphanion was busy with other questions deep within himself. He would have liked to look them squarely in the face, to confront them with what he had found words to express, to make them the subject of discussion. But he kept them to himself, so that they were constantly being shouldered out of his mind by their actual talk. Only now and then, by chance as it were, did he come to terms with them, only to lose them a moment later in the confused onset of his silent thoughts. "What about the two M's—Memento Magnitudinis? . . . What have I done for the two M's? . . . How do I stand now in regard to the two M's? . . . How do they fit in with what I've just been saying? When I'm sixty will it be the line marked out for me by the two M's that I shall then consider as having been the great fulfilment of my life, the supreme realization of my vanished youth?" His silent colloquy ended on another note: "This evening, or to-morrow, when our intimacy will have regained something of its former warmth, I may be brave enough to trot out the two M's. I may even be brave enough to ask him what he thinks about it all."

A little later, somewhere between the Horses of Marly and the corner of the avenue de Marigny, on the right-hand sidewalk of the Champs-Élysées, Jerphanion said:

"Do you know, sometimes at La Rochelle when I thought about these things, I used to get a sudden rush of blood to the head. I've a vague sort of idea that you once said or wrote much the same about yourself, but I'm not sure. . . . It used to come over me with a rush that I was entirely wasting my time simply and solely because I was not in Paris. Nothing else mattered. At that very moment I might be having some extremely interesting discussion with a colleague—the younger ones are not all fools—or I might be in some house where there was good music going on, listening to Beethoven, Franck, or

Debussy admirably played . . . or I might be sauntering down by the docks reading some perfectly staggering book . . . and suddenly everything would seem absolutely empty and without meaning. I got the impression that all action, no matter how rich it might be in itself, was completely devoid of interest just because it was not taking place in Paris. At such moments I would feel that a glass of beer that I had drunk in some Parisian café was endowed with a quite incomparable significance and importance. You see what I mean, don't you? It was as though all the actions, all the moments of one's life, even the most secret and intimate movements of one's mind, derive value from the fact that they are or are not situated topographically close to the centre of human activity, a value far in excess of any they might otherwise possess. So much was this so that, walking in a mood of pleasing melancholy some evening by the harbour of La Rochelle, I would feel that my time was being utterly wasted, would feel that the moment was out of place, like a marble pillar set in a farmyard . . . or, if I happened to be saying something rather subtle, rather particularly well worded, to a companion equipped to understand it, I would suddenly say to myself: 'What's the use? Why cudgel one's brain for the right phrase if it's not going to be spoken in Paris?' . . . It wasn't as something personal and capricious that I felt it, as something that at bottom I knew to be false, but as a sort of scientific truth, independent of my private preferences and at times extremely tiresome. And this curious sense of value attached to a particular place had the effect of making me feel that things happening in Paris, however unimportant in themselves, were all aglitter, suffused and irradiated by a sort of continuous glow. I had only to think of two or three friends meeting, say, at the corner of the rue Laffitte and exchanging there on the pavement the most empty nothings, to see them, and everything to do with them, as though caught in the converging beams of searchlights, existing, as it were, in so concentrated a profusion of bright rays that their every 'How are you?' and 'It's not very hot today, is it?' appeared to give off a shower of sparkling rays. . . ."

"How can you doubt my feeling the same? Why, the fact that I do is surely the chief explanation of my having chosen to live like this in spite of every inconvenience. I'm quite sure that what you describe corresponds to something very deep in the human spirit . . . deeper and more intense than any effect of merely physical or climatic conditions. At all periods men have had this sense of the virtue of some particular place . . . of a magnetic field in which actions receive a charge ten times more powerful than any produced by their own peculiar essence: ancient Rome; the Versailles of Louis XIV. What happens within that field matters intensely; what happens elsewhere is nothing. . . . It's a terrible thing when a civilization becomes concentrated in that way, but it's a glory too. Think, for instance, how you'll be feeling in a minute or so when we sit down outside some café for a drink, and how I shall feel too, though for me there will be an extra delight in the fact of your being so much in sympathy with my mood. . . ."

"Yes. . . . I think that's really why, though I didn't consciously plan any such thing, I arranged to meet you at the Châtelet and brought you the way I have. Today I have no craving for the suburbs. I want to drink my fill of the city's centre."

"But if we go on as we are, we shall eventually come to the suburbs."

"You think so? My idea was that after reaching the Place de l'Étoile, we should take the avenue du Bois. It's a fine day, and there should be a lot of people there."

"Why not Longchamp? I've never known you so 'Parisian'—in inverted commas! Where do you want to lunch? At the Cascade? I've got a better idea than that. Let's turn down the avenue Matignon here and rejoin the faubourg Saint-Honoré. We'll walk up it as far as the rue Royale and find a table in front of one of the two most 'central' cafés in the whole world. After that we'll keep to the boulevards. In your present state of mind you seem to me to be on the verge of falling a prey—though on a higher level than most people—to the mysticism of the boulevardier, which is something we were probably

quite wrong to laugh at as we used to do. After all, it may have concealed a sensitive response to this magnetic field of yours. It's a pity
that its adepts, in the heat of their enthusiasm, talked such a lot of
rot. It's all rather difficult."

Chapter

2

When they were seated outside Weber's, Jallez learned that Jerphanion would "almost certainly" be appointed to Orléans at the beginning of the October term.

"I was in two minds about telling you, because things aren't finally settled yet. . . . I'm terribly keen. . . . If the fellow who's got the job at the moment goes, I'm to take his place. But Paris being impossible, he wants Versailles, and Versailles will become vacant only if the man there's retired, and that's not yet definitely fixed. I'm like a cat on hot bricks. For me Orléans would, to all intents and purposes, be Paris. Only two hours by express, and more trains a day than I can remember. No, that's not strictly true; I know exactly how many there are. I almost learned the time-table by heart in a café at La Rochelle. It would mean the beginning of a new life for me. I should take a season ticket and try to keep a lodging in Paris. I might even make it my headquarters. It would only mean a little extra care in arranging my hours and my budget. I should let nothing stand in my way. The idea of such a future fills me with excitement. We could see quite a lot of each other, couldn't we, old man? It would be like being back at the College. Naturally, we should each have his job to do, but, on the other hand, there wouldn't be those awful exams hanging over our heads. All things considered, we should be just as free as we ever were."

Jallez congratulated his friend—and himself too, since such an event would have the happiest effect upon their friendship. Still, he was anxious to know whether, for Jerphanion, the "future" meant nothing more than a mere return to the capital. He put a few discreet questions. What about that "active life" which he had so often heard the other plan and contemplate? Would having a lodging in Paris help that, or would Jerphanion be willing to side-track it, provided he could ensure himself a more exciting and happier daily existence than he enjoyed at present?

Jerphanion betrayed signs of embarrassment. He admitted that he had taken a few "first steps" in politics at La Rochelle.

"I've thought it all over carefully. The only way to become active politically, quite apart from any personal aims and objects, is by joining some sort of an organization. I got into touch with a committee, the members of which were good enough to let me join temporarily without forcing me to take any final vows. I addressed them once or twice. I found it extraordinarily interesting to watch local politicians at close range. My experience at Bergerac wasn't enough. Besides, I wanted to try my wings."

"What committee was it?"

"You'll laugh when I tell you—the Radical-Socialist. . . . If I'd wanted to I could have been a candidate at next year's election. But the only thing I really want is to get clear of La Rochelle. My ambitions, you notice, are strictly limited."

Jallez smiled at some unexpressed thought. "Weren't there," he asked very quietly, "any Socialists there? Or have you broken with them?"

Jerphanion did not show so much as the quiver of an eyelid.

"I could give you many subtle reasons for my action," he said, "if you'd really like to hear them. . . . I'm in no way estranged from the Socialists. If I ever enter active politics, I shall be on the best possible terms with them. But I don't want to join the party, and, as a matter of fact, they don't want men like me. If I've got to belong to any regular organization, I'd infinitely rather be a very advanced member of some party which allows perfect freedom of thought and does not regard a complicated attitude as a crime. I'm pretty sure that the Socialists are wrong on a number of points, and that they do themselves harm by sticking to them. If I belonged to them, I could never criticize them openly."

"But can you do so any more easily if you're not?"

"Perhaps. And, in any case, I'm not sure that I care."

But it was only later, about four o'clock, when they were taking their ease in front of a small café on the boulevard Bonne-Nouvelle, that Jerphanion said suddenly, like a man making up his mind to jump into a cold bath:

"I've kept the best news to the last—I'm going to get married."

Chapter

3

WHY I'M GOING TO GET MARRIED

The effect of his words was all that he could have wished. Jallez said nothing. The sudden complexity of his feelings seemed to have taken from him all power of speech.

"Yes . . . I didn't write about it before, partly because it wasn't certain, partly because I wanted to tell you and get your immediate impression. It's really all terribly simple. If I've anything to be ashamed of, it's that my story's so ordinary. I got to know the girl at La Rochelle, though neither she nor her parents are natives of the place. She's the daughter of a civil servant, of a local tax-collector. She's been pretty well educated; the mother, I think, had money of her own, and the father's had quick promotion. But don't run away with the idea that I'm making a sound, sensible match. There are several children, and that, combined with the fact that the parents like living comfortably, means that there won't be much in the way of a marriage portion. Please realize, too, that we didn't meet, as we ought to have done, in some provincial drawing-room. There's no old matchmaker in the picture. No, our acquaintance began in the Paris train, and at first we kept our friendship secret. We were very shy. We used to meet with a good deal of romantic mystery, and considerable discomfort, in the less frequented parts of La Rochelle, at night under the ramparts, or down by the docks, or in some sailors' bar, or at a suburban tramway terminus, or at some country restaurant where nobody went in the middle of the week.

"There was a charm about it all which no one who's not lived in the provinces could realize, and then only if he'd come originally from Paris, with Paris always at the back of his mind. My adventure was rather like a child's game in which the element of play was the most important ingredient, a game touched with nostalgic pain, and capable of affecting the most diverse circumstances of my daily life. For instance, I'd imagine myself a boy again, coming out of school about five o'clock of a winter's afternoon, straight into the main street of the town. I would make an effort to realize how many people there were about, how thick the traffic was, how numerous the lights. I would be struck with amazement at the number and variety of the shop-fronts, as though I couldn't take in everything at once. I would suddenly discover houses, cafés, side-streets, seeing them as a never-ending stream. 'What, another street-crossing!' or 'What an amazing perspective of lamps!' Another day I would amuse myself by adventuring into a quarter that had all the appearance of lying on the outskirts of the town—a sort of modern suburb, all tall new houses and tramway lines—delighted to discover more roads than I had thought existed there. Or again, on the pretext of buying some little thing, I would go into one of the big local shops, take the lift, elbow my way through the crowd, hang about the counters, far from any window, in a radiance of artificial light. The point of the game was pretending to be in a great city, cheating my longing for the sights and sounds of a great city. But there's one longing that it's difficult to cheat by make-believe, one illusion that it's almost impossible to get—the feeling that one can lose oneself, can escape one's individuality and become a nameless element in a multitude, unrecognized and unremarked. My love-affair with this young woman made it possible for me to try, really to try, to achieve that mood. I became extraordinarily ingenious, we both did, in discovering the mysterious possibilities of La Rochelle, the resources of anonymity in its public places, since there was never any question of our being able to escape somewhere indoors. Our idyll remained innocent. There was nothing about it that anyone mightn't have known. But I am pleased to think that it had this gently romantic air. If it had begun according to all the ghastly social rules, which are worse in the provinces even than here—apparently accidental meetings under the watchful eyes of Mamma—and all the rest of it—I should have got heartily sick of it. . . . My future wife is very pretty and really quite informed. She has quite definite tastes of her own, is not devoid of character, likes certain things and dislikes others. The provinces have been not so much the fixed centre as the passing background of her life. Paris has always stood for her as the true heart of civilization. There's nothing comic about her—and that's saying a good deal when you think what she might be."

"And you're very much in love?"

"Yes."

"May I know her name?"

"Odette Clisson. I look forward to introducing you to her one day very soon."

"When do you think of getting married?"

"At the beginning of September. By that time my new appointment will have been settled. I shall have a month for a short honeymoon and the business of getting into our flat."

Jallez's amazement had given place, little by little, to a sort of friendly interest. While he voiced his not very exuberant congratulations, thoughts crowded on him. "What does all this really mean? Does it just represent the sudden, the almost unexpectedly sudden, collapse of a man into ordinariness after the brief flare of enthusiasm which marked our earlier companionship? Or is there something more behind it? Perhaps he's deliberately minimized the whole affair; perhaps, in reality, it's all much finer, much less flat, than he's led me to suppose. Why not? There might well be an exquisite side to a love-idyll such as he has described, with its background of a small provincial town twisted for the purposes of passion into the semblance of a huge and kindly city, a quality both rich and satisfying. It is not difficult to imagine those small cobbled streets pinched between ramparts and silent ale-houses and little dock-side houses like the ones I've so often seen at Saint-Malo. I can visualize it all: some corner tucked away at the end of one of the docks, with a cargo boat tied up to the bollards, and the quay-side littered with ropes that get in the way of one's feet; a street running down to the sea; an open-air restaurant on the town's edge where, on Sundays, the sailors go to dance, deserted on week-days, and made for lovers' meetings. Why should I, who know so well how friendship can find its highest flights during a quiet and unexciting walk, demand for love some rare and special setting? Why be so romantic about it? A perfectly ordinary spring day, replete with all its traditional and rather flat 'poetical' associations, fruit-blossom and brimming streams, birds and moonlight, may well be bursting with lyric rapture. And so it is with love. Why shouldn't the daughter of a provincial civil servant be tempting to enamoured youth, be wholly his and caught up in the intoxicating ecstasy of life? Who, looking at Hélène Sigeau's home and circumstances, would ever have suspected hidden depths? If it comes to that, what outward evidence is there in me, in us, of the life that goes on within?"

Jerphanion had no suspicion that his friend's mind was working along these more or less sympathetic lines. To himself he said: "I'd much better have said nothing at all than explain myself so badly. A laundryman telling a pal at some local hop that he had just got engaged would have made a better job of it. I must have seemed clumsy and rather shamefaced, awkward and flat. The important thing was to make Jallez realize that I could get married, and get married in just this way, without necessarily behaving like a fool. There were a number of reasons I might have given. They would, perhaps, have sounded odd to him, and even cynical, but they would have prevented my becoming an object of scorn. But I just hadn't the courage to put them into words. And now it's too late. What little courage I had has gone. If I spoke now, it would look as though I were trying to correct the bad impression I had made, seeking excuses for something already done."

He had, in fact, spent the last three or four days in "working up" these reasons in readiness for the explanation he knew he would have to make to Jallez. But the only result of his labours had been to leave him uncertain of how far those reasons were genuine, and how far they had been furbished up for the purpose of disarming the objections of his rather frightening friend.

Why *was* he getting married? He was half inclined to banish the question from his mind as useless. He had reached the point of wondering whether indeed it wasn't a rule of life that the more important a question was for the individual, the more impossible it became to say anything of value about the motives that had dictated it. "It's all quite natural. An important decision involves the whole man; that is to say, the reasons that lie behind it are infinite in number. It's impossible, therefore, to pick out a few from the sum total and make a case for them. We should be terrified if we really thought that we were taking such an important step for reasons so few, so utterly insufficient. We should feel guilty of unpardonable irresponsibility. No, rather than that, we persuade ourselves that we are acting in obedience to a host of reasons deep within us. So little do we let our minds dwell on the determining factors that not seldom we are consciously swayed at last by something that in itself is perfectly trivial. Not that the single consideration is alone responsible for what we do, but at any given moment it releases the spring as a result of which, in the twinkling of an eye, we pass from one set of circumstances already established to another, seemingly of the same sort, but differing from it in some highly important detail which our conscious mind glosses over. For instance, the established circumstance in my particular case was that I found myself deeply in love with, and beloved by, a young girl; that I met her constantly in conditions of romantic secrecy; that I found in her a friend and companion; that I discovered suddenly that murmured nothings and stolen kisses were not enough; that I desired her wholly. To say to myself, and to her, that I was going to marry her seemed a mere detail added by a scarcely perceptible flick of the mind to what had gone before. Similarly, if she had come to see me in my lodgings, it would have needed but a tiny shift of the emotional pattern to change the quality of the kisses we had always exchanged so far and to make me into her lover. In both cases thought plays little part in the business, but that doesn't alter the fact that the tiny additional detail has become more important than everything else put together. On that detail—though at the moment of its occurrence it may seem to be merely amusing, half accidental, capricious even —may depend a considerable part of one's future, or, for that matter, all of it. If my lodgings in La Rochelle had not been so lacking in discreet opportunities, had not been so open to the public gaze, she might have come to see me there, in which case the probability is that she would have become my mistress. Had the set of circumstances represented by that fact really materialized, I might have found them wholly satisfying. The idea of marriage would have seemed to belong to a totally different sequence of events situated vaguely and problematically in the future, to be a matter of no urgency or even probability in the immediate future. Or again, had La Rochelle been a larger city, with hotels respectable enough to be visited, if chosen with care, by the daughter of a local bigwig without fear of recognition. . . ."

Why was he getting married? He felt now pretty certain that he could answer the other question "how it was that he was getting married"—that is to say, as a result of what circumstances—emotional as well as material—and with a full realization that each stage of the process had followed on, for good or ill, quite "naturally" from those that had preceded it.

He couldn't, however, help regretting certain formulas which had been an integral part of the brief he had worked up for his friend's benefit and then been too cowardly to employ, formulas which, apart from the fact that they sounded well, would not have been without an explanatory value. They were, of course, nothing but intellectual exercises, but even intellectual exercises have a way of expressing underlying realities. This, for instance (though it was so daring that he could with difficulty bring himself to dig it from the recesses of his consciousness and display it before his friend, who might well doubt its sincerity and see in it nothing but a piece of self-conscious exhibitionism couched in the worst possible taste, unworthy of the solemnity of the occasion, and insulting to the other party to the contract): "I'm getting married because I like pleasantness, because I'm feeling lustful, because it's convenient. . . . Pleasantness? Yes, I have a weakness for pleasant things and pleasant actions. Marriage is extremely pleasant. To ask the hand of a young girl is pleasant. All the circumstances surrounding and accompanying the act of marriage, are pleasant. (If one isn't careful, they may become merely fatuous.) Given the existence of a woman with whom one is in love, getting married differs from not getting married precisely by the addition of a 'pleasant' factor. . . . Because I'm feeling lustful, and because it's convenient? One implies the other. For some months now I've been going through a period of acute sexual appetite and it looks as though the condition is likely to remain permanent. I crave the sexual act constantly, I want to enjoy it at my leisure, and at quite unexpected times. Nor am I insensitive to its material background. So long as I haven't a woman of my own, always available, any satisfaction I may get will be desultory and incomplete. Mood and practicability rarely coincide. The charm of certain settings which come frequently to my imagination would be enhanced by a feeling of security. Outside marriage they could hardly be come by at all, or only as the result of a very rare concatenation of circumstances. They would involve more money, more planning, more preparation, more concentration than I am prepared to devote to them. Nor is monopoly to be sneezed at. All things considered, it is as reasonable to want to have a woman of one's own as to have a house, a library, or a car of one's own. (The advantages for a woman of having a man of her own are, in the present state of society, too obvious to merit discussion.) The act of marriage transforms possession in fact into possession in law, in sexual as in other matters. True, the security is not quite the same as in the case of a house, and involves a certain loss of liberty—more for the man than for the woman. Still, there's a good deal to be said for it."

A few vague references of this description did, in fact, creep into Jerphanion's conversation in the course of the afternoon.

"I've told you all my secrets," he said next day as they were lunching together in the rue Montorgueil; "but you've not repaid me in kind. You've said absolutely nothing. How are things with you?"

Jallez assured him that, unfortunately, so far as his love-life was concerned, there was absolutely nothing to report.

"If I'd spent a year in La Rochelle, I can quite easily imagine that I too might be contemplating marriage with a charming young friend who had saved me from loneliness. . . . As to my work, that falls into three different sections: poetry, of a very concentrated and abbreviated kind; prose poems, also very abbreviated, which are a medium for another kind of concentrated emotional experience—in all this, of course, you will see the influence of Baudelaire—finally, essays, combining great precision of expression and a strong lyric feeling—or, at least, that's my intention. I've published next to nothing because—oh, for fear that what I produced might fall flat. If that happened I should be discouraged from going on. At present I have a feeling of gentle affection for what I write, a feeling that is unaffected by my powers of self-criticism. And failure might spoil that."

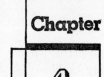

Chapter

4

MIONNET FEELS HIMSELF ABANDONED

For the last fortnight Mionnet had been staying with the Lacchinis in their villa at Frascati, whither they had moved for the first part of the summer. The second half of August and all September they would spend at a large estate which they owned in the Abruzzi. The Abbé had been given a room on the first floor with a south-west aspect. A big tree, the branches of which actually brushed his window, blocked out most of the view, but tempered the heat of the sun.

He had hesitated a long time before accepting Mme Lacchini's invitation, which, in a slightly different form, had been of long standing. For some time now the Hôtel Helvétia et de la Paix had become impossible. One fine day a new valet de chambre of a very odd sort had made his appearance. The man had all the appearance of a sheriff's officer, and it didn't need a particularly acute nose to smell "black police" a mile off. From that moment Mionnet noticed that whenever he went out his room was ransacked and his clothes gone through. Papers had a way of disappearing, or, what was worse still, of vanishing for a time and being suddenly replaced, without any explanation being given of these curious vagaries. He set about testing his suspicions, deliberately leaving about faked letters that contained nothing but a lot of nonsense. They would be spirited away, to turn up again forty-eight hours later with an air of complete innocence in some place where Mionnet knew perfectly well he had never put them.

"Come and take up your quarters with us," Mme Lacchini had said. "Our servants are absolutely reliable. We've got a spare room that's doing nothing."

"With us" meant the Villa Ludovisi. Mionnet had excused himself from accepting. He did not like the idea of losing his liberty of movement, and he was afraid of compromising his position by seeking too openly the protection of a family whose opposition to the heads of the Curia was so well known. Besides, Mme Lacchini's excessive sympathy made him uneasy. It reminded him of Mme de Quingey, and he was in no mood, for the moment at least, to encourage an increasing intimacy.

He tried taking a furnished room quite close to Santa Maria Maggiore, but soon grew to dislike the district, finding it too far removed from the centre of the city. It had a provincial air and belonged to no period and no particular style. The room itself was uncomfortable. The single tap, for all its shining newness, provided only a thin trickle of water, and even that no more than once or twice a day. The thin walls afforded no protection against the overpowering heat. His landlady may have had nothing to do with the police, but she was coarse and indiscreet. He felt that his refusal to gossip made him at once, in her eyes, an object of suspicion.

When, on the eve of departing for their house in the Alban Hills, the Lacchinis had renewed their offer of hospitality, he had yielded, feeling that to accept an invitation to the country during the hot months was something very different from living with the family in Rome itself.

The question of domicile was not, however, his most besetting preoccupation. The principal cause of his worry lay in Paris.

After his third interview with Ginorini, realizing that the business upon which he had embarked was of an extremely delicate nature, he had taken several days to think things over. Finally he had written to Manifassier in terms left purposely vague. He mentioned his meeting with a highly suspect individual who might, however, turn out to be well informed, who had given him a certain amount of information which it might be worth while verifying, and who had made him the offer of a document of a very special sort, which it might be impossible to use and for which he was asking an absurd price.

It was some time before Manifassier's answer arrived, and when it did, it contained no definite instructions, though Mionnet realized that his own had hardly been of a kind to elicit any.

Meanwhile he had spoken once more to three of the persons who, from the earliest days of his inquiry, had shown the greatest readiness to answer questions. "This," he told them, "is what I have found out about the MacWrench affair. Is my information, so far as you can remember, likely to be accurate—especially in the matter of dates?" None of the three agreed in all particulars with the other two. One queried the year. "It was certainly later than that . . . I can prove it by . . ." The second maintained that there never had been an appeal: "It was a perfectly clear case of guilty—there was no getting away from it. It's quite likely that he never served his sentence, because there are ways and means of coming to terms with Heaven—but that's the most that can be said." The third refrained from questioning Mionnet's facts, but refrained equally from substantiating them.

He confided his uncertainty to M. de Fontmonge, and asked that gentleman for his advice.

"Now that I know the dates," he said, "there must be some way of verifying the details by reference to the official records. Do you think I could manage to do that without attracting too much attention to my movements and to the nature of my inquiry?"

"No. You mustn't do that. I'll try to get the information for you. But it won't be easy even for me. You realize, don't you, that Rome's a place where far fewer things happen than in Paris? Nothing goes unnoticed here. If the authorities began to suspect that I was making serious efforts to dig up that old scandal—just passing on a good story is quite another matter—they're quite capable of demanding my recall."

Three days later M. de Fontmonge, with an air of embarrassment which was foreign to him, said:

"Apparently it's impossible to find out anything."

Mionnet was on the point of exclaiming: "Nonsense! You can't be serious!" but noticing his informant's expression, he held his peace. He merely said, pursing his lips a little:

"It's all very odd."

M. de Fontmonge continued, this time in a firmer tone of voice: "We should have to move heaven and earth to get hold of any official documents . . ." (his accent achieved wonders with the word "official"). "Personally, I can't afford the risk. And I don't know anyone who could take the necessary action without raising a hornet's nest. My advice to you is: leave that dirty linen alone." He frowned. "You'd much better keep clear of the business."

Mionnet was honoured with another visit from Ginorini.

"Well, have you verified what I told you about MacWrench? Do you still think I'm trying to cheat you?"

"No, I haven't—not yet. . . . Apparently it's impossible to find any proof."

Ginorini gave a chuckle. Then he shrugged his shoulders and sighed. Obviously he had just been about to say something, but had changed his mind. When he spoke, it was very quietly:

"Very well, then, buy those newspaper pages. You'll be able to verify them all right."

"Show them to me. If I find them sufficiently interesting I'll buy them."

"Oh dear me, no! Once you've seen them, you'll tell me you haven't any further need of them."

"I certainly won't buy them without seeing them first. For all I know, they may be just taken from some comic sheet . . . or from some publication got up for purposes of blackmail" (he did not know the Italian for "blackmail" and left the word untranslated). "They may be completely valueless."

Ginorini gave vent to another sigh.

"All right, but buy the photo and I'll throw the pages in. If it's only the method of payment that's bothering you, I'll come to an arrangement. But you must make up your mind quickly. I've had another offer for the negative and all the other compromising documents in my possession. I'm a man of honour, and, once the bargain's made, I shall keep nothing back. You'll have missed the chance of a lifetime."

Mionnet wrote once more to Paris. His envelope contained two separate letters. One of them was couched in the impersonal style of a report. What it said in substance was: "A certain G—, a pretty shady ecclesiastic, who says he was once a member of the black police, has furnished me with the following information about the affair to which I referred in my letter of the . . . an affair which, in the early days of the present pontificate, threatened to send the Cardinal Secretary of State sky-high. . . . It should be noted that the dates correspond exactly with those of the mutilated newspapers in the public files. . . . I have tried to get official confirmation. . . . Certain reasons made it impossible for me to undertake the inquiry myself. The man I commissioned to make it for me either failed or got frightened. The net result is that though the matter in question seems to belong to a class admitting of material proof, such proof has so far escaped me. Is it your wish that I should get it no matter what the risk? It's quite on the cards that you might be able to confirm the dates by other means. This fellow G— gave me the information free, hoping in that way to persuade me to buy a document about the nature and value of which I am extremely sceptical. If it is genuine—and it's not going to be easy to prove that it is—it provides perfectly definite proof of the particular charge in question. But it is so dubious a weapon that you might refuse, on principle, to have anything to do with it, and in any case the problem of how to make use of it would be an extremely delicate and difficult one to solve. The price asked is fantastic. I could probably beat the man down a good deal. I must add that, should you decide to buy, my gentleman offers to throw in certain of the mutilated newspaper pages (see what I said about them above), which he claims to have in his possession."

The other letter, marked: *"Destroy when read,"* was a confidential note addressed personally to Manifassier. In it Mionnet wrote very much more freely, giving his personal views on Ginorini, describing the photograph, and making no bones about his personal feeling of embarrassment in the matter. "I have a feeling that, all things considered, the picture may be genuine. But the fellow's a rat, and carrying out a deal of this kind with him will make me feel grubby. I realize, too, that the mere fact of getting hold of such a document puts me within measurable distance of becoming a blackmailer. At the same time, one mustn't forget that the complicated intrigues of the Roman scene and the curious give and take that goes on between persons of very different moral standards have a way of making credible here the employment of methods which would be incredible elsewhere. In Rome men of honour have fewer scruples than in France about using weapons, when necessity arises, which they know would be used unhesitatingly against themselves. The problem for us is not so much whether we should or should not take advantage of a document of this particular kind—I can't really see us descending to such a dirty level—as whether we could find anyone of a type to jump at such a tasty morsel and, while using it for his own purposes and entirely on his own responsibility, bring about a train of events with which we should be honestly in sympathy." He then mentioned the sum demanded by Ginorini, adding that it could probably be halved.

He awaited the reply impatiently, and it was long in coming. It showed no sign of that excitement which he expected his own missive to have aroused. A careful examination of it left him with two predominant impressions: first, that Manifassier had troubles of his own and was beginning to take a detached view of the Roman tangle, even tending to regard it all as something trivial and faintly ridiculous; secondly, that the President himself was showing less interest than he had done in this particular field of diplomatic activity, and that Gurau was no longer prepared to be as helpful as formerly. They were willing to leave him in Rome. His mission, which was not sufficiently expensive to bother about, was to be allowed to drag on. They were prepared, perhaps, should the occasion arise, to make use of him for some special task. Meanwhile he was to be left unemployed and with no cause for complaint, since he would be paid regularly.

The prospect was not a very alluring one. To accept a position of diminishing importance was neither to his liking nor, he thought, to his ultimate interest. The only excuse for his occupying so false a position was that it should be important. He wrote to Manifassier as follows: "I have an idea that you don't really know what to do with me here. I never asked for this job. It is quite possible that the results I have already obtained, or look like obtaining, may appear less than was expected, or may be leading to tiresome complications. I have done my best to follow instructions, and it's not my fault if I've been left without proper guidance. I don't want to go on unless I can feel that what I'm doing is useful and is regarded as useful there."

Chapter

5

A SURPRISING SUMMONS

It was some days after the dispatch of this letter that M. Lacchini, on returning one evening from Rome, whither he was in the habit of going three times a week on business, took him aside.

"I have been charged with a commission to you of rather a curious nature. The Cardinal Secretary of State wishes to see you."

Startled out of his usual attitude of calm detachment, Mionnet showed sudden pallor.

"The Cardinal?" he stammered. "You must be joking."

"I most certainly am not."

The banker smiled. "I've no idea why he wants this interview. He's probably heard something of your activities. Cheer up, he can't eat you."

"When is it to be? . . . And, more important, where?"

"Where? In his office at the Vatican, I imagine."

"Not at Castel Gandolfo?"

"I rather think not. I'm not at all sure he's there yet."

"When does he expect me?"

"I am to be told later the day and the hour. What he wants to be sure of at the moment is your willingness to oblige him."

"But—tell me what you think I ought to do."

"It would, I think, be difficult for you to refuse. Very difficult."

Mionnet appeared to be thinking deeply.

"What's your own view of this invitation?" the banker asked him.

"I'm trying to make out what's behind it."

"What's behind it is that he's begun to take an interest in you. He's paying you a compliment."

"You really think so?"

"The surprising thing about it all is not so much his being up in your movements and behaviour as his feeling the need of making your personal acquaintance."

"It's not, then, the sort of thing he might have been expected to do?"

"I think not."

"All right then. Tell him—tell him that I'll come . . . I don't see what else I can do."

M. Lacchini took a long look at Mionnet, who seemed genuinely put out.

"What are you afraid of? We're no longer living in the days when popes were absolute monarchs. Nobody's going to throw you into a dungeon."

Chapter

A TIRESOME LETTER

"What a complication! This is the last straw!"

       Seated in the garden of the Frascati villa, at a little table on which his breakfast had been served, Mionnet had just finished reading a long letter from Manifassier which had been handed to him a few minutes previously.

Dear Sir:

Your sense of grievance is fully justified. We have undoubtedly treated you with scant consideration. Your last letter has made me realize how long a time you have been in Rome, how shockingly we have left you without instructions or even answers, and how natural it is that you should feel abandoned and discouraged. Your situation is one that must often arise in the case of men on service of various categories—of colonial governors, military officers, etc. They set off fired with enthusiasm, to take up posts of difficulty and danger, exert themselves to make the most of their job, start large-scale enterprises, and run a thousand risks, only to realize that the people at home ignore their existence and ask no better of them than to let themselves be forgotten. There is a lesson to be learned by all of us from what has occurred. The whole trouble, it seems to me, is this; that here, at the centre of things, the chief, whoever he may be, is always up against immediate problems on which he has to concentrate his attention for the greater part of each day. If he thinks once every three months of the man he has sent off to bury himself in the bush, who hangs about there, always ready for action, waiting for the authorization or the instructions of which he so urgently stands in need, he feels that he is doing all that duty demands of him. It's not surprising, is it, that in those circumstances, the man in the bush sees chance after chance slip through his fingers and feels his keenness growing cold? What we need at the seat of government are men at the head of things who should be protected against the claims of mere routine and able to give all their attention to their agents at the other end of the chain, seeing the passage of time with *their* eyes, sharing *their* determination, *their* impatience. But that's an ideal state of affairs that won't come about overnight.

In our particular case the general awkwardness to which I have referred is complicated by the odd sort of arrangement that has been forced upon us by circumstances, by obligations of courtesy, and by various other considerations. It has come about by a queer twist that the President, my own chief, and I are all collectively responsible for you and for the means of keeping in touch with you. No one could call the President a scatterbrain, but I think you will agree that it is only natural, living as he does in a whirl of endless occupations and preoccupations, that he should, not forget a piece of departmental business—I can assure you that he is far from forgetting yours—but persuade himself that it is only a few days since he last turned his mind to it when in fact it is six weeks. My own chief, even in the early days, was never directly concerned and, as things have turned out, is less so now than he ever was. He turned the whole thing over to me, and it is I who am chiefly to blame for what has happened. My excuse must be that for the last few weeks all my time has been given up to what has long been a pet scheme of mine—the starting of a new magazine dealing with politics and sociology. Several friends are helping me, but you know how it is with things of this sort. The main brunt always falls on one pair of shoulders, and in this case they happen to be mine. Looked at from a distance, it may seem a trivial matter (a lot of things have a way of seeming trivial when looked at from a distance). But it thrills me; it occupies my attention to the exclusion of everything else. Honestly, whenever I've thought of you with a vague feeling of guilt—and that's been not seldom—I, like the President, have felt convinced that your last letter to me or my last answer to you was but a day or two old. Enough of explanations—all I ask is that you should bear with me.

You have deserved better of us after giving proof, as you have done, of so much remarkable activity and skill. The last results you reported were brilliant enough to bring the house down! I only hope our negligence hasn't spoiled everything. No sooner did I realize how unpardonably slack I'd been than I did all I could to make up for lost time.

Here, in two words, are your instructions and the considerations on which they are based. We agree with you that this photograph business is frightfully delicate, and the idea that we should be asked to make use of such a weapon makes our hair stand on end. But we agree also that if other hands can be found pure enough or saintly enough to wield it, without involving us, for the attainment of noble ends, it would be a pity to put difficulties in their way. The great point is to get hold of it and keep it in readiness for them should occasion demand. No doubt sooner or later the right man will turn up to avail himself of this liberal aid. At least we shall have time to look about us. The people here, I think, have ideas about the whole business not very different from yours and are contemplating other ways and means of approach which might be employed without prejudice to any new suggestions you may feel moved to make. The immediately important thing is that this document shouldn't be allowed to escape us. The price is terrifying. Try to tempt him to part with it for ten thousand lire, cash down. I am sending the money to you today, under separate cover, in the form of a cheque which you can cash without fear of indiscretion at the Banca Commerciale Italiana, 112 Via del Plebiscito. I needn't warn you, before handing over the money, to try to make sure by an examination of the negative (he must part with that, of course) that the photograph is genuine—a point I can't help feeling very uneasy about. It has been suggested here that it might be well if you first paid a visit to a French photographer named Buché, who has a studio in the Via dei Condotti (we can't discover the number), and either get him to go with you to the interview (telling him nothing of what it's all about) so that he can examine the negative simply and solely as a technical expert (don't let him see the print for fear he might recognize the principal figure), or, if his presence looks like embarrassing Ginorini or seems to you undesirable, make him explain as far as possible the points to look for in establishing the authenticity of a negative and the ways of discovering faked details. In whichever way you decide to use him, say you come from M. Courson, and offer to pay him for his trouble. Courson has already written to him (don't worry, he knows very little of what's on foot, and the photographer, who has already rendered discreet services of a like nature in the past, will not ask awkward questions). It is essential that he examine the negative either before or after its purchase.

Mionnet's interview with Cardinal Merry del Val was timed for five o'clock of the same afternoon.

Chapter

7

MERRY DEL VAL

Never had Mionnet felt so nervous, so little master of himself or of his powers of observation, as when he entered Monsignor Merry del Val's study.

So awkwardly did he go through the movements of genuflexion, of kissing the ring, and of seating himself that he struck his thigh painfully against the arm of the chair. At first his eyes could take in nothing. He would have found it impossible to say whether the room in which he had been received was large or small. The problem of its size became an obsession to him during the first few minutes, all the time that he was doing his best to listen to and answer the questions put to him: "Is it large? Is it small?" He told himself that it was absurd to worry about so trivial a matter, but that didn't alter the fact that his mind continued to work as though he had been commissioned to give an accurate statement of the cubic contents of the apartment: "What are the dimensions from floor to ceiling? What is the width in feet of that panel?"—though he found that he had lost all idea of what a foot looked like at the very moment when, for some inscrutable reason, it seemed essential to him to make a meticulous reckoning, as essential as that his body should have light and air. "Three feet, six, nine . . . no. . . ." He strove hard to remember the exact appearance of places the dimensions of which were familiar to him, of his room in the Hôtel Helvétia, of his room in Paris, trying to visualize them, to calculate how many times they would go into the space in which he now found himself for the first time. "The wall of my room in Paris would come just about where that scrolled pattern is . . . no, it wouldn't . . . that moulding would be nearer it. . . ."

So far his impressions of the Cardinal had been of the sketchiest.

He seemed separated from him not so much by a veil, which would merely have blurred his physical characteristics, as by something much more abstract yet much more effective as a barrier. The Cardinal's bulk and material appearance had been dissipated as though by magic. He could see the man's features, but they remained, as it were, without significance. He couldn't "get hold" of them enough even to begin to draw conclusions about their owner. They were isolated within a defensive, neutral zone as rarefied as interstellar space, across which the organ of sight could pass only by dint of being divorced from all intelligent direction.

Mionnet fixed his attention on a piece of furniture, a peculiar object that might have figured in a museum or the room of some amateur collector. It was made of wood and leather. The wood had the smoothness and roundness of age. Reddish reflections showed in its rich brown surface. The leather, shining, mottled, and marked here and there with traces of old gilt, reminded him of the belly of some fish. The legs and inset panels were of wood, but there was a large expanse of leather, of plaited leathern strips, such as is to be seen on the backs of old chairs. The object appeared to be a cross between a chest, a press, and a prie-Dieu. It was massive, but not without touches of elegance. Peasants might have used it—or kings. There was about it a Merovingian or a Visigothic air, with an added touch of Renaissance exuberance.

Mionnet retained sufficient lucidity of mind to say to himself: "It's Spanish. It must be some piece of furniture he brought with him from Spain."

The fact that he could make so definite a deduction—the first since he had entered the room—eased his discomfiture. He found that he could listen more attentively to what was being said. He began to find some sort of meaning to his own words. He was aware of an increasing ability to pay attention to the man before him and to draw certain inferences from his appearance.

After first saying a few words in French, Merry del Val asked his permission to continue the conversation in Italian. No doubt his visitor was by this time familiar with the language, though if he would prefer to use French he was at perfect liberty to do so.

These early exchanges took place during the time that Mionnet was suffering from his initial state of mental paralysis. He noted, however, that the Secretary of State spoke French "like a foreigner." Later, although he made no pretence of being able to estimate the degree of excellence of the Cardinal's Italian, he was struck by his host's clear-cut enunciation and by the ease with which, as he listened to him, he could recognise the various words and follow the flow of the phrases, which for the most part were short, unencumbered by parentheses, and uninterrupted by any attempt on the part of the speaker to attain precision or subtlety of expression. This clear-cut quality, this laconic mode of utterance, had about it something rather frightening and vaguely imperious. But the effect was not embarrassing, because the voice in itself was charming.

"I hear that you are studying diplomatic history. It is a subject in which I am deeply interested. I began my career by teaching diplomacy. I should have liked to devote my time to research. As things have turned out, however, I am far too much concerned with the difficulties of present-day politics to find time for pondering those of the past. What precisely is your subject?"

"The foreign policy of the Papacy during the nineteenth century, Your Eminence. But the field is too vast, and I shall have to concentrate on one corner of it."

"You will find the pontificate of Pius IX most likely to reward your efforts. There is a great deal of work to be done on it. The policy of Pius IX has never received fair treatment. He could not have fought otherwise than he did against the errors of his century. Had he been more accommodating, he would still not have been able to lessen the evils to which the Church has been exposed, because, no matter what he had done, covetousness and hostility would always have been in the field against him. Thanks to the resolute line he took, the Church was enabled to retain its rights and take up the struggle again at a later date. . . . I suppose you were afraid of bothering me with the details of your work when you first arrived in Rome. I could have suggested certain lines of approach."

It was at once clear that the charm of this voice was due, in the first place, to a number of purely physical concomitants: clearness of enunciation, freedom from all hesitation and uncertainty, a deep-throated but by no means coarse resonance, the rounded quality of certain syllables that had the effect almost of an organ swell, without, however, breaking the even progress of the vocal line. But it owed something, too, to a very considerable, and seemingly perfectly natural, element of superiority and courtesy. There was no noticeable effort to dominate, nor yet to charm. The speaking tone was never raised, nor by a show of emotion did it try to force the assent of an interlocutor. What it seemed to say was: "This is how things are. It is all perfectly clear; no argument is possible. I am merely drawing your attention to facts. You are far too intelligent, far too well informed, not to see that I am right."

While he spoke, the Cardinal gazed squarely at his visitor. He had magnificent brown eyes beneath thick brows, eyes quite devoid of that hot and sensual quality usually associated with those of Spaniards. They were lustreless, not liquid, but neither were they muddy. From time to time they deepened to the colour of burnt wood, and from time to time their owner looked away, fixing his gaze intently on some object before him as though seeking some analogy with which to point his speech. The nose was finely modelled. The full lips echoed the strong accent of the brows. These two features were the only visible evidence that the man was not devoid of natural instincts.

"And what, may I ask, are your impressions of Rome?"

At first Mionnet replied with a few amiable generalities that committed him to nothing. But as the Cardinal seemed in no haste to interrupt him, he felt obliged to elaborate his comments. Especially did he try to explain the effect on a newcomer of that curious interpenetration of the old and the new city, which no amount of reading could have led him to expect.

Very politely, in two or three sentences which he accompanied with a smile (his smile was rather cold, though the lips were full, but, for all that, it brought light to the face) the Cardinal made it clear that he found no little interest in the tourist attitude which the Abbé had adopted. He asked him whether he knew Madrid. He said that Madrid was a delightful city, but altogether different from Rome. Rome, despite the calamities which had fallen upon her through the ages, had always managed to conserve something of the past, retaining through its long history of two thousand years important vestiges of each separate period. Madrid, apart from a few scattered details, might have been built yesterday. And yet behind it lay long centuries of wealth and glory. He mentioned various places and the names of several streets.

He smiled again. His smile was of finer quality than the lips which gave it life. That the Cardinal Secretary of State should be willing to smile, should be ready to waste time talking of such trivial matters, seemed evidence of his humanity. Here was no fanatic, no inquisitor indifferent to the passing claims of existence. His smile, too, drew attention to his well-tended mouth and gave a glimpse of white and regular teeth, many of which were generously filled with gold, a detail which at that period and especially in Latin countries, produced an effect of transatlantic luxury which the visitor found subtly attractive.

Having to this extent humoured the newcomer, the Cardinal intimated that what really interested him was the impression that Rome had made on the priest rather than on the tourist. Had he felt that curiously "Catholic" grace which the city has it in her power to bestow?

"A man may make his prayers to God in the tiniest chapel of France or Spain. But perhaps only in Rome can he realize the full wonder of the Church."

He even went so far occasionally as to wonder whether anyone could really be said to be a "man of the Church" unless he had been to Rome. (The faintest of smiles took the edge from what might have seemed a statement lacking in charity towards the immense and unseen army of humble clerics scattered through the world—some in country parishes which they would never leave; some in lands given over to heresy; some far away beyond the sundering oceans.)

"Quite clearly he looks on himself as superlatively 'of the Church,' as the Churchman *par excellence*," thought Mionnet, who was now able to see clearly enough. "It's odd."

But why odd? Mionnet would have found himself hard put to it to explain. But there was, somehow, a need to explain the fact that here, facing him, in the year of our Lord 1913, sat the essential Churchman. It was, in a way, so different from what in his calmer moments he might have expected. There was something puzzling about the general impression made by the man, by his worldly air that twenty-five years in the priesthood had in no wise modified, by his appearance of easy nonchalance, almost of aloofness. Then, too, there was the still perfect oval of the face, such as is seen as a rule only in those gifted by nature with genuine beauty and protected, by the habit of always making the best of themselves, against the ravages of age. Nor was the colour of the skin without its part in the total effect. The observing eye was held, fascinated, by its smoothness, its fine, unbroken quality. In a sense it seemed to have no connexion with the crudities of flesh and blood, but to have been chosen, for reasons of texture alone, to express, as in certain works of classic inspiration, a purely plastic and semi-abstract purpose. There was something in it of wax, something of ivory, with a rich golden tint deeply ingrained and a dull, lustreless surface like that of the brown eyes. On a wrinkled face such a colour would have brought to mind some pictured Christ or some Spanish martyr, would have evoked the burning faith, the tormented asceticism, the divorce from life, the withdrawal of the individual, that marks the religious state when it has become a permanent habit of the mind. But on this unlined and quiet countenance it was but an added puzzle, stressing that impression of self-mastery and aristocratic detachment which was apparently typical of the Cardinal.

Mionnet, however, replied that since his first arrival in Rome he had in fact noticed several circumstances that had the effect of deepening his sense of "the Church," making of it a more living reality, bringing home to him the suppleness that belonged to it of right. (He had by this time mastered his earlier nervousness and was now once more capable of marshalling his words, giving direction to his observations, even introducing veiled insinuations into his speech.) At first, he said, he had felt rather at sea, but by degrees he had qualified his first superficial judgments and come to a more profound knowledge of things. (To all of this the Cardinal listened with an air of polite agreement.) But he felt bound to admit that there was still one point in his apprehension of the general atmosphere that was still far from perfect. He certainly realized better now than when he had first come the vital complexity of the Church, but he still had to make a definite mental effort, had, as it were, to apply his acquired knowledge of history, in order to understand how it was that across the centuries, and despite the changes of outward fashion, the life of the Church had been one and indivisible. This effort was more noticeable in Rome than elsewhere. In other places one felt free to generalize on big, bold lines; but here, in Rome, the particular features of each period, the marked originality of each successive age, so obvious even at first sight, had been brought home to him with all the directness of immediate evidence.

The Cardinal seemed so acquiescent that at first Mionnet wondered whether, perhaps, he had not fully grasped his meaning. He was soon, however, reassured on this point.

The Secretary of State admitted that in the course of centuries the activity of the Church had varied, had, no doubt, been marked by many errors.

"But—" (he fixed on Mionnet a piercing gaze, and his voice took on an incisive quality) "we have always ready to hand one certain means of determining when people are mistaken and when they are not, when, that is, they have strayed from the way, and when, despite all appearances to the contrary, their feet are set on the right road. Have they—that is the question—set the destinies of the Church before and above all other considerations? No matter what changes the centuries may have seen, that is the touchstone. This or that pope in the past, respected though he may have been for his private virtues, diverged from the true line, because, without any evil intention, he delivered the Church over to the temporal powers. Another, far from blameless in his personal life, was a great pope because his work was always dominated by a due sense of the Church's undying destiny. All concatenation of circumstances must be judged in the same way, and in the same way we must decide who should be treated by the Church as a friend, who as an enemy, and for how long."

Not once, while he spoke, did he raise his voice, but every word seemed heavily charged with meaning. His phrases were not of the ready-made kind that we speak glibly for the edification of a stranger in whom we have no interest, letting him take or leave them as he wills. "What he says, he says with authority," thought Mionnet, now and then meeting the other's glance; "he speaks what he thinks, and he speaks for me." He continued to read the strange face before him. Above the thick brows rose a fine forehead, almost unlined, in colour something between wax and ivory. This forehead swept upward in an even curve until it merged with the shining ivory of the skull set between two expanses of hair dressed with all the elegance of a "young noble." The effect of baldness had been merely to enlarge a central parting that had been traced with care. Mionnet saw vividly in imagination the photograph and Ginorini's plump fingers disengaging it from its wrappers of tissue paper. "He certainly is very like the man in the picture . . . but then, of course he would be, even if the thing were faked. . . . That this man here before me might have participated in such a scene is not utterly incredible . . . but that doesn't for a single moment alter the fact that he's a very extraordinary individual."

"What is really thrilling," continued the Secretary of State, once more fixing upon him those lustreless eyes beneath their thick brows, set in the midst of that lustreless and well-formed face, "is to discover as a matter of personal experience that the Church is a work of God achieved by men. Its continuity is the result of its divine origin. The vicissitudes through which it has passed are due to the fact that human hands have built it. The melody flows from the inspiration; the impurity of this or that note must be attributed to the instrument. The trouble, when dealing with particular situations of the kind you must be constantly having to deal with in the course of your researches—or elsewhere" (he hurried a little over the words "or elsewhere" and looked away)—"is to determine with due sense of proportion between what is to be attributed to the Church as a divinely inspired institution and what must be regarded as the work of human agents. It is a fine intellectual exercise."

The word "exercise," as he spoke it, seemed to take on a peculiar significance, to belong to some highly technical and specialized vocabulary.

"And in judging of the purely human element one must be careful not to rush to conclusions. The world is not a monastery. One must take the passions of mankind into consideration, sometimes, even, submit to their promptings. Faced by the fact of an apparent evil, one should always ask oneself: 'Didn't it, perhaps, save the world from an evil still worse? Wasn't it possibly productive of an ultimate good?'"

Rightly or wrongly, Mionnet had a feeling that the man's Jesuit training sounded behind these words. But the interesting thing about them was that they were no mere repetition by a disciple of a lesson learned long since. Here was a man with a long and impressive experience of life, occupying one of the most powerful situations that the world could offer, who put into words that admitted of no argument all that the handling of men, backed by long training in a rigid doctrine, had taught him.

Having said this much, the Secretary of State allowed a subtle change to creep into his voice. He became more confidential, descended, as it were, from the lecturer's rostrum, and adopted the attitude of a man discussing things with an equal whose agreement he hopes to win.

"The application of this general rule will ensure sound and untroubled judgment in matters which have perturbed some of the greatest minds. But it is no good applying it partially. The heresy of the modernists is a good example of what I mean. According to them, the doctrines of the Church are the product of a living organism. The important thing, they maintain, is not so much fidelity to the letter of a dogma regarded as fixed and unchangeable, as the continuity of the Church's spiritual life. Tyrrell, whom I knew well, was one of those who held this view. I am no theologian, and I took no part in that particular controversy. The actual point at issue was, I think, the least of the charges that could be made against the modernists. Their real error lay in refusing to listen to the living voice of the Church when she declared that she wished to have nothing to do with their personal theories, with their so-called scientific outlook borrowed from the enemies of Christendom, with the odds and ends of philosophy which they had picked up from the fashionable pundits of the times, when, in short, she pointed out that their continued activity constituted a mortal threat to her own life and continuity. They, a mere handful of cranks, had the cheek to set their private judgment against the whole tradition of the faith, and that, too, after maintaining that truth must be sought in the Church and in the Church alone! The rule is no less applicable to the problem raised by the Separatist activities in France. You will find people here and there to tell you that the situation could have been saved at the cost of a little tact, of a few concessions. They don't seem to realize that such a surrender would have led, inevitably, to far worse evils, until a point would have been reached when there would have been no remedy. On the other hand, by acting as it did, the Church may have suffered much, but from those sufferings, willingly undergone, great blessings are destined to emerge . . . not all of which are yet visible."

Mionnet was conscious of a confused tumble of thoughts. Foremost among them was a sense of pride: "He is showing me the most secret corners of his mind. I am being made aware of the very springs that have controlled all his past acts, all his past life, that will make clear his every movement in the future. Holding, as he does, the second most powerful position in the Church, and knowing, or guessing, that I have been sent here to intrigue against him, he has yet decided to justify himself in my eyes rather than to crush me utterly and drive me underground. Nor, in doing so, has he resorted to specious fallacies, to mere refutations of detail, or clever lies. No, he has set the problem before me in its most general terms, has asked me, as man to man, to join with him in viewing it from the loftiest standpoint. He regards me as capable of such detachment. He is a judge of men, and he has done me this signal honour. . . ." To this thrill of pride was added a feeling of admiration. Was not the Secretary of State's choice of weapons in itself worthy of the highest tribute? Was it not evidence of a great mind? But more than this, Mionnet yielded to the temptation, common to us all when some highly placed individual admits us to intimacy, of being surprised to find that he has refused to confine himself to mere formalities. We are flattered by being made witnesses of the genuine processes of his thought, by the realization that the great man actually attributes importance to certain general ideas, and that he has allowed his acts to be influenced by them. What from other lips would seem utterly banal takes on the quality of revelation. It is as though we had felt sure that men so eminent would turn out to have acted from mediocre, shameful, or, at best, opportunist motives; that if they gave real thought to a problem, it would be only for reasons of private interest or calculation; that if they invoked the authority of general ideas, it would be in the manner of men absent-mindedly enunciating truisms which had no real connexion with their acts. It is true, too, that general ideas seem to acquire added value when a man who has done important things and handled great interests shows that he takes them seriously. We feel rather as we do when the cashier of a bank pays out gold for a note; his act has a symbolic significance. What till then has been a mere token is seen to have real, negotiable value. It was not strange, therefore, that Mionnet should feel more genuinely thrilled by this expression of opinion on the part of Merry del Val than he would have done had the same things been said, perhaps with even greater subtlety, by one of his own colleagues of the Catholic Institute.

But there were more reasons than this why he should be moved by what he had heard, reasons that struck down to the depths of his being, not to be explained merely in terms of flattery or illusion. What it came to was this: that Merry del Val had just shown how, on certain essential points, they might be said to see eye to eye. It wasn't, perhaps, too much to assume that this community of outlook went further than the Cardinal had been able to express, that it might be extended to cover many things hidden deep down in the recesses of his thought, things which a great man might never be able to confide to anyone, but the nature of which he might be willing to indicate, for the benefit of a companion of sufficient mental endowment, to be guessed, at such a man's own risk, by the method of analogy and innuendo.

"If we were entirely free to ask each other questions about matters of the deepest import and to answer fully and frankly, who knows what might be the result? . . . We might find that we both of us tended to write 'yes' and 'no' in the same places."

He looked at the Cardinal's hands. They were beautiful and well kept, though there was something abnormal about the curve of the fingers. In movement or repose they were set off by the fine quality and cut of the black sleeves. His attention was held by the man's clothes; he took in the whole effect from feet to neck and shoulders. Rumour had not been wrong. There was evidence in every detail of studied elegance, just a little too obvious, however, and faintly feminine.

"My neat get-up must look pretty crude to him, pretty undistinguished. There's probably not a single point in which I resemble him. Our backgrounds are utterly different. And yet, he's one of the very few men I should like to resemble, one of the very few in whose shoes I should like to stand."

He watched the full lips speaking. More than once he anticipated some remark of the Cardinal's, more than once proffered an added commentary. But what excited him to the pitch almost of intoxication was this idea—arrogant, no doubt, but reaching far beyond mere arrogance—that between the Cardinal and himself there had obtained, almost since the first words of their interview, the kind of relation that the "man in the street" could not even guess at, so far was it above his head as to seem almost astronomical in its remoteness: a shared lucidity, a silent exchange possible only between men of genius and their peers, beyond the need to explain or define. It was as though, simple caution apart, they realized that the language of every day, used by and intended for the undistinguished mass of humanity, would too coarsely deform the delicacy of their thoughts. This, for Mionnet, was the touchstone of the true aristocratic spirit. His heart swelled within him at the thought that he had been allowed to react to it in its fullest splendour, here at Rome, in the Vatican, in the very heart of the Church.

But men of the highest caste, between whom such shared lucidity becomes, at times, a realized possibility, are sometimes, too, forced by circumstance into mutual opposition. That this should be so may be madness, but not necessarily. It is true of athletes; has always been true of princes. Such opposition in no way makes occasional collaboration impossible, though when those outside the magic circle find evidence of it, they fume with indignation, so far is it beyond their power to understand.

"In any case," Mionnet said once more to himself in no uncertain tones, as though fighting against the evidence before him, and striving to recapture something of the mood of which he had been conscious during his visit to the Sistine Chapel, "once men of this stamp have recognized one another, there are certain weapons they could never dream of using." (He no longer employed the phrase: "Save Merry del Val"; it seemed to him now both pretentious and stupid.)

"If you are to be still some time in Rome"—the Cardinal got up and fixed his visitor with his lustreless gaze, while the light of the room played over the perfect waxen surface of his face, as water slips over lacquer without soaking in—"you must come and see me again. Ask my secretary, Monsieur Perez, to arrange an audience. There are many things we might discuss which we have had no time today to mention. There is so much, don't you think, to interest one in the present state of the world?"

Chapter

8

HOW A MAN REFUSES TO MAKE USE OF CERTAIN WEAPONS

The next day, after careful consideration, Mionnet wrote the following short note to Manifassier:

"I have given up all idea of buying the document I mentioned to you. The present owner would certainly not be ready to accept the cut price you have fixed as your limit, and I am inclined to agree with you that, even assuming the thing to be genuine, it is not worth more. Apart from this, however, I am of the opinion that the authenticity of the document (of which I am becoming more and more doubtful) could not be established with sufficient certainty to make its employment fool-proof. Each time it was shown the whole history of its provenance would have to be gone over again from the beginning. Besides, there are people—those perhaps whom we most want to convince —who would remain incredulous no matter what evidence you adduced, or who would be so conscious of the dirtiness of the transaction that they would deliberately refuse to accept any proof. If this were so, we should merely be spoiling our own case.

"I am afraid you may find this, my considered view, at variance with what I have written on previous occasions. Please do me the justice of believing that I have reached it only after very careful reflection and because I am anxious to avoid taking any false steps.

"I think I see a way of achieving something valuable by quite other methods, slower, perhaps, but a good deal less dangerous, and, may I add, more worthy of the interests at stake. I hope soon to be in a position to explain myself more fully.

"I am leaving the ten thousand francs on deposit at the bank. I should like to know whether I am at liberty to use them to settle up for certain services I have received, or whether I can draw on them for the payment of a few of the subsidies we have discussed. It might be advisable to do a good deal more than we have done along those lines, provided we carry through the scheme systematically."

Chapter

⑨

PIERRE DE LHERM ON HIS FARM
AND, LATER, WITH HIS NEPHEW

Pierre Crouziols, generally known as Pierre de
Lherm, maternal uncle of Jean Jerphanion, emerged
at a single stroke from sleep to wakefulness in the "concealed" [1] bed
where he lay alone. This concealed bed was one of the many wooden
objects which occupied two of the four walls of the kitchen. The
others were a combined sideboard and dresser, a clock-case, and several built-in presses. They were all of beechwood left in its natural
colour.

The opening of the bed was raised about eighteen inches above the
floor of stamped earth, and could be closed by means of two hinged
panels, both of which together were scarcely more than three feet wide
and about shoulder-high. The mattress rose slightly above the bottom
edge of the opening and extended for some distance into the thickness
of the wall at either end. The bolster and pillow lay at the right-hand
extremity and were invisible from the room. In summer Pierre Crouziols slept with the panels of his sleeping-cupboard open, although
he never did without the heavy, patterned coverlet. He wanted a great
deal of warmth in bed, especially in the region of his feet. In this his
nephew resembled him.

Not that Pierre Crouziols liked waking in the middle of the night
in a sweat. But he could manage to sleep only when he was well covered, and plenty of bed-clothes seemed beneficial to his physical health.
He was subject to stiffness of the joints and extremely sensitive to any
moisture in the air. In his native mountains the days are often very
dry, but the nights, even in August, have a way of being damp.
Though the bed was built into the wall and snugly tucked in with

[1] This is the Scottish name for a similar article of furniture—TRANSLATOR'S NOTE.

332

many thicknesses of blanket, the night air in the kitchen could be very penetrating.

It was his habit to wake at once and, without any conscious exercise of the will, to sit straight up with his arms extended towards his knees. It may have been partly the morning light filtering into his fastness that woke him, but it was also the sense of time, which never left him even while he slept. He dreamed a good deal, especially towards dawn. In these dreams at the tail-end of the night, this consciousness of time played a considerable part, together with a vague feeling that he had got to get up soon to do some job or other. Nevertheless, he hated getting up early and would much rather have lain awhile dozing, had his way of life permitted him to do so. The winter months, in so many things productive of discomfort, had the one great advantage that they allowed him to indulge in the luxury of lying late and emerging slowly into wakefulness to an accompaniment of much stretching and yawning, and without doing violence to his feelings. The sharp movement of sitting upright suddenly, as though moved by a spring, was always followed by a minute or two of profound misery which he thought would never end, although he knew from experience that this interlude was of extremely short duration.

On this particular morning the first job to be done was to go and fetch a load of clover from the Laoun meadow. After that there was firewood to be gathered in the Bès copse. That done, he must cut wheat in the small field of Coustettes, which, by reason of its exposure, and perhaps, too, of its soil, was always a week ahead of the other grain crops. About ten o'clock—he would know when that was by the position of the sun over the mountains, or, in the last resort, by the chiming of the Saint-Julien bells—he would be able to find time to get back to the house, where, after a hurried snack, he would proceed to change the cows' bedding and to tidy up the manure heap.

He did his shaving in a little earthenware basin which he placed on the kitchen table. Then he took from the ashes of the fire a covered bowl containing what was left over of last night's soup. It could scarcely be called warm, though it just missed being completely cold.

A stalk of cabbage, a potato, and a piece of bacon, were floating in it. Pierre cut himself a hunk from the brown loaf which he had baked himself the previous week. He made no noise, trying not to wake his wife and daughter, who slept on the floor above and would not begin to stir for another hour.

Across the fields behind the house he climbed the hill to the Laoun meadow. Each field had its name. All the meadows and woods had names. The very small ones sometimes shared a name with their neighbours, but since each patch of ground belonged to a different proprietor, there was no danger of confusion. The Laoun meadow belonging to Lherm was one place, the Laoun meadow belonging to Beïrou another. The whole countryside was parcelled out in this way, showing to the eye a hundred different faces. A child of six sent on an errand would be sure of finding his father, his grandfather, or his uncle at the precise spot indicated. No need to say: "Take that path over there, and then it's the first turn to the left and the first to the right."

The day had only just dawned. As yet there was little cheerfulness in the light. At such an hour it was as well not to think of the hundred and one things to be done before nightfall. Darkness was many hours distant, but the work was never-ending. No man so conscientious but that something would be left unfinished to prey on his mind. One of these days he must really take a pick to the meadow above the house and open up twenty yards or so of the glazed land-drains that brought water from the Igaous stream to the pond. There must be a big leak somewhere, for only a trickle was reaching its destination. The animals had got to drink. No good being short of water when the hot weather came. One of these days, too, he must find time to go up to the roof and replace those tiles that had slipped. There had been no rain since the new moon, but in a few weeks now the storms would begin. With the roof in its present state, some of the gutters were as leaky as an old cow, and in very awkward places, too.

By this time the sun had risen above Meygal. There was just the faintest hint of red in it. The sky was clear. The wind was blowing from the direction of the sun—that is to say, from midway between east and north. At the moment it was chilly and made him shiver a bit, but in an hour or two it would grow milder, and though it probably wouldn't die down, it would steadily increase in warmth.

There was very little dew on the clover, and what there was seemed to be rapidly evaporating. No storm likely in the immediate future. Neither last evening nor during the night had Pierre felt any pain in his legs, not even the faintest twinge. Any physical discomfort he might have this morning—and his body was always conscious of a vague discomfort—was the kind that afflicted him on hot, dry days when the wind was in the east. It was only on very rare occasions that about ten in the morning he didn't feel a slight pain in the head with a shooting sensation behind the eyes, just as though someone had clapped a lid on his scalp and were rapping on it. It would be foolish, though, to assume that this sort of weather would stay constant. Winds from that quarter had a way of veering. It might be blowing like this in the morning straight from the east, with a clear, greyish sky, but by afternoon there would be wisps of cloud coming in from the direction of Mézenc, at first scarcely perceptible, no more than the mark left by a duster on a well-polished window-pane. But as the day grew older, there would gradually form, high up in the sky, a misty substance like the filament spun by certain insects, and little by little the whole of the heavens would be covered. These cloudy wisps were the famous "veils of the south wind," heralding an onset at present a good half-day off. With cunning persistence it would drive the east wind from the field, and there it would be, next morning, eddying up, soft and enervating, from beyond the sky-line. Folk said it came from the coasts of the south, or even from across the sea from Africa. While it lasted, the trees and grass would wilt, would look feverish and withered. Two or three days would pass before it grew to the dimensions of a gale, and sometimes, before that happened, a storm would burst, shattering the skies from end to end. It all depended on the year. Some years the heat brought on a storm at once, and then the weather would change suddenly and they would have four or five days of rain and westerly winds. But at other times it seemed as though nothing could make the rain fall, and then the devilish, arid wind from the south would sweep the district like the fiery breath of a furnace, while the great storms would pass afar off with a flicker of lightning and distant rumblings, as though a battle were raging far away across the frontier. Weather today wasn't what it used to be. There was no relying on anything. The seasons seemed all mixed up.

This year it had been a fairly dry summer. Since the rain had been so careful to hold off, it would be a good thing if it held off still longer until the harvest was in. But Pierre Crouziols had his doubts. He believed in the malevolence of nature. The peasant is right never to rejoice. It is when everything seems to be going well that disasters happen. It is when the crops are in full ear that the storms come and strip them and lay them flat, or when they are scythed, that a cold rain from the south-west rots them where they lie. But worst of all is the hail, for it can destroy a whole year's work in twenty minutes and has a way of coming without warning. At times it will push malice to the point of devastating one man's crop while sparing that of his neighbour. When the farmer hears it rattling up a mile away with a noise like all the chariots of hell, he mutters every oath he knows; but his women tell their beads and make the sign of the cross in the hope of diverting it to somebody else's fields. They may be right— more right, certainly, when it's a matter of hail, which seems to choose its line of advance, than where only drought is concerned. If drought is sent by the good God as a punishment, it is sent to thousands of poor folk. Nor does rain come to one man alone. But thunder, like hail, seems to choose its path. When the visiting priest starts off his sermon on Sundays at the eight o'clock Mass, he is always careful to work in the story of the peasant who persisted in harvesting his hay on a Sunday, instead of going to church, on the grounds that he feared a storm was coming up, only to get caught by the thunder just as he was loading his crop; or that other one of the farmer, several times guilty of the same sin, who saw his cattle die one after the other of "pestilence."

How much truth was there in all that sort of talk? At bottom, of course, religion is true; there can be no doubt of that. Everyone agrees about religion, except perhaps a few daring spirits in the big market towns and the cities, and if they laugh at it, that's probably only because they want to appear cleverer than their neighbours, or because they're vicious and would like to be up to all sorts of dirty tricks and don't want to think too closely about what's coming after. . . . What's coming after? Yes, the next world. . . . Pierre Crouziols did his best to think as little about it as possible. He wouldn't like to swear that everything the priests said was strictly true; after all, neither they nor anybody else had ever been there to see; or, rather, those who had had never come back to tell us what it was like. Still, there must be something in it all, and it was as well to be careful. When it's a question of possible trouble in the future, one loses nothing by acting as though one did believe, even though the business should turn out to be a fraud, and taking a few precautions. Just as well to lead a decent life, to behave properly, do wrong to no man, bring up one's children in the right way, go to Mass on Sunday, be careful not to swear too much when one's in a temper with the animals or when things go wrong, or at least, if swear one must, to see to it that one uses only good mouth-filling words which have no reference to God but which nevertheless relieve one's feelings: "Damned old bitch!" or "Son of a bitch!" or "Pesty old bastard!" or "Damned bitch-begotten old cow." . . . If one doesn't say worse than that, things probably won't go too badly with one when one's dead. After all, one has done one's best and one couldn't do more. . . It would be rather a comfort to know what clever nephew Jean thought about it all. He didn't look as though he bothered much about going to church. That time he'd spent three weeks of his holiday here he'd only been once, on Assumption Sunday, and then only because he didn't want to hurt his mother's feelings. Education seemed often to have that effect. Most of the school-teachers, especially the young ones, were free-thinkers nowadays. The priests would explain it of course by saying that learning made a man proud, particularly if he was the kind whose head could be turned easily. After all, it was the way the Devil had tempted our first parents. Still, Pasteur, the fellow who'd invented that cure for hydrophobia, had been a good Catholic all his life, and Voltaire had died begging God for forgiveness and crying like a lost soul because the priest wouldn't bring the absolution quickly enough. Victor Hugo had attacked religion, but, for all that, he had said time and time again that a man must believe in the good God. There was some excuse for school-teachers: they'd got to keep their end up with the teaching Orders. If one of them went to Mass it would be a little like Malosse, the grocer, going to buy his coffee from Mallon, who kept the rival shop. The priests were in much the same boat too: if it wasn't that they got something out of folk going to church, if it wasn't for the candles, the collections, the fees for Masses and baptisms and marriages and burials and Christmas offerings, they might be less concerned about the welfare of men's souls and less certain in their predictions about what would, or would not, happen in the next world.

Pierre Crouziols had by this time finished raking together the necessary quantity of clover and was busy tying it up into a large truss ready to hoist on to his back. He loved the smell of freshly cut clover, and he was responsive to the cheerfulness of the early morning hours. Once one stopped thinking of the weather and of the various dangers and responsibilities connected with harvesting, it was impossible not to feel that a cool and gusty wind from the east coming as prelude to a day of great heat gave a zest to life, even though one was no longer young. It made one feel a longing to be happy and carefree without asking why, as one used to do before the years had brought their burden. That was the good side of a farmer's life. But raking was irksome; gathering the scythed hay and binding it was irksome. Work didn't go on for ever, of course; all jobs came to an end some time. This job would come to an end when darkness fell, and others like it. But every time one took the strain, there was a sense of discomfort in the small of one's back; every time one bent or struggled with the bits that somehow had got left out of the truss, or pressed with one's knee to draw the binding tight, there was a little stab of pain. Yesterday's weariness was always lurking in the background ready to jump out at one and strike at one's limbs. The slightest movement would be enough to summon it. Later in the morning, when one's muscles had warmed up a bit, yesterday's stiffness wouldn't, so to speak, be so noticeable, but that didn't mean that one wouldn't, all the same, have to make a deliberate effort to go on with one's work. To make matters worse, on this particular morning Pierre Crouziols had not slept well, with the result that each time he exerted himself he began to sweat and his head felt empty. Getting up so early is bad for the digestion. He had a slight feeling of nausea in the pit of his stomach. The cold cabbage soup he had taken when he got up prevented him from feeling really ill, but it lay heavy, for all that, and gave him a certain amount of acidity. In an hour or so it would start his belly rumbling. One day he had heard a great paunchy fellow from Le Puy say: "Oh, I know all about those country stomachs of yours!" If he'd had a country stomach like Pierre's, maybe he wouldn't have done justice to quite so many banquets, wouldn't have put on so much fat either—quite apart from any question of hard manual labour. No one can have a good digestion if he's got to be moving about all the time. Pierre could not remember a single afternoon when his food had settled without giving him a certain amount of discomfort, and most of the men and women he knew suffered in the same way. The field worker's life is too hard. The body can't expend all that energy and still retain enough to digest its meals and keep the organs in good running condition. Only city folk, less driven and less exposed to the elements, can keep really well. The size of their stomachs proves that. If, for the most part, they don't live to be older than countrymen, that's because they don't know how to observe moderation. They abuse their natural good health; they drink too much, eat too much, and lie too often with their wives. They don't always stop at their wives, either.

They're too full-blooded, and they usually die of apoplexy.

Besides, the air up in the mountains was too bleak. Pierre Crouziols suffered from it more or less continuously all the year round. In the depth of winter he was never warm except when he was in bed. Now and then a day of dry frost and bright sun would be pleasant enough, but in the mountains those were just the days when, for no particular reason, his back and arms would start giving him hell. Nor did he find the long-drawn-out rains of late winter and early spring any more agreeable. Endless days of rain made him melancholy. He hated damp clothes and the icy trickle that always ended by getting down his neck and into his sleeves and turned the straw stuffing of his clogs into a clammy sort of pulp. (The times he most liked during the bad season were those he spent making clogs for a dealer in the neighbouring market town. His workshop was a stuffy little corner next the stable, with the pig feed simmering beside him in a great iron cauldron. There was a delicious sense of warmth. The wood shavings and the cooking mash smelled good. At such times he would forget his troubles and think of nothing but cutting and scraping away with his tools at the sweet-smelling wood from which a clog was so soon to emerge. The manual labourer's work is, as a rule, so restful compared with that of the farmer, so much less physically exhausting. It knows nothing of that most wearisome thing of all—worry for the future, anxiety about possible bad weather, about some sick animal, about the threatening possibility of hail. . . .)

The summer, taken merely as a season, has fewer inconveniences, but then only the man of means and the city-dweller can enjoy it. People from the towns—the lucky devils—refer to the summer as "holidays," but for all the countrymen the summer is the most exacting of all the divisions of the year, and in the mountains more than in most places, because it is shorter than elsewhere and the same amount of work has to be compressed into fewer weeks.

What's the good, some people said, of being born in the mountains, of being bred from mountain stock on both sides, if one couldn't make a better job of it than that? But what better job could one make?

All very well for people to talk. Isn't one bound to be better off in the plain, provided it's not too hot, with good soil that can be ploughed deep? Down in some great valley, for instance. In a valley one usually has enough water for the fields and the live-stock and the house. The valley of the Rhône, one hears it said, is too windy and too narrow, with too much stone in the earth. But over by Brioude there are wide stretches of splendid soil. Carting in the level lands is an easy job compared to what it is in the mountains. Driving from the house to the fields is child's play, while up here the carrying of the least little load means a terrible struggle for the horses, and as bad downhill as up. The roads in the plain are better. They are built of earth or sand and not, as here, of rocks as big as a man's fist, when they're not as big as his head, so that they're as like as no matter the dried bed of a torrent.

On one occasion Pierre Crouziols had been as far as Clermont, Clermont in the Auvergne, which is called by some people Clermont-Ferrand. He had not visited the famous Limagne,[1] but he had seen it in the distance, had heard its praises sung. He found no difficulty in believing everything he was told about it. There was a country, if you like, where people needn't be pitied. When the cares of his mountain farm became too heavy to be borne, Pierre Crouziols would dream of the Limagne, conjuring up pictures of soft black earth and level fields, of roads without hills, and a surface hard enough to prevent the cart-wheels sinking deeply, and never rutted by the rain. He saw in imagination houses, not built on steep slopes and exposed to all the winds of heaven, as here, but surrounded by fields and closely shaded by clumps of great trees, chestnuts and oaks. How good life must be there! It was consoling merely to know that somewhere a country like the Limagne existed! What weather, too, from one year's end to the other! Pierre had spent only a few days at Clermont, during the early spring, but he had never felt so well. Not a twinge had he had in legs or arms. But that wasn't all; his whole body had felt comfortable. He had slept better. His digestion had been better, and that although he had eaten and drunk far more than usual, for he had

[1] The Auvergnat plain.—TRANSLATOR'S NOTE.

been fêted like an honoured guest. For four whole days he had, as it were, hardly noticed that he had a stomach or a belly at all.

Unfortunately a man couldn't change the country in which he was born, short, that is, of packing up, when he was young, and going off to the city—which was quite another question. How could one move away in middle life and start farming somewhere else? Such a thing was inconceivable. Not that it wasn't terribly tempting! One might, of course, find a purchaser for one's property; that, perhaps, wouldn't present insuperable difficulties. But what would it be like, arriving down there, dropping out of the blue into the Limagne? . . . How would one do it? . . . With all one's household goods piled on an ox-cart, or by train? And how dig oneself in among all those settled farms? How manage to buy a house and fields? How get used to different faces and different ways? How learn the different seasons, the different ways of ploughing and sowing and doing the hundred and one other things that a farmer must do—learn the prevailing winds, the weather signs, the market days, the names and surnames of new neighbours, the way of greeting them, the details of their families? . . . The worst part of all would be the feeling that one was a stranger, that one was intimate with no one, had no one with whom to exchange a friendly story. . . . And then there would be the difficulty of the dialect, which would be altogether different. In the market at Clermont Pierre had found it almost impossible to understand the country talk. The people of Auvergne pronounced their words in the most extraordinary way, and there were a great many he had never heard before at all. When one's only paying a short visit, one just laughs at such difficulties; but suppose it was for always! . . . In time one might learn to understand the way they talked, but one would never be able to talk like it oneself. And to one's dying day the people there would listen to one with a smile as though one were a sort of freak.

That sort of thing can only be done if one comes into a property in some strange place, or marries a wife from some distant village, and only then if one is young.

In the days of his youth Pierre had gone with a friend three winters running to the "mines." Together they had trudged the whole distance, as far as Saint-Étienne, as people did in those days. They had signed on for the winter months. They lived in a furnished room about a quarter of an hour's walk from the mine. They took their midday meal with them each morning, and the bacon and cheese had a flavour of coal dust. Pierre could taste again, as though it had been but yesterday, the curious consistence of crushed coal and bacon. They had found there several other young fellows from their native district, and that had helped to make them feel less wholly exiled. One of the great advantages was that one could drink wine at every meal—and not just coloured water either, but the real stuff. Of course one couldn't have as much as one wanted, because it cost money, but a reasonable quantity.

Augustin, Aurélie's son, had gone to Canada. He wrote home that he had been working at clearing forest land where the trees were three times the height of any in France. He said, too, that after long periods of drought he had seen prairies three times the size of their parish at home all on fire, the flames moving with the speed of a galloping horse.

Only men with nothing to keep them at home, and a bit weak in the head, would deliberately leave the country of their birth. Merely to go to Paris to get a steady job or start a business was easy enough to understand, but it was silly just to go off into the void. Much better stay where God had put one, however bad the conditions.

Besides, there were always those who were worse off than oneself, those who lived still higher up in the mountains, round about Raffy, for instance, or in Saint-Jeure, among the Protestants, or at Fay-le-Froid or among the Mézenc moorlands. With them winter began earlier and ended later. They were often snowed up in their houses for weeks together, and sometimes when it was sunny here they were fog-bound and moving about muffled up to the eyes. To them Saint-Pierre and Saint-Julien seemed like places in the promised land where hardship was unknown. The only fuel they had for their fires was peat or dried cow-dung. Sometimes the soil from their fields would slide down the mountain side and have to be carted up again on their backs; and on their backs, too, they had to carry down into the valley their thin harvestings of rye, as Pierre carried his truss of clover.

This country had at least the merit of being good to look at. He would have found it very difficult to put into words exactly what he meant by the phrase, which certainly had nothing whatever to do with the fruitfulness of the soil or the size of the crops. It was beautiful —that was it; that was the word used by travellers who stopped at Saint-Julien. His nephew Jerphanion was always using it, and he was a man of education, who had seen all sorts of places and had some claim to know what he was talking about. A year or two back he had invited one of his Paris friends to come and see him here, a companion of his at the great Training College, a distinguished young fellow, but one who'd been hail-fellow-well-met with everybody. And the day before he left he had said that he had never seen a more beautiful country.

Pierre Crouziols, generally known as Pierre de Lherm, knew of course that "beauty" didn't put butter in one's soup, but it was pleasant to have it about one, for all that. Having deposited his truss of clover on the barn floor, he started out to gather firewood from his little copse over at Bès, and on the way he indulged in another dream, quite a different dream from the one that had to do with the Limagne. He often summoned it to his aid, and it took the form of imagining what it would be like to have nothing to do but enjoy this beautiful country-side which was so hard on those who had to work. He usually saw the scene as placed vaguely in the "olden time," or in some quite un-defined period. However that might be, the one changeless feature of the dream was that Pierre was a great lord, owner of innumerable acres, the master of the whole parish. The people living about all paid their rents to him. He did no work. When he walked abroad folk doffed their caps. He hunted. He road on horseback. He had all the time he wanted in which to look at the fields, the forest, and the lovely mountains.

Perhaps there was some basis for his dream; who could tell? In his family the name de Lherm had come down from father to son. Only an hour's walk from this very spot there was a low hill called Herm with the ruins of an old castle—one could see it quite clearly if one looked southwards. Centuries ago great lords had lived there. Where were they now? What had happened to their blood in the many revolutions that had passed across the face of the land? All alone, gathering faggots in his wood, Pierre had a perfect right to dream that he was descended from the lords of Herm. As lord of Herm he would fear neither winter nor summer. If the climate brought a stiffness to his joints, there would always be something he could do about it. Great lords are not like peasants. They enjoy beautiful things. Pierre would have liked to tell his nephew Jean Jerphanion of his dream, if only he had dared.

That same nephew, hearing that Pierre de Lherm had not finished cutting his wheat up in the Coustettes meadow, but would go back there after dinner, decided to accompany him. He felt suddenly that he would like to play at being a harvester, and he longed for a good talk with his uncle, whom he admired in an odd sort of way as well as liked. He was not blind to the fact that Pierre Crouziols had many not wholly admirable weaknesses, that he worried too much over the trivial incidents of his country existence, that he got angrier than was strictly necessary when one of the harnessed oxen didn't back quickly enough, or when he jabbed his pitchfork against a stone. But taken by and large, he was a fine, reliable old chap. And there was something rather mysterious about him. Not in the ordinary routine of his days— no mystery there, apparently, not the least suspicion of such a thing, and not in the things he said, either. No, the mystery had to be read, as it were, between the lines of what he did and what he said. It took the form of a certain detachment from the mechanical ordering of his labours, in a kind of concealed spiritual freedom. For instance, he would suddenly get interested when one started talking of things that had nothing to do with his personal experience, like the United States or the X-ray. There was something mysterious, too, in the feeling one had with him of a difficult, sensitive nature, of a stubborn refusal to accept things. A sensitive peasant; a sensitive man of the mountains. From beginning to end of every year at Saint-Sylvestre he lived a hard life; but he would never shirk anything, never turn over to someone else the work he ought to do himself. He lived hard, and he knew that he lived hard.

No, one certainly couldn't take Uncle Crouziols for granted.

Jean was no bad hand with a pitchfork, but he was more careful than a real harvester would have been not to hurt himself, gathered smaller armfuls of the cut grain, cut his hands more often on the stubble and the thistles. But the most noticeable thing was that he hadn't got the habit of bending. For him, in the words of lazy workers, "the ground was too far away." The stiffness in his joints became very soon more than he could bear. But that was rather an advantage for a man who liked talking as much as he did.

His uncle, anxious though he was to get through as quickly as possible with this damned little field of Coustettes, so inconvenient with its early-ripening grain, was glad enough for an occasional pause. They would sit down, the two of them, on a tumbled stretch of the low earthen wall, and Jean would start talking, trying to keep the conversation along the lines he had mapped out. But today his uncle quite kindly but firmly refused to be led. Either he didn't answer or he spoke of other things. Jean would have liked to discover how his uncle had reacted to the great public events of the last year, and what his impression of them was. But today Pierre de Lherm took no interest in great public events; what he wanted to hear about was his nephew's approaching marriage.

"So you're getting married in two weeks?"

"Yes, about that."

Jerphanion tried to get back to his subject, but his uncle would not leave the question alone.

"Will it be at your wife's home?"

"Yes."

Jerphanion felt sure that he could hold his uncle's attention by side-tracking the conversation onto the "Three-Years Act"; but all in vain.

"Going to be married in church?"

"No."

"Ah!"

The older man seemed more thoughtful, more interested, than disapproving. He was anxious, it appeared, to hear his nephew's reasons for such a decision. But so averse was Jerphanion to discussing this particular point that he seemed ready to talk at length on any other aspect of his plans—even to take the initiative in bringing them forward. He spoke of his future father-in-law, who, he admitted, was a "very nice fellow."

His uncle narrowed his eyes, assuming a confidential and knowing expression.

"Your girl got a little something put away?"

Jerphanion made a stammering sort of reply to hide his embarrassment and save his self-respect. But deep down he felt disappointed: "Is that all he's worrying about?"

Chapter

10

GURAU: CURRENT AFFAIRS:
AUTUMN IN THE RUE DE CHAILLOT

Before going out (the Autumn day was very tempting, and the ex-Minister was more anxious now than
he used to be to enjoy every moment that remained of the good
weather), Gurau discussed one or two matters of business with Manifassier, mentioning them without method, just as they occurred to
him.

"I've had a look at the number of your magazine that reached me
yesterday. Your young friends are pretty down on me."

"Oh, sir . . ."

"They're careful enough not to come out into the open, but they
get in a good many sly digs at me and my colleagues. Well, it's just
youth. Far be it from me to reproach the young with being hard on
their elders . . . they'll change only too soon. . . . I'd like to see them
when they're fat and forty—a good deal fatter than I am now. Just
you wait. They'll be falling over each other to get good jobs, pulling
strings here, there, and everywhere, and they'll understand a heap
of things then that they don't understand now. . . . What I've really
got against the young is that, generally speaking, they make no effort
to distinguish between those of their elders who sell the pass, who go
over to the enemy, and those who really work hard to inject just as
much idealism into the real world as it will stand—and it will stand
only very occasional, carefully spaced, small, doses. . . . The only people
the young admire unreservedly are the failures and the impotent.
It's a convenient point of view, and probably their way of preparing
in advance for the profitable betrayals to come. . . . Oh yes, and
there's another thing: you must get busy about this Colonel Duroure,
or rather this Duroure who's so desperately anxious to be a colonel. I

thought he was one already, but I gather he's only a Lieutenant-Colo-nel. Sammécaud's taking the matter up, and so is de Champcenais, I believe. He's written them both heart-rending letters. If he doesn't get his promotion, he'll be put on half-pay, he says, or something like that. It's all in the file. Sort it out for yourself. He published some time ago a technical pamphlet which had a certain amount of influence on the voting for the Three-Years business. That's not much of a recommendation where we are concerned, but it ought to carry a good deal of weight with the War Office people."

He issued a few more instructions of the same kind. Then:

"I was thinking this morning, for no particular reason, about that Abbé of ours in Rome, that big, clever chap . . ."

"Mionnet?"

"Yes. What's happened to him? You never speak of him these days."

"He was here on holiday for a month—when you were away in Touraine."

"Did you see him?"

"Yes."

"Didn't he ask to see me?"

"He inquired very politely about you. But he's a reasonable sort of fellow, and he didn't want to put you out unnecessarily."

"Did he see Poincaré?"

"Yes."

"Why didn't you tell me about all this before?"

"Frankly, sir, you didn't seem to be particularly interested. It's quite natural that you shouldn't be. I wasn't going to bother you while you were taking things easy in Touraine, and since you got back and I've been seeing you, the thing slipped my memory. Besides, he's returned."

"What a mysterious chap you are! Well, what's this future bishop of yours been up to?"

"He didn't tell me much, and I didn't feel justified in forcing his confidence. I've got the impression that Poincaré, as a result of what he reported, has given him fresh instructions."

"You don't know what they are?"

"Not precisely. I only know that there was a moment when the President was getting very much worked up about a certain della Chiesa. . . ."

"Della Chiesa?"

"Yes . . . an Archbishop . . . of Ferrara, I think it is, about whom Mionnet had been talking. His name's cropped up once or twice in some of the letters I've seen. . . . But I've been taken off that job. Yes, really, didn't you know? Mionnet still drops me a friendly line occasionally, though. Still, any reports he may send go straight to headquarters."

"Headquarters? . . . And what do you mean by that? Pichon?"

"Perhaps. Perhaps not."

"What are you suggesting? Do you really think that Poincaré would try the same game on Pichon that Caillaux played with me over those Berlin dispatches?"

Gurau asked the question without bitterness. He even made it plain that such a possibility would not altogether displease him.

"I've no idea," said Manifassier. "If he did, it wouldn't be nearly so serious. It's quite possible that Pichon knows about the Rome business, but is willing to turn it over to the President in order to keep him busy."

Gurau lowered his voice:

"Look here, it's suddenly occurred to me. Don't you think that the President is perfectly capable of running a sort of diplomatic service of his own, of having an organization of private and personal agents . . . in the most important countries . . . Russia, obviously, and perhaps London as well?"

Manifassier pursed his lips.

"It's possible. . . . It would be in the old kingly tradition."

"When kings were absolute," rejoined Gurau in high good humour.

"That's, of course, what I mean. . . . On the other hand, he's a great stickler for etiquette. I should be very much surprised to find that he hadn't arranged things to look all right and proper. The Quai d'Orsay may have been short-circuited in fact, but the forms will be observed."

Gurau pondered his words for a few moments. "And this della—"

"Della Chiesa?"

"Yes, who is he?"

"A possible successor to Merry del Val. I think the idea is to engineer some sort of palace revolution. I know that there's been a plan on foot to send a certain eminent monk to negotiate on the spot with della Chiesa, Mionnet being left watching in Rome, where, also, a good deal of money's been distributed. I don't know whether the scheme has been abandoned or merely postponed, but I rather think our people want to try approaching Merry del Val direct before involving themselves in it too deeply. . . ."

"That business of the photograph, you mean? . . . But surely that was given up long ago!"

"Oh, that's no longer even mentioned. No, what I'm referring to is something on the lines of a friendly approach . . . a frank exchange of views. . . . Mionnet mentioned some such possibility in the days when he still confided in me."

It was Gurau's turn to make a face.

"It all seems rather childish to me. Have you yourself any faith, really, in these palace intrigues? When we were at the Quai d'Orsay can you remember a single instance of that kind of play-acting having the slightest effect?"

"That was probably because we didn't believe in it. It's not been our habit in this country, not at least since the establishment of the Republic, to work in that way. We've become more bureaucratic, more careful of appearances, even where so-called secret diplomacy is concerned. But take the English, for instance. There's no plotting they would stop at. Side by side with their perfectly correct diplomatic service they run a system of secret agents—though they'd always disavow them if it came to a show-down—whose activities are as improbable as those in any cheap mystery story."

"Do you really think so?"

"I'm quite sure of it."

At this point Gurau broke off the interview to betake himself to the pleasures of an Autumn morning, sauntering along the near-by streets as far as one of the great arterial avenues, keeping to the sunny side of the road, stopping to buy a packet of cigarettes or a paper, or both, conscious occasionally of a faint chill in the air, savouring the peculiar charm of a day of mid-autumn in Paris, caught between the 15th of October and All Saints' day, an evanescent, fugitive charm, dependent as it was on the accidents of the weather, but striking a responsive chord in the heart of the observer. The light seemed more limpid than that of summer, because objects were more clearly defined and had taken on a sharper brilliance. "See," they cried, "there's still happiness, still hope, in the world!" With some such glory, perhaps, the houses shine in the early hours of a summer morning, but one never sees them then, and by eleven o'clock the streets are crowded and no longer glamorous. In the wide thorough-fares, too, the avenue Marceau, the avenue de l'Alma, there was a special quality in the sound of things that seemed to tell of autumn; the ordinary noises of the street, instead of becoming, as at other seasons, muted in the confused undertone, seemed to swell to a final crescendo, to close on a clash of cymbals or a trumpet-call. The note of a taxi horn, the rattle of milk tins before a dairy, were, it might be, muffled by the damp stillness that seemed to have crept into the city from some woodland fastness. But the real secret of the day's magic was bred of a combination of three things: the tempera-ture of the human body, the temperature of the day, and the move-ment of the streets. It was but a short while ago that Gurau had noticed a similar, though subtly different, coming together of such elements —physical sensation, the peculiar quality of the season, and the sense of country things—against the lush setting of Touraine.

In his enjoyment of these various pleasures there was, if not deliberate affectation, at least a degree of self-conscious surrender. His attitude was rather that of a man who wishes to make it clear to a somewhat neglectful friend that he is not feeling abandoned, that he is quite capable of enjoying life without the delights of companionship. These easy saunterings were each a challenge to the spirit of power. It was as though he said in so many words: "I can do perfectly well without you. It is some months now since I lost you, and it doesn't look as though you will come my way again for a while, but see how contentedly I can bear the separation."

It was his habit, when he had no other call upon his time, to end these walks with a visit to Gisèle in the avenue du Bois. At this hour of the day Mme Godorp had finished her many duties and would be ready either to receive him in the intimacy of her boudoir or to accompany him on a renewed ramble, by car or on foot, in the environs of the Bois.

GURAU, GERMAINE, AND THE FUTURE

It was on one of these days, just as he had left his flat, that he came face to face with Germaine at the corner of the rue Pauquet and the rue Bassano. They were on the point of passing one another without the faintest sign of recognition. But the make-believe would have been too crude, and both showed, by a faint smile, that they realized the absurdity of the situation. They exchanged greetings, shook hands, and began to walk together in the direction that Germaine seemed to be taking, down the slope of the rue Pauquet towards the avenue Marceau.

They addressed each other with polite formality, asked of each other's news; but all the while they were careful to make it clear that neither had lost sight of the other, that they had each of them even been at some pains to think occasionally how the other was getting on.

"It didn't surprise me to hear that you had turned down that part in Marquis's play. . . ."

"I was pretty sure you wouldn't want to stay at the Quai d'Orsay with things going as they are at present."

Gurau had an impression that Germaine had taken more trouble than she used to do to understand the political situation with which he was faced and to draw her conclusions about the rather delicate position in which he found himself in regard to Poincaré.

But he was soon to get a much more definite shock.

The "few steps" of their original intention had lengthened. They were now in the avenue Marceau, walking up and down the west side of that thoroughfare between the rue Pauquet and the rue Pierre-Charron, beyond which point Germaine seemed unwilling to go.

In reply to his inquiry what she was doing at present, she said that she was rehearsing at the Vaudeville (she did not, however, add that it was for a play of Mareil's), but that she hoped to be through with that soon, since she was very anxious to attend a course of lectures which Bergson was giving, and didn't want to miss too many of the earlier ones.

She had spoken quite simply, without any apparent desire to produce an effect. Snobbery, if it came to that, had never been one of her failings. Gurau remembered that she had taken a degree in Philosophy, but that didn't prevent him from feeling a certain amount of surprise at finding how eager she was to attend Bergson's lectures, and at hearing her mention it in the natural and direct tone she might have used to explain that she was about to undergo a cure.

"You're taking up philosophy again, then?" he said with a smile that expressed friendly interest rather than ironic intention.

"I have been led to take an interest in certain things," she said with the same serious air and choosing her words with care, "almost, as it were, by accident. . . . Don't you agree that it's all terribly important? I'm right, am I not, in thinking that you've never given much thought to these subjects—the occult, I mean?"

"Spiritualism?"

She seemed slightly put out.

"Not spiritualism exactly . . . I'm not interested in that . . . no. . . . I'll give you an example of what I mean. Some time ago, it must be two years at least, I had occasion to consult a woman . . . I went out of sheer curiosity after something a friend told me about her. . . . The woman in question told me a lot of very accurate things, not only to do with the present and the past, but about the future as well. Still curious, I tried several others, and they all told me more or less the same. . . ."

Gurau listened to her indulgently. "It's odd," he thought, "how keen women are on mysteries, at least on the odds and ends of mystery that may concern them personally. They're all the same, irrespective of what sort of education they've had, and in spite of the feminine character being, on the whole, rather matter-of-fact."

Germaine was still speaking:

"Some of the things I was told have already happened, or partially happened. In so far as they concerned the present or the past they might have been explained, of course, by thought-transference. . . . You know me well enough to bear me out when I say that I am not a credulous person, not even a believing Christian. . . . The things I refer to were unlikely to have been in my mind already, weren't, I mean, the kind of things that happen simply because one's adopted a mental disposition, even without meaning to sometimes, which results inevitably in their happening . . . nor were they the sort that one can foresee simply by letting one's brain work on one's knowledge whether of oneself or of other people. . . . If somebody foretells that I shall leave the man with whom I am living, well, that's simple; it may merely mean that they have read my feelings—better than I have myself. But imagine for a moment that this taxi coming down the avenue swerved onto the pavement and crushed us both . . . and suppose that a year ago one of these women had told me: 'I see you on the pavement of a wide avenue talking to a man you once knew very well, but whom you've not seen for a very long time . . . and I see a taxi charging onto the pavement and crushing both of you. . . .'"

"I hope nobody did tell you that!"

And, though he did his best to laugh, Gurau eyed the oncoming taxi with no little apprehension.

"Oh no, you can be comfortable on that score, but, incidentally, I should like to point out that though you're not superstitious, you don't like the idea that I might have been told it. . . . As a matter of fact, my woman referred a good deal to you, but you were only in my past. It may interest you to know that you didn't figure at all in my future."

"Ah, so much the worse," he said, half jokingly, half serious, and conscious, while he spoke, of a faint pang.

"So much the worse, I agree," replied Germaine, her tone balanced between politeness and sincerity. . . . "But"—and here politeness won the day—"that these fortune-tellers didn't see you, there can be no doubt. . . . There's nothing in anything they told me that need worry you in the slightest. All I meant to do when I used that illustration was to make you realize that if a prediction of that sort came true, it couldn't be explained by saying that they had read my thoughts or my intentions. . . . You agree, don't you? Whoever foretold that must have had a genuine vision of things to come. . . . Well then, I've not studied the question deeply, and I've not got the kind of brain that takes easily to philosophy, but it seems to me that one can't get away from the fact that if an old woman can read the future like that, a whole lot of other problems arise. . . . What we were taught at school just doesn't work. Some women, of course, just love being superstitious; the more contrary to good sense a thing is, the happier they are. But I'm not like that. I've given a good deal of thought to the matter, I've asked other people how they explain it. I've had one or two of Maeterlinck's books lent me—I'd only read his *Life of the Bees*—and I've been advised to read Bergson. I do remember vaguely some of the things we used to be told at school, about the datum of immediate experience, you know, and free will and determinism and things like that."

"Allow me to congratulate you!"

"But I find him rather stiff reading . . . or rather I don't quite see how what he writes links up with the point I'm particularly interested in. Probably he's easier to follow in a lecture, and after I've been once or twice I may pluck up courage to ask a few questions at the end of the hour. . . . I only hope he won't snub me."

"I can see that you're taking all this very seriously. . . ."

To himself he thought: "All this keenness to get things clear, to arrange her thoughts logically, is extraordinarily unfeminine, or, I should say, doesn't square with what we men regard as typically feminine. . . . It may be that our view of women is too conventional."

"I'm quite determined to go through with it," replied Germaine. "It's not that I want to put on airs. I shouldn't be such a fool, you know me well enough to believe that—but I want to get things straight. I can't rest until I know what to believe and what not to. It's a purely personal matter, a question of my own private point of view."

She added:

"When we met I was actually on my way to one of these women who lives in the rue Pauquet, a particularly famous one. She's already told me one or two things, but she said very early that my future wasn't at all clear. Each time I go she tries to see a little more. Admittedly it's in her interest to do so. They're rather like doctors, these women, always trying to make one go again and again. But I think she's honest. You ought to pay her a visit yourself one of these days."

"Why should I?"

"In a career like yours, in which you've always got to be fighting somebody or something, and in which you must feel constantly discouraged, you might derive considerable strength from prediction."

"Provided it was favourable."

"Oh, but it would be in your case, I'm certain of that."

There was more in the conviction of her tone than a mere desire to be agreeable. Hearing it, Gurau took comfort, though there was no reason to suppose that Germaine had caught the gift of "clairvoyance."

Chapter

12

**GERMAINE AND MAREIL
FACE TO FACE WITH THE UNSEEN.
THE MAN COVERED WITH BLOOD**

They parted. Germaine walked a short distance up
the slope of the rue Pauquet towards the house in
which her business lay. She was already a little late for her appointment. She began to hurry. Had any further meeting, any further incident, occurred to make her stop, she would have been very much
vexed.

Her present state of mind contained one element of which she had
said nothing to Gurau—the need she felt of bolstering up, at intervals
which must not be indefinitely prolonged, the sense of confidence
upon which she had grown to rely. After each visit she said to herself:
"That'll do now, I won't go back, and I won't try another woman,
not for a year or two, anyway. Whether what she told me is true or
false, it has given me a definite direction for some time to come. I've
only got to keep to it. She didn't tell me when all the good things
she promised were going to happen. I must just wait patiently. She
saw the whole of my future bathed in radiant light. Why give her an
opportunity of unsaying what she has said already?" She was not one
of those vague creatures who can never make up their minds when
they are faced by the necessity of choosing. She felt perfectly well
able to make a choice when occasion arose. All she asked of fortune-
tellers was that they should give her a feeling of general confidence.

But after a short while the level of her confidence began to drop.
She had a perfectly clear recollection of the predictions already made,
and though she didn't, if it came to that, weaken in her belief, she
had lost something of the stimulus that they had originally given her.

For a while she struggled against temptation. "Just to hear the same
thing all over again won't help me much. I can do that without going

to a fortune-teller." She warned herself against indulging too far her curiosity about the future. She mistrusted what more the oracle might have to say: "A misfortune which I didn't see clearly last time. . . ." She tried to prove to herself that she was sufficiently well balanced to find support for her optimism in the pleasant predictions and not to let herself be influenced by the bad. "Once these things start worrying me, I shall give it up." But ultimately she always yielded, and hurried off to her clairvoyant with fear and trembling.

On each occasion she crossed the threshold in the mood of a gambler entering the "rooms," not knowing which excited her the most, desire of winning or fear of losing. When, the interview over, she came out with her gains, her anxieties were calmed for the time being. "She still sees a royal future for me. . . . Things look brighter, she says, even than they did before. . . ."

More than once when her fortune was told she had been warned that there would be an estrangement between herself and Mareil. "I see you separated from the man with whom you are now living." But no date had been even approximately given for this particular development. "Will it be soon?" she had asked. "No, not very soon." "Within the next few years?" "I can't see clearly enough to say." Nor was it possible to get any definite statement about which was to leave the other. Prompted by pride, she thought: "The initiative, of course, will come from me"; only the next instant to realize how very much fonder she was of Mareil than she had ever suspected. "I don't believe I could ever really leave him . . . so it must be he who is going to take the first step." Whereupon another possibility presented itself to her mind: "Only if he deceived me could I bring myself to do such a thing. In anger and resentment I might find the necessary strength of mind." A more flattering variant was that somebody might fall desperately in love with her. "Jealousy would make Henry horrid. He would become hateful to me. Then he'd try to bluff by pretending to leave me, and from sheer exhaustion I should let him go."

She had waited a long time in the hope of getting further details. Mareil had been told something, if not all, about her habit of consulting the oracle, and had shown strong disapproval. "If what these women tell you is true, you can do nothing about it, and destiny must take its course. Why spoil the present by trying to know what unhappiness the future, possibly the very distant future, may have in store?" "But it's not always unhappiness. What I've been told isn't unhappy at all." (Naturally, she had said nothing about the prophesied estrangement.) "Hm, well, all I can say is you're very lucky. . . . But why, in that case, take the bloom off good things to come? Personally, I should prefer things to come as a surprise. . . . On the other hand, they may be lying to you, and why poison your peace of mind with a lot of illusions and old wives' tales?"

He was, however, extremely superstitious. He avoided fifty-franc notes like the plague. Even five-hundred ones were suspect in his eyes. He had a strong dislike of Mondays and of the number 22. A Monday falling on the 22nd was, to him, the height of misfortune, only to be counteracted should he have the good luck to meet a hunchback, a piebald horse, or a nigger as he left his front door. He was careful to avoid the use of certain words. But worst of all was his habit of catching other peoples' superstitions as some men catch colds. He could be made miserable by hearing someone say: "Surely you don't wind your watch with your left hand? Don't you know it's unlucky?" After a while, it is true, these borrowed beliefs had a way of fading out of his consciousness, unless some coincidence had meanwhile cropped up to confirm them. Short of that, he was thrown back on his own private stock, which seemed to him far superior in common sense and plausibility.

So far as knowing the future was concerned, he had long ago come to the conclusion that the possibility of such a thing ran counter to the general view of life which he had formed for himself as the result of his early studies and youthful reading. He was not naturally given to philosophy, but that did not mean that he was incapable of taking an interest in general ideas. If in his plays he was careful never to put forward anything that might look like metaphysical speculation, it was from a native caution and a fear of being laughed at. The ardent protestations of his heroes and the emotional anguish of his heroines were vaguely determined by the semi-scientific, semi-sceptical view of life which was the common property of his more cultivated contemporaries, a not very precisely defined attitude in which universal determinism was modified, in matters of human concern, by chance. Foreknowledge of events was, somehow, made to square with an assumption that the future was unpredictable, since every event was held to be so complex and so individual that no amount of scientific knowledge could ever master all of its many causes or determine its nature in advance as might have been done with, say, an eclipse. He had, therefore, smiled indulgently at the naïve faith which Germaine had accorded, from her very first visit, to the unverifiable predictions of her old women. Like Gurau, he saw in this love of the marvellous a fundamental characteristic of the feminine mind. Women were his passion, but he hated to see them over-intellectual, and such amiable weaknesses appealed to him as providing a corrective to the effects of higher education and forming no small part of their charm as a sex.

One evening, however, dining with a certain Mme Eliphas, he had met Mougeon, the doctor, and the conversation had turned on the speed of light. What precisely that was he had learned at school and had seen mentioned many times since in articles on popular science. There was no reason, therefore, why its mention should have surprised him. But on this evening, for the first time, his mind had really come to grips with it, and after dinner he had got Mougeon to confirm the fact that 300,000 kilometres per second did genuinely mean something to him and was not merely a convenient figment of the mathematical mind. The doctor, who, without being a man of any great originality, was careful to keep abreast of modern developments, even went so far as to tell him that certain foreign physicists were inclining to the old view that light was composed of extremely small particles, which meant, of course, that one could envisage this enormous speed, not as the movement of waves through space, but as the rate at which our world was being bombarded by innumerable projectiles. Mougeon expounded the theory more than willingly. He was surprised and flattered that a distinguished dramatist should find such details interesting. Though his own devotion to physics was complete, he was inclined to think that in the eyes of most people the physicist ranked somewhere midway between the mechanic and the pedant, and that the art of moving lovely ladies to tears by depicting the troubles of the heart demanded far more genius than the solution of scientific problems and ranked very much higher as an accomplishment.

Why, when he got home, before going to sleep, and again next morning, had Henry Mareil, dramatist of love, thought so much about the speed of light? Why, in particular, had he tried by the unaided exercise of his own mental powers, to visualize the spatial reality of 300,000 kilometres and the velocity of a projectile many million times smaller than a grain of dust traversing that distance in the space of a single second, in just the time, that is, that he could count "one—two"? That he should do so was one of those fantastic facts which, God be thanked, occur from time to time to remind us that the human spirit, thus capable of free speculation and irresponsible adventure, is indeed nobly parented. Henry Mareil went to considerable intellectual trouble to "imagine" the speed of light. It should not, of course, be forgotten that the question of speed interested him more than it had done in the past. He had bought a car which he drove himself and which was a source of much pleasure to him when everything was going well. His speedometer was to him exactly what the face of a clock is to a child who has just learned to tell the time, a toy and a bubbling source of trivial but deliciously exciting problems. ("What have I been travelling at this last quarter of an hour? . . . I'm just coming to a milestone now. . . . At what speed shall I take this hill?")

The result of his meditations—which were neither continuous nor methodical—was very typical of his easy-going nature. He had no dislike of complex and ephemeral thoughts so long as he had not got to make any intellectual effort to grasp them and examine them in detail. In strict fact, there was no result, nothing but a vague impression, so vague as to be hardly conscious, that all this talk about the speed of light wasn't concerned with anything that could be considered possible. Naturally, there could be no question of accusing contemporary science of making a mistake. One was left, therefore, with the necessity of admitting that when scientists spoke of "distance" in connexion with the movement of some star or the speed of light, they were dealing with something that had no relation to the normal spatial measurements of our daily life such as we come in contact with, for instance, when we are driving a car, or when we shoot with a pistol at a target. The "space" manipulated by scientists was something real —there could be no doubt of that—but it had very little to do with the space known to the ordinary unprivileged mortal. The degree of its reality was very, very small; it was little more than a formula in their calculations. Essentially, the speeds to which they referred were "magic." Essentially, all those operations of nature, as was clear from their statements about them, were to be regarded as "magic." Common sense was bound to reject them. The cleverness of men of science consisted precisely in this: that they could find a paper formula which authorised them to state categorically that these various things were to be explained by natural causes—were, in fact, not magical at all. At any moment they could, if they so wished, produce similar proofs of events in any other field. For instance, they would be able to give proof on paper that something which would happen only a year hence could be already seen. They would explain everything in terms of light-speed. The ordinary man might combat their conclusions in the name of common sense, but his objections would be no more valid than they would be today if he maintained that a tiny grain of dust could not *in reality* make the circuit of the globe eight or ten times in the space of a heart-beat.

No one, naturally, would deny the findings of science. But one was justified, surely, in accusing the man of science of arrogance if he maintained that common sense should reject those instances of magic which he had not yet taken under his wing? To say that a clairvoyant could read the thoughts of somebody not present, or not situated in the present, didn't, certainly, hold water, but the moment men of science took the trouble to explain it on paper by a mathematical formula, it would. What they had done for space they would do for this business as well, and prove by juggling with plusses and minuses that time didn't exist or that it could be retraced. And if anyone, in the name of common sense, refused to admit their conclusions, he would be dubbed a lunatic.

This day marked for Mareil the point at which the opposition that, ever since his youth, he had set up in his mind against the marvellous and the supernatural broke down. He did not hesitate for a moment over his own pet superstitions. (The reason why the 22nd is a bad day may not be clear, but because the reason for a thing is not clear, it doesn't follow that the thing itself is false. The only point that matters is that the belief is confirmed by experience.) If, in the ardour of his new enthusiasm, Mareil did not admit the truth of religion, that was because there were so many religions, and unless they could be added together to form a sort of composite truth, they must necessarily cancel out. Besides, they didn't confine themselves to affirming certain facts such as the existence of God or life after death—which, if it came to that, would have to be a good deal better established than they were—but tried to impose on the credulousness of mankind a lot of obviously legendary stories and a whole mythology which had clearly taken form in the minds of a primitive people. Once admit the Virgin and the saints, Adam and Eve, and all the things that Jewish prophets and Christian doctors had said about angels and cherubim, devils and the seventh heaven, and there was no reason why one shouldn't do the same for the stories retailed by Brahmins about Siva, the sacred cow, or the elephant who bears the world on his back; or by some Negro medicine-man about gods with pointed navels or phalli in a constant state of erection.

What he was inclined to admit now, however, was that there was a certain residuum of truth concealed in the various practices and beliefs common to all ages, which the religions of the world have either absorbed or have smothered and attacked from fear of competition.

There are hundreds of religions, but at bottom there is only one magic. That this is so can hardly be due to chance. If all religions have features in common, are all of them built on a basis of real value, that basis is precisely the belief, more or less vague, which underlies the many practices of magic and sorcery to be found in all sections of mankind and at every period of its history—the belief, for instance, in the power of human thought to operate at a distance, in the control of matter by mind, in the reality of spirits and an invisible world, in survival after death, and in the actuality, at any given moment, of the future.

Nature is a state of unbelievable chaos. Things believed by people separated by millions of miles have curious points of contact. It may be that the present, the past, and the future are less distinct than we normally assume them to be. A woman with "second sight," fishing in that troubled sea, may hook up, more or less by chance, odds and ends of events which are ahead of our lives. And why not? After all, a member of an orchestra may play a phrase ten pages ahead of his fellow-musicians. It is conceivable that thought may be able to travel at the rate of "three hundred thousand kilometres per second" towards the future and then return to the body, which meanwhile, herded with its companions, has moved but a few feet.

Mareil gave up laughing at Germaine. But he quite definitely refused to pay a visit on his own to any of her fortune-tellers. Germaine, however, insisted. "I want to know what they'd tell you. . . . You mustn't let them know who you are . . . and you mustn't say that you know me. It'll be interesting to see what happens. I want to know whether they'll repeat to you some of the things they've told me, or whether they'll see something different."

To this he made his usual reply: "If my future is to be happy, I'd rather have the pleasure of surprise; if bad, what's the use of meeting trouble half-way?"

Sometimes he teased her:

"Ask your sibyl whether there's going to be a war, and whether we shall win. That's a matter of interest to everybody. Being an event of some size, it should be visible at a considerable distance."

"That's where you're wrong. Madame Lysis once explained to me that she never saw generalized futures, but only as they effected single persons"—and Germaine's voice began to tremble.

"Then I can't even ask her," continued Mareil in high good humour, "whether she sees me as a Territorial guarding a bridge, because that's not at all my line of country! We shall have to introduce her to General Joffre. I suppose she could manage to tell him whether he was going to die before taking part in a battle? . . . A war must be of some importance in the life of a commander-in-chief!"

She changed the conversation, since she had no control over her face and would turn pink or go pale according to her mood of the moment. What actually was troubling her was something that Mme Lysis had told her quite recently, repeating it on three separate occasions with various embellishments:

"I see a big change in store for you. . . . I see you meeting a tallish, elegant-looking man, rather older than yourself. . . . He speaks with difficulty. . . . But the chief thing about him is that he is covered with blood. . . ."

"With blood? How frightful!"

"No, there's nothing frightful in it for you. . . . The blood has been caused by some wound produced at long range by a firearm."

"But not because of me? You don't mean that somebody has tried to kill him because of me?"

(She imagined Mareil challenging a rival to a duel, or else driven by his jealousy to commit a murder.)

"I don't think so."

"What's the cause of the wound, then?"

"I don't know. . . . The man in question is not free. . . . He is married. . . ."

"You don't mean—that his wife has tried to kill him?"

"Scarcely. . . . The weapon is a very long way off. . . . There are a great many people round him."

Germaine began to think vaguely of a war. The clairvoyant continued:

"You are tending him. You are not in love with him at first, but you become so later."

"Is it somebody I have already met?"

"That I can't tell you. . . . But the change I spoke of takes place then. This man gets his freedom for your sake. He abandons his wife and his children. He is very rich, fabulously rich."

Germaine's thoughts turned at once to "Monsieur Roger Sammécaud." "He's certainly very rich. He is elegant. . . . He is married and he has children. . . . He has never been able to forget me, that's it. One of these days we shall come together again; he will make up his mind to give up everything for me. But what about the wound? Perhaps he will try to kill himself first. . . ."

Chapter

13

GERMAINE BAADER AND MARIE DE CHAMPCENAIS RUB SHOULDERS IN THE BEYOND

The visit which Germaine had been on the way to make when she fell in with Gurau was intended to elucidate this very point. On the occasion of her last interview the clairvoyant had said:

"Bring me if you can some object belonging to the gentleman you are thinking of. . . . I will then try to make out whether it is the same one as I saw covered with blood."

Germaine had with her the brooch which Sammécaud had given her. Mme Lysis, her eyes half-closed, took the object and began to feel it. Then she laid her right hand on her forehead.

"It is difficult. . . . This is not something that strictly belongs to him. I cannot see the gentleman's face. It is very strange . . . what I see is a woman."

"What woman?"

"A woman he once loved. It really is very extraordinary! She is standing there behind you. She is rather like you, but it is not you. . . . What I mean is that she is fair, as you are, only rather less so. She has been through much suffering."

"Is it his wife?"

"No. . . . But it may be some woman he abandoned for your sake. I am not sure. She is looking towards the brooch with eyes full of sadness. Oh, she is very, very close to you."

Germaine shivered. She could feel this invisible woman there behind her, pressing against her. But even if she had thought that by turning her head she could have seen her, she would not have turned it. She bent forward slightly as though the woman had touched her shoulder. Why had she appeared like this if not to cross Germaine's destiny, to revenge herself upon her?

Suddenly her fit of shivering increased in intensity. She had just remembered that, four or five months before, she had been to see a woman who read the cards, somewhere near the Buttes-Chaumont. Like all devotees of the prophetic art, Germaine was in the habit of exchanging addresses and recommendations with her friends and with women whom she met in the waiting-rooms of the various practitioners she frequented. "Do go and see so-and-so; she really is extraordinary . . . and she gives such good advice, especially in affairs of the heart." In this way, without abandoning her favourite fortune-teller, she had made the round, by degrees, of all the clairvoyants who had any reputation at all. What had been this one's name? Something like Serpollet or Cerfeuil. And where had she lived? In some little street leading from that larger one with the trees, which stretched uphill in a fine sweep. Her flat had been clean, but terribly full of furniture! The card-reader of the Buttes-Chaumont had begun by telling her all the usual things. Then: "Strange. . . . Have you ever been here before? . . . No . . . I should have recognized you. Still, it's very odd. There is something about you which seems familiar. I don't recognize you, but I recognize something. Wait. . . ." The woman Serpette, or Serpillière, had stared in front of her, stretching out her hand. "Don't move. I see someone quite close to you. . . . A woman I know. Yes, one of my clients. . . . It's all very curious. You have done her some wrong. She is looking at you very reproachfully. . . ." The woman Cercotte—yes, that was it, Cercotte—had broken off, bowing her head as though in an effort of concentration. "Strange. I have a feeling that I have seen you, too, just where this other woman is now. . . ." Mme Cercotte's hand moved, as though in an effort to wave away an encroaching mist. . . . "Yes, it was you who were standing like that, rather nebulous, half hidden, as it were, by mist, behind her; and, on that particular occasion, *she* had come to consult me. She was seated on the same chair that you are occupying. . . ." Having said that, the prophetess had gone through the movements of waking from her trance. Perhaps she had realized that she had told too much. She had refused to give any further explanation. "You say I spoke to you of one of my clients? I must have been wrong. . . . Anyhow, I don't know her name."

And now, as she listened to Mme Lysis describing the shadowy form, Germaine felt quite convinced that it was the invisible woman of the room in the Buttes-Chaumont who had come to meet her in the rue Pauquet and was actually standing behind her, so close that she had almost touched her shoulder. In a husky voice, shaken, and different from her ordinary tones, she asked:

"Is it the woman who is going to be responsible for the blood?"

"I don't think so . . . but I can't say definitely. . . . It's all very confused."

MARIE FINDS NEW HAPPINESS

In this way Germaine Baader and Marie de Champ-cenais, who in life had never met, came together in the invisible world of the spirit. Marie, however, was quite unaware of the fact, since, for some time now, she had given up going to the woman Cercotte or to any of her rivals.

She had found her way back to religion. The change had come about very gradually. There had been no blinding vision of Grace. There had been no need for her to return to beliefs which she had never really abandoned, and she was not the kind of woman to see the content of her faith in the light of a problem. For her this return to God had manifested itself in a growing conviction, reached gropingly and with slowly increasing certainty, that she could obtain a more satisfying and surer spiritual happiness by redoubling her religious observances and by giving more time to her daily hours of contemplation, even by allowing her every mood to become impregnated with a sort of religious sensibility.

She had no reason not to believe that Grace was working in her by stealth. The changes of which she was conscious had very little to do with thought or will. She was aware of them only after they had occurred.

A day came when she realized suddenly that the church at Auteuil had taken on for her a new significance. It had ceased to be merely the place where one went to hear Mass in a crowd of more or less worldly parishioners and in a mood less of devotion than of fashionable observance. The first stage in her changed attitude was when, on Sunday morning, she found a definite pleasure in submitting to the discipline of refusing to go to one of the two showy and convenient

Masses—High Mass and Midday Mass—and patronizing instead the eight o'clock service, which was severe and often chilly, and frequented for the most part by aged spinsters of the neighbourhood and domestic servants. This discipline had become more meritorious when the family had left the apartment in the rue Mozart—as being too modest—for the house which the Comte de Champcenais had just had built in the rue du Ranelagh, close to La Muette.

A little later, coming out of church about twenty minutes to nine and finding herself on the pavement of the Place d'Auteuil, she had realized that a long, empty morning stretched before her and that she was in no mood to fill it with a secular saunter. She was aware, too, of a sense of regret for the music and ceremonial of High Mass. One day, having come, as usual, on foot, she arranged to be met by her carriage after the eight o'clock service and be taken to Notre-Dame, where she knelt in prayer until the High Mass began, and remained until it was finished. This arrangement of her Sunday mornings became habitual, though occasionally Saint-Eustache or even the Sacré-Cœur took the place of Notre-Dame. Another of her innovations was to stop on the way to her chosen place of worship and to spend the hour of prayer immediately preceding the High Mass in one of the side chapels of a church met with by accident in her wanderings, or in some almost abandoned chapel.

At the same time she learned how to induce the right state of mind for prayer and to keep it unbroken. She would choose a chair with its prie-Dieu in some quiet corner, far removed from the press of people, if there happened to be many present, and there she would kneel and cover her eyes with her hand for a few moments before reciting a due number of Aves and Pater Nosters, which she repeated in no particular order. Sometimes she inserted a Credo, sometimes a simple, "childish" prayer the origin of which she had forgotten but which she had been taught in her convent days. She made no effort to attain any definite concentration in these prayers, to keep her mind on the words, or to fight against the hypnotic effect of the murmured phrases by summoning to her aid a special intensity of spirit. She merely let herself relax, knowing that there is more than one way of praying. All that she had ever read or heard tell of the mystics convinced her that they had just been people who never forced their mood, but let themselves be swept along, confident in their faith. Gradually, as she spoke the words to herself, they lost their first clear significance until they sounded like the whispering of a distant voice. Neither the sound nor the sense any longer held her attention; all that remained with her was the consciousness of duration, of the time occupied by each prayer and by each phrase of her prayers. This feeling alone marked for her the divisions of her hour, flowing over her in a succession of waves. Her prayers, themselves scarcely noticed, set up a deep rhythm, an endless accompaniment of sound, against which a series of day-dreams took possession of her mind, sweeping it onward. In this respect she was particularly favoured. In the first place her reveries never seemed to be incongruous, never were such as to break the charm of the moment, and then, too, she never attempted to analyse or to question them, never tried to find them at fault. The house of God has many mansions, and it seemed to her that in a soul like hers, filled, however vaguely, by the grace of prayer, many thoughts might be allowed to come and go at will without scandalizing her Father in heaven. She made no effort to thrust into forgetfulness the echoes of her past. From her part in it she had been abundantly absolved, and if it came back at all, it was not to plague her, since she could resist so easily the temptations it laid in her path.

As time went on, Marie discovered that there was no reason to deprive herself during the week of these moments which she now regarded as the happiest of her life, and which had the additional virtue of filling her days with a sweet, delicious, lethargy.

She got into the habit of going at least once each day into a church for spiritual recreation. Paris may not be so rich as its history and its size might lead one to suppose in religious buildings of real architectural importance, but its churches, whether large or small, beautiful or ugly, offer considerable variety. There is scarcely a mood, scarcely a demand of æsthetic taste in the whole scale from the most vulgar to the most discriminating, which cannot somewhere or other within its limits find the background that it craves.

Architecture, however, and what the jargon of the day called "artistic sensation," did not interest Marie, nor were her demands in any way obsessive. She could find satisfaction in many different places. She could grasp at once the peculiarly religious quality of any church, and, provided she could find comfort for her spirit, the outer decoration of the place never worried her.

She would enter the building, and while she moistened her fingers in the holy-water stoup, would breathe in the atmosphere of the place and make it her home. Sometimes, if there were many people present, or if the service were noisier than usual, she felt a momentary disquiet. But as a rule she found herself welcomed by a silent, empty shell and by the memory of hours she had already passed there. Without giving too much thought to the matter, she chose a spot for her devotions, being guided as a rule by the way the light fell, by the promise of privacy in some particular chapel, by the peace and quiet of some cleared space of floor against one of the pillars of the nave. She would slip along a row of chairs, settling herself by choice somewhere near its middle. That done, she was ready to pursue the sequence of her prayers. Sometimes, but rarely, she had some special favour to ask, but she avoided, when possible, coming into the presence of God in the guise of a beggar. She would rather give thanks than formulate demands. It seemed to her that God had, in general, shown much indulgence towards her. He had allowed her to descend into the pit, almost to its depths, to become not only a great sinner, but a criminal. There she had wandered for many months. God might have left her there for ever, but, in fact, He had brought her out from it again, and without too great a sense of violent shock. Even her break with her lover, painful though it had been, had not been violent. It was he who had abandoned her, and he had done it so skilfully, or perhaps helped by God's pity for the sinner, that she had felt herself alone only when the deed had been done beyond recall. There had been nothing left for her then but to acquiesce, to accept as a penance the tears that had welled up suddenly in her heart.

That, at least, was how, looking back, she saw the course of her life. The adventure of her heart had taught her what life might hold in store for the poor and humble, what utter degradation might mean for those less fortunate than herself. But what she had not realized was that the chief element in her own salvation, the force that had kept her from yielding to the deceptive peace of final surrender which alone she could never have resisted, had been born of her wealth and her family connexions. They had acted, those two things, as buoys to float her to the surface. When one is as rich as she was, and as well connected, it needs something approaching genius, a constant endeavour, a ceaseless struggling against the buoys, to remain for long in the dark and oozy depths of misery.

Marie had found a simpler, a sweeter explanation. God, having permitted her to touch the utter confines of despair, doubtless that she might learn a lesson in humility, had brought her back again, had even granted to her compensation for the ordeal to which He had exposed her. For she felt at once better and happier than she had done before her fall—better from the point of view of religion, better, too, in her attitude towards her neighbour. She was more charitable. She was never happy now unless, in her journeying from church to church, she could find occasion to give alms to some poor man or woman. She even went out of her way to find objects for her charity among the poor traders of the gutter, lest she should find too easy a way of discharging her duties by giving only to professional beggars. She devoted more money, more time, and, in particular, more feeling, to good works. In the ladies' committees to which she belonged she filled all the most useful posts, or, at least, those involving the least agreeable tasks, such as house-to-house investigation.

When budgeting for her expenses in the old days before her "fall," she had never made any allowance for household matters, leaving them, together with such things as subscriptions and charitable gifts, to her husband. In fact, apart from the cost of certain definite articles, she had scarcely known how much she did spend. The small sums needed for day-to-day alms—and even those were few in number— were all that she ever debited to her private income. When, however, she entered upon the period of her "redemption," she asked the Count's permission to take over personally the control of all monies earmarked for charity. He seemed surprised at the request, but could hardly refuse. "All right, if you really want to. How much will you need?" "I don't know. How much do we give at present?" "Well, I've never actually reckoned it up." (He was a little ashamed to mention too low a figure, since his income, always huge, was still growing. The declared profits accruing to him, for instance, in 1913 must have amounted to more than three million, to say nothing of a good deal not included in his public accounts. . . .) "But I suppose, on an average, it must come to roughly fifteen hundred a month, perhaps two thousand . . . possibly more. There are a good many unforeseen demands on me which I never tell you of." "In our position we ought to give away a great deal more." (Though she had little head for figures, she had a shrewd suspicion of the kind of level on which they lived. During the building and furnishing of the house in the rue de Ranelagh, she had necessarily become aware of certain considerable payments. She knew, for instance, that "the plumbing alone had come to sixty thousand francs" and that "more than eighty thousand had gone on new carpets." She had herself spent about thirty thousand, with the full knowledge of her husband, on modern pictures. And then there was all the furniture. But large though these sums were, they had apparently made but a very small hole in the Count's resources.) "Would you mind letting me draw, as a beginning, up to three thousand a month? . . ." (Her entertainment allowance had been increased from two to three thousand since they had moved from the old apartment.) "If I want more, I'll ask for it."

No, in all fairness she must admit that God had refrained from pun-
ishing her in any way—not even in the matter of Marc. The boy had
returned to England, where he would continue his education, certainly until 1915, and perhaps until he had to start his military service.
It was suiting him admirably. So far as appearances went, he might
have been the son of a Highland laird, thoroughly hearty and a little
uncouth. His English, though rather jerky, was more fluent than his
French. The structure of words and sentences suffered less from a
staccato mode of utterance in his acquired than in his native tongue.
The strong tonic accent of the north, the suppression of weak termina-
tions, and the abundance of monosyllables, all fitted well into his natural mode of speech. He acquitted himself with distinction in all outdoor sports, and his dislike of reading was no disadvantage in the
eyes of his companions. Their only grievance was that he was apt to
hit a bit hard when he got involved in a fight. But it was generally
agreed that there was no real harm in him. His personal habits seemed
to be above reproach, and he took not the slightest interest in women.
His attitude towards drink was, perhaps, not quite so detached, and
his letters recounted more than one drunken frolic. But, for all that,
his reports remained good.

Whenever Marie thought of Roger Sammécaud, she felt bound to
condemn him for the ill he had done her (including the pain she had
been caused by his abandonment of her). But even while her mind
worked thus, she accused herself of unfairness in not taking into account the almost providential role he had played in the whole business of Marc. "It was he who grasped everything at the very first
glance, who took all the decisions. Events have proved him abundantly
right. Without him, where would the boy have been now?" She was
still haunted by a vague impression that Sammécaud had become, in
some mysterious way, Marc's "father," and that her surrender in the
Forêt d'Arces had been both the recognition of a pre-existing relationship and a thank-offering. There were times, even, when her invention went still further, when the romantic twist of her mind took
a mystic direction. By an imperfect analogy with the popular belief

that the soul of a dead child may pass into the body of the small brother or sister about to be born, she built up for her own satisfaction a private fairy-story, the gist of which was that the child they had got rid of during that terrible night at La Noue had somehow transmitted its identity to Marc. The new and highly gifted identity had been grafted onto the wilder shoot, with the result that Marc had become, not only in the spirit but even in the flesh, Roger's child and her own. (With subtle ingenuity she proved to her own satisfaction that the change in Marc had dated from that moment, a belief made the easier by the fact that her miscarriage had taken place no more than two months after Marc had been settled in England, and that the first letter of encouragement written by the headmaster of Southlea had reached her a few days after that terrible night.) Thus what had, in effect, been a criminal action became transformed into a magical operation resulting in a transfer of paternity and the grafting of one child's soul onto another child's body.

These figments of her imagination all helped to wean Marie from an idea of punishment in which she was in any case little fitted by temperament to believe. Being herself without cruelty, she found it impossible to think that vengeance could be an essential part of the order of the universe. She was, consequently, less surprised than another might have been to find herself forgiven and absolved, though that did not blind her to the fact that she had been right in accusing herself of the most terrible of sins. If now she tried to find for them a mystical explanation, it was less from a desire to excuse her actions than to acquit Providence of guilt.

For free though she might be of any sense that she had been punished, she was profoundly conscious of humiliation. She never even tried to persuade herself that she had not been deeply humbled. When the guilty past rose before her, it was in the form, not of remorse and spiritual torment, but of a persistent wind of humiliation, from the buffetings of which she did not turn aside. That was why when incidents from her past, and not seldom the most impure incidents, came back to haunt her hours of prayer, she made so little effort to drive them from her mind. Deep in her heart she went even further. Could she have lived that past over again, with full freedom of choice, she would probably not have wished any of those horrible incidents—with one signal exception—away. If she had had to justify to other ears an attitude that might have looked like an insolent refusal to repent, she would almost certainly have said that but for her misfortunes she would never have been saved from pride and hardness of heart. But she would not have admitted that she had found a certain satisfaction in all that had happened. Only in the secrecy of her thoughts did she say: "I have had the experience! I know now what it is like." And the "experience" to which she referred was not just any experience. In her varied life there were a great many that she was glad not to have known. But this particular one was hers and hers alone, was something that had been awaiting her since the beginning of time. Had she grown old without knowledge of it, something would always have been lacking. The woman whose path had been marked by the Café des Bouffes du Nord, by visits to the old herbalist, by the rue de l'Évangile, and the night of La Noue, felt at peace with herself. She was like some worn and weary housewife who can sit back with the consoling sense that she has at last got through with a menacing and heavy task which, sooner or later, had to be tackled.

It was to this feeling that she owed the sureness of touch and firmness of tone with which she carried out her new duties of visiting the poor. She knew precisely how to speak to them. No spectacle of poverty, however dire, betrayed her into insincerity. She never, now, had to be careful to avoid an exhibition of pride or condescension, and those into whose houses she went felt the difference. They could never have imagined an experience of the kind that lay behind her tact, nor were any signs of it visible in the calm serenity of her face. They attributed all to her natural goodness. Even when she was not there, they said, speaking of her: "Ah, that's a good lady!" They loved her—those at least of them in whom grinding destitution had not destroyed all trace of sweet and kindly thoughts.

She was less successful with the poor people of Courveillens. Perhaps it was that she had not the same understanding of rustic misery. Perhaps it was that the objects of her charity felt at sea and mistrustful unless they could detect in the kindness of others a necessary minimum of contempt.

Chapter

15

"FOUR DAYS OF LOVE AT BRUGES WITH AN EGYPTIAN PRINCESS"

At about this time Sammécaud was seated in a first-class compartment of a Belgian train. The train was Belgian, but the coach was German. It was handsomely upholstered in dark red, the seats were large, flat, and well-sprung, and the windows wide. Being efficiently warmed and almost hermetically sealed, it produced an impression of secure and comfortable cosiness. All around were noise and cold, but they remained outside. A thin mist lay upon the countryside, blotting out all detail save close at hand. The glass of the windows, though not obscured, was faintly veiled. Sammécaud was alone. A lamp above his head made it possible for him to read, but it did not spoil the charm of the winter's day, which it would have been a pity to miss.

Sammécaud felt completely happy. He was in the first stages of an adventure which bore all the signs of being infinitely agreeable. He found no sacrilege, however, in the thought that these preliminary moments were probably more completely delightful than any of those to come could possibly be. When one has passionately looked forward to something, there is always the risk that, even though it may not be disappointing, it may involve complications and unforeseen difficulties. Worst of all, once it has begun, it is no longer whole and unbroken: it slips between one's fingers. The more exquisite it is, the more heart-rending is it to see the small part that remains dwindling so fast away. But during the few hours that immediately precede a looked-for happening, when everything has been arranged, all is certain, yet nothing has actually begun, then is the keenest point of enjoyment. The period of waiting is just long enough to be exciting, yet not too long to be depressing. It corresponds admirably to the time necessary to go over once again in imagination all the joys to come, or to add to them the final, perfect, pleasure.

"The indispensable condition," he thought, leaning back against the handsome red cushions, "is that there should be no anxiety in anticipation. The event must be as sure of realization as such things can be, given the uncertainties of human existence. Many things are reasonably sure—often, alas, the least agreeable things. If some bore threatens to pay you a call and makes it quite clear that he will try to borrow money, it is extremely unlikely that he will let you down. Of course, there is always a certain amount of anxiety inevitably involved in looking forward to some hoped-for happiness—in the idea, in fact, that the future, however close it may be, is not yet safely grasped—but such anxiety is not of a kind to spoil the last exquisite moments. It is little more than a hint upon the palate, and the diluted bitterness of its flavour serves but to enrich the taste of waiting."

Sammécaud remembered another occasion on which he had been waiting—at the station of Laroche. His mood then had been genuinely anxious, almost feverish. The moments had been difficult to endure. In what had consisted the difference? In the first place, to be compelled to do nothing while waiting is, of all things, the most exhausting. Then, the place of waiting must be reasonably cheerful. To be rolling along in a railway carriage upholstered handsomely in red velvet is—quite apart from the pleasing features of the background, which figures as a padded casket for impatience—to get the impression that one is being efficient, is utilizing every moment, and that the distance separating one from the desired object cannot fail to be overcome, depending as it does upon one's own powers of attack which one is employing, lazily perhaps, but quite definitely, to attain the necessary end. "When, in a short time, we shall have reached the station at Bruges, in spite of all my precautions I shall almost certainly be more nervous than I am at this moment." But he had to admit also that, since the long-distant day he was remembering, he had made considerable progress, and in nothing so much as in having learned not to demand of life more than life can give (conditional, of course, on one's taking oneself all necessary steps): to demand only a limited degree of success.

Once in possession of this essential piece of knowledge, one finds that all else is simple. The mistake is to expect life to furnish one of those great set pieces of complicated construction, depending on a multitude of circumstances, feelings, and interests, and condemned to struggle endlessly against all sorts of evil chances—for instance, ten years of happiness (the very thought is enough to make one laugh!), or even a great mutual passion (with all the incidentals such a thing implies!). Real life behaves like an artist, and an artist never attempts to work with an amorphous mass of material. He contents himself with a comparatively tiny piece of marble, or with a small rectangle of canvas and a few tubes of colour. Life raises protesting arms to heaven when one begins to talk of ten years of happiness, or of a splendid love. And if one refuses to abate one's demands, and things, as is only to be expected, turn out ill, it is life one blames. A little reflection ought to have shown one that the demand was impossible. Even if life does manage to achieve the miraculous and to find two persons whose actions and sentiments will remain in harmony over a number of years without either being over-conscious of constraint or of sacrifice, how can it guarantee them against the thousand and one accidents that may cut across their careful planning? It is hardly to be expected that the whole universe will conspire to further the scheme of happiness envisaged by two individuals.

But ask of life one blissful week—nay, less than that, three or four days—and the words mean something; the problem enters at once the field of practical politics. Not that it's easy; even the comparatively tiny achievement represented by an easel picture is not easy—but it's not a great dashing enterprise, and it is designed to arouse the interest of the cultured man. It soon becomes apparent that four days may contain a world. Why talk of fleeting pleasures or of emotions that are no more than skin-deep? In the space of four days a man may experience the most violent of sentiments, may gather profound impressions the echoes of which will perhaps haunt his imagination for years to come. Provided those four days are completely successful, they may contain a crushed essence of many experiences, each thrown into strong relief by the others, such as life, except when she is in artistic mood, produces only with sparing hands and at long and weary intervals.

"In all the long time that Marie and I were together," thought Sammécaud, leaning back comfortably against the red and springy velvet, "there was only one adventure that came within measurable distance of perfection—that week in London. It would have been even better if, at the time, I had been able to look on it as a masterpiece sufficient in itself, something complete and framed and glazed, if we hadn't, she and I, spoiled it by thinking of the past and the future. Then, and then only, and almost in spite of myself, I found the secret formula. At the moment I failed to make the most of it, because, charming scrap of life though it was, it was all mixed up with one of those stories that stretch over months and years, that are too diffuse to "compose" into finished pictures and must, inevitably, turn out badly. It was spoiled, though in a different way, as my adventure with Germaine Baader was spoiled. There I failed from lack of preparation. There are men who enjoy such things only when they do lack preparation; but they are not the fastidious ones of the world. A masterpiece needs work and concentration."

The train drew up in a clean and dimly lit station. There were very few people about, and it soon drew out again. "Thank God, nobody got in!" The time-table showed no other stop before Bruges.

"Four days of love at Bruges with an Egyptian princess. . . . What a title! It says everything that needs to be said. One has only to let the words tell their tale, to see, conjured up, one of life's most successful efforts, a masterpiece duly mounted and framed."

It came to Sammécaud that, having fumbled empirically and strayed into blind alleys for half his life—more than the effective half, unfortunately—he had at last found his particular brand of "truth," had adjusted himself to the direct line of his destiny.

Others may be perfectly right in deciding to pursue different ends. Sammécaud had no desire to make converts except among a few women chosen, from time to time, at his own discretion. Indeed, it was highly desirable that his own peculiar brand of truth should not be accepted by the generality of men. There was a risk that it might become cheap. Handled by too many, it might die of exhaustion.

He was an artist. That he had long felt. But what he had only just begun to realize clearly was that he must realize himself in definite achievement, in a series of "works." They would be neither pictures, those works, nor books; not *written* chapters, as in the case of a Loti, a France, a d'Annunzio, a Barrès, but in chapters lived.

Where, of course, those men had the pull, those gods of his worship, Loti, d'Annunzio, and especially Barrès, was that they were authors twice over. They had written their delectable chapters, to be sure, but only after they had lived them first. Sammécaud yielded them the palm with a good grace. If he couldn't excel doubly, in literature and in life, he was wisely content to confine his efforts to life. Had he been free to choose between the offered alternatives, he would certainly have chosen life. And had his gods, too, been forced to choose, he felt pretty sure that their choice would have been the same as his. Thus he was more truly their disciple than the host of petty scribblers who called them master.

The work of the artist in "life" consisted precisely in preparing, at duly spaced intervals, and with the most meticulous care, one of those "chapters." The content, in each case, must be expressible, the complex individual savour made sensible, in a "title." The title was of the very first importance, for in it lay the quintessence of the theme, the clue which enabled the artist to gauge the value of what he proposed. Before deciding to embark on an adventure the elements of which were there beneath one's hand, one must first seek a "title." If it were not attractive in itself, if it did not strike the right note, one could be sure that the adventure would not be worth pursuing.

"Four days of love in Bruges with an Egyptian princess." No doubt whatever about that. Either the title was misleading, or the adventure was bound to be delicious. Each word was significant. Substitute four months for four days, and at once disaster loomed. Substitute for a *real* princess a sham one, some international courtesan in search of a rich prey, and at once the whole thing became ridiculous. Set the four days and the real princess against the background of a humdrum town, and everything would look different. In the present case Bruges was better than either Venice or Granada. In Venice or in Granada the Egyptian princess would be neither in her natural setting nor sufficiently far from it. She would be "alien," perhaps, even, a shade "provincial." Her dark beauty would be a little too dark; everything would be just "off key," vaguely cheap and nasty. Seen against the dead graces of the Flemish city, she would at once gain by contrast, would shine in the northern mists like an Orient pearl. It takes a man of breeding to appreciate such subtleties.

The train sang its pæan of bright light, driving onwards through the dwindling day, piling the gathering dusk on either side upon the distant plain.

A "chapter" with its title is the fruit of careful planning and happy circumstance. The connoisseur, intent on life, gathers in their flight the scattered buds of opportunity. He it is who takes them up unbruised and sets them in a posy. The handsome cushions of red velvet seemed richly dight with offerings of gems and flowers and opportunities.

Why had he not earlier made harvest of the gifts of life? Sammécaud could not find consolation for all the time that he had wasted. At his age, with all the advantages of his bodily powers, his mental endowment, his social prominence, his money, he ought by now to have had behind him a glittering chain of "chapters." Not one alone, but three, but four, should have had the word Venice in their titles. There should have been a whole Venetian suite of passionate memories spread over long years, tangled in wanton locks of brown and gold and red. Many rounded arms, freckled, milky white, or touched with sunny warmth, should have marked in retrospect the year's seasons and the city's many corners. The Rialto, the Schiavoni, the Zattere . . . for each separate heroine there should have been some special window, some remembered balcony, seen against water and palaces. . . . He, who adored Venice, for whom the mere fact of Venice was enough to preserve the world from utter triviality, had no single memory of Venetian love! And Florence? And Naples? And Granada, the city he had seen but once in passing? In such places the artist in life should surely have been able to stage a hundred different triumphs. Essentially nothing else for a man of his tastes mattered at all. To wear himself out in business may be all right for the poor man, the ugly man, the man with no beauty in his soul. . . . But for him, Sammécaud? . . . In passionate pilgrimage alone could lie his key to free and rich existence. . . . There are in the world so many outstanding places just waiting to stage some precious episode of love subtly diversified: Saint-Moritz, for instance, in the Engadine; Portofino-Kulm . . . even Stockholm or Saint Petersburg, with their promise of long nights of snow-bright passion. In Dresden, it seems, there are curious subtleties of beauty. A man with highly placed connexions would find it not impossible to get an introduction at court and watch, as in the glass cases of a museum, the preserved vestiges of the great age. "A love-affair at the Saxon court" had points as a title, and such an episode might well last three months, for it wouldn't be a question of three months lived constantly in the company of one woman—a dangerous experiment that might well end in satiety or misunderstanding—but of many, varied meetings: flirtations in the State apartments; ten minutes of whispered nothings in some rococo boudoir; glances exchanged across a crowded, brilliant room; notes confided to a gold-laced flunkey whose understanding look would say: "His Highness may rely on me"; meetings hardly granted and tenderly pursued, and, between whiles, balls and the opera, long drives into the country, hunting parties, discriminating visits to museums, long, idle mornings in the shops of antique-dealers, day-dreams in old streets or on the slopes of ancient bridges. . . . .

What chances he had missed! But there was still the future, and
he must miss no more.

He was no longer young, of course, but he still felt comfortably far
from old age, and in a polite society maturity misses fewer chances
than it gains privileges. His health was reasonably good. He had
to be careful what he ate; could stand up less than of yore to fatigue
and excess; was occasionally troubled by a liver attack which he had
to combat in the strict intimacy of his room—but none of these things
was a serious handicap. . . . In the lists of love, naturally, he had
little aptitude for the breaking of records; but the women with
whom he peopled his fantasies of the future were not such as to
swoon with delight at the idea of some Hercules of the market-place.

Love, to be sure, figured directly or indirectly in almost all the
titles of these exquisite adventures, but it was as part of an artistic
convention, of a charming law of style, not as a crude physiological
craving. The picture took shape in the imagination, and somewhere
in it, naturally, a woman would be found, to gather up in her
features the half-lights and the melancholy, to give to the ineffable
a name of intimacy. But, if it came to that, and by way of a change,
one episode might well be called: "A day's shooting on the Upper
Nile with the Duke of Gloucester," on condition that the Duke was
a real aristocrat, still young, affable, and refined, a good companion,
whimsical and faintly touched with eccentricity. . . . There would
be stories of an evening round the camp-fire beneath the tropical
stars and gin to drink (in spite of the liver). . . . Or there might be
"A week in the Atlas Mountains with Lyautey"; long treks on small
Arab ponies, talks in which reminiscences of campaigning would
take turn with discussions on Wagner; meetings with native chiefs;
distant rifle-shots; and, at night, just brushed in as a vague background to this tale of action, some adventure, perhaps, with a little
dancer. . . .

One of the advantages of the period of life at which Sammécaud

now found himself was that he had been able to shake himself free
of certain restrictions. His wife, preoccupied with the education of
her growing children, left him more time to himself. The children
themselves, especially his two sons, though their problems might involve him in the necessity of taking more important, more carefully
thought-out decisions, no longer demanded the ceaseless watchfulness of paternal solicitude. He could think of them now at a distance, could even, from the slopes of Atlas, write them letters about
the joys of an active life (letters at which they would be less inclined
to smile when they had read the heading: "In Camp something-or-
other Kebir"). Business, unfortunately, took more of his time than
ever, especially since Champcenais, lured into the Zülpicher waters
—and troubled waters at that—and ambitious of navigating the main
reaches of capitalism, had shown signs of regarding the oil concern
as no better than a small family farm and was leaving Sammécaud
to grapple with most of the details of the cartel. But even here he had
for some time past been planning to shelve most of his responsibilities. He was looking about for someone who not only could take his
place in the office, but could be trusted to look after the general concerns of the whole cartel. For a moment he had played with the idea
of Haverkamp. But he had soon come to the conclusion that the
founder of Celle, apart from the fact that he was already fully occupied and was less energetic than formerly, was hardly the man to
take a real interest in anything that he did not fully control, no matter how tempting the fees might be. Either he would neglect the
cartel or else he would get it ultimately into his own hands, a prospect that by no means appealed to Sammécaud.

He had toyed also with the idea of Pierre Lafeuille. But with all
his talents and all his cleverness, Pierre Lafeuille was not really the
man for the job. He was too insignificant, too much lacking in force-
fulness, too much the little gentleman, with the little gentleman's
liking for backstairs intrigue. He was exceedingly fearful of soiling
his hands or involving himself in the rough and tumble of the market-
place. It would never occur to him to work all night on a problem

should time press, and though he might disdain the petty shifts of vulgar fraud, he was capable of far more serious dishonesties. In short, he was too much the middle-class business man, too deeply wedded to his office table and his files. (Sammécaud, with his tendency to give knock for knock in matters of business, knew that, whatever his faults, they were not those of the middle-class outlook.)

What he was looking for was the ideal managing director: a man of character and energy, bred in the shops, accustomed to command, with a touch of the sergeant-major about him. Someone who would be able to handle the men, who wouldn't mind taking his turn with an oil-can and a piece of cotton waste, a man of the people, courageous, reasonably keen on money, and quite determined to feather his nest. "I'm ready to give him sixty thousand myself, and I'll get the cartel to guarantee him forty thousand more. In addition to that he can be sure of getting at least a hundred thousand on the sly from secret commissions and bribes. It's an enormous sum of money, to be sure, but he'll be enormously useful to me." It would be silly to count pennies where really essential matters were concerned. "What's a hundred thousand or a hundred and fifty thousand francs more or less on my overhead? Just one item the more on the annual balance-sheet, a matter of minor adjustment in my investments. Regarded from the only point of view that really matters, the point of view of my own happiness, it's just not worth bothering about. My children will have more than enough, provided, that is, that the whole world doesn't go smash. At any moment some catastrophe beyond my power to control may strip them of a hundred times more than I could ever give them by scraping and saving. And anyhow, what do they want with so much extra capital?"

The great thing was to live. He had plenty of money, and money still meant power. But how long would he have it? The prophets of disaster might, after all, be right in predicting a social cataclysm and the expropriation of the possessing classes. But where they were wrong was in failing to taste to the full, with exquisite sensibility and secret gratification, all that the present time could still afford them.

Why spoil the moment, charged with its treasure of memories? After all, nothing else counted. Those who did so were fools; above all, they lacked the artistic sense. As though, at any period of the world's history, men had been able to count on having everything, including security! Sammécaud would have been as pleased as most to live in a time of settled order and wide civilization; a time of authority sufficiently based on law to need no plotting and planning for its maintenance within the social hierarchy, sufficiently wise to eschew perilous adventures abroad. It would have suited him well to live in one of the old monarchies of polished manners and exquisite scepticism, the enemy alike of revolution and of war, patron of pomp and pleasure, safeguarded by an efficient police service with a due sense of social differences, benevolently despotic, tolerant of reasoned liberty, to be feared only by the fanatic and the criminal. (The Austrian Empire, seen from a pleasant distance, and less rickety than it was in fact, would have given a very fair illustration of his ideal.) He sympathized with much in the point of view of the Action Française, though he hated its pompous dogmatism, its lack of easiness and humour, the almost Huguenot fury of its Catholic enthusiasm.

The world must be accepted for what it was. The older he grew in thought and experience, the more convinced he was that the age deserved better than to be summarily damned. The man of skill and patience could extract a good deal of pleasure from it. It was easy enough, of course, to grumble at things as they were, easy and modish too. In so far as it was modish, Sammécaud gave it a certain amount of lip service. For instance, the artist could not but deplore the invasion of modern life by vulgarity and barbarism. It was permissible to think with a nostalgic thrill of past ages when the art of living had been at its height, to call down curses, too, on the calamities that a possible future might have in store (such, for instance, as this abominable collectivist regimentation which a lot of rogues and fools who made their living out of deceiving the people were so busy painting as the glory of a new Golden Age). But no amount of regret for the past or fear for the future should keep the wise man from plucking the rare and delicate fruits of life where still they could be found.

Once more Sammécaud assured himself that there were more good things left in the world than the whiners seemed to think; that just because their existence was precarious—the last few apples hidden among the thinning branches—it was the part of wisdom to dwell lovingly upon their fugitive beauties and grow intoxicated on a draught that soon might vanish. One need go back in imagination no further than a single generation to realize how many irreplaceable delights had been allowed to disappear unpossessed and unenjoyed by those who now complained that, since the '60's or the '80's, the world had grown grey and empty. Loti had seen things that no one would ever see again: Japan barely emerged from her Middle Age, Pekin still the glory of the old Empire, the South Seas still an earthly paradise, Turkey before the coming of the Young Turks. . . . He at least, for all his grudging humour, had known how to see and enjoy. But what of all those others who, living then with leisure and wealth at their disposition, had been satisfied with the humdrum flatness of a middle-class existence—not without an occasional derisive appreciation of the rich and coloured centuries that had gone—arguing that the grey world in which they found themselves had nothing left to offer, that nothing any longer was worth while? "I," thought Sammécaud, "I shall go to Constantinople, spoiled though it doubtless is by the domination of a lot of so-called progressives in black coats . . . because in ten years, in twenty, the Constantinople of 1913 or '14 will seem like a vanished fairyland, and a sail up the waters of the bay with a fair veiled Turkish girl like a fantastic adventure which all the money in the world will not serve to buy. I shall go to Stamboul and taste the pleasures of love. I shall drift upon the waters in an open boat with some woman in my arms, and beneath a crescent moon rising above the Sweet-Waters of Asia, I shall gently draw aside her veil. . . . I want to go to Moscow while there are still Grand Dukes and extravagant orgies and night drives in sleighs and kissing princesses in sumptuous furs who adore the French. . . ." It came to him too that Africa of the Mussulmans, of which he had been told such wondrous things, which was so easy to reach, would not long hold out against the assaults of modernism. There one might still find without too much difficulty "chapters" of mingled pleasure and romance worthy of the *Arabian Nights*. "God! To think of all the time I've lost! Nowhere in the world is safe from the creeping tide of boredom, of twopenny-halfpenny progress, of the vulgar garishness of democracy. . . . A grey morality may invade more than Europe! . . . Old age will come, and death. I must delay no longer. Until now—and I ought to be ashamed to admit it—I have scarcely ever travelled except on business. What a fool I've been! Had there been oil in Tunis, I should have gone there. All very well for Champcenais or Desboulmiers—but not for me." He could have bitten his fingers to the bone from sheer vexation and regret. "But I will take my revenge. It's all really so easy to do." The one good mark that the present age deserved was for the unprecedented freedom of movement it had placed at the disposal of the lover of life. It had allowed many marvels to vanish, but how simple now to see what yet remained, to travel to the places of the earth where adventures could yet be found! "If tonight we found Bruges too cold at this time of year, we could buckle our bags and catch a night train, with excellent sleeping-car arrangements, for the South, and wake tomorrow morning on the Italian lakes! We need ask no one's leave. I don't even know that passports are still necessary for Russia and Turkey. Wherever we went we should find good hotels, at all times and in all places my notes and gold would be accepted with unfailing courtesy. Not so long ago, arriving in Bucharest, one could tip the porter with what was left of one's French change. Let's hope that those times will come back. Europe is as open to us as our own flat. We saunter from room to room without even troubling to put on outdoor clothes. Is that nothing? Perfect freedom from all the material stupidities of life, from the fuss and bother which made travelling such an ordeal for our ancestors; absence of that prosaic weariness that was always intruding on their romance and on their loves? Doesn't all this constitute a victory for those who still practise the art of living? Isn't it rather unfair, after all, to have eyes only for what the present age has deprived us of?"

He thought of the telephone call that had been put through to him the previous evening in Brussels: "I am at Ostend. I had a good crossing. I shall spend this evening and part of tomorrow with some friends of mine here. That's the best arrangement, I think. I shall get to Bruges by the train arriving about six, a little after six . . . you can find the exact hour in the time-table. Heavens! How cold this country of yours is!"

"That telephone call," he thought in his railway carriage with the red velvet cushions, while the first lights of Bruges began to appear, "would have spared many a lover of the olden time that last hour of anxiety before the chosen hour of meeting, his heart beating at the thought of a boat missed, of some final delay, which would be explained in a letter arriving a week too late. . . . There is nothing now that I need fear. What's the very worst that could happen? A forced stay overnight at Ostend? Even so, I could still see her before midnight. Ostend?—a mere twenty minutes in the train."

Thanks to the arrangements he had made, he could rely on a margin of three quarters of an hour in which to go from the station to the hotel, look at the rooms he had reserved, tidy himself, and get back in time to meet the "Egyptian princess." Three quarters of an hour was just right, long enough to spare him the inconvenience of having to hustle, not too long to constitute a trying wait.

Outside the station he found the hotel porter with the hotel omnibus.

"I think there's a message for you," said the man.

It could only be some change in her plans. Sammécaud felt uncomfortable during the short drive to the hotel. He experienced something like a sensation of relief when he read that his princess had been delayed and would come by the next train, arriving an hour later.

It was signed Eugénie. The Egyptian princess was called Eugénie. On learning this fact when they had met for the first time in Paris,

Sammécaud had been conscious of a slight feeling of disappointment, which he had not been able wholly to conceal, for she had said to him, in her soft, full voice, which gave almost the impression of being swaddled in down: "Eugénie . . . you think it is not Oriental enough? My mother was born at the time when the opening of the Suez Canal by the Empress of the French was being celebrated. She was named after the Empress, to whom my grandfather was presented. Later, when a name had to be found for me, I was given my mother's. You would have preferred an Arab name? My family is neither Arab nor Turkish. It is Coptic. I am a Christian."

Thinking things over, he had decided that this name, Eugénie, represented the happy mingling of elements, one at least of which was redolent of history. It is not uncommon for princesses to bear names which in the case of a woman of the middle classes might sound dowdy or countrified.

Having made up his mind that this Bruges "chapter" must, whatever happened, be a success, he refused to attach any undue importance to this small delay. He gave orders for the room to be filled with flowers. He examined every corner of the hotel. He had decided on it by chance and congratulated himself on having chosen well. The architecture and the decoration, the emptiness of the lounge at this time of the year, an occasional piece of old furniture in the corridors and the rooms, all combined to give the illusion of being guests in the town house of some great Flemish magnate of the Renaissance; of some host who had carried discretion to the point of keeping himself invisible.

"It was a happy thought of mine. This is just the kind of setting, differing only in the local colour of the various countries of Europe, for the romantic adventures of my dreams."

He asked to have the room specially warmed, gave instructions that oysters from Ostend and hare from the Ardennes should be added to the menu, and chose a Moselle and a Chambertin. "Madame" would decide whether they should dine downstairs or in their own room.

These many concerns occupied him until it was time to take the omnibus once more to the station. He sat as near the inside lamp as possible in order to read a descriptive pamphlet on Bruges. The evening was damp but mild. There was no wind. The princess would shiver a bit, just for the sake of appearances, but she would have to admit that it was pleasanter here than in London.

The train came in. The princess appeared at the door of her carriage, swathed in furs. She got out and, true to his anticipation, went through the form of shivering. But she admitted that it was really "all imagination." She had often, she said, been colder getting off the ship at Alexandria. Besides, with all the furs that she had bought in London, she could face anything.

Chapter

ONE HOUR OF LOVE WITH A WOMAN DOCTOR OF RATHER PECULIAR TASTES

"Well, honestly, what do you think of my poem?"

He spoke rather like a shy pupil in the presence of a master whose word, once given, could not be disputed. His expression was both apologetic and appealing, and not without a touch of almost childlike confidence.

She answered, stirring her tea the while:

"Oh, not too bad, passable. I still don't like the last stanza but one. It's so clumsy as to be—how shall I put it?—almost pitiable."

"I've rewritten it seven or eight times since Tuesday."

She raised her spoon and delicately sipped its contents. Her face seemed to show nothing but haughty, disdainful boredom.

"That I can well believe. . . . The probability is you will never do better. It just shows, you see, what a difference there is between a man of genuine talent and a man—of none. There's a point beyond which mere hard work will never take you."

There was no trace of bitterness in his reply. He spoke like one calmly discussing a question of fact:

"I did think, though, that I'd improved it a little. The stanza does anyhow express more or less what I mean. The clumsiness you speak of is part and parcel of the effect of starkness and ugliness I was aiming at. There are passages in Baudelaire, some of my favourites, which have a similar air of awkwardness."

"I can see no comparison."

He said nothing, but bent his head above the paper before him, almost as though he were bowing. Meanwhile she had lit a cigarette. She had changed her chair for a divan, on which she lay half reclined, her right elbow resting on a cushion, one leg stretched out, the other bent and partly hanging over the edge. Her loose dress left most of the calf visible. Her face, crowned by black hair drawn tightly back on either side of a central parting, expressed calm superiority. The features were regular and not unhandsome, giving rather the effect of a Madonna. There was about them a hint of gentleness, even of sweetness, which though unemphasized was none the less noticeable. The same was true of her voice.

He read through once again the stanza in question and the whole of the end of the poem. Then he made a sound which might have been intended for a sigh, but ended as a sniff.

"Do you think I ought to publish it in the paper?"

"Why not? . . . No good being too modest."

He blushed, she tittered. Both sound and expression were barely noticeable. She went on:

"Since it's you who are putting up the cash people will merely say that old Léon de Solendre's paying you a few ridiculous compliments. He's always afraid of not giving you your money's worth. He's already referred to you in print as the French Meredith, and the paper managed to survive that, which proves that it's got considerable power of resistance, and that you're paying up pretty handsomely. The contributors can always have a good laugh among themselves, behind your back."

She deliberately lowered her voice to a rich contralto, stressing the note of mockery.

He seemed to be thinking over her words. Then, with considerable hesitation, as though something long repressed were forcing its way from the depths of his being:

"There's a question," he said, "that I'd like you to answer. If I hadn't got money, should I ever be able to get my poetry published?"

"I don't know. I've never considered the point. The *Hippocampe* wouldn't publish it, for the very good reason that the *Hippocampe* wouldn't exist. But someone else might . . . though I doubt it."

"May I point out that the *Mercure* has printed three of my sonnets?"

"I don't think Vallette can ever have read them. He just wanted to be polite to an amateur who was known to be a patron of literature."

To this he said nothing. He appeared once more to be plunged deep in thought. Both of them sipped their tea. She smoked, looking at him the while beneath lowered lids, her whole attitude eloquent of a carefully assumed feminine insolence.

He spoke again, still in a tone of quiet deference:

"Still—I'd like to know how you explain this . . . I know it's not the same thing, but, well—you see, where business is concerned, I've shown that I have quite definitely intellectual qualities—no one, I think, would deny that."

"What connexion is there between business and literature?"

"Hang it all, if the mind's at work in both, there must be some. I'm sure I've heard you use the same argument in your own case. . . . You are a woman doctor—I beg your pardon, a *doctor* . . . quite distinguished in your field; in fact, considering your age, very distinguished! . . . You once said, if you remember, that precisely the same qualities were at work in your professional life as in your writing."

"Did I really say that?" she mocked.

"Yes."

"Are you quite sure you got my meaning?"

"I think so."

She shook the ash from her cigarette, frowned, and resumed on an almost shrill note:

"It's quite possible . . . but, then, *my* business has a good deal in common with literature. It's nothing, after all, but psychology with a little scientific jargon thrown in. When I get my clients to tell me all their little manias, their adventures in public lavatories and secluded corners—" she broke off with a gust of laughter that seemed to shake her body—"as though, by the way, I didn't know that they got a kick out of confiding in a woman with some pretensions to looks and who doesn't wear spectacles . . . that's the reason why most of 'em come . . . well, I could transcribe word for word certain dialogues which go on in my consulting-room and have a nice little slab of literature ready made. You, I think, could hardly say as much!"

"Business on the scale that I operate on has a good deal to do with psychology, you know."

She changed her tone:

"You're arguing like a fool! I might just as well say that when my dog begs for a bit of sugar, he's indulging in psychology. I still fail to see the slightest connexion between your success as a swindling industrialist and financier and your lack of it as a dilettante poet. But I know what you're after! You want me to pay you a few compliments. You're almost as appealing as my dog when he wants a lump of sugar. You'd like to think that I admired you as a great big business man—which I very well might do, let me tell you, since I know nothing whatever about business."

She paused for a moment without even looking at him.

"As a matter of fact, I don't admire you one little bit. I'm quite certain that you owe any success you may have had to circumstances and the luck of your birth. I don't say you haven't been helped by a certain natural cunning and a complete lack of sensibility. You're quite capable of knowing which side your bread's buttered. You'd give your broker an order on the day of your mother's funeral without turning a hair."

"So," he asked without any visible trace of irony, as though he awaited her answer before making up his mind on a point, "you don't think I've got any superior qualities at all?"

She looked long at him, a curious smile on her lips. She made another little grimace which said as plainly as words: "I'd like to, but I can't." She started to swing the toe of the foot which was hanging over the edge of the divan. With her right hand she played with a bell-pull which lay at the end of its cord among the cushions. She looked closely at the pear-shaped wooden object as though discovering some peculiarity about it. From her expression a stranger might have thought there was no one else in the room. She seemed overcome by boredom. With her other hand she drew towards her a book which lay near by in a grey paper dust-cover secured with elastic. But she did not open it.

He, meanwhile, as quietly as possible had slipped to his knees between the tea-table and the divan. He took in his hands the foot that was swinging to and fro in front of his face, holding it by the piece of curved leather that joined the heel to the sole, without, however, interfering with its movement. Next he rather timidly kissed the lowest extremity of the leg. Then, leaning rather farther forward, he touched with his lips the other leg, which was outstretched along the divan.

She took no more notice than if her dog, of which she had just been speaking, excited by the moving shoe, had started to bite it. She poured out a second cup of tea, lit another cigarette, and opened her book.

He ventured a few kisses rather higher up, raising the edge of her skirt in order to reach her knees. Without even taking the trouble to look at what was happening, she mechanically pulled down her skirt again, making a movement with her hands as though to brush away something that was annoying her. Her fingers struck him on the temples and on the cheeks; her nails slightly scratched his skin. He withdrew his head, but as soon as she moved her hands once more, he took advantage of the respite to approach again with his lips the region of her knees.

She let him go on as though the book whose leaves she was turning were absorbing all her attention, or as though she were too lazy to struggle against what was no more disturbing than the tickling of a fly. A slight frown showed between her brows. Meanwhile his kisses moved higher and higher. He continued to lift her skirt and made a faint effort to separate the legs of the young woman, who must, indeed, have been deeply absorbed in her book or too lazy to protest, since she made no attempt to resist, though resistance would have been more than ever easy. For some seconds his appearance was that of a worshipper, wearisome perhaps, but still tolerated.

Suddenly, without the slightest warning, she struck him full in the face with the book she was holding and threw him backwards with a violent thrust of her thighs. In a voice that expressed boredom rather than anger she cried:

"You're no good to me! Do you hear? You're no good to me! Get away and leave me in peace!"

She stared at him. There was a mocking curiosity in her gaze, mingled with an odd air of sympathy. The discomfort which showed upon his face had little, apparently, to do with the actual facts of the situation. It was as though what worried him proceeded from causes that lay deeper than the eye could see. In particular he seemed moved by some obscure sense of delight. In both his own case and hers, what was happening appeared less the result of any natural sequence of events than of some secret and undisclosed connivance.

"So you're all worked up, are you?" she said. "Want to work off your filthy cravings on me? Well, you'd better try your luck with women who are less difficult to please."

She seized the bell-pull and rang. "I've sent for my maid. Whether she'll be able to put up with you, I have no idea. But she, too, knows that you're rich. The prospect of a good tip may persuade her to overcome her natural repugnance."

At this moment the maid entered. She was by no means old or ugly, though rather thin. She looked extremely respectable and rather knowing.

"Madame rang?"

"I really must beg your pardon, Georgette. Monsieur de Champcenais is in one of his states. Would you, I wonder, be willing to submit to certain advances? . . . I'm afraid you won't find it very attractive, but it'll soon be over."

"Just as Madame wishes."

"Thank you, Georgette. You can use my consulting-room. There's a chaise-longue in there. . . . Once more, I beg your pardon."

Turning towards the Count, and in a bullying tone that was in marked contrast to the kindly way in which she had addressed her servant, she said:

"Get out. And don't be too long. We've still got a lot of work to do on the next number. If you dawdle, I shall come and fetch you."

Which is precisely what she did, throwing the door of the consulting-room suddenly open. In her hand, as though she had picked it up by accident, she held her dog's leash, which had a whip at its handle end. At the sight which met her she assumed an air of fury and outraged decency, striking at the Count—being careful, however, to miss Georgette—and driving him from the room to an accompaniment of foul-mouthed abuse. When she had given him time to recover and had made him sit down beside her on the divan, she patted his shoulder and proceeded to address him in the friendliest terms:

"Take it easy, old thing, take it easy. Have a drop of tea, or some port if you'd rather. What's the matter?"

His manner, too, seemed subtly to have changed. He still spoke calmly, collectedly, but there was a genuineness in his tone which it had lacked before. It was as though now, at last, he were expressing what he really felt.

"Oh, nothing much," he said; "only I've got a sort of feeling that you really do despise me a bit."

"My dear, don't be absurd. If I despise anything, it's just human nature in general, yours and mine and everybody's. . . . Though I'm hanged if I know why I say that, because I don't really mean it. What I actually despise is human nature as it shows itself in, say, a butcher boy or one of your financier friends who make love much as they go to the lavatory. I have the highest esteem for all vicious tendencies. I'm vicious myself."

Smilingly he shook his head, his eyes on hers.

"Oh no, you're not."

"How can you say that!"

"No, you're a woman doctor, doctor and writer too, who takes a professional interest in vicious persons and happens to be intellectually curious about vices in general."

She drew away from him, curled her legs beneath her on the divan, propped herself against the cushions, and offered to his gaze her smiling, Madonna-like profile, her eyes gleaming behind their lashes.

"And you really believe that! So did I, once, because I was a fool, because something of my Puritan upbringing was still operative, because I wanted to make excuses for myself. I've got a theory about these things. When a doctor decides to specialize, I believe it's because a particular field of investigation fits in with some purely personal leaning of his own, because by concentrating on it he can satisfy or appease or stimulate or tranquillize some deep-seated instinct. That isn't so all the time, of course, because there are always a few people who don't know their own minds, who have no fixed temperament, who take the easiest way and let themselves drift. Men like that choose a line for no particular reason. They may be influenced by the kind of work that happens to come their way in hospital, by the advice of masters, or by the fact that there is some family business waiting for them to step into. . . . The doctor who specializes in stomach troubles is usually a man who suffers from his stomach and hopes by that means to get early information about new methods of treatment and hitherto undiscovered drugs. That makes you smile, eh? You think the explanation rather too simple?"

"Too simple?—well, perhaps. I can't help thinking that you're leaving a good deal out of account."

(He was speaking freely now, as though to an equal. It was clear that he was perfectly capable of defending his point of view and contradicting his opponent.)

"I'm pretty sure I'm right, though. . . . Another reason is that, being always plagued by his stomach, he wants to think about it the whole time, to interrogate his own symptoms. He's in exactly the same position as an old pensioner who likes nothing so much as talking about his ailments to other old pensioners on a seat in the public gardens. The subject is one that they find inexhaustibly interesting. Similarly, a man who specializes in heart trouble is one who suffers from his heart, or thinks he does, or has a subconscious fear that he may be going to. And if he isn't so simple as to think that by dint of devoting every moment of the day to diseases of the heart, of seeing endless patients, trying out all the newest dodges on other people, and reading everything that's printed on his subject, he stands a greater chance of healing a lesion or preventing it from developing, even of performing a miracle, his subconscious *is* simple enough to think so."

"Do you know," said Champcenais, "I should never have dared to think that sort of thing about doctors . . . or if such an idea had occurred to me, I certainly should never have dared to mention it, least of all to you."

"I'm pretty sure that the same is true about other professions. It's the only way of explaining the kind of idiocies one's always coming across—for instance, when people deliberately run the risks they're most terrified of. I know a case of a young officer who chose the army simply and solely because he was afraid of war. Ever since his childhood the various circumstances of his family—his elder brother was killed as a private in Dahomey—had combined to give him a sort of haunting obsession that he would die on the battlefield. It's more than likely that deep down he argued—everyone is guilty of such foolishness at times—that as an officer he would run fewer risks. . . ."

"But you wouldn't say that was normally true of all army officers?"

"Bah! What we call normal is nothing but the average of variations from the abnormal. Take the case of doctors again. It's long been a truism that all alienists are a little mad, and no one can deny that they frequently end by being certified. But the popular error lies in believing that they become mad by having to look after mad people and listen to their talk . . . that madness is catching, like other diseases. . . ."

"Still, it seems to me perfectly reasonable to take such a view."

"Oh no, the reverse is really the truth. It's because they feel themselves interested in madness and threatened by it that they become alienists. They want to understand, to study, to fight against, all the fantastic notions that are already buzzing about in their own heads. Similarly with venereal disease. Out of four fellow-students of mine who specialized in that, two got the clap, with every kind of complication, during their first years at college, and the third picked up a bad dose of syph off a street woman."

"Did they confide all this to you?"

"Yes, and to others too. The thing became a popular joke. And so you see, having already studied up their symptoms in the books and learned all about what were good signs and what were bad . . . they'd only got to go on working along the same lines to become specialists. My own particular weakness shows itself in exactly the same way. I realize that now, and I'm proud that I realize it. . . . There are only two kinds of people, those who realize what's the matter with them and those who don't. . . ."

"To which kind do I belong?"

"To the first, of course. Otherwise I shouldn't be talking to you like this. . . . The others are poor wretches, no better than slaves or machines or insects. They belong to a definitely inferior type; I can't think of them as in any way my equals. No matter what extraordinary things they do, I just feel sorry for them, but much as one feels sorry for animals, and sometimes I don't even feel sorry. Don't you remember, at the time of the Russo-Japanese War, and more recently still, how we used to be told in article after article about the Japanese soldiers, whole waves of them, going forward to certain death without the slightest hesitation or the slightest regret, without thinking, even, because they had no idea of the value of human life. . . . They were held up to us as models of superb heroism, of sublime indifference to danger. . . . What damned nonsense! I suppose they'd say that the locusts in Algeria, throwing themselves, millions of them, into the advancing flames, are also to be admired for their sublime unconsciousness of danger! If I could get all the slave populations of the world together and herd them into the crater of some volcano to die heroically like the locusts and so wipe out the type completely, I'd do it without a moment's compunction!"

"How ferocious you are, my dear!" said Champcenais with a sympathetic chuckle. "I'm not sure that people like that haven't their uses. . . . Doesn't it occur to you that humanity may be in a bad way when there are no longer folk ready and willing to get killed without thinking?"

"On the contrary, it'll be a time of blessed peace! . . . All the evils of the world, my friend, have arisen just because there were always people ready to get themselves killed without thinking."

Zülpicher's partner shook his head. The subject of their discussion had awakened in him certain ironical echoes which he could not have put into words, even here, without a faint feeling of embarrassment and outraged modesty.

"What it comes to is this: I know I'm vicious and that I chose my profession because I had a weakness for vice. Even as a small girl I was excessively conscious of sex. I couldn't keep my mind off it, and it was a source, for me, of incessant difficulties. Like other small girls, I used to mess about with myself, but there was always at the back of my mind an uncomfortable feeling that made it impossible for me to find any real relief that way. Do I shock you?"

"Of course not. I was trying to picture you as a little girl at grips with her dawning femininity—hardly a picture for a school-book! But Baudelaire, I think, might have found it interesting."

"One fine day the idea came to me that sexual pleasure demanded a partner; that without one it didn't really exist. After that I just couldn't have gone on alone. In my case the 'partner' was of my own sex, a nice little girl of my acquaintance. There were others, too, a little older than myself, who gave me a few lessons. But I couldn't get any real pleasure out of it—it gave me a sense of insurmountable disgust."

"So, you see, you're not so vicious as you'd like to make out!"

"Don't flatter yourself! All that proved was that I wasn't equally gifted for every kind of vice. . . . When one's driving a car and comes to a cross-road, it's sometimes necessary to follow the main road for a bit before turning off down the lane one's looking for. . . . My sexual appetite led me quite naturally and directly to men. But because there weren't any handy and because I couldn't find any satisfaction in substitutes or make-believe, I passed several very uncomfortable years. Do you know I think I realize now exactly why it was that I decided to be a doctor? I must have argued that for a girl like me, well brought up in a good middle-class family, the only really convenient way of being made love to, from both a material and a moral point of view, was to adopt the life of a student or a doctor. Whether the men I should find would be fellow-students or professors didn't matter a jot. It was borne in on me that in the world of my choice, promiscuity was less frowned on than elsewhere, and that it would be easier for me to avoid having a child. You see, I knew perfectly well that the particular hell lying in wait for a young woman who played about with men was the unwanted child. So I matriculated, and a long time after, because even a vicious girl can be shy, I had my first experience of a man—of two men, to be accurate, and no more, and neither of them for long, but quite long enough to teach me another horrible fact, the most horrible of all: these transports for which I had longed so ardently gave me no pleasure at all, or, if pleasure so much as showed the tip of its nose, it was only to withdraw it the moment after."

"Perhaps it was your lovers who showed themselves lacking in technique . . ." and then, with an air of mock humility, he added: "as I did myself just now."

"No; they were both men of experience, and it was a matter of self-respect with them to overcome my frigidity. The first was one of the house surgeons, the second a young professor. Neither of them, I must admit, had the slightest notion of what psychologic complexes meant. They were pure materialists. The only subtleties whose existence they would admit were all confined to the physical plane and consisted in ingenious variations of the kind referred to, in their more chaste manifestations, by authors of text-books on physics or mechanics, such, for instance, as duration, speed, acceleration, distance covered, the nature of surfaces, the coefficients of friction, contact, fluids, or lubrication. . . ."

Champcenais burst into a guffaw.

"You're a marvel! I never knew that a page of physics could contain such a string of obscenities."

"They scarcely even took account of the indirect effects produced by that curious device known as the nervous system. There's no doubt at all in my own mind that what turned my attention to nervous ailments, and particularly to the special kind in which I have specialized, was just this fresh disappointment. I wanted to know; I was drawn by a feeling of sympathy for all those odd cases among which my own belonged. I longed to spend all my time examining these abnormalities. I don't say that I was quite as simple as the stomach-doctor we were supposing just now and actually hoped to find a cure, whether direct or not, for my own difficulties in the course of such investigations; I think my motives were more subtle, more cunning, than that; I hoped—how shall I put it?—that in the course of picking over all this dirty linen I should discover some sort of satisfaction and appeasement. And that is what more or less happened. I certainly am not cured—if, indeed, there ever was anything to be cured, which I now deny. What I mean is that I haven't reverted to what are usually called normal standards—and Heaven be thanked I haven't. But I have had a number of opportunities which I never should have had if I'd lived the sort of life I'd been born into, which I shouldn't even have had—not, at any rate, under such good conditions—if I'd gone on the streets. Besides, there are many reasons why I shouldn't have liked the streets. . . . To cut a long story short, what love-affairs I have, I have with my patients."

Champcenais jumped. His face grew dark and sullen.

"Not with all of them, by any means," she went on, correcting herself. "And those with whom I do don't, for the most part, realize it. They're much too much occupied with their own troubles."

He still looked annoyed and had moved slightly away from her.

"Why, what's the matter? What do you think I mean?"

She sidled closer, leaned over him, stroked the back of his head with her hand.

"What a great jealous old silly it is! Can't you understand anything unless it's underlined? What's got into that head of yours? Do you think I allow Tom, Dick, or Harry to do to me, or to begin doing to me, what you did just now? Don't be a fool . . . I'm not a guinea-pig. . . . You're pretty ungrateful, I must say, if you don't realize that I regard you as my lover—as my only lover."

She flung her arms round his neck and kissed him on the temple. Then she moved away from him again and sat for a while as though absorbed in her own thoughts. When she spoke again, the note of mockery had crept back into her voice.

"I'm afraid that even you didn't succeed in giving me much pleasure today. I hate having to say it, but we're always frank with each other, aren't we? . . . No, when you did what you did, it was with you that my mind was occupied, with the state I wanted to get you into. . . . When you really gave me pleasure, or, rather, when I found pleasure for myself, was when I went to fetch you and found you engaged on all sorts of beastlinesses with Georgette, and chased you out of the room with my whip. That did give me a thrill, from the roots of my hair to the tips of my toes—you never suspected it, did you?— with every satisfaction that only copulation as a rule produces. . . . But don't, by the way, get the idea that Georgette's used to doing that sort of thing. She knows what I feel about you, and she's very fond of me. That's why she consented. But I don't keep a brothel, you know."

Champcenais seemed a little less ruffled, though there were still traces of uneasiness in his expression, which he concealed beneath a renewed access of tender humility.

"I've no right, dearest, to call you to account for anything you do. To me you have always been kindness and sweetness itself. Please forgive my little outburst of masculine jealousy; regard it in the light of a compliment."

She replied with the air of a woman trying to be scrupulously honest.

"I don't want to pretend that butter wouldn't melt in my mouth. I'm not playing the old game and saying that 'you're the very first.'

On the other hand, you're not the nth $+$ one. I've had very, very few real 'friends' like you—so few, indeed, that if I told you the number of such friends, you'd think I was trying to fob you off with the age-old feminine lie. What has really happened is this—and I'll be perfectly honest with you—that very occasionally, when some man not altogether repulsive physically has come here to talk about some special mania of his own, with that wealth of detail, that desire to cross his t's and dot his i's which is the common symptom of such cases—you don't really know anything about these things; you're not a person who has manias, but only someone who has discovered his peculiar 'line' rather late in life—I've sometimes, under the pretence of wanting to see what the dotted i's were like and thereby appreciating more fully the gravity of his case, asked him for a little demonstration. You find that amusing, eh?—in spite of your retrospective jealousy; the idea excites you?"

"I'm wondering just how far these patients are taken in. . . ."

"Oh, my reputation is such that I can do anything. My clients are all personally recommended, and it's generally known that my methods are unorthodox. Besides, you can't imagine how scientifically detached I can become in such circumstances; even when I'm getting the greatest kick out of it, when my inside feels as though it's all turned upside down. I can hear the change in my voice, I know that it goes all thin and trembly, but they don't. Outwardly I remain severe and judicial. . . . As a matter of fact, in these demonstrations I usually play no more than a spectator's part; but even if it so happens that I have to take a hand in the business—and it never goes very far—you'd be surprised, my dear, to see how I manage to give the whole thing the appearance of a purely technical operation. A doctor, on the track of some painful symptom, can feel the breast of a woman patient without in any way infringing the laws of chastity. But what I'm telling you is still more remarkable, in that I, a woman, can examine a man in order to verify something he has told me about the erotic peculiarites from which he suffers, and, while taking every necessary step, appear to be approaching the matter in a completely chaste frame of mind; but most remarkable is this—let me repeat that it's only very rarely that I embark on this sort of little game, and only with very carefully chosen subjects—that fundamentally my mood is far from chaste. . . . No, I'm wrong, it very often is chaste in spite of myself. You see, the real risk for me is that the whole thing will be spoilt by professional indifference, by the complete absence of surprise. One has to keep up a minimum degree of innocence, and it's not easy! I expect you're kicking yourself for not having managed a consultation of this sort the first time you came to see me. . . . But I've no use for bogus patients. I get no kick from them, and I'm pretty good at smelling them out."

"Can you be sure of that? Do you really think that it's only women who can simulate successfully in these cases?"

"No, I'm not always sure . . . but on the rare occasions that I've treated myself to one of these little whims, I've always been sure. . . . But all this is a very uninteresting digression . . ."

"I don't find it so."

". . . which I embarked upon in order to correct certain misconceptions under which you were labouring. You're quite on the wrong tack, you see, if you think of me as having love-affairs with my patients. All I meant to say was that my own particular vice finds satisfaction in the contact set up between them and me, making due allowance, of course, for the various caprices, unforeseeable demands, and disappointments, which inevitably ensue. For the most part there is nothing physical at all in such contacts—the intimacies in which I have allowed you to indulge are entirely misleading. But very occasionally, without any apparent break in professional decorum, and without the patient having the slightest idea what is happening, it does sometimes occur that he—or she, for sex in this aspect of the affair doesn't seem to matter—succeeds in imparting to me the sharp, the extreme, sense of his abnormality. In such circumstances I seem somehow to achieve a complete realization of it. The sensitive point of my attention, if you understand what I mean, and the sensitive point of his complication come into juxtaposition . . . it's as though I had

stretched my finger to the very heart of his vice and felt it beating. . . .
When that happens I experience the actual sensual spasm. . . . I'm
not speaking metaphorically, the complete satisfaction of physical passion with every objective accompaniment of female consummation, a
thing that I have never found in normal intercourse. . . . You see
now just how vicious I am, and how little right I have to despise you
where matters of that kind are concerned. . . . But how is this peculiarity of mine to be explained? You don't need to be told that I've
tried and tried to find an answer. Just now there are several new
theories being worked out in Austria and Switzerland. I have to keep
abreast of these things. There's a substratum of truth in most of them,
mixed with a good deal of special pleading. They trace everything
back to things that have happened to us in very early childhood. What
they don't explain is the part played in it all by what I may call a sort
of specialized cerebral ingenuity. Take your own case, for instance;
you, I imagine, always passed for a perfectly normal man?"

"Certainly, and but for you, I should have continued so."

"Which is but one proof the more. You had probably never found
complete satisfaction, never discovered the particular erotic act which
was necessary for your temperament. . . . It's all a question of brain
structure, but I don't see how it can be tacked onto things that happened to you in childhood. I have my own theory. People like us are
essentially literary, literary in the only true sense. Love for us means
taking part in a play, or, to be strictly accurate, seeing others take part
in one. We regard the act of love in the light of a religious drama.
Physical consummation for us is the applause that greets the dramatic
crisis. That, by the way, is why so many literary folk have been per-
verts where passion is concerned. There are some for whom the play
is always the same, fashioned to meet their needs and never moving
outside strictly defined limits. For others, like me, the situation is
more generalized. I can appreciate many different sorts of drama,
even those designed for the satisfaction of somebody else, and played
by somebody else. I appropriate the scenario for my own—sometimes,
when everything goes well. I step right into the situation, and then

that little burst of final applause comes quite naturally. One of the reasons may be that I have never succeeded in creating a drama of my own. You see, I don't fit into any of the regular categories that are used to define these individual dramas. I am not a sadist, in spite of the way I treat you and the pleasure I get from it. Nor am I a masochist, though sometimes it is in identifying myself with your masochism, or somebody else's, rather than in exploiting it, that I mount to the seventh heaven. I know the delights of the 'voyeur,' and often indulge in them, though I'm far from being one. Fetishism appeals to me, and onanism too—in others, for, speaking personally, I avoid it. When I meet a girls' school out walking, I get a terrific kick out of thinking of all the delicious naughtinesses that go on in the dormitory after lights-out. The fact that Lesbianism disgusts me, so far as I am concerned, doesn't prevent my thoroughly enjoying a Lesbian's confidences and sharing her satisfactions."

"Doesn't it all really boil down to this, my dear, that you're highly imaginative—a woman of letters in the truest sense, if you will—and that doing things interests you far less than visualizing them?"

"Maybe. Rousseau says something of the sort about himself in the *Confessions*. . . . And so, you wicked creature, you're bent, are you, on demolishing all my beautiful theory of drama? . . . Imaginative? . . . Let me think that out a moment. . . . No, it's too simple an explanation. Merely imagining a sexual act, visualizing it, doesn't give me any thrill at all, no more than if I were performing it. The twice-weekly embraces of the couple in the flat upstairs? What a hideous thought! . . . Consider, on the other hand, a perfectly definite fact; the extreme pleasure I take, for instance, in your company . . ."

"I am flattered."

". . . in discussing with you your sexual satisfaction, working it all out as man to man, sharing your enthusiasm, each of us taking his due part as though we were playing a sonata for violin and piano in which every note has to be given its true value, making your case my own, settling comfortably into your skin, getting the sense of you, taking everything into consideration. And then how delicious it is to talk of all this, allowing to words complete freedom, complete access, letting them feel their way into the intimacies of mind like venturesome hands exploring the body. There is the same sort of pleasure in that, the same sort of satisfaction, as comes from bodily contacts, as when hands, fumbling and hesitating, find their way into places left ordinarily unvisited."

She leaned over him again, gazing into his eyes, stroking his forehead.

"But there's one thing I want to know that you have never told me, something that I want to be sure of. What do you think of in those moments of pleasure? . . . What is the key to your own little private drama? Do you try to conjure up the memory of some thing, some person?"

She smiled at her own banality as she added:

"I don't mind betting it's some woman!"

Chapter

17

QUINETTE'S PROGRESS

For more than a year Quinette had killed nobody.

He had not even planned to kill. Consequently he was in a particularly miserable state of mind. In fact, he was going through a difficult period.

As with love, so with murder. Certain habits, certain cravings, soon get the upper hand. It amazed Quinette sometimes to think that there were only three corpses in his past—three and no more: Leheudry, the never-to-be-forgotten Leheudry, precious as the memory of a first love; Sophie Parent, who had kept the paper-shop in the rue Vandamme; the caretaker at 142 A, faubourg Saint-Denis. True, there had almost been another, Mlle Alberte, but, to be strictly accurate, three was the sum total. It really was amazing when he came to think of it, so large a place had murder, the science of murder, the subtle preparation of murder and its no less subtle realization, come to play in his life and imagination.

Three only. In a sense even three was too many. All the common sense in Quinette's nature had risen in remonstrance. Not once, but ten, but fifty times he had sworn never to start playing that game again, and he had almost kept his word. A moment's thought, a review of the various dates in question, a pondering of the many postponements, was all that was necessary to convince him that his good resolutions had been serious, had almost, all appearances to the contrary, been effective. There may be people with whom murder has become a mania, savage beings who, having once tasted blood, can never again do without it and embark blindly on a succession of crimes to which nothing but final punishment will put a term. Quinette did himself the justice of admitting that, however open to

417

criticism his conduct, sometimes even his good intentions, may have been, he was not like them.

After Leheudry's murder and the rather hysterical excitement that had come in its train, had he not lived for a long time with one object, and one only, before him—to get quit of the business altogether, to mobilize every element of the wide-spreading universe in an effort to achieve the best possible, the only really satisfactory, solution— namely, the utter obliteration of Leheudry? And that had meant the obliteration, too, of all those scattered, those innumerable, those indefinably dangerous traces which even the humblest of mortals leaves behind him in the society of his fellow-men; traces all of which, unfortunately, one can never be sure that one has destroyed, just as one can never be sure that one has destroyed all the parasites in a bug-infested room (when the mattress has been cleansed, there are always a few left in the woodwork of the bed; and when one has burned that, one finds a few nests left behind the wall-paper). Could it be that, during that time, Quinette had never been absolutely sincere when he swore that never would he get himself into such a fix again? "I shall be only too glad to get clear!" And why should he begin again? What fate was driving him on? He was not an assassin. To have killed once, as the result of an extraordinary train of circumstances, does not make a man an assassin, any more than the fact of having once been drunk makes a man into a habitual drunkard. Even the sense of well-being that he had experienced, the increase of all his mental powers, the vanishing of boredom, the miraculous reawakening of virility, could not really, for a man of his well-balanced temperament, weigh in the scales against the advantages of an honourable existence. Occasional intoxication may bring a feeling of sublime exaltation that sets the spirit soaring above the flat drabness of everyday life. But that is no real reason for becoming a drunkard.

"I ask no more than to be freed from the terrors of that nightmare." He had got rid of the last vestige of the abominable Leheudry, who had had to die only because his presence had become insupportable— of the last vestige, that is, but one—the memory. That he must keep to himself. Not that it actually incommoded him. Reduced to the narrow limits of something in his past, Leheudry was no more than a not uninteresting titillation of the imagination, a pleasing diversion in moments that otherwise might have been tedious. What it came down to was that he had done something that nobody knew about, something removed from the inquisitive gaze of the world. He was no longer a mere nobody. Other people may feel what morality and books refer to as "remorse." When one has killed a man for purposes of theft, or to satisfy a base desire for vengeance, it is natural enough to feel remorse. But mere killing is not enough to provoke the feeling. One may even feel proud of having killed when the motives have been good. Some years ago an old man who lived in the rue Dailloud had taken to the tiresome habit of dropping into Quinette's shop. Quinette had never liked being on terms of casual intimacy with his neighbours. But the old man used to make himself at home there with his pipe, settling down for long bouts of gossip. He had served in the war of '70 and loved to talk about his battles. He boasted of having killed a lot of "Pruscos."

Even had he wanted to start again on his course of crime, Quinette would have been prevented from doing so, if the worst came to the worst, by the clever way in which he had got in with the police. He had originally taken the step in order to cover his tracks, but it now served another purpose—as a prophylactic against the future. A man who feels himself to be more or less a member of the police is separated by an insurmountable barrier from anything that smells of crime. He has, as it were, dug an official ditch between crime and himself.

But, alas, a day had come—did he really mean "alas"? . . . yes, from a certain point of view, he did—when the bookbinder had been forced to the conviction that in the whole wide-spreading universe not a trace of the Leheudry business remained. The crime had vanished as completely as the body. Ouf! What a weight off his chest! What a blessed sense of relief! What a long vista of days to come made bright by a certainty of Heaven-sent security!

But that weight lifted off his chest was rather like a large stone that has been embedded in the earth. One lifts it and one sees a scuttling swarm of hideous insects which it had kept from sight, which, till then, had lain imprisoned beneath it.

The fear once gone, desire once more was active. The heart of a man is a pendulum that lets no second run to waste, but swings, in the twinkling of an eye, through the dead past.

Quinette's case resembled that of a thoroughly good young man who, in spite of all the terrible things he has been told about street women, at last overcomes his repugnance and goes with one. In the days immediately following, various symptoms, reinforced by an all too plausible presumption, convince him that he has caught a dose of syphilis. For weeks he is the victim of mental torment. The period after which he can consider himself immune grows longer and longer because, in some book that he had not previously consulted, he finds reference to cases in which the disease has not manifested itself for six, eight, even ten weeks! During the terrible period of waiting he continually discovers in himself symptoms which give him a further forty-eight hours of intense panic. No good to warn him against prostitutes and make him promise never to be such a fool again. All he wants is to be free of his terrors. Never again, he says. What is a moment's pleasure compared to such agony of mind? Anyhow, what is physical pleasure when seen in the light of a whole lifetime? If prostitutes had to rely on him, they'd soon starve, street-walkers and the rest of them, even the little work-girls. He'll be chaste now until he marries; if need be, until he dies. And then, at the end of ten weeks, just to make sure, he goes to see a doctor. And the doctor says: "There's absolutely nothing wrong with you; you can sleep quietly in your bed. It's only one case in ten thousand that's so long retarded." From that moment life changes completely for the good young man in the space of a few hours. He breathes freely once more, straightens his back, regains his old confidence, his old love of adventure, his former desire for excitement. Gone are the fears that have been besetting him; his eyes are on the future, and the pleasures of the body have once again the power to tempt. His senses wake to the fact that they have been lying dormant. To achieve that considerable, that indispensable thing called pleasure, to know again that instant of intense delight which now once more comes to life in memory, he is willing to take a small risk, a risk that really amounts to very little and can be diminished still more as the result of experience. And the good young man realizes with satisfaction that during the time he was in despair and swore to observe an eternal chastity, a mysterious self deep down in him had never really believed either the despair or the promises of prudence; had decided that they didn't, in fact, concern him at all, and on that basis had made definite provision for the future, such, for instance, as putting aside a certain amount of money, noting the address of a well-conducted establishment, or embarking with a little work-girl on a flirtation which, though so far it had amounted to nothing, needed but a touch to develop satisfactorily. And perhaps, in his new lightness of heart, the good young man may decide to lose none of his chances, but to visit the well-conducted establishment and to proceed with his flirtation as well.

The moment that Quinette received from Marilhat the assurance that the affair of the Bagnolet quarries had been definitely shelved, the owner of the paper-shop in the rue Vandamme and the caretaker of the faubourg Saint-Denis ought, strictly speaking, in the language of the journalists, to have felt their heads loose on their shoulders. Not that their heads were particularly threatened. Let us say, rather, that they ought to have felt in every limb a little shudder of approaching annihilation.

During all this time Quinette was slightly light-headed. He hardly knew himself. He redoubled his caution in matters of detail, but that did not prevent him from indulging in bouts of almost delirious rashness. "If there were any justice in the world," he said to himself later when he looked back on these days, "I ought to have been discovered ten times over." What were the wretched clues of the Leheudry affair or the miserable traces left by Leheudry in the world around him compared with the swarm of clues and traces that hung about a

Sophie Parent, shopkeeper, married woman, owner of a savings-bank deposit? He found a certain excuse for his conduct in the thought that Sophie Parent was, in a way, one of Leheudry's traces, and that the process of obliteration might be held to include her. As to the caretaker of 142 A, hadn't she, too, known Leheudry? Strictly speaking, she also was one of his traces. Death had been waiting for her, really, while her hateful acquaintance had been breathing his last.

But they were poor excuses at best. It had been a time of madness, a period of aimless drifting of which the fleeting moments had passed unreckoned. The most sensible of men might well doubt himself. Two murders, each following hard on the heels of the other, marked by appalling blunders in execution, or rather by a deliberate shutting of the eyes to errors, to the loop-holes through which danger might come. Once they were done, once he had recovered a certain lucidity, he could scarcely bring himself to swear: "If only I get out of this scrape, never, never again! This is definitely the last time!" For it seemed impossible that he should go undetected, and unworthy of him to make resolutions which he would never keep.

All of which, however, did not alter the fact that part of himself, far below the surface, was continuing its own mysterious life, much as, during some revolutionary outbreak, an economist in Government employ may quietly carry on with his work while in the streets men are fighting and setting fire to public buildings; bringing his statistics up to date, completing his documentation, accumulating relevant observations on a number of problems viewed theoretically and with absolute detachment; coolly analysing the various experiments which, beyond his study walls, are being brought to the test of practice to an accompaniment of mad and feverish hysteria; calmly drawing from them lessons for the future. . . . The chief of these problems, upon which, for the moment, all his attention was directed, was that of *obliteration*. How best could all trace of a deed or of an individual be removed? Admittedly, the technique of obliteration which he had employed in the case of the caretaker and the shopkeeper after their deaths had, from the experimental point of view, taken the whole question a step further. But with the solution of each problem, new ones had sprouted. How could one be sure in advance that any given person could be obliterated quickly and efficiently? How know for certain that their remains would not resist removal like the bodies of those fat flies which one squashes on a window-pane? The squashing is a matter of seconds, but it may take an hour to wipe the window clean.

It is not surprising that when a man's mind is working on points so remote and involving such different methods of approach, the effects upon his conduct of such concentrated attention may seem mutually maladjusted and even contradictory.

Having regard to the long period of apparent good sense through which the bookbinder had passed since these events—the longest he had known since he had abandoned his old ways of life—an observer might have been led to suppose that the frightening experience had indeed borne good fruit. The lesson had all the greater chance of being lasting since, although the technique of *obliteration* had made marked progress so long as it was merely a question of getting rid of the bodies of two women, it had found itself up against insuperable difficulties in the matter of social repercussions. Quinette had found it impossible so to order things that the caretaker and the shopkeeper should seem never to have existed. The shelving of the two cases by the police authorities was not, in itself, sufficient guarantee that they had been finally forgotten. Some trace left by Sophie Parent might well assume sudden and alarming proportions. This prolongation of the period of danger was enough, apart from anything else, to justify continued watchfulness.

Month after month had gone by during which he had led a blamelessly white, or, more strictly, chequered, existence. Not a drop of blood had he shed, not a trap had he laid, nor hatched a single scheme for further deeds of violence in the future. His life had relapsed into an ordered routine, divided between work, reading (his earlier love of inventing things had not returned), and memories of the most innocent kind (unaccompanied now by any form of ritual observance). He might have been a colonel on half-pay comforting his old age with memories of the things he had seen and done long ago and far away, or some old soldier of the war of '70. Now and again, at carefully chosen intervals, he kept up his contacts with the police, just sufficiently to ensure their friendly attitude. "I'm not feeling very happy in my mind; I've been getting threatening letters. I'd rather you didn't employ me in any very risky business. You see, at heart I'm an unadventurous and peace-loving chap." He was bored, there could be no doubt of that, but he put up with his boredom. His virility, if not exactly dormant, manifested itself only in a very capricious fashion; but an occasional burst of activity was enough to keep him from worrying.

And then, suddenly, had come the relapse: Mlle Alberte. All those long months of quiet good sense had gone up in flame; a prolonged abstinence with all the advantages it had brought had been swept away in the twinkling of an eye.

The whole business had been curiously confused. The oddest feature about it was, not that a craving long repressed had suddenly burst once more into life and taken complete possession of his will; not even that, thinking himself cured, he should have suffered so swift a relapse; such things are commonplaces of existence. No, the really strange feature of the case was the way in which, from its very inception, it had been marked by a mixture of cold calculation and thoughtlessness, of elaborate precaution and childish rashness. There had been something approaching genius about the method he had chosen for finding a suitable female subject who could be gradually drawn into the required relationship of intimacy and then "disposed of" without too much difficulty. He had simply filed an advertisement with a matrimonial agency: "Gentleman highly desirable every way, 45, widower, no children, comfortably off, desires acquaintance, view marriage, lady widow or single, similar age, without encumbrances, good education." The idea, too, of introducing himself as M. Des-

chaumes—a rejuvenation in more countrified form of M. Dutoit [1]
—Civil Engineer, had been no less happy. But to take up, as he had
done, with Mlle Alberte, who was alone in life only so far as her
sleeping-arrangements were concerned, who was watched over by
a whole tribe of relations; to let himself be drawn into the family
circle and to figure there as a desirable suitor—that surely had been
madness. A sudden access of lucidity at the very last moment, comparable to the awakening of a somnambulist, brought about by some
casual remark of poor Mlle Alberte, had saved Quinette from a
blunder which, this time, would have been irreparable, and had restored the lady to her loving relatives and to the solitude of her night
hours.

It had taken him months to recover from the fright of that incident. But the "double" who, deep within him, played the part of the
cool-headed Government economist had not failed, on this as on
other occasions, to draw the requisite lesson from what had occurred.

It was probably this same "Government economist" who, a little
later, had had the idea of renting, in the valley of the Bièvre, half-way
between Bièvre and Jouy-en-Josas, a tiny country house standing
about a mile from any other habitation.

In order that this estate, which was really very small, should not
unduly strain his resources, Quinette decided to earmark for its upkeep the income, amounting to very little, which had come to him
from bonds, valuables, and cash inherited, on each separate occasion
or, as it were, in direct succession, from Leheudry, the caretaker of
142 A, and Sophie Parent. To speak more accurately, it was the
proceeds of these "legacies" which he now decided to use, for he had
negotiated as much as he could do with safety, reinvesting what they
had fetched in City of Paris bonds and State securities. The rest he
had burned.

Until then he had availed himself of this money only with the
greatest repugnance and had kept it in reserve. There had seemed to
him something shocking in using it for his own personal advantage.

[1] As who should say "Mr. Thatch" and "Mr. Roof."—TRANSLATOR'S NOTE.

He did not wish to think of himself as of a man who kills for money. But to make use of these funds for the upkeep of his country estate seemed somehow different.

It was on the 21st of January that he set a term to this period of uncertainty and left with Messrs. Mathieuw and Castro, publishers of the weekly paper *Home and Marriage,* the following very carefully composed advertisement:

"Gent. 45. disting. engineer without encumb. wishes acq. view marriage lady widow or single sim. age good educ. pleasing app. agreeable nat. lonely. Write enclosing photo. No. 2,821."

The 21st of January was the feast of Saint Agnes. He had chosen it partly for this reason. Though not superstitious, he attached importance to certain sentimental refinements. He found something attractive about the name Agnes, perhaps because it reminded him of the word *"agneau"* (lamb). He couldn't help thinking of the little creature's long bleating cry.

Chapter

18

JALLEZ SPENDS AN EVENING WITH JERPHANION AND HIS WIFE

The evening before his departure for London, Jallez was invited by Jerphanion to dinner. The occasion was to be in the nature of a house-warming.

After hunting high and low, Jerphanion had at last found a satisfactory small flat. He had taken it from January, but had got possession a few weeks earlier and had thus been able to move his furniture in during December.

He had spent his first term living with his young wife in furnished rooms at Orléans. The possibility of settling in Paris had constituted for the couple the chief advantage of his new post, and he had made frequent trips to the capital in search of a convenient place. Paris would be his headquarters, and there his wife would be permanently installed. He had so arranged his work as to be able to spend four nights of every week there. At Orléans he would keep nothing but a single small room, which he could get for twenty-five francs a month. With the intention of burning his boats he had taken out a quarterly season ticket on the Paris-Orléans line dating from the 1st of November.

The Paris flat would have to combine several advantages not usually to be found in one and the same place. It must be situated within easy distance of the d'Orsay or, better still, of the Austerlitz station. It must have four principal rooms, be neither too inconvenient nor too gloomy—and it must be cheap. At that time, in most of the districts of Paris, four-roomed flats were exceedingly difficult to find. It was a transitional type between the "three-roomed," which constituted the highest ambition of the modest middle class, and the "five-roomed," which was already appearing in response to the demands of a public drawn from a higher social stratum. The demand was not great, but the supply was even less. It was most frequently to be found in the big new blocks that were springing up in such places as Auteuil and Passy, where it would meet the needs of young married people in easy circumstances, or of old comfortably-off couples looking for somewhere to spend the evening of their days after seeing their children settled. The most that the Jerphanions could afford to pay in rent was twelve hundred francs a year. They had to budget for a season ticket, though it is true they got this at cut rates, the room in Orléans, meals which Jean would have occasionally to get away from home, and all the small expenses that a married household inevitably involves.

Jallez had seen Jerphanion several times in the course of the winter, though less often than might have been expected, seeing how intimate they had been, since Jerphanion had been much occupied in looking for a flat, in buying furniture, and in the hundred and one cares of his new life. Jallez had met his young wife. Four or five times the three of them had lunched or dined together at restaurants. Jallez had decided that young Mme Jerphanion was pretty, shy, and generally charming. In fact, his first impressions had been favourable. Obviously she was no fool, and her conversation was neither excessive nor petty. On the other hand she seemed determined and quick-tempered, perhaps even a little obstinate. The two young people gave the impression of being deeply in love.

Jallez found the house where his friend lived close to the stopping-place of the bus that plied from the Place Pigalle to the Halle aux Vins. It stood near the start of the boulevard Saint-Germain, north of the Place Maubert, on the left-hand side. It had been built about forty years previously, just after the boulevard itself had been laid out. The entrance hall was quite attractive, with its purplish marble, its rather dirty pictures, its door-mat, and its gas lamp.

"First floor, right-hand side," said the caretaker; "there's no mezzanine."

"I can't tell you what a pleasure it is for me to see you here this evening. You're the first person we've had to dinner—our very first guest. Take off your things. You must make allowances for the meal and, indeed, for the whole place. We've worked like slaves, but there's still an awful lot to do."

Little Mme Jerphanion appeared at the door of the drawing-room and made the guest welcome. She was wearing a simple but becoming silk dress, consisting of a dark skirt and white blouse. She seemed very shy in her new role as hostess. After a few minutes she asked to be excused on the ground that she wanted to keep an eye on the dinner, but her husband explained that he was going to show Jallez over the flat, and thought it would be nice if she went with them. She vanished, therefore, for a very short while, rejoining them just as the explanatory tour was about to begin.

Of the four rooms that the flat contained, the two biggest gave on to the boulevard, with a more or less northerly aspect. The windows, unfortunately, were overshadowed by the balcony of the floor above, thereby losing a good deal of light, but owing to the fact that the street was a broad one, the effect of the rooms was considerably brighter than is usual in Parisian flats. These two front rooms communicated by a double door, which the Jerphanions left open. The larger was used for meals, the other, slightly smaller, served as a drawing-room.

"Furnishing was terribly difficult," said Jerphanion. "I very nearly called you into consultation. I agree with you that in every age people ought to use contemporary stuff, and that it's absurd for us moderns to surround ourselves with things made in the time of Louis XV or Louis XVI. . . . But you've no idea of the horrors that go by the name of 'modern.' . . . Perhaps if one was rich enough to deal direct with the designers and could make one's own conditions . . .

I don't know. But at the prices we can afford the results would be incredibly frightful. I'd like you to have a look at what passes for a 'modern' drawing-room, not at the Autumn Salon, where price doesn't enter into the question, but in the shops one visits as a customer."

Jerphanion confessed that he had leaned towards having a dining-room furnished in "country style," for many reasons, the chief being that it would have created a particular sort of atmosphere and reminded him of the things he most loved. But his wife had dissuaded him. (Her thoughts, probably, though she had not put them into words, ran somewhat as follows: "When a girl settles in Paris after spending all her early life in a little provincial town, she doesn't want to surround herself with things imitated from what she has seen so often in the houses of her peasant neighbours.") They had fallen back, therefore, on a Louis XVI suite in mahogany, faked of course, and distinctly disputable in the matter of style. It was "smart," it was solid, and it gave an air of gaiety to the room. The lead given by the dining-room had, of necessity, been followed by the drawing-room next door, which, too, was furnished with Louis XVI pieces, as little genuine as those of its neighbour, though of pleasant design and not too new (they probably dated from about the same period as the building).

The two back rooms, separated from the front of the flat by the entrance hall, were smaller. They looked on to an inner court which even Jerphanion had to admit was "gloomy and not very attractive." Access to both was obtained from a passage leading straight from the boulevard, though one of them could also be entered by a door in the entrance hall. It was this one that Jerphanion had chosen as his study. He had furnished it with a set of bookshelves, an oak table, and two chairs. A "salamander" stove was glowing in front of the chimneypiece. When he had saved a bit more, he said, he was going to add an old chest and an armchair.

This talk of saving provoked Jallez to sudden thought. "He told me that his wife hadn't a penny. But it must have cost him something to settle in here. He can't have done it all on his salary, unless, of course, he's bought all the stuff on credit; but that, somehow, isn't like him."

They next visited the bedroom. Of all four rooms it was the smallest and the least comfortable. The young couple had made the best of a bad job by keeping it charmingly simple, and it contained nothing but a divan-bed and an old wardrobe which Mme Jerphanion said had been a present from her parents. Jallez carried his tour of inspection to the point of examining even the washing-alcove, which was small and had no running water. His host and hostess had shown great ingenuity in dealing with its limited resources, and it was equipped with a washstand, a tub, a shower-bath arrangement, and two pails. The back wall was fitted as a hanging cupboard, which was concealed by a pink curtain. The floor was covered with linoleum designed in blue and white squares.

While on the subject of the lack of running water, Jerphanion remarked that the house, like almost all those he had seen, was completely innocent of modern comforts. As Jallez had no doubt observed, there was nothing but gas throughout, except in the bedroom, from which it had been excluded for reasons of safety, with the result that they had to be satisfied with an oil-lamp there. A plan for installing electric light was under discussion. The landlord had given the tenants permission to take the running water from the kitchen to the washing-alcove at their own expense, but problems of plumbing had made it impossible to do so. The heating problem had been solved by the stove, which, after much discussion, they had installed in his study as being the most central room of the flat and the one in which Jerphanion had to sit for long periods at his work.

"You may have noticed that though it's a coldish day, the front rooms are really quite warm."

Jerphanion spoke with obvious delight of all the many contrivances, of the various things that he and his wife had or had not been able to do with the flat. Jallez listened to it all with a sense of pleasure that was neither assumed nor perfunctory. As he moved from room to room, taking in detail after detail, he became increasingly aware of an emotion which he found it difficult to define or to trace to its source. So many elements went to compose it! Seeing thus a very dear and very intimate friend in his own home, the first real home he had ever had, the home he had created by his own efforts; watching him with the young wife who represented so new, so personal a term in the equation of his existence; deducing from a thousand little signs—the eagerness with which they talked and the way they interrupted one another—what delight they took in showing off their little arrangements; glimpsing the joys and the disappointments they had known in making them; realizing the anxious moments through which they passed if they so much as suspected that the visitor did not altogether approve; coming to understand that the vague tendencies and possibilities which had always existed in connexion with this friend, fluttering, as it were, from the beginning, about his destiny, were now at last taking form and becoming crystallized for other eyes to see and other minds to judge, sweeping aside alternative possibilities and chances which might otherwise have held the field. All this was sincerely moving. One might, of course, argue that a mere flat, situated in this or that street, arranged in such and such a fashion, was a temporary expedient with no claim on eternity. . . . Still, there was something decisive about the anfractuosities of these four rooms. . . . ("My little place in Montmartre offers no comparison; it's nothing but a halting-place between journeys.") Besides, there was no getting away from the fact that a woman of flesh and blood is a symbol of some degree, at least, of durability. This sudden setting and fixing of the future in an anfractuosity was the sign of youth's ending, the first far warning bell of death's approach. And that being so, surely one had a right to look around with care, mark the shape and details of the anfractuosity in question, and, though it brought a lump to the throat, feel to the full its importance in the scheme of things? Nor did it do to forget that Jerphanion was poor ("as, indeed, am I"), since it is an undoubted fact that people who have little money to spend do manage to impart to their homes a peculiarly moving, because direct, quality of appeal. The print of the shaping finger is more clearly to be seen than where money is plentiful; the difficulties overcome, the urgency of choice, are forced more crudely upon the attention. When a man is rich, he makes use, even though he may not realize it, of advisers and intermediaries. The shops he goes to bring to the solution of his problems certain cut and dried formulas. Money may give increased freedom, but it also breeds indifference. It persuades him who has it that many things are "just as good," that few errors are past repair. "When Jerphanion and his young wife chose this paper for the dining-room, they probably thought that a mistake in judgment would mean disaster."

Jallez had no idea, could not possibly have guessed, how much of the actual work of his hands, how much ingenious invention, Jerphanion had put into the arrangement of his home, nor what agonies of spirit he had gone through in the process. Without aptitude himself for manual labour, and unused to apply an exacting standard to its results, he had no conception what a vast field of opportunity, but also of dangerous temptation, this tiny establishment had represented for his friend, who had a natural feeling for craftsmanship and could find it a stimulus to intoxicating enthusiasm or an overbearing tyrant: "This is shoddy work and must be done again. That could be done if only one had the courage to try or was willing to sacrifice to it hours that ought to be spent in intellectual work. This is appalling (useless to try to persuade oneself that one'll get used to it) and must be altered no matter what the cost. That, alas, cannot be altered —short of scrapping everything and beginning again—and must be endured as a horror to be for ever before one's eyes. This, though a small blemish in fact and hardly noticeable, will grow in importance and become an obsession if it is neglected." All the virtues are involved: conscientiousness, the craving for perfection, horror of the approximate, hatred of mess—weapons to be turned against one's own breast. . . . Not a proverb, such as "The best is the enemy of the good," but is borne out by tormenting experience. . . .

Jallez's emotion was not lacking in an element of introspection. "Which of us two has chosen the better way? I, too, might have married Juliette. I still might. Being alone isn't always fun. There's something to be said for having always at one's side a loving companion with the same interests as oneself. What pleasure there must be in shared delight over something newly bought, in mutual concessions, in trying to please another, in trying to read in the eyes of the loved one the cause of sudden sadness or of cooling ardour! Why should one assume that such things are mere foolishness? Of course they may make a man vulgar or dull. It's all a question of the characters with which the two given people start, and of their power to maintain a constant vigilance. That Jerphanion and his wife are, at this moment, both charming and happy there can be no possible doubt. But what will they be in ten years? *That* is the real question."

The meal pursued its leisurely course. It was served by a neatly dressed maid going about her work under the watchful eye of Odette Jerphanion, who was constantly alert for the first sign on the face of her guest or her husband that things were not quite right, or that some detail was lacking. They took their coffee and liqueurs in the drawing-room like comfortable middle-class householders. They sat late, talking of many things, among others of the district in which the young couple had settled, and which was familiar both to Jerphanion and to Jallez, since it was less than a mile from where they were to the steep slope of the rue d' Ulm. But things look very different, they agreed, according to the angle from which they are viewed. Jerphanion reminded Jallez of something he had once said about the part played in the lives of Parisian children by "moves," and he remembered, while he spoke, the impressions which had flowed in on him one evening at the Saint-Papouls'. What he liked, he said, about this part of the city was the airiness and the feeling of space on every side. He spoke of Orléans as of a scattered township, lacking in concentration and intensity. If one didn't know of its illustrious past from books, one would think of it as barely a century old, with its little drab brick houses. One would take it for a place built exclusively to be the home of not very affable people of leisure and retired country shopkeepers. He related how their friend Caulet, who came originally from Orléans, had said in answer to some joking remark that he, Jerphanion, had made about the Beauce country and its metropolis: "You know nothing whatever about it. The Beauce is a very remarkable district, with a profound character of its own unlike that of any other. Its people, both in temperament and in manners, are as different from their neighbours as the Chinese are from the French. . . . As to Orléans, it is a city as secret as the tomb —Lyons, where you lived, is a limpid stream by comparison—and, like all centres of an extremely advanced civilization, given to excesses and subtle refinements of indulgence, secret orgies, black Masses, and unnatural vices decked in the exotic flowers of a decadent æstheticism. It is a sort of modern Byzantium which, from prudence as much as from perversity, hides its true nature behind a veil of mystery; a Lesbian courtesan dressed in fustian and flannel." According to Caulet, Chartres and its cathedral belonged to a period at which the Beauce, several centuries in advance, as it always had been, of every other part of western Europe, had already exhausted the resources and the charms of Christianity, including those that were to be discovered by a belated romanticism. "You will find us of the Beauce," he had concluded, "waiting for you on the highway of history, several stages farther on."

The talk having turned on certain recent attacks made against schoolmasters in the pages of a number of ultra-patriotic newspapers, Jallez asked for news of Clanricard.

"He got married," answered Jerphanion, "just after Christmas."

"To whom?"

"Mathilde Cazalis."

Jallez, who had not forgotten a confidential talk they had had one day as they climbed the stone steps that lead to the top of Montmartre, while the west wind blew in their faces, and the song of the sailor in *Tristan* sounded in their ears, was not quite sure how to take this.

Had Clanricard's marriage been a source of bitterness to his friend? It didn't seem likely. Did Odette Jerphanion know what part Mathilde Cazalis had played, or almost played, in her husband's life? That, too, was improbable. Anyhow, their faces betrayed nothing. Odette Jerphanion even went so far as to say that she knew Mathilde from having met her once with Clanricard a few days before their marriage. She had thought her, she said, very charming, very vivacious, very simple. Clanricard too, with his clear, honest eyes, had made a very good impression on her.

Jallez indulged in a little day-dreaming. He tried to imagine Mathilde in Odette's place. Which was the better of the two women? Odette seemed made of finer material, was more attractive, had more depth in her character. Her cultural background might not be as solid as the other's, but it was less hidebound and richer in unexpected qualities. So far as character was concerned, and her chances of contributing to a man's domestic happiness, honest Mathilde Cazalis was less of an unknown quantity than this little Odette with her air of taut, emotional, self-sufficiency. But who could say what would have happened if things had turned out differently? There was a whole side of Jerphanion's character about which Jallez knew little, about which even Jerphanion himself probably knew as yet scarcely more; all that part which a psychologist might have referred to as his "matrimonial potentialities." Until they have been tested on the touchstone of experience, a man's characteristics do not admit of generalization. It might well be that Jerphanion belonged to that intellectual type for which all that matters in a companion is an easy-going nature, good humour, adaptability, and the domestic virtues, for which the rarer qualities are of little importance. On the other hand it was conceivable that he might need a less facile mate, someone of a stronger individuality, with whom his relations would be based on a greater profundity of character. There was no end to what he might be!

But at this point his sober and well-balanced thoughts were scattered by something which was at once the sailor's song from *Tristan,* the wind blowing down a side-street while one climbs a long flight of city steps, the gradual unfolding of the vast urban landscape dressed all in spring, and a thousand fleeting intuitions, the sharp, fleeting stabs of which had always for him symbolized wisdom and youth, the sense of eternal values, resistance to the temptations of everyday things, refusal to admit that life could ever be less glorious than once it had been. It seemed to him suddenly that this free wind of heaven was somehow confined within the walls of this Louis XVI dining-room. It caught at him with a different emotion from the one of which he had been conscious two hours earlier. He had to remind himself that he was on the wing for London; that for him, at least, however the case might be with others (and he wished to condemn nobody), there would be no confinement of the future within the narrow limits of an anfractuosity, no hint, indeed, of any anfractuosity to come; no flat of four or of five rooms looming on the horizon; no mounting tale of duties like the lengths of a bounding frame, or like printer's type within the tightened form. The vision that rose before his eyes was of a ship, of a wind-tossed sea, of an enormous and unknown city, where he might learn at will to be lost or not as the mood should take him. Casual passers-by would be about him, men and women, faces for ever new, and streets that beckoned with all the charm of aimlessness, streets crying out to be chosen just because no necessity imposed them on the choice, buses at his call to take him no matter where—the pageant of the world and all the curious places of the earth. He would lean upon some bridge's balustrade and watch life flow beneath him with the stream, while high above him from the turret's top, his own bright oriflamme would wave like a wind-borne cloud bearing in letters on its folds the one word: "Liberty."

He spoke of his coming visit to London, saying that he expected from it much delight. He had never been there before, and this gap in his experience had been growing less and less easy to endure, had, from far back, tormented him. The greatest city in the world! The idea of "the greatest city in the world" held his imagination in thrall. He kept wondering, with curiosity unappeased, with a sort of anxious impatience, how this or that would look in "the greatest city in the world." Would that greatness be apparent in every tiny detail? Quite possibly. Walking the streets of Paris, one has but to raise one's eyes to be conscious of a hundred details which could be just so nowhere else but in Paris, with all that Paris implied of extent and density, etc. . . .

This trip had long been planned. He had been in two minds about the subject of inquiry he should propose to his editor. Should it be: "Do the English think there's a war coming?" or "How do the English go about their city?" The first subject would have made a longer stay possible, would have enabled him to write a greater number of articles and have justified him in running up a larger expense account to cover the necessary costs of entertainment and social activities. . . . On the other hand it would mean seeing a very large number of people, many of whom would be highly placed officials difficult of access, and spending almost all his time making contacts.

"I don't deny that it might be interesting to meet all those people and to penetrate into their various circles. But I came to the conclusion that it would be a bad way of making my first acquaintance with London. I should start off wrong, and I might never be able to retrace my steps. Just think what it would have been like if our first introduction to Paris had been made in the light of endless official calls on important gentlemen, with all the preliminary business with secretaries that that would have entailed, the hanging about in anterooms, the telephone calls, the constant dressing up in formal clothes and stiff collars. . . . If we'd begun like that we should never afterwards have found the Paris that we love. And then what a bore it would have been straining oneself to write that sort of article. After all, one can describe a motor-bus without fear of protest, but there's always the danger that a member of a ministry may lose patience, may accuse one of misrepresentation. . . . Just at the moment I'm feeling carefree and frivolous. I don't want to have my mind occupied with the possibilities of war."

"Nor do I," said Jerphanion, correcting the phrase a moment later to: "Nor do we. . . ." He glanced across at his wife, then shifted his gaze to take in the whole stretch of the two communicating rooms. "We've not got much use for a war at the moment, as you may imagine! . . . But do you think the danger's worse now than it was a year ago? Or two, three years ago?"

"No," said Jallez in reassuring tones.

"We've all talked about it so much that it probably won't happen."

"So," went on Jallez, "I chose the alternative subject. Thinking things over, I came to the conclusion that it was just my line. I shall be able to see London exactly as I should have done if I'd gone there simply and solely for my own pleasure: I shall nose about just as the fancy takes me. I'm proposing to spend a whole week there, more if the money holds out. So as not to spoil my time there, I shall write my articles when I get back. I shall only have to get hold of a few train and bus maps and make some pencil jottings, to be able to work the stuff up later."

Jerphanion asked him whether he still liked the life of a journalist with its constant supervision; whether he found he had enough time to himself and could keep an open mind.

"Oh, it's just a matter of arranging things as one wants them. I make very little money, and that's the great thing. One's got to be able to resist temptation. Régis Gignoux, who was an intimate friend of Charles-Louis Philippe, has been very kind. He wanted me to join the staff of the *Figaro*. Somebody, I gather, had been favourably impressed by certain articles from the pen of our dear Charles Saint-Front. Gignoux's got a very good job on the *Figaro*. Thanks to him, I received a very attractive offer: four hundred and fifty francs a month, with good prospects. The *Figaro's* all right, though a shade too reactionary and worldly for my taste. But they treat their people generously and the conditions of work are civilized. I've no doubt I could have settled down there very comfortably—and then, of course, Charles Saint-Front isn't exactly me. . . . Still, I don't mind admitting that this new campaign of theirs against Caillaux put me off a bit. But the real trouble was that they expected me to turn out stuff regularly. I should have become a cog in the newspaper machine. All the efforts I've made so far to escape that fate would have gone for nothing. No, I prefer the uncertainty and the difficulties of my present career."

Jerphanion remarked that he had been reading several of his more recent articles, one series in particular which had been devoted to popularizing certain recent scientific theories, printed under the rather bogus title of "Forward with the Sciences."

"I thought they were extraordinarily good, really quite remarkable; so lucid. They gave one such a feeling of being on firm ground. One said to oneself as one read: 'This is accurate.' I must say I don't think the fellows whose ideas you were explaining, whose thoughts you were voicing, had much to complain of."

"No, I don't think they had. In fact, several of them told me that they'd quite altered their views about journalists. But then, of course, when they found I was a Normal College man with a degree in philosophy, they were much less distrustful of me than they might have been, and took more trouble than if they'd been dealing with somebody else."

"Still, I don't suppose they were ready with all those perfectly phrased statements you put into their mouths. It all seemed to come so pat, and just exactly when the reader wanted a convenient summary and something to stimulate his imagination."

"Of course they weren't; that's my job."

"Well, done like that," Jerphanion remarked seriously, "it's a jolly good one. After all, somebody's got to do it. I don't mind confessing that I did feel a bit nervous when I first saw what you were up to—and I expect you did too. How could one help it, remembering the kind of thing that most papers demand of their contributors? But your last lot of articles were as straightforward and honest as though you had been writing them as a set of lectures for a class in philosophy, even if the manner was, if I may say so, a trifle exuberant. . . ."

"That's what we call in the trade: 'making the subject live.' "

"And that means at least the same quality of brain-work. Two of them in particular interested me—the one on Jean Perrin and the atom, and the one on that doctor—I shall remember his name in a moment . . ."

"Viaur?"

"Yes, Viaur. . . . He was about the only person you mentioned who was new to me, though now I come to think of it, I believe I have come on odds and ends of articles here and there dealing with his work. I didn't attach much importance to them at the time. I got the idea that it was just another of those more or less bogus affairs that are always cropping up in the papers."

"Yes, there's been a lot of stupid comment, and it's done him a good deal of harm. Still, you didn't need to go to the specialist medical and scientific journals to find one or two quite sound expositions of his theory. For instance, there was an excellent article last autumn in *L'Illustration,* with photographs and diagrams. . . ."

"I missed it. Then," Jerphanion asked rather shyly, "you do think there's something in it? As much as there is in the other new movements you've been writing about?"

Jallez replied that it was quite impossible to be sceptical about the experiments on which Viaur based his argument. He had himself been able to examine them, thanks to the kindness of the doctor, who, despite several unfortunate adventures with the journalist tribe, had been extremely helpful.

"I spent two days with him. He was good enough to put me up in the hotel attached to the Casino at Celle. . . ."

"It makes it all rather funny, doesn't it, his being resident physician at a place like that?"

"I suppose so. But seeing him on the spot, I found him rather an attractive figure. The whole thing became, in a way, more credible. It seems more natural that such a revolutionary idea should have come to someone who wasn't fixed in the professional rut. . . . Celle itself is quite unbelievable. . . . He showed me everything I wanted to see. Even half the experiments he worked out for me—I actually conducted some of them—would have been enough to carry conviction. But they're merely pointers to the general theory of the part played by the nervous system in living organisms which Viaur has been developing. He's not at all dogmatic about it, and would be the first to admit that the whole thing's in the experimental stage. . . . His investigations have opened up an enormous field involving the whole subject of biology. He doesn't claim for a moment that he's found the ultimate solution. All one can say is that the facts have got to be explained somehow, and that if one doesn't accept his theory it's up to one to find a better. The facts themselves are beyond question; it's very puzzling."

"And you're quite sure there's no suspicion of trickery?"

"In what I saw for myself? Absolutely none. As it happens, I had a long conversation with one of his chief opponents. I said to him: 'These are the various facts that I have seen for myself. Either they're genuine or they're faked. If they're genuine, what I want to know is how are they to be fitted into the general scheme of our knowledge without having recourse to Viaur's theories? If they're faked, I should be obliged if you could explain to me by what known method of trickery they could have been produced.' "

"And what was his answer?"

"Very vague. What it boiled down to was that though he couldn't describe, couldn't even guess at, the actual trickery involved, it was quite obvious, *a priori,* that there had been trickery. Note the beautiful simplicity of the argument: '*A priori,* it is clear that the earth does not revolve. If it did, we should all fall smack on our faces. So what's the good of trying to argue? The earth doesn't revolve because it's impossible that it should.' It's odd, isn't it, that after three centuries of experimental science we should find the same attitude obtaining?"

Jerphanion thought over what had just been said. Odette Jerphanion, who had read the article by her husband's friend, was all attention. Her sympathy went out to Dr. Viaur. The adventure of this little unknown man appealed to her, in the first place because it was romantic. She hated to think that he had been misunderstood and persecuted, but it was only what was to be expected. More than that, however, there was something in the general tendency of the experiments that appealed to her. The mechanistic interpretation of life has never found favour with women any more than the deterministic. Every champion who sets lance in rest for an attack on such sharp and arid doctrines may be quite sure that the women are behind him. Odette Clisson had been devoted to Bergson without having any very clear idea of his teaching. She felt instinctively that Viaur was playing his part, too, in an attempt to show the universe as less overwhelming.

"I'm not really qualified to have an opinion," said Jerphanion in his most cautious tones. "On the whole I'm inclined to discount the idea of trickery. The question that really interests me is this: 'Are the facts sufficiently general to be capable of the important interpretation he sets on them?' . . . Science, after all, is concerned with generalizations. . . ." (The enunciation of this axiom increased his self-confidence.) ". . . There have always been what the cheapjack at the fair calls 'phenomena.' But half a dozen exceptional cases are not enough to make hay of our accepted theories."

Jallez was smiling in the way that had always made his friend feel nervous.

"Look here. Suppose you were shown a man who could raise himself thirty feet in the air by his own efforts, without any apparatus and without any suspicion of trickery, in exactly the same way that a fish can rise through water; and suppose that, being naturally excited by what you had seen, you asked some medical man who had been present at the incident what he thought of it; would you be really satisfied if he said that the case in question was exceptional, and that therefore it was not worth worrying about?"

Jerphanion burst out laughing.

"You're right. I admit that I was arguing like a fool."

"And suppose the doctor, in order to calm your fears, added: 'Not only is it exceptional, it is pathological as well,' wouldn't you laugh in his face? Le Verrier might just as well have argued that the irregularities in the movement of Uranus were pathological, and have decided not to worry his head about them."

"True. . . . And I agree that the chief revolutions in science have been brought about as the result of facts which contemporaries have been satisfied to regard as unimportant anomalies. . . . That's obvious. . . . For the men of the eighteenth century who amused themselves with attracting pieces of paper with a magnetized rod, electricity was nothing but a sport of nature. . . . Still, there's one thing I'm not clear about."

"What's that?"

"In those other interviews you had—the one with Jean Perrin, for instance—you noted a number of facts which completely destroyed all the generally accepted theories of physics, which raised the whole question of the structure of matter, and so on. . . . Now, there was a short period during which contemporary opinion refused to admit them, but that passed, and they were ultimately accepted as true. . . . On the whole, scientific opinion since the days of Galileo has been moving forward. It has got into the habit of being 'revolutionized' from time to time. It expects such shocks, and adapts itself to them more or less good-humouredly. Think, for instance, of the success that Curie had, and you can't deny that radium was a knock-out!"

"Certainly it was."

"Well, don't you think—and this is where my argument of a moment ago looks rather less idiotic—that the great difference between a case like Curie's and a case like Viaur's lies in this: that the facts involved by the first, however revolutionary they may be, can be reproduced at will by any investigator, whereas the second lot are destined to remain exceptions and anomalies?"

Jallez thought this over a moment or two; then:

"There are certain experiments in atomic physics," he said, "which have never been repeated and never could be except by a very small number of people. . . . There are facts, too, of a very special nature or necessitating mathematical calculations of an extremely complicated kind, which have to be accepted on the word of a single experimenter.

. . . I maintain that if Viaur's colleagues, instead of denying his findings or shaking their heads, had taken the trouble to work over the same ground, a number of them would have got results. The process would have been thoroughly explored. And don't forget, too, that the human organism is very much more complex than the atom. It's natural, surely, that a phenomenon taking place in a highly developed organism should be more difficult to repeat or to reproduce than one belonging to atomic science, since there are many more accompanying conditions."

"But then why didn't Viaur's colleagues make the effort?"

"Now you're asking!"

Jallez seemed to be plunged once more in his thoughts. After a moment or two, however, he smilingly asked Odette Jerphanion whether their talk wasn't boring her. It would have seemed so natural to him that she should have had enough of it. It is one of men's weaknesses that they are apt to go on talking of things that interest them without thinking about the women. She protested vigorously.

"Have you, too, got a little prejudice against women?" she asked him. "Some women, I admit, especially of an earlier generation, might give you a certain amount of justification. Not that I think myself better educated than they were—I've only got a very humble degree, and I started a thesis which I never finished; but I love listening to all sorts of discussions which I know would have seemed very tedious to my mother, if, indeed, she had made any effort to understand them."

"You certainly don't belong to the days when young girls were brought up in convents and boarding-schools and turned out like well-mannered little savages. Things are very different now. We're getting back to a belief in education for women."

" 'Getting *back*'? Do you really mean that?"

"Of course I do. In the seventeenth and eighteenth centuries there were always a number of women, even in the middle classes, who enjoyed to the full the educational facilities of their time. Read their letters. There's a tone about their talk, no matter what the subject—a grown-up quality. Hothouse education for little nit-wits, the bedding out of little plants of feminine frivolity, the idea that women are fitted only to gossip about clothes, children, and, as a great concession, a few second-rate books, are all products of the nineteenth century."

"But what about *Les Femmes savantes,* then?"

"For once in his life Molière was uninspired and set himself to champion a cause that was already lost. . . . A few blue-stockings had got on his nerves. Besides, he wanted to flatter the little reactionary shopkeepers in the pit."

Jallez then reverted to the case of Dr. Viaur and explained that he had been deeply pondering the contradiction to which Jerphanion had referred. How does it come about that a period which is ready, apparently, to offer hospitality to every kind of daring scientific speculation can be, at the same time, in certain respects so mulishly obstinate?

"I suppose the reason is that, when one comes to think of it, no period is open to every kind of idea. . . . Each period is limited by its own peculiar prejudices and blind spots. Science works in blinkers, and turns its head first one way, then another. It sees the world, as it were, in slices, and the truths that belong to the slice it happens to be concentrating upon at the moment stand a good chance of being recognized and accepted without any very great opposition. All others are as though they did not exist. Where we moderns are so simple is in believing that there can ever be a time at which someone won't refuse to accept the proofs and evidence of experience. Galileo failed to convince his contemporaries; Harvey's theory about the circulation of the blood took a hundred years to become a commonplace of medicine, whereas the contentions of both men can be proved to our satisfaction in five minutes. Things, we think, aren't like that now. We believe that if a theory is scientifically demonstrable, it must win the day. Nothing can stop the triumph of truth. Actually, however, the general situation has changed very little. All that has changed really, that has swung round, is the slice of acceptable knowledge as compared with the slice that is still denied. A number of very simple discoveries made by the nineteenth century in the fields of physics, chemistry, and physiology might just as easily have been made by the sixteenth. The scientists of those days had all the necessary equipment and showed in many of their speculations that they were daring and inventive. But the only discoveries that touched their imaginations, that were certain of general acceptance if they could be proved, happened to be mathematical. Everything else came up against a dead wall of obstinacy and incredible stupidity. The same holds true of even later periods. Think what happened in the time of Descartes and Pascal. In all that concerned the inventions of mathematicians, no matter how fine-drawn, how paradoxical, men showed themselves fully capable of adult ratiocination. But where it was a matter of physics or physiology, they behaved like mistrustful, frightened children. Today it so happens that physics is full in the fairway of acceptable truth. It matters little whether the discovery in question concerns electricity, radio-activity, the structure of matter, or any other phenomenon, that they are in violent opposition to the classical theories on which we have been brought up, or even at variance with the most popular theories of a year or two ago—twelve months, I should say, at most will elapse before they are fully admitted by the world at large. In such matters everyone seems prepared to accept everything. Don't forget, too, that there is a regular routine of discovery . . . a beaten track of revolution. You may demolish the principle of the conservation of matter provided you do so as physicist and don't try to work outside the field of physics. No one will treat you as a visionary or a humbug. You have but to speak and the world will listen. But so much as suggest that a man can control the action of his heart by the action of his will in the same way as he controls his breathing—and God knows that's not much compared to the upheavals that have taken place in the realm of physics—you will be regarded as a fanatical quack."

They discussed the question at length. It seemed to Jallez that some of Jerphanion's objections were the result of a slight misunderstanding, and he restated his point of view in a different form. He pointed out that at any given period a certain group of scientific truths might flourish and hold the field without in any way increasing the general probability of acceptance for truths of another kind. Truths help one another up the ladder of public opinion so long as they recognize one another as mutually related, but if an outsider dares to show his nose, they combine to kick him to the bottom. For a discovery to be generally admitted, it must have some recognizable connexion with the "reigning family." Careful examination will show that the discoveries of modern physics don't seriously, appearances notwithstanding, threaten a certain family of "reigning" truths which trace their lineage back to Descartes—who saw the world as so much movement of matter in space. But, rightly or wrongly, the experiments of a man like Viaur do seem to menace the supremacy of that same reigning family —and he would be the first to admit it.

"There seems to be an impression about—unfairly perhaps, but that doesn't matter—that science is being swung round on a psychologic course at the expense of pure physics. And this idea that the whole of scientific knowledge will have to take account of psychology is peculiarly distasteful. It is regarded as undermining more completely the accepted canon than any mere talk of electrons or radium could do. Remember, too, that a scientist may be a spiritualist or even a practising Catholic in his private life. That has nothing to do with his work. But as scientist he will be as frightened as any of his materialist colleagues if he is asked to make allowances for possible psychological considerations in his investigation of material manifestations. If Viaur, who, I believe, is a good churchman, is free of this particular fear, it is because he is possessed of a very unusual degree of originality."

That fact alone—according to Jallez—was sufficient to explain a great deal of the opposition to these views. There were others of a more strictly medical nature, inspired by motives that were often not wholly conscious. Once you admitted a discovery like Viaur's, didn't it mean realigning medicine in a way that might be extremely dangerous for the doctors?

Odette Jerphanion remarked that she didn't quite see why.

"Just think for a moment. Don't you see that it threatens the whole fabric of the profession—the mystery, the rigmarole of consulting-room and laboratory, and the giant that stands behind it all, the Pharmacopœia, that huge arsenal of drugs? Hundreds of treatises will be blown sky-high, thousands of theses made worthless. Tons of medicaments will become useless. If Viaur is right, the art of directing the patient's will, of acting morally upon his system, will turn out to be more important than all the present accumulation of material knowledge and manufactured remedies. The faculty realizes that, at least in certain cases, the 'healer' will have to be treated on equal terms with the doctor, if not as more important (and it doesn't follow that the same man will be able to combine both characters in his own person); that natural talent and pure 'gift' will be on a level with acquired skill. It is the revenge of Jacob the medicine-man. If Jacob the medicine-man can work on my will more efficiently than Professor Péan, I shall prefer Jacob the medicine-man, no matter what all the Academicians in the world may say. And the danger is all the greater because the man in the street has always had a secret yearning for the 'healer,' has always had a soft spot in his heart for Jacob the medicine-man. He has never quite got rid of the idea that there is something mysterious about his body. Consequently, official medicine has been forced onto the defensive. It is a matter of simple instinctive reaction. It is the old story of the priestly caste with its hereditary secrets finding itself suddenly up against the 'inspired' layman."

"Does Viaur himself realize all this?"

"Pretty well, by this time. He has even tried to limit the consequences of his method. All his more recent articles have a sort of refrain: 'We mustn't exaggerate.' He is trying to reassure the pundits. But it's too late now. He should have preached caution earlier, instead of which he allowed a whole lot of rather sensational write-ups to appear. . . ."

"But if he is right, he's bound to win in the end, no matter how long he may have to wait. Whatever you may say, no great scientific truth can remain indefinitely suppressed today."

"That may be so—when it belongs to the reigning family, but not otherwise. . . . We know only the truths that have made good. I shouldn't be surprised to hear that within the last century dozens of truths have been sent flying. . . . What'll happen to Viaur I don't know . . . I should like to think that he would come out on top, but I'm not at all sure that he will. Considering the revolutionary nature of his discovery, the excitement's already cooling. The first effect of surprise is wearing off. The number of his disciples is not increasing. Those who have so far remained unconvinced are not likely to change their minds now. With men like that, official science always wins in the end. . . ."

"But won't articles like yours help?"

"With the general public, a little; but not with his colleagues. . . . And they're the people who hold the trump cards. It's not with scientists as it is with artists. The general public can't do much to help them . . . and the effect of the general public on other scientists is more irritating than anything else. Just imagine their feelings at finding this little nobody in the limelight, at hearing him spoken of in the same breath as illustrious members of the Institute."

"Do you think, then, that you've done him harm?"

"No, because on the whole it's a good thing to rattle them a bit. . . . If I don't blow his trumpet, they certainly won't. I've got no choice in the matter. What must be avoided, though, is the sensational newspaper stuff, the kind of article that is full of scientific howlers. The essential thing is that he shouldn't lose courage."

"Is he a sound chap?"

"Yes."

"Really sound?"

"Oh, I don't say there aren't great gaps in his mental equipment. Where general ideas are concerned, world views, and the like, he's not very brilliant. But that's not unusual with scientists. . . . Remember Pasteur and his philosophy! . . . But such details apart, I regard Viaur as a genius in his own particular field."

"Then he won't lose courage."

"That's another of those agreeable superstitions. . . . A man may be a genius and entirely lacking in grit; or as obstinate as a mule and next door to an idiot. The inventor of a tie-clip—and a bad tie-clip, at that—will move heaven and earth for twenty years and reduce his family to poverty, all for the sake of his wretched tie-clip. On the other hand, Ampère, who gave new life to two or three departments of science, got sick of his greatest discoveries after a while and ceased to think of them. Having created electrodynamics, he threw up the sponge and took to writing verse."

Chapter

19

A WANDERER IN LONDON

Jallez's first act on arriving in London was to post
a letter at the box in the station. It was addressed to
Juliette. He had written it on the English train. It was very short, and
its composition had not prevented him from having a good look at
the countryside. It had served merely to give him a sense of rending
pain. It lay, as it were, like a scar upon the passing fields.

In the course of his journey he had become aware of an unexpected
clearness of vision comparable to the state of mind which accompanies
insomnia, when a whole portion of our life is seen suddenly in perspective, foreshortened and in sharply defined focus.

The portion that had thus assumed a perfect clarity of outline for
him, with no detail lost in the general vista, had been the one containing the whole of his adventure with Juliette from its first moment to
its last. (Perhaps the evening spent with Jerphanion and his young
wife had had the effect of stirring some of the problems that had lain
so long unregarded in his deep consciousness. Perhaps, too, the news
of Clanricard's marriage to Mathilde Cazalis had had its share in producing this effect.)

Then the spot-light of his mind had shifted until it concentrated
itself upon the months just past. He became suddenly aware of decisions which he would never have dared to formulate in his normal
mood of every day, so fearful had he ever been of having to accuse
himself of injustice, of inventing pretexts for what he would have
recognized as being, at heart, pure selfishness. "She has been deceiving
me for some time, of that there can be no doubt. It is probable that
her disloyalty dates from a good way further back. But now I can no
longer shut my eyes to the fact. Her behaviour the other evening with

Etiemble—when I was so depressed—was conclusive." (Etiemble was a literary friend without kindliness or character, though gifted with a certain charm.) "She swears she loves me. That may be true. She's a baffling and impulsive creature, capable of feeling and acting in the most contradictory ways. If I don't take advantage of this moment of lucidity to break with her finally, I know exactly what will happen: I shall end by marrying her. That would be a weakness unworthy of me. By doing that I should be betraying my future, and piling up unhappiness."

While he wrote the letter, his mind was still carrying on a silent soliloquy: "She'll talk about suicide. She'll really believe that she wants to kill herself. But at bottom she will have no such intention. Her self-love is much too strong. Besides, her very romanticism would keep her from it; with her, day-dreaming is a constant substitute for action—whenever, that is, action would cost her an effort. What an odd girl she is, a combination of the best and the worst! She'll probably suffer a good deal—though even about that I'm not sure. The chances are she'll invent some extravagant consolation for herself, as she did when she got married that time. There's something in me—a hard little core of egotism—which never forgave her that. No, that's not quite true; I did forgive it, over and over again; but somehow I ceased to believe in her fundamental seriousness. And then that terrific lie! What determination, what skill, she shows in lying! Sometimes, I admit, it seems to make her unhappy; she's miserable when she hasn't told me the truth—but only about trivial matters. Where really important things are concerned, she'll lie till all's blue."

Before slipping the letter into the box, he questioned his conscience once more: "What possible alternative is there? To wait until I've got definite proof? For that I should have to resort to the lowest police methods. She's so appallingly cunning! The odds are I should find nothing, and then in a sudden fit of idiotic remorse I might take her in my arms and implore her forgiveness."

He had given no address. In a postscript he had said: "I shall be moving about and my letters won't be forwarded. I shan't be back for a fortnight. No use writing to me just yet."

He wanted to persuade himself that he was not suffering. He pretended to be proud of his determination and his cleverness. Oh yes, it was a shrewd move to break with her thus on the eve of a journey, to avoid the first violence of despair, especially where so impulsive a creature was concerned.

The letter dropped to the bottom of the box with an air of finality. He plunged into London as into a new life.

The twelve days he spent in London were a breathing-space. He lived them in a mood of calm exaltation, without striving to determine whether it masked a deep disquiet.

He stayed in three different places: in a hotel close to Charing Cross, in another hotel on Shaftesbury Avenue, and in a furnished room which he managed to rent for a few days in some lodgings close to the British Museum. These three addresses were all more or less in the same district. But he could set out each day on foot to explore the heart of the city, and there were always at hand the subway and the buses, which he was there ostensibly to study. He used them frequently, but deliberately refused to think about the articles he would have to write later.

London delighted him from the very first moment. He could not have said precisely why. The chief reason probably was that it was so utterly different from Paris. He felt free to take up with this new love unoppressed by the thought that he was being false to the old.

No sooner had he arrived than he found himself once more in the presence of his idea of "the greatest city in the world." It was there waiting for him on the platform like a registered trunk, and it never left him. He was conscious of no disappointment. His very first impressions were true to the picture he had painted in his mind of "the greatest city in the world." He was aware of a feeling of great spaces, of the weight and spread of things establishing their effect with slow, unhurrying power. The place imposed its sense of vastness on the spirit, but with no sense of scramble or impatience.

The streets opened to his view long fading vistas, twisting and crossing in an endless complexity. But there was something about them that seemed to murmur: "There are many more of us, many, many more!" The crowd was but the fringe of a crowd. One would have to go far, he felt, before one would find its greatest density, its fullest flow. The traffic gave him the impression of ever moving outwards to far distances, noisy but indifferent. He had the sense of many things turning their backs on him, not from contempt, but simply because it was no part of their job to be a spectacle for sightseers. All the important things of life seemed to be happening a long way off. The houses were not high, but their very paucity of storeys contributed to the impression of a hive stretching endlessly on every hand.

Jallez spent his first few days drinking in this sense of the place until it almost intoxicated him. He would start out with no fixed goal in view as he had so often done in Paris, but with this difference: that here he was less influenced in his choice of route by casual circumstance, was less inclined to take one street rather than another because of some momentary curiosity, was brought up less sharply by a meeting of many ways, had less the sense of standing on a turntable operated from beneath his feet by some hidden switchman. In Paris he would find himself going where he had had no intention of going, attracted or repelled in unexpected fashion, changing direction from one moment to the next like a rocket at each explosion. In London he set out, as it were, on a compass bearing, nosing his way inward on a predetermined route. He would feel a vague desire to go "this way"— "this way" being decided by eye and by general "feel." Sometimes it would be straight ahead down the road he was already in; but sometimes the line of advance would be drawn in imagination right through some intervening block of buildings, and then it was necessary to find a way round, circling the block first by this street, then by that, rejoining the main direction by a twisting, tortuous route. Something, too, in the light, in the way the sky showed above the roof-tops, played its part in determining the choice of ways, and something in the power of certain districts to attract, less because of any

hidden mysteries they might contain than because of the vast difference of tone that seemed to mark them off from their neighbours.

The choice once made, Jallez would drive stolidly onwards like a
sailor holding to his course. He kept as closely as possible to his determined line and covered as much ground as he could. In the course of
a single walk he would see the town under a dozen different aspects,
each, in its way, absorbing: business thoroughfares abutting on streets
of residential houses withdrawn and silent; slums giving place to
miles of shops, here a square, there a church at the corner of an irregular open space, then quiet roads again and long lines of low, tiny
houses, each with its humble flight of steps; walls that enclosed some
emptiness but left it shapeless, and houses once more, but higher now,
threaded by twisting lanes where merely to keep direction was a task
in itself. What he found pleasure in was the endless succession of
streets and houses, this never ceasing maze of paths and alleys; the
sense of weariness at the day's end and the knowledge that streets and
houses still lay around him in inexhaustible profusion. The end of his
expedition was never the end of London. Drink though he might
his fill of the city in any one direction, the cup was never drained. Always before him went the feeling of infinite space, and he drove onwards through the dense agglomeration like a ploughman opening a
furrow, a sailor cleaving the waves. When he turned back on his steps,
the sense of the infinite closed in behind him like a wall, and as he
walked he felt on shoulder and on flank, firm, distant, comforting, the
pressure of unbreached infinity.

There was also, about the places he passed through, not perhaps an
identity of appearance so complete as to bemuse the wanderer, but a
tendency to escape definition, a sort of diffused individuality to which
no place-name could be given, no positive trait attached, a refusal to
fall into a succession of identifiable sections built up in due proportion. "Paris too is large," thought Jallez, "and I could walk there as I
do here, pushing straight ahead to those outer suburbs that still have
something in them of the city. But even if I were careful to hold my
course to the far line of the horizon I should be for ever coming on

districts so individual, each with such strongly marked features of its own, portions, as it were, of engulfed market-towns, of places individualized and separate, that I should never get, to quite the same extent, this feeling of a seamless garment of metropolis through which the walker moves like a tailor's scissors, of something solid into which he bites like the share of a plough or the sharp stem of a ship."

Another of his satisfactions came from the people he met. They too, in various ways, made him feel that he was indeed in the greatest city in the world. As individuals they were, without exception, less remarkable than those he might have met with elsewhere, as though the fact of belonging to so great a concourse diminished each man's claim to be regarded as a separate entity. And less than elsewhere, too, did they seem to take notice of the stranger. There were far fewer signs in their faces of that easy distraction of attention—always more noticeable in cities than in villages—which marks the response of the man in the street to the stranger, as clearly as the swing of the straw shows the movement of the stream. Anonymity is the great gift of every city. Even in La Rochelle Jerphanion had enjoyed it. But though unknown, the stranger may excite attention. In London Jallez discovered a new, a heightened form of anonymity. He was not only unknown, but unnoticed too. The field was too vast for his influence to be felt. It was too quickly absorbed into the surrounding life to have the least little effect upon the floating straws, even those in closest proximity to him. Utterly alone in the midst of a crowd, he felt, more than he had ever felt before, relieved of the pressure of identity. The young man wandering down some Baker Street of London, N.E., had moved far since the days of the rue des Amandiers, had moved farther in the direction of release, tranquillity, escape.

Jallez took advantage of his present mood to ponder again one of the themes beloved of his secret soul: escape—but whither? Into what new life? Suddenly he saw in imagination those wild places of the Mézenc to which Jerphanion had introduced him. He dreamed of wandering, no longer with a friend, but quite alone, across those mountain wastes, or astride one of those country ponies which he had seen so often ambling with their silent riders. There must be in the world many such empty countrysides where solitude, though perhaps no more profound, would stretch more widely—the great spaces of the ocean, for instance, which, though he had never seen them, he could so well visualize from books. The sense in such places of having cut completely adrift must be a heady draught indeed. He was far from underrating what they had to offer, nor yet what joy might come of a long walk at night across those houseless landscapes he had so often glimpsed from speeding trains, when the barking of the distant dogs should have ceased and no sound be heard but the blowing of wind in the grass, and high in the darkness would gleam a single star, so bright that to the watcher it might seem a planet.

He denied to none of these things, nor to others too, the power to bring him the peace he craved, the feeling that he had escaped from himself, that he was, as never before, lost; nor would he refuse their healing balm. But why was it that a thing so simple, so almost childish, as the sense of being lost in the greatest city in the world should be, beyond comparison, so much more satisfying? It was the words rather than the ideas they denoted that were alike, the ideas rather than the actual experiences to which they referred, so true is it that the great spreading texture of human life changes everything. One can be lost more completely in its folds than in the wildest waste. On barren heaths the wanderer is thrown dangerously on himself. Everything depends upon his mood; if it is not just right, what guarantee is there that it will yield itself idly to the winds of the mountain, will allow itself to be drawn into reverie, into entranced contemplation of the universal present by the strange brightness of the sun above the peaks, by the empty line of the horizon, by the hypnotic effect of nearness and of distance? It is more than likely that it will be attacked by the troublesome thoughts of every day, by those gnawing worms that men call "worries." Should that happen, instead of feeling "lost," he will be but too strongly held, and by bonds that of all he hates the most. But when for an hour he has walked along a street, an atom in a vast concourse of men and buildings, a speck in the seething life of millions, it is not in vain that he can speak—that he speaks to himself—of tranquillity and of being lost. There is nothing then for him to fight against; no need for him to throw off the obsessions of his spirit. The necessary work is all done for him. His solitude then has nothing in common with the solitude of lonely country walkers. He is never alone, but the companionship of which he is conscious is unlike any companionship that he has ever known. His spirit has the impression of moving constantly in a medium which is of the same stuff as itself, but which yet remains a medium—that is to say, something which surrounds it, from which it can draw sustenance, which, quite definitely, conditions it, which may, perhaps, be directing it to higher ends, but which never dictates, demands no oath of fealty, and is of the same general nature as one of those natural fluids which, though it limit and confine, has a certain elasticity and, better still, seems completely indifferent whether we try to elude its influence or not. Enriched by this experience a man is made aware that there is a sort of cosmic fashion in which he can enter into relation with the worlds of spirit and of his fellow-men, whereas normally the spiritual and the social present themselves to him only in the guise of despotic ordinances, compelling him to conform, even in the depths of his secret conscience, to formulas of their own devising.

"It is also true," he reflected, "that one stands a greater chance of receiving this benefit in its purest form if one is bound by no other considerations to the great human texture in which one moves. Here, if I want to, I can ignore all social duties, all claim exerted by the sense of social solidarity, or, rather, I can touch them lightly in passing, confining myself by contractual obligations which are valid but for the moment (my relations, for instance, with this bus conductor), and so keep my liberty of action and my anonymity unimpaired." He wondered whether the ultimate wisdom in a civilization for ever oppressed by an abnormal sense of civic obligation and exaggerated consciousness of a historic past, having its hands always full of duties to be apportioned and disasters to be made good as occasion demands, isn't to try to be at all times, just as he was here and at this single moment, infinitely alone, yet infinitely companioned, setting forth freely on a compass bearing to explore the greatest city in the world, in which, as an individual, he counts as nothing at all.

It was the east of London, the north-east, and the north-north-west that he most often chose for his voyages of discovery. Sometimes, too, he penetrated to the south-west, though the knowledge that he was hemmed in by Hyde Park and its extensions on one hand and by the Thames on the other did much to diminish his sense of limitless expanses. This he found, in perfection, to the south-east, by reason of the Docks. The West End gave him no such feeling; not that it lacked open spaces, but that there was about them no atmosphere of mystery. The whole quarter was marked and laden with features too easily identifiable; they forced themselves on his attention as he walked, so that he never got the sensation of being "lost."

His happiest finds were in the neighbourhoods of Bethnal Green and Whitechapel. There is a spot on the farther side of the City for which Jallez came to feel a particular degree of affection—the short length of wide roadway called Aldgate. Little by little he grew to think of Aldgate as of a door; a door opening onto limitless space; a harbour mouth leading to the great ocean of the city and its suburbs. For in London, more even than in Paris, he felt the suburbs as throbbing outliers of the urban; as though some deep tide were at work carrying to the far limits of the world the marvellous undertow of the town. The long streets dwindled to a misty distance; the roofs and chimneys dipped into sudden valleys, crowded together in unexpected groups, or lay like thin metal strips along the sky. But the deep drag of the suburban waters never ceased to make their influence felt beneath the curving shoulders of the world.

He liked going to Aldgate by the subway. Once there, he would walk about aimlessly sniffing the air. Then he would leave Aldgate as a ship leaves harbour between the jetty heads, setting his course on a point to the east or north-east to which he was drawn by some quality in the light or some feeling in his bones.

The intoxicating pleasure which he derived from London was with him always. It underlay every impression of detail. Naturally, after the first few days, he grew as eager as in Paris to proceed from the general to the particular, to discover for himself the historic monuments, the streets, the shops, the crowds, the passing faces, the high ground, and the buried secrecies. He knew most of the buses by their numbers and itineraries; was familiar with the tubes and subway in all their ramifications; the trams of the riverside and the East End; the innumerable Lyons tea-shops and A.B.C.'s; the public-houses with their private and saloon bars, and the clientele who frequented them, marked, in the more respectable streets, by an air of secrecy, of being there on sufferance, and blossoming into carefree noisiness only as one approached the almost marine horizons of the suburban east. He visited the Tate and the National Gallery; he saw the antiquities of the British Museum. He watched great teams of horses shaking their shaggy fetlocks in the steep alleys that lead from the Monument and the Tower towards the river, and sniffed the sour, intoxicating smell of beer and fog which, taken in conjunction with the sound of wheels on cobbled causeways and the lift of the sky above the low-roofed houses, had come to mean for him the sudden dip of London to the Docks, the slope of the town towards the hidden ships. He climbed to the top of the Monument, of St. Paul's, of Primrose Hill—from this latter point of vantage the view of a London seen, as it were, in retreat beyond wide sweeps of grass gave him a peculiar thrill. He fell in love for several minutes, and twice in the course of a few hours, with young girls whom he met in his wanderings or glimpsed in shops. One, in particular, took his fancy. He saw her standing by the lake in Battersea Park, whither he had gone late one afternoon. For a long while he hung about, gazing at her, smiled once and was given a smile in return, was in two minds about asking her to go for a row. But he was afraid that his bad English might make her laugh. Besides, he was not at all sure that shyness, and that kind of mental reservation with which he hedged about his world of mysteries, might not prevent him from enjoying to the full a pleasure which would have sounded against the deep bass of London like the sweet tinkle of a sheep-bell. He decided, therefore, to take a boat by himself in the deepening dusk of Battersea Park, already thickening with the creeping river mists.

Chapter

THE BLACK FLAG

His return journey would have been entirely uneventful had it not been for a very odd impression of which he became aware almost as soon as the boat left Folkestone harbour, and the effect of which grew on him during the crossing. It seemed to arise out of none of the ideas which had been occupying his mind in the course of the past few days. He had no reason to suppose that it had insinuated itself into his consciousness while he walked the streets of London, nor yet that it was the logical conclusion of some train of argument worked over earlier. On the other hand, it was too absurd to suppose that it owed its origin to the very ordinary sight of the few dozen English and the twenty-four or so French and other Continental nationals in whose company he was crossing the Channel.

The thing began as follows: He was standing by the starboard rail beside an Englishman of thirty or thirty-five. A few of his neighbour's countrymen were grouped a little way off and, like him, were gazing at the sea, which was neither very rough nor particularly interesting, but merely moving with a slight swell beneath a sky that was cloudy, with occasional bursts of sun. In the direction in which the Englishman was looking lay the horizon, partly obscured by mist; behind him lay the coast of the mainland, still invisible. Jallez was suddenly struck by the look of intense boredom on his face. The light blue eyes, fixed in a grimace of staring concentration, seemed to sweep the horizon in a search for some object—for some object that should relieve their possessor's boredom. Jallez followed their gaze and assured himself that there was, in fact, nothing at all between sea and sky. Then, almost automatically, he scanned the other faces near him as though to compare them with the one that had fixed his attention. He began to wonder whether he was not, perhaps, the victim of an illusion which he had himself imposed upon the scene in the same way that the eyes, when tired, will veil what lies before them behind a layer of coloured specks. It seemed to him that every face was marked by an expression of boredom, by almost an identical expression of boredom. They were all of them starting out on a journey, but the crossing was too short to become tiresome. Seen all together in such circumstances, there was really no good reason, either present or threatened, why they should be bored.

Jallez took a few paces along the deck, surprised by what he had seen, seeking an explanation. Do what he would, he could not help feeling every time that he glanced at a new face that he was on one of those boats which, in ancient days, had been driven forth from one bank of a river to the other laden with people all suffering from the same infectious disease—and that the disease in this case was boredom.

"But why should they be specially bored? What is the meaning of my vision?"

A too facile association of ideas suggested that he might be in the presence of that boredom commonly attributed to the English. "I am on a ship filled with English people; it is a well-known fact that the English are easily bored. That is the reason they are such great travellers."

But the explanation did not satisfy him. The boredom of which he had just become so oddly conscious could not be dismissed as a peculiarly English weakness. It occurred to him that his stay in London had perhaps, without his realizing it, made him susceptible to impressions of boredom, even when they were no more than suggested, as a sojourn in a very damp climate may make us sensitive to dampness, however mild, in other places.

But the impression continued to spread in his consciousness, increasing in extent as he pondered it. He tried to put it from him, but, in spite of all his efforts, it held him still and seemed to grow. "When we reach the mainland shan't I find them all looking just the same? Aren't they all suffering from the same disease? Now that I've learned to see it, shan't I be struck by its marks on every face I meet?"

This idea, which perhaps he had touched on in his former broodings, though without attaching any importance to it, now burst upon him with the dramatic suddenness of a lightning-flash illuminating vast stretches of darkness.

"Boredom over Europe! Boredom over the world! This ship that bears me is steaming under the black flag!"

Chapter

21

THE LITTLE PROFESSOR WITH THE MONGOL CHEEK-BONES

Maykosen stood watching while his handsome English leather suitcases were being brought to the room that he had chosen because it overlooked the Cathedral. From its window the belfry was visible, rising from a confusion of court-yards and roofs. Its occupant, no doubt, would be able to hear the curious fanfare of trumpets which accompanied the striking of the hours, with a few notes repeated at the halves and quarters. To hear this fanfare sounded from the clock-tower was one of the reasons that had prompted this visit of his to Cracow—or, rather, to hear it again, to rediscover the little tune which for the last ten years had been haunting his memory without ever achieving the precision of a memory; its mingling of pomp and dreamy vagueness, its hint of the spacious days of chivalry, its quality of seeming always new, so that one could hear it all a long night through, yet at every repetition strain one's ears to miss no detail of the sound. "I shan't get much sleep tonight," one would say. "Well, that can't be helped. This time I must learn it by heart."

The business of his luggage ended, he set forth to keep his appointment with the man he was so anxious to meet.

It was his friend Guerassimov, once head of the Okhrana[1] but now disgraced and living in retirement, who had first put the idea into his head. Invaluable Guerassimov! To him Maykosen owed his knowledge, unsurpassed in Europe, of the secret history of the Russian court, of the authority wielded by that dirty moujik who had got the Emperor in his pocket and had quite possibly had the Empress in

[1] The tsarist secret police.—TRANSLATOR'S NOTE.

his bed—if, indeed, that was the worst of his villainy. "Mark my words," Guerassimov had said some time ago (just after Stolypin had been murdered, to be precise), "now they've got this moujik as a convenient instrument, that precious band of U.R.P. members,[1] spiritualists, Montenegrin princesses, and the rest, will end by sending the Empire sky-high. Stolypin's murder is only a beginning. They're far more dangerous than the revolutionaries." Unfortunately it was not easy to make use of such information even in the columns of American newspapers. He tried to rouse the interest of William II in a conversation he had had with him. What he had heard fell easily into line with his own views. He had always tried to convince the Kaiser that it would be short-sighted policy to take advantage of the misfortunes of Russia and to rejoice at the dangers that threatened her. His main obsession was still that Europe had committed every conceivable mistake; that her national rivalries counted as nothing in the scale against the necessity of saving her common heritage; that an internecine war was the one thing above all others that must be avoided. Each time that he had been in a position to sow this good seed in the brain of anyone of importance, whether in Berlin, in Paris, or in London, he had surprised even himself by the vigour he had put into his pleading, so out of tone did it seem with the cynicism of his normal attitude. He exploited to the full the good impression that he had already made on William II, in order, if possible, to get him to see that the interests of Germany no more depended on the internal collapse of Russia than it did on the military defeat of France. The Kaiser's reaction depended on his mood of the moment. These stories of the Russian court brought to his lips a smile that might have meant almost anything. Perhaps, with so many other sources of information at his disposition, he but half believed them. Perhaps his view of the world of St. Petersburg was tinged with

[1] Union of Russian People, a secret organization of the extreme Right which, before the Revolution, had considerable power and was widely feared. It was violently nationalist and was responsible for the organization of many pogroms and for the harrying of the intelligentsia.—TRANSLATOR'S NOTE.

a contempt that nothing would alter. Who could tell? Be that as it might, he had quite definitely refused to take any steps to open the eyes of his "cousin" Nicholas II.

Then, no longer ago than the previous winter, Guerassimov had said to Maykosen: "Since you're so fond of Cracow, why not run down and have a look at this fellow I've been telling you about? I know he's living there. The Austrian police are so easy-going that he doesn't even have to bother much about concealing himself. I shouldn't be at all surprised to hear he'd given you an interview. They're all the same, these revolutionaries, just a lot of actors showing off. You'd get stuff for a damn good article out of it. His name's hardly known abroad, though he's spent most of his life there. Even in Russia people scarcely ever think of him. You told me yourself that you'd very rarely heard him mentioned. As a matter of fact, he's the head of an extremely dangerous organization. He's got more than one attempt at assassination on his conscience—some of them directed against me, though luckily they didn't come off. In '05 he engineered a number of riots. He is the founder of a new party, more extreme and more energetic than any of the others. Violence is its object, but meanwhile it keeps a number of representatives in the Duma. For a long time past, the Okhrana has had several secret agents working among his friends. I've even heard it said that he's in Government pay himself, but I never got any definite information on that point while I was with the police. Still, it's perfectly possible; I never knew more than a tenth part of all the baseness and treachery that I felt was going on behind my back. The authorities never really forgave me for doing what I did against that disgusting moujik. If Kourlov employed this fellow as one of his agents, he very naturally refrained from telling me anything about it. Can one be surprised at anything when the police of the Empire are in the hands of men like Maklakov and Djunkovski? . . . If he does see you, it might amuse you to tell him that you're a friend of mine. I should like to see his face! I've more than one bone to pick with his pal Bourtzev."

Maykosen felt for Russia, his nominal fatherland, apart from a certain amount of professional curiosity, almost as much contempt as did William II. He flattered himself that he knew it inside out. He had kept in close contact with it. During the Japanese war he had seen the functioning of the Russian machine at fairly close range. In his wanderings about Europe and America he was for ever meeting people who expressed loud enthusiasm for Russian music, Russian literature, and the Russian ballet, who were ready to forgive the Russian soul a great deal for the sake of its charm and its innocence. He had heard the view expressed in many drawing-rooms that if Europe was destined to come under the domination of one of the countries that seemed to be the heirs of the future, it had far better be Russia than Germany. Maykosen was in love with neither alternative. But the prospect of a Russified Europe conjured up for him a revolting vision of servility, extortion, debauchery, barbarous luxury, simulated innocence, and, above all, of treachery, treachery in every department of life, from the lowest to the highest. Every Russian whom he knew was busily engaged in treachery against someone or something. Its simplest form was a rich ingenuity, and most of the Russians he knew had qualified in its school, first conspiring, at the cost of endless lying, against an authority to which they had taken an oath of allegiance, and then selling their fellow-conspirators to this same authority at the cost of lying still more. How many of them were there who did not figure on two or three secret lists? To betray their party to the police, the police to the Minister, the Minister in power to the Minister who would be in power next, was for most of them the A B C of their craft, and productive of a comfortable melancholy. Even his dear friend Guerassimov probably had things in his past which would raise the hair on the head of most easy-going gentlemen. The rot had been there from the beginning. Maykosen's own ancestors, the Baltic barons, had tried to introduce into the Russian chaos a degree of Teutonic and Nordic tidiness. Peter the Great had applied the red-hot iron. But all in vain. The incurable Russian rottenness remained in Maykosen's opinion one of the great problems of the future. If Europe could be saved from a suicidal war, could Russia ever be saved from the canker that was eating her heart? Impossible for a new race of Baltic barons to start the work all over again. Any such effort would provoke an outcry from the English. And if Russia couldn't be saved from her canker, what chance was there of ever cleaning up the Continent?

These being his feelings, he had no illusions about the man he had come to see. In dealing with him he must proceed with the utmost caution. He was prepared to believe nothing from one who probably, at the very least, combined the roles of terrorist chief in exile, agent of the tsarist police, and spy in the pay, quite possibly, of Austria (since that country's tolerance of him within her frontiers was, to say the least, curious). But he was not forgetful of the fact that his own standing as a great international journalist and his friendship with the great ones of the earth laid on him the duty of keeping his records up to date and occasionally adding a rare specimen to his collection.

Guerassimov had advised Maykosen not to announce his coming by letter (the bird might take fright and spread his wings). He had, however, provided him with a sure means of finding his man once he had got to Cracow.

The appointment was for the following afternoon. They were to meet outside the big café on the Promenade—the Kunstverein. The lack of privacy made the choice seem an odd one. Not that it was otherwise displeasing to Maykosen. He adored this particular street, with its trees, its gay cafés, its general charm, which made of it the one place where a man could feel most at ease in a city which combined the dreamy gentleness of Poland with the Austrian gentleness of life—that gentleness vaguely submissive and cringing which Vienna had made universal from Trent and Agram to the Carpathian border.

He found the man he was looking for seated in a solitary corner of the café terrace. He could not yet be fifty but his face showed a fine network of wrinkles. He was bald and wore a little chin tuft. But what at once riveted Maykosen's attention were the "Mongol" cheek-bones (as he styled them to himself) which showed beneath the deep-sunk and slightly elongated eyes. This telltale feature of the dweller in the Asiatic steppes had stood for him, since childhood, for everything he most hated in the Russian character. As soon as he noticed it in anyone, he was conscious of a shudder of repulsion and distrust. To these bastard Europeans he much preferred the genuine Easterners, who at least had the merit of not disguising their barbarian stock beneath the trappings of Western civilization.

The man, who was carelessly but cleanly dressed and looked like a minor civil-service clerk, held out his hand with an expression of shyness and introduced himself with a sort of tight-lipped primness:

"Lenin."

"Alfred Maykosen."

The man called Lenin was rather short. There was an air of refinement about his smile; his eyes were bright and sharp, with an expression of keen directness which might have passed for frankness. "Obviously a man of some character," thought Maykosen, summing up his first impressions, "and not nearly so repellent as he might be with those Mongol cheek-bones."

Since talking to Guerassimov, Maykosen had made several inquiries about the man he now saw before him, and had formulated a number of questions to put to him, though he had no intention of limiting his freedom of approach by confining himself within any prearranged program. Unless he happened to be asking questions about some particular point—and today he certainly was not—he always laid it down as a rule to let the other fellow make the running and reveal his own character in conversation. He was very skilful at turning the accidents of the moment to account.

He apologized for taking up the time of as busy a man as he knew Lenin to be. He did not say that the main object of his journey had been to make his acquaintance.

"I happened to be passing through Cracow, of which I am very fond. I'm on my way to the South."

They chatted for a while of Cracow. Lenin declared that the public libraries were very rich in books and much quieter to work in than those of larger cities. He was enthusiastic for the surrounding country, which towards the Carpathians, he said, was very beautiful. Unfortunately, however, he had little time for walking. As soon as the summer came, he meant to settle down in some mountain village as he had done the year before.

The conversation was conducted in German, since Maykosen had thought it wiser not to reveal his Russian origins. Lenin was occasionally at a loss for a word. His voice was clear-cut, without those soft overtones which Maykosen so hated in his one-time compatriots. He expressed himself clearly, almost brusquely.

He explained that he had spent part of the previous winter in Paris, and that on the way back he had stayed for a while in Germany.

This led to an exchange of views on Paris, Berlin, London, and Geneva, cities of which Lenin appeared to have an intimate knowledge. They compared impressions. Maykosen, who himself led a wandering existence, could not help feeling a certain amount of sympathy for this fellow-vagabond.

The conversation continued, touching idly on various subjects. Maykosen offered his companion a cigarette. He made a number of mental notes with a view to building up later a portrait of his new acquaintance, though, at the same time, reflecting that it might well turn out that the man was not worth the expenditure of so much labour. The Cathedral fanfare had already sounded once in the distance. Maykosen hummed the air delightedly to himself: "I know it now—or almost."

In a series of rather hurried questions, which he made to seem less so by the tone of detachment in which he put them, he asked whether it wasn't his interlocutor's impression that, for the last year or so, the internal affairs of Russia had been quieting down. Hadn't there been a considerable lessening of revolutionary agitation?

Lenin replied evasively, accompanying his words with a faintly ironic smile.

Maykosen pressed his point. Wouldn't it be true to say that Stolypin had, in fact, succeeded? Hadn't his policy of reform on one side and of energetic repression on the other produced a certain number of results? How did he, Lenin, envisage the future?

Lenin was finally prevailed upon to admit that the present situation had at least the advantage of being no longer ambiguous. Most of the alleged revolutionaries had taken fright. A few had enlisted under the banner of reformism and were playing at honest bourgeois politics in the Duma. The drawing-room circles of St. Petersburg, scared out of their former audacities by the events of 1905, were less open now than they had been to subversive theories. All of which was to the good. The Revolution had never really counted on that type of support.

"But on what can it count, then?"

"On the working class, which is learning organization and getting ready to fight."

At this point Lenin embarked on a long rigmarole to which Maykosen had to force himself to listen. The Baltic Baron had a feeling that the other was now well mounted on his hobby-horse. He was revealing himself as what he really was—a theoretical and boring fanatic, boring even in his dreams of violence. What could be more dreary to contemplate than a proletarian insurrection in the slums of a great industrial city—than a series of isolated street battles in dirty, rainy alleys between the police and a lot of grubby and dishevelled rioters, with the inevitable accompaniment of aimless destruction, crude looting, and wordy speechifying, alternating with hooliganism? Maykosen had already had enough experience of modern warfare to know that it is not a pretty sight. He had said as much to anyone who would listen. He had still less belief in the beauties of this last word in revolutions over which the little professor with the Mongol cheek-bones—and he really had begun to look like a little professor—was so avidly licking his lips in anticipation —those thin lips which combined with the dark fire smouldering in the slightly slanting eyes to give a terrifying and maniacal look to the man's expression. Despite the fact that he had no particular wish to remember what he had just been told, the Baron made a mental note to the effect that, if ever his article came to be written, he must be careful to underline the greasy, sordid character of the "proletarian" revolution as envisaged by those most qualified to organize it.

In the hope of transferring the conversation to a less gloomy level, he introduced the subject of the scandals of the Russian court. Was Lenin well informed about them? What did he think would be their outcome?

The professor with the Mongol cheek-bones made just the grimace that might have been expected of him: the grimace of a respectable little bourgeois bookworm who knows that such horrors are to be expected when a régime goes to pieces, but finds in them nothing psychologically interesting, nothing of human drama to excite his attention. It was clear, too, that he attached no importance to the question. Clearly this scrap of history in the Michelet manner found no place in his intellectual system. The idea that such things might change the destinies of nations would have seemed to him tantamount to doctrinal heresy.

He decided that it was his turn now to lead the conversation, and declared, somewhat in the manner of enunciating a challenging paradox, that it was ridiculous always to go on thinking about what was happening in Russia; that there were other countries in Europe than Russia; that whether or not Russia was ripe for revolution, there were plenty of other places where it might break out.

Maykosen agreed that that was true. But he hinted that he had reason to suppose that his interlocutor was especially interested in preparing a Russian revolution. That being so, the aspect of the affair to which he had referred could not be regarded as entirely negligible.

Lenin returned to his main thesis, elaborating and correcting what he had previously said—that the proper task of the Russian revolutionaries was undoubtedly to prepare revolution in their own country —that is to say, to intensify the local conditions favourable to an outbreak, but at the same time to keep a careful eye on those general conditions which would make possible the detonation of local charges. The great mistake—due to short-sightedness—would lie in concentrating attention exclusively on local conditions when formulating any prognosis of the situation.

Maykosen, rather surprised, but deeply interested, asked whether he thought there were serious chances of revolution in Europe. Was he, perhaps, thinking specially of France?

"I am thinking of no country in particular. What I mean is that, as I have more than once demonstrated, it won't be long before a general war breaks out as the result of conflicting imperialisms. Such a war is an inevitable stage in the development of the capitalist system. It will also be its death-knell."

"In what sense?"

"In this sense: that a general war is bound, automatically, to take on the nature of a revolution of the type described by Marx. It will mean a mutual destruction of imperialisms, and then the collapse within each separate country of the capitalist system, of which imperialism is the supreme expression. In this way a revolutionary situation will be created. The function of the militant revolutionaries in each country will consist in carefully watching the evolution of this situation as it affects their own people, and in choosing the favourable moment for decisive intervention. Don't forget that when that moment comes, millions of proletarians will be serving in the army, will, that is to say, be in possession of arms, and therefore capable of immediate employment. The revolutionary party of the first country in which the situation comes to maturity will obviously have to act without waiting for their neighbours. But it is more than likely that their action will hasten the process of ripening in countries other than their own."

By now Maykosen was sincerely interested, less by the exposition of theory than by the forecast of what was likely to occur.

"Do you think that's going to happen soon?" he asked.

"The European war?"

"Yes."

Lenin thought for a moment.

"My opinion about that has changed several times," he said. "The actual circumstances may vary considerably, though within strictly defined limits. It is not possible to say with scientific exactitude precisely how long the present stage of the system will last. At the moment I am inclined to think that the decisive conflict of imperialisms will not come about for some years. . . ."

"Heaven send you're right!" exclaimed Maykosen. "But I can't help thinking you're a little optimistic."

Lenin smiled at this charge of optimism.

"I am by no means an optimist," he said dryly; "but I can't help feeling that certain of the combatants are not yet ready, while others are frightened. The general effect will be to postpone matters. Then, too, one's got to take into consideration the slowness of the English in coming to a decision. I've no doubt whatever that England wants to have done once and for all with German commerce and the German Navy, two growing threats to her supremacy with which she can no longer put up. But she'll hesitate a bit longer before definitely taking sides. I'm not at all sure that we shan't first of all see one or two limited conflicts, fought out in relatively secondary theatres, in which the chief imperial powers won't come directly to grips at all— something in the nature of the recent Italo-Turk and Balkan wars. . . . What I'm particularly prepared for is an attack by Austria on Servia."

"But in that case wouldn't Russia take a hand?"

"Perhaps. But Russia will move only if France backs her, and it's quite possible that France and Germany will come to a tacit agreement to avoid any immediate hostilities that might look like becoming general."

The Baron smiled up at the sky; his expression was that of a man who is amused rather than convinced. He was thinking of William II, of certain talks he had had recently with the Emperor who had one arm shorter than the other, conversations which had been as lacking in reticence as was this one with the little revolutionary with the Mongol cheek-bones; conversations in the course of which the Emperor had most certainly expressed his mind freely. Maykosen silently compared the two men. The Emperor and the little revolutionary started from widely divergent points of view, and the sources of information which each had at his disposition were hardly to be compared. Their general deductions, however, were not so different as might have been expected. The Baron remembered, in particular, two phrases which the Kaiser had uttered in his hearing last winter: "I believe now that a war is inevitable; but I don't think it will break out for another two or three years," and: "Poincaré has not yet got France where he wants her. . . . He'll prevent Russia from making a fool of herself for some time yet." The resemblance, however, proved nothing more than that at any given moment certain ideas are in the air and may be put into words by an Emperor and a militant revolutionary alike. The fact only went to show that in these matters one could never be sure; that on every rung of the social ladder there might be men living in the same state of expectation, that an Emperor, with his ministers, his diplomats, his secret agents, and his meetings with friendly and allied sovereigns, was no better equipped to tell the future than a poor devil of a professor-conspirator seated in front of a café in Cracow.

"I notice one thing," said Maykosen in a tone of light mockery, "and that is that you don't seem to think that your friends and colleagues among the Socialists of the various European countries are going to be able to do much to prevent an outbreak of hostilities. Am I right?"

Lenin replied coldly:

"I have no reliance on them."

"Is it that you think they actually want a war as a necessary preliminary to revolution?"

"No . . . most of them are too stupid for that."

He broke off, almost as though he felt he had gone too far.

"You ask what they'll do. They'll do precisely what they have always done: hold meetings, make speeches, adopt inflammatory resolutions. . . . When the mine goes up, the most I expect of them—of those of them who are members of Parliament, and almost all of them are—between now and then they probably all will be," he added on a note of sarcasm—"is that they will refuse to vote the war credits. . . . That"—he slipped into French—"will be merely a compromise *(cela ne fera ni chaud ni froid)*"—then, once more speaking in German: "That's about all they're capable of."

Maykosen continued, picking his words very carefully:

"But—you?"

"What about me?"

"Don't you want a war? . . ."

"No, I do not want a war," Lenin replied sharply. "Why should I? I am doing, and I shall continue to do, everything in my power to hinder mobilization and prevent a war. I've no wish to see millions of proletarians cutting one another's throats in the interests of capitalist stupidity. Let there be no mistake. It's one thing to foresee war as an objective probability and to hope that once the scourge is let loose, one may be able to make good use of it, but quite another to hope for it and to be active in bringing it about. Do you understand my meaning?"

Maykosen assured him that he understood him perfectly. But for the moment he was preoccupied in listening to the fanfare of the Cathedral belfry—the notes falling as from a dead age of chivalry upon the city's quiet; all of them, the whole tune. He even hummed it to himself, anticipating each turn of the air, to prove to his satisfaction that he really knew it by heart.

That night, sitting in his room with the window open, he put down on paper the substance of the talk he had had. Against the blackness of the night sky, in which a hint of red still lingered, he could see the dark, cliff-like silhouette of the Cathedral. At each quarter-hour the fanfare drifted in through the wide-open window, unchecked, like a king exercising his right of entry into a vassal's house.

One of the phrases that he remembered set him thinking: "I must explain that to the Kaiser" (it concerned the mechanism of revolution as something arising automatically out of a war of conflicting imperialisms) . . ."as clearly as I possibly can. . . . I will tell him that that is the view of one of the greatest living specialists in revolution. Presented to him in that form, as starkly as a mathematical formula, the idea may make an impression on him."

Chapter

A SWIRL OF LEAVES BEFORE THE COMING STORM

Ever since the beginning of the domestic upset, Macaire had remained in the kitchen, apparently occupied with his own trivial affairs. He had carried prudence to the extreme point of twice accepting a few crumbs of the cake left over from the previous evening, before it was sent up with the early coffee to Mlle Bernardine and the Marquise, though he had no appetite. Then, suddenly, he took advantage of the cook's opening the back door to an errand-boy who was delivering several parcels which smelt of groceries. He slipped down the service staircase and along the landings like a scrap of wind-blown paper. On reaching ground level he found the postern of the courtyard gate open, as he very well knew it would be at this hour of the day. The concierge was busy polishing the big brass knob. As he rubbed hurriedly against her skirts in passing, she exclaimed: "Where are you off to, you little beast?" but did not interrupt her work for so unimportant a cause. Besides, by that time Macaire was well away.

Without the slightest hesitation he made a sharp right-angled turn which brought him into the rue de Chanaleilles, and then another into the rue Barbet-de-Jouy, where he met an archbishop *in partibus* on his way to the archiepiscopal palace. He had no idea of the stranger's importance, being content to class him with the generality of men dressed like women who wore enormous hats and seemed more or less indifferent to a dog's existence. He could not, however, help noticing the unaccustomed smell of leather and dress material which was richly exuded by the man-woman, like water flushed over the pavement by a caretaker with her pail.

A short run down the rue de Babylone, a perilous passage almost between the very wheels of a motor-car, and he was in the rue Monsieur. He had not swerved as much as a hair's breadth from his predetermined course. Even the wheels of the motor-car had caused him but a moment's uneasiness. He knew exactly where he wanted to go, and not the most romantically evocative whiff of urine had caused him to diminish his pace. At last he found himself before a very high gateway flanked by very high columns and closed by very high doors set in very high walls which, had he been a dog with no particular end in view and with plenty of time on his hands, would have constituted two entrancing worlds ripe for discovery, two golden books to be perused at leisure. In his present state, however, one question and one only pressed for an answer: when would the great doors be opened? A little way off to the left was a much smaller entrance. But it was very carefully guarded. To slip through when it was left ajar would merely result, as he knew from experience, in a kick from a boot or a blow from a leather strap, or, if he pressed his attack, in a wild chase which would end in the same way. Macaire decided, therefore, to wait until the main gate was opened. He was extremely clearheaded and yet aware, at the same time, of a sensation of delirious intoxication. Now and again he could not help giving vent to a little whimper.

He was desperately in love; not with all the bitches who happened to be at that moment in a responsive state all over Paris, not even with some casual bitch he had met and smelled out in his wanderings and would forget in five minutes; but with one bitch in particular. She lived hidden away in the depths of this impressive dwelling. Five days ago, on his way back from an evening visit to the shops of the neighbourhood, he had come across her in the rue de Varennes being led by an extremely distinguished lady (he knew she was distinguished by the clothes she wore and by the dizzy sweetness of the smells she spread around her). His attention had first been caught by the odour of love proceeding from this bitch; next by the sight of her. At any time he would have judged her beautiful, but his heart would not to this extent have been stirred. It was the odour that had, as it were, marked with a bright phosphorescence the loveliness of her form—the long, delicate paws, the subtle curve of her back, the clean silhouette of her muzzle. Not a line of her body but showed clearly beneath her close-clipped coat. She was much larger than Macaire. For the last five days he had thought of nothing but of how he might be with her long enough, and sufficiently free from interruption, to possess her entirely. Several things that he had noticed led him to suppose that his advances would be not wholly unpleasing. But he could conjure up no clear impression of the delights awaiting him, practised though he was in the ways of love, even if his previous experiences had been lacking in variety and sown with difficulties. Whimpering to himself, he thought of the fierce joys to come, joys of the body and joys of the spirit inextricably combined. Enemies, he knew, he might have to deal with, people who would try to hold him from his triumph, jealous rivals. But one thing never occurred to him—that there might be intimate, physical obstacles to the achievement of his designs.

In a carriage of the subway—a second-class carriage, for since his return from England he had not been able to balance his budget and was making a violent effort to economize—Jallez sat watching his fellow-travellers. His experience on the boat from Folkestone had left him with a haunting obsession. Whenever now he found himself in a public place where people are left to their own devices, their private thoughts, the sensations of the moment; whenever he saw around him a certain number of his "contemporaries" free to give to their surroundings, unconsciously, "the colour of the times," he found his attention wide awake. He began to wonder about this "colour." "Isn't it just that I've got hold of an idea which I'm running to death? Isn't this colour just the ordinary emanation of normal middle-class people occupied with their own private troubles—the same sort of thing I might have noticed ten years ago?" How be sure? An old man could give no clue, would merely talk a lot of nonsense about everything having been gay when he was young. "Even Jerphanion notices nothing. When the question is put to him, he says that on the whole he thinks . . . well, he'll take another good look. For the moment I'm inclined to think that his mind's occupied, to the exclusion of everything else, with his honeymoon and his car. Lucky fellow! . . . Is it merely my imagination, this oozing to the surface of men's faces of the hidden menace of the times . . . this clammy sweat of history? If, for instance, a man who had lived during the easy years in the middle of last century were suddenly shown these people whom I see around me, would he, once he had got over the surprise occasioned in him by the way they dressed and the general appearance of their world, say: 'What's the matter with them all? What are they waiting for?' I must try to get a look at some photographs of crowds of an earlier epoch, accurate pictures and drawings of the past, if any such exist."

"You won't find what you require in that material, madame; it wouldn't look at all well. It's a line we only carry in very cheap stuffs."

Juliette had come too early; the shop was still too empty. She missed the crowding and the jostling to which she had been looking forward; the sensation of being carried up a sloping shore by wave after breaking wave; the feeling that her eyes, her whole body, were caught in a web of dazzling, blazing lights, that she was moving among multiple reflections of herself from department to department and floor to floor. The shop-girl was stupid and common, with a tiresome air of thinking herself pretty and a pretentious way of announcing what was and was not being worn. Juliette caught sight of her own face in a square of mirror to her right between two piles of ribbon. "No one could say I wasn't nice to look at. All the terrible crying I've done doesn't show at all. . . . Why am I not as happy as the hundreds of women who are no better than me? . . . I am too good, too gentle. I don't make the most of myself. He had no right to say I'd deceived him, no proof. Anyhow, it was nothing but an excuse. He could perfectly well have married me as soon as I was free; he could perfectly well have given up all this travelling. When a woman's felt herself scorned, it's only natural that she should want to prove to herself that she is capable of inspiring love in another; that someone else is ready to make sacrifices, to change his whole life, for her sake. He would never have changed his life for me. He's heartless, entirely wrapped up in himself. It was always I who did the sacrificing. Even now what is it that stops me from accepting Lucien's offer? I loved Pierre so! I love him still in spite of everything he's done to me. This time I did nearly kill myself. Oh, how I longed to die, just to die! He would have seen then whether I was lying when I talked of taking my life from sheer despair . . . whether I was acting. But I'm such a coward. There's some actions I can't bring myself to take. But this time it wasn't a question of not having the courage, nor the other, when he had already abandoned me! If only it had been a question of just saying yes. . . . But the having to do something was what stopped me, the having to plan it all, the thought of the pain. . . . And then he'd have been too pleased, too glad to get rid of me."

Seated on the left-hand pavement, thumping the ground with his tail in short, sharp movements which betokened his nervousness, Macaire was uttering a series of little sounds in which tenderness seemed mixed with pain, as though someone whom he loved were twisting his paw. He watched, from his position on the opposite side of the roadway, the two tall doors that were of the same colour as his master's library. Twice he had been driven from the pavement just opposite the smaller entrance by a man who seemed set there on purpose to watch for him—a rough, dangerous man of a peculiar type that Macaire had come to know well. They were not, the representatives of this type, quite the same as "masters," of whom, indeed, they were frightened, as could be seen by the way their whole attitude and tone of voice changed when the masters came where they happened to be, or sent for them. The masters were always calling them, but they never called the masters. They were not badly dressed, and they gave off none of the strong smells that a dog associates with the inferior beings one meets with casually in the streets. But neither their clothes nor their smell were the same as the masters'. They smelled mainly of good food, meat and sauces; the inferior beings of the streets (apart from body odour, which, after a while, had a quality of its own), more or less like the dirty glasses that got brought down to the kitchen. . . . Two other dogs were prowling a little way off. They, too, had been attracted by the bitch. They avoided Macaire, trying to escape his watchful eye. In all probability they did not feel themselves weaker than he—in fact, just the contrary. But when they had first put in an appearance, he was already in position, sighing for his lady love. They knew him. They wouldn't fight him unless driven to do so, and even then not enthusiastically. They would very much rather slink up to the bitch without his seeing them. For the moment they considered themselves as being in an alliance against Macaire, and therefore as friends. But if he were out of the way and they should become rivals, they would turn and rend one another with all the savagery in their natures.

How extraordinary to be outside Saint-Germain l'Auxerrois at this time of the morning! Probably Clémence wasn't even up yet. The truth was, when things had reached a certain point, one just couldn't go on. Better burn one's boats. What saint's day was it? Hell, what did it matter anyhow! Even the Marquis had got sick of his exercises. He no longer flapped about like a seal in the bathroom, though if everything one heard was true, he probably went through a good many exercises of another kind, and with no more clothes on, with that little whore of his. To hell with all the saints! They were nothing but a pack of old fools! Most of them had been hunchbacks or cripples or had had smelly feet. When a priest stank of scent like the Abbé Daniel, the odds were he had other things than sanctity to think about. It'd be more interesting to read about the lives of dancers, provided nothing was left out. Mary Magdalene and Saint Augustine —ah, there, now, was a couple that had known how to get the most out of life: fun first, virtue afterwards—that had been their motto! Should she go into the church? No! Unless, of course, she could find a nice austere old confessor to whom she could say: "I admit that I have wanted to give myself to the footman . . . that I have lusted after the caretaker's son . . . that I wanted to offer the porter money to go to bed with me. . . . I admit to having envied street-women who are had by several men in the course of a single night . . . to having dreamed of getting drunk on champagne and committing every sort of beastliness in the arms of a man with handsome moustaches . . . and I admit to having lost my faith in God! I admit that I no longer believe in the existence of anything beyond the grave. We are dust and rottenness in life, and dust and rottenness we remain after death. That's all there is to it!" "What horrible influence has been at work in you, my child? With whom have you been living?" "I read nothing but pious works, meet only the most distinguished persons. We belong to the real old nobility; there's nothing bogus about us. And we're very rich too, now that an old wholesale grocer, whose daughter we degraded ourselves by allowing to marry into the family, has had the decency to kick the bucket."

The Marquis would have liked to say something rather knowing in order to make it plain that he saw how well this piece of silk material harmonized with the panelling. But though he had soon learned the language of Parliament, he had never, despite his long residence in Paris, been able to master the idle chatter of the arts. Still, the great thing was that she should be pleased, and she certainly seemed so, chattering without stopping, for ever jumping up and down and flinging her arms round his neck. Ten times at least she had made him admire the fitting-room—not that he wasn't delighted to do so or made any protest—the old-rose boudoir where she conducted interviews with her really smart customers: "I've put some very special crêpe de chine aside for you, Madame la Comtesse . . ." and the workroom, which was "so convenient, though it was a bit dark and meant using rather more electric light." The bills for all this, when one reckoned up the total, would, of course, be a bit startling. He must pay them off by degrees or Clémence might begin to grow suspicious of such a heavy outlay. Perhaps he could pass it off as part of his re-election expenses. The tactful thing would be to get Paulette to make up a sort of trousseau—silks, lace, and needlework—for him to give his wife on her birthday. The difficulty was to manage so that Paulette could take Clémence's measurements. Why shouldn't he bring her here quite casually? With the place all freshly furnished like this, she couldn't think it not up to her standard. But she might wonder how he had found it, and, anyhow, such an introduction might be in doubtful taste. Better get hold of some old things of hers and let Paulette guess the size from them. He must take the maid into his confidence: "I want to make your mistress a present, but she mustn't know anything about it. . . ." If only the wretched maid didn't burst out laughing! But, after all, there was no reason why she should; she couldn't know anything.

The family was quite sure that it was "only a matter of a few hours." Obviously that was what the two doctors thought; if they said differently, it was only because they wanted to break the news gently. The papal benediction had arrived; it would be read to him as soon as he appeared to be having a lucid moment and could be said to be conscious. Roland would land at Marseilles tomorrow, but he couldn't get home until late the day after—probably too late. It was something to be thankful for that, seeing he had been buried in the heart of the African desert, he had managed to get back for the funeral. The other children had come already. A sister and a brother of the dying man's had arrived from the provinces. Other relations, living in Paris, called in every day for news. Friends, too. The reception rooms of the flat were full of hushed movement: people coming and going and whispering together in groups. One phrase was repeated again and again: "And still so young, really. He always looked so healthy too. Such a short illness—everyone thought it was just influenza." But it appeared now that he had been suffering from albumin for some time. People began to remember that his father had died before he was sixty after a quite unimportant illness. The doctors had tried blood-transfusions and injections of camphorated oil. For the last forty-eight hours he had been more or less in a state of coma varied by more active periods during which those near him suspected that he was suffering. At such times he had been clearly conscious though he had avoided talking and had seemed to want not to be spoken to. To the question: "Are you in pain?" or "Are you in pain, darling?" he had answered: "No, not much," in a voice so weak, so nearly exhausted, that it had given the lie to the words. He had made it obvious finally that he would prefer to be alone, and since he had received extreme unction the day before, his family had interpreted the wish as a desire to be left alone with his God and had done their best to obey him. They had left the communicating door open and had remained within call in the next room. The religious sister in attendance had sat where she could see the pillow of the dying man through the opening. At short intervals one or other of them had tiptoed into the room to see how he was. They thought he did not notice this, though in fact he was perfectly aware of what was happening. If he made no protest, that was because he was too weak. Besides, any argument, however slight, would have been worse than these hushed comings and goings. His appearance gave no clue to the various things that were happening in his mind. When he seemed excited or twisted with pain, the truth was that though he really was suffering, it was with a dull, numb pain, of which he was conscious only as through muffling veils. When he seemed insensible, it was true that he could only with difficulty have said what was going on round him, but his awareness continued to be active, to be even abnormally acute, though, as it were, inside a padded cell. Thoughts were passing through his mind, quite clearly defined thoughts arranged in perfectly logical sequence, but they reached him wrapped in some deadening material. He felt much as he had done sometimes when he had been suffering from fever. His head ached, but his brain was very active. If he had said out loud all he was thinking of, those standing by would have said "delirium." But he was far from being delirious. Of that he was quite sure. He had the impression that now, for the first time in his life, his brain was working freely and with accuracy. Formerly, it seemed to him, he had thought always under some sort of direction, and, as it were, in public. He was like a man who has suddenly discovered that he can draw a deep breath.

"My article had no political intention whatever. I know nothing of politics, and don't want to. I am quite sure that, whatever the régime I had lived under, I should have thought exactly as I think now and got on with my work. . . . But take my word for it, no period can stand too long an interval of peace, too much of the drug of prosperity. The virile virtues atrophy. Heroism becomes nothing but a word to provoke laughter. Mention one of our actual contemporaries to whom the name 'hero' could be accurately applied. Egotism is unchecked. The search for pleasure has become the first law of life. Degradation seems to be proceeding at so headlong a pace that the pleasure sought takes on more and more the character of the sensual and the morbid. Woman is looked on now as nothing but a means to self-indulgence; love has become nothing but a series of bodily contacts. It has always been so whenever life has become too easy. . . . You'll hardly deny that our literature is going rotten on us, and that it accurately reflects our social manners. I'm beginning to feel that I've had enough of it—don't you?"

The three young writers who were sitting with Allory in his study agreed that the age was thoroughly disgusting. Jacques Verdanzat was of the opinion that a good war would do no harm, and pointed out that the sentiment did him credit since he would be among the first to be called up. Not that he looked on war as a heroic cure for the ills of the times. His own opinion—if he might speak quite frankly —was that it would thin things out. . . . There were too many people in the world. Every profession was overcrowded. Men were trampling on one another. A few hard knocks would undoubtedly improve matters.

"Always provided," put in a novelist and journalist called Octave Perrelaud, "that one's among those who come through."

"Bah! One's got to take the luck of the game. Even though the chances of not coming through were equal, that would be better than vegetating till seventy."

Allory said nothing, but he smiled. Nevertheless he was rather shocked. He took a nobler view of war.

Macaire, having succeeded in reaching the far end of the garden, was squatting under a laurel bush. When the great door had opened, one of the two rivals had crept in behind him. By a lucky chance it was this rival who had been seen and chased and kicked and had run back out again howling. The men had shouted something which showed they knew that another dog had got in, and they had started to look for him. Macaire stayed quietly under his laurel bush. There was still a certain amount of excitement, and he dared not move. Quivering in every limb, he looked at the huge house which concealed the bitch. He kept himself from whimpering.

Mascot was seated facing Laulerque in his office at the book-shop, much as on the day of the attempt on Briand's life. But the hour was much earlier—a quarter past twelve. The assistants had gone out to lunch. The two men were alone. But from long habit they leaned their heads together and spoke in low voices.

"I must apologize," said Mascot, "for having bothered you at so inconvenient a time. But I shan't be at home this evening, and I wanted to warn you at once."

"Monsieur Karl has gone?"

"Yes."

"And you're throwing up the sponge?"

"I see no point in mixing myself up in a terrorist campaign for the sake of Servian nationalism."

"You're sure that's what it is, definitely?"

"After what Karl told me! . . . Even if a doubt remained, I have no right to go on. Think!"

"So I see."

Laulerque sighed. "I'm completely broken up—more so even than I seem. This is the end of everything."

Mascot made no reply. He fingered his lips and tapped the table in a series of meaningless gestures.

Laulerque went on:

"What can one believe in? To what cause can one devote oneself? Luckily I've not abused the Socialists so much that I can't join up with them now."

"Oh—the Socialists! . . ."

"What's on your mind?"

"Nothing that isn't on yours. Nothing that we haven't discussed a hundred times. They're just like the rest of 'em . . . like our friends the Balkan conspirators . . . out for themselves. They wouldn't hesitate a moment to let loose a war on us if they thought it convenient to do so. But they wouldn't lift a finger to prevent one. I know the German species pretty well. They'll obey without a murmur. Why, half their leaders are reservist officers."

"What about 'my' house?"

"Do nothing. . . . I'm pretty sure they won't use it any more. Your 'tenant' belonged to the same side as Karl. Presumably Karl's ratted on them. . . . Even if the worst comes to the worst, you don't stand to lose anything. Hang on to it."

"Yes, I suppose I'd better wait and see. But that's not the only thing. Don't you remember when you 'recruited' me you said we'd only have 'two or three years to wait. . . .' You think it's come, then?"

Mascot remained silent for a moment; then:

"Karl does."

"Has he said so?" exclaimed Laulerque, jumping in his chair.

Mascot spread his arms, extended his hands, and moved them in a deprecating gesture.

"Karl is not infallible. He's already told us a lot of nonsense. He maintains that at the court of Vienna, and elsewhere, the general opinion is that it's been timed for this summer, and that other people too, including our southern friends, are of much the same opinion.

According to him, the only question as yet undetermined is who shall fire the train. It appears that there has recently been a meeting between William II and the heir to the Austrian throne, the Archduke Franz Ferdinand. The Archduke, we are told, is in favour of war. The Servian nationalists would like to get rid of him, not so much for that reason as because he is ambitious to incorporate the Slavs of the Empire into a kingdom something after the model of Hungary, enjoying a considerable amount of liberty, and if that happens it will mean that the ground will be cut from under the feet of the Servian party. . . . The same situation is at the bottom of his sympathy for a war policy; that's to say, he wants to smash Servia and so get rid of a dangerous competitor in popular favour. Perhaps, too, he would like to annex the country to his new kingdom, to subject it to the same fate as Bosnia and Herzegovina. . . ."

"But if that's so . . . wouldn't getting rid of the Archduke by the Servians be a step towards preserving peace?"

"That's not the impression I get. If he is sacrificed, it will not be as an enemy of peace, but as an enemy of Servia—and that, in my opinion, would serve only to precipitate matters."

Laulerque crumpled up in his chair in a state almost of collapse. "Then there's nothing for us to do but bow our heads to what's coming? . . ."

He added between clenched teeth in a tone of suppressed rage:

"And I swore I'd do anything, anything at all, rather than . . ."

About the same time, Clanricard and Mathilde, dinner over, were settling down in their tiny flat in the rue Hermel to talk of Laulerque. Mathilde felt no embarrassment; it needed no effort for her to preserve a tone of detached and friendly kindliness. Why shouldn't she be detached? Had there ever been anything that could be called a serious attachment between her and their amusing, slightly mad companion? Had he been there in the room with them, she would have behaved no less naturally. Clanricard, on the other hand, had to make a considerable effort to deal calmly with the name of Laulerque and his remembered presence when they occurred in the course of a conversation with his wife. He was on his guard, however, against a pettiness of mind and a purely selfish sensibility which he found typical of a culture built on a basis of bourgeois private property. He remarked out loud that Laulerque, though mysterious as usual, didn't give the impression he once had done of being a man who had found an object in life, who could feel certain of being able to do something useful for a cause. "And what about me?" he reflected silently; "what about my own case?" There was to be a meeting of his lodge the evening after next, a "lodge night," as it was called. He knew what the resolution was to be. The thought of it was pleasant, was, in a way, a source of comfort. When he was with his Masonic friends it was as though he were suddenly cut off from the world of the uninitiated. Another sort of world, narrow, perhaps, but close and secret, hedged him round, a world marked by comradeship and complete equality, not unlike the world of soldiers or monks, in which he knew a quite extraordinary freedom of thought such as no outsider could even imagine. The Brethren, so often intolerant and narrow in their dealings with strangers, observed as between themselves an almost playful respect for plain speaking and even for extreme audacities of speculation. He could never resist a certain feeling of surprise that quite ordinary men could be capable of such unordinary attitudes. "Between ourselves, there are no truths that cannot be spoken." The result was an atmosphere of privilege and refreshment for which Clanricard was profoundly grateful. If he had been deprived of it he could have found nothing similar elsewhere. The meetings of the "little group" were the only occasions at all like it. But with Sampeyre, as Clanricard realized as soon as he started to work out the analogy, there were always certain precautions that one had, half unconsciously, to observe. For one thing, women were present; for another, the tone of the talk was desultory; it was impossible to thrash out ideas to the end, especially for a man who was at all shy. On lodge nights there was a lot of nonsense talked, to be sure; a good deal of what was said was pretentious and ignorant. But there was such virtue in the twin conventions of freedom and tolerance that very often ideas, in themselves quite undistinguished, engendered from mutual contact a peculiar sort of pleasing freshness in which the spirit, condemned at all other times to live under stranger laws, seemed to breathe the air of its native country, to hear a whisper from the Promised Land. The *form* which thought took at such times seemed infinitely more valuable than its content. But there was still the question of results to be considered. Where was it all leading? What influence would it have on the affairs of the world? So far as that side of the business was concerned, Clanricard had to admit to a sense of disappointment. The lodge far more nearly resembled an academy than a secret society. Did it, unwittingly, form part of a larger, unsuspected whole? He doubted it—doubted it profoundly.

In the avenue du Bois Mme Godorp and Gurau were seated at luncheon with a few friends. There were several painters present, a number of representatives of the world of fashion, including two foreign couples, and a sprinkling of journalists and men of letters. The conversation at table had turned almost exclusively on questions of painting and of art in·general. But a little later, apropos of the avenue du Bois, in which the house was situated, and of Alphand, its creator, someone had expressed the opinion that since the time of Haussmann and of Alphand—that's to say, since the beginning of the Third Republic—almost nothing had been done to increase the beauty of Paris or to make it worthy of its position as a great modern city. Mention was made of everything that had been done under the Second Empire to transform the older plan, of the changes brought about in every district, from the environs of the Bois to the working-class quarters of the east; from the slopes of Montmartre to the Observatory.

"What little there is to mark Paris out as a capital is due entirely to the work of a single generation achieved in a period of about fifteen years."

Dates were mentioned and discussed, each guest making a great show of erudition.

Gurau pointed out that the beautifying of Paris had resulted in almost every instance from the preoccupation of the Imperial Government with considerations of police strategy. Popular uprisings must be deprived of the shelter formerly afforded them by a network of narrow streets; Paris must be turned into a city where cavalry charges, rifle- and artillery-fire could be most effectively employed. Someone else chipped in with the remark that, if that were so, one must admit that progress sometimes owes its happiest achievements to curiously indirect motives. At this point the conversation turned into an amusing game, the object of which was the rebuilding of Paris on ideal lines. The foreigners present were asked to give their opinion. What avenues should be cut through? What vistas created or restored to their former glory? The company dealt in turn with the boulevard Haussmann, the rue de Rennes, the Institut, the Trocadéro, the Eiffel Tower, the Champ de Mars, and the outer boulevards. Attention was next turned to the old streets at the centre of the city and the slum districts, the final conclusion being that the task would be endless and so beset by obstacles that it was quite hopeless to expect that it would ever be finished.

"What we need," put in a painter with a turn for humorous exaggeration, "is a war which would reduce half Paris to ruins. Short of that . . ."

Nobody echoed this sentiment, but nobody seemed to be outraged by it. Nobody even thought of remarking that a war which would reduce half Paris to ruins might be rather disastrous for France.

In the rue Vaneau luncheon had been quite spoiled, if not entirely overlooked, as a result of the general feeling of anxiety. Neither Mlle Bernardine nor Macaire had been seen since the morning. Until half past twelve nobody had bothered much about them. But it was now two o'clock. Had they gone out together? On this point there was a good deal of conflicting evidence. The cook, scenting blame, asserted that it was quite impossible that Macaire should have slipped out by the back door. Étienne said that Mlle Bernardine had been alone when he saw her go out. M. and Mme de Saint-Papoul had visions of an accident. Bernardine was so often absent-minded in the matter of crossing streets. They'd noticed, too, that she'd been behaving, of late, more oddly than ever. Though they were afraid of speaking of their forebodings out loud, each wondered secretly whether the old lady hadn't perhaps gone completely mad and become involved in Heaven knew what disaster. The Marquis had already rung up first the local police stations and then Headquarters, in each case being careful to explain who it was who was making the inquiry. "Has nothing been seen of the dog either?" Having described his sister, he described the dog. He had an uncomfortable feeling that the constable on duty who had taken down the details had not got the two descriptions quite clearly distinguished in his mind.

Macaire was going through a particularly unpleasant time. From his place of concealment under the laurel bush, from which he had not stirred—time had ceased to have any meaning for him, even if it were that of a meal—he had seen one of his rivals—the larger and dirtier of the two—wandering quite openly, and apparently unconscious of danger, on the gravel sweep that lay in front of the house. How had he managed to get there? Up and down he prowled, his tail wagging and a purposeful look in his eye. He sniffed at the steps leading up to the front door. He even had the cheek to whine. No one appeared to have noticed him. Macaire was torn between a desire to fly at him and fear of the scene to which a dog-fight would inevitably give rise. But his irritation at such idiotic behaviour was greater even than his jealousy. It would be lovely, of course, to see his rival caught and given a thorough good hiding by the servants. But would it end there? It was only too probable that his terror-stricken rival would seek asylum in the laurel bush. . . . The pangs of love were quite bad enough without these additional complications.

As to Mlle Bernardine, she was neither in the Morgue nor at the bottom of the Seine, as her relations were beginning to think probable.

She was in the Louvre Museum, seated on a bench near the exit. She had had no luncheon, but the omission left her entirely unmoved. She had been wandering for hours through the picture galleries and the rooms devoted to antique statuary. Nor for a moment did she attempt to conceal from herself the object of her visit. She had come to look at the nudes. And if she had chosen the Louvre as the scene of her adventure, it was because, just when she was feeling at her worst, she happened to be immediately opposite the entrance, in the Place de Saint-Germain l'Auxerrois; because, too, she didn't know where else to find examples of what she sought. To be sure, if there had been some other place where, by paying something at a turnstile, she could have seen, while herself remaining invisible, real naked men and real naked women engaged in every kind of filth and beastliness, she would willingly have gone there, though she would have felt terrified at the idea of having to pass the turnstile. But no one had ever told her of such places; so she had to be satisfied with the Louvre Museum for want of somewhere better. The place had certain advantages. There was nothing particularly immoral about being seen entering it, and once inside, the only precaution she need take was to be sure that she was alone before going up to a particularly disgusting picture or staring her fill at the less modest portions of a gladiator or a Hercules. Her recollections of the place were lost in the dim past. She had forgotten what a gorgeous riot of nudity it contained. How many naked women there were, glancing provocatively at lovers with smouldering eyes or exploring hands! How many magnificent yet terrifying male organs! From this point of view she was not disappointed. More than once her eyes were nearly starting out of her head. But what good was that! What mockery this mere looking was, however delightful in itself! Seated on her bench, exhausted and worn out, she told herself in a mood of frustrated violence that she was ready to do "anything," meaning by "anything" any carnal abomination. To make quite sure, she would go to confession afterwards. Confession was not meant for animals. Anything! But with whom? She knew perfectly well that she could not offer herself to the first well-dressed man she met in the street. Mad she might be, but not so mad as that. Even if she made eyes at one of the hundreds of ordinary men who thronged the pavements, neither handsome nor ugly, neither old nor young, he would only burst out laughing, taking her for some old lunatic. The sole chance of success for her would be if she chose one of those degraded beings—she wasn't quite sure how to describe them—loafers, casual labourers—the sort of men who distributed prospectuses or sold evening papers. But they would almost certainly be filthy, covered with vermin, and eaten up with appalling diseases; besides, their manners would be so rough and their language so coarse that, on the whole, she'd rather die. Ready for anything—easier said than done. On her bench, not far from one of the attendants, who kept an uneasy eye on her—for he was beginning to be sure that if this old woman was not dangerous she was certainly odd—Bernardine realized with complete lucidity that her present situation was one of those which, though it admits of easy solution in imagination or in a book, in, for instance, a "vicious" novel, can find in actual life no possible satisfaction. A day as hideous as this—and there might be others in store for her—must be lived to the end, must be dealt with by her own unaided strength. She must face it on her knees, or die.

M. de Lommérie, already on the threshold of death and, to all appearances, in a semi-comatose condition, was still, deep within himself, pursuing a rapid train of thoughts, each one of which seemed to be tripping on the heels of its immediate predecessor. But they took the form of visual images rather than of logical formulas, and only he could understand them fully. They referred one and all to the problem which life had been to him, as it is to all men. He was like a schoolboy two minutes before the end of a written examination. At the far end of the room they are beginning to collect the papers. No matter whether the problem has been solved or not, his attempt must be given up. There is just time to read it all through once more, very hurriedly. M. de Lommérie had a feeling that he had got it wrong. The right solution was not the one he had given. What was the right one? It was hard to find at the last moment. Besides, his head was aching terribly. One of the others had almost certainly found it, but which one? No time now for him to get the answer whispered across to him. Why had he chosen this method rather than another of treating the problem? How funny it all was! This concern for decency, for respectability, for the conventions. All the things he had done, thought, and said without really believing in them. What use had his money been to him? He couldn't, in the popular phrase, "take it with him." What consolation had he found in faith? Could he take that with him? How odd this adventure was on which he was embarked! Who could have foretold it a week ago? Oddest of all to think that he would almost certainly not meet his respectable acquaintances in heaven. Either there was no such place as heaven, or they would not be there. Had he any real friends who could help him now to die? The family was all very well in its way; at least it was something. "If only they'd leave me in peace! If I had nothing to leave them they'd be less considerate. I should probably be lying in a hospital. Roland is the nicest; but he's a fool. He'll be certain to get himself killed in the next war— and that won't be long in coming. It's all very sad, but if there weren't so many people like him, there wouldn't be any wars. We're all liars, every one of us! And it's to ourselves chiefly that we lie. They thought I didn't hear just now when the papal benediction was read. I know all about that. I've got shares in two hotels at Lourdes. All I want now is to be left in peace. I think I'm in considerable pain. Anyhow, I'm going to die; that won't be difficult."

Haverkamp, in his office at the headquarters of the Celle-les-Eaux Company, now situated in the avenue de l'Opéra close to the corner of the rue des Pyramides, thought with regret of the days when he had first occupied his fifth-floor attic on the boulevard du Palais with its view of the Palais de Justice. Business was bad. The spa was fluttering on a broken wing. The overhead was too high. He had failed to find purchasers for the last lot of villas he had put up, and a good many building plots remained unsold. Other enterprises in which he had money were complaining of excessive competition and were not managing to make both ends meet. His "Limoges factory" was rather like one of those charming little country estates, complete with kitchen garden, the owner of which is two francs out of pocket every time he eats a home-grown salad. The two Benoit-Cotru sons had turned out to be villains, and old Nanthiat had had to be pensioned off. For more than a year now things had been in a very odd state. The price of houses had not gone up; rather it had gone down; and the same was true of real estate. That's not much fun for a man who has arranged his whole career on the assumption of a continual rise in house values. It had all begun, apparently, with the slump in stocks three years ago. What did it all mean? Was it a sign of impending disaster? If only what was coming would come! Everyone knew that when business was slack the only thing to be done was to wipe the slate clean and begin afresh. Well, the sooner the wiping began, the better!

Champcenais went into a book-shop on the boulevard des Italiens with which he had got into the habit of dealing regularly. Business was far from bad with him; in fact, the ease with which he was making money was a little disquieting. Without being a pessimist, he was not one of those people whom success makes careless of the future. There were special reasons why petroleum should be booming. The consumption of fuel was steadily increasing. But petroleum was now the least of his concerns. His chief activity lay in the manufacture of armaments, and results in that field were excellent. Every country in Europe was busy buying machine-guns, armour-plate, torpedoes, and shells. . . . Conditions in the industry couldn't be better. The chief producers all over Europe, though naturally out to attract custom to themselves, had come to a more or less definite arrangement to keep prices up, and even in some cases to share the available orders. The various governments, intent on getting quick delivery, were not disposed to haggle. Subsidies to newspapers and, in certain countries, bribes paid to politicians, officials, and army chiefs were having the effect of keeping discussion to a minimum. High wages had reduced labour troubles. Champcenais had even found that it was possible to buy the support of some of the trade-union leaders, provided it were done tactfully. "If only things go on like this it'll be all right!" he reflected. He had never really wanted war, not even when it had seemed the only cure for social unrest. But now he was actually afraid of the possibility. Not that, viewed superficially, a war wouldn't mean a golden age for the munition-makers. But war contained too large an unknown quantity to be viewed with complacence. A state of increasingly armed peace would be very much better. But he did not disguise from himself the fact that the game couldn't go on indefinitely. Sooner or later the nations, faced with the alternative of war or bankruptcy, would choose war, if only to justify the sacrifices they had made to be prepared. He sometimes thought that if the manufacturers were really wise they would work for the convening of a new Hague Conference and the signing of a pact for limitation of armaments. He had hinted as much to Zülpicher, who had taken the suggestion as an example of French humour and had laughed in his face. But then, Zülpicher believed that war was inevitable. According to him, they would be better em-ployed, instead of uttering amusing paradoxes, in starting to work out means of dealing with the complex situation which was bound to arise, and not waiting until the conflict was on them, and im-provising machinery at the last moment. They ought, for instance, to think out some way of ensuring unbroken communication between the industrialists of the warring countries; for some communication there would have to be if they were not to be embarrassed by a shortage of raw material, the awkward topographical situation of many of the factories, and the general complications resulting from hostilities.

On leaving the book-shop, Champcenais became aware of a con-siderable commotion all the way along the boulevard. People walk-ing on the pavements were stopping and collecting by the curb. The very carriages were slowing up, coming to a standstill, and taking position on either side of the thoroughfare. There was a sound of music. From the direction of the Opéra a battery of artillery in full field equipment was approaching, marching in column. There were guns and limbers, ammunition carts and regimental wagons; there were the colours. It must be a whole regiment on the way back from manœuvres. The colonel, perhaps carrying out orders, perhaps acting on his own initiative because he knew that this sort of demonstration would be approved by the authorities, had arranged to march down the Boulevards at the most crowded hour of the day. Everything in the column was bright and polished, though a light coating of dust gave to the whole an air of meaning business. The sound of the horses and the wheels, the rattling of the caissons, was as unusual here on the boulevard as the absence of all the normal traffic noises. The crowd cheered and applauded; hats and caps were raised. The shrill notes of women's voices were distinctly audible. The crowd was under the impression that guns were passing by the dozen, that thousands of shells were concealed in the jolting box-seats. The shining metal, the shipshape order of everything, gave convincing proof of efficiency. The very noise was evidence of power. Those who heard it were moved to a sense of gratitude. It acted like a tonic against the ravages of fear; an iron tonic. "We are strong!" "How strong we are!" More than one old man emerging from the Crédit Lyonnais, where he had been drawing his dividends, moved suddenly by a memory of '70, felt the tears welling in his eyes.

Champcenais had no difficulty in resisting the general intoxication. There was nothing to get excited about in the war material before him. It hadn't even the merit of having come from his factories. Besides, what possible significance had a dozen and a half of guns in the Europe of 1914?—the merest driblet. And yet here were thousands of gaping fools all down the boulevard acting as though they believed that with those few troops they could defy the world. Poor devils!

Bernadine was seated in the corner of a small confectioner's shop.

She was eating a piece of tart and had ordered a glass of wine. Weariness had proved too much for her. Her feeling of misery had, fortunately, become entirely physical. She was not quite sure what part of the town she was in. Just before coming into the shop, she had noticed several poor women. She had reflected that, victim of despair though she might be, it was still comforting to think that she had a bed and a comfortable room of her own to go to, and money in her purse.

The bitch was coming down the steps led by a woman who looked like a cook. The rival had vanished some time ago. The bitch and the woman did not make for the gate. Probably they would confine their activities to a walk round the garden. The intoxicating smell swept in great waves over the whole garden, became a sort of flood in which Macaire, under his laurel bush, felt himself engulfed. He became intolerably excited; desire blinded him to every other consideration. Nevertheless, his mind remained sufficiently clear to warn him that, despite appearances, the psychological moment had not yet arrived. The woman who looked like a cook was not going to let go of the lead and was certainly not going to stand by and watch the ravishment of her charge. But no matter how obedient to reason a dog may be, there are extremities of emotion in which his self-control begins to waver. The bitch, at the end of her lead, was going to pass quite close to the laurel bush. With difficulty Macaire choked back his whines. A sudden movement, a sudden yelp, showed that the bitch, too, had become aware of his presence and by no means disapproved of it. The amorous waves proceeding from her had become like a rushing tide that overcomes a sea-wall in its tumultuous onset. They were accompanied by another emanation, no less powerful, appealing not to the nostrils, but directly to heart and head, telling of consent. This new flood was, if anything, more irresistible than its forerunner. The bitch stopped, tugging at her lead, and was making pretence of the most innocent of needs. The woman in charge of her, yawning, absent-minded, and apparently unaware of the threatening danger, stopped too, without looking behind her. Her attention was occupied by the upper windows of a neighbouring house. Macaire pounced. The bitch, far from retreating, did her best to respond to the attack. The worst would there and then have occurred but for the fact that Macaire realized that his small size made necessary a series of acrobatic movements to which neither he nor his partner were accustomed. There followed an unfortunate interval of fumbling, and, worse still, one or two sharp cries drawn from Macaire by exasperation and the unkindness of fate. They were loud enough to make the woman turn her head. She saw what was happening and burst into a torrent of indignation. She aimed at Macaire a series of kicks and struck at him with the loose end of the lead. He dashed off at full speed towards the gate and, overjoyed to find that the postern was by chance ajar, slipped between the legs of the man who was holding it open, though not without getting a final kick which bruised the whole of his right flank.

Holding a program in his hand, Sammécaud settled into his seat in the eighth or tenth row of stalls of the Érard Concert Hall. There were not many people present. He had come to listen to a performance of chamber music. He had a weakness for these intimate, rather melancholy concerts, provided they took place between five and seven. At a later hour they would make rather too gloomy an end to the day. He liked, after applauding with discrimination the final *presto quasi allegro,* to walk out into the animation of the streets with the comfortable feeling that he had just enjoyed a pleasure accessible only to the very few.

On her way from a visit of charity in the rue Basfroi of the Saint-Antoine district, Marie had discovered the Church of Sainte-Marguerite. She had entered and had found it charming. It was as empty as a village church, and as quiet. Here and there the setting sun struck through the windows. It was a true refuge, seemingly separated by endless miles from the world of men. She determined to say a prayer there every time her round of visits brought her to the neighbourhood. In her sudden passion for the place she went still further: "It is my own special church," she thought, "the harbour of my spirit." A peace desended upon her, bred of a sense of these suburban streets, full as they were of memories of her deepest humiliation; of the gentle unpretentiousness of the interior, so little suburban in character, so little like those great pseudo-Gothic barns usually to be found in working-class districts.

"Can't you tell me any more about this man covered with blood?"

"I see him drawing closer to you . . . to us, perhaps. Yes, I have an impression that since I first mentioned him, what he represents has come appreciably nearer. It is all very much more distinct, less misty. That, of course, may be due to the fact that I've grown accustomed to the vision. Repeated sessions do, naturally, make a thing like this more distinct. It's as though it were much less far away. It's all very difficult."

"And the woman who's standing behind me?"

"It's odd. . . . I seem to see her on her knees, hiding her face in her hands . . . she's in some place that looks like a church. But she is not thinking of you. You have nothing to fear."

Quinette took a train from the Sceaux station, whither he had gone by a subway. It was not a very comfortable time for travelling. The carriages were filled with suburban workers going home. The change at the Grande-Ceinture—why couldn't there be a direct train?—would be an infernal nuisance. The only advantage was that at this time of day he would attract less attention when he got out at Bièvres. One could never be too careful about rousing suspicions. Quinette had managed to find a vacant corner. He had opened his evening paper and put on his spectacles, but solely in order to keep up appearances in front of his fellow-travellers—a way of avoiding attracting their attention, and a defence against their indiscreet efforts at conversation. But he was careful to be extremely polite, to apologize for any clumsiness of which he might be guilty. When he turned the page of his paper he took pains to avoid flicking the face of the man sitting opposite. But he was more intent on his thoughts than on what he was reading. They concerned a very special problem which he would have to face as soon as he reached his little house in the valley. "If one takes a hammer and pounds up bones previously burned, and then buries them, will they become unrecognizable in the earth?" How long would it take? That was the ticklish problem. To argue from the analogy of cemeteries was to argue fallaciously. "Cemeteries have time on their side."

Jerphanion, too, was rumbling along in a train, but in the opposite direction. He glanced at the first suburban houses just as he had done long ago when he first arrived from Saint-Étienne. Since then, and it wasn't so very many years, the city had encroached on the surrounding plain. The open country ended sooner, and there was a noticeable thickening of the houses on the outskirts. Jerphanion, too, was pondering a technical problem. He was impatient to reach the Austerlitz station because, naturally, he wanted to see his young wife again, but almost as much because he wanted to change into old clothes and hurry round to the tiny garage which he rented for his car in the rue du Cardinal-Lemoine. Ever since the previous Sunday he had been obsessed by the idea that his engine was misfiring, that there was something wrong with the spark. This sense of there being something the matter with the car had faintly spoiled his time at Orléans, keeping him in a constant state of irritation. By dint of hard thinking he had come to the conclusion that though the magneto was irreproachable, the two plugs—his engine was a two-cylindered one—wanted a thorough cleaning. He had bought the car second-hand, paying for it no more than three thousand francs (most of which had been lent him by his father-in-law and his father). One can't expect perfection in a car three years old and costing only three thousand francs. Jerphanion went over in his mind with great precision the operations of taking out the plugs, cleaning them, and replacing them. He could hear with anticipatory pleasure the regular, exciting, comforting, companionable sound which the two-cylinder engine would make when, the plugs duly cleaned, it would start up with four or five turns of the crank.

M. de Lommérie had reached a state in which he felt separated not only from those around him, but from himself as well. He was escaping from his own personality. The essential *he* was withdrawing, sliding away, becoming more and more distant. He was, as it were, "leaving himself in peace." What a strange, exhausting adventure! How terribly he would suffer were it not for the fact that he was no longer strong enough to react to suffering! How well worth while it would have been to take careful note of what was happening to him, but, by a stupid coincidence, it so happened that he was beyond taking note of anything. Well, so much the worse; it would be another thing lost. He was becoming a child again, a tiny little baby, but his head was heavier than it should have been in one so young, and he thought of his body as of something hateful and ignominious. If only the whole mass of corruption, the corpse-wrapping of poison-infested flesh would slough off and fall away! . . . There would still be people in the world after he had gone, people and events. Things would go on happening, on and on and on. . . . Let those left behind get out of the mess as best they could!

MURDER, FAR OFF, OF AN ARCHDUKE

It was on his return from an early Sunday morning excursion in the mountains with his revolutionary friends belonging to the Russian colony living in Cracow that Vladimir Ilitch Ulianov, better known as Lenin, having stopped for a moment at an inn in Zakopane for a drink of water before returning to Peronin, learned from the innkeeper a piece of news which a friend of the latter's who was a postman had just told him on the strength of an official telegram which had passed through his hands. The Archduke Franz Ferdinand, heir presumptive to the throne, had just been assassinated at Sarajevo by Bosnian or Servian conspirators. Hardly anybody at Zakopane had yet heard the news. But already there was a sense of emotional tension in the air. The man who would have been in a few years, perhaps in a few months, Emperor, for the Galicians no less than for the other subject peoples of the huge Empire, had fallen, struck down by emissaries of a race which was known to be living in a condition of open hostility to the Dual Monarchy. The innkeeper dared not ask his customer what he thought would be the outcome, though he knew him for an important and well-informed, though perhaps a dangerous, individual. Vladimir Ulianov made a sound something like "Ho! Ha!" and proceeded to ask whether the occurrence had taken place the day before or that same morning. No one, however, could answer his question, and he said nothing more.

Lenin and his friends talked of what had happened most of the way back from Zakopane to Peronin. Two of them were of the opinion that if the assassination of the Archduke had really taken place in the circumstances alleged, and it certainly looked as though it had, it might well start that war between Austria and Servia which had so long been threatening, and, as a result of the close bonds uniting Servia and Russia, Austria and Germany, Russia and France, a general European conflagration. Lenin declared that he did not believe it would. In the first place, he was not at all sure that the death of the Archduke would be altogether looked at askance in Vienna. The plot to which he had fallen a victim might, of course, have unsuspected ramifications. But, more important still, Europe was not prepared to regard it as an "incident." Certainly it was more critical than anything that had happened for some time, but it could only produce a war if the great imperial powers were of a mind to take up the challenge here and now. He was inclined to lay it down as an axiom that in the modern world, dominated as it was by a purely economic determinism, the role of foreign policies and of diplomacy was merely that of the seconds in a duel whose business it is to arrange the date and place of the meeting, with mutual exchange of courtesies and many expressions of willingness to adjust their plans to the convenience of their opponents. "This week is not very suitable? Well, then, let us put it off for a few days." Speaking for himself, he was of the opinion still that the great powers were not yet ready to risk their all.

"Look here," he said jokingly, "I'm ready to bet on 1917. If I lose I'll stand you all to champagne—in Cracow or anywhere else you like."

Before reaching Peronin, where they were all going to take a late meal together, they had already changed the subject. They discussed the case of Malinovsky. Some of Lenin's friends maintained that he was decidedly suspect, and that his vulgar showing off was utterly detestable. Lenin, however, insisted on defending him, though in rather a playful manner.

"There may be more than a little of the guttersnipe in him," he said, "but he's useful to us."

"More than a little?" replied the others. "Hm! And how is he useful? Only the future will show that."

Jallez had not gone out until the early afternoon. He had stayed in his room all morning to finish an article on the subject of Antwerp which he wanted to get off to his paper (it was the second of a series he was doing on the Great Ports of Europe).

He meant to slip his article into the post, to eat at any restaurant he might find, and then treat himself to a saunter along the quays, looking at the innumerable sailing ships with their varied, multicoloured rigging, which at that time made of Rotterdam the first of all the harbours of the Continent for sailing vessels, and the most brightly chequered.

As he walked along the Spaensche Kade, he noticed, at the door of a hotel, pinned to a notice board, a slip of paper which at first he took for a menu.

The paper in question was a bulletin issued by a news agency. It announced the murder, that very morning, at Sarajevo, of the heir to the Austrian throne, the Archduke, and his wife, by a Bosnian student.

Jallez had only the vaguest ideas about the Archduke. But it needed very little perspicacity to realize that the news was hardly a message of hope to Europe. "What a tiresome business!" he thought.

More than once in the course of the day he turned it over in his mind. Somehow he couldn't dismiss it. This news from the Balkans hung about him like "a weight," as people say. But for some years now the peoples of Europe had grown into the habit of living their lives, going about their business, and taking their amusement with a weight about their necks.

He took advantage of the lovely day. Midsummer was not far off. He bought some newspapers and saw in them a few brief comments on the event. But, as he could not read Dutch, he made little of them. After dinner he loitered long by the waterside, watching the slow fading of the pearl-coloured twilight from sky and river.

Maykosen, who was in the town of Monnickendam, not far off, where he had gone to make a study of the Zuyder Zee problem, heard the news only some hours later (from the proprietor of his hotel, who had got it from a guest to whom it had been telephoned by somebody in Amsterdam). His reaction was immediate and violent. His diagnosis was rapid. "The Sect has struck; or, probably, one of its more or less dissident branches. I wonder how deeply the Archduke H. is involved." His mind turned at once to William II. "How's he going to take this? What's he feeling at this moment?" He had not seen him for some time. He had heard rumour of a mysterious meeting that had taken place shortly before at Konopischt between the Kaiser and the man who had just been murdered. "It'll be more than ever a shock for the Emperor. . . . What did they talk about at Konopischt? . . . I must go to Berlin and try to get an hour with him as soon as I possibly can." Without being fool enough to think of himself as William II's chosen guide—he knew too well how many influences were at work around that versatile man—Maykosen had the impression that the Emperor, when they were too long apart, tended to get out of control and do foolish things.

After luncheon he packed his luggage and fell back on Amsterdam, where he could keep in closer touch with the news and where he would be in a better position to make a sudden departure.

Gurau did not get the news until Monday morning when he bought the papers at Tours station. He had spent Saturday and Sunday with Mme Godorp, taking the opportunity to pay several duty visits to his supporters in the constituency, for which he had just been re-elected with a handsome majority. He was now on his way back to Paris.

The event did not alarm him unduly. Still, he realized its seriousness, and it awakened in him certain lively regrets. When, on the day immediately following the recent elections—which had resulted in a marked drift to the Left, due mainly to popular dislike of the Three-Year Act—Poincaré had imprudently, or very maliciously, asked Ribot to form a government, Ribot the solemn, pompous mainstay of the Right Centre, Gurau had been prominent among those who had brought about the fall of that paradoxical Ministry which had suffered the unprecedented ignominy of being forced to resign on the occasion of its first appearance before the Chamber. In his own opinion he had been mainly responsible for the whole affair. In view, too, of the fact that he had not forgotten Poincaré's earlier promises and, in spite of certain divergences of opinion, had remained on cordial terms with the President, he had regarded it as almost a foregone conclusion that he would be entrusted with the formation of the next government. A hint dropped by Poincaré during the consultations which had led to the construction of Ribot's ephemeral Cabinet had led him to think that the President even then had his eye upon him as the natural successor to a combination which had been condemned even before it took office.

In fact, however, it was Viviani whom Poincaré had summoned. It needed but that to fill Gurau's cup of bitterness to the brim. Viviani was his contemporary in politics; Viviani's program was almost a reflection—at least superficially—of his own; Viviani was a charlatan who had a gift for nothing but words, and whose lack of any real culture, any genuine intellectual background, even, if it came to that, of determination, could not really have taken Poincaré in for a moment. To Gurau the choice had all the appearance of a personal insult. To be sure, one of Viviani's first acts had been to offer him the portfolio of Foreign Affairs—after making the courteous gesture of praying the "much respected" Léon Bourgeois, who had accepted it from the hands of Ribot (another of Bourgeois's disconcerting contradictions), to retain it—but he had haughtily refused the proffered seat in the Cabinet. Upon which Viviani had promptly taken it himself! Nor was that all. In his address to Parliament the new Prime Minister had, in dealing with the very ticklish question of the Three-Year Act, stolen from Gurau the extremely astute formula which the latter had used to such effect in his electoral campaign: "Since it has been passed into law, let us at least give it a fair trial. If we do not, our opponents will accuse us of bad faith and say that we are plotting the downfall of France. We will accept it as a fact and let it stand or fall by its results."

That had been too much. Gurau had withdrawn into an attitude of reserve more disdainful even than before. He let it be understood that he was sitting with folded arms while governments fell like ninepins all around him, biding his time.

And now this news from Sarajevo awoke in him, though at first rather vaguely, a feeling that swept aside considerations of personal pride. "Perhaps I ought to have accepted. I was the only man who, in certain circumstances, could have preserved the peace of Europe, seeing that Caillaux—whom I have not forgiven, but who, at least, did work for peace—has been put out of the running for a long time owing to this absurd business about his wife. Caillaux and I were the only two men who could have stood up to Poincaré. Viviani is just a windbag. . . . There are times when personal considerations should go by the board." Apart, too, from his private grievances against Poincaré, Gurau had been conscious of a renewed and growing distrust of the man's policy. During the last year a number of incidents had occurred to give countenance to his sense of uneasiness. He even called to mind things in the past, the importance of which, at the time, he had been careful not to exaggerate, such, for instance, as Delcassé's appointment as Ambassador to the court of St. Petersburg. Seen now in retrospect, they took on a new significance as carefully planned steps in a consistent plan of campaign. "Young Geoffroy was right after all." What use was to be made by the plotters of what had just happened at Sarajevo? "If I were at the Foreign Office, I wouldn't let Poincaré out of my sight from now onwards. If necessary, I'd make him put his cards on the table. I'd try to throw light on all this private diplomacy of his, with its system—if there really is one—of direct reports from agents like this fellow Mionnet who are responsible to him personally. My unfortunate experience with Caillaux would have come in useful. Poincaré may be terribly dictatorial, but I could have frightened him by threatening to appeal to the constitution."

Once again he felt something of that enthusiasm to do battle with rising dangers which had belonged to the old days of his interviews with Maykosen, when the Foreign Office had still for him the freshness of a new-wed bride.

"I must really make an effort to see Jaurès this afternoon."

He found Jaurès in one of the lobbies. Jaurès was quite definitely worried. In his opinion it was nothing but childish to do as some were doing and try to reduce the whole incident to the dimensions of a piece of international gossip. On the other hand he was strongly against yielding to panic.

"When things like this happen, the danger is primarily psychological. A *casus belli* doesn't grow naturally. The Schnäbele [1] incident began as a joke, but it nearly caused a war by becoming a psychological sounding-board of a peculiarly detestable kind. How are the Austrians going to react to this little drama? That's the question. It's not we who are primarily concerned except in so far as we can 'muffle' the sounding-board. That's a thing we must do by every means in our power."

He admitted that he too was gravely suspicious of Poincaré.

"I sometimes wonder whether he hasn't really been playing a game with all of us, hasn't been making us, in our various spheres, serve his own private purposes. . . ." He stopped, seemed for a moment to be plunged in thought, and then, in a low voice, but without beating about the bush:

"I'm not blaming you," he said, "but you ought to have taken it on, you know."

[1] The incident referred to took place towards the end of the '8o's. A French police inspector named Schnäbele, stationed on the frontier, made friends with his opposite number on the German side of the line, who one day invited him to a companionable meeting. The French official accepted without suspicion, but no sooner had he appeared at the agreed meeting-place than he was arrested on the charge of violating German territory. He was kept in prison, and a grave international situation looked, at one time, like developing. The French Government of the day, however, took a strong line, and the unanimity of French public opinion made it clear that national feeling had been deeply stirred. Schnäbele was ultimately released, and the danger passed.—TRANSLATOR'S NOTE (from information supplied by M. Henry Dauray).

Gurau went pale.

"Taken on what?" he asked.

"The Foreign Office, when Viviani made you the offer."

"You say that to me? You, who invariably vote against Viviani?"

Jaurès began to laugh.

"My obligations are rather different from yours. . . . We could have done with a man like you in such a post at such a time. . . ." Without the slightest trace of irony he added: "particularly in view of the experience you have had in the past."

"You make me feel very sorry, Jaurès, almost guilty. . . ."

"Well, we must just keep a watchful eye on 'them' from outside— and in cases of this kind Parliament is always outside. But it's not going to be easy. For my own part, I shall remain in the closest possible touch with the working-class organizations, and with our friends abroad."

"Those in Germany are about the only ones who really count. It's not very likely that the Socialists of Austria-Hungary or Russia will be able to do much."

"I agree."

"Do you really expect great things from the Germans? Don't you think they're pretty canny, pretty well inclined to purr when the Kaiser strokes them?"

Jaurès fidgeted, moving his head and shoulders several times from left to right. He was obviously trying to get things clear in his mind before committing himself to an answer. Gurau, who was watching him closely, noticed that in the last few months his hair had grown noticeably greyer, almost white.

"Let's be fair," Jaurès said at length. "They're not, temperamentally, as highly strung as we are. It takes more to put them in motion; their reactions are slower. I agree with you, too, that they'll hesitate a good deal before openly challenging the law. They're a little too prone to discipline, too much official-ridden. . . . Still, they're sound enough at bottom. Their organization is excellent, and their leaders have them well in hand. Obviously they're not going to start up their whole vast machine without very good reason. But once it gets going, it will prove irresistible—as a brake at least. The German Army will never be able to mobilize unless the Socialists are willing."

"I only wish I could share your confidence. . . ."

"And then," went on Jaurès in response to a sudden uprush of optimism from the deep springs of his nature, "we mustn't leave altogether out of account the other sections of the International, even in those countries that are not directly involved. None of them, perhaps, could completely stop the war plans of their governments, but a general movement, a mounting wave, all over Europe, of proletarian anger, would almost certainly give pause to the cabinets and chancelleries. . . . In that, I think, lies the chief hope of peace."

Chapter

24

EXTRACTS FROM A CONFIDENTIAL RE-PORT ADDRESSED BY MIONNET TO PRESIDENT POINCARÉ,[1] DATED JULY 4, 1914

. . . .

I happened to be at Bologna when the news of the Sarajevo murder reached me, and was therefore in a position to study the initial reactions of people there to the incident before following up developments in Rome, whither I returned the day following. But first let me say a word or two about the previous situation, taking it up where my last letter left it. I have scrupulously observed Your Excellency's instructions in the matter of the attitude to be adopted towards the Cardinal Secretary and the Archbishop of Bologna. My chief difficulty, as I have already pointed out to Your Excellency, was, in view of the efficiency of the Roman police, to keep the Secretariat in ignorance of the fact that I had made personal contact with della Chiesa. The best way seemed to me to tell M. de V., when I last saw him, that I was preparing to go to Bologna to meet a certain Capuchin, R. (there really is such a man), a known enemy of France and agent of Germany, in the hope of being able to buy him off. The Cardinal would see no objection to this, since he has the lowest opinion of the man in question. Once on the spot, I think I covered my tracks successfully. My interview with the Archbishop took place, not at the Palace, but in the house of a sympathizer lying outside the town. I am quite convinced, from what I heard, that there is no longer any question of engineering M. d. V.'s fall. The question is no longer one of practical politics. I had been warned by friends in Rome that I should find this so. It appears that the Pope's health is a good deal less satisfactory than the general public is led to suppose. Those in the know

[1] Sent under double cover. The outer envelope addressed: "Monsieur Joseph Dillon, Palace de l'Élysée, Paris"; the inner: "Sent by the Abbé Mionnet, Rome. To be handed unopened to H. E. President Poincaré in person"; followed by the Abbé's signature.

have unimpeachable information on this point from one of the Vatican doctors. In high Church circles the rule is always to look ahead and make arrangements for the future. Consequently it is the next Conclave that everyone is discussing in secret, uncertain though its date may be, and shocking though such a state of mind may seem. The great ambition of della Chiesa's party now is to make him, not Secretary of State, but Pope. If they can do that, they settle the whole problem of Merry del Val at a single stroke. They are already intriguing busily. It is assumed as certain that Merry del Val will stand and that he can count on the votes of all the *zelanti,* unless, of course, Pompili or even Gaetano di Lai play him the dirty trick of offering themselves as candidates. Della Chiesa reckons on the support of the *politicanti,* who, almost certainly, will form the majority of the Sacred College owing to the extreme line which the present Pope has pursued. But he is nervous of Maffi. Maffi's friends are urging him to stand, and he would have behind him all those Italians, whether bishops or politicians, who are trying to bring about a reconciliation between the Vatican and the civil power. What his attitude is towards France I do not know, but I suspect it of being fairly neutral. Della Chiesa himself made it quite clear to me that he was relying on French support for his candidature, and that he would know how to show his gratitude. I have ready for Your Excellency, should you wish to see it, a full and almost word-for-word account of my interview with the Archbishop of Bologna, written the evening after it took place. I was not, I must confess, very favourably impressed by the man himself. He seemed to me definitely shifty. There is nothing in him of the high breeding which marks the Secretary of State. One must not, of course, forget that his sickly appearance and physical deformity tell against him. To sum up on this, to me rather premature, matter of the next Conclave. The success of Merry del Val is by no means impossible, and, since I have managed to establish with him rather better relations than at one time seemed likely, it would, I think, be wise, while keeping in close touch with della Chiesa, not to commit ourselves so far with him as to let M. del V. conclude that we are to be regarded as definitely opposed to his own candidature. I intend, therefore, with Your Excellency's approval, should another opportunity arise for an interview with M. d. V., to make it clear to him that our attitude at any forthcoming Conclave is not yet finally determined, and that the votes which we shall be able to influence—whether of its French members or of the Italians "subsidized" by us—need not necessarily be regarded as earmarked for his opponents. That will have the effect of making him more inclined to court our friendship in the months immediately ahead, for my impression is that he is extremely anxious to become pope. At the same time it will leave us free to bring all our influence to bear, between ballots, and as a last resource, on his candidature, should it appear that he is certain of being elected without us and despite us. I feel more and more convinced that it would be the worst possible blunder for us to alienate ourselves permanently from a man of such outstanding ability whose youth makes it more or less certain that he will occupy the See of Peter for a very long time. Either we must bring him down or we must make him our friend. There is no middle way. The course I suggest would have the further advantage of lessening the ill effects should my relations with della Chiesa, by some unfortunate accident, come to light. The Cardinal would merely conclude that, quite naturally, we were playing a cautious game and sampling the various candidates *before definitely deciding on the policy to be adopted*.

And now to return to the repercussions here of the Sarajevo incident. It has caused a painful impression everywhere, and among people of all shades of opinion. Laymen in this country have, generally speaking, no more love for Servia than they have for Austria and would gladly see both countries go to the devil. But Italians have unfortunate memories in the matter of regicide, or of anything approaching regicide, and they are forced to admit that Austria's anger is fully justified, and that the idiocy of the southern Slavs has furnished her with an admirable excuse to demand satisfaction. But I am forgetting that Your Excellency must already be well informed about lay opinion and can hardly require my comments. In Vatican circles the traditional sympathy for Austria has shown itself in no uncertain manner. Servia, as an outpost of the Orthodox "heresy," need expect no kindly feelings there. If she is to be taught a salutary lesson, the Church will unhesitatingly approve—will even go so far as to look on it as a gesture of defence made on the frontiers of the Catholic world. In view of the extreme urgency of the situation I did all I could to get a further audience with M. d. V. He received me for a few moments yesterday, the 3rd of July. He spoke with indignation of the murder, and of the Servians with profound contempt as "a little nation of savages," turbulent as well as heretical, whose insolence would never cease to grow at the expense of European civilization as a whole, so long as they thought they could do what they liked with impunity. Russia, already looked at askance as the headquarters of the Orthodox heresy, as the persecutor of Catholic Poland, and as the natural protector of the Balkan schismatics, is now suspected, in addition, of harbouring dangerous political designs. It is hinted that Servia would be less insolent if she was not sure of Russian support. The Cardinal said nothing to me about France's attitude in all this. He did, however, as a parting shot, remind me of a conversation that he had had with me this winter in the course of which he pointed out that the policy of religious appeasement was by no means general in France, and that neither the results of the last elections nor the tendencies of the Government now in power were of a sort to diminish what I had referred to as the "prejudice" entertained by the Vatican against our country. Let me add that something he said in passing convinced me that he, too, regards the health of the Pope as very uncertain.

. . . .

The general opinion here seems to be that, as much for reasons of prestige as of security, Austria will feel bound to make some sort of demonstration against Servia. Most people hope that the other countries will be sensible enough to give her a free hand provided she does not overstep the limits of reasonable policy and abstains from making still worse a situation which is bad enough as it is.

. . . .

Chapter

25

MAYKOSEN SEES WILLIAM II

"Sit down, my dear fellow. I don't think you've seen my yacht before, have you? Rather lovely, eh?— beautiful lines, but as sound an ocean-going boat as you could want. I can't spare more than a few minutes. With things as they are just now, I've got to see an enormous number of people. I've put off sailing more than once already. I don't want to go far until I see how matters are shaping."

William II was dressed from head to foot in dazzling white. On the whole, he seemed to be in a gay mood. His appearance was that of a man who is preoccupied, but not to excess. He was scarcely more jumpy than usual. Before the armchair, or, rather, the chair with arms, in which he was seated, stood a table covered with maps and leaflets.

"What view do you take of the situation?" asked the Emperor.

Maykosen got ready to reply, but the Kaiser left him no time to utter so much as a word. Sharply, and in a low-pitched, rather worried voice, he put a further question:

"Do you think this was the Sect's doing?"

"Not directly, Majesty. I have the impression now that the organizations of the South have got completely out of hand. The blow was struck by one of them."

The Emperor seemed to be unconvinced.

"One can never be sure," he said.

"But, Sire," put in Maykosen quietly, "if it was the Sect, we have to assume a really monstrous complicity. Besides, why should it have done precisely that?"

William II shook his head.

"There has been a lot of talk about our meeting at Konopischt. I know that people are saying that the Archduke and I decided on war." He shrugged his shoulders (he had got into the habit of raising his "good shoulder" rather higher than the other). "I myself have been threatened. I was told that I should be murdered if I went to the funeral. There can be no doubt that it's all part of an anti-dynastic movement. These creatures want to get rid of the lot of us. To accomplish that end they don't mind whom they associate with. They make use of any revolutionaries who happen to be handy. And the revolutionaries, meanwhile, make use of them. It is an alliance of devils."

"This is a bad start," thought Maykosen. He didn't see now how to bring back the conversation into the channels he had prepared. Luckily, William II's mind took a sudden jump.

"I only hope," he broke out with a spurt of anger, "that the Tsar won't be such a fool as to support these ruffians. He must see that he's in the same boat as the rest of us. What are they saying in England?"

Maykosen declared that he had reason to believe that the murder had been universally condemned in England, but that people were hoping it would not give rise to European complications.

The Kaiser moved sharply in his chair.

"Not give rise to complications! . . . What extraordinary people they are! It's for them to see that France and Russia don't make complications. I can hardly suggest to Austria that she should turn the other cheek. As it is, I find the old Emperor's moderation quite amazing. Only yesterday I received from him another letter, couched in terms of the most admirable common sense. What do you want me to say to him? If I were in his position, plunged as he is into such terrible mourning—for it's the very head of the dynasty that has rolled in the dust—I certainly should not be so patient!"

Maykosen employed all the tact of which he was master to discover what it was that this letter from Franz Joseph had contained, and what, more generally, might be the intentions of the Austrian Government.

The Kaiser made no direct reply to his questions. Instead he banged the leather top of the table with his hand and shouted in a voice in which fury was the predominant note:

"Servia and all this scum must be taught a lesson! You're familiar with the Balkans, and you know what a worthless lot they are. But one can sometimes turn a hooligan into a policeman. Not only must Servia be taught a lesson; she must be eliminated as a factor in the political situation. Has it occurred to you that the old Emperor may die tomorrow, especially after the blow he has just received? What will happen to the Dual Monarchy with this danger left hanging on her flank? In the long run Rumania and Bulgaria may be able to help us. Meanwhile Austria must be left an absolutely free hand to punish the offender. Anything she does will be done in the interests of European peace. Of that there can be no possible doubt."

Maykosen, who knew that the Emperor could not be brought into a calmer state of mind by any frontal attack, agreed that "there could be no possible doubt." He pointed out, however, that the nations of Europe were in a very nervous state. What at all costs must be avoided was the danger of a general conflagration being started as a result of this "punishment," however justifiable such punishment might be in itself. The conditions, therefore, in which it was to be administered would be of enormous importance.

The Kaiser replied with a frown that England, where the monarchic sentiment was so strong and the love of order so marked, would hardly be likely to take up arms in defence of a regicide. Besides, the English did not want a war with Germany. He had good reasons for saying that. The same was not true either of France or of Russia. But they were not ready; both were short of heavy guns. Poincaré, who might well be credited with the worst designs against Germany, wanted to wait until his Three-Year Act should have produced results. Similarly Russia could do nothing until she had achieved some sort of internal reform and completed her system of strategic railways.

He concluded by shaking his head, slowly this time, and remarking quietly and almost with the hint of a smile:

"In two or three years they may be ready to take the risk; but not now."

As he spoke he leaned back a little in his armchair, only two feet of which remained on the ground, and began rocking to and fro. Maykosen had a view of him in profile. The Kaiser, plunged in thought, was gazing before him in the direction of a small English sporting print which hung on the wall of the cabin. His eyes looked bright between their lids; a touch of mockery showed on the lips beneath the moustache. The general impression that he gave was one of humanity; there was a sort of air of delicacy about him; he looked almost cordial. Of his charm there could be no doubt.

"Say what one may," thought Maykosen, "his personal decision's going to count for a very great deal. Well, I can but try!"

He was careful not to contradict anything the Kaiser said, but confined himself to reminding him of the increasing importance assumed of recent years at the Russian court by certain "sinister forces." Where such a pack of adventurers and cranks were in control, anything might happen.

"Not a few of them," he said slowly, so that the full meaning of each word should sink into his hearer's attention, "are fools enough to think that a war might save them from the dangers of revolution."

The Kaiser interrupted him with a remark that showed how far he was from finding such a manner of thinking wrong-headed. Maykosen felt that he had just waked in the mind of William II, precisely as he had intended to do, one of those fantastic ideas which alternated with others in the control of his imagination. The days when the Emperor despaired of bringing to a peaceful understanding the old dynasties of Europe and persuading them to accept him, of their own accord, as suzerain, he was inclined to envisage as "second best" the possibility of a short but terrible war, as a result of which the nations would get rid of the elements making for their internal unrest and restore order and authority within their borders; at the end of which, moreover, Germany, victorious of course, but magnanimous in her victory, should preside over a general reconciliation of Europe, purged, for generations to come, of its Socialists, terrorists, mysterious conspirators, regicides, and other enemies of the human race.

"If Your Majesty would permit," went on Maykosen in a tone which he hoped would awaken curiosity in his interlocutor, "I should like, in this connexion, to relate an interview which I had recently with one who is perhaps at the present moment the most dangerous revolutionary in Europe, and the most modern in his methods."

The name Lenin would have meant nothing to the Kaiser, so he did not use it, but spoke of a secret meeting in a rather "remote country," admitting that he had been able to bring it off only in return for a solemn promise that he would reveal to no one at all details of either place or person. All he could say was that, in his opinion, there was no specialist in revolution now living better qualified to speak on the subject than the individual in question.

This mysterious piece of information, leaving, as it did, a free field for the Emperor's romantic imagination, prepared him to give more weight than ever to what was coming.

Maykosen revealed the fact that, in the opinion of this eminent specialist, the best, indeed the only, way of ensuring revolution in Europe was by indulging in a general war. Maykosen summed up Lenin's arguments, being careful to present them in the most striking light possible. He added—and this was a pious invention of his own—that the revolutionary in question, who was at the head of a powerful and widespread international organization, had expressed an ardent hope that the Sarajevo business would precipitate a catastrophe.

The Emperor appeared to be deeply impressed. He rested his cheek on his hand, and stared at the ground. He believed in Maykosen, and liked him. Maykosen's opinion had greater weight with him than that of many others; greater weight, indeed, than Maykosen, never inclined to undervalue himself, suspected. This Baltic Baron had, on more than one occasion, shown evidence of possessing a gift of prophecy. This Baltic Baron had never failed him yet; had never played a dirty trick on him (and that was more than he could say of a great many people, from the Chancellor down to the most obscure journalist). This Baltic Baron had, with great ability, rendered him more than one difficult service, and had never asked a single pfennig in return. "I love and admire Your Majesty. I take the liberty of considering that Your Majesty has the best political brain of the century and is the only man capable of bringing salvation to the world. Your Majesty condescends to use me, and occasionally to make me the confidant of important schemes. I ask no other reward." Furthermore, the Emperor, sensitive as he was about the figure he cut in the eyes of his contemporaries, and profoundly responsive to a "bad press," was sincerely grateful to Maykosen for certain "excellent" articles and for the irreproachable tact with which he had always dealt with him in the leading papers of England and America.

After a long pause of silent thought, and in a very friendly tone, he said:

"My dear Maykosen, you know how very highly I think of you. You are not a German, but you are quite incapable of giving any advice to me, the Emperor of Germany, which would run counter to the interests of my country. It may be that you see things more clearly than I do myself."

"Oh, Majesty! . . ."

"Yes. . . . You meet more people, and in more varied ranks of life, than I do. You are less open to deception than I am. As a free lance, you can remain cool and impartial. What would you do in my place?"

"Since Your Majesty does me the very great honour of asking my opinion," began Maykosen, resolved to keep both his manner and his matter within strictly moderate limits, "I should try, in the first place, so to arrange matters that the punishment of Servia should be, if not decided, at least accepted by *all* the great powers; that any action taken by Austria should, so to speak, be 'authorized' by Europe."

"An international conference, eh? It would take too long. Austria would never have the patience to wait. . . ."

"Diplomatic exchanges would be quite enough."

There was a slight pause; then, in a rather lower voice, the Kaiser continued:

"And what if they fall on us in two or three years, when they have completed the encirclement of Germany and are thoroughly prepared?"

"Another of his manias," thought Maykosen, "and one that his advisers are careful to back as sound policy: the preventive war." Aloud he said:

"I implore Your Majesty not to take at their face value certain obsessions of your entourage. A circle is often broken more quickly than it is formed. As to preparedness—no one is ever 'prepared.' The most that can be said is that one is more or less prepared than one's enemy. The important thing is to convince one's enemy that he will never be more prepared than one is oneself, and that competition in armaments is therefore useless."

The Kaiser shook his head, smiled, got up, and held out his hand to Maykosen, who had also risen.

"There are many things I could say in answer to that. The situation is far from simple. But I shall think over what you have told me. If, as I hope, I go for my cruise, you must come and see me when I get back."

As he shook his hands, he added:

"You are a true friend, a true friend."

Arriving next morning in Berlin, Maykosen had an interview with a high official of the Wilhelmstrasse with whom he had long been on terms of friendship and who was well aware of the high favour enjoyed with the Kaiser by the Baltic Baron.

"You know," remarked this gentleman, "that the Chancellor, Bethmann-Hollweg, is strongly of the opinion not only that Austria ought not to communicate to the powers her intentions in regard to Servia, but that she ought, officially at least, to keep us in the dark too."

Maykosen, who remembered clearly every moment of the previous day's interview, went pale.

"But he thinks she ought to take action of some sort?"

"Certainly!"

"Does Bethmann-Hollweg want a war?"

"I don't think so."

Maykosen gave a harsh laugh. "Has he gone mad, then?"

"No . . . on the contrary, he thinks that the only chance of avoiding the interference of a third power, and, consequently, the danger of a general conflagration, lies in rapid action by Austria, and the appearance, at least, of our not being involved. It's a possible point of view. It's his opinion that neither Russia nor any of the other powers, faced with a *fait accompli,* will touch off the fuse any more than they did in '08 at the time of the Bosnia-Herzegovina affair. There will be negotiations, the usual hunt for a formula—and all the trumps will be in our hands. If we were to start by asking everybody's opinion, God knows where we should end!"

Maykosen was in a state of tense nervous excitement.

"And what," he asked, not without a hint of sarcasm, "is Vienna saying about all this?"

"You know what the Viennese are! First they want us to tell them what to do, then they're all for taking matters into their own hands. A little later they change their minds again, and later still they want to fix things up with Budapest before acting. One thing only is certain: they want to finish with Servia this time once and for all."

Chapter

26

THE GATEWAY OF HISTORY

It was only when he read in the papers that the, on the whole, conciliatory reply sent by Servia to the Austrian ultimatum of July 23 had been rejected, and that Austria, determined to prolong negotiations no further, was preparing to send an army against Belgrade, that Gurau felt the cause of peace in Europe to be finally lost.

It was Sunday morning. He had been spending the night in the avenue du Bois, with Gisèle. He confided his fears to her, and she looked at him with her great sad eyes. He felt grateful to her for not indulging in that morbid excitability which, for the last ten days, had got hold of so many people, and especially of so many women.

He put through telephone calls to as many of his political friends and colleagues as could be reached in that way. Two of them said—though it probably wasn't true—"we knew it yesterday evening." All of them, allowing for individual differences on points of detail, shared his own view of the situation: Austria had decided, whatever the cost, to make war on Servia. She was willing to take the risks, and there could be little doubt that Germany was behind her. Was it safe to assume that the Central Empires, in their present mood of fierce aggressiveness, wanted a general war? That, despite the opinions expressed by the morning papers, seemed rather less certain. But it was going to be very difficult for Russia to refuse her support to Servia, and very difficult for France to abandon Russia. In the present state of public opinion any tendency to moderation on our part would be regarded as a surrender to threats. Besides, so far from preserving peace, it would result, probably, in merely increasing the insolence of the enemy. The best that could be hoped was that some last-minute miracle would occur to solve the difficulty. Some thought that this miracle should take the form of an energetic pronouncement by France and Russia: "It's no good your trying to frighten us. If you want to fight, here we are"; others, that an intervention by England might have the necessary salutary effect. But there was a feeling abroad that both parties knew that nothing was really any good, that the hour of disaster, awaited so long and so often deferred, had sounded at last in spite of every human effort to retard it, as a result of a blind law of fatally accumulating forces and of hostile tension drawn out to its breaking-point. Both parties agreed that Poincaré's and Viviani's journey to Russia had been ill-timed—unless they had been able to make the Tsar see sense—a very unlikely occurrence—and that the sooner they returned, the better.

During the last few days Gurau had seen Jaurès more than once. Jaurès was rushing about in a mingled mood of heroic confidence and despair. In spite of everything, he refused to abandon his belief in the efficacy of popular demonstrations in all the countries involved. He expected wonders of a great meeting of the Second International which was to be held in Brussels on the 29th. Gurau, who had seen at close range how governments work, who knew only too well how little weight was attached at decisive moments by statesmen to the distant, scattered noises of the streets and the faint echoes of meetings ("How many were there? . . . Four thousand? . . . Bah! Merely a matter for the police!"), did not share the illusions of which Jaurès, perhaps half-deliberately, was the dupe. Not that he didn't admire him for doing his duty to the very end. Had he, Gurau, been at the Foreign Office, he would have done no less.

This duty, which he had been spared, of which he had been deprived, appeared now clear before his eyes in its every detail. He was conscious of the same kind of hallucination as that which leads us to go through the movements of driving a car when we are travelling as the passenger of someone less efficient than ourselves. First of all, he would have stopped Poincaré from going to Russia (there would have been no difficulty about finding excuses); would have locked him up somewhere; would have applied a soothing hand to Russia while at the same time keeping a wary eye on her, requesting her to hold herself ready while forbidding her to make the slightest gesture towards the world beyond her frontiers without first coming to a complete agreement with France. "Either that or we shall not stand by you." With England he would have kept in the closest possible touch, and proposed with her a joint representation to Germany couched in more or less the following terms: "Do you want war? If not, then let us all get round a table and talk things over. Let us take advantage of this alarm to discuss the whole wretched armament race which is landing us all in bankruptcy and will eventually, no matter what we do, result in war. . . ."

At this point in his reflections he felt unfortunately bound to ask himself a question: "Suppose, meanwhile, Austria entered Belgrade and crushed Servia. Should I have been sufficiently cool and collected to continue in the same vein? Even if I had, should I have been able to resist the attacks of the press and the fury of public opinion?—'String the traitor up! . . . On, on to Berlin, Gurau!' I should have had to reckon with a whole country in the throes of patriotic fervour. Everyone would have been at me, from the fashionables, the stock-exchange men, and the editors down to the crowds in the subway; from factory-owners and university professors to every petty workman in every petty town. That would be something very different from a miserable little meeting which is so easily ignored, which at times, indeed, can be a definite convenience, since it acts as a harmless safety valve for the dissidents, while at the same time providing the doctrinaire element with an alibi for its ideals."

A little later he was conscious, deep within himself, of another thought: "Perhaps, after all, I'm lucky not to have to shoulder the responsibility."

The same thought occurred to him with still greater force when he ventured out on the Boulevards that afternoon, about five o'clock, to "take," as the papers say, "the temperature of the Parisian crowd."

The atmosphere was a discreet but heady compromise between that of a summer afternoon and a patriotic demonstration. Along the roadway, strangely empty of vehicles, there passed from time to time small processions of young people, headed by a flag. They were singing, very much out of tune, the *Marseillaise* and the *Chant du Départ,* though in neither did they get far beyond the first few lines. They were shouting: "Long live France! Long live the Army!" and sometimes, though not often: "Down with Austria!" or "Long live Servia!" Whenever they met a soldier on leave, they made a regular ovation. There was nothing very serious about all this, but such a thing had never happened before in his experience. Outside the cafés people were applauding these processions, getting up from their chairs and joining in the shouting. Perhaps the most noticeable thing of all was that they talked among themselves. They "fraternized." In front of the bulletin boards outside the *Matin* offices a small crowd had collected, gazing at the portraits of Joffre and other generals that were pinned to them. There was little noise, but the watchers, gathered in groups, discussed the news, always in the same tone, a tone which, whatever the actual words used, meant one thing and one thing only —the passing of a "divide," the movement from one slope of a hill to the other; from the slope where men had thought: "Pray God it doesn't happen!" to the other, where they said openly to their neighbours: "The swine want it, do they? Well, then, let them have it!" A short distance beyond the *Matin* building, on the right-hand pavement, he came on a small collection of men in cloth caps—a dozen at most—who, while a patriotic procession was passing, cried, rather timidly: "Down with war!" adding almost at once: "Long live the Social Revolution!" which had the unfortunate effect of isolating them from the rest of the crowd and making their manifestation seem like something aloof and special, set apart and non-contagious.

"And Jaurès still thinks that the people of France are with him! (But does he really think so?) What would happen if he came out here and started talking? Even the members of his party who voted for him, and of whom there must be some among all these people, would pretend not to recognize him, would turn away their heads, would seem to be saying to their neighbours: 'Don't take any notice of him, that's just his way—a lot of hot air'—Peter's denial repeated again and again down the whole length of the street."

But Gurau was rapidly becoming conscious of something still more painful. He felt himself yielding to the general intoxication, the feverish delight of this public manifestation, the extraordinary emotional facility of it all. It was so simple: it was enough just not to resist; enough just to say yes; enough to replace the arduous thinking on events, the exhausting effort to appraise the situation, by a blind acceptance of the immediate future there before him, blowing on his face like a hot wind from the desert, rushing to his head, caressing him with its burning fingers, touching his lips with fiery kisses, filling his brain with visions and with ghosts. What peace in having no longer to kick against the pricks! What excitement in being able to dream confusedly of all those wonderful things that destiny would shower on him in armfuls, if only he could accept! Terrible things, cruel things, glorious things, things of an unheard-of intensity; yes, unheard-of, so intense that the very nerves would crack under the strain. That would be life at last! No threat, even for a moment, of boredom. Boredom? Get thee behind me, Boredom! Get thee behind me, age of Boredom, the long emptiness of inglorious peace. History begins today. From the shadows we emerge to set our feet in the gateway of History. And suddenly we see that History is a place of virgin soil, dazzling, burning, a sort of stretch of golden sand quivering in the sun's rays, so that the feet that touch it are burned in their passage, though he who treads there is encompassed by splendour and enthusiasm, moving in a haze of triumphant smoke. What is the pleasure of watching a great fire—the engines, the ladders, the spouting hosepipes, the crash of walls amid the flames, what the thrill of some street accident with its dead and wounded, seen perhaps once in a lifetime, compared with the daily excitements of this new adventure? No wonder that the people whose portraits adorn the history books look so happy and excited. He had never realized that History, so thrilling to read, could be so good to live! For it was good, no use denying it, and so easy to come by! It needed but the slight effort necessary to cross this almost invisible threshold, where a man's feet moved almost of their own free will. Why make all this fuss, then, about plunging into History?

Chapter

27

PORTRAIT OF FRANCE IN JULY '14

Thus it was that this nation of decent folk, of men rather badly dressed, not too well washed, and somewhat undersized, prepared to march once again into the pages of History.

The west end of Paris got ready with a bright air of gallantry. Beautiful women, crossing the Place de l'Étoile in their cars, gazed dreamily at the Arc de Triomphe. Retired colonels who had seen the war of '70 and served in the campaign of Madagascar screwed their monocles into their eyes and raised their walking-sticks in a gesture of swagger. Racecourse habitués, their grey top hats set at rather a more rakish angle than usual, made a point of discussing the favourite's chances as calmly as though their hearts were not already beating to the sound of the charge and the booming of the guns.

The farther one went towards the east, however, the more definitely did one become aware of a troubled undercurrent. One was vaguely conscious of ideas in the light of which complacency felt sick. Perhaps one was permitting them to raise their uneasy heads now for the last time, before letting one's feeling sink to the level of everyone else's, before calmly, like everyone else, crossing the threshold of a heroic age into that great echoing hall of heroisms, that side-show of freaks, both men and women, on whose behalf the newspapers were already playing the showman: "Just about to begin. . . . Fifteen wild savages in a state of nature. . . . Step up, ladies and gentlemen!"

History was no stranger to us. From the open-air restaurants of Montmartre men had already seen, in former days, the Prussian batteries spouting flame from beyond Saint-Denis or Stains. From the open-air restaurants of Belleville their fellows had watched the militiamen marching to be swallowed up in the battle of Champigny. From a certain mound near Charonne, just above the ruined buildings, anxious eyes had followed the flashes on the far slopes of Châtillon and been terrified at times by the sight of a shell crashing into some house on the left bank. Men had helped the gunners drag their pieces up the rue du Télégraphe and set them on the ramparts. Later still had come a time when changed circumstances had meant changed targets for the guns of Paris, when the foe had been no longer Prussian, but French troops marching from Versailles. But at such a distance of time the details were all confused. It sufficed for those others to remember, those crowded, indistinguishable subjects of the Kaiser, square-heads beneath spiked helmets, that they were men without fear in their hearts, ready at a word to march.

City of taut nerves. City in which the memories of History had had no time to fade, of History in its last new garb. City placed always at the point of danger. When the wind blew from the east—on summer days when the children played ball on the slopes of Romainville—it could come in a short three hours from the enemy lines, nor find its way impeded. The plain lay open to its onset; "Blow freely above my spaces," said the plain. City that must sleep always with one eye open. Strange must have been the thoughts of those who set her there, the kings of long ago; and of those others, older still, half-wild men with long moustaches and great spears and bodies swathed in skins. Farther off, in the deep heart of the land, they might have found high mountains to serve them in the place of walls. Ah, if only the kings had been cunning, had built their Paris among the slag-heaps and the mines, the Prussians might have whistled for their victory. But could anyone seriously regret the choice? Could anyone think of Paris, of the Paris of the Parisians, set among the slag-heaps and the mines? A fine thing that would have been! If things are as they are, it is because a destiny has guided them.

This exposed city, with her flank ever open to the attacks of History —again and again she has tried to clothe her nakedness with walls;

but always they have been breached—this city is where she is because a fate has set her there, and it would be ungracious to complain over-much, since there is so much beauty in her choice of a site, marked out at a meeting-place of many ways. The rivers called for her, and the open plains. The folk, wandering at first, and later settled on their lands, craved her presence. The people of the mountains found it good that their capital should be builded in a valley low and fruitful. Thinking of her, men have been ever influenced more by considera-tions of convenience, of splendour, of adornment, than of possible danger. Famous throughout the world as a place of pleasure, she has ever known a destiny of peril. At her back, wide-stretching miles rise to slow uplands; before her the plains of the north-east lie bare, so that she resembles one of those churches that we see perched on a cliff-top's farthest edge, gazing out to sea—a Notre-Dame du Péril.

And, like her metropolis, all France is a meeting-place of ways, a country ill placed for security, but proud of her post of danger and of honour, a country set on the extreme point of a lean and bony con-tinent which narrows away from the great cow's flanks of Asia until at last it fronts the Western Ocean. But though she stands at this far end of a mass of land, she is neither cabined nor confined; is neither the cul-de-sac of Europe, a backwater whither the flood of wandering folk have drifted when all other lands were full, nor an island to which men have, as it were, swum when naught but safety mattered, or when the spirit of adventurous daring drove them onwards in search of new worlds to conquer.

All the peoples who moved slowly through the centuries from east to west were bound, unless they settled elsewhere on their journey, to come at last to France. Not a race, not a wandering tribe, but some time or other found itself within her borders and stood on her high terraces above the Ocean, feeling the chill air on naked bodies, sniffing the winds that blew from far immensities, and all the damp sweetness of the gardened land. Many of them turned back again like wild beasts that, from the prison of fair meadows, long for the freedom of open spaces; but in the hearts of all of them the moist sweetness left its memory, so that, when the desire to wander seized upon them once again, it was always to these Western gardens, to these Ocean terraces, that they tried once more to come.

Vaguely France has always known of this lure she exercises, has taken thought, though casually, with herself, has felt, now and again, a passing fear of these invading strangers. Sometimes the knowledge has filled her with pride. She has found it but natural that her lands should be more constantly sought than any others of the world, nor thought it hard to pardon those who, from time to time, have disturbed her peace.

But on her perilous situation, which so often has cost her dear, she has never brooded with a dark, aggressive pride; has never said to herself: "I am the rampart of a continent; through me the world breathes in the airs of Ocean"; nor, when what was once for her "the world" became the "Old World," did she say: "The part of bastion to a continent thrust forth to meet the challenge of new lands is mine and must be mine to play alone, whatever the cost. Shamelessly have all the races of the Old World invaded my privacies, crept into my bosom, mixed the stream of their lives with mine; therefore now, tirelessly and of right, warm with their blood and avid with their greed, will I greet what is to come from worlds still young." By force and forethought she might have made of all her coastline between the Pas-de-Calais and Brittany, between Finisterre and the Pyrenees, a lurking trap, facing two ways, to catch and hold the wanderer, with, at its back, netted by roads and canals and railway lines, a land fed by skilled farmers, rich in factories laboriously installed, dotted with overcrowded harbour towns; a double-headed tentacle planted there at the far limit of Europe, into whose clutches the Atlantic must, willy-nilly, have surrendered her rich and aimless freights, her fleets of treasure ships at sea without a goal. But to accomplish such an end she would have had to pursue, through long generations, one of those great plans, at once blindly wrought yet cunningly devised, which set a seal on nature's work by forcing things to a determined shape, feeling a slow way to achievement, harnessing necessity to wily ends, leaving to chance no right but that of choosing between two or three alternative channels dug to make doubly sure that the rich waters shall flow in set courses and not escape elsewhere.

But to realize such an ambition she would have needed what she has never had, a grandiose self-seeking that never leaves a task but at completion. Obstinate she may have been, and mad at times, but of the unswerving schemer she has never shown a trace. When the delirium of glory has seized on her, it has always been with the desire to accomplish some deed islanded in History, without past or future, some enterprise envisaged against every rule of caution, and for ever at the beck and call of chance: a Europe called to arms, a young Corsican leading the nation to the world's far ends, just because, with his men from Brittany and Auvergne, he wished to build again, and on a greater scale, the realm of Charlemagne. Or it might be that suddenly she held it to be a point of honour to conquer at one blow more distant lands than Spain had ever done. But since, with the prize all but in her grasp, she grew sick of adventure, nothing of Canada has remained to her but an isle of fisher-folk, and of the West Indies but a strip of land barely large enough to flaunt her flag. Finding no satisfaction in schemes fashioned with an eye to the future, she has taken pleasure in what came her way, and, flushed with the excitement of the moment, has grown to see in passing triumphs a compensation for the longer view. She constructed the Suez Canal, and all but made its twin in Panama; but the ideal of linking her own two seas, north and south, by waterways she has obstinately regarded as a madman's dream to which never again would she set her hand. She has equipped with railways all the new countries, taking in exchange their gold, but she has never seriously considered joining Paris and the Western Ocean with what should have been the great trunk line of Europe. And with an easy negligence she still faces the wide new world, not with a string of overpeopled harbour towns fitted to draw to her the trade of all the world, but with desolate plains, and woods, and fields of vine.

Once, perhaps, in a century her pride has found a vent; but between whiles she has let it sleep, preferring the self-love that turns in upon itself. Prudent and capricious she has been by turns; more sensible than any of her neighbours, but victim, now and then, of fits of petulance. She has always been more willing to lose her money by believing in the illusions of others than by using it to back her own, which she has ever seen with too clear a vision. Economical by temperament, she has been led to waste her substance on ill-planned schemes. Intending peace, she has more than once been forced into a war by some movement that has caught her unawares.

True it is that, through the ages, samples of all the hardiest and most adventurous races of Europe have drifted into the hexagon of France, as later they were to filter across into the vast quadrilateral of America, but they never, unlike those men beyond the seas, found an empty land awaiting them. From the first they were confronted by the squat folk of the mountains already thick upon the ground, a stubborn people content to live on little, good fighters and tenacious of their rights in a land where they had settled long before anybody else. To these, the earliest inhabitants, words meant nothing. It mattered little to them that their country was the point at which all roads of the Old World met, the great assembly-ground of the West, the sea strand on which the men of countless lands could breathe free air, a terrace set above the Ocean. They cared only about holding what they had, and sending the intruders back whence they had come. And when, in their despite, the intruders stayed, it was, in their turn, to become even more sensitive than their predecessors to the call of the new homeland; to pretend that they had never known any other.

This mixture of blood has been common to all the provinces of France, but it was achieved without bitterness, and in no two places have its ingredients been exactly the same. Brittany, Normandy, Auverge, Burgundy, Gascony and Provence, all are alike in so far as all contain the product of a mixed heritage. But in some places the squat men of the mountains still form the heart of the race, having absorbed each new wave of migration, while elsewhere it is some other intruding stock that has become predominant, though never twice the same, nor in the same proportions. The one constant rule has been that each of the new peoples came soon to forget its origins. There was room for every mixture of strain, and, in places, for pockets even of the unsullied aborigines. Here and there the old blood has kept itself pure in some hidden cranny, and ten thousand years of History are seen to have been as nothing. The accidents of the land have permitted this interplay of race; have, to some extent, conditioned it by the variety of its features, its natural divisions, its watersheds, its slopes, so that in places certain arrangements have been almost automatic, while in others natural obstacles have forced life to adapt itself to the requirements of the surrounding earth.

France is a land of valleys, majestic, almost royal of contour, but not drawn on a scale of vastness. No one of them is central to the whole country, nor drains it from end to end. It is a land, too, of many mountains, easy of access, yet forming many self-contained areas. The highest of them make its frontiers and repel invasion. The great plains are few, and lie far apart, so that the mixture of races obtaining in one rarely overflows into another, and intercommunication is exceptional. This fact has led to the coexistence of many agglomerations, no one of which has remained definite for long. It is a land of many provinces, yet few small cantons shut away from the world, since, with minor exceptions in the mountain tracts, communities have been separated by obstacles rather than by imprisoning walls, while what walls there have been have never been impenetrable. Since, therefore, the soil is fruitful, many peasant communities have taken root, varying in kind, yet all, in different ways, settled and obstinate. Jostled in the course of History they may have been, but they have clung desperately to their homes, refusing, whatever legend may say to the contrary, to be uprooted. Some individuals have migrated to the cities, but they have never taken their roots with them. Now and again the ancient stock may have shown a trace of withering, but it has never been torn from its native earth.

True to the lie of the land, these peasant communities have set their boundaries, marking canton from canton, village from village, but also field from field, each man staking his claim to what would suffice him for a livelihood. No work, however hard, on the rolling plough-lands has broken the spirit of these tillers of the soil, nor has the power of overlords, sweeping like a harrow over the vast acres, dispossessed these farmers of their fields. France is a land of peasant proprietors some of whom may have been called serfs when the word was in fashion, but none of whom have ever really been slaves.

Her people come from a race of peasants who, through the centuries, have loved their tiny holdings—each district having its own methods of demarcation and enclosure, jealously held to since the first settling of the tribes. Knowing they are in matters of boundaries, great disputers in questions of division, curious in all matters of usage and strict in its meticulous observance. Ready at all times they are to listen to the law's interpreters, or to peer through spectacles at its written authority. The "Code," for them, is an animal only less attractive than the cow. They like to see lines of ownership sharp drawn, and so, to avoid injustice and, better still, to avoid inequality, they incline to make all shares the same. Privilege, the lion's part, the superior claim of the eldest born—these things are anathema to them, and similarly all rights that are not clearly based, the justification for which has been lost in the misty distances of the past and cannot be hammered out in talk around a table. In this category they include the claim of any one man to issue orders to another, to demand tithes of his produce, or to live off his labour. They are a race of small-holders, of jurists, of equal shareholders in the family estate, of free men. A race which has created the communes of France, yet has always striven to have community of ownership in as few things as possible.

These are the men who love work, so it be in their own fields and for their own advantage; who delight in the vision of the task as it emerges to the call of their tools and grows to perfection, even preferring the small profit made in the sweat of their brows, but without fear or favour, to the wage which a man must take blindly, which may come conjoined with fraud and treachery in its concealing envelope. Handymen all of them, Jacks of all trades since the days of the cave-dwellers. Still, they have had to accept the age of factories, though it went against the grain for them to do so. No people were ever less intended by nature to form part of the long stream that, morning and night, crowds the suburban thoroughfares. Work, yes —since work is man's destiny; sixteen hours a day if need be when the harvest calls—but not the slavery of the shops. To war, likewise, they will submit, since war, so they are told, is sometimes necessary— but not to the barrack yard. At the heart of the proletarian here in France has ever dwelt the essential farmer; beneath the soldier's uni- form has always beat the heart of a rebel drilled by authority and furiously resentful.

It was they who made the great Revolution, not to bring to birth some vague new world fated to end in disenchantment, but to reform injustices of ancient date, to have done, once and for all, with old wrongs, to make it possible for men to discuss everything under the sun freely around a table. They had no quarrel with their King, nor would ever have driven him from his throne and killed him had he but listened to the voice of reason and consented to be the guardian of the law and the protector of free men. Since then they have made other, smaller revolutions, partly, no doubt, because their nerves were on edge, partly, perhaps, on occasion, to satisfy a taste for violence left as a heritage from '89; but whatever the cause, it has never lain in the desire to set all things in ruin. Rather has it sprung from a longing to protest against the violation by others of a contract, to re- establish order on a firmer basis. At bottom the French peasant pro- prietor is neither a conservative nor a revolutionary. He may lose respect for institutions which have outlived their usefulness, but he sees no reason to believe that what men have never tried must neces- sarily be better than what they have always known. Anarchy he de- tests, and would rather, if it came to a choice, suffer from an excess of discipline, hoping that a chance may come later of restoring a truer balance. Law and order he does not worship, but in so far as they can justify themselves, he loves them.

When it seemed probable that the age of factories had come to stay, those whom the world now calls "proletarians" saw that they had been fooled; that the cities were poor substitutes for their native villages, that the Great Revolution had foreseen nothing of what was to come; that it had taken very few years for new masters and new abuses to arise in the place of those from which their fathers had shaken themselves free. And since they could not go back to their villages, where none knew them, they talked, like their brothers in other countries, of the possibility of making a new beginning, calling it the "Social Revolution." But no more than formerly did they wish to hurl themselves blindly into the arms of a new world. Their object was mainly that of redressing wrongs, of suppressing the policy of the lion's share and the claim of primogeniture, of re-establishing an equality of inheritance, of clothing once more in flesh and blood the essential landowner who had lain dormant beneath the skin of the proletarian.

France has long been the most lay-minded of countries, for she was the first to discover that civil society can function in its every part without the meddling of priests, and that prayers may be offered to God, morning and evening, by the member of Parliament, the chief of police, and the paterfamilias. She might well have been, too, the least religious, capable as she is, like the Chinese, of dispensing with everything that is not of this world, yet at the same time of finding this world a pleasant place in which to live. But she has always liked to take stock of things, nor has ever lacked a passion for creation and for vast, sweeping movements of the intellect, with the result that she has been able to approach God by way of the mind, to build for Him the loveliest churches in the world, and to give Him an honourable place in the great systems of her philosophy.

Furthermore, she has ever been the one country in which people of vision, with an interest in maintaining ancient privileges, have seen clearly and calmly the value of religion in the purely social scheme. Having at first decided that it would be enough to keep it alive among the masses as a quieting influence, without themselves having to submit to its unnecessary discipline, these people soon made the second discovery that, in a land where even the smallest fry were gifted with extreme subtlety of intelligence, the best way of maintaining piety among the lower orders was to give an example of it themselves. They resumed, therefore, the practices of their faith, and, as often happens in such cases, found that belief followed automatically. But since the smaller fry, with their genuine subtlety of intelligence, had, from the beginning, seen through the whole manœuvre and realized the contempt for themselves which it implied, they refused to take the sequel at its face value. Pricked to suspicion by the attitude of the clergy in every political struggle, they grew accustomed, by degrees, to looking on religion as one of those weapons employed by the possessing classes to keep them in poverty and subjection. Consequently, in the great cities and in many parts of the country men lost their faith as well as the habit of religious observance, and, finding that none of those disasters befell them which had been foretold, grew obstinate in their attitude of agnosticism. So much was this so that France became almost the only country—Italy being a bad second—in which religion was identified in men's minds with a definite political and social outlook; where, for instance, a Socialist leader who should happen to mention the name of God at a meeting would have been suspected of having lost his reason.

But it is also the one country in which religion might be taken seriously, because it is the one country in which it is quite impossible for a mind with any claim to seriousness to retain or to discover a belief in God without first asking itself whether it is being tricked by considerations of social utility, and because the natural intelligence of the French people, averse as it is to all mental slovenliness and superficial cleverness, keeps them from remaining in a state of complacent satisfaction, suspended half-way between faith and incredulity. France, indeed, has produced a peculiarly national type of mysticism, which has always been more exacting than any other, since it has never ceased to be on its guard against the hysteria of the flesh and the visions of an exaggerated sensibility.

There is no human excellence of which this people—with the mixed blood of all Europe in its veins—has not shown itself to be capable, or, at least, of becoming so. But, except in certain outstanding instances, such, for example, as literature, fashion, and the arts of the kitchen, it has rarely tried to assert itself. Too often have Frenchmen been satisfied with the mediocre, or rather with a facile and careless achievement. Every now and then, in a sudden burst of activity, they have realized that some particular department of human endeavour was important and glorious, and that it was intolerable that they should be contented to occupy a back place among its practitioners. When that has happened, suddenly, with a promptness which their rivals have found disconcerting, they have forced their way to the front, amazed to find pre-eminence, after all, so simple a matter. For instance, after long remaining satisfied to be a country well in the wake of its neighbours, in which an occasional painter of fine, if rather academic, inspiration broke through the tradition of an easy pictorial grace, France all at once decided to show the world what a genuine national school might achieve, with the result that, to the amazement of all, she has produced most of the first-rate painters of Europe for over a century. Without any apparent difficulty, painting has become a peculiarly French art, notwithstanding the fact that the Frenchman is still, of all Europeans, the least susceptible to colour. Similarly, during the last thirty years, she has grown sick of occupying an inferior place in the world of music. Without even having the time to teach her own people to sing or her village bands to play in tune, she is now well on the way to claim a monopoly in the contemporary field.

It is, therefore, as well for a man to be on his guard in describing and summing up the French nation, or in foretelling its future. A good rule, before committing himself to any statement, would be to realize that, in her case, a number of contradictory formulas are simultaneously true. In matters relating to the past, contradictions have a way of seeming natural or of escaping attention altogether. No one, for instance, finds it difficult to accept the fact that this nation of peasants, in whose veins runs the blood of a stocky mountain ancestry, should have given birth to a proud aristocracy and been the one country in the world where life for a privileged few reached its highest expression of subtlety and elegance; nor yet that a race given, above all others, to a close domesticity should have carried to perfection the arts of social intercourse, of conversation, and of fine manners. No one is surprised that these small-holders and careful tradesmen with a reputation for miserliness should, ever since the Middle Ages, have countenanced and financed so many works of mere magnificence that their country can show thousands of grandiose cities and luxurious buildings, a few dozen of which would have satisfied any of its neighbours. No one is surprised when it learns that this nation of doubters and mockers built the cathedrals and organized the Crusades; that these confirmed stay-at-homes and fastidious sensualists have waged so many wars merely to please a king or an emperor; that the inventors of patriotism, the cry of *"Vive la Nation!"* and the mania of Monsieur Chauvin could also declare themselves, almost in the same breath, to be the champions of Universal Peace and the International Republic; that a people so pleased with itself and so completely absorbed in its own affairs could more than once have set itself to preach a gospel through the length and breadth of Europe.

Preach a gospel? Yes, the worst of it has always been that, with their fatal gift for turning the moment to account, they have ever been too ready to begin the old game over again. It took them, in 1914, not longer than a week to convince themselves that if History was calling them to arms, it was as the result of no sinister concatenation of mishaps and misunderstandings, no mere interplay of the Forces of Economics and the Influences of the Powers that Be. It did not take them six days to persuade themselves that the bugles were blowing to the last great battle for Liberty, Justice, and Civilization. The voice of History, they decided, was summoning them to take a part in the supreme struggle, begun a hundred and twenty years earlier, but again and again interrupted and postponed, of Democracy against Absolutism, to join in the marshalling of the Peoples against the Kings and the Emperors. The object to be attained was not so much the defeat of the Germans and the Austrians as the striking of the fetters from their limbs. Even at the meetings and in the papers of the revolutionary Left, now that the cry of History had sounded, all references to imperialist guilt, to the joint conspiracy of the capitalist governments, to the indifference which good working-class men should show to the criminal call of patriotism, were soon seen to be out of fashion. All these over-recent cries of an academic ideology writhed like strips of tinfoil in a furnace and vanished, touching the flames with a faint and fugitive discoloration. No longer was it a question of the class war, of Socialism, of conflicting theories, but only of a Crusade, of the freeing of the Holy Sepulchre.

Eastwards, welded to the land of France, its spear-head, its terraced watch-tower on the Ocean fringe, lay the Continent. Europe, lean and bony, rich and turbulent, close-knit yet divided, one but never united, a place of Kings, of Emperors, and of Peoples. Neither the Kings, the Emperors, nor the Peoples knew really why they set such store on battle, nor for what end they fought. None of them had ever clearly viewed the miracle of this continent, nor stopped deeply to consider the more fragile miracle that had determined its position in the world. This Europe, their Europe, which had become the mother and the teacher of all the countries of the earth, the source of all thought, of all invention, the guardian of all the high secrets of mankind, was less precious to them now than was a flag, a national song, an accident of language, a frontier line, the name of a battle to be graven on a stone, a deposit of phosphates, the comparative statistics of ocean tonnage, or the pleasure of humiliating a neighbour.

And that is why, on the 1st of August, at half past four in the afternoon, Jean Jerphanion, a man sprung from the ancient stock of France, and one among the many million inhabitants of Europe, standing with his young wife beside his uncle Crouziols, heard the bell of Saint-Julien Chapteuil, a canton similar to a hundred others, sounding for the peasants of this age-old land the tocsin cry of "Mobilize!"

Jallez and Jerphanion meet by arrangement in Paris. The capital as a "magnetic field." Jerphanion's plans. His coming marriage.—Mionnet, left in the lurch by his chiefs in Paris, is summoned to an interview by Merry del Val. Manifassier sends him instructions about the photograph, but Mionnet, after his talk with the Cardinal Secretary of State, is loth to make use of it.

Life and preoccupations of Pierre de Lherm. The nature of his daydreams. His curiosity about his nephew's marriage.—Gurau hands over matters of routine to Manifassier, and lets himself enjoy the fine autumn weather. He meets Germaine, who confesses to him her interest in fortune-tellers. Mareil's attitude to the "beyond." The man covered in blood.—Germaine and Marie come together in the world of the spirit, though Marie, who has turned once more to religion, is unaware of the fact. Her pilgrimage of churches, and her gratitude to God. March.—Sammécaud, having at last discovered a true solution of the problem of existence, goes to Bruges preparatory to "living" the first chapter of a new adventure.—Champcenais takes part in a strange love scene with a woman doctor who makes him the recipient of a very curious confession.—Quinette's new role. His three corpses. He inserts an advertisement with the object of making the total up to four.

The Jerphanions' flat. Preoccupations of a householder. Jallez dines with his friends and discusses Viaur's experiments.—Jallez in London. His breach with Juliette, and discovery of the "greatest city in the world." Voyages of discovery. The journey back across the Channel. The Black Flag.—Maykosen, while in Cracow, meets a Russian revolutionary who looks like a professor, and renews an old pleasure in a fanfare of trumpets.

Macaire in love. Jallez notices the signs of boredom. Juliette goes shopping. Strange conduct of Mlle Bernardine. The Marquis pays a visit to Paulette's dressmaking establishment. Last moments of M. de Lommérie. Three young writers discuss with Allory the need for a war. Anxieties of Macaire. Mascot and Laulerque see their dream shattered. Clanricard and Mathilde at home. Freemasonry. Gurau listens while his friends talk of the rebuilding of Paris. The Saint-Papouls are worried. Mlle Bernardine among the nudes. M. de Lommérie sees the whole of his life in a single flash. Haverkamp reflects bitterly on the state of business. Champcenais watches a battery of artillery march down the Boulevards. Bernardine in a confectioner's shop. Macaire is sent flying just when he is in sight of the goal. Sammécaud at a concert. Marie discovers the Church of Sainte-Marguerite. Germaine learns that the man covered in blood is drawing nearer. Quinette and Jerphanion, each in a separate train, wrestle with problems of a technical nature. Death of M. de Lommérie.

Lenin, Jallez, Maykosen, and Gurau hear of the Sarajevo murder. Jaurès expresses his views.—Mionnet, in the course of a confidential report to Poincaré, explains the double game he is playing with Merry del Val and Giacomo della Chiesa.—Maykosen and William II.—Gurau fells that the cause of peace is lost; the comfort that comes from non-resistance to the course of events, and the intoxication of heroism.

How the honest folk of France prepare to march once more into History. Paris. France as the meeting-place of races and the epitome of Europe. The squat men of the mountains. Pride and self-love. Contradictions of the French temperament; its excellences. How the thought of war becomes transmuted into the idea of a struggle for Liberty, Justice, and Civilization.

INDEX OF CHARACTERS
SECOND INSTALMENT
Note regarding the use of this INDEX

This Index will figure at the end of every volume, and will be extended as necessary. An Index of the characters in the first five volumes will be found at the end of the fifth volume, *The Earth Trembles.*

Large roman numerals refer to the Book.

Small roman numerals refer to the chapter.

Arabic numerals refer to the page.

If there is *no page reference,* this means that the character takes part in the *whole* of the chapter indicated.

When a chapter or a page is given *in brackets,* this means that the character is involved, but does not take part personally in the action.

EXAMPLES

I, x. Refer to Chapter x, Book I, where the character plays an important role.

I, xviii, 149. Refer to page 149, Book I (Chapter xviii), where the character appears only incidentally.

II, (xi). Refer to Chapter xi, Book II; a chapter which, as a whole, involves the character, though he is not personally present.

II, xv, (391). As above; the character is involved only on page 391.

In the case of important events the reference is preceded by a brief summary of the event.

Proper names extraneous to the action, and intended to remain so, are not included in the Index.

ACADÉMIE FRANÇAISE, XI, iv.—The cause of peculiar symptoms in Allory, XI, v.—XI, xii.—An election, XI, xv.—XI, xvi, (138).—XI, (xvii).—XIII, xi, (95).

ACTION FRANÇAISE, XIII, viii.

AGNES, writes to Marc of her love for Lucien Ravenaz, of her scruples and her mental torment, XII, viii.—Marc's reply and advice, XII, (ix).—XII, x, (389). —XII, xii, (403, 409).

INDEX OF CHARACTERS

ALBÉRAND, DOCTOR, XIII, VIII, (75-6).

ALBÉRAND, GASTON, XIII, VIII.

ALBÉRAND, MADAME, XIII, VIII, (76), 79.

ALBÉRAND, MESDEMOISELLES, XIII, VIII, (76), 79-80.

ALBERTE, MADEMOISELLE, XI, XXVII. —XIV, (XVII).

ALLORY, GEORGE, his first symptoms of "Academic fever," XI, IV.—The symptoms fully developed—his day-dreams, fantasies, and recollections; Uncle Joseph, Napoleon Malaparte; "I too will be one of the Forty," XI, V.— XI, (XII).—Awaits the result of the election, XI, XV.—XI, XVI, (138).—Its terrible effect on him; his envy of the "unrecognized genius," XI, XVII.—First meetings with Bergamot; a walk at night in the Champs-Élysées; the story of Claude, XI, XVIII.— Is introduced by Bergamot to the Chessboard Club and there meets Mme Raymond(e), XI, XIX.— His first visit to the latter, XI, XX.—Begins to keep a private diary, XI, XXI.—Confesses to Mme Raymond(e) his most intimate desires, XI, XXII.—Meets Michèle and Mme de Lammermont, XI, XXIII.—His thoughts in a taxi on his way to the avenue Victor-Hugo, XI, XXV.—Is left alone with Michèle and achieves his desires, XI, XXVI.— Mme Raymond(e) tells him what happened at the avenue Victor-Hugo after his departure, XI, XXVIII.—Writes to Michèle and arranges to meet her, XI, XXX.—As a result of their walk in the Bois he falls desperately in love with her, XI, XXXI.—His private diary continued, XI, XXXII.—Tries to shoot himself, XI, XXXIII.—Michèle tells him of a plan to get her married, XII, XV. —Talks with three young writers about the coming war, XIV, XXII, 489-90.

ALLORY, MADAME, XI, V.—XI, XV. —XI, (XVII).—XI, XXI, (191).

APOLLINAIRE, GUILLAUME, dines with Ortegal, XII, (XVI).—XII, XXII, (515).

ASSISTANT AT THE BOOKSHOP IN THE ODÉON ARCADE, XI, XXIX, (265-6).

ATTACHÉ AT THE ROME EMBASSY, XII, XXIII, (519-22).

AUGUSTIN, Aurélie's son, XIV, IX, (343).

BAADER, GERMAINE, has several new ideas about her "destiny," and finds her friendship for Marthe growing warmer, XI, XII.— Meets Gurau in the rue Pauquet and talks to him about fortune-telling, XIV, XI.—Beginnings of her interest in the occult; prediction of the "man covered with blood," XIV, XII.—Her meetings with Marie in "the beyond," XIV, XIII.—Questions Mme Lysis, XIV, XXII, 505.

BABINSKY, PROFESSOR, XII, XIX,

(482).—XII, xxv, (543).—XIII, (vi).

BARRÈS, MAURICE, XI, v, (44).—XI, xxv, (227).—XII, xxii, (504).

BASTIDE, LOUIS, seventeenth in mathematics, XIII, ix.

BASTIDE, MADAME, XIII, (ix).

BASTIDE, MONSIEUR, XIII, (ix).

BENOÎT-COTRU, his sons, XI, xiii, (111-13).—XIV, xxii, (500).

BERGAMOT, brings a manuscript to Mme Raymond; his appearance, XI, iii.—XI, v, (42).—Makes advances to Allory, walks with him in the Champs-Élysées, and tells him the story of Claude, XI, xviii.—Introduces Allory into the Chessboard Club, where he tries to interest him in roulette, XI, xix.—XI, xx, (185, 187).—XI, xxii, (206).—XI, xxiii, (207-8). XI, xxxi, (280).—Goes with Michèle to see Allory in hospital, XI, xxxiii.—XII, xv, (437, 441).

BERLETTI, XIII, xxi.—XIII, xxiii, (191).

BETHMANN-HOLLWEG, XIII, xxi, (183).

BITCH IN LOVE, THE, XIV, xxii.

BLONDE, THE SHINING, XII, iv, (338-9).—XII, v, 350.

BONFIGLI, XIII, xxi.—XIII, xxiii, (191).

BOURGEOIS, LÉON, XIII, xi, (94-5).—XIV, xxiii, (512).

BOURGET, PAUL, XI, (iv.)—XI, v, (35, 44).—XI, xxv, (227).

BRESCHE DES BROONS, HERVÉ DE LA, XIII, viii.

BRIAND, ARISTIDE, XI, xvi, (137).

—XII, xxiii, (519, 522).—XIII, viii, (78).—XIII, (ix).—XIII, xiii, (110-11).—XIII, xxiii, (188).

BROTHER OF JALLEZ, THE, XI, (xi).

BROTHER OF MADEMOISELLE ALBERTE, THE, XI, xxvii.

BUCHÉ, XIV, vi, (314-15).

BÜLOW, VON, XIII, xxi, (183).

CAILLAUX, JOSEPH, XI, iv, (24).—XI, (xiv).—XI, xvi, (137).—XII, xxi, (495, 496).—XIII, xiii, (110, 111).—XIV, x, (350).—XIV, xxiii, (513).

CAMUS, DR., XI, xiii, (118).—XII, ii, (311).

CARPENTER OF CELLE, THE, XIII, xxvii, (241).

CAULET, XI, xi, (80).—XIV, xviii, (435).

CAZALIS, MADAME, XI, xii, (107).

CAZALIS, MATHILDE, XI, viii, (72).—Laulerque makes certain proposals, XI, x.—Nervously goes to her first meeting with her lover, XI, xii.—Confides in Sampeyre and asks his advice, XII, xxiv.—Married to Clanricard, XIV, xviii, (435-6).—See also CLANRICARD, MATHILDE.

CERCOTTE, MADAME, XIV, xiii, (370-1).—XIV, xiv, (372).

CHALMERS, in the bosom of his family, XI, (xi).

CHAMPCENAIS, HENRI DE, XI, (xvi).—Hunts for Baudelaire's forbidden poems on his way to an interview with Senator Testevel, XI, xxix.—XIII, xi, (100).—

XIV, x, (349).—XIV, xiv, (377).
—XIV, xv, (390).—His hour of
love with a woman doctor, and
their confidential conversation,
XIV, xvi.—Watches a battery of
artillery marching down the
boulevard des Italiens, XIV, xxii.
500–2.

CHAMPCENAIS, MARC DE, XIV,
(xiv).

CHAMPCENAIS, MARIE DE, XI, xxix,
(268).—XIV, (xiii).—Her return to religion, and the new
pleasures it brings her, XIV, xiv.
—XIV, xv, (383, 385).—Discovers the Church of Sainte-Marguerite, XIV, xxii, 504–5.

CHAMPEAUX, HENRY, XIII, xxvii,
(233).

CHARLES, XII, (viii).—XII, (ix).

CHESSBOARD CLUB, XI, iii, (14, 15,
20).—Bergamot introduces Allory as a visitor; its atmosphere
and members, XI, xix.—A
"world apart" for those who frequent it regularly, XI, xxiii,
(214–16).—XI, xxxi, (274–5).

CHIESA, GIACOMO DELLA, XIII,
(xxiv).—XIII, xxx, (277).—
XIV, x, (350–1).—XIV, (xxiv).

CHILDREN OF AGNES, THE, XII,
(viii).—XII, ix, (385–6).

CHIQUETTE, XI, xxiv, (217).

CHURCH, THE, XIII, (vii).—XIII,
(xviii). — XIII, (xx). — XIV,
(vii).

CLANRICARD, XI, viii, (72).—XI,
xii, (107, 109).—XII, (xxiv).—
XIII, ix, (83–4).—Married to

Mathilde, XIV, xviii, (435–6).
—XIV, xix, (452).—Discusses
Laulerque with Mathilde and
thinks about Freemasonry, XIV,
xxii, 492–4.

CLANRICARD, MATHILDE, née CA-
ZALIS, XIV, xix, (452).—XIV,
xxii, 492–3.—See also CAZALIS,
MATHILDE.

CLAUDE, XI, (xviii).—XI, xx,
(187).—XI, xxxi, (280).—XII,
xv, (437).

CLAUDEL, PAUL, XII, xvi, (445).

CLEMENCEAU, XI, xiv, (132–3).—
XI, xvi, (137).—XIII, xx, (174).

CLISSON, ODETTE, Jerphanion
speaks of her to Jallez, XIV,
iii).—XIV, ix, (346–7).—See
also JERPHANION, ODETTE.

COCHIN, DENYS, XIII, i, (ii).—
XIII, ii, (16).

COLLEAGUE OF JERPHANION'S, A,
XIII, xiv, (114).

COTINESCU, dines at the de Fontmonges'; his anecdotes, XIII, xx.
—XIII, xxiii, (191).

COURSON, FRANÇOIS, XI, xiv, (129).
—XII, xxi, (495, 496, 497).—In-
forms Manifassier how things are
going at Rome, XII, xxiii.—XIII,
i, (3, 5).—XIII, v, (36).—XIII,
xvi, (120).—XIII, xvii, (131,
135).—XIV, vi, (315).

COURTELINE, GEORGES, XI, (xv).—
XI, xvi, (138).

COUSIN OF MARGARET, THE, XI,
(vi).—XI, vii, (61).

CROUZIOLS, PIERRE, described; his
way of life, his preoccupations,

his dreams; interest in his nephew's marriage, XIV, ix.—XIV, xxvii, 549.

CUSTODIAN OF THE ARCHIVIO SEGRETO, THE, XIII, xix, 161.

DANIEL, ABBÉ, XIV, xxii, (485).

DAVID, CLÉMENTINE, XI, (v).—XI, xxi, (193).

DAVID, UNCLE JOSEPH, as theme of one of Allory's "mental panoramas," XI, (v).—XI, xxi, (193).

DAVID (the tax-collector), XI, (v).

DELCASSÉ, XI, xiv, (126, 133).— XI, xvi, (137).—XII, xxiii, (522).

DESBOULMIERS, XIV, xv, (394).

DESCHAUMES, dines out, XI, xxvii. —See also QUINETTE.

DIDIER-VIGNAC, SABINE, XII, viii, (380).

DIDIER-VIGNAC, SOLANGE, XII, viii, (380–2).—XII, ix, (385).

DOCTOR, MME RAYMOND'S, XI, (11).

DOG, THE YELLOW, XIII, xix, 158.

DOGS IN LOVE, XIV, xxii.

DOUGÉRIN, MONSIGNOR, XIII, vii, (65).—XIII, xvii, (138).—XIII, xx, (169).—Dines at Fagiano's with Monsignor Z— and Mionnet, XIII, xxii.

DOUMER, PAUL, XIII, xi, (101).— XIII, xx, (174, 175).

DRESSMAKER OF CELLE, THE, XIII, xxvii, (241).

DUC OR DUCLE, XIII, viii, 76–80.

DUCATELET, PROFESSOR, XII, ii, (311).

DUFOUR, MADAME, XII, xxii, (512, 515).

DUPUY, PAUL, XI, xi, (78).

DUROURE, LIEUTENANT-COLONEL, review in the *Temps* of his pamphlet "The Army and the Next War," XIII, (xii).—XIV, x, (348–9).

EDDINGS, XIII, xxx, (278).

EDITOR OF THE "PARIS-JOURNAL," XII, xxii, (499).

EDMÉE, XI, v, (38).—XI, xvii, (139).

ELIPHAS, MADAME, XIV, xii, (362).

EMPUIS, MADAME, XIII, xxvii, (241).

ENAULT, LOUIS, XI, v, (35–6).

ESPARS, MADAME DE L', XI, xii, (105).

ETIEMBLE, XIV, xix, (453).—XIV, xxii, (484).

ETIENNE, XIII, xi, (101).—XIII, xiii, (111).

ETIENNE (footman at the de Saint-Papouls'), XIV, xxii, (486).

EUGÉNIE (the princess), Sammécaud on his way to meet her in Bruges; her arrival, XIV, xv.

EZZELIN, JULIETTE, her letter to Jallez while he is in Cologne, XII, (xxii).—See also VÉRAND, JULIETTE.

FAGUET, EMILE, XI, v, (30–1, 42, 44).—XI, xii, (104).—XI, xvii, (141).—XII, xv, (431).

FAMILY, THE CHALMERS, seen as a collective monster, XI, (xi).

INDEX OF CHARACTERS

FATHER OF PAOLINA, XIII, xxv.

FONTMONGE, BARON DE, XIII, VII, (65).—Meets Mionnet and gives him some advice, XIII, XVI.— XIII, (XVII).—XIII, XVIII, (140). —Invites Mionnet to dinner, XIII, xx.—XIV, IV, (305-6).

FONTMONGE, BARONESS DE, gives a dinner-party, XIII, xx.

FONTMONGE, MADEMOISELLE DE, described, XIII, xx.

FONTMONGE (the son), XIII, xx.

FRANCE, in July 1914, XIV, XXVII.

FRANCE, ANATOLE, XI, V, (44).— XII, XI, (395).

FREEMASONRY, XII, XXIII, (518).— XIII, III, (20, 21).—XIII, XXVI, (220).—Atmosphere of a lodge night, XIV, XXII, (493-4).

GENEVIÈVE, XII, XXII, (512, 515).

GENTILCŒUR, XI, XI, (86).—XII, XVI, (443).

GENTILCŒUR, MADAME, XI, XIII, (117).

GEOFFROY, makes representations to Manifassier similar to those which were discussed between them during the autumn of 1911, XI, XIV.—XII, XXI, (496).—XIV, XXIII, (513).

GEORGETTE, XIV, (XVI).

GIGNOUX, RÉGIS, XIV, XVIII, (439).

GINORINI, introduces himself to Mionnet, offers him an alleged photograph of Merry del Val, and tells him the story of Mac-Wrench, XIII, xxx.—XIV, (IV). —XIV, VI, (314-15).—XIV, VII, (323).

GODORP, GISÈLE, founds a salon in the hope of helping Gurau with his career, XI, XII.—XI, XIV, (131-2).—XII, (XXI).—XIII, II, (16).—XIII, IV, (28-9).—XIV, X, (353).—XIV, XXII, (494).— XIV, XXIII, (511).—XIV, XXVI, (529).

GOLDBERG, XIII, xx, (169).

GONZALEZ, XII, XVI, (447-8).

GUARDIAN OF THE BITCH, THE, XIV, xx, 503-4.

GUERASSIMOV, XIV, (XXI).

GUILLAIN, XIII, (XI).

GURAU, MAXIME, XI, IV, (24).— Focus of, and reason for, Gisèle's sudden worldliness, XI, (XII).— Is he going to resign and so bring down the government? XI, (XIV).—XI, XVI, (137).—Lives up to Manifassier's idea of him— with a difference, XII, (XXI).— XII, (XXIII).—Confides to Poincaré his anxieties about Rome and asks advice of the Comte de Mun, XIII, I.—Sounds the Marquis de Saint-Papoul, XIII, II.— XIII, (III).—XIII, IV.—Dines with Mionnet at the Saint-Papouls', XIII, V.—Asks Jaurès whether he ought to accept the Foreign Office; their long conversation, XIII, XI.—XIII, XIII, (110-11).—XIII, XVI, (129).— XIII, XVII, (131).—XIII, XXIII, (188-9).—XIII, xxv, (206-7).— XIV, IV, (308).—XIV, VI, (313). —Gives instructions to Manifassier and goes for a walk on a fine autumn morning, XIV, X.—

Meets Germaine Baader, who tells him of her interest in the occult, XIV, xi.—XIV, xii, (359).—Talks at Mme Godorp's of improvements in Paris, XIV, xxii, 494-5.—Hears of the assassination of the Archduke and discusses the news with Jaurès, XIV, xxiii.—Feels that the cause of peace in Europe is lost, and yields to the intoxication of History, XIV, xxvi.

GUYARD, ROMUALD, discusses with Isabelle the subject of her "permanent" client, XI, xxiv.—Accepts, with Isabelle, an invitation to coffee from the Le Burec family, XI, xxvii.—His thoughts as he waits for Isabelle at a dance-hall, XI, xxxiii.

H., ARCHDUKE, is he the chief of the Sect? XIII, xxvi.—XIV, xxiii, (511).

HACHENARD, DR., expresses enthusiasm for Viaur's experiments, advises him, and arranges to be present at his tests, XII, xxv.—Helps Viaur to stage a demonstration in his laboratory for the benefit of two medical pundits, XIII, vi.—Helps again at a public lecture in a medical school, XIII, xxvii.

HAVERKAMP, FRÉDÉRIC, buys a factory at Limoges; his financial difficulties; consults Dr. Viaur, XI, xiii.—XIII, viii, (74-5, 78).—XIV, xv, (390).—Is depressed about business prospects, XIV, xxii, 499-500.

JALLEZ, PIERRE, receives a letter from Jerphanion, who is stationed at Reims, XI, (viii).—Replies to Jerphanion, telling him of his work and his manner of life; dinner in the bosom of the Chalmers family, XI, xi.—XI, (xvi).—Describes to Jerphanion a visit to Ortegal, XII, xvi.—Writes to Jerphanion from the Rhineland and gives him his views on the Alsace-Lorraine question, etc. Receives a letter from Juliette. His thoughts as he wanders about Cologne, XII, xxii.—Receives a letter from Jerphanion on "modern youth," XIII, (xiv).—Parts of his reply, XIII, xv.—Meets Jerphanion again in Paris during the summer of 1913, XIV, i.—Asks him about his plans, XIV, ii.—Hears of his forthcoming marriage, XIV, iii.—XIV, ix, (344).—Dines for the first time with the Jerphanions; is shown over their flat; his reflections; talks about Viaur, XIV, xviii.—Arrives in London and sends a letter to Juliette breaking off his relations with her; his method of discovering London, XIV, xix.—Crossing the Channel on his way home; Boredom, XIV, xx.—Observes the faces in the subway, XIV, xxii, 482-3.—Hears, at Rotterdam, of the assassination of the Archduke, XIV, XXIII.

JANITRESS AT 142A FAUBOURG SAINT-DENIS, THE, XIV, (XVII).

JANTEAUME, PROFESSOR, attends a demonstration of Viaur's, XIV, VI.

JAURÈS, JEAN, XI, XIV, (126).—XII, XI, (395).—XII, XXI, (496).—Consulted by Gurau; their conversation; "Are we still a democracy?" XIII, XI.—His views on the Sarajevo assassination, XIV, XXIII.—XIV, XXVI, (530, 532–3).

JERPHANION, JEAN, writes to Jallez from Reims; his views on officers, military discipline, and cathedrals, XI, VIII.—As seen by Private Mouillevin, XI, (IX).—Hears from Jallez, XI, (XI).—XI, XII, (107–9).—Fragment of a letter from him to Jallez, XI, XVI.—Goes to a love tryst, XI, XXXIII.—Recèives a letter from Jallez, XII, (XVI).—And another one about Germany, XII, (XXII).—XII, (XXIV).—Writes to Jallez on "modern youth," XIII, XIV.—Receives Jallez's answer, XIII, (XV).—Meets him again in Paris during the summer of 1913, XIV, I.—Discusses his plans, XIV, II.—And his approaching marriage, XIV, III.—Helps his uncle, Pierre de Lherm, with the harvest, XIV, IX.—Entertains Jallez for the first time in his flat; questions him about Viaur's theories, XIV, XVIII.—XIV, XIX,

(452, 457).—XIV, XXII, (482–3).—Thinks about the spark-plugs of his car, XIV, XXII, 506–7.—XIV, XXVII, 549.

JERPHANION, ODETTE, née Clisson, plays the hostess to Jallez; her housewifely preoccupations; her interest in intellectual discussion, XIV, XVIII.—XIV, XIX, (452).—XIV, XXII, (506).—XIV, XXVII, 549. See also CLISSON, ODETTE.

JESUITS, THE, XIII, III, (20–1).—XIII, XIX, (165–6).—XIII, XXII, (187).

KARL, MONSIEUR, XIV, XXII, (490–2).

KATCHOWSKY, XII, XVI, (448).—XIII, XXVIII, (248).

KREUZ, MARGARET-DESIDÉRIA, tells Laulerque of her approaching departure, XI, VI.—XI, (VII).

LACCHINI, MADAME, described; welcomes Mionnet, XIII, XVII.—XIII, XIX, (164).—XIII, XX, (169).—Gives a dinner and evening party to which Mionnet is invited, XIII, XXI.—XIII, XXIX, (266).—XIII, XXX, (269, 276).—XIV, (IV).

LACCHINI, MONSIEUR, XIII, XVII.—XIII, XIX, (164).—XIII, XX, (169).—XIII, XXI.—XIII, XXIX, (266).—XIII, XXX, (269, 276).—XIV, (IV).—Tells Mionnet that Merry del Val wishes to see him, XIV, V.

LADY OF MONTE CARLO, THE, XI,

XXIII, (212).—XI, XXXI, (275).

LAFEUILLE, PIERRE, XII, XXI, (493).
—XIV, XV, (390–1).

LAMBERT, introduces Wazemmes to the Action Française, XIII, VIII.

LAMBRON DE CRAUZE, VICOMTESSE, XI, XII, (93–7).—XIII, II, (16).

LAMMERMONT, COMTESSE DE, her circumstances; introduced by Mme Raymond to Allory, XI, XXIII.—XI, (XXV).—Plays backgammon with Mme Raymond while Allory is with Michèle, XI, XXVI.—XI, (XXVIII).—XI, (XXX).—XI, (XXXI).—XI, XXXII, (281).—XI, XXXIII, (290).—XII, (XV).

LAMMERMONT, MICHÈLE DE, introduced to Allory at the Chessboard Club; her appearance, XI, XXIII.—XI, (XXV).—Shows Allory a collection of butterflies, XI, XXVI.—XI, (XXVIII).—Allory writes apologizing for his behaviour and asking her to meet him, XI, (XXX).—She walks with him in the Bois and forgives him, XI, XXXI.—Unknown to herself, figures for him as Queen of the Underworld, XI, (XXXII).—Goes to see Allory in hospital, XI, XXXIII.—Tells Allory that she is probably going to get married, XII, XV.

LAPIERRE, DENISE, XII, IV, (339, 343). — XII, V, (348–50). — Spends an evening with Viaur in the gardens at Celle, XII, XVIII, (474–6).—XII, XXV, (539–40).— XIII, VI.—XIII, XXVII, 240.

LARICHE, COMTE, elected to the Academy, XI, XV.—XI, XVI, (138).—XI, XXI, (193).

LAULERQUE, ARMAND, learns of Margaret's approaching departure, XI, VI.—Goes shopping, XI, VII.—Makes certain proposals to Mathilde, XI, (X).—XI, (XII).—XII, (XXIV).—Urged by Mascot to sever his connexion with the "Organization," XIV, XXII, 490–2, (492–3).

LAVARDAC, JEANNE DE, XI, VIII, (65).

LAVARDAC, ROBERT DE, XI, VIII, (65).

LAVOLLÉE, ÉTIENNE, XI, IV, (23).—XI, V, (29, 30–1).—As seen by Mme de Ruje, XI, XII, (104–5).—XI, (XV).—XI, XVI, (138).

LEBAIGUE, MONSIGNOR, XIII, (V).—XIII, VII, 68–70.—XIII, X, (90).—XIII, XVI, (120).—XIII, XVII, (138).

LEBRUN, ALBERT, XI, XIV, (122).

LE BUREC, EUGÉNIE, called NÉNETTE, behaves with doubtful taste, XI, XXVII.

LE BUREC, MADAME (Popaul's wife), XI, XXVII.

LE BUREC, PAUL, called POPAUL, his habits and appearance; acts as host to Romuald and Isabelle, XI, XXVII.

LE BUREC (the father), XI, XXVII.

LE BUREC (the young brother), XI, XXVII.

LEHEUDRY, AUGUSTIN, XIV, (XVII).

LEJARS, XII, VII, (367).

LEMAÎTRE, JULES, XI, V, (36, 44).

INDEX OF CHARACTERS

LENIN, explains to Maykosen, at Cracow, how revolutions are started, XIV, xxi.—Learns, at Zakopane, of the Sarajevo murder, XIV, xxiii.—XIV, xxv, (525).

LEVISSON, JAN, XIII, (xxviii).

LÉVY, LÉON, XI, xiii, (111, 115).

LIBRARIAN AT THE VICTOR EMMANUEL LIBRARY, XIII, xix, (163). —XIII, xxiii, (191).—XIII, xxix, 263–5.

LIBRARIAN OF THE SANT' ANSELMO LIBRARY, XIII, xix, (160).

LOMMÉRIE, MONSIEUR DE, is very seriously ill; his thoughts during his last moments; his death, XIV, xxii.

LOMMÉRIE, ROLAND DE, XIV, (xxii).

LONDON, "the greatest city in the world," XIV, xviii, (437–9).— Discovered by Jallez; its sensation of density; its suburbs, XIV, xix.

LYSIS, MADAME, XIV, xi, (358).— XIV, xii, (367–8).—Sees the "spirit" of Marie standing behind Germaine, XIV, xiii.—XIV, xxii, 505.

M—, visited by Mionnet for forty-eight hours during the winter of 1913, XIII, vii.

MACAIRE, takes enormous risks in order to win the bitch's heart, XIV, xxii.

MACWRENCH, XIII, xxi, (184).— Object of prolonged research by Mionnet, XIII, (xxix).—Gino-

rini's account of him, XIII, (xxx).—XIV, (iv).

MAGLOIRE, DOM CHARLES, XIII, vii, (69–70).—XIII, (xvii).— XIII, xviii, (140).—Takes a fancy to Mionnet and acts as his guide; his ideas, XIII, xix.—XIII, xx, (169).—XIII, xxiii. (191).— XIII, xxix, (263).

MAID OF M. DE FONTMONGE, XIII, xvi, (125).

MAIEUL, FRANÇOISE, seriously ill, XIII, ix.

MAIEUL, MADAME, at her daughter's bedside, XIII, ix.

MAILLECOTTIN, EDMOND, XI, xxiv, (217).

MAILLECOTTIN, ISABELLE, discusses with Romuald matters of common concern and plans for the future, XI, xxiv.—Goes with Romuald to see the Le Burec family and criticizes them severely, XI, xxvii.—Meets Romuald at a dance-hall, XI, xxxiii.

MALAPARTE, NAPOLEON, his significance in Allory's past, XI, (v). —XI, xvii, (140–1).

MANGUY, Vicar-General, XIII, vii, (66).

MANIFASSIER, LÉON, on his way to the British Embassy meets Geoffroy, who asks for his good offices with Gurau; their joint visit to Mme Godorp, XI, xiv.—Coming back from Touraine by train reflects sadly on Gurau's changed attitude, XII, xxi.—Courson talks to him about the position of affairs at Rome, XII, xxiii.—XIII,

I, (3).—Makes contact with Mionnet, XIII, IV.—Dines at the Saint-Papouls', XIII, V.—XIII, XVI, (120).—XIII, XVII, (130–1). —XIII, XVIII, (140).—XIII, XXIII, (188–9).—XIII, XXV, (206–7).— XIII, XXIX, (269).—XIV, (IV). —Sends Mionnet instructions in the matter of the photograph, XIV, VI.—XIV, (VIII).—Takes his orders from Gurau, XIV, X.

MARCEL, gives Mme Raymond cause to be anxious about his health, XI, II.—XI, III.—XI, XIX, (184).

MAREIL, HENRY, XI, XII, (100).— XIV, XI, (355).—His attitude towards the occult, XIV, (XII).

MARILHAT, XIV, XVII, (421).

MARQUENART, XIII, XXVII, (235–7).

MARQUIS, XIV, XI, (354).

MARTHE, XI, XII, (101).

MARTIN, XII, I.—XII, II, (305).— XII, III, (322).—XII, IV, (332–3).—XII, XVII, (453).—XII, XVIII, (471, 474).

MASCOT, tells Laulerque that he is going to leave the "Organization," XIV, XXII, 490–2.

MASSON, FRÉDÉRIC, XI, IV, (24–5).

MASSON, SIMONE, XI, XII, (93, 95).

MAURRAS, CHARLES, XIII, (XI).

MAYKOSEN, ALFRED, sends William II a long report on the internal situation of France after Poincaré's election to the Presidency, XIII, XIII.—Sends a further report on the foreign policy of Italy, the attitude of the Vatican, and the nature of the "Organization," XIII, XXVI.—Meets Lenin at Cracow; the cathedral fanfare, XIV, XXI.—Learns while at Monnickendam of the murder of the Archduke, XIV, XXIII.—Has an interview with William II on the Imperial yacht, XIV, XXV.

MAZOYER, XI, V, (50).

MERRY DEL VAL, a cause of anxiety to France, XIII, (I).—XIII, IV, (29).—XIII, V, (39–42).— XIII, XVII, (135).—XIII, (XVIII). —XIII, (XIX).—XIII, (XX).— XIII, (XXI).—XIII, XXII, (186). —XIII, (XXIII).—His origins and upbringing; beginnings of his success; his relations with the Vatican and with the German party; his private life, XIII, (XXIV).—XIII, (XXVI).—XIII, (XXIX).—The photograph and the MacWrench affair, XIII, (XXX).—XIV, IV, (307).—Summons Mionnet to an interview, XIV, (V).—XIV, VI, (315).—Receives him in his rooms at the Vatican; described, XIV, VII.— XIV, X, (351).—XIV, (XXIV).

MÉZAN, COMTE DE, discusses his rumoured connexion with the Jesuits; gives Saint-Papoul news of Mionnet, XIII, III.

MILANDIER, XII, IV, (335).—XII, XXV, (544).

MILLERAND, ALEXANDRE, XIII, XI, (101).

MIONNET, ABBÉ, XIII, (III).— Saint-Papoul sounds him as to

his willingness to undertake an unofficial mission to Rome, and puts him in touch with Manifassier, XIII, IV.—He dines with the Saint-Papouls; receives instructions from Poincaré, XIII, v.—His trip to M—; is called on by the Abbé Robert, XIII, VII.—Arrives in Rome and looks for a hotel, XIII, x.—His first impressions of Rome; his wanderings; he calls on M. de Fontmonge, XIII, XVI.—Pays his first call on the Lacchinis, XIII, XVII.—Spends a long morning in the Vatican Museum and reflects on the former greatness of the Church; "Save Merry del Val," XIII, XVIII.—Introduces himself to Dom Charles Magloire, who constitutes himself his guide, XIII, XIX.—Dines at the de Fontmonges', XIII, xx.—And also with the Lacchinis, XIII, XXI.—His meeting with Monsignor Z— and Monsignor Dougérin at Fagiano's, XIII, XXII.—Receives a questionnaire from Poincaré, XIII, XXIII.—Replies to it in a long report, XIII, XXIV.—Takes a walk on the Palatine and meets the "scagnozzo," who introduces him to Paolina, XIII, xxv.—Embarks on investigations in various libraries on the subject of the MacWrench affaire, XIII, XXIX.—Is accosted by Ginorini, who importunes him to buy a curious document, XIII, xxx.—Writes to Manifassier about the photograph, XIV, IV.—Is summoned to an interview by Merry del Val, XIV, v.—Receives fresh instructions from Manifassier, XIV, VI.—Is received by Merry del Val at the Vatican, XIV, VII.—XIV, VIII.—XIV, (x).—Sends a confidential report, dated July 4, 1914, to Poincaré; the Sarajevo murder; della Chiesa and the next Conclave, XIV, XXIV.

MIRAUD, VICTOR, XIII, VIII, (78).

MISTRESS OF ORTEGAL, XII, (XVI). —XIII, XXVIII, (246).

MODEL, ORTEGAL'S, XIII, XXVIII.

MOËVRE, COMTESSE DE, XI, XII, (97).

MONK AT THE MONASTERY OF SANT' ANSELMO, THE OLD, XIII, XIX.

MONTAGNINI, MONSIGNOR, XIII, (xx).

MONTECH, MONSIEUR DE, XIII II, (16).

MOTHER OF MADAME RAYMOND, XI, II.—XI, III.

MOTHER OF PAOLINA, XIII, xxv.— XIII, xxx, (267).

MOUILLEVIN, PRIVATE, extract from one of his letters, XI, IX.

MUN, COMTE ALBERT DE, XIII, I.— XIII, II, (15–16).—XIII, v, (39).

NANTHIAT, gives advice to Haverkamp, XI, XIII, (113).—XIV, XXII, (500).

OHNET, GEORGE, XI, v, (36).

OLD MAN OF THE RUE DAILLOUD, XIV, XVII, (419, 424).

"ORGANIZATION, THE," XI, (VI).—
As reviewed by Maykosen, XIII,
(XXVI).—XIV, XXII, (490–2).—
XIV, XXIII, (511).

ORTEGAL, his studio, his mistress,
his character, and his art; the
"Ortegal mystery," XII, (XVI).
—At work; his career; the distorting mirror; the fan; the free
play of genius, XIII, XXVIII.

PAILLETON, DR., XII, IV, (335–7).
—XII, VII, (372).—XII, XVIII,
(474).—Lunches with Viaur and
expresses his views on nervous
diseases, XII, XIX.—Examines
Vidalencque, XII, XX.—XII, XXV,
(539, 543).—XIII, VI, 45.

PAMS, XII, XXIII, (518).

PAOLINA, XIII, XXV.—XIII, XXIX,
(266).—XIII, XXX, (267).

PARENT, SOPHIE, XIV, (XVII).

PARENTS OF JALLEZ, THE, XI, VIII,
(64).—XI, (XI).

PARIS, as a magnetic field, XIV,
(I).—As a threatened capital,
XIV, XXVII, (535–7).

PAULETTE, XIV, XXII, 486–7.

PÉGUY, CHARLES, XIII, XI, (94).

PÉREZ, XIV, VII, (328).

PÉRIER, DR., attends Françoise
Maieul, XIII, IX.

PERRELAUD, OCTAVE, XIV, XXII,
489.

PERRIN, JEAN, XIV, XVIII, (441,
444).

PÉTIAUX, XII, II, (308–10).

PICHON, XIII, XXV, (206–7).—XIV,
X, (350).

PIUS X, XII, XXIII, (527).—XIII,
(I).—XIII, IV, (29).—XIII,
(XVII).—XIII, (XIX).—XIII,
(XX).—XIII, (XXI).—XIII, XXII,
(185, 186).—XIII, (XXIII).—His
relations with Merry del Val;
his election; his lack of interest
in politics, XIII, (XXIV).—XIII,
XXX, (278).—XIV, (XXIV).

POINCARÉ, RAYMOND, arranges his
future and embarks on a polit-
ical flirtation with Gurau, XI,
(XIV).—PrimeMinister,XI,(XVI).
—His ambitions, XII, (XXIII).—
Warned by Gurau about the po-
litical activities of the Vatican,
XIII, I.—XIII, (II).—XIII, (III).
—XIII, (IV).—XIII, (V).—XIII,
VII, (58).—XIII, VIII, (71).—
XIII, X, (91).—XIII, (XI).—
XIII, (XIII).—XIII, XVI, (129).
—XIII, XVII, (131).—His ques-
tionnaire on the subject of Merry
del Val, XIII, (XXIII).—XIII,
XXIV, (204).—XIII, XXV, (206–7).
—XIII, XXVI, (220).—XIII, XXIX,
(261).—XIV, IV, (308).—XIV,
VI, (313).—XIV, (X).—XIV,
XXIII, (511–16).—XIV, (XXIV).
—XIV, XXV, (523).—XIV, XXVI,
(530).

POISSON, OCTAVE, XIII, VIII.

PORTER AT THE HOTEL IN BRUGES,
XIV, XV, 395.

PROFESSOR OF MATHEMATICS AT THE
COLLEGE OF CHAPTAL, XIII, (IX).

PUJAC, XIII, XXVII, (232).

QUINETTE, at a dinner party, XI,
XXVII.—His career since 1908; his
anxieties; his progress; his search

for another victim, XIV, XVII.—
On the way to his little house at
Bièvres, XIV, XXII, 505–6.

QUINGEY, MADAME DE, XIV, IV,
(304).

QUINGEY, MONSIEUR DE, XIII, VII,
(66).

RAVENAZ, DR. LUCIEN, XII, (VIII).
—XII, IX, (384, 386–7).

RAVENAZ, MADAME, XII, (VIII).

RAYMOND or RAYMONDE, MADAME,
at home, XI, II.—Her visitors,
XI, III.—Meets Allory at the
Chessboard Club, XI, XIX.—Is
visited by him and makes cer-
tain suggestions, XI, XX.—Ap-
pears in Allory's private diary as
Mme X, XI, (XXI).—Gives her
mind to Allory's case, XI, XXII.
—Introduces Michèle to him, XI,
XXIII.—XI, (XXV).—Plays back-
gammon with the Comtesse de
Lammermont, XI, XXVI.—Tells
Allory what happened after he
had left the avenue Victor-Hugo,
XI, XXVIII.—XI, (XXXI).—XI,
XXXII, (281).—XII, XV, (433,
441).

REGNIER, HENRI DE, XI, V, (29).
—XI, XII, (104).

ROBERT, ABBÉ, gives Mionnet a
curious warning, XIII, VII.—
XIII, XX, (176).

ROBERTET, PROFESSOR, attends Viaur's demonstration, XIII, VI.

ROME, Mionnet's arrival, XIII, X.—
His first walks; the hills; the
modern city; the Vatican, XIII,
XVI.—Mionnet visits the Vatican,

XIII, XVIII.—XIII, (XIX).—The
Palatine; the dust of history and
the green of trees, XIII, XXV.—
XIII, (XXVI).—XIV, VII.

ROSTAND, EDMOND, XII, XII, (401).

ROTHWEIL, LÉON, dreams of the
delights of antiquity, XI, XXXIII.

ROUJON, XI, V, (27, 28).—XI, XII,
(104).

RUJE, MADAME DE, advises Allory
to stand for the Academy, XI,
IV.—XI, V, (26, 27, 29, 30).—
Her "stable," XI, XII.—Supports
Allory with her presence during
the election, XI, XV.—XI, XVII,
(139, 141).—XI, XIX, (175).

SAINT-PAPOUL, BERNARD DE, XIII,
IV, (29).

SAINT-PAPOUL, BERNARDINE DE,
XIII, IV, (29).—XIII, V, 35.—
Passes through an acute psychological crisis; her aimless wanderings; the contemplation of
nudity, XIV, XXII.

SAINT-PAPOUL, MARQUIS DE, XI,
XVI, (138).—XIII, I, (II).—Consulted by Gurau on the subject
of a mission to Rome, XIII, II.—
Asks Mézan for news of Mionnet, XIII, III.—Sounds Mionnet
about the proposed mission, XIII,
IV.—Puts him in touch with
Gurau, XIII, V.—XIV, XXII,
(485).—Approves of Paulette's
new premises, XIV, XXII, 486–7.
—Tells the police of the disappearance of Bernardine and Macaire, XIV, XXII, 495–6.

SAINT-PAPOUL, MARQUISE DE, XIII, IV, (29).—XIV, XXII.

SAINT-PAPOUL, RAYMOND DE, XIII, IV, (29).

SAMMÉCAUD, BERTHE, XIV, XV, (390).

SAMMÉCAUD CHILDREN, THE, XIV, XV, (390).

SAMMÉCAUD, ROGER, XI, XII, (100).—XIV, X, (349).—XIV, XII, (368).—XIV, XIII, (369).—XIV, (XIV).—In a Belgian train on his way to meet the Egyptian princess, XIV, XV.—At a concert, XIV, XXII, 504.

SAMPEYRE, XI, X, (74–5).—Listens to Mathilde, advises her, and gives her a word of warning, XII, XXIV.—XIV, XXII, (493).

SCAGNOZZO, THE, offers his services to Mionnet and introduces him to the parents of Paolina, XIII, XXV.—XIII, XXX, (267).

SCHARBECK, XI, XIII, (114).

"SECT, THE," see "ORGANIZATION, THE."

SELLIER, XII, II, (310).

SÉRASQUIER, MONSIGNOR, entertains Mionnet at M—, XIII, VII.—XIII, (XVI).—XIII, XVIII, (148, 153).—XIII, XX, (169).—XIII, XXII, (186–7).

SISTER-IN-LAW OF MLLE ALBERTE, XI, XXVII.

SOLENDRE, LÉON DE, XIV, XVI, (399).

SOUTH AMERICAN WOMAN, THE, XII, XXI, (494).

STRIGELIUS, MARC, hears from Agnes that she may get a divorce, XII (VIII).—Answers her letter and gives her his advice, XII, IX.—First sketch of his "method," XII, X.—His philosophy, XII, XI.—His fear of "drying up" and his project for a method of automatic composition, XII, XIII.—First application of his method; "The Lesson of a Cenotaph," XII, XIV.

TELLIÈRE, XI, XI, (86).—XII, XVI, (443).

TESTEVEL, SENATOR, champions the cause of national defence, XI, (XXIX).

TINCHON, XI, XI, (84, 85.)

TURPIN, XI, XIII, (111).

VALENSINE or VALENSINI, MONSIGNOR, XIII, XIX, 162–3.

VALLETTE, ALFRED, XIV, XVI, (399–400).

VAQUEZ, PROFESSOR, XII, XXV, (543).—XIII, (VI).

VATICAN, THE, XII, (XXIII).—Subject of a conversation between Gurau and Poincaré, XIII, (I).—XIII, (IV).—XIII, (V).—XIII, (XVI).—XIII, XVII, (136–8).—Mionnet visits the museum and meditates on the past grandeurs of the scene, XIII, (XVIII).—XIII, (XX).—The German party, XIII, (XXI).—XIII, (XXIII).—Election of the last Pope; appointment of Merry del Val as Secretary of State; influence of the German party; the "triumvirate," XIII, (XXIV).—XIII, (XXVI).

VÉRAND, JULIETTE, XIV, XVIII, (434).—Jallez breaks with her by letter, XIV, XIX, (452–4).—Her meditations while shopping, XIV, XXII, 483–4.

VÉRAND, MADAME, XII, XXII, (512).

VÉRAND, MONSIEUR, XII, XXII, (512).

VERDANZAT, JACQUES, XI, XVII, (144).

VIAUR, DR. ALBERT, examines Haverkamp; his appearance, XI, XIII.—His first examination of Vidalencque, XII, I.—His training, researches, and experiments, XII, II.—His second examination of Vidalencque and his discovery of the suspended heart-action; XII, III.—Takes a walk in the forest and reflects on marriage in an attempt to escape from his obsession, XII, IV.—Sketches a rough program of procedure, XII, V.—His views on human knowledge, XII, VI.—His notes for future research, XII, VII.—Questions Vidalencque about his heart, XII, XVII.—Continues his experiments and becomes discouraged; his walk with Denise Lapierre, XII, XVIII.—Lunches with Pailleton and asks him to examine Vidalencque, XII, XIX.—Is present at the examination, XII, XX.—Confides his secret to Hachenard, XII, XXV.—Demonstrates his work for the benefit of Professors Robertet and Janteaume, XII, VI.—Again, some months later, before a learned audience at the medical school, XIII, XXVII.—Is the subject of a conversation between Jallez and Jerphanion, XIV, (XVIII).

VIDALENCQUE, consults Dr. Viaur, XII, I.—XII, II, (320).—Viaur notes that he can stop his heart at will, XII, III.—XII, IV, (330).—Tells Viaur how he learned the trick, XII, XVII.—Is made the object of several experiments by Viaur, XII, XVIII.—XII, (XIX).—Examined by Pailleton, XII, XX.—XII, (XXV).—XIII, VI.—XIII, XXVII, 240.

WAZEMMES, FÉLIX, XI, XIII, (111, 115).—Joins the Action Française, XIII, VIII.

WILLIAM II OF GERMANY, XII, XXII, (501).—Receives a long report by Maykosen from Paris, XIII, (XIII).—XIII, XXI, (183).—Maykosen reports to him from Rome on the Italian situation and the "Sect," XIII, (XXVI).—XIV, (XXI).—XIV, XXII, (492).—XIV, XXIII, (511).—Receives Maykosen on his yacht in July 1914, XIV, XXV.

WOMAN DOCTOR WITH LITERARY TASTES, THE, has a curious love-scene with Champcenais, to whom she gives a frank description of her life, XIV, XVI.

YOUNG GIRL OF BATTERSEA PARK, THE, XIV, XIX, (461–2).

YOUNG GRADUATE ON THE STAFF OF

L'Humanité, THE, XIII, XI, (97–102).

Z, MADAME, XI, XII, (104–5).
Z—, MONSIGNOR, dines at Fagiano's with Monsignor Dougérin and Mionnet, XIII, XXII.—XIII, XXIII, (191).
ZÜLPICHER, CHRISTA, theme of a new poem by Henri de Champcenais, XI, XXIX, (269).—Mysteriously mixed up in a strange scene, XIV, (XVI).
ZÜLPICHER, MONSIEUR, fragment of his conversation with Champcenais, XI, XVI.—XIII, XI, (100).—XIV, XV, (390).—XIV, XVI, (408).—XIV, XXII, (501).

A NOTE ON THE TYPE IN
WHICH THIS BOOK IS SET

This book is set in Granjon, a type named in compliment to ROBERT GRANJON, but neither a copy of a classic face nor an entirely original creation. George W. Jones drew the basic design for this type from classic sources, but deviated from his model to profit by the intervening centuries of experience and progress. This type is based primarily upon the type used by Claude Garamond (1510–61) in his beautiful French books, and more closely resembles Garamond's own than do any of the various modern types that bear his name.

Of Robert Granjon nothing is known before 1545, except that he had begun his career as type-cutter in 1523. The boldest and most original designer of his time, he was one of the first to practise the trade of type-founder apart from that of printer. Between 1549 and 1551 he printed a number of books in Paris, also continuing as type-cutter. By 1557 he was settled in Lyons and had married Antoinette Salamon, whose father, Bernard, was an artist associated with Jean de Tournes. Between 1557 and 1562 Granjon printed about twenty books in types designed by himself, following, after the fashion of the day, the cursive handwriting of the time. These types, usually known as "caractères de civilité," he himself called "lettres françaises," as especially appropriate to his own country. He was granted a monopoly of these types for ten years, but they were soon copied. Granjon appears to have lived in Antwerp for a time, but was at Lyons in 1575 and 1577, and for the next decade at Rome, working for the Vatican and Medici presses, his work consisting largely in cutting exotic types. Towards the end of his life he may have returned to live in Paris, where he died in 1590.

THIS BOOK WAS COMPOSED, PRINTED, AND BOUND BY H. WOLFF, NEW YORK · THE PAPER WAS MADE BY S. D. WARREN CO., BOSTON.